Three Complete
Amelia Peabody
Mysteries

ELIZABETH PETERS

Three Complete Amelia Peabody Mysteries

Crocodile on the Sandbank
The Curse of the Pharaohs
The Mummy Case

BARNES
&NOBLE
BOOKS
NEW YORK

This edition published by Barnes & Noble, Inc.,
by arrangement with Elizabeth Peters,
c/o Dominick Abel Literary Agency.

1993 Barnes & Noble Books

ISBN 1-56619-035-5

Printed and bound in the United States of America

M 9 8 7 6 5 4 3 2 1

Contents

Crocodile
on the
Sandbank

To my son Peter

The love of my beloved is on yonder side
A width of water is between us
And a crocodile waiteth on the sandbank.
—*Ancient Egyptian Love Poem*

Author's Note

Although my major characters are wholly fictitious, certain historic personages make brief appearances in these pages. Maspero, Brugsch and Grebaut were associated with the Egyptian Department of Antiquities in the 1880's, and William Flinders Petrie was then beginning his great career in Egyptology. Petrie was the first professional archaeologist to excavate at Tell el Amarna and I have taken the liberty of attributing some of his discoveries—and his "advanced" ideas about methodology—to my fictitious archaeologist. The painted pavement found by Petrie was given the treatment I have described by Petrie himself. Except for discrepancies of this nature I have attempted to depict the Egypt of that era, and the state of archaeological research in the late nineteenth century, as accurately as possible, relying on contemporary travel books for details. In order to add verisimilitude to the narrative, I have used the contemporary spelling of names of places and pharaohs, as well as certain words like "dahabeeyah." For example, the name of the heretic pharaoh was formerly read as "Khuenaten." Modern scholars prefer the reading "Akhenaten." Similarly, "Usertsen" is the modern "Senusert."

Chapter One

 WHEN I first set eyes on Evelyn Barton-Forbes she was walking the streets of Rome—

(I am informed, by the self-appointed Critic who reads over my shoulder as I write, that I have already committed an error. If those seemingly simple English words do indeed imply that which I am told they imply to the vulgar, I must in justice to Evelyn find other phrasing.)

In justice to myself, however, I must insist that Evelyn was doing precisely what I have said she was doing, but with no ulterior purpose in mind. Indeed, the poor girl had no purpose and no means of carrying it out if she had. Our meeting was fortuitous, but fortunate. I had, as I have always had, purpose enough for two.

I had left my hotel that morning in considerable irritation of spirits. My plans had gone awry. I am not accustomed to having my plans go awry. Sensing my mood, my small Italian guide trailed behind me in silence. Piero was not silent when I first encountered him, in the lobby of the hotel, where, in common with others of his kind, he awaited the arrival of helpless foreign visitors in need of a translator and guide. I selected him from amid the throng because his appearance was a trifle less villainous than that of the others.

I was well aware of the propensity of these fellows to bully, cheat, and otherwise take advantage of the victims who employ them, but I had no intention of being victimized. It did not take me long to make this clear to Piero. My first act was to bargain ruthlessly with the shopkeeper to whom Piero took me to buy silk. The final price was so low that Piero's commission was reduced to a negligible sum. He expressed his chagrin to his compatriot in his native tongue, and included in his tirade several personal comments on my appearance and manner. I let him go on for some time and then interrupted with a comment on *his* manners. I speak Italian, and understand it, quite well. After that Piero and I got on admirably. I had not employed him because I required an interpreter, but because I wanted someone to carry parcels and run errands.

My knowledge of languages, and the means which enabled me to travel abroad, had been acquired from my late father, who was a scholar and antiquarian.

There was little else to do but study, in the small country town where Papa preferred to live, and I have an aptitude for languages, dead and alive. Papa preferred his languages dead. He was a devoted student of the past, and emerged from it only occasionally, when he would blink at me and express surprise at how I had grown since he last noticed my existence. I found our life together quite congenial; I am the youngest of six, and my brothers, being considerably older, had left the nest some time before. My brothers were successful merchants and professional men; one and all they rejected Father's studies. I was left, then, to be the prop of my father's declining years. As I have said, the life suited me. It allowed me to develop my talents for scholarship. But let not the Gentle Reader suppose that I was ill equipped for the practical necessities of life. My father was disinclined toward practicalities. It was left to me to bully the baker and badger the butcher, which I did, if I may say so, quite effectively. After Mr. Hodgkins the butcher, Piero gave me no trouble.

My father died, eventually—if one may use so precise a word for the process that took place. One might say that he gradually shriveled up and ran down. The rumor, put about by a pert housemaid, that he had actually been dead for two days before anyone noticed, is a complete exaggeration. I must admit, however, that he might have passed away at any point during the five hours I spent with him in his study on that particular afternoon. He was leaning back in his big leather chair, meditating, as I assumed; and when, warned by some premonition, I hurried to his side, his wide-open eyes held the same expression of mild inquiry with which they had always regarded me. It seemed to me quite a respectable and comfortable way in which to pass on.

It came as no surprise to anyone to discover that he had left his property to me, the aforesaid prop, and the only one of his children who had not an income of its own. My brothers accepted this tolerantly, as they had accepted my devoted service to Papa. They did not explode until they learned that the property was not a paltry sum, but a fortune of half a million pounds. They had made a common mistake in assuming that an absentminded scholar is necessarily a fool. My father's disinclination to argue with Mr. Hodgkins the butcher was due, not to lack of ability, but to disinterest. He was very much interested in investments, "'change," and those other mysterious matters that produce wealth. He had conducted his business affairs with the same reticence that marked his habits in general; and he died, to the surprise of all, a wealthy man.

When this fact became known, the explosion occurred. My eldest brother James went so far as to threaten legal proceedings, on the basis of unsound mind and undue influence. This ill-considered burst of temper, which was characteristic of James, was easily stopped by Mr. Fletcher, Papa's excellent solicitor. Other attempts ensued. I was visited by streams of attentive nieces and nephews assuring me of their devotion—which had been demonstrated, over the past years, by their absence. Sisters-in-law invited me, in the most affectionate phrases, to share their homes. I was warned in the strongest terms against fortune hunters.

The warnings were not unselfish; they were, however, unnecessary. A middle-aged spinster—for I was at that time thirty-two years of age, and I scorned to disguise the fact—who has never received a proposal of marriage must be a simpleton if she fails to recognize the sudden acquisition of a fortune as a factor in her new popularity. I was not a simpleton. I had always known myself to be plain.

The transparent attempts of my kin, and of various unemployed gentlemen, to win my regard, aroused in me a grim amusement. I did not put them off; quite the contrary, I encouraged them to visit, and laughed up my sleeve at their clumsy efforts. Then it occurred to me that I was enjoying them too much. I was becoming cynical; and it was this character development that made me decide to leave England—not, as some malicious persons have intimated, a fear of being overborne. I had always wanted to travel. Now, I decided, I would see all the places Father had studied—the glory that was Greece and the grandeur that was Rome; Babylon and hundred-gated Thebes.

Once I had made this decision, it did not take me long to prepare for the journey. I made my arrangements with Mr. Fletcher, and received from him a proposal of marriage which I refused with the same good humor that had characterized the offer. At least he was honest.

"I thought it worth a try," he remarked calmly.

"Nothing ventured, nothing gained," I agreed.

Mr. Fletcher studied me thoughtfully for a moment.

"Miss Amelia, may I ask—in my professional capacity now—whether you have any inclinations toward matrimony?"

"None. I disapprove of matrimony as a matter of principle." Mr. Fletcher's pepper-and-salt eyebrows lifted. I added, "For myself, that is. I suppose it is well enough for some women; what else can the poor things do? But why should any independent, intelligent female choose to subject herself to the whims and tyrannies of a husband? I assure you, I have yet to meet a man as sensible as myself!"

"I can well believe that," said Mr. Fletcher. He hesitated for a moment; I fancied I could see him struggle with the desire to make an unprofessional statement. He lost the struggle.

"Why do you wear such frightful clothes?" he burst out. "If it is to discourage suitors—"

"Really, Mr. Fletcher!" I exclaimed.

"I beg your pardon," said the lawyer, wiping his brow. "I cannot think what came over me."

"Nor can I. As for my clothes, they suit the life I lead. The current fashions are impractical for an active person. Skirts so tight one must toddle like an infant, bodices boned so firmly it is impossible to draw a deep breath. . . . And bustles!

Of all the idiotic contrivances foisted upon helpless womankind, the bustle is certainly the worst. I wear them, since it is impossible to have a gown made without them, but at least I can insist on sensible dark fabrics and a minimum of ornament. What a fool I should look in puffs and frills and crimson satin—or a gown trimmed with dead birds, like one I saw!"

"And yet," said Mr. Fletcher, smiling, "I have always thought you would look rather well in puffs and frills and crimson satin."

The opportunity to lecture had restored my good humor. I returned his smile, but I shook my head.

"Give it up, Mr. Fletcher. You cannot flatter me; I know the catalogue of my faults too accurately. I am too tall, I am too lean in some regions and too amply endowed in others. My nose is too large, my mouth is too wide, and the shape of my chin is positively masculine. Sallow complexions and jetty black hair are not in fashion this season; and I have been informed that eyes of so deep a gray, set under such forbidding black brows, strike terror into the beholder even when they are beaming with benevolence—which my eyes seldom do. Now, I think I have dealt with that subject. Shall we turn to business?"

At Fletcher's suggestion I made my will. I had no intention of dying for a good many years, but I realized the hazards of travel in such unhealthy regions as I proposed to visit. I left my entire fortune to the British Museum, where Papa had spent so many happy hours. I felt rather sentimental about it; Papa might just as well have passed on in the Reading Room, and it would possibly have taken the attendants more than two days to realize he was no longer breathing.

My last act before departing was to engage a companion. I did not do this for the sake of propriety. Oppressed as my sex is in this supposedly enlightened decade of 1880, a woman of my age and station in life can travel abroad alone without offending any but the overly prudish. I engaged a companion because—in short, because I was lonely. All my life I had taken care of Papa. I needed someone, not to look after me, but the reverse. Miss Pritchett was a perfect companion. She was a few years my senior, but one never would have supposed it from her dress and manner. She affected dainty frilled gowns of thin muslin which hung awkwardly on her bony frame, and her voice was a preposterous high-pitched squeal. She was clumsy; her stupidity was so intense it verged on simplemindedness; she had a habit of fainting, or, at least, of collapsing into a chair with her hand pressed to her heart, whenever the slightest difficulty occurred. I looked forward to my association with Miss Pritchett. Prodding her through the malodorous streets of Cairo and the deserts of Palestine would provide my active mind with the distraction it needed.

After all, Miss Pritchett failed me. People of that sort seldom fall ill; they are too busy pretending to be ill. Yet no sooner had we reached Rome than Miss Pritchett succumbed to the typhoid, like the weak-minded female she was. Though she recovered, she delayed my departure for Egypt for two weeks, and it was manifest that she would not be able to keep up with my pace until after a long convalescence. I therefore dispatched her back to England in the care of a clergyman and his wife, who were leaving Rome. Naturally I felt obliged to pay her salary until she was able to secure another post. She left weeping, and trying, as the carriage left, to kiss my hand.

She left a vacuum in my carefully laid plans, and she was the cause of my ill humor when I left the hotel that fateful day. I was already two weeks behind schedule, and all the accommodations had been arranged for two persons. Should I try to find another companion, or resign myself to solitary travel? I must make my decision soon, and I was musing about it as I went for a final visit to the desolate Cow Pasture which was the seat of the ancient Forum of Rome.

It was a brisk December afternoon; the sun was intermittently obscured by clouds. Piero looked like a cold dog, despite the warm jacket I had purchased for him. I do not feel the cold. The breezy day, with its alternating shadow and sunshine, was quite appropriate to the scene. Broken columns and fallen stones were obscured by tumbled masses of weeds, now brown and brittle. There were other visitors rambling about. I avoided them. After reading a few of the broken inscriptions, and identifying, to my satisfaction, the spots where Caesar fell and where the senators awaited the arrival of the Goths, I seated myself on a fallen column.

Piero huddled at my feet with his knees drawn up and his arms wrapped around the basket he had been carrying. I found the hard, cold seat comfortable enough; there is something to be said for a bustle, in fact. It was compassion for Piero that made me order him to open the basket the hotel kitchen had provided. However, he refused my offer of hot tea with a pitiful look. I presume he would have accepted brandy.

I was drinking my tea when I noticed that there was a cluster of people some distance away, who seemed to be gathered around an object that was concealed from me by their bodies. I sent Piero to see what it was, and went on drinking my tea.

After an interval he came bounding back with his black eyes gleaming. Nothing delights these gentry quite so much as misfortune; I was therefore not surprised when he reported that the "turisti" were gathered around a young English lady who had fallen down dead upon the ground.

"How do you know that she is English?" I inquired.

Piero did not reply in words; he went through an extraordinary series of grimaces to indicate a certainty so profound it requires no evidence. His eyes rolled, his hands flew about, his shoulders rose and fell. What else should the lady be but English.

English or not, I doubted that the lady was dead. That was only Piero's Latin love of the dramatic. But so far as I could see, no one in the crowd was doing anything except stare. I rose to my feet, therefore, and after brushing off my bustle,

I approached the group. My parasol proved useful in passing through it; I had to apply the ferrule quite sharply to the backs of several gentlemen before they would move. Eventually I penetrated to the center of the circle. As I had surmised, no one was behaving with sense or compassion. Indeed, several of the ladies were pulling their escorts away, with comments about infection and criticism of the fallen lady's probable character.

She was so pitiful as she lay there on the cold, damp ground that only a heart of stone could have been unmoved. There are many hearts of that composition, however.

I sat down upon the ground and lifted the girl's head onto my knee. I regretted very much that I had not worn a cloak or mantle. However, that was easily remedied.

"Your coat, sir," I said to the nearest gentleman.

He was a stout, red-faced person whose extra layers of flesh should have been enough to keep him warm, without the fur-lined greatcoat he wore. He carried a handsome gold-headed stick, which he had been using to poke at the fallen girl as a lecturer in a waxworks indicates the exhibits. When I addressed him, he turned from his companion, to whom he had been speaking in an undertone, and stared at me.

"What—what?" he snorted.

"Your coat," I said impatiently. "Give it to me at once." Then, as he continued to stare, his face getting redder and redder, I raised my voice. "Sir— your coat, at once!"

I put the coat over the girl. Having assured myself that she was only in a faint, I was at leisure to look at her more closely. I was not a whit distracted by the whalelike sputterings of the red-faced gentleman whose coat I had appropriated.

I have said that I am a plain woman. For this reason I have a quite disinterested love of beauty in all its forms. I could therefore disinterestedly admire the girl who lay unconscious before me.

She was English, surely; that flawless white skin and pale-golden hair could belong to no other nation. She was naturally fair of complexion; now, in her fainting state, her face was as pallid and pure as marble. The features might have been those of an antique Venus or young Diana. Her lashes were several shades darker than her hair, forming a pleasing contrast. She was dressed, quite inappropriately for the chilly weather, in a summer frock and thin blue cloak; both cloak and gown were sadly worn, but had once been expensive—they were of costly material and showed good workmanship. The gloves on her small hands had been neatly mended. The girl presented a picture of poverty and abandonment that excited my curiosity as much as it aroused my compassion; I wondered what had reduced a young woman of obvious refinement to this state. I surmised that she suffered chiefly from cold and hunger; the thin white face was pinched and sunken.

As I watched, her dark-gold lashes fluttered and lifted, disclosing eyes of an exquisite deep blue. They stared dreamily about for a time, and then fixed themselves on my face. The girl's expression changed; a touch of color came to her thin cheeks, and she struggled to sit up.

"Be still," I said, putting her down with one hand and beckoning Piero with the other. "You have fainted and are still weak. Partake of some nourishment, if you please, before we proceed to further measures to relieve you."

She tried to protest; her helpless state and the circle of staring, unfriendly eyes clearly distressed her. I was perfectly indifferent to the observers, but since she seemed embarrassed, I decided to rid myself of them. I told them to go. They did so, except for the indignant gentleman whose coat was over the girl.

"Your name and hotel, sir," I said, cutting short a loud protest. "Your coat will be returned later this evening. A person of your excessive bulk should not wear such heavy clothing in any case."

The lady by his side, who had the same rotund outlines and hard red face, exclaimed aloud.

"How dare you, madame! I have never heard of such a thing!"

"I daresay you have not," I agreed, giving her a look that made her step back. "I do not doubt that it is too late to awaken in you any faint sense of Christian compassion or normal human emotion, so I shan't try. Take yourself away, madame, and this—I can hardly say 'gentleman'—this male person with you."

As I spoke I was administering bits of food from my basket to the fallen girl. The fastidious manner in which she ate, despite her obvious hunger, confirmed my assumption that she was a lady. She seemed better when she had finished a piece of bread and the remainder of my tea; and since the crowd had retired to a distance I was able, with Piero's assistance, to raise her to her feet. We then proceeded, by carriage, to my hotel.

II

The doctor I summoned assured me that my diagnosis had been correct. The young lady was suffering from starvation and cold only. There was no sign of infection, and she was recovering quickly.

A plan had taken shape in my mind, and I considered it, striding up and down the drawing room of my suite, as is my habit when engaged in thought. It did not take me long to reach a decision. Frail as the girl appeared, she must have a stout constitution in order to have resisted, in her weakened state, the putrid air and water of Rome. Clearly she had no friends or relatives to whom she could look for relief, or she would not have sunk to such a state. Equally clearly, she could not be left in that state.

Having made up my mind, I went to tell the young lady what was to be done.

She was sitting up in bed, taking soup from the hand of my maid, Travers. Neither of them appeared to be enjoying the process. Travers is a living contradiction to the theories of the physiognomists, for her face and shape do not at all reflect her personality. She is a round, cheery-faced little person with the soul of a dried-up old spinster. She did not approve of my taking in a "stray," as she would have said, and her sour look expressed her feelings. To be fair, that was the only way in which Travers *could* express her feelings. I do not permit verbal complaints.

"That will do," I said. "Too much food might be ill advised at present. Go away, Travers, and be sure you close the door tightly."

When she had obeyed, I studied my patient and was pleased at what I saw. My flannel nightdress was considerably too large for the girl. She would need clothing—dainty, delicate things, to suit her fairness—garments of the sort I had never been able to wear. She would look charming in pale shades, blue and pink and lavender. There was color in her face now, a delicate rose flush that made her even prettier. How on earth, I wondered, had such a girl come to her present pass?

My stare must have been more intent than I realized. The girl's eyes dropped. Then she raised her head and spoke, with a firmness I had not expected. Her voice settled any lingering doubts as to her class; it was that of a well-bred young lady.

"I am more indebted than I can say," she began. "But be assured, ma'am, I shall not take advantage of your charity. I am quite recovered now; if you will direct your maid to return my clothing, I will rid you of my presence."

"Your clothing has been thrown away," I said absently. "It was not worth the trouble of laundering. You must remain in bed for the rest of the day in any case. I will order a seamstress to come tomorrow. There is a boat leaving for Alexandria on Friday next. A week should be sufficient. You will need to do some shopping, of course, but first I had better see what you have with you. If you will tell me where you have been staying, I will send a man around for your boxes."

Her face was very expressive. It had registered a variety of emotions as I spoke; the blue eyes had flashed with indignation and then narrowed with suspicion. But the ultimate emotion was openmouthed bewilderment. I waited for her to speak, but she merely opened and closed her mouth, so I said impatiently. "I am taking you to Egypt with me, as my companion. Miss Pritchett failed me; she took the typhoid. I had agreed to pay her ten pounds a year. Naturally I will be responsible for equipping you for the journey. You can hardly travel in a flannel nightdress!"

"No," the girl agreed, looking dazed. "But—but—"

"My name is Amelia Peabody. You will call me Amelia. I am a spinster of independent means, traveling for pleasure. Is there anything else you wish to know about me?"

"I know all I need to know," the girl said quietly. "I was not entirely unconscious when you came to my rescue, and I hope I am able to recognize true kindness of heart. But my dear Miss Peabody—very well, Amelia—you know nothing about *me!*"

"Is there something I should know?"

"I might be a criminal! I might be vicious—unprincipled!"

"No, no," I said calmly. "I have been accused of being somewhat abrupt in my actions and decisions, but I never act without thought; it is simply that I think more quickly and more intelligently than most people. I am an excellent judge of character. I could not be deceived about yours."

A dimple appeared at the corner of the girl's mouth. It trembled, and was gone. The blue eyes fell.

"You *are* deceived," she said, so softly I could hardly hear. "I am not what you think. I owe it to you to tell you my story; and when you have heard it, then—then you will be justified in ordering me out of your sight."

"Proceed," I said. "I will be the judge of *that.*"

"I am sure you will!" The dimple reappeared, but did not linger. Her face pale, her eyes steady, the girl began to speak.

THE GIRL'S STORY

My name is Evelyn Barton-Forbes. My parents having died when I was an infant, I was brought up by my grandfather, the Earl of Ellesmere. I see you recognize the name. It is an ancient name and an honorable one—although many of the holders of the title have not been men of honor. My grandfather . . . well, I cannot speak fairly of him. I know he is regarded by many as miserly and selfish; though he possesses one of the greatest fortunes in England, he has never been known as a philanthropist. But he was always good to me. I was his pet, his little lamb, as he called me. I think perhaps I was the only human being to whom he never spoke harshly. He even forgave me for being a girl and not the heir he so ardently desired.

I suspect you are a feminist, Miss—Amelia? Then you will be indignant, but not surprised, to know that although I am the only child of my grandfather's eldest son, I cannot inherit his title or estates. There are few exceptions to the rule that only male descendants may inherit. When my father died prematurely, the next male heir was my cousin, Lucas Hayes.

Poor Lucas! I have not seen a great deal of him, but I always liked him, and I cannot help but pity him because Grandfather was so cruelly unfair to him. Of course Grandfather would never admit to prejudice. He claims to dislike Lucas because of his extravagance and wild habits. But I feel sure such tales are only rumors. Grandfather really hates my unfortunate cousin for the sin of being his father's son. You see, his mother, Grandfather's eldest daughter, ran away with—

with an Italian gentleman. . . . (Excuse my emotion, Amelia, you will understand its cause presently. There; I am better now.)

My grandfather is British to the core. He despises all foreigners, but especially those of Latin descent. He considers them sly, slippery—oh, I cannot repeat all the terrible things he says! When my aunt eloped with the Conte d'Imbroglio d'Annunciata, Grandfather disowned her and struck her name from the family Bible. Even when she lay dying he sent no word of comfort or forgiveness. He said the Conte was no nobleman, but a fraud and a fortune hunter. I am sure that is untrue. The Conte had very little money, to be sure, but that does not mean his title was not genuine. However, Lucas, on reaching maturity, felt it wise to change his name, since his true one maddened Grandfather. He calls himself Lucas Elliot Hayes now, and he has abandoned his Italian title.

For a time it seemed that Lucas had succeeded in winning Grandfather by his assiduous attentions. I even wondered whether Grandfather was considering a marriage between us. It would have been a happy solution in a sense, for, the estate and title being entailed, Lucas would eventually inherit them. But without my grandfather's private fortune, which was his to dispose of, the earldom would be a burden rather than a privilege; and Grandfather made no secret of his intention of leaving that money to me.

Yet if there was such a scheme, it came to nothing. Hearing of some new misbehavior, Grandfather flew into a rage and sent Lucas away. I am ashamed to admit I was relieved. Fond as I was of Lucas, I did not love him; and being a foolish, sentimental girl, I fancied love must precede marriage. I see you frown, Amelia, to hear me use such terms of myself. They are too mild, as you will soon learn.

For love came, as I thought; and it proved my utter undoing.

While Lucas was with us I had become interested in drawing. Lucas said I had considerable natural skill, and before he left he taught me what he knew. Afterward, I was desirous of continuing, so Grandfather, who indulged me more than I deserved, advertised for a drawing master. Thus Alberto came into my life.

I cannot speak of him calmly. The handsome features and shining dark hair, which seemed to me angelic, now take on a diabolical aspect. His soft voice, with its tender broken accents—for he spoke English rather badly—come back to me, in retrospect, as the sly whispers of a fiend. He—he. . . . Let me be short and succinct. He seduced me, in short, and persuaded me into an elopement. At his instigation I fled my home; I abandoned the old man who had loved and sheltered me; I flung away every consideration of religion, moral training, and natural affection. I cannot speak of Alberto without loathing; but, believe me, dear Amelia, when I say that I blame myself even more. How true are the old sayings, that evil brings its own punishment! I deserve my wretched fate; I brought it on myself, and I cannot blame those who would shun me. . . .

Forgive me. I will not give way again.

The end of the story is soon told. I had taken with me the few jewels, suitable for a young girl, which Grandfather's generosity had bestowed upon me. The money procured from the sale of these jewels did not last long as we made our way across Europe toward Rome. Alberto insisted that we live in a style that was worthy of me. The lodgings we took in Rome were *not* worthy of me, but by then my money had run out. When I asked Alberto what we were to do, he was evasive. He was also evasive about marriage. As a good Catholic he could not entertain the idea of a civil ceremony. But I was not a Catholic. . . . Oh, his excuses were feeble, I see that now, but I was so naïve. . . .

The blow finally came a week ago. Alberto had been increasingly elusive; he was out a good part of the day, and when he returned he would be intoxicated and sullen. I awoke one morning, in the shabby, freezing attic room to which our poverty had reduced us, to find myself alone. He had had the courtesy to leave me a gown and cloak and a pair of shoes. Every other object I possessed had gone with him, from my ivory brushes to my hair ornaments. He had also left a note.

The sight of this ill-spelled, badly written document was the final blow; its crudities stung me even more than the message it contained, though this was blunt enough. Alberto had selected me as his prey because I was a wealthy heiress. He had expected that my grandfather would react to our elopement by cutting me out of his will; and through communication with the British authorities in Rome he had learned that this had in fact happened. He had believed, however, that with time the old man, as he disrespectfully called him, would relent. His most recent visit to the consul—whom he had always refused to let me visit—had destroyed this hope. My poor grandfather had suffered a most violent stroke, as a result of my cruel abandonment. He had retained his senses only long enough to make a new will, cutting me off with a shilling, and had then fallen into a coma that was expected to end in death. Finding his expectations frustrated, Alberto saw no reason to waste any more time with me. There were, as he explained, more enticing prospects.

You may only faintly imagine my state of mind, Amelia. I was ill for several days, grudgingly nursed by the horrid old woman who owned the lodging house. She did not want a corpse on her hands, I suppose, for charity had no part in her actions. As soon as I was well enough to speak, she discovered that I was penniless. This very day she evicted me from the last refuge I had, poor as it was. I went out, fully determined to end a life which had become unbearable. What other option had I? I had no money and no means of procuring employment. For all I knew, my darling grandfather might already be dead. If some miracle had spared him, the dear old gentleman would rightfully refuse to take me back, even if I could communicate with him; and I would rather die than admit to anyone that I had been so cruelly betrayed. My wrongdoing was bad enough; my folly I would admit to no man. No, I had no choice, or so it seemed then; but you need not fear, your kindness has saved me from that ultimate crime. I will not take my own life. But

I can no longer stay here. Your countenance is as benevolent as your mind; it betrays no sign of the loathing and disgust you must feel, but you need not spare me. Indeed, I would welcome words of contempt, for punishment relieves some of my feelings of guilt. Speak, Amelia—Miss Peabody—speak, I beg you. Chastise me, and I will welcome your reproaches in the spirit of Christian humility in which I hope to end my miserable existence.

III

When she had finished, Evelyn's blue eyes were swimming with tears, and her voice was unsteady; but she had kept her promise to remain calm. She had spoken with vigor and decision throughout the last part of this shameful narrative.

I was silent, trying to decide which of many things I should say first. My silence was painful to the girl; she drew a long, shuddering breath. Her hands were clasped so tightly that the knuckles showed white; the slender shoulders under my flannel nightdress were braced as if for a blow. I was in a state of some mental confusion. The words that finally came from my lips were not at all those I had meant to say.

"Tell me, Evelyn—what is it like? Is it pleasant?"

Evelyn's astonishment was hardly greater than my own; but having once begun, I had to explain more fully. I hurried on.

"You will forgive me for probing into what must be a source of pain for you; but I have never had the opportunity of inquiring. . . . One hears such conflicting stories. My sisters-in-law whisper and shake their heads and speak of the cross a wife must bear. But I have seen the village girls in the meadows with their sweethearts and they seem—they look—in short, they do not seem to find . . . Dear me! How strange, I seem to be at a loss for words. That does not often occur. Do you understand what I am trying to ask?"

For a moment longer Evelyn stared at me, her wide eyes brimming. Then an extraordinary grimace crossed her face. She covered it with her hands; her shoulders shook convulsively.

"I must apologize," I said resignedly. "Now I suppose I will never know. I did not intend—"

A choked sound from Evelyn interrupted me. She lowered her hands. Her face was flushed and tear-streaked. She was gasping—with laughter.

I took it for hysteria, of course, and moved alertly forward. She caught my lifted hand.

"No, no, you needn't slap me; I am not at all hysterical. But, Amelia, you are—you are so—Is that really all you can think of to ask me, after such a story as mine?"

I considered the matter.

"Why, I really do not think there is anything else to ask. The shameful behavior of your abominable old grandfather and your villain of a lover require no comment. I presume your other family connections are equally cold-hearted, or you would have appealed to them."

"And you are not repelled by my ruined character?"

"I do not consider that it is ruined. Indeed, the experience has probably strengthened your character."

Evelyn shook her head. "I can't believe you are real!"

"There is nothing extraordinary about me. However, I suppose—yes, I am sure that it would be wise for you to make certain I am what I claim to be before you accept the position I offer. My father had friends in academic circles; I can give you references to a clergyman here in Rome, and the consul knows of my—"

"No. I do not need to make such inquiries." With a gesture, Evelyn indicated that I should take a seat on the bed beside her. I did so. She studied me earnestly for a few moments. Then she said,

"Before I answer your question, Amelia, perhaps you will answer one for me. Why did you say, 'I will never know'? Referring, of course, to the question—"

"Well, it is unlikely that I shall ever have firsthand experience. I am fully acquainted with the use of the mirror and the calendar. The latter tells me that I am thirty-two years old; the former reproduces my plain features without flattery. Moreover, my nature does not lend itself to the meekness required of a wife in our society. I could not endure a man who would let himself be ruled by me, and I would not endure a man who tried to rule me. However, I am curious. I had thought. . . . But no doubt I spoke out of place. My brothers assure me that I constantly do so."

"If I have not answered your question," Evelyn said, "it is not because I consider it unfair, but because I find it difficult to give a balanced answer. At this time, my recollection of the hours I spent—shall we say in Alberto's arms?—makes a shudder of disgust pass through me. But at the time—at the time. . . ." She leaned forward. Her eyes were brilliant. "Oh, Amelia, under the right circum- stances, it is—in a word—perfectly splendid!"

"Ah. I suspected as much. Well, my dear Evelyn, I am indebted to you for the information. And now shall we consider a more pressing question? No doubt you will wish to inquire of those references I mentioned before making a decision as to—"

"No." Evelyn shook her head vigorously. Her golden curls danced. "I need no references, and no time to consider. I would love to be your companion, Amelia. Indeed—I think we will get on very well together."

With a quick, graceful movement she leaned forward and kissed me lightly on the cheek. The gesture took me quite by surprise. I mumbled something and left the room. I never had a sister. I began to think that perhaps a gesture that had begun as an act of charity might benefit me as much as it helped its object.

IV

I may say, without undue egotism, that when I make up my mind to do something, it is done quickly. The lethargic old city of the Popes fairly quaked under my ruthless hand during the following week.

The week brought several surprises to me. I had looked forward to adopting Evelyn and dressing her, rather as if she had been a pretty, living doll. I wanted to buy for her all the dainty, impractical garments I could not wear myself. But she was not a doll, and she soon made that fact apparent. I don't know quite how she accomplished it, for she never openly contermanded an order or contradicted me; but she eventually acquired a wardrobe that was charming and simple and astonishingly inexpensive. And, in the process, I somehow acquired half a dozen new frocks of my own, which I had had no intention of buying. They were not the kind of frocks I would have chosen for myself. One evening dress, which I certainly did not need, was of the most astonishing shade of crimson, with a square neckline cut several inches lower than anything I had ever worn. The skirts were draped back over a bustle, displaying a sequined underskirt. Evelyn chose the fabric and bullied the dressmaker quite as effectively, and much more quietly, than I would have done. I thought the gown quite absurd; it squeezed my waist down to nothing and made my bosom look even more ample than it unfortunately is. But when Evelyn said, "Wear it"; I wore it. She was an amazing girl. She also discovered a weakness, so secret I was not aware of it myself, for embroidered batiste; the dozens of fine undergarments and nightgowns I had meant to get for her ended being made to my measurements.

I was in something of a daze during that week. I felt as if I had picked up a pathetic, half-drowned kitten from a pond and then had seen it turn into a full-grown tiger. Enough of my natural instincts remained, however, to allow me to take certain practical steps.

I am not at all a man-hater, despite the innuendos of a certain person whose name has not yet entered into this narrative. I had found, however, that few persons of the male sex were to be trusted, and Evelyn's story had merely confirmed this theory. It was obvious that Alberto was an untruthful person. The story he had written to Evelyn about her grandfather was not to be believed without investigation. I therefore went to our consul in Rome and made inquiries.

I was disappointed for several reasons to learn that on this account, if no other, Alberto had spoken the truth. The Earl of Ellesmere was personally known to our consul; and of course the health of a peer of such rank was a matter of general concern. The elderly earl was not yet dead, but word of his demise was expected at any moment. He had been in a deep coma for days.

I proceeded to tell the consul about Evelyn. He had heard rumors of this affair; that was clear, from the way his face changed to its blank diplomatic mask.

He had the temerity to remonstrate with me when I explained my intentions with regard to the girl. I cut him short, naturally. I had only two reasons for mentioning Evelyn at all. Firstly, to ascertain whether or not any of her kin had made inquiries about her. Secondly, to inform someone in authority of her future whereabouts in case such inquiries should be made in the future. The answer to the first question was negative. The diplomatic mask notwithstanding, I could see by the consul's expression that he did not expect any such inquiries; he knew the old Earl too well. I therefore gave him my address in Cairo and departed, leaving him shaking his head and mumbling to himself.

On the twenty-eight of the month we boarded the ship at Brindisi and set sail for Alexandria.

Chapter Two

 I will spare the Gentle Reader descriptions of the journey and of the picturesque dirt of Alexandria. Every European traveler who can write his name feels obliged to publish his memoirs; the reader may refer to "Miss Smith's Egyptian Journals" or "Mr. Jones's Winter in Egypt" if he feels cheated of local color, for all the descriptions are the same. The sea voyage was abominable, but I was happy to see that Evelyn was a good traveler. We made our way to Cairo without incident and settled down at Shepheard's Hotel.

Everyone stays at Shepheard's. Among the travelers who meet daily in its magnificent dining room one may eventually, it is said, encounter all one's acquaintances; and from the terrace before the hotel the indolent tourist may watch a panorama of eastern life pass before his eyes as he sips his lemonade. Stiff English travelers ride past, on donkeys so small that the riders' feet trail in the dust; followed by Janissaries in their gorgeous gold-embroidered uniforms, armed to the teeth; by native women swathed to the eyebrows in dusty black, by stately Arabs in flowing blue-and-white robes, dervishes with matted hair and fantastic headdresses, sweetmeat vendors with trays of Turkish delight, water sellers with their goatskin containers bloated with liquid and looking horridly lifelike. . . . But I see I am succumbing to the temptation of the traveler, and will stop; the procession is unending and fascinating.

There were not many English travelers in Cairo that winter. The fighting in the Sudan had apparently alarmed them. The mad Mahdi was still besieging the gallant Gordon at Khartoum. However, Sir Garnet Wolseley's relief expedition had reached Wadi Halfa, and the gentlemen we met at Shepheard's reassured us—or rather, reassured Evelyn—when she expressed doubts as to the wisdom of traveling south. The fighting was still hundreds of miles below Assuan, and by the time we arrived there the war would surely be over—the Mahdi taken and his barbaric army crushed, the gallant Gordon relieved.

I was not so sanguine as the gentlemen. The mad carpenter of the Sudan had proved himself an extremely potent general, as our losses in that area proved. However, I said nothing to Evelyn, for I had no intention of changing my plans to suit the Mahdi or anyone else. I planned to spend the winter sailing up the Nile, and sail I would.

Travel by water is the only comfortable method of seeing Egypt, and the narrow length of the country means that all the antiquities are within easy reach of the river. I had heard of the pleasure of travel by dahabeeyah, and was anxious to try it. To call these conveyances houseboats is to give a poor idea of their luxury. They can be fitted up with any convenience the traveler chooses to supply, and the services available depend solely on his ability to pay. I intended to go to Boulaq, where the boats are moored, and decide on one the day after our arrival. We could then inspect some of the sights of Cairo and be on our way in a few days.

When I expressed this intention to some of our fellow guests in the lounge of the hotel after dinner, a burst of hilarity greeted my remarks. I was informed that my hopes were vain. Choosing a dahabeeyah was a frustrating, time-consuming process; the native Egyptian was a lazy fellow who could not be hurried.

I had my own opinions on that score, but I caught Evelyn's eye and remained silent. She was having an astonishing effect on me, that girl; I thought that if I continued in her company much longer, I might become mellow.

She was looking very pretty that night, in a frock of pale-blue silk, and she attracted considerable attention. We had agreed that her real name was not to be mentioned, since it was well known to many Englishmen; she was therefore introduced as Evelyn Forbes. Tiring, finally, of the clumsy efforts of some of the ladies in the group to discover her antecedents, I used fatigue as an excuse for early retirement.

I awoke early next morning. An ethereal, rose-tinted light filled the room, and I could see Evelyn kneeling by the window. I thought she was brooding over past events; there had been moments of depression, quickly overcome, but not unnoticed by me. I therefore tried to remain motionless, but an inadvertent rustle of the bedclothes caused her to turn, and I saw that her face was shining with pleasure.

"Come and look, Amelia. It is so beautiful!"

To obey was not as simple as it sounds. I had first to fight my way through the muffling folds of fine white mosquito netting that encircled the bed. When I joined Evelyn, I shared her pleasure. Our rooms overlooked the garden of the hotel; stately palms, dark silhouettes in the pale dawn, rose up against a sky filled with translucent azure and pink streaks. Birds fluttered singing from tree to tree; the lacy minarets of mosques shone like mother-of-pearl above the treetops. The air was cool and exquisitely clear.

It was as well that our day began with such beauty and peace, for the wharves of Boulaq, where we went after breakfast, were not at all peaceful. I began to understand what our fellow travelers had warned me about. There were over a hundred boats at their moorings; the confusion and noise were indescribable.

The boats are much alike, varying only in size. The cabins occupy the after part of the deck, and their roof forms an upper deck which, when furnished and canopied, provides a charming open-air drawing room for the passengers. The crew occupy the lower deck. Here is the kitchen, a shed containing a charcoal stove, and a collection of pots and pans. The dahabeeyahs are shallow, flat-bottomed boats with two masts; and when the huge sails are spread to catch the brisk northerly breeze, they present a most attractive picture.

Our problem, then, was to decide which boat to hire. At first even I was bewildered by the variety. It did not take long, however, to realize that some of the boats were impossible. There are degrees of uncleanliness; I could tolerate, indeed, I expected, a state of sanitation inferior to that of England, but . . . ! Unfortunately, the bigger boats were usually the better kept. I did not mind the expense, but it seemed a trifle ridiculous for the two of us—and my maid—to rattle about in a boat that contained ten staterooms and two saloons.

At Evelyn's insistence we had hired a dragoman that morning at the hotel. I saw no reason why we should; I had learned some Arabic phrases during the voyage to Alexandria, and had every confidence in my ability to deal with an Egyptian boat captain. However, I yielded to Evelyn. Our dragoman was named Michael Bedawee; he was a Copt, or Egyptian Christian, a short, plump, coffee-colored man with a fierce black beard and a white turban—although I must confess that this description would fit half the male population of Egypt. What distinguished Michael was the friendliness of his smile and the candor of his soft brown eyes. We took to him at once, and he seemed to like us.

With Michael's help we selected a boat. The *Philae* was of middle size, and of unusual tidiness; Evelyn and I both liked the looks of the reis, or captain. His name was Hassan, and he was an Egyptian of Luxor. I approved of the firm set of his mouth and the steady gaze of his black eyes—and the glint of humor in them when I assayed my few words of Arabic. I suppose my accent was atrocious, but Reis Hassan complimented me on my knowledge of his language, and the bargain was soon concluded.

With the pride of ownership Evelyn and I explored the quarters that would be our home for the next four months. The boat had four cabins, two on either side of a narrow passageway. There was also a bathroom, with water laid on. At the end of the passage a door opened into the saloon, which was semicircular, following the shape of the stern. It was well lighted by eight windows and had a long curved divan along the wall. Brussels' carpets covered the floor; the paneling was white with gold trim, giving a light, airy feeling. Window curtains of scarlet, a handsome dining table, and several mirrors in gold frames completed the furnishings.

With the ardor of ladies equipping a new house, we discussed what else we should need. There were cupboards and shelves in plenty, and we had books to fill the shelves; I had brought a large box of father's books on Egyptian antiquities, and I hoped to purchase more. But we should also need a piano. I am totally without musical ability, but I dearly love to hear music, and Evelyn played and sang beautifully.

I asked Reis Hassan when he would be ready to depart; and here I received my first check. The boat had just returned from a trip. The crew needed time to rest and visit their families; certain mysterious overhaulings needed to be done on the vessel itself. We finally settled on a date a week hence, but there was something in Hassan's bland black eyes that made me wonder. . . .

Nothing went as I had planned it. Finding a suitable piano took an unreasonable amount of time. I wanted new curtains for the saloon; their shade clashed horribly with my crimson evening frock. As Evelyn pointed out, we were in no hurry; yet I had a feeling that she was even more anxious than I to be on our way. Every evening when we entered the dining room I felt her shrink. Sooner or later it was more than probable that she should encounter an acquaintance, and I could understand why she shrank from that.

Our days were not wasted; there is a great deal to see and do in Cairo. The bazaars were a source of constant amusement; the procession of people passing through the narrow passages would have been entertainment enough, without the fascination of the wares on display. Each trade occupies a section of its own: saddlers, slipper makers, copper and bronze workers, carpet sellers, and vendors of tobacco and sweetmeats. There are no real shops, only tiny cupboards, open at the front, with a stone platform or mastaba, on which the merchants sit cross-legged, awaiting customers. I could not resist the rugs, and bought several for our drawing room on the *Philae*—soft, glowing beauties from Persia and Syria. I tried to buy some trinkets for Evelyn; she would only accept a pair of little velvet slippers.

We visited the bazaars and the mosques and the Citadel; and then planned excursions somewhat farther afield. Of course I was anxious to see the remains of the ancient civilization, but I little realized what was in store for me that day, when we paid our first visit to Gizeh.

Everyone goes to see the pyramids. Since the Nile bridge was built, they are within an easy hour-and-a-half drive from the hotel. We left early in the morning so that we should have time to explore fully.

I had seen engravings of the Great Pyramid and read extensively about it; I thought I was prepared for the sight. But I was not. It was so much grander than

I had imagined! The massive bulk bursts suddenly on one's sight as one mounts the steep slope leading up to the rocky platform. It fills the sky. And the color! No black-and-white engraving can possibly prepare one for the color of Egyptian limestone, mellow gold in the sunlight against a heavenly-blue vault.

The vast plateau on which the three pyramids stand is honeycombed with tombs—pits, fallen mounds of masonry, crumbling smaller pyramids. From the midst of a sandy hollow projects the head of the Sphinx, its body buried in the ever-encroaching sand, but wearing more majesty on its imperfect features than any other sculpture made by man.

We made our way to the greatest of the three pyramids, the tomb of Khufu. It loomed up like a mountain as we approached. The seeming irregularities of its sides were now seen to be huge blocks, each one higher than a man's head; and Evelyn wondered audibly how one was supposed to mount these giant stairs.

"And in long skirts," she mourned.

"Never mind," I said. "We shall manage."

And we did, with the help of six Arabs—three apiece. One on either side and one pushing from behind, we were lifted easily from block to block, and soon stood on the summit. Evelyn was a trifle pale, but I scarcely heeded her distress or gave her courage its due; I was too absorbed in the magnificent view. The platform atop the pyramid is about thirty feet square, with blocks of the stripped-off upper tiers remaining to make comfortable seats. I seated myself and stared till my eyes swam—with strain, I thought then; but perhaps there was another reason.

On the east, the undulating yellow Mokattam hills formed a frame for a picture whose nearer charms included the vivid green strip of cultivated land next to the river, and, in the distance, shining like the towers of fairyland, the domes and minarets of Cairo. To the west and south the desert stretched away in a haze of gold. Along the horizon were other man-made shapes—the tiny pyramid points of Abusir and Sakkarah and Dahshoor.

I gazed till I could gaze no more; and was aroused from a reverie that had lasted far too long by Evelyn plucking at my sleeve.

"May we not descend?" she begged. "I believe I am getting sunburned."

Her nose was certainly turning pink, despite the protection of her broad-brimmed hat. Remorsefully I consented, and we were lowered down by our cheerful guides. Evelyn declined to enter the pyramid with me, having heard stories of its foul atmosphere. She knew better than to try to dissuade me. I left her with some ladies who had also refused the treat, and, hitching up my skirts, followed the gentlemen of the party into the depths.

It was a horrid place—stifling air, debris crunching underfoot, the dark barely disturbed by the flickering candles held by our guides. I reveled in every moment of it, from the long traverse of the passage to the Queen's chamber, which is so low that one must walk bent over at the waist, to the hazardous ascent of the Grand Gallery, that magnificent high-ceilinged slope up which one must crawl in semidarkness, relying on the sinewy arms of the Egyptians to prevent a tumble back down the stone-lined slope. There were bats as well. But in the end I stood in the King's Chamber, lined with somber black basalt, and containing only the massive black coffin into which Khufu was laid to rest some four thousand years ago; and with the perspiration rolling down my frame, and every breath an effort, I felt the most overpowering sense of satisfaction I had felt since childhood—when William, my brother, dared me to climb the apple tree in the garden, and I, perched on the highest bough, watched him tumble out of a lower one. He broke his arm.

When I finally joined her outside, Evelyn's face was a sight to behold. I raked my fingers through my disheveled hair and remarked, "It was perfectly splendid, Evelyn. If you would like to go, I would be happy to see it again. . . ."

"No," Evelyn said. "Not under any circumstances."

We had been in Cairo for a week by then, and I really had hopes of getting underway within another fortnight. I had been to Boulaq several times, assisting Reis Hassan—bullying him, as Evelyn quaintly put it. In recent days I had not been able to find him on the boat, although once I saw a flutter of striped petticoat that looked like his disappear over the stern as I approached.

After Gizeh, Hassan was left in peace. I had a new interest—but to call it an interest is to understate my sentiments. I admired, I desired—I lusted after pyramids! We went back to Gizeh. I visited the Second and Third pyramids there. We went to Sakkarah to see the Step Pyramid. There are other pyramids at Sakkarah. Being built of rubble within a facing of stone, unlike the solid-stone pyramids of Gizeh, the smaller Sakkarah pyramids are only heaps of debris now that the outer facing stones have been taken away for building purposes; but I did not care. They were, or had been, pyramids, and pyramids were now my passion. I was determined to get into one of these smaller mounds, whose burial chamber is beautifully inscribed with hieroglyphic picture writing, and I would have done it, too, but for Evelyn. Her outcries, when she saw the funnel-shaped well into which I proposed to lower myself, were terrible to hear. I pointed out that with two men holding the rope I should do quite nicely; but she was adamant. I had to yield when she threatened to follow me down, for I saw that she was appalled at the idea.

Travers was no more sympathetic to my pyramid inquiries. She mourned aloud over the state of my clothes, some of which had to be given away as beyond repair, and she objected to the mementos of bats which I inadvertently carried away from the interiors of the pyramids. One morning, when I proposed a trip to Dahshoor, where there are several splendid pyramids, Evelyn flatly refused. She suggested that instead we visit the museum of Boulaq. I agreed. It was not far from the wharves; I could go and assist Hassan after the museum.

I was looking forward to meeting M. Maspero, the French director of antiquities. My father had been in correspondence with him, and I hoped my name would be familiar. It was; and we were fortunate to find Maspero at the museum. He was usually away, his assistant informed us, digging for the treasures which had made him known throughout the scholarly world.

This assistant, Herr Emil Brugsch, I knew by reputation, for it was he who had been the first European to gaze upon the famous cache of royal mummies that had been discovered a few years earlier. While we waited for M. Maspero, Brugsch told us of the robber family of Thebes who had discovered the hiding place of the mummies ten years before. The discoverer, a shifty character named Abd er-Rasool Ahmed, had been searching for a missing goat amid the rocky cliffs near his village of Gurnah. The goat had fallen into a crevice, or shaft, forty feet deep; upon descending, Ahmed made an incredible discovery—the mummies of the great pharaohs of Egypt, hidden in ancient times to keep their sacred bodies safe from the thieves who had looted their original tombs!

His eyes never leaving my face, Herr Brugsch explained, with affected modesty, that he was responsible for the detective work that had eventually discovered the mummies. Collectors had sent him photographs of objects bearing royal names, and he had realized that these must have come from a tomb. Since the known royal tombs were in Thebes, he had alerted the police to watch out for a peasant from that city who had more money than he could have come by honestly. Thus suspicion was focused on the Abd er-Rasool family; and, the thieves having fallen out in the meantime over the disposition of the loot, one of them betrayed the secret to Brugsch.

I did not care for this gentleman. His brother is a respectable and well-known scholar, and Mr. Emil has been employed by Maspero and his predecessor, M. Mariette, for many years; but his bold stare and hard face affected me unpleasantly, as did his calloused description of the interrogation of the unfortunate Abd er-Rasool brothers. Not a muscle in his tanned face moved as he described beatings with palm rods, and heated pots being placed on the heads of the suspects. Yet I could not help but be fascinated by an eyewitness account of the incredible discovery. Brugsch admitted that his sensations, as he was lowered into the pit, were not wholly comfortable. He was armed, of course, but his weapons would not have availed against treachery, and all the inhabitants of the area hated the representatives of the government. And then his feelings, as he stood in the stifling gloom of the little cave, amid a jumble of royal dead . . . ! He knew the bodies must be moved at once, in order to prevent their being stolen, and he accomplished this difficult task in only eight days. He was describing the northward voyage of the barge—the banks of the river lined with mourning women, rending their garments and pouring dust on their heads as the bodies of the ancient kings floated by—when Maspero joined us.

The director of antiquities was a stout, genial man with twinkling eyes and a short black beard. A true Frenchman, he bowed over my hand and greeted

Evelyn with admiration. He spoke of my father in the highest terms. Seeing how busy he was, we soon excused ourselves, and he begged pardon for not showing us over the museum himself. Perhaps he would join us later, he said, glancing at Evelyn.

"You have made another conquest," I said softly to Evelyn, as we walked away. "M. Maspero could hardly keep his eyes away from you."

"Nor Herr Brugsch his eyes from you," Evelyn replied with a smile. "He was anxious to escort you; did you see his scowl when M. Maspero told him he had work for him to do?"

"Don't try to give your admirers to me," I retorted. "I am not in need of such mendacious flattery; and if I were, Herr Brugsch would not be my choice."

I was glad the director was not with us when we began our tour. Courtesy must have prevented me from telling him what I thought of his museum. Not that the place wasn't fascinating; it contained many marvelous things. But the dust! And the clutter! My housewifely and scholarly instincts were equally offended.

"Perhaps you are not being fair," Evelyn said mildly, when I expressed my feelings. "There are so many objects; new ones are discovered daily; and the museum is still too small, despite the recent enlargement."

"All the more reason for neatness and order. In the early days, when European adventurers took away what they discovered in Egypt, there was no need for a national museum. Then M. Mariette, Maspero's predecessor, insisted that Egypt should keep some of its national treasures. The cooperation between Great Britain and France, to regulate and assist this unfortunate country, has resulted in the French being given control over the antiquities department. I suppose they must have something; after all, we control finance, education, foreign affairs, and other matters. But we could do with a little English neatness here, instead of French nonchalance."

We had penetrated into a back room filled with objects that seemed to be leftovers from the more impressive exhibits in the front halls of the museum—vases, bead necklaces, little carved ushebti figures, flung helter-skelter onto shelves and into cases. There were several other people in the room. I paid them little heed; in mounting indignation, I went on, "They might at least dust! Look at this!"

And, picking up a blue-green statuette from a shelf, I rubbed it with my handkerchief and showed Evelyn the dirty smudge that resulted.

A howl—a veritable animal howl—shook the quiet of the room. Before I could collect myself to search for its source, a whirlwind descended upon me. A sinewy, sun-bronzed hand snatched the statuette from me. A voice boomed in my ear.

"Madam! Do me the favor of leaving those priceless relics alone. It is bad enough to see that incompetent ass, Maspero, jumble them about; will you complete his idiocy by destroying the fragments he has left?"

Evelyn had retreated. I stood alone. Gathering my dignity, I turned to face my attacker.

He was a tall man with shoulders like a bull's and a black beard cut square like those of the statues of ancient Assyrian kings. From a face tanned almost to the shade of an Egyptian, vivid blue eyes blazed at me. His voice, as I had good cause to know, was a deep, reverberating bass. The accents were those of a gentleman. The sentiments were not.

"Sir," I said, looking him up and down. "I do not know you—"

"But I know you, madam! I have met your kind too often—the rampageous British female at her clumsiest and most arrogant. Ye gods! The breed covers the earth like mosquitoes, and is as maddening. The depths of the pyramids, the heights of the Himalayas—no spot on earth is safe from you!"

He had to pause for breath at this point, which gave me the opportunity I had been waiting for.

"And you, sir, are the lordly British male at his loudest and most bad-mannered. If the English gentlewoman is covering the earth, it is in the hope of counteracting some of the mischief her lord and master has perpetrated. Swaggering, loud, certain of his own superiority . . ."

My adversary was maddened, as I had hoped he would be. Little flecks of foam appeared on the blackness of his beard. His subsequent comments were incomprehensible, but several fragile objects vibrated dangerously on their shelves.

I stepped back a pace, taking a firm grip on my parasol. I am not easily cowed, nor am I a small woman; but this man towered over me, and the reddening face he had thrust into mine was suggestive of violence. He had very large, very white teeth, and I felt sure I had gotten a glimpse of most of them.

A hand fell on his shoulder. Looking up, I saw Evelyn with a young man who was a slighter, beardless copy of my adversary—dark-haired, blue-eyed, tall, but not so bulky.

"Radcliffe," he said urgently. "You are alarming this lady. I beg you—"

"I am not at all alarmed," I said calmly. "Except for your friend's health. He seems about to have a fit. Is he commonly subject to weakness of the brain?"

The younger man now had both hands on his companion's shoulders. He did not seem concerned; indeed, he was smiling broadly. He was an attractive young fellow; from the way Evelyn looked at him I suspected she shared my opinion.

"My brother, madam, not my friend," he said cheerfully. "You must forgive him—now, Radcliffe, calm yourself. The museum always has this effect on him," he explained, looking at me. "You must not blame yourself for upsetting him."

"I certainly should not blame myself if my harmless behavior brought on such a violent, inexcusable breach of common courtesy—"

"Amelia!" Evelyn caught my arm as a roar of rage burst from the bearded person. "Let us all be calm, and not provoke one another."

"I am not provoking anyone," I said coolly.

Evelyn exchanged a glance with the young man. As if some message had passed between them, they both moved, the young fellow tugging at his agitated brother, Evelyn using a gentler but equally firm grip to pull me away. The other visitors were watching us with ill-bred curiosity. One lady pulled her companion out of the room. Another couple followed, leaving a single spectator, an Arab in flowing robes, headcloth, and bright-green goggles, who continued to watch the antics of the incomprehensible foreigners with amused contempt.

Rapid footsteps in the hall heralded the arrival of M. Maspero, who had apparently been alarmed by the uproar. When he saw us his pace slowed, and a smile spread over his face.

"Ah, c'est le bon Emerson. I should have known. You have met one another? You are acquainted?"

"We are not acquainted," said the person called Emerson, in a slightly modified shout. "And if you make any attempt to introduce us, Maspero, I shall fell you to the ground!"

M. Maspero chuckled. "Then I will not risk it. Come, ladies, and let me show you some of our finer objects. These are unimportant—a miscellany only."

"But they are most interesting," Evelyn said in her gentle voice. "I admire the soft colors of the jewelry."

"Ah, but these trinkets are not valuable—no gold, only beads and amulets, made of faience, common as sand. We find such bracelets and necklaces by the hundreds."

"Faience?" Evelyn repeated. "Then the lovely coral, the delicate blue-green which resembles turquoise, are not the real stones?"

The black-bearded male person had turned his back on us and was pretending to sneer at a collection of ushebtis; I knew he was eavesdropping, however. His brother was not so rude. The young fellow stood looking shyly at Evelyn, and when she asked about the jewelry he started to answer. The ebullient Maspero anticipated him.

"Mais non, mademoiselle, they are imitations of coral, turquoise, lapis lazuli, made from a colored paste common in ancient Egypt."

"They are lovely, all the same," I said. "And the very age of them staggers the imagination. To think that these beads adorned the slim brown wrist of an Egyptian maiden four thousand years before our Savior was born!"

Blackbeard whirled around. "Three thousand years," he corrected. "Maspero's chronology, like all his work, is inexcusably inaccurate!"

Maspero smiled, but I think his next act was prompted to some extent by the annoyance he was too courteous to express directly. Lifting a necklace of tiny blue and coral beads, he handed it to Evelyn with a courtly bow.

"Keep it as a memento of your visit, if you treasure such things. No, no"—he waved away Evelyn's protests—"it is of no consequence; I only regret I have nothing finer for such a charming lady. For you, too, Mademoiselle Peabody"—and another string of beads was pressed into my hand.

"Oh, but—" I began, with an uneasy glance at the blackbearded person, who was shaking like an engine about to burst.

"Do me the honor," Maspero insisted. "Unless you fear the foolish tales of curses and avenging Egyptian ghosts—"

"Certainly not," I said firmly.

"But what of the curses of M. Emerson?" Maspero asked, his eyes twinkling. *"Regardez*—he is about to say unkind things to me again."

"Never fear," Emerson snarled. "I am leaving. I can only stand so many minutes in this horror house of yours. In God's name, man, why don't you classify your pots?"

He rushed off, pulling his slighter companion with him. The young fellow turned his head; his gaze went straight to Evelyn and remained fixed on her face until he had been removed from the room.

"He has almost the Gallic temperament," said Maspero admiringly. "One observes the magnificence of his rages with respect."

"I cannot agree with you," I said. "Who is the fellow?"

"One of your fellow countryman, dear lady, who has interested himself in the antiquities of this country. He has done admirable work excavating, but I fear he does not admire the rest of us. You heard his abuse of my poor museum. He abuses my excavation methods with the same ardor. But, indeed, there is no archaeologist in Egypt who has been spared his criticism."

"I don't care to speak of him," I said, with a sniff.

"We think your museum is fascinating, M. Maspero," Evelyn added tactfully. "I could spend days here."

We spent several hours more inspecting the exhibits. I would not have said so for the world, but I felt a certain sympathy for the odious Emerson's criticisms. The exhibits were not arranged as methodically as they might have been, and there was dust everywhere.

Evelyn said she was too tired to go down to the boat that day, so we took a carriage back to the hotel. She was pensive and silent during the drive; as we neared Cairo, I said slyly,

"Mr. Emerson's young brother does not have the family temper, I believe. Did you happen to hear his name?"

"Walter," said Evelyn, and blushed betrayingly.

"Ah." I pretended not to notice the blush. "I found him very pleasant. Perhaps we will meet them again at the hotel."

"Oh, no, they do not stay at Shepheard's. Walt—Mr. Walter Emerson explained to me that their money all goes for excavation. His brother is not supported by any institution or museum; he has only a small yearly income and, as Walter says, if he had the wealth of the Indies he would consider it insufficient for his purposes."

"You seem to have covered quite a lot of ground in a very short time," I said, watching Evelyn out of the corner of my eye. "It is a pity we can't continue the acquaintance with the younger Mr. Emerson, and avoid his insane brother."

"I daresay we shall not meet again," Evelyn said softly.

I had my own opinion on that score.

In the afternoon, after a rest, we went to shop for medical supplies. The guidebooks advise travelers to carry a considerable quantity of medicines and drugs, since there are no doctors south of Cairo. I had copied the list of suggested remedies from my guide, and was determined to do the thing properly. If I had not been a woman, I might have studied medicine; I have a natural aptitude for the subject, possessing steady hands and far less squeamishness about blood and wounds than many males of my acquaintance. I planned to buy a few small surgical knives also; I fancied I could amputate a limb—or at least a toe or finger—rather neatly if called upon to do so.

Our dragoman, Michael, accompanied us. I thought he seemed quieter than usual, but I was occupied with my list: blue pills, calomel, rhubarb, Dover's powder, James's powder, carbolic acid, laudanum, quinine, sulfuric acid, ipeca-cuanha. . . . It was Evelyn who asked Michael what the trouble was. He hesitated, looking at us in turn.

"It is my child, who is ill," he said finally. "She is only a girl-child, of course."

The faltering of his voice and his troubled countenance betrayed a paternal emotion that contradicted the words, so I modified what had begun as an indignant comment into an offer of assistance. Michael protested, but it was clear that he would welcome our help. He led us to his home.

It was a narrow old house with the intricately carved wooden balconies that are typical of Old Cairo. It seemed to me appallingly dirty, but compared with the squalor and filth we had seen elsewhere, it could have been worse. The sickroom where the child lay was dreadful. The wooden shutters were closely barred, lest evil spirits enter to harm the child further, and the stench was frightful. I could scarcely see the small sufferer, for the only illumination came from a clay lamp filled with smoking fat, with a wick of twisted cloth. My first move, therefore, was to go to the windows and throw them open.

A wavering shriek of protest arose from the women huddled on the floor. There were six of them, clad in dusty black and doing nothing that I could see except add to the contamination of the air and keep the child awake by their endless wailing. I evicted them. The child's mother I allowed to remain. She was a rather pretty little thing, with great black eyes, and was herself, I suspected, not more than fifteen years of age.

Careless of her dainty gingham skirts, Evelyn was already seated on the floor by the pallet where the child lay. Gently she brushed the tangled black curls from its face and dislodged a cluster of flies swarming around its eyes. The mother made a gesture of protest, but subsided after a frightened glance at me. Evelyn and I had already had cause to be horrified at the way these people allow insects to infest the eyes of the children; I had seen pitiful infants so beset by flies that they looked as if they were wearing black goggles. If they attempted to brush the stinging, filthy creatures away, the mothers slapped their hands. One sees tiny children who have already lost the sight of one or both eyes through this dreadful custom; and, of course, infant mortality is extremely high. One authority claims that three children out of five die young.

I looked at Michael's agonized face, and at the flushed face of the small sufferer, and I decided this was one child that would not succumb if I could help it. How fortunate that we had just come from purchasing medical supplies!

The cause of the child's illness was not hard to discover. She had fallen and cut herself, as children will; infection had entered the wound, which naturally had not been washed or cleaned. One small arm was puffed and swollen. When I cut into the swelling, after disinfecting the knife as best I could, the infected matter spurted out in an evil-smelling flood. I cleaned and dressed the wound, then lectured the distracted parents on the necessity of keeping it clean. Evelyn was a tower of strength. It was not until we got back to the hotel that she was quietly and thoroughly sick. I dismissed Michael for the remainder of the day, telling him to go home and keep his horde of female relatives out of the child's room.

By evening Evelyn was feeling better, and I insisted that we dress and dine downstairs, instead of having a bowl of soup in our room, as she wished to do. Although she never complained, I knew she was often depressed on her own account. We had as yet heard no word of the Earl's fate, but Evelyn expected news of his death daily, and it fretted her tender heart to think of him dying alone. For my part, I felt the old reprobate was meeting the end he richly deserved.

In her soft-rose evening dress, with its wide lace cuffs and ruffled under-skirt, Evelyn looked quite charming; the wistful droop of her mouth only added to her appealing appearance. I put on my crimson satin, feeling we needed something bright and cheerful, although I still felt self-conscious in the dress. We made a fine show. Several of our gentlemen acquaintances followed us into the lounge after dinner, and attempted to win a smile from Evelyn. Suddenly I saw a rosy flush spread over her face. I suspected the cause even before I followed her gaze to the doorway. There stood young Walter Emerson, looking very handsome in evening dress. He had eyes only for Evelyn, and crossed the room so quickly that he nearly stumbled over a low table.

He had brought his brother with him. I had to stifle a laugh at the sight of the irascible Emerson, he wore a look of such gloom. His evening clothes looked as if they had been pulled out of a traveling bag and put on without the benefit of pressing; his collar seemed to be too tight. He had lost all his swagger and shambled along behind Walter like a great black bear, darting suspicious glances at the elegantly garbed travelers around him.

After greeting me hastily, Walter turned to Evelyn and they were soon deep in conversation. The other gentlemen, being ignored, faded away; and I was left face-to-face with Emerson. He stood looking down at me with an expression of sullen dejection.

"I am to make my apologies," he growled.

"I accept them," I said, and indicated the place next to me on the sofa. "Do sit down, Mr. Emerson. I am surprised to see you here. I understood that social life was not to your taste."

"It was Walter's idea," said Emerson bluntly. He sat down, edging as far away from me as the limited confines of the sofa would allow. "I hate such things."

"What things?" I inquired, enjoying myself hugely. It was delightful to see the arrogant Emerson cowed by society.

"The hotel. The people. The—the—in short, all this."

He waved a contemptuous hand at the handsome chamber and its finely dressed occupants.

"Where would you rather be?" I asked.

"Anywhere in Egypt but here. Specifically, at the site of my excavations."

"In the dust of the desert, away from all the comforts of civilization? With only ignorant Arabs for company—"

"Ignorant perhaps; but lacking the hypocrisies of civilization. Good God, how it maddens me to hear the smug comments of English travelers concerning the 'natives,' as they call them! There are good and bad among the Egyptians, as there are in any race; but by and large they are an admirable people, friendly, cheerful, loyal, intelligent—when taught. . . . For centuries these people were oppressed by a vicious, cruel despotism. They are riddled by disease, poverty, and ignorance, but through no fault of their own."

He was recovering his confidence. His fists clenched on his knees, he glared at me. I rather liked him for his defense of an oppressed people, but I could not resist baiting him.

"Then you should approve of what we British are doing in Egypt. By assuming responsibility for the finances of the country—"

"Bah," said Emerson vigorously. "Do you think we are acting out of benevolence? Ask the inhabitants of Alexandria how they enjoyed being shelled by British gunboats, two years ago. We are not so uncivilized as the Turk, but we have the same purpose—our own self-interest. And we are letting those imbecile French mismanage the antiquities department! Not that our own so-called scholars are any better."

"Are they all wrong?" I inquired. "All but you?"

My irony went unnoticed. Emerson considered the question seriously.

"There is one young fellow—Petrie is his name—who seems to have some idea of method in archaeology. He is excavating in the Delta this winter. But he has no influence; and meanwhile every year, every passing day sees destruction that cannot be remedied. We are destroying the past! Digging like children for treasure, wrenching objects out of the ground without keeping proper records of how and where they were found. . . ."

I glanced at Evelyn. I could not hear what she and Walter were discussing, Emerson's voice was too loud, but she seemed to find the conversation enjoyable. I turned my attention back to Emerson, who was still ranting.

". . . scraps of pottery! Something should be done with pottery, you know. One should study the various types—discover what kinds of pottery accompany certain kinds of ornaments, weapons, furnishings. . . ."

"For what purpose?"

"Why, there are a dozen purposes. Pottery, like other objects, changes and develops with time. We could work out a basic chronological sequence which would enable us to date not only the pottery, but other objects found with it. And it is not only pottery that can be useful. Every object, every small scrap of the past can teach us something. Most of these objects are now tossed into rubbish heaps, or carried off by ignorant tourists, lost forever to science. Maspero saves only the impressive objects, and half of those are lost or smashed or stolen, in that reputed museum of his."

"I understand," I said. "For example, studies might be made of anatomical remains. The race to which the ancient Egyptians belonged might be ascertained, and the racial mixtures. Are they the same stock today as they were in ancient times? But scholars do not collect bones and mummies, do they, except to display the latter as curiosities."

Emerson's jaw dropped. "Good God," he said. "A woman with an inquiring mind? Is it possible?"

I overlooked the insult, having become interested in what he was saying. I was about to pursue the subject further when there was a dramatic interruption.

Evelyn was sitting next to the sofa, with Walter leaning on the back of her chair. She suddenly started to her feet. Turning, I saw that her face had gone white as linen. She was staring with a fixed look of horror toward the entrance to the room.

I glanced about. The room was crowded with people, but I saw nothing that might explain her agitation. Before I could make a more searching perusal, Evelyn had collapsed onto the floor. When Walter, clumsy with agitation, managed to reach her and raise her in his arms, she was in a dead faint, from which she was restored with some difficulty.

She would not answer our questions; she was only capable of reiterating her desire to return to our rooms.

"Let me carry you," Walter begged. "You are no burden; you cannot walk—"

He put out his arms. She shrank back, as if he had offered to strike her.

"No, no," she gasped. "Amelia will help me. I can walk, indeed I can. Pray do not touch me."

Poor Walter was as white as Evelyn. But there was nothing to be done but accede to her wishes. She walked, falteringly, but without any assistance except mine, to the stairs. As we started up, I had only time to assure Walter that I would let him know next morning how Evelyn was, if he cared to come by.

My maid was waiting when we reached our rooms. Evelyn rejected her attentions, which were given grudgingly enough; she seemed to shrink from any company but mine, but still refused to tell me what was wrong. At her request, I dismissed Travers, telling her to go to bed.

"I believe I will send Travers home," I said, seeking to strike a casual note, since Evelyn would not talk of the matter uppermost in both our minds. "She hates everything—the country, the Egyptians, the boat—"

"And me," said Evelyn, with a faint smile.

"She doesn't think highly of me, either," I said, pleased to see Evelyn regaining her spirits. "We can manage without her quite nicely. I shall make arrangements tomorrow. Evelyn, won't you tell me now—"

"Later," Evelyn said. "I will explain later, Amelia, when I have. . . . Won't you return to the saloon? You were having such a nice talk with Mr. Emerson. I am sure he is still there. You might reassure him and his. . . . You might reassure them, and make my apologies. I am well; I only need rest. I will go straight to bed. I really am quite well."

This speech, delivered in a rapid monotone, was quite unlike the girl I had come to know. I looked at her searchingly; she refused to meet my eyes. I started to speak, fully prepared to break down a reticence which now alarmed me; then came a loud knock at the door of the sitting room.

Evelyn started convulsively. A renewed pallor spread over her face. I stared at her, too bewildered to speak. Who could this visitor be, who knocked so peremptorily? And at such an hour! It was not too late for evening social activities, but it was certainly too late for anyone to be coming to our rooms. I could not believe that Walter's anxiety would drive him to such a step. Moreover, it was clear from Evelyn's demeanor that she suspected who the visitor might be, and that her suspicion caused her deep dread.

Her eyes met mine. Her shoulders straightened, and she set her lips in a firm line before she opened them to speak. "Open the door, Amelia, if you will be so good. I am being a miserable coward. I must face this."

I suppose her speech conveyed a clue to my mind. I remember I felt no surprise when I opened the door and saw the man who stood there. I had never seen him before, but his swarthy complexion, his sleek black hair, his bold good looks confirmed the suspicion Evelyn's manner had aroused.

"Ah," I said. "Signor Alberto, I presume."

Chapter Three

ALBERTO placed one hand on his heart and bowed. His look, as well as his manner, verged on insolence; and as his eyes moved from my face toward the inner doorway where Evelyn stood, pale and still as a statue, it was all I could do not to slap him.

"You invite me in?" he asked, looking at me. "I think you prefer I would not speak of matters close to our hearts except in the privacy."

I stepped back; silently I motioned him in; gently I closed the door behind him. I wanted to slam it. Alberto rushed toward Evelyn.

"Ah, my lost darling, my heart's beloved! How can you desert me? How can you leave me with agony for your fate?"

Evelyn raised her hand. Alberto stopped, a few feet away from her. I really believe the rascal would have taken her into his arms if she had not moved. Now he cocked his head on one side and said, in tones of deep reproach, "You push me! You crush me! Ah, I understand. You have found a rich protectress. She gave you gifts and you abandon the poor lover who give only love."

My parasol was standing in the corner. I went and got it. Evelyn was silent throughout; I think she was too thunderstruck at the man's insolence to speak. I approached Alberto and jabbed him in the waistcoat with my parasol. He jumped back.

"That will do," I said briskly. "You abandoned this lady; she did not abandon you, although she would have been wise to do so. How dare you come here after writing that abominable message to her, after taking all her possessions—"

"Message?" Alberto rolled his eyes. "I leave no message. Going out, to seek employment, so I buy food for my beloved, I was strike by a horse while I cross the street. Weeks I lie in the terrible hospital, in delirious, crying out for my Evelyn. When I recover, I stagger to the room which was my paradise. But she is gone! My angel has flow away. I leave no message! If there is message my enemy must leave it. I have many enemy. Many who hate me, who try to steal my happiness, who envy me my angel."

He looked meaningfully at me.

I have rarely seen such an unconvincing dramatic performance. Yet I was not sure it might not convince Evelyn; love has a most unfortunate effect on the brain, and I feared some lingering fondness for the rascal might still move her.

I need not have feared. Evelyn's color had returned; indeed, her cheeks were flushed becomingly with an emotion that I recognized to be anger.

"How dare you?" she said in a low voice. "Have you not done me enough harm? Oh, you are right to reproach me; I deserve your contempt. Not for having left you, but for ever coming away with you in the first place. But how dare you come here and insinuate such things about this lady? You are not worthy to occupy the same room with her. Begone, and never trouble my sight again!"

Alberto staggered back a few paces. He was counterfeiting shock and anguish, but the ferrule of the umbrella, which I had against his stomach, might have assisted his retreat.

"You cannot speak with true meaning. You are sick. No—you do not understand. I come to marry you. I offer you my hand and name. There is no other way for you. No other man marry you now, not when he know—"

He was an agile fellow; he jumped nimbly back as I tried to bring the parasol down on his head, and when I raised it for a second attempt, Evelyn caught at my arm.

"Pray don't break a good parasol," she said, with a curling lip. "He is not worth it."

"But he is trying to blackmail you," I said, panting with rage. "He is threatening you with exposure unless you agree—"

"He may publish my infamy to the world," Evelyn said coldly. "Believe me, Amelia, he has no more power over me. If any lingering trace of fondness had remained, this would have ended it."

Smoothing down his hair, which had been disarranged by his rapid movement, Alberto stared at us in affected horror.

"Blackmail? Threat? *Dio mio,* how you do not understand me? I would not—"

"You had better not," I interrupted. "The first sign of trouble from you, you rascal, and I'll have you put in prison. Egyptian prisons are vastly uncomfortable, I am told, and I have a good deal more influence with the present government than you do."

Alberto drew himself up.

"Now you threaten me," he said with satisfaction. "No need for threat. If the lady do not want me, I go. I come only for honor. I see now. I understand. There is another! It is true, no? Who is he, this villain who steal my darling's heart?"

Evelyn, who had born up magnificently, now showed signs of breaking— which was no wonder.

"I can't stand any more of this," she whispered. "Amelia, can we not make him go away? Can we call for help?"

"Certainly," I said.

I passed Alberto—who drew back nervously—and threw open the door. There is usually a floor attendant on duty, and I meant to summon him. But there was no need. Sitting on the floor, across the hall from our door, was our dragoman, Michael. I did not stop to ask why he was there. He leaped to his feet when he saw me, and I beckoned him in.

"Take this man by the collar and throw him out," I said, gesturing at Alberto.

Michael looked surprised, but he did not hesitate. As he reached out for Alberto, the latter stepped back.

"No need, I go, I go," he exclaimed. "I leave Egypt. My heart is broke, my life is—"

"Never mind that," I said. "One question before you go. How did you find us here, and how did you get the money to follow us?"

"But I go to the British consul at Rome, what else? I work way on boat—I am seasick, I am cold, but I work to follow my heart's—"

"Enough of that. Go, now, or Michael will—"

"I go." Alberto drew himself up. He rolled his eyes one last time at Evelyn; then Michael took a step forward, and Alberto bolted out the door with more speed than dignity.

"I follow, to be sure he is gone," said Michael.

"Thank you," Evelyn said gratefully. "Your little girl, Michael—how is she? Did you want us to come to her again?"

"No," Michael said. "No, lady. I come to tell you she is better. She wakes up, she asks for food. I come to thank you; to tell you when you want anything from Michael, you ask, even if it is his life. Now I will follow the evil man."

With a gesture that oddly combined humility and dignity, he departed; and as the door closed, Evelyn broke into a storm of weeping.

The storm was soon over. While I rushed around searching for smelling salts and handkerchiefs, Evelyn recovered herself and insisted that I sit down. She relieved me of my parasol, which I was still holding.

"You are more upset than you will admit," she said. "Let me order you a glass of wine."

"No, there is no need. But perhaps you—"

"No." Evelyn sat down and looked at me steadily. "My predominant emotion, strangely, is one of relief. I feel as if I had exorcised some evil spirit."

"It was Alberto you saw in the lounge, when you fainted."

"Yes. You will not believe me, Amelia; but when I saw him standing there, watching me with that insolent sneering smile, I thought him a demon of the mind, conjured up to remind me of my past. I was so happy just then, with—with—"

"With Walter. Why do you shrink from speaking his name? Do you love him?"

"I cannot use that word; not after. . . . But, yes; I could love him, if I had the right to love any decent man."

"Oh, come, you are being absurdly melodramatic! We are almost in the twentieth century; abandon your old-fashioned morality."

"Do you think Walter would ask me to marry him if he knew of my past?"

Well . . ." I shrugged uncomfortably. "He seems a nice young man, but he is a man, after all. But why should he ever know?"

There was no need for Evelyn to answer. He would know because she would tell him. Candor was an integral part of her nature. She smiled sadly at me.

"Let us change the subject, Amelia. All I meant to say was that I was foolishly relieved to find Alberto mere flesh and blood. We have finished with him now; but how amazing that he should actually follow me here!"

"Yes, I wonder . . ."

"What?"

"If perhaps your grandfather had not recovered after all."

Evelyn gasped. "Heavens, Amelia, how cynical! And how clever of you. Oh, how I hope it may be so!"

"Do not hope too much. I daresay there are other, equally cynical reasons that may explain Alberto's appearance here. I shall take steps, tomorrow, to see what I can find out. I must also go to Boulaq and hurry Reis Hassan. The sooner we leave Cairo, the better for both of us."

"Yes," Evelyn said, smiling wistfully. "It is becoming crowded with people whom I do not wish to see. But Walter will not be here much longer. He and Mr. Emerson are leaving in two days."

"Where do they go?"

"I cannot remember the name. It is several hundred miles to the south; the remains of the city of the heretic pharaoh."

"Amarna," I said. "Yes. Well, child, let us go to bed. It has been a tiring day."

But the day was not yet over.

Evelyn dropped off to sleep almost at once. She was worn out, poor girl, by her emotional experiences. I could hear her quiet breathing as I lay sleepless under my canopy of white netting. Her bed and canopy were across the room from mine, which stood near the window. There was a small balcony outside. I had left the shutters open, as I always did; the netting protected us from insects, and the night air was particularly sweet and cool. Moonlight streamed in through the window, illumining the objects in its path but leaving the corners of the large room deep in shadow. A ray of silver light shone distractingly on my bed.

I am not often unable to sleep, but the events of the day had given considerable food for thought. Oddly enough, I found my self principally preoccupied with the exasperating Mr. Emerson and his peculiar ideas. Peculiar—but stimulating. I thought about them for some time; and then forcibly turned my thoughts to more important matters.

Walter and Evelyn. . . . Now there was a worrying subject. If she had been what she pretended to be, an impoverished gentlewoman serving as my companion, a marriage between the two might have been eminently suitable. But I suspected that the elder Mr. Emerson controlled his young brother; that there was not sufficient income to support a wife for Walter and an archaeological expedition for Emerson, and that, if a choice had to be made, Emerson would have the deciding vote. And poor Evelyn was right; she would have to tell Walter the truth, and I doubted that any man would take it in the proper way. He might marry her and then spend the rest of his life nobly forgiving her. Nothing can be more infuriating than being forgiven over and over again.

I turned restlessly in my bed. The springs squeaked and something outside the window—a night bird, or an insect—squeaked as if in answer. I turned over on my side, with my back to the brilliant moonlight, and lay still, determined to woo sleep. Instead, my thoughts turned to Alberto, and I began to speculate about his motive for following Evelyn. I could not credit the creature with the slightest degree of altruism or love; he must have another reason for pursuing her. I thought of several possible answers. No doubt he had other prospects in mind when he deserted her. Perhaps one such scheme had brought him to Egypt, the destination of so many travelers from Italy, and, finding Evelyn under the protection of a wealthy woman—for so I must seem to him—he had decided to see what could be gotten from me.

With such thoughts churning around in my mind I was no nearer sleep than I had been. They distracted me from the usual night noises, however; I was unaware of extraneous sounds until one sudden noise, close at hand, struck my ear. It was a squeaking sound from one of the boards of the floor. I knew it well; the faulty plank was between my bed and the window, and my foot had pressed it several times that day.

I turned onto my back. I was not alarmed; I assumed that either I had been mistaken about the origin of the sound or that Evelyn had waked up and crept to the window for a view of the moonlit garden.

Standing over the bed, so close that its body brushed the folds of white netting, was an incredible apparition.

It appeared to be swathed in a white mist, like an emanation of fog. This blurred the features, but the general outline of the figure was plain enough. It might have walked out of the main hall of the Boulaq museum, where Maspero kept his prized, life-sized statues of ancient Egyptian ladies and gentlemen. Like the painted statues, this apparition had the hues of life, though they were faded by the cold moonlight. The bronzed body, bare to the waist; the broad collar of orange and blue beads; the folded linen headdress, striped in red and white.

I was thunderstruck. But not by fear—no, never suppose for a moment that I was afraid! I was simply paralyzed by surprise. The figure stood utterly motionless. I could not even detect the rise and fall of its breast. It lifted an arm, then, in a gesture of unmistakable menace.

I sat up and, with a shout, reached out for the thing. I do not believe in apparitions. I wanted to get my hands on it, to feel the warmth and solidity of human flesh. Unfortunately, I had forgotten the confounded mosquito netting.

(My Critic reminds me that "confounded" is not a word a lady should use. I reply that some strong expression is called for, and that I have avoided others far stronger.)

It was the netting, of course, that had given the apparition its ghostly aura, and it fit so well with the presumed supernatural appearance of the thing that I had forgotten its existence. I plunged head foremost into a muffling cloud of fabric; the bed sheet and the skirts of my nightgown wound about my limbs. By the time I had fought my way out of these encumbrances I was gasping for breath—and the room was empty. I had succeeded only in waking Evelyn, who was calling out agitatedly and trying to escape her own netting.

We met at the window; Evelyn caught me by the shoulders and tried to shake me. I must have looked like a wild woman with my hair breaking loose from its night braids and streaming over my shoulders. My determined rush toward the window had persuaded Evelyn, as she later confessed, that I was bent upon self-destruction.

After I had assured myself that there was no trace of the visitant on the balcony or in the garden below, I explained to Evelyn what had happened. She had lighted a candle. By its flame I saw her expression, and knew what she was about to say.

"It was no dream," I insisted. "It would not be surprising that I should dream of ancient Egyptian ghosts; but I believe I know the difference between reality and sleep."

"Did you pinch yourself?" Evelyn inquired seriously.

"I had not time to pinch myself," I said, pacing angrily up and down. "You see the torn netting—"

"I believe you fought a gallant fight with the bed sheets and the netting," Evelyn said. "Real objects and those seen in dreams blend into one another—"

I let out a loud exclamation. Evelyn looked alarmed, fearing she had offended me; but it was not her disbelief that had prompted my cry. Bending over, I picked up from the floor the hard object that my bare instep had painfully pressed upon. In silence I held it out for Evelyn's inspection.

It was a small ornament, about an inch long, made of blue-green faience, in the shape of the hawk god, Horus—the kind of ornament that often hangs on necklaces worn by the ancient Egyptian dead.

II

I was more determined than ever to leave Cairo. Of course I did not believe in ghosts. No; some malignant human agent had been at work in the moonlit room, and that worried me a good deal more than ghosts. I thought immediately of Alberto as a possible culprit, but there really seemed no reason why he should undertake such a bizarre trick. His was not the type of the murderer; he was vicious, but weak. And what would it profit him to murder either Evelyn or myself?

A criminal of another kind might hope to profit, however, and I came to the conclusion that my visitor had been a would-be thief, a little more imaginative than his fellows, who hoped by his imitation of an ancient Egyptian to confound a wakeful victim long enough to effect his escape. It was a rather ingenious idea, really; I almost wished I could meet the inventive burglar.

I decided not to summon the police. The Egyptian police are perfectly useless, and I had not seen the man's face closely enough to identify him, even supposing that the authorities could track one man through the teeming streets of Cairo. The man would not return; he had found me wakeful and threatening, and he would look for easier prey.

Having come to this conclusion, I was somewhat easier in my mind, so I explained it all to Evelyn, hoping to calm her nerves. She agreed with my deductions, but I think she still half believed I had been dreaming.

I did take the precaution of investigating Alberto's activities. I was unable to discover where he had been staying. There are hundreds of small inns in Cairo, and presumably he had used one of these, for he certainly had not been observed in any of the European hotels. I did learn, however, that a man of his description had taken a ticket on the morning train for Alexandria, and I decided that we could dismiss Alberto from our thoughts.

Walter was not so easy to dismiss. He called next morning, as early as was decently possible. Evelyn refused to see him. I understood, and commended, her motives; the less she saw of him, the easier the eventual parting would be. Not knowing her true feelings, Walter naturally misunderstood. I assured him that physically she was recovered and then informed him she could not receive visitors. What else could he assume but that she did not want to see *him*? He even went so far as to ask whether it was some act of his that had brought on her fainting fit the night before. I assured him that this was not so, but the poor lad was unconvinced. Looking like a wan Byronic hero, he asked me to say goodbye to Evelyn for him. He and his brother were leaving next day for their dig.

I felt so sorry for the young fellow I almost blurted out part of the truth; but I knew I had no right to violate Evelyn's confidence. So I went upstairs, to console the other half of the pair of heartbroken lovers, and a tedious business it was too, when a little common sense on both parts would have settled the matter to the satisfaction of all.

With Michael's assistance I contrived to hurry the boat crew. Michael's newborn devotion was complete; he did everything he could to assist us, although at times I think he shared the opinion of the men—that I was an interfering, illogical female. One of my acquaintances at Shepheard's had informed me I had made an error in selecting a Christian as my dragoman, for the Copts are not accepted as readily as coreligionists by Moslem crews and captains. However, Reis Hassan and Michael seemed to get on well enough, and the preparations proceeded apace. The piano was moved into the saloon, and the curtains were hung; they looked very handsome. The crew began to straggle in from their home villages. I sent Travers off to England, and saw her go with no regrets.

We were very busy during those days, shopping for more supplies and visiting Michael, where we played with the little girl and practiced our Arabic on the ladies of the household; having the piano tuned, paying final visits to Gizeh (I went in the Great Pyramid again, but Evelyn would not), going to the museum several more times, and making calls on the British authorities. I found another of my father's old acquaintances in the finance ministry; he scolded me for not having called earlier so that he could have the opportunity of entertaining me. He was very kind; so much so, that I began to feel uncomfortable at the way his eyes examined me. Finally he burst out,

"My dear Miss Amelia, you really have changed; are you aware of how much you have changed? The air of Egypt must agree with you; you seem much younger than you did when I last saw you in Sussex."

I was wearing a dress Evelyn had selected for me, a mustard-yellow foulard trimmed in green, with draped skirts.

"Fine feathers, my dear sir," I said briskly. "They are becoming even to elderly hens. Now, I wonder if you could help me—"

I had come, of course, to find out about Evelyn's grandfather. I could see that my friend was surprised at my interest, but he was too much of a gentleman to ask the cause. He informed me that word of the earl's death had reached him within the past fortnight. He knew no details, only the bare fact; it was not a subject of consuming interest to him. I was inhibited because I could not ask the questions I needed to ask without betraying Evelyn's secret. I did not want her identity to become known in Egypt, since we proposed to spend the rest of the winter there. So I had to go away with my curiosity partially unsatisfied.

However, I was able to meet Major—now Sir Evelyn—Baring, the consul general and British agent, who came into the office as I was leaving it. He reminded me of my brothers. Solid British respectability lay upon him like a coating of dust. His neat moustache, his gold-rimmed pince-nez, the rounded configuration of his impeccably garbed form, all spoke of his reliability, capability, and dullness. However, he had done an admirable job of trying to restore financial stability to a country heavily in debt, and even when I met him he was known to be the chief power in Egypt. He was faultlessly courteous to me, assuring me of his willingness to be of assistance in any possible way. He had known my father, he said, by reputation. I was beginning to get an image of my dear papa sitting quietly in the center of a web whose strands extended all over the globe.

We planned to leave on the Friday. It was on the Thursday evening that our visitor arrived, and conversation with him made clear several points that had hitherto been cloudy—and raised new problems not so easily solved.

We were in the lounge; I had insisted we go down. Evelyn had been pensive and sad all day, brooding about her grandfather and, I suspected, about the thought of Walter speeding southward away from her. The Emersons did not hire even a small dahabeeyah; Walter had explained that they rented space on a steamer which carried their supplies, and that they slept on deck with the crew, rolled in their blankets. I thought of my delicate Evelyn living in such conditions and could not wholly regret the loss of Walter.

We were both tired, having been occupied all day with such last-minute details as always occur when one prepares for a journey; and I believe I was dozing just a little when an exclamation from Evelyn aroused me. For a moment I thought we were about to have a repetition of the evening of Alberto's appearance. Evelyn had risen to her feet and was staring toward the door. Her expression was not so much one of alarm, however, as of disbelief; and when I turned to see the cause of her amazement, I beheld a young gentleman coming quickly toward us, a broad smile on his face and his hand extended in greeting.

He seemed for a moment as if he would embrace her. Propriety prevailed; but he took her limp hand in both his big brown ones and wrung it enthusiastically.

"Evelyn! My dear girl! You cannot imagine the relief, the pleasure. . . . How could you frighten me so?"

"And you cannot imagine my surprise," Evelyn exclaimed. "What on earth are you doing here?"

"Following you, of course, what other reason could I have? I could not rest while I was in doubt as to your safety. But we forget ourselves, Evelyn." He turned to me with the same broad smile. "I need not ask; this must be Miss Peabody. The kindly, the noble, the greathearted Miss Peabody, to whom I owe my dear cousin's recovery. Oh, yes I know all! I visited the British consul in Rome; that is how I traced your here. And knowing what that gentleman did not, of the circumstances that had brought Evelyn to Rome—no, Cousin, we will not speak of them, not now or ever again; but knowing of them I am able to give Miss Peabody's conduct the credit it deserves. My dear Miss Peabody! Excuse me, but I cannot restrain my enthusiasm; I am an enthusiastic fellow!"

Seizing my hand, he wrung it as thoroughly as he had wrung Evelyn's, beaming like a younger edition of the immortal Pickwick all the while.

"Really, sir," I said. "I am quite overwhelmed—"

"I know, I know." Dropping my hand, the young gentleman burst into the jolliest peal of laughter imaginable. "I do overwhelm people. I can't help it. Please sit down, ladies, so that I may do so; then we will have a pleasant talk."

"Perhaps you might even consider introducing yourself," I suggested, tenderly massaging my fingers.

"Forgive me, Amelia," Evelyn exclaimed. "Let me present my cousin, Mr. Lucas Hayes."

"*I* will let you; whether *he* will be silent long enough to be presented, I don't know." I looked keenly at the young man, who was smiling broadly, undisturbed by my sharpness. "But I fancy it is no longer Mr. Hayes. Should I not say 'your lordship?' "

A shadow clouded Evelyn's face. The new earl leaned over and patted her hand.

"*You* will say Lucas, I hope, Miss Peabody. I feel I know you so well! And it may be painful for Evelyn to be reminded of her loss. I see the news has reached you."

"We only learned of it a few days ago," Evelyn said. "I had tried to prepare myself, but. . . . Please tell me about it, Lucas. I want to hear everything."

"You are sure you wish to?"

"Oh, yes. I must hear every detail, even if it is painful to me; and although I know I should not, I cannot help hoping that he forgave me, at the end . . . that he had time for one kind word, one message. . . ."

She leaned forward, her hands clasped, her blue eyes misty with tears. She looked very pretty and appealing; the young earl's face reflected his admiration.

"Evelyn, I am sure he felt kindness, even though. . . . But I will tell you all. Only let me marshal my thoughts."

While he marshaled them I had leisure to study him with a curiosity I made no attempt to conceal. He was a tall, broad-shouldered young chap, dressed with an elegance that verged on foppishness. His patent leather boots shone like glass; his waistcoat was embroidered with rosebuds. A huge diamond glittered in the midst of an immense expanse of snowy shirt front, and his trousers were so close-fitting that when he sat down I expected something to rip. The candid cheerfulness of his face was very English, but his swarthy complexion and large dark eyes betrayed his father's nationality. I looked then at his hands. They were well shaped, if rather large and brown, and were as well tended as a woman's. I always think hands are so expressive of character. I had noticed that Emerson's were heavy with calluses and disfigured with the scars and scratches of manual labor.

There is no use trying to conceal from the reader that I found myself illogically prejudiced against my new acquaintance. I say illogically, because his manner thus far had been irreproachable, if ebullient. His subsequent speeches proved him to be a man of honor and of heart. Still, I did not like him.

Lucas began his explanation.

"You know, I imagine, that after your—your departure, our revered progenitor fell into such a rage that he suffered a stroke. We did not expect that he would recover from it, but the old gentleman had amazing powers of recuperation; I have noted that a vicious temper does seem to give its possessors unusual strength. . . . Now, Evelyn, you mustn't look at me so reproachfully. I had some affection for our grandfather, but I cannot overlook his treatment of you. You must allow me an occasional word of criticism.

"When I heard what had transpired, I went at once to Ellesmere Castle. I was not the only one to respond; you, who know our family, can imagine the scene of pandemonium I found on my arrival. Aunts and uncles and cousins of every degree had descended, like the scavengers they are—eating and drinking as hard as they could, and trying every despicable stratagem to get into the sickroom, where the sufferer lay like a man in a beleaguered fort. I couldn't decide which of them was the worst. Our second cousin Wilfred tried to bribe the nurse; Aunt Marian sat in a chair outside the door and had to be pushed back whenever it was opened; young Peter Forbes, at his mother's instigation, climbed the ivy outside the window of the sickroom and was only repelled by the footman and your humble servant."

The waiter coming by at that moment, Lucas ordered coffee. He caught my eye and burst into another of those hearty peals of laughter.

"My dear Miss Peabody, you have a countenance as expressive as an open book. I can read your thoughts; shall I tell you what you are thinking? You are thinking that I am the pot that calls the kettles black—that I am as thorough a scavenger as the rest. And, of course, you are absolutely correct! I respected our grandfather for his good qualities. He had a few; if I had more time, I might be able to recall one of them. . . . No, dear Miss Peabody, frankness is my worst failing. I cannot pretend to emotions I do not feel, even to improve my position in the world, and I will not be such a hypocrite as to pretend I loved our Grandfather. Evelyn is a little saint; she would find some excuse for a man who knocked her down and trampled on her. . . ."

He broke off as I made a warning gesture. Evelyn's face was flushed; her eyes were fixed on her hands, folded tightly in her lap.

"Evelyn is a saint," Lucas repeated more emphatically. "Only a saint could have loved Grandfather. But I could not help feeling sorry for the old gentleman just then. It is pitiable to lie dying and have no one there who loves you.

"I was in a stronger position than my fellow scavengers, for I was the heir, and the doctors and lawyers who surrounded my grandfather knew this. While he was incapable of speech or movement, the authority was mine, and I exercised it to rid the house of the family. If curses have any effect, I am due to perish miserably. But I did not care for that; and I cannot help but think that the silence and peace I produced in the castle helped Grandfather's recovery. For, to the astonishment of the doctors, he began to mend. Within a few weeks he was tottering around his room swearing at the nurses and throwing crockery at his valet as was his endearing habit. However, the doctors had warned him that any exertion or emotion might bring on another stroke and this one would certainly be fatal.

"One of his first acts, Evelyn, on your departure, was to call his solicitor and make a new will. You know that; you know that he left you five pounds with which to buy a mourning ring. He had made me his heir—not through affection, but because he detested the other relatives even more than he did me. When he recovered sufficiently, I at once spoke to him of the impropriety of his treatment of you. I had no objection to inheriting, but there was plenty for both of us, and I could not enjoy my share if I thought you were in need.

"Needless to say, my interference was received without favor. Indeed, I had to abandon the attempt for fear of bringing on another seizure. Dear Grandfather hinted to me that I ought to leave, but I had the concurrence of his medical advisers when I remained in spite of the hints. He was still rather feeble, and it was necessary to spare him as much as possible. I was the only one with the proper authority to fend off annoying visitors, and I exercised it to the full.

"I honestly did believe that he was beginning to soften toward you, until . . . It happened one afternoon when I was away from the house. It was virtually the first time I had left, and I had business. . . . Ah, well, let me be candid. I needed amusement. It had been a dreary month. I blame myself; for in my absence Grandfather dragged his poor old bones from his bed and set the servants to packing your belongings. Nothing of any value, alas; only your clothing and ornaments, and the dozens of little trinkets and mementos he had given you. Not a single one was missed; I was told that Grandfather stormed in and out of your rooms gathering up objects and throwing them into boxes. A demonic energy had seized him; by the time I returned home, the boxes had been packed, corded, and dispatched by the local carter. The castle was swept clean of any object that could remind him of you; and he had collapsed, like the old bundle of bones he was. The house was in an uproar, with doctors arriving and conferring, the servants in hysterics, and snow falling heavily, as in a scene from a dreary novel. It was frightful!

"From that evening, Grandfather never recovered. By morning he was much worse, and although he tried once or twice to speak, he never uttered a consecutive sentence. But, dearest Evelyn, I am convinced he wanted to speak of you. I am sure he forgave you and wanted you back. I hope you will believe that."

Evelyn's head was bowed. Crystal drops splashed down onto her hands.

"A very affecting narrative," I said drily. "Evelyn, you will spoil that dress. Satin water-stains badly."

Evelyn took a deep breath and dabbed at her eyes. Lucas had the effrontery to wink at me. I ignored him.

"Well," I said "that solves one problem, does it not, Evelyn? The motives of our visitor become more comprehensible. The individual to whom I refer had not heard of the final fatality, but was informed of the preceding recovery. Hope springs eternal."

"You need not be so tactful," Evelyn said dully. "Lucas must know to whom we refer. His manner has been generosity itself, but I will not insult him by glossing over my dreadful—"

"You will insult me if you ever refer to the matter again," Lucas interrupted. "The past is finished; unless I should be fortunate enough to encounter a certain individual someday in a quiet spot. . . . Evelyn, let me finish my narrative. You have heard the distressing part, let me proceed to happier matters."

"Happier?" Evelyn smiled sadly.

"Happier, I hope. I hope you cannot be insensible to my actions, my feelings. . . . As soon as the obsequies of our ancestors had been celebrated, I set out in pursuit of you. And here I am, only waiting for your consent to share our fortune—I cannot call it mine—and, if you will, our title, our lives, and our name!"

He leaned back in his chair, beaming on both of us like a youthful Father Christmas.

I really did have a hard time maintaining my dislike of Mr. Lucas; my prejudices struggled and were almost subdued. The offer was magnificent, noble; and it was made with a delicacy I would not have believed possible.

Then the meaning of Lucas's last phrase penetrated my brain, and I exclaimed, "Sir, are you proposing marriage?"

"I don't think my words are open to any other interpretation," said Lucas, grinning broadly.

Evelyn sat openmouthed and staring. Twice she tried to speak; twice her voice failed her. Then she cleared her throat, and on the third attempt succeeded.

"Lucas, this is too much. I cannot believe—you cannot mean—"

"Why not?" Leaning forward, he captured her hands in his. "We were meant for each other, Evelyn. Common sense, worldly values and, I hope, mutual affection design us for one another. Oh, I know you don't love me. I know your heart is bruised and fearful. Let me offer it a refuge in my heart! Let me teach you to love me as I adore you."

His intense dark eyes shone with an ardent light; his handsome features were set in an expression of tenderness. I really did not see how a girl could resist him. But, as I had learned, Evelyn was made of sterner stuff than she appeared. And, as I was about to learn, the sentiment that had entered her heart was stronger than I had supposed.

"Lucas," she said gently. "I cannot tell you how much your offer moves me. All my life I will honor and revere you as one of the noblest gentlemen of my acquaintance. But I cannot marry you."

"If you fear censure—" Lucas began.

"I do fear it—for your sake rather than my own. But that is not why I refuse your generous offer. I will never marry. There is an image enshrined in my heart—"

Lucas dropped her hands. His expression was one of disbelief.

"Not that wretched—"

"No." Evelyn flushed. "Certainly not."

"I am relieved to hear it!" Lucas looked thoughtful. Then his face cleared. "Dearest Evelyn, I am not disheartened. I was prepared for a refusal, although the reason you cite does rather take me by surprise. However, it does not alter the facts of the case. Such a sudden affection—forgive me, Cousin, but it is the truth—cannot be a deep affection. With time, I will overcome it. In lieu of parent, I turn to Miss Peabody, and ask her permission to pay court to you in the proper fashion!"

He did turn to me, his hand on his heart and a broad smile on his lips. I couldn't help smiling back, although it was a rather sour smile.

"I can hardly prevent you from enjoying the society of your cousin," I said. "But you will have to work fast, Mr. Lucas; we leave tomorrow morning for a trip down the Nile. So you have only a few hours in which to press your suit."

"Tomorrow morning," Lucas exclaimed. "I have no undue modesty about my powers of persuasion, but really—!"

"I am sorry," Evelyn said, in her gentle voice. "Lucas, I cannot encourage you. I will never change my mind. But I regret that we will not enjoy your company for a longer time."

"Really, Evelyn, we must discuss this," Lucas said. "I am as stubborn as you are, and much louder; I do not intend to abandon my hopes. But my dear girl, you don't suppose that I am making marriage a prerequisite to the enjoyment of the rights that are morally yours, even though they have not been established legally. Half of our grandfather's fortune belongs to you. I will settle it upon you immediately when we return home. That is where you belong, at home. You can have your own establishment, anywhere you like—if the Dower house at Ellesmere does not suit you, we will find another—"

He stopped speaking. Evelyn was shaking her head.

"My grandfather had the right to dispose of his property as he chose. I cannot take what is not mine, Lucas, and if you try to give it to me, I will give it back. Further, I have agreed to spend the winter with Amelia. One companion has already deserted her; I will not do so, she is depending on me."

"Then in the spring . . . ?"

"I do not promise that."

"No, but. . . . I see your argument with regard to Miss Peabody; it would indeed be a poor return for her kindness to abandon her now, at the last minute. Altogether, it is a good idea. Winter in Egypt, recover your health and spirits; in the meantime we can work out a good lie with which to confound our friends at home when they wonder where you have been all this time."

"No, Lucas, really—"

"A good lie is absolutely essential, my love. Never mind what they suspect; together we will outface them."

"Lucas, you bewilder me," Evelyn exclaimed. "You pay no heed to anything I have said—"

"I do, I do. But I do not take it as final. No, my dear cousin, Egypt is a splendid place in which to spend the winter; I have always wanted to come here. If I cannot convince you of my sincerity by spring, I will abandon my hopes. Come, Miss Peabody, you are our Minerva, our font of wisdom; what do you say?"

"Oh, I am to be allowed to say something? Well, my dear Lord Ellesmere, then I must confess you have some justice on your side; and you, Evelyn, cannot refuse your cousin's desire to assist you. If you will not accept all the money he wants to give you, you can in clear conscience accept a respectable annuity. If you wish to go home—"

"Oh, Amelia, how can you say so?"

"Very well," I said, sniffing to conceal my pleasure. "Then we will carry out our trip down the Nile. When it is over, you will consider your cousin's offer. Does that seem fair to both of you?"

Lucas snatched my hand and shook it enthusiastically. Evelyn nodded. She was not favorable to the idea, but was far too fairminded to object.

"However," I continued. "Mr. Lucas will have to conduct his courtship from a distance. I can hardly offer him a room on our dehabeeyah. It would not be proper."

"I had not thought you the sort of lady who worried about propriety," Lucas said, with a meaningful look. "However, I shall hire my own dehabeeyah and be on your trail as soon as possible. You shan't escape me so easily, ladies. I shall sail where you sail and moor where you moor!"

"That sounds very romantic," I said coolly. "I hope you will not be disappointed; it is not so easy to arrange these things in Egypt."

"So I have been informed." Lucas rose, squaring his shoulders. "Therefore I must get at the business immediately."

"You can do nothing tonight," I said.

"Ah, your underestimate me, dear lady! Tomorrow, when I accompany you to your boat, I will hire one for myself. Nor is it too late, tonight, to acquire a dragoman. The lobby still teems with the wretched fellows, and I am told they are essential to travelers. Perhaps you could recommend a good one."

"No," I said.

"Michael might know of someone," Evelyn said, with a smiling glance at me.

"He has gone home," I said.

"He is sure to be somewhere about," Evelyn said gently. "He never leaves until we have retired. Indeed, I think the fellow sleeps here, he's so devoted to you since you saved the life of his child. He would do anything for you."

"You are the one he is devoted to," I said. "I cannot imagine where you get these notions, Evelyn."

Michael had taken quite a fancy to Evelyn and was, as she had thought, still in the hotel. We found him and, taking our leave of his lordship, left the two of them in conversation.

I was really vexed with Evelyn for helping her cousin to further his plans; if I had not known her so well, I would have imagined she wanted to encourage him. But that was Evelyn's weakness. She was too kind, and too truthful. Both, I have found, are inconvenient character traits.

Chapter Four

 I had thought to avoid Mr. Lucas by making an outrageously early departure next morning. I underestimated him. The rosy streaks of dawn were scarcely brushing the sky when we descended into the lobby of the hotel, to find Lucas waiting, with an armful of flowers for Evelyn and a knowing smile for me. He insisted on accompanying us to Boulaq, and as the little boat carried us across to the waiting dahabeeyah he stood on the shore waving both arms like a semaphore and showing all his teeth in a smile.

With much bustle and a babble of cheerful voices the men took their places. The mooring ropes were loosed; the oarsmen pushed off from the bank; the great sail swelled as it took the wind; and we were off, with a six-gun salute from our crew, answered by other boats along the bank.

We sat on the high upper deck, with an awning to protect us from the sun. Rugs, lounge chairs, and tables had transformed this area into a comfortable drawing room, and the waiter, young Habib, at once appeared with mint tea and cakes. Evelyn lost her thoughtful look and sat up, pointing and exclaiming at the sights. The worst pessimist in the world must have responded to the happiness of such an excursion on such a day. The sun was well up, beaming down from a cloudless sky. The gentle breeze fanned our cheeks. The palaces and gardens on the riverbank glided by as smoothly as in a dream, and with every passing minute new beauties of scenery and architecture were displayed to our eager eyes. In the distance the shapes of the pyramids were etched against the sky; the air was so clear that they seemed like miniature monuments, only yards away.

We sat on the deck the whole of that day; the experience was so new and so enchanting it was impossible to tear ourselves away. At dinner time delectable smells wafted up from the kitchen near the prow. Evelyn ate with a better appetite than I had seen her display for days; and when we retired to the saloon as the evening fell, she performed Chopin beautifully on the pianoforte. I sat by the window watching the exquisite sunset and listening to the tender strains; it is a moment that will always remain in my memory.

We had many such moments as the days went on; but I must curtail my enthusiasm, for I could write another of those repetitious travel books about the trip—the eerie singing of the crewmen as we lay moored at night; the exchanges of salutes with the Cook's steamers plying the river; the visits to the monuments of Dashoor (pyramids) and Abusir (more pyramids).

Most travelers hurry up the river as fast as possible, planning to stop at various historic sites on the return voyage. The voyage upstream is the difficult one, against the current, which, as the reader knows, flows from south to north; one is dependent upon the prevailing northerly wind, and, when this fails, as it often does, upon the brawny arms of the men. After we watched them tow the heavy boat through an area of sandbanks in a dead calm, we could not bear to inflict this labor on them any more often than was absolutely necessary. To see the poor fellows harnessed to a rope, like ancient slaves, was positively painful.

I had private reasons for wishing to push on as quickly as possible. The energetic Mr. Lucas would find difficulty in hiring a dahabeeyah as promptly as he hoped, but I did not underestimate his stubbornness, and I fancied a few weeks of peace and quiet before he caught us up.

However, my study of history had told me that the common method of travel is the wrong way. The monuments near Cairo are among the oldest; in order to see Egyptian history unroll before us in the proper sequence, we must stop on our way south instead of waiting till the return voyage. I wanted to see Twelfth Dynasty tombs and Eighteenth Dynasty temples before viewing the remains of the later Greek and Roman periods. I had therefore made out an itinerary before we left Cairo and presented it to Reis Hassan.

You would have thought I had suggested a revolution, the way that man carried on. I was informed, through Michael, that we must take advantage of the wind, and sail where, and as, it permitted.

I was beginning to understand a little Arabic by then, and I comprehended a few of the comments Michael did not translate. According to the reis I was a woman, and therefore no better than a fool. I knew nothing about boats, or wind, or sailing, or the Nile; who was I, to tell an experienced captain how to run his boat?

I was the person who had hired the boat. I pointed this out to Reis Hassan. I hoped I need not say who won the argument. Like all men, of all colors and all nations, he was unable to accept an unpalatable fact, however; and I had to argue with him every time I proposed to stop.

Except for running aground on sandbanks, which is a common-enough occurrence, we made admirable time. The wind was good. I therefore encountered some stiff resistance from the reis when I told him we would stop at Beni Hassan, which is some 167 miles south of Cairo. Brandishing my copy of M. Maspero's history, I explained to him that the tombs at Beni Hassan are of the time of Usertsen of the Twelfth Dynasty; chronologically they follow the pyramid of Gizeh, where we had been, and precede the antiquities of Luxor, where we proposed to go. I doubt that he understood my argument. However, we stopped at Beni Hassan.

The village was typical. I would have reported a man who kept his dog in such a kennel. Small mud hovels, roofed with cornstalks, looked as if they had been flung down at random on the ground. These huts are clustered around an inner courtyard, where the cooking is carried on; there is a fire, a stone for grinding corn, a few storage jars, and that is all. The women spin, or grind, or nurse their infants. The men sit. Children, chickens, and dogs tumble about in an indiscriminate mass, equally dirty, equally unclad; and yet the children are pretty little things when they are not disfigured by flies and disease.

When we appeared, the village seethed as if someone had stirred it with a stick. We were besieged by outstretched hands—some empty, begging for the inevitable backsheesh; some holding objects for sale—antiquities, stolen from the tombs, or manufactured by enterprising merchants to delude the unwary. It is said that some Europeans and Americans engage in this immoral trade.

Evelyn recoiled with a cry as an indescribably horrid object was thrust under her very nose. At first it appeared to be a bundle of dry brown sticks wrapped in filthy cloth; then my critical gaze recognized it for what it was—a mummy's hand, snapped off at the wrist, the dried bones protruding; black from the bitumen in which it had been soaked in ancient times. Two tawdry little rings adorned the bony fingers, and scraps of rotten wrappings were pushed back to display the delicacy in all its gruesome reality.

The seller was not at all put off by our mutual exclamations of disgust; it required Michael's added comments to convince him that we would not own such a repulsive object. Many travelers buy such mementos, even entire mummies, which are exported from the country like bundles of wood instead of human remains.

Evelyn's sensitive face was pensive as we went on. "How strange and pitiful," she said musingly. "To reflect that that horrid object was perhaps once clasped ardently by a husband or lover! It was very small, was it not, Amelia—a woman's hand?"

"Don't think about it," I said firmly.

"I wish I could stop thinking about it. My reflections should dwell on the frailty of the flesh, on human vanity, and the other precepts of Christian faith. . . . Instead I shudder at the horror of what it is, after all, only a bit of cast-off flesh—the discarded garment of the soul. Amelia, if it had touched me I should have died!"

We went up to the tombs. You may rest assured, dear reader, that I had not wasted my time during the voyage. I had with me the Reverend Samuel Birch's little books on the study of Egyptian hieroglyphs; and my hours of pouring over these sources were repaid in full when I was able to point out to Evelyn the group of hieroglyphic signs which spells the name of the chief of this district during the Twelfth Dynasty. There is no thrill equal to seeing the actual signs, painted on crumbling rock walls instead of printed on a page; finding in them meaning and sense. . . .

But I fear I am being carried away by my scholarly enthusiasm. The tombs had considerable interest even for casual tourists, the painted scenes on the wall are gay and pretty, showing the activities in which the dead man loved to indulge during his lifetime, as well as the industries pursued on his estates. His serfs blow glass and work gold into jewelry; they tend the flocks, fashion pottery, and work in the fields.

Some years later these same splendid tombs were savagely mutilated by native Egyptians extracting fragments of the paintings for sale to antiquities dealers. But even when we saw them I was aware of some of the abuses Emerson had talked about. Fragments of paint and plaster were constantly flaking off the walls, which were dulled by the smoke from the candles carried by the guides. Visiting travelers were no more careful than the uninformed Egyptians; as we stood in one tomb I watched an American gentleman calmly walk away with a fallen bit of stone that bore a pretty picture of a young calf. I shouted at him, but Evelyn prevented me when I would have pursued him to retrieve the fragment. As she pointed out, someone else would have taken it anyway.

The name of Emerson has now returned to the narrative; but the reader must not suppose that it was absent from our thoughts during the halcyon days of sailing. Evelyn did not refer to Walter, but when I introduced his name the eager light in her eye, the unguarded way in which she turned toward me told me that, though absent from her tongue, the name was not far from her thoughts.

As for myself, I thought often of Emerson, though not of course, in the same way Evelyn regarded his young brother. No; the thought of Emerson was a stinging mosquito, which produced an itching spot that constantly demanded to be rubbed. (The Critic comments upon the inelegance of this comparison. I insist upon leaving it in.) Emerson's criticisms kept recurring to me; I saw evidence of neglect and vandalism to the monuments wherever we went, and I itched (you see the appropriateness of my analogy), I positively itched to be in charge of the entire antiquities department. I would have settled things properly!

We got to know some of our crew quite well. The cook was an elderly, toothless black gentleman from Assuan, who produced the most delicious meals upon two small charcoal burners. The waiters, Habib and Abdul, were handsome boys who might have stepped straight out of an ancient Egyptian painting, with their broad shoulders and long, slim bodies. We got to be very fond of them, especially Habib, who laughed in the most infectious manner whenever I spoke to him in Arabic. The crewmen I could only vaguely distinguish by their complexions, which ranged from black to café-au-lait; they looked identical otherwise, in their flowing striped robes and white turbans.

I acquired a new name during the voyage. The Egyptians have nicknames for everyone, and some of them are quite amusing and disrespectful. Maspero told us of a friend of his, an American gentleman named Wilbour, who is the proud possessor of a magnificent white beard. The Arabs call him "Father of the Beard." My name was equally descriptive; they called me the Sitt Hakim, the lady doctor. I felt I deserved the title; scarcely a day went by when I was not patching up some scrape or cut, although, to my regret, I was not called upon to amputate anything. When we stopped in the native villages I was always being approached by dark-eyed mothers, some no more than children themselves, carrying their pitiful babies. I had used virtually all my stock of eye medicines by the time we left Beni Hassan—and knew, unfortunately, that my efforts were like a single drop of water in a desert. The key to the regeneration of Egypt lies in the women. So long as they are forced into marriage and motherhood long before they are ready for such responsibilities—sold to the highest bidder like animals, untrained in even the rudiments of sanitation and housekeeping, untaught, unassisted, and degraded—so long will the country fail to realize its potential. I determined that I would speak to Major Baring about this as soon as we returned to Cairo. I didn't suppose that the man had any notion of matters outside of his account books; men never do.

With such reflections and studies the days passed delightfully. Evelyn's companionship added immeasurably to my enjoyment. She was the perfect friend: sensitive to beauty, responsive to my moods and to the frequent distressing sights of poverty and disease; interested in learning all she could of the history that unrolled before us; cheerful; uncomplaining. I found myself dreading the spring. It would have been so pleasant to look forward to years of Evelyn's company; we could have lived like sisters, enjoying the domestic comforts of England, and traveling whenever we got bored with domesticity. But that was clearly not to be expected. Whether Evelyn yielded to her cousin's suit or not, she would certainly marry one day; and I rather believed that Lucas would prevail. He had every argument on his side. So I decided to enjoy the moment and forget about the future.

After Beni Hassan, the next site of interest to historians is near a village called Haggi Qandil. The region has a more famous name; it is sometimes called Tell-el-Amarna, and it was the city of the heretic king Khuenaten—if indeed he was a king, and not a queen in disguise, as some archaeologists have claimed. I had seen copies of the strange portraits of this monarch, and had to admit that his form bore more resemblance to the feminine than to the masculine.

Even more intriguing was the speculation on the religious beliefs of this peculiar personage. He had abandoned the worship of the old gods of Egypt and given his devotion to the sun, Aten. Did he worship only this god? Was he the

Crocodile on the Sandbank **53**

first monotheist of whom history gives us a record? And what connection could there be between this supposed monotheism and the monotheism of the Hebrews? Moses was raised at the court of Egypt. Perhaps the elevated faith of Yahweh derived, ultimately, from the iconoclastic religion of an ancient Egyptian pharoah!

Evelyn was rather shocked when I proposed this idea, and we had a pleasant little argument. I gave her a lecture on Khuenaten; she was always anxious to learn.

"He abandoned the royal city of Thebes," I explained, "and built a new capital dedicated to his god, on land that had never been contaminated by other worship. Herr Lepsius discovered some of the boundary inscriptions placed on the rocks around the city of Khuenaten. There are also tombs in the cliffs, rather interesting ones; the drawings are quite different in style from the usual tomb decorations. If the wind suits, I think a visit there might be profitable. What do you say?"

I was leafing through my copy of Brugsch's *Geographical Dictionary* (Heinrich Brugsch, the archaeologist, not his disreputable brother) as I spoke; but I watched Evelyn out of the corner of my eye, and saw the betraying color rise in her cheeks. She put down her pencil—she was quite a good little artist, and had made a number of nice sketches along the way—and gazed out across the river toward the cliffs.

"What is the name of the place, Amelia?"

I riffled busily through the pages of Brugsch.

"The ancient name of the place was—"

"The modern name is El Amarnah, is it not?"

"There are three villages on the spot, el-Till and el-Haggi Qandil and El-Amariah. A corruption of these names—"

"Yes, yes, I recall—I recall Walter speaking of it. That is where he and Mr. Emerson are working. You would have no reason to remember that, of course."

I decided that Evelyn was being sarcastic. She seldom allowed herself this luxury, so I overlooked it on this occasion.

"Is that so?" I said casually. "Well, I suppose there is no reason why we should necessarily encounter the Emersons. The site is large and the tombs are scattered. We will take it as settled, then. I will speak to Reis Hassan."

Owing to a difficulty with the wind, we did not reach the village of Haggi Qandil for two days. Indeed, we had some trouble reaching it at all; if I had not been determined, Reis Hassan would not have stopped. He mentioned unfavorable winds, disease in the village, the remoteness of the archaeological remains from the river, and a number of other irrelevant arguments. You would have thought the good captain would have learned by now the futility of arguing with me; but perhaps he enjoyed it. Honesty compels me to admit that Hassan may have had some reason on his side. We ran aground on a sandbank outside the village and had to be carried ashore by the villagers. We left Reis Hassan staring gloomily at his crew, who were trying to free the boat and making very little progress.

Michael, our dragoman, led the way into the village. It was a typical Egyptian village—perhaps a trifle more wretched than others. The narrow streets were heaped with refuse of all kinds, steaming under the hot sun. Dust and windblown sand coated every surface. Mangy dogs lay about the streets, their ribs showing. They bared their teeth at us as we passed, but were too miserable even to rise. Half-naked children stared from eyes ringed with flies, and whined for backsheesh.

Michael plunged into the crowd, shouting orders, and eventually we were presented with a choice of donkeys. We chose the least-miserable-looking of the lot, and then I proceeded to a ritual which had caused considerable amusement along the way, and which puzzled even our loyal Michael. Following my orders, interpreted by Michael, the reluctant owners took the filthy cloths from the animals' back, swabbed them down with buckets of water, and smeared on the ointment I supplied. The donkeys were then covered with fresh saddle cloths, supplied by me, which were laundered after every use. I think it was the only time in the lives of these little donkeys that the cloths were ever removed; sores and insects proliferated under them.

The scowls on the faces of the donkeys' owners turned to broad smiles as I tipped them liberally for their unusual effort; I took the opportunity to add a short lecture on the economic advantage of tending one's livestock, but I was never sure how much of this discourse Michael translated. With the now laughing attendants running alongside, we trotted off across the desert toward the tombs.

The cliffs, which run closely along the river in other areas, fall back here, leaving a semicircular plain some seven miles long by four miles wide at its greatest extent. The cultivated land is only a narrow strip less than half a mile wide; beyond, all is baking yellow-brown desert, until one reaches the rocky foothills of the cliffs into which the tombs were cut.

We were bouncing along in fine style, squinting against the glare of the sun, when I beheld a figure coming toward us. The air of Egypt is so clear one can make out details at distances impossible in England; I saw at once that the person approaching was not a native. He wore trousers instead of flapping skirts. My internal organs (if I may be permitted to refer to these objects) gave an odd lurch. But soon I realized that the man was not Emerson. Evelyn recognized him at the same time. We were side by side; I heard her soft exclamation and saw her hands clench on the reins.

Walter did not recognize us immediately. He saw only two European travelers, and ran toward us with increased speed. Not until he was almost upon us did he realize who we were; and he stopped so abruptly that a spurt of sand shot up from under his heels. We continued to trot decorously toward him as he stood swaying and staring like a man in a dream.

"Thank God you are here!" he exclaimed, before we could greet him. "That is . . . you are really here? You are not a vision, or a mirage?"

His eyes were fixed on Evelyn's face; but his agitation was so great I deduced some other cause of trouble than frustrated love.

"We are really here," I assured him. "What is wrong, Mr. Walter?"

"Emerson. My brother." The lad passed his hand across his damp forehead. "He is ill. Desperately, dangerously ill. . . . You have no doctor with you, of course. But your dahabeeyah—you could take him to Cairo . . . ?"

His brother's danger and Evelyn's unexpected appearance had turned the poor boy's brains to mush. I realized that I must take charge.

"Run back to the boat and get my medical kit, Michael," I said. "Hurry, please. Now, Mr. Walter, if you will lead the way . . ."

"A doctor . . ." mumbled Walter, still looking at Evelyn as if he didn't believe in her.

"You know there is no doctor nearer than Cairo," I said. "Unless I see Mr. Emerson, I cannot tell whether he is fit to be moved. It would take days to get him to Cairo. Lead on, Mr. Walter."

I jabbed him with my parasol. He started, turned, and began to run back in the direction from which he had come. The donkeys, aroused by my voice, broke into a trot. Skirts flying, parasols waving, we dashed forward, followed by a cloud of sand.

Emerson had situated himself in one of the tombs that had been dug into the rock wall of the hills bounding the plain. The entrances looked like black rectangles against the sunbaked rock. We had to climb the last few yards, along a sort of path that led up the cliff. Walter devoted himself to Evelyn; the donkey attendants would have helped me, but I swatted them off with my parasol. I needed no assistance. I was panting a trifle when I finally reached the entrance to the tomb, but it was—yes, I confess it—it was with agitation rather than exertion.

The lintel and jambs of the entrance were covered with carved reliefs. I had no time for them then; I entered. Once inside, I cast a quick, comprehensive glance about, and understood why Emerson had chosen to take up his abode in the resting place of the ancient dead, rather than pitch a tent. The room was long and narrow—a passageway, as I later discovered, rather than a chamber. The far end was lost in shadow, but diffused sunlight illuminated the area next to the entrance. Wooden packing cases served as tables. Some were covered with tins of food, others with books and papers. A lamp showed how the room was lighted by night. A few folding camp chairs were the only other pieces of furniture, save for two camp beds. On one lay the motionless form of a man.

He lay so still that horror gripped me; I thought for a moment that we had come too late. Then an arm was flung out and a hoarse voice muttered something. I crossed the room and sat down on the floor by the cot.

I would not have known him. The beard, which had been confined to lower cheeks and jaw, spread upward in a black stubble that almost met his hairline. His eyes were sunken and his cheekbones stood out like spars. I had no need to touch him to realize that he was burning with fever. Heat fairly radiated from his face. His shirt had been opened, baring his throat and chest, and exposing a considerable quantity of black hair; he was covered to the waist with a sheet which his delirious tossing had entwined around his limbs.

Evelyn sank to her knees beside me.

"What shall I do, Amelia?" she asked quietly.

"Dampen some cloths in water. Walter, you must see that we do not run out of water; send the men for more. I don't suppose he can eat; has he taken water to drink?"

"He won't take it," Walter said.

"He will take it for me," I said grimly, and began to roll up my sleeves.

By the time Michael arrived with my bag, we had managed to make Emerson more comfortable. Constant application of water to his face and breast had lowered his temperature somewhat, and I had forced a few drops past his cracked lips. He knocked my bonnet off and sent me sprawling before I succeeded; but resistance merely increased my determination. I then gave him a stiff dose of quinine, lying flat across his chest and pinching his nose shut, while Walter held his arms and Evelyn sat on his legs. Not surprisingly, he fell into an uneasy sleep after these exertions, and I was able to turn my attention to arrangements for the future. Michael was sent back to the dahabeeyah for bedding and supplies. Evelyn went with him, to help him select the personal things we would need. I ordered her to remain on board, but she refused, with the quiet determination she showed at certain times. So I directed Walter to pick out a nice tomb for us.

He was staring at me in the most peculiar fashion. He did not speak, but he kept opening and closing his mouth. If he had not been such a handsome fellow, he would have reminded me of a frog.

"There is a nice tomb close by, I trust," I repeated, resisting the desire to poke at him with my parasol. "Go along, Walter, we mustn't waste time; I want the place all swept out and tidy by the time our luggage arrives. Where are your workmen? Some of them can take care of that matter."

"Nice tomb," Walter repeated stupidly. "Yes. Yes, Miss Peabody, there are several other tombs nearby. I don't know whether you would call them nice. . . ."

"Walter, you are incoherent," I said. "This is no time to lose your head. I understand your concern, but there is no need for it now. I am here. I have no intention of leaving until Mr. Emerson is on his feet again. I have always wanted to spend some time with an archaeological expedition; it should be a delightful experience. There is no point in moving your brother, for the crisis will come in the next few hours, long before we could reach the nearest town. I believe there is no cause for alarm. He has a strong constitution; and at the risk of sounding repetitious, may I say again that I am on the job."

Walter was sitting on the floor next to me. He watched as I wrung out another cloth and slapped it on Emerson's chest. Then, quite without warning, he leaned forward, took me by the shoulders, and kissed me soundly on the cheek.

"I believe you, Miss Peabody; there is no cause for alarm with you here. I believe you would square off at Satan if he came around and inconvenienced you!"

Before I could reply he had jumped to his feet and bolted out.

I turned back to my patient and wrung out another cloth. There was no one there but myself and Emerson, and he was sleeping; so I permitted myself to smile. Some Eternal Designer had robbed Peter to pay Paul; one Emerson had an extra share of charm and the other had none. Poor Evelyn; no wonder she had succumbed! Luckily Emerson presented no such danger to any woman.

I had to admit, though, that he looked rather pathetic in his present state. A fallen colossus is more pitiable than a felled weakling. As I went on wiping his hot face, some of the lines of pain smoothed out, and he gave a little sigh, like that of a child sinking into restful sleep.

The crisis of the fever came that night, and we had our hands full. Neither Evelyn nor I saw our beds until dawn. Walter had made some of his workers clean out a tomb for us, and Michael fitted it up quite comfortably; but I would not leave my patient, and Evelyn would not leave me. Or perhaps it was Walter she was reluctant to leave. I had no time or energy to inquire, for Emerson became delirious toward sunset, and it took all my strength and Walter's to keep him from harming himself, or us. I acquired a handsome bruise across one cheek when Walter's grip on his brother's arm failed for a moment. I have never seen a man carry on so; you would have thought him an Egyptian soul traversing the perils of the Afterworld, and us crocodile-headed monsters trying to keep him from Heaven. Well, we kept wrestling him back onto the bed, and I forced more medicine down him; and in the early hours of the morning he fell into a coma that must end, as I knew, in death or recovery.

In a way, those succeeding hours were worse than the violent struggles of the earlier time. Walter knelt by the bed, unaware of anything except his brother's gasping breath. The fever rose, in spite of our efforts. My hands were sore from wringing out cloths, and my bones ached—especially those of my left hand, for at some point before he dropped into his coma Emerson had seized it and would not let go. It was terrifying to feel the hard grip of that hand and see the immobility of the rest of his body. I had the superstitious feeling that he was clinging as if to a lifeline, and that if I forced his fingers apart he would drop into the bottomless abyss of death.

As the night wore on I grew giddy and light-headed with lack of sleep. The scene was uncanny: the smoky lamplight casting its shadows over the taut faces of the watchers and the sunken countenance of the sick man; the utter stillness of the night, broken at long intervals by the wavering howl of a jackal, the loneliest, most desolate sound on earth.

Then, in the darkest hour before dawn, the change came. It was as palpable as a breath of cold air against the face. For a moment my eyes failed, and I felt nothing. I heard a sound, like a strangled sob, from Walter. When I opened my eyes I saw him lying across the foot of the bed, his face hidden and his hand resting on his brother's arm. Emerson's face was utterly peaceful. Then his breast rose in a single long inspiration—and continued to move. The hand that held mine had gone limp. It was cool. He would live.

I could not stand; my limbs were too cramped with crouching. Walter had to half carry me to my bed. He would sit with Emerson the rest of the night, in case there was a relapse, but I had no fear of that. I fell into slumber as one falls into a well, while Evelyn was bathing my hands and face.

When I woke later that morning I could not imagine for a moment where I was. Stone walls instead of the white paneling of my cabin; a hard surface below instead of my soft couch. I started to turn, and let out a cry of pain; my left hand, on which I had tried to raise myself, was swollen and sore.

Then memory came back; I levered myself up from the pallet on which I had slept and fumbled for my dressing gown. Across the room Evelyn still slept the sleep of exhaustion. A beam of light streaming through a gap in the hastily curtained doorway touched her fair hair and made it glow like gold.

When I stepped out onto the ledge in front of my improvised bedchamber, the heat struck like a blow. In spite of my anxiety I could not help pausing for a look. Below me a panorama of desert rolled away to the blue curve of the river, with the western cliffs beyond like ramparts of dull gold. The huts of the village were cleansed by distance; half hidden by the graceful shapes of palm trees, amid the green of the cultivated fields, they looked picturesque instead of nasty. Midway between the village and the cliffs a huddle of black shapes, busy as ants, moved amid a great dusty cloud of sand. I surmised that this was the site of the current excavation.

I walked along the ledge to the next tomb, whence I could hear sounds of altercation. My anxiety had been unnecessary. Emerson was himself again.

I wish it clearly understood that my feelings that bright morning were those of pure Christian charity. For Emerson I felt the comparison and interest one always feels toward a person one has nursed.

These sentiments did not last two minutes.

When I entered I saw Emerson half out of bed, restrained only by Walter's arm. He was partially clad; his nether limbs were covered by the most incredible garments, pink in color. He was shouting at Walter, who waved a small dish under his nose like a weapon.

Emerson stopped shouting when he saw me. His expression was hardly welcoming, but I was so glad to see his eyes aware and sensible, instead of flaring wildly with fever, that I gave him a cheerful forgiving smile before I inspected the contents of the dish Walter was holding.

I forgot myself then; I admit it. I had picked up several forceful expressions from Father, and I used them in his presence, since he never heard a word I said; but I endeavored to avoid them in other company. The sight of the sickly gray-green contents of the dish were too much for my self-control.

"Good Gad," I burst out. "What is that?"

"Tinned peas," said Walter. He looked apologetic, as well he might. "You see, Miss Peabody, they are an excellent cheap source of food. We also have tinned beef and beans and cabbage, but I thought this might be more—"

"Throw it out," I said, holding my nose. "Tell your cook to boil a chicken. One can obtain chickens, I hope? If this is what you eat, no wonder your brother had fever. It is a wonder he doesn't also have dysentery and inflamed bowels."

Walter brought his hand to his brow in a military salute and marched out.

I turned to Emerson. He had flung himself back onto the bed and pulled the sheet up to his chin.

"Go on, Miss Peabody," he said, drawling offensively. "Comment on my other organic failures if you will. I understand I am to thank you for saving my life. Walter is inclined to dramatize things; however, I thank you for ministering to me in your inimitable fashion. Consider yourself thanked. Now go away."

I had intended to go, until he told me to. I sat down on the bed and reached for his hand. He jerked it away.

"I wish to take your pulse," I said impatiently. "Stop acting like a timid maiden lady."

He let me hold his wrist for a few moments. Then he pulled his hand free.

"I wish Miss Nightingale had stayed at home where she belongs," he growled. "Every wretched Englishwoman now wants to become a lady of the lamp. Now, madam, if your instincts are satisfied, take yourself away or—or I shall rise from my bed!"

"If that is what you intend, I shall certainly remain. You cannot get up today. And don't think to frighten me by threats. I watched you all night, remember; your anatomy is not prepossessing, I agree, but I am tolerably familiar with it."

"But my pavement," Emerson shouted. "What is happening to my pavement? You fiend of a woman, I must go and see what they are doing to my pavement!"

"My pavement" had been a recurrent theme in his delirium, and I wondered what he was talking about. The only allusion that occurred to me was the description in the Gospel of Saint John: "When Pilate therefore heard that saying, he brought Jesus forth, and sat down in the judgment seat in a place that is called the Pavement. . . ." However, although I considered Emerson quite capable of blasphemy, I doubted that he would compare his illness with that divine Martyrdom.

"What pavement?" I asked.

"My painted pavement." Emerson looked at me consideringly. "I have found part of Khuenaten's royal palace. Pavements, walls, and ceilings were painted. Some have miraculously survived."

"Good—that is, how amazing! Do you mean that the royal heretic's palace once stood where that waste of sand now stretches?"

"You know of Khuenaten?"

"Yes, indeed. He is a fascinating personality. Or do you think he was a woman?"

"Balderdash! That is typical of the fools who manage archaeological research today. Mariette's notion, that he was taken captive by the Nubians and cas——that is, operated upon—"

"I have read of that theory," I said, as he stuttered to a halt. "Why is it not possible? I believe the operation does produce feminine characteristics in a male."

Emerson gave me a peculiar look.

"That is one way of putting it," he said drily. "It seems more likely to me that Khuenaten's physical peculiarities are an artistic convention. You will note that his courtiers and friends are shown with similar peculiarities."

"Indeed?"

"Yes. Look there." Emerson started to sit up and clutched the sheet to him as it slid. He was a *very* hairy man. "This tomb belonged to a high noble of Khuenaten's court. Its walls are decorated with reliefs in the unique Amarna style."

My curiousity aroused, I reached for the lamp. This motion produced a scream of rage from Emerson.

"Not the lamp! I only use it when I must. The fools who light the tombs with magnesium wire and lamps are vandals; the greasy smoke lays a film on the reliefs. The mirror—take the mirror. If you hold it at the proper angle it will give you sufficient light."

I had observed the mirror and wondered at this unexpected sign of vanity. I ought to have known. It took me some time to get the hang of the business, with Emerson making sarcastic remarks; but finally a lucky twist of the wrist shone a beam of reflected light through the doorway in which I stood, and I stared with wonder and delight.

The reliefs were shallow and worn, but they had a vivacity that at once appealed to me. There seemed to be a parade or procession; all the small running figures followed the mighty form of pharaoh, ten times the size of lesser men. He drove a light chariot, handling his team of prancing horses easily; in the chariot with him was a slightly smaller crowned person. Their heads were turned toward one another, it seemed as if their lips were about to touch.

"He must have loved her very much, to give her such a prominent place at his side," I mused aloud. "I am inclined to agree with you, Emerson; no man who was less than a man would violate tradition by showing his devotion to his beautiful wife. Even her name, Nefertiti—'the beautiful woman has come' . . ."

"You read the hieroglyphs?" Emerson exclaimed.

"A little."

I indicated, without touching it, the oval cartouche in which the queen's name was written, and then moved my finger toward the empty ovals which had once contained the names of Khuenaten.

"I have read of this—how the triumphant priests of Amon destroyed even the royal heretic's name after he died. It is strangely disturbing to see the savagery of their attack. How they must have hated him, to obliterate even his name!"

"By doing so they hoped to annihilate his soul," Emerson said. "Without identity, the spirit of the dead could not survive."

The incongruity of the conversation, with a gentleman in pink undergarments, did not strike me until Evelyn appeared in the doorway, and as abruptly disappeared. From without, her timid voice inquired whether she might come in.

"Oh, curse it," Emerson exclaimed, and pulled the sheet over his head. From under it a muffled voice bade Evelyn enter.

Evelyn entered. She was properly dressed in a pale-green cotton frock, and looked as neat and dainty as if she had had all the amenities of the dehabeeyah at her disposal instead of a basin of tepid water. She was a little flushed. Knowing her as I did, I concluded that she was amused, although I could not imagine why. Emerson pulled the sheet down to the bridge of his nose. Over its folds a pair of blue eyes regarded Evelyn malevolently. She did not look at him.

"Do come in, Evelyn, and look at these carvings," I exclaimed, flashing my mirror about expertly. "Here is the king riding in his chariot and his queen beside him—"

"I am sure they are fascinating, Amelia, but do you not think it might be better to wait for a more propitious time? Mr. Emerson needs rest, and you are not really dressed for a social call. . . ." There was a suspicious quiver in her voice. She suppressed it and went on, "Walter seems to be having some trouble with the chicken you ordered."

"I suppose I must take charge, as usual." With a last lingering glance at a group of running soldiers, I replaced the mirror.

"So long as you are taking charge, you might have a look at my pavement," Emerson said grudgingly. "You stand here chattering like a parrot, and every moment the paint is chipping away—"

"You were the one who uncovered it," I reminded him. "What are you planning to do to protect it?"

"I've had a wooden shelter built, but that is only a small part of the problem. The question is, what preservative can we apply that won't damage the paint? It is crumbled to powder; an ordinary brush simply smears the surface. And the varnishes that have been used in such cases are atrocious; they darken and crack . . ."

"But you, of course, have found a solution," I said.

"A solution is precisely what it is. A mixture of weak tapioca and water, brushed on the painting—"

"You said brushing marred the paint."

Emerson looked as dignified as a man can look under such adverse circumstances.

"I brush it on with the edge of my finger."

I stared at him with reluctant admiration.

"You are determined, I'll say that for you."

"It is slow work; I have to do it myself, I can't trust any of the workmen. I have only covered part of it." He groaned feelingly. "I tell you, woman, I must get up and see to my pavement."

"I'll see to your pavement," I said. "Stay in bed or you will have a relapse and be ill for weeks. Even you must see that that would be foolish."

I did not wait for an answer, it would only have been rude. I started along the ledge. Evelyn caught my sleeve.

"Amelia, where are you going?"

"To see Mr. Emerson's pavement, of course. Have you ever known me to break my word?"

"No, but . . . Do you not think you might assume a more appropriate costume?"

In some surprise I glanced down. I had forgotten I was wearing my dressing gown and slippers.

"Perhaps you are right, Evelyn."

As the reader has no doubt realized, female fashion has never interested me. However, while in London, I had learned of the Rational Dress League, and had had a dress made in that style. It was of slate-colored India cloth, with a plain, almost mannish bodice and a few simple frills at the cuffs as its only ornament. But the daring feature of this costume was the *divided skirt*. The two legs were so full that they resembled an ordinary kilted skirt and did not give me nearly the freedom of action I desired, but they were a good deal more practical than the so-called walking dresses then in vogue. I had kept this garment at the very bottom of my trunk; in Cairo, I had not had quite the courage to wear it. Now I took it out, shook out the creases, and put it on.

As I scrambled down the rocky, hot path, I appreciated the divided skirt; but I still yearned for trousers. At the foot of the slope I found Walter arguing with the cook, a morose-looking individual with only one functional eye. I never did make out what the argument was about, but I settled it, and saw the chicken, which the cook had been waving under Walter's nose, plucked and in the pot before I proceeded. Walter offered to accompany me, but I sent him back to his brother. Emerson needed a watchdog; I did not.

I found the place where the workers were employed and introduced myself to the foreman, Abdullah. He was a stately figure of a man, almost six feet tall; his flowing snowy robes, long gray beard and voluminous headcloth gave him the look of a biblical patriarch. He was not a native of one of the local villages, but came from Upper Egypt and had worked with Emerson before.

Abdullah directed me to the pavement, which was some distance away. It was easy to find, however, because of the low wooden roof that had been erected over it.

There was a great stretch of it—twenty feet across by perhaps fifteen feet long—miraculously, magnificently preserved. The colors were as fresh as if they had just been applied—exquisite blues, glowing reds, and cool greens, with touches of white and deep blue-black to emphasize details. Birds flew with out-stretched wings in luxuriant gardens where flowers bloomed. Young animals, calves and kids, frolicked amid the undergrowth, kicking up their heels. I could almost hear them bellowing and bleating with the sheer joy of living.

I was still squatting on the ground, looking, when Evelyn and Walter found me.

"Amelia, it is the hottest part of the day; the workers have stopped for food and rest, and all sensible people are indoors. Come back and have lunch."

"I won't eat a bite of that miserable-looking chicken," I said. "Evelyn, look; only look. I have never seen anything like it. And to think that the gold-trimmed sandals of the beautiful Nefertiti may have walked across this surface!"

"It is exquisite," Evelyn agreed. "How I would love to sketch it!"

"What a splendid idea!" Walter exclaimed. "And how pleased my brother would be to have a copy, in case of accident. I am the official expedition artist, among other things, and I am very bad at it."

Evelyn promptly disclaimed any skill, but Walter continued to press her. I grew tired of their mutual raptures after a time and staggered to my feet.

We had an atrocious lunch—stringy, tough chicken and some unidentifi-able vegetables cooked into a tasteless mass. My devoted Michael was at hand; I took him aside for a whispered conference. I decided to put off discussing future arrangements with Evelyn and Walter until that evening. It was rather hot, and after my disturbed night I was ready to take a siesta.

Michael was a jewel. When Evelyn and I came out of our tomb in the late afternoon, the place was transformed. Tables and chairs, even a small rug, had been spread out along the ledge, making a charming little piazza or balcony—a balcony with a view such as few property owners enjoy. The cool breeze of evening fanned our cheeks, and across the river the most splendid sunset I had ever seen, even in Egypt, turned the sky to a glowing tapestry of light. From below, a succulent odor wafted up to my appreciative nostrils. Michael had brought food as well as furniture, and was supervising the criminal of a cook.

I sank down luxuriously in one of the chairs. Michael came trotting up the cliff with tall glasses of lemonade. Walter soon joined us. I was about to ask when I might check on my patient, when a sound of rattling pebbles turned all our heads around.

Emerson stood in the door of his tomb. He was fully dressed and looked comparatively respectable, except for his face; it was as gray as the shadows in the darkening western cliffs; and one of his hands was tightly clenched on the stone jamb.

Men are never of any use in an emergency. I was the only one who moved; and I reached Emerson just in time to catch him by the shoulders and prevent his head from striking against the rock as he fell. It was hard, prickly rock; I could feel a thousand sharp points through my skirts as I sat down, rather more suddenly than I had planned, for Emerson was a considerable weight. I was forced to hold him tightly against me with both arms, or he would have tumbled off the ledge.

"There is absolutely no limit to this man's arrogant stupidity," I exclaimed, as Walter came rushing to us. "Fetch Michael and help your brother back to bed, Walter. And for pity's sake," I added angrily, as Emerson's unconscious head rolled against my breast and bristly black hairs scratched me through the fabric of my bodice, "for pity's sake, get rid of this beard!"

Chapter Five

 EMERSON was luckier than he deserved. His injudicious act did not bring on a relapse, but it was obvious that he would be too weak to assume command for some days. Clearly something had to be done; equally clearly, I was the one to do it.

I brought Emerson out of his faint, forced another dose of quinine down him, and left Abdullah sitting on his legs to keep him down. His curses floated out across the valley as I left him.

Without, the sky had darkened. A glittering web of stars covered the indigo-blue vault; the afterglow transformed the cliffs into glowing ghost shapes, the shadows of rock. Side by side Evelyn and Walter sat looking out across the valley.

I had intended to discuss my plans with them; but one look told me they wouldn't care. I did not need to see their faces, their very outlines were eloquent.

I had decided there was no purpose in removing Emerson to a more civilized milieu. By the time we reached Cairo he should be on the road to recovery—unless the removal from his beloved antiquities induced a stroke from sheer rage, which was more than likely. I had told Michael we would remain where we were for approximately a week, by which time Emerson should be out of danger. Michael assured me that the boat crew would be delighted to rest for a week, so long as they were paid. He was distressed that I refused to stay on the boat, traveling back and forth to the excavations daily. I saw no need for this, it would simply be a waste of time.

For the next two days everything went smoothly. At least I thought it did. Later I discovered that there had been ominous signs, if anyone of intelligence had been watching for them. Unfortunately I was not. I was totally preoccupied with my—that is, with Emerson's pavement.

His notion of tapioca and water was good, but I improved on it, adding a teaspoonful of starch and two of bismuth to each quart of water. He had been correct about the impossibility of using an ordinary brush to apply the mixture. I had used my right hand, my left hand—and was almost ready to remove shoes and stockings in order to use my toes—when Evelyn intervened.

She had been copying the painting, and was doing splendidly. I was amazed at her skill; she caught not only the shapes and colors, but the vital, indefinable spirit underlying the mind of the ancient artist. Even Emerson was moved to admiring grunts when she showed him her first day's work. She spent the second morning at the task, and then went up for a rest, leaving me at work. Having covered the edges of the painting, I had set some of the workers to building walkways across the pavement; the supports rested on blank spaces where pillars had once stood, so there was no defacement of the painting, but I had to watch the men closely. They thought the process utterly ridiculous, and would have dragged planks across the fragile surface if I had not supervised them every moment.

They had finished the job and I was lying flat across the walk working on a new section when Evelyn's voice reached me. Glancing up, I was surprised to see that the sun was declining. My last useful finger was beginning to bleed, so I decided to stop; bloodstains would have been impossible to remove from the painting. I crawled back along the boards. When I reached the edge, Evelyn grasped me by the shoulders and tried to shake me.

"Amelia, this must stop! Look at your hands! Look at your complexion! And your dress, and your hair, and—"

"It does seem to be rather hard on one's wardrobe," I admitted, gazing down at my crumpled, dusty, tapioca-spotted gown. "What is wrong with my complexion, and my hair, and—"

Making exasperated noises, Evelyn escorted me back to the tomb, and put a mirror in my hands.

I looked like a Red Indian witch. Although the wooden shelter had protected me from the direct rays of the sun, even reflected sunlight has power in this climate. My hair hung in dusty elf-locks around my red face.

I let Evelyn freshen me and lead me out to our little balcony. Walter as waiting for us, and Michael promptly appeared with cool drinks. This evening was an occasion, for Emerson was to join us for the first time. He had made a remarkable recovery; once he grasped the situation he applied himself to recuperation with the grim intensity I might have expected. I had agreed that he might dress and join us for dinner, provided he wrapped up well against the cool of evening.

He had acrimoniously refused any assistance in dressing. Now he made a ceremonious appearance, waving Walter aside; and I stared.

I knew the beard was gone, but I had not seen him since the operation. I had overheard part of the procedure that morning. It was impossible *not* to overhear it; Emerson's shouts of rage were audible a mile away, and Walter had to raise *his* voice in order to be heard.

"Excessive hair drains the strength," I had heard him explain, in a voice choked with laughter. "Hold his arms, Michael; I am afraid I may inadvertently cut his throat. Radcliffe, you know that fever victims have their hair cut off—"

"That is an old wives' tale," Emerson retorted furiously. "And even if it were not, hair on the head and hair on the face are not the same."

"I really cannot proceed while you struggle so," Walter complained. "Very well . . . Miss Peabody will be pleased."

There was a brief silence.

"Peabody will be pleased that I retain my beard?" Emerson inquired.

"Miss Peabody claims that men grow beard in order to hide weak features. Receding chins, spots on the face . . ."

"Oh, does she? She implies my chin is weak?"

"She has never seen it," Walter pointed out.

"Hmph."

That was all he said; but since silence followed the grunt, I knew Walter had won his point.

Seeing, as I now did, the beardless countenance of Emerson, I understood why he had cultivated whiskers. The lower part of his face looked a little odd, being so much paler than the rest, but the features were not displeasing—although the mouth was set in such a tight line I could not make out its shape. The chin was certainly not weak; indeed, it was almost too square and protuberant. But it had a dimple. No man with a dimple in his chin can look completely forbidding. A dimple, for Emerson, was out of character. No wonder he wished to hide it!

Emerson's defiant eyes met mine, and the comment I had been about to make died on my lips.

"Tea or lemonade?" I inquired.

When I handed him his cup, a half-stifled expletive burst from his lips. Walter followed his gaze.

"My dear Miss Peabody, your poor hands!"

"There must be some better way of going about it," I muttered, trying to wrap my skirt around the members in question. "I haven't given the matter much thought as yet."

"Naturally not," Emerson said gruffly. "Women don't think. A little forethought would prevent most of the suffering they constantly complain about."

Walter frowned. It was the first time I had seen the young fellow look at his brother with anything but affectionate admiration.

"You should be ashamed to speak so, Radcliffe," he said quietly. "Miss Peabody's hand was swollen and painful for hours after you passed the crisis of your sickness, you held it so tightly; and I had to carry her to her bed because her limbs were cramped from kneeling beside you all night long."

Emerson looked a little uncomfortable, but I think I was even more embarrassed. Sentimentality always embarrasses me.

"No thanks, please," I said. "I would have done as much for a sick cat."

"At least you must stop working on the pavement," Walter said. "Tomorrow I will take over the task."

"You can't do the pavement and supervise the workers at the same time," I argued, conscious of an inexplicable annoyance.

Emerson, slouching in his chair, cleared his throat.

"Abdullah is an excellent foreman. There is no need for Walter to be on the spot at all times. Or is there, Walter?"

How he had sensed the truth I do not know, but Walter's uneasy silence was answer enough.

"Come," Emerson insisted, in a voice of quiet firmness. "I knew this evening that something was worrying you. What is it? Fruitless speculation will be worse for me than the truth, Walter; be candid."

"I am willing to be candid, but it isn't easy to be explicit," Walter said, smiling faintly. "You know how one becomes sensitive to the feelings of the men. There are so many meaningful signs—the singing of the work crews, the way in which they move about, the joking and laughter—or the lack thereof. I don't know how long it has been going on. I only sensed it today."

"Then it has not been going on long. You are too experienced to be unaware, preoccupied though you are." Emerson glanced meaningfully at Evelyn, who sat listening with her hands folded in her lap. "Are the men hostile? Are they hiding something they don't want us to know about?"

Walter shook his head; the dark hair tumbled over his high brow, giving him the look of a worried schoolboy.

"Neither of those, I think. Your illness disturbed them; you know how superstitious they are, how ready to find evil demons behind every accident. But I can't really account for the feeling. There is a general laxity, a slowing down, a—a stillness. As if they knew something we don't know—and are afraid of it."

Emerson's brows drew together. He struck his hand on his knee.

"I must see for myself."

"If you venture out into that sun tomorrow, you will be back in bed by noon," I said firmly. "Perhaps I can have a look around myself. But I hate to neglect my pavement, even for a day."

"Peabody, you are not to touch the pavement tomorrow," Emerson said. "Infection is in the air here; you will lose a finger or two if you continue to rub them raw."

I am not accustomed to be spoken to in that tone. Oddly enough, I was not angered by the order, or by the name. Emerson was looking at me with a kind of appeal. His mouth had relaxed. It was, as I had suspected, a well-shaped organ.

"Perhaps you are right," I said.

Evelyn choked on her tea and hastily set the cup down.

"Yes," I continued. "No doubt you are right. Then I will supervise the workers tomorrow and see what I can ascertain. What are you digging up at present, Walter?"

The conversation became technical. Evelyn showed us the progress of her drawing; this time Emerson unbent far enough to mutter, "Not at all bad," and suggest that Evelyn might copy some of the tomb reliefs when she had finished the pavement.

"A trained artist would be a godsend on expeditions like this," he exclaimed, his eyes flashing with enthusiasm. "We cannot save all the relics; we are like the boy with his finger in the dike. But if we had copies of them before they are destroyed . . ."

"I would like to learn something of the hieroglyphic signs," Evelyn said. "I could copy them more accurately if I knew what they meant. For example, there seem to be a dozen different kinds of birds, and I gather each has a different meaning. When the inscriptions are worn it is not always possible to see what the original form was; but if one knew a little of the language . . ."

Emerson beetled his eyebrows at her, but it was clear that he was impressed; before long he was drawing birds on his napkin and Evelyn was attempting to copy them. I looked at Walter. His ingenious face was luminous with pleasure as he watched his admired brother and the girl he loved. Yes, he loved her; there could be no question of that. She loved him too. And at the first declaration from him, she would ruthlessly destroy their happiness because of a convention that seemed more absurd the more I considered it. Knowing what was in store, my heart ached at the sight of Walter's face.

We sat late on our little balcony that night, watching the afterglow fade and the stars blaze out; even Emerson was companionably silent under the sweet influence of the scene. Perhaps we all had a premonition of what was to come; perhaps we knew that this was our last peaceful evening.

I was brushing my hair next morning when I heard the hubbub below. Within a few minutes Walter came running up the path and shouted for me. I went out, fearing some disaster; but his expression was one of excitement rather than alarm.

"The men have made a discovery," he began. "Not in the ruins of the city—up in the cliffs. A tomb!"

"Is that all? Good Gad, the place is overfurnished with tombs as it is."

Walter was genuinely excited, but I noticed that his eyes strayed past me to where Evelyn stood before the mirror, listening as she tied a ribbon around her hair.

"But this one has an occupant! All the other tombs were empty when we found them—robbed and rifled in antiquity. No doubt this new tomb has also been robbed of the gold and jewels it once contained, but there is a mummy, a veritable mummy. What is even more important, Miss Peabody, is that the villagers came to me with the news instead of robbing the tomb. That shows, does it not, that the fancies I expressed last evening were only fancies. The men must trust us, or they would not come to us."

"They trust Mr. Emerson because he pays them full value for every valuable object they find," I said, hastily bundling my hair into its net. "They have no reason to resort to antiquities dealers under those conditions."

"What does it matter?" Walter was fairly dancing with impatience. "I am off, I cannot wait to see, but I thought you might like to accompany me. I fear the trail will be rough . . ."

"I fear so, too," I said grimly. "I must apply myself to the question of appropriate costume. My rationals are an improvement on skirts, but they do not go far enough. Do you think, Evelyn, that we could fashion some trousers out of a skirt or two?"

The trail *was* rough, but I managed it. A few of the villagers accompanied us. As we walked, Walter explained that the tombs we were inhabiting were known as the Southern Tombs. Another group of ancient sepulchers lay to the north, and were, logically enough, referred to as the Northern Tombs. The newly discovered tomb was one of this group.

After several long miles I finally saw a now-familiar square opening in the cliffs above us, and then another beyond the first. We had reached the Northern Tombs, and a scramble up a steep slope of detritus soon brought us to the entrance to the new tomb.

Walter was a different man. The gentle boy had been supplanted by the trained scholar. Briskly he gave orders for torches and ropes. Then he turned to me.

"I have explored these places before. I don't recommend that you come with me, unless you are fond of bats in your hair and a great deal of dust."

"Lead on," I said, tying a rope in a neat half-hitch around my waist.

I had Walter thoroughly under control by then. He would not have argued with me if I had proposed jumping off a pyramid.

I had been in a number of ancient tombs, but all had been cleared for visitors. I was somewhat surprised to find that this one was almost as clear, and far less difficult than Walter had feared. There was a good deal of loose rubble underfoot, and at one point we had to cross a deep pit, which had been dug to discourage tomb robbers. The villagers had bridged it with a flimsy-looking plank. Other than that, the going was not at all bad.

Walter too was struck by the relative tidiness. He threw a comment over his shoulder.

"The place is too well cleared, Miss Peabody. I suspect it has been robbed over and over again; we will find nothing of interest here."

The corridor ended, after a short distance, in a small chamber cut out of the rock. In the center of the room stood a rough wooden coffin. Lifting his torch, Walter looked into it.

"There is nothing to be afraid of," he said, misinterpreting my expression. "The wrappings are still in place; will you look?"

"Naturally," I said.

I had seen mummies before, of course, in museums. At first glance this had nothing to distinguish it from any other mummy. The brown, crumbling bandages had been wrapped in intricate patterns, rather like weaving. The featureless head, the shape of the arms folded across the breast, the stiff, extended limbs—yes, it was like the other mummies I had seen, but I had never seen them in their natural habitat, so to speak. In the musty, airless chamber, lighted only by dimly flaring torches, the motionless form had a grisly majesty. I wondered who he—or she—had been: a prince, a priestess, the young mother of a family, or an aged grandfather? What thoughts had lived in the withered brain—what emotions had brought tears to the shriveled eyes or smiles to the fleshless lips? And the soul—did it live on, in the golden grain fields of Amenti, as the priests had promised the righteous worshiper, as we look forward to everlasting life with the Redeemer these people never knew?

Walter did not appear to be absorbed in pious meditation. He was scowling as he stared down at the occupant of the coffin. Then he turned, holding the torch high as he inspected the walls of the chamber. They were covered with inscriptions and with the same sort of reliefs to which I had become accustomed in the Southern Tombs. All centered on the majestic figure of pharoah, sometimes alone, but usually with his queen and his six little daughters. Above, the god Aten, shown as the round disk of the sun, embraced the king with long rays that ended in tiny human hands.

"Well?" I asked. "Will you excavate here, or will you remove the poor fellow from his coffin and unwrap him in more comfortable surroundings?"

For a moment Walter looked unnervingly like his shaven brother as he tugged thoughtfully at his lower lip.

"If we leave him here, some enterprising burglar will rend him apart in the hope of finding ornaments such as were sometimes wrapped in the bandages. But I don't hope for much, Miss Peabody. Some tombs were used for later burials, by poor people who could not build tombs of their own. This looks to me like just such a late mummy, much later than the period in which we are interested, and too poor to own any valuable ornaments."

He handed his torch to one of the villagers and spoke to the man in Arabic—repeating the comment, I assumed. The man burst into animated speech, shaking his head till the folds of his turban fluttered.

"Mohammed says our mummy is not a commoner," Walter explained, smiling at me. "He is a prince—a princely magician, no less."

"How does he know that?"

"He doesn't. Even if Mohammed could read the hieroglyphs, which he cannot, there is no inscription on the coffin to give the mummy's name. He is only trying to increase the backsheesh I owe him for this find."

So Mohammed was the discoverer of this tomb. I studied the man with interest. He looked like all the other villagers—thin, wiry, epicene, his sunbaked skin making him look considerably older than his probable age. The life span in these villages is not high. Mohammed was probably no more than thirty, but poverty and ill health had given him the face of an old man.

Seeing my eye upon him he looked at me and grinned ingratiatingly.

"Yes," Walter said thoughtfully. "We must take our anonymous friend along. Radcliffe can unwrap him; it will give him something to do."

Emerson was delighted with the find; he fell on the mummy with mumbled exclamations, so after making sure his temperature and pulse were normal, I left him to his ghoulish work. When he joined us on the ledge that evening, however, he was vociferously disappointed.

"Greco-Egyptian," he grumbled, stretching his long legs out. "I suspected as much when I saw the pattern of the wrappings. Yes, yes; the signs are unmistakable. I am familiar with them from my own research; no one has done any work on this problem, although a chronological sequence could be worked out if one—"

"My dear fellow, we are all of us familiar with your views on the deplorable state of archaeology in Egypt," Walter broke in, with a laugh. "But you are wrong about the mummy. Mohammed swears it is that of a princely magician, a priest of Amon, who placed a curse on this heretical city."

"Mohammed is a scurvy trickster who wants more money," growled Emerson. "How does he know about heretics and priests of Amon?"

"There is another project for you," Walter said. "Investigating the traditions and folk memories of these people."

"Well, his folk memory is wrong in this case. "The poor chap whose wrappings I removed this afternoon was no priest. It frankly puzzles me to find him here at all. The city was abandoned after Khuenaten's death, and I did not think there was a settlement here in Ptolemaic times. These present villages did not occupy the site until the present century."

"I doubt that the tomb was used by the official who had it built," Walter said. "The reliefs in the corridor were not finished."

"What have you done with our friend?" I asked. "I hope you are not planning to make him the third occupant of your sleeping dormitory; I don't think he can be healthy."

Emerson burst into an unexpected shout of laughter.

"Being dead is the ultimate of unhealthiness, I suppose. Never fear; the mummy is resting in a cave at the bottom of the path. I only wish I could account for his original position as easily."

"I might have a look at the tomb in the morning," I said. "That would leave the afternoon for working on the pavement—"

"And what do you expect to find?" Emerson's voice rose. "Good God, madam, you seem to think you are a trained archaeologist! Do you think you can walk in here and—"

Walter and Evelyn broke in simultaneously in an attempt to change the subject. They succeeded for the moment, but Emerson was sulky and snappish for the rest of the evening. When I tried to feel his forehead to see if he had developed a temperature, he stalked off to his tomb, fairly radiating grumpiness.

"Don't mind him, Miss Peabody," Walter said, when he was out of earshot. "He is still not himself, and enforced inactivity infuriates a man of his energy."

"He is not himself," I agreed. "In normal health he is even louder and more quarrelsome."

"We are all a little on edge," Evelyn said in a low voice. "I don't know why I should be; but I feel nervous."

"If that is the case we had better go to bed," I said, rising. "Some sleep will settle your mind, Evelyn."

Little did I know that the night was to bring, not a cure for troubled minds, but the beginning of greater trouble.

It is a recognized fact that sleepers train themselves to respond only to unfamiliar noises. A zoo keeper slumbers placidly through the normal nightly roars of his charges, but the squeak of a mouse in his tidy kitchen can bring him awake in an instant. I had accustomed my sleeping mind to the sounds of Amarna. They were few indeed; it was one of the most silent spots on earth, I think. Only the far-off ululation of an occasional love-sick jackal disturbed the silence. So, on this particular night, it was not surprising that the sound at the door of our tomb, slight though it was, should bring me upright, with my heart pounding.

Light penetrated cracks in the curtain, but I could see nothing without. The sound continued. It was the oddest noise—a faint, dry scratching, like the rubbing of a bony object on rock.

Once my pulse had calmed, I thought of explanations. Someone on the ledge outside the tomb—Michael, keeping watch, or Walter, sleepless outside his lady's chamber? Somehow my nerves were not convinced by either idea. In any case, the sound was keeping me awake. I fumbled for my parasol.

The frequent mention of this apparatus may provoke mirth in the reader. I assure her (or him, as the case may be) that I was not intending to be picturesque.

It was a very sturdy parasol, with a stiff iron staff, and I had chosen it deliberately for its strength.

Holding it, then, in readiness for a possible act of violence, I called softly, "Who is there?"

There was no response. The scratching sound stopped. It was followed, after a moment or two, by another sound, which rapidly died away, as if someone, or something, had beat a hasty but quiet retreat.

I leaped from bed and ran to the doorway. I confess that I hesitated before drawing back the curtain. A parasol, even one of steel, would not be much use against a feral animal. The scratching sound might well have been produced by claws; and although I had been told that there were no longer any lions in Egypt, they had abounded in ancient times, and an isolated specimen might have survived in the desolate region. As I stood listening with all my might I heard another sound, like a rock or pebble rolling. It was quite a distance away. Thus reassured, I drew back the curtain and, after a cautious glance without, stepped onto the ledge.

The moon was high and bright, but its position left the ledge in shadow. Against this dark background an object stood out palely. It was at the far end of the ledge, where it curved to pass around a shoulder of rock; and I was conscious of an odd constriction of my diaphragm as I glimpsed it.

The shape was amorphous. It was of the height and breadth of a man, but it more resembled a white stone pillar than a human form, split at the bottom to present an imitation of a man's lower limbs. Stiff, stubby appendages like arms protruded at shoulder height, but they were not arms; humans arms were never so rigid.

As I stared, blinking to cure what I thought must be a failure of my vision, the shape disappeared. It must have moved around the corner of the path. A faint moaning sigh wafted back to me. It might have been the sigh of the wind; but I felt no movement of air.

I retreated to my bed, but I did not sleep well the rest of the night. The first pale streaks of dawn found me wide awake, and I was glad to arise and dress. I had managed to convince myself that what I saw was a large animal of some kind, raised on its back legs as a cat or panther will rise; so the full horror of the night did not strike me until I stepped out onto the ledge, which was now illumined by the rising sun. As I did so, something crackled under my foot.

Sunrise in Egypt is a glorious spectacle. The sun, behind the cliffs at my back, shone fully upon the western mountains; but I had no eye for the beauties of nature then. The sound and feel of the substance my foot had crushed was horribly familiar. With reluctance I bent to pick it up, though my fingers shrank from the touch of it.

I held a small fragment of brown flaking cloth, so dry that it crackled like paper when my fingers contracted. I had seen such cloth before. It was the rotting bandage which had once wrapped an ancient mummy.

Chapter Six

 I stood on the ledge for some time, trying to think sensibly. Emerson had spent some hours with the mummy. Fragments of the fragile cloth, caught on the fabric of his garments, might have been brushed off when he sat down at dinner the night before. But as soon as the idea entered my mind, common sense dismissed it. There was a regular trail of the stuff leading down the ledge as far as I could see. If Emerson's clothes had been so untidy I would have noticed. Further, Emerson's chair was some six feet away from the door of our chamber. He had never approached our door last night; and the largest heap of fragments was there, as if it had been deposited by a creature who stood for a long time on our threshold.

I don't know what instinct moved me to action—fear for Evelyn's nerves, perhaps, or concern for the superstitions of the workers. At any rate, I dashed inside, snatched up a cloth, and swept the horrible fragments off the ledge. Evelyn was still sleeping; and from below, the fragrance of coffee reached my nostrils. Michael was on duty early.

I was not the only early riser. As I stood by the campfire sipping my tea, Emerson came down the path. He gave me a surly nod and paused for a moment, as if daring me to order him back to bed. I said nothing; and after a while he went on and disappeared into the cave where his precious mummy had been deposited.

He had not been within for more than a few seconds when the sweet morning air was rent by a hideous cry. I dropped my cup, splashing my foot with hot tea; before I could do more, Emerson burst out of the cave. His inflamed eyes went straight to me. He raised both clenched fists high in the air.

"My mummy! You have stolen my mummy! By Gad, Peabody, this time you have gone too far! I've watched you; don't think I have been unwitting of your machinations! My pavement, my expedition, my brother's loyalty, even my poor, helpless carcass have fallen victim to your meddling; but this—this is too much! You disapprove of my work, you want to keep me feeble and helpless in bed, so you steal my mummy! Where is it? Produce it at once, Peabody, or—"

His shouts aroused the rest of the camp. I saw Evelyn peering curiously from the ledge above, clutching the collar of her dressing gown under her chin. Walter bounded down the path, trying to stuff his flying shirttails into his waistband and simultaneously finish doing up the buttons.

"Radcliffe, Radcliffe, what are you doing? Can't you behave for five minutes?"

"He is accusing me of stealing his mummy," I said. My own tones were rather loud. "I will overlook his other ridiculous accusations, which can only be the product of a disturbed brain—"

"Disturbed! Certainly I am disturbed! Of all the ills on earth, an interfering female is the worst!"

By this time we were surrounded by a circle of staring faces; the workers, coming in from the village, had been attracted by the uproar. They could not understand Emerson's remarks, but the tone of anger was quite comprehensible; their dark eyes were wide with alarm and curiosity as they watched Emerson's extraordinary performance. Foremost in the crowd stood Mohammed, the man who had led us to the tomb the day before. There was the most peculiar expression on his face—a kind of sly smirk. It interested me so much that I failed to respond to Emerson's latest outburst, and turned away, leaving him waving his fists at empty air. Mohammed saw me. Instantly his mouth turned down and his eyes widened in a look of pious alarm that would have suited an angel.

Seeing the futility of communication with Emerson when he was in this state, Walter turned to the cave where the mummy was kept. He was soon out again; his expressive face told me the truth before he spoke.

"The mummy is gone," he said, shaking his head in disbelief. "Only scraps of the wrappings remain. Why would anyone steal such a poor specimen?"

"These people would steal their grandmothers and sell them if there were a market for decrepit old ladies," Emerson growled.

I had observed that his fists of rage, though violent, were soon over. Afterward he seemed greatly refreshed by the outburst and would, in fact, deny that he had ever lost his temper. He now spoke to me as if he had never made his outrageous accusations.

"What about breakfast, Peabody?"

I was meditating a suitably crushing retort when Walter spoke again.

"It is really incomprehensible. The men could have made off with the mummy when they first found it. And what has become of the bandages you removed?"

"That, at least, is easily explained," Emerson answered. "I could not unwrap the bandages. The perfumed resins in which the body was soaked had glued the wrappings into a solid mass. I had to make an incision and open the thorax. As you know, Walter, the body cavities often contain amulets and scraps of—Peabody! Miss Peabody, what is the matter?"

His voice faded into a dim insect buzzing, and the sunlight darkened. A ghastly vision had flashed upon my mind. If the moon had been higher—if I had seen the nocturnal visitor more distinctly—would I have beheld the violated body, gaping wide?

I am happy to say that this was the first and last time I succumbed to superstition. When I opened my eyes I realized that Emerson was supporting me, his alarmed face close to mine. I straightened, and saw a dark flush mantle his cheeks as I pushed his arms away.

"A momentary weakness," I said. "I think—I think perhaps I will sit down."

Walter quickly offered his arm, and I did not disdain it.

"You are wearing yourself out, Miss Peabody," he said warmly. "We cannot allow such sacrifices. Today you must rest; I insist upon it."

"Hmmm," said Emerson. His eyes expressed neither concern nor appreciation, but rather speculation as they examined my face.

As the day wore on I could not help recalling Evelyn's remark of the previous evening. I had discounted her mention of nervousness then; now I could not deny that the atmosphere was uneasy. I myself was unable to settle down to anything. After working on the pavement for a time I went to the site where Walter and Abdullah were directing the workers.

There were more than fifty people at work. The men were removing the sand that had covered the foundations of temples and houses, shoveling it into baskets which were then carried away by children, boys and girls both. It was necessary to dump the sand some distance away, lest it cover future excavations. The work was tedious, except when the men reached the floor level, where abandoned objects might be found; yet all the workers, children and adults alike, usually worked cheerfully and willingly. They are very musical people, the Egyptians, although their wailing, yodeling singing sounds odd to European ears; but today no brisk chorus speeded the work. The children who carried the baskets were slow and unsmiling.

I joined Abdullah, the foreman, where he stood on a little rise of sand watching the diggers.

"They do not sing today," I said. "Why not, Abdullah?"

Not a muscle moved in the dignified brown face; but I sensed an inner struggle.

"They are ignorant people," he said, after a time. "They fear many things."

"What things?"

"Afreets, demons—all strange things. They fear ghosts of the dead. The mummy—they ask where it has gone."

That was all he could, or would, say. I went back to my pavement in some perturbation of spirit. I could hardly sneer at the ignorance of the natives when I had experienced equally wild thoughts.

The reader may well ask why I had not spoken of my adventure. I asked myself the same question; but I knew the answer, and it did not reflect creditably on my character. I was afraid of being laughed at. I could almost hear Emerson's great guffaws echoing out across the valley when I told him of seeing his lost mummy out for a midnight stroll. And yet I felt I ought to speak. I knew I had not seen an animated mummy. My brain knew it, if my nervous system did not. I spent the rest of the day brushing tapioca and water over my lovely pavement and carrying on a vigorous internal debate—common sense against vanity.

When we gathered on the ledge for our customary evening meeting, I could see that the others were also distraught. Walter looked very tired; he dropped into a chair with a sigh and let his head fall back.

"What a wretched day! We seem to have accomplished nothing."

"I shall come down tomorrow," said Emerson. He looked at me. "With Peabody's permission or without it."

Walter sat upright.

"Radcliffe, why do you address Miss Peabody so disrespectfully? After all she has done for us . . ."

It was unusual for Walter to speak so sharply—another indication, if I had needed one, of the strained atmosphere.

"Oh, I don't mind," I said calmly. "Sticks and stones may break my bones, you know. As for your returning to work tomorrow . . ."

I looked Emerson up and down. The clinical appraisal annoyed him, as I had known it would; he squirmed like a guilty schoolboy, and exclaimed, "What is your diagnosis, Sitt Hakim?"

Truthfully, I was not pleased with his appearance. He had lost considerable flesh. The bones in his face were too prominent, and his eyes were still sunken in their sockets.

"I disapprove," I said. "You are not strong enough yet to be out in the sun. Have you taken your medicine today?"

Emerson's reply was not suitable for the pages of a respectable book. Walter sprang to his feet with a hot reproof. Only the appearance of Michael, with the first course of our dinner, prevented an argument. We went early to bed. I could see that Emerson fully intended to return to the excavations next day, so he needed his sleep, and after my disturbed night I too was weary.

Yet I did not sleep well. I had disturbing dreams. I awoke from one such dream in the late hours of the night, and as my sleep-fogged eyes focused, I saw a slim white form standing by the doorway. My heart gave such a leap I thought it would choke me. When I recognized Evelyn, I almost fainted with relief.

She turned, hearing my gasp.

"Amelia," she whispered.

"What is it? Why are you awake at this hour? Good Gad, child, you almost frightened me to death!"

She looked ghostly as she glided toward me, her bare feet making no sound, her white nightdress floating out behind her. I lighted a lamp; Evelyn's face was as pale as her gown. She sank down on the edge of my bed, and I saw that she was shivering.

"I heard a sound," she said. "Such an eerie sound, Amelia, like a long, desolate sigh. I don't know how long it had been going on. It woke me; I am surprised it didn't waken you too."

"I heard it, and it became part of my dream," I answered. "I dreamed of death, and someone weeping over a grave . . . Then what happened?"

"I didn't want to wake you; you had worked so hard today. But the sound went on and on, until I thought I should die; it was so dreary, so unutterably sad. I had to know what was making it. So I went and drew the curtain aside and looked out."

She paused, and went even paler.

"Go on," I urged. "You need not fear my skepticism, Evelyn. I have reasons, which you will hear in due course, for believing the wildest possible tale."

"You cannot mean that you too—"

"Tell me what you saw."

"A tall, pale form, featureless and stark. It stood in shadow, but . . . Amelia, it had no face! There was no sign of nose or mouth or eyes, only a flat, white oval; no hair, only a smooth-fitting covering. The limbs were stiff—"

"Enough of this equivocation," I cried impatiently. "What you saw resembled . . . was like . . . seemed to be . . . in short—a Mummy!"

Evelyn stared at me.

"You saw it too! You must have done, or you could not accept this so readily. When? How?"

"One might add, 'why?' " I said wryly. "Yes, I saw such a form last night. This morning I found scraps of rotted wrappings on the ledge outside our chamber."

"And you said nothing of this to Walter—or to me?"

"It sounded too ridiculous," I admitted, "particularly after I learned that the mummy we discovered had mysteriously disappeared in the night."

"Ridiculous, Amelia? I wish I could think so. What are we to do?"

"I will have the courage to speak now that I have you to support me. But I shudder to think what Emerson will say. I can hear him now: 'A walking mummy, Peabody? Quite so! No wonder the poor fellow wants exercise, after lying stiff for two thousand years!' "

"Nevertheless, we must speak."

"Yes. In the morning. That will be time enough for my humiliation."

But the morning brought a new sensation, and new troubles.

I was up betimes. Emerson, another early riser, was already pacing about near the cook tent. A pith helmet, set at a defiant angle, proclaimed his intentions for the day. I glanced at it, and at his haggard face, and sniffed meaningfully; but I made no comment. Breakfast was prepared; we returned to our table on the ledge, where Evelyn and Walter joined us; and the meal was almost finished when Emerson exploded.

"Where are the men? Good God, they should have been here an hour ago!"

Walter withdrew his watch from his pocket and glanced at it.

"Half an hour. It appears they are late this morning."

"Do you see any signs of activity in the direction of the village?" Emerson demanded, shading his eyes and peering out across the sand. "I tell you, Walter, something is amiss. Find Abdullah."

The foreman, who slept in a tent nearby, was nowhere to be found. Finally we made out a small white figure crossing the sand. It was Abdullah; he had apparently been to the village in search of his tardy work force. We were all at the bottom of the path waiting when he came up to us. He spread out his hands in an eloquent gesture and looked at Emerson.

"They will not come."

"What do you mean, they won't come?" Emerson demanded.

"They will not work today."

"Is there some holiday, perhaps?" Evelyn asked. "Some Moslem holy day?"

"No," Emerson answered. "Abdullah would not make such an error, even if I did. I would think the men are holding out for higher pay, but . . . Sit down, Abdullah, and tell me. Come, come, my friend, let's not stand on ceremony. Sit down, I say, and talk."

Thus abjured, Abdullah squatted on the bare ground, in that very same posture in which his ancestors are so often depicted. His English was not very good, so I shall take the liberty of abridging his remarks.

A conscientious man, he had set out for the village when the workmen failed to appear on time. The squalid little huddle of huts presented a disquieting appearance. It was as deserted and silent as if plague had struck. No children played in the dusty streets; even the mangy curs had taken themselves off.

Alarmed, Abdullah had gone to the house of the mayor—who was, I learned for the first time, the father of Mohammed. He had to pound on the barred door before he was finally admitted, and it took him some time to extract the facts from the mayor. At first he said only that the men would not come. Upon being pressed, he said they would not come the next day either—or any other day. His son was with him; and it was from Mohammed that Abdullah finally received a statement. As Abdullah repeated this, his face retained its well-bred impassivity, but his eyes watched Emerson uneasily.

The workers had been disturbed by the mummy Mohammed had found. The man repeated his absurd claim—that the mummy was that of a princely priest-magician, a servant of the great god Amon whom Pharaoh Khuenaten had toppled from his spiritual throne. The deposed god's wrath found a vessel in his priest; through him, Amon had cursed the heretic city and anyone who set foot on its soil to resurrect it, forever. The villagers knew that none of them had made off with the mummy. Its disappearance could be accounted for in only one way; restored to the light of day, and animated by its discovery that new heretics were at work to uncover the accursed city, it had taken to its feet and left the camp. But it had not left the city—no, indeed. It walked by night, and on the previous midnight it had visited the village. Its moans had awakened the sleepers, and a dozen men had seen its ghostly form pacing the streets. The villagers were too wise not to heed the warning, which Mohammed helpfully interpreted: no more work for the infidels. They must leave Khuenaten's unholy city to the desolation of the sands, and take themselves off. Unless they did so, the curse would be visited on them and all those who assisted them in the slightest way.

Emerson listened to this bizarre hodgepodge without the slightest change of expression.

"Do you believe this, Abdullah?" he asked.

"No." But the foreman's voice lacked conviction.

"Nor do I. We are educated men, Abdullah, not like these poor peasants. Amon-Ra is a dead god; if he could once curse a city, he lost that power centuries go. The mosques of your faith stand on the ruins of the temples, and the muezzin calls the faithful to prayer. I do not believe in curses; but if I did, I would know that our god—call him Jehovah or Allah, he is One—has the power to protect his worshipers against demons of the night. I think you believe that too."

I had never admired Emerson more. He had taken precisely the right tone with his servant, and as Abdullah looked up at the tall form of his employer, there was a glint of amused respect in his dark eyes.

"Emerson speaks well. But he does not say what has become of the mummy."

"Stolen." Emerson squatted on his lean haunches, so that he and Abdullah were eye to eye. "Stolen by a man who wishes to cause dissension in the camp, and who has invented this story to support his aim. I do not name this man; but you remember that Mohammed was angry because I brought you in to be foreman instead of giving him the position. His doting father has not disciplined him properly; even the men of the village resent him."

"And fear him," Abdullah said. He rose to his feet in a single effortless movement, his white robes falling in graceful folds. "We are of one mind, Emerson. But what shall we do?"

"I will go down to the village and talk to the mayor," Emerson said, rising. "Now go and eat, Abdullah. You have done well, and I am grateful."

The tall foreman walked away, not without an uneasy look at Emerson. Evelyn glanced at me. I nodded. I had not wished to speak in front of Abdullah, but the time had come to tell my story. Before I could start, Walter burst out.

"What an incredible tale! You would think I should be accustomed to the superstitious folly of these people, but I am constantly amazed at their credulity. They are like children. A mummy, walking the village streets—could there be anything more absurd?"

I cleared my throat self-consciously. This was not a good prelude to the tale I was about to tell.

"It is absurd, Walter, but it is not imagination. The villagers are not the only ones to see the Mummy. Evelyn and I both saw such a shape here in the camp."

"I knew you were hiding something," Emerson said, with grim satisfaction. "Very well, Peabody, we are listening."

I told all. I did not tell the story well, being only too conscious of Emerson's sneer. When I had finished, Walter was speechless. My support came, unexpectedly, from Emerson himself.

"This proves nothing, except that our villain—and we have a good notion as to his identity, have we not?—has gone to the trouble of dressing up in rags and wandering around in order to frighten people. I confess I am surprised; I had not thought Mohammed would be so energetic, or so imaginative."

As he spoke the last word, a memory popped into my mind. In the hotel in Cairo another imaginative miscreant had penetrated my room, dressed as an ancient Egyptian. I started to speak and then changed my mind; there surely could be no connection between the two events.

"I am off to the village," Emerson said. "I have dealt with these people before; I think I can persuade the mayor. Walter?"

The distance to the village was several miles. I am sure I need not say that I made part of the expedition. Evelyn remained behind, feeling herself unequal to the exertion; with Abdullah and Michael in camp, she was amply protected. Emerson, who had opposed my coming with his customary temper tantrum, was annoyed that I kept up with him easily. Of course I could not have done so if he had been at his normal strength, and I was increasingly concerned for him as he plodded through the sand.

The brooding silence of the village was most disturbing. I thought at first we would not be admitted to the slightly more pretentious hovel that housed the mayor of the village, but Emerson's repeated blows on the rickety door finally produced a response. The door opened a mere crack; the sharply pointed nose and wrinkle-wrapped eyes of the old sheikh peered out. Emerson gave the door a shove. He caught the old gentleman as he staggered back and politely set him on his feet. We were in the house.

I wished immediately that I was out. The stench of the place was indescribable. Chickens, goats, and people crowded the dark little room; their eyes shone like stars in the shadows. We were not invited to sit down, and indeed there was no surface in the place on which I would have cared to sit. Obviously the chickens roosted on the long divan that was the room's most conspicuous piece of furniture.

Emerson, arms folded and chin jutting, carried on the discussion in Arabic. I could not understand what was being said, but it was easy to follow the course of the conversation. The mayor, a wrinkled little old man whose pointed nose almost met his bony chin, mumbled his responses. He was not insolent or defiant; this attitude would have been easier to combat than his obvious terror.

Gradually the other human inhabitants of the place slipped away; only the goats and the chickens remained. One friendly goat was particularly intrigued with the sleeve of my dress. I pushed him away absentmindedly, trying to keep track of what was transpiring between the speakers, and slowly the truth dawned on me. The mayor could hardly bear to be in the same room with us. He kept retreating until his back was up against the wall.

Then someone slipped through the narrow aperture that gave entry into the back room—the only other chamber this mayoral palace contained. I recognized Mohammed. With his appearance the conversation took a new turn. His father turned to him with pathetic pleasure, and Mohammed took over his role in the argument. He *was* insolent; his very tone was an offense. Emerson's fists clenched and his lips set tightly as he listened. Then Mohammed glanced at me and broke into English.

"The Mummy hate stranger," he said, grinning. "Stranger go. But not women. Mummy like English women—"

Emerson was on him in a single bound. The poor old father squealed in alarm; but it was Walter who plucked his infuriated brother from Mohammed's throat. The man collapsed, moaning, when Emerson's fingers were detached, but even in the bad light I saw the look he gave his assailant; and a chill ran through me.

"Come away," Walter said in a low voice, holding his brother's rigid arm. "Come away, there is nothing more we can do here."

We did not linger in the village, but traversed its single narrow street as quickly as we could. When we reached the clean emptiness of the desert, Emerson stopped. His face was shining with perspiration; under his tan he was a sickly gray in color.

"I think I owe you both an apology," he said thickly. "That was stupid of me; I have ruined any chance we might have had of convincing the mayor."

"I heard what the fellow said," Walter replied. "I don't blame you, Radcliffe; it was all I could do to control myself. I feel sure Mohammed is out to drive us away; your action was ill advised, but I don't think it mattered."

"I am amazed at his effrontery," I exclaimed. "Doesn't he realize what he risks from the authorities in opposing you?'"

Emerson's face darkened.

"Egypt is more unsettled than those complacent fools in Cairo realize. The mad dervish in the Sudan has stirred up the peasants; most Egyptians secretly yearn for his success and gloat at every British defeat. I wouldn't give a shilling for the lives of foreigners here if the Mahdi should approach the First Cataract."

"But surely there is not the slightest danger of that! Gordon is still making a valiant defense at Khartoum, and Wolseley's expedition is about to relieve him. How can untrained native rebels succeed against British troops?"

Emerson's answer was all the more convincing because I secretly believed it myself; but I would not give him the satisfaction of looking as if I agreed.

"Those untrained rebels have already massacred half a dozen British armies, including that of Colonel Hicks. I have the gravest fears for Gordon's safety; it will be a miracle if the relief expedition arrives in time. The whole business in the Sudan has been a masterpiece of blunders from start to finish. In the meantime, we seem to be facing a minor rebellion here, and I won't tolerate it."

Stumbling a little, he started walking.

"Where are you going?" I asked. "The camp is this way."

"There are two other villages on the plain. If the men of Haggi Qandil will not work, we will try el Till and al Amarnah."

"I fear it will be useless." Walter caught up with his brother and tried to take his arm. Emerson shook it off. "Radcliffe, stop and listen; you aren't fit to walk all over the desert today, and you can be sure that Mohammed's story has reached the other villages as well. They battle among themselves, but they are of the same stock. Your efforts will not avail there any more than they did at Haggi Qandil."

Emerson's feet were dragging, but his chin was set stubbornly. I decided to end the matter before he fell flat on his face.

"Let him go, Walter," I said. "You know he is too stubborn to listen to reason. What we need now is a council of war; we must consult Abdullah, and also Michael, who is an astute man. I can think of several things we might do, but we may as well wait until after your brother has fainted, then he won't be in our way, arguing and shouting. I think we can drag him back to camp from here. If not, Abdullah and Michael can come for him."

Emerson was still on his feet when we reached the camp. Walter took him into their tomb for restorative action; then we met for the suggested council of war.

This was the first time Michael had heard of what was happening. He spent his nights on the dahabeeyah, considering the three-mile walk trivial; as a Christian and a stranger he was not welcome in the village. Squatting on the rug at my side he listened without comment; but his fingers strayed to the gold crucifix around his neck, and he kept touching it throughout the remainder of the discussion. I asked him for his suggestions.

"Leave this place," he said promptly. "I am protected from demons"—

and his fingers closed over the crucifix—"but in this place are also evil men. The boat waits; we all go, the gentlemen too."

"Surely you don't believe in demons, Michael," Evelyn said in her gentle voice.

"But, lady, it is in the Holy Book. God lets demons and afreets exist; how can we say the Holy Book is a lie? I do not fear demons, no, I am a true believer. But this is not a good place."

Abdullah nodded vigorously. His faith was not Michael's, but beneath both Christianity and Islam lie the dark superstitions of the pagan religion.

"Michael has made one of the proposals I intended to make," I said, nodding at Michael, who beamed with gratified pride. "You must face the fact, gentlemen, that you can do no more here at this time. I suggest you withdraw and recruit workers from some other part of Egypt. They will not be subject to the influence Mohammed can bear; and when the local villagers see that the work is proceeding without incident, they will realize that the idea of a curse is nonsense."

Walter was clearly impressed with the argument, and with the additional point I had not made—his brother's health. He looked at Emerson, who said nothing; but his chin jutted out so far that I had to repress an urgent desire to strike it.

"There are other sites in Egypt that need work," Evelyn added. "Many of them, from what you tell me. Why not try another place until the resentment has died down here?"

"An interesting suggestion," Emerson said. His voice was very quiet; it grated like a grinding stone. "What do you say, Abdullah?"

"Very good, very good. We go. Work at Sakkarah, Luxor. I know tombs in the Valley of the Kings," he added, with a sly glance at Emerson. "Royal tombs, many not found yet. I find you good king's tomb and we go to Thebes, where is my home, where I have friends who work gladly."

"Hmm," said Emerson. "There certainly are undiscovered tombs in the Valley of the Kings. It is a tempting suggestion, Abdullah. You seem to forget, however, that one cannot excavate in Egypt without permission from the Antiquities Department. I had a difficult enough time wringing this concession out of Maspero; he certainly will not allow me to dig in any spot where he hopes to find interesting objects. There is also a minor matter of money to be considered. Walter—what is your opinion?"

Walter had been looking at Evelyn. He started when his brother addressed him, and faint color stained his tanned cheeks.

"Why, Radcliffe, you know I will do whatever you wish. But I urge one thing most strongly. Whether you and I go or stay, the ladies must leave. Not that our situation holds any danger; but it is unpleasant, and the ladies have already given too much time to us. They must depart; today, if possible."

A tear glimmered in my eye as I gazed at the gallant young fellow. He was a true Briton, ordering the girl he loved out of danger and remaining loyal to his billy goat of a brother. Evelyn clasped her hands and gazed at me beseechingly. She felt the same loyalty to me, and would not oppose my decision. There was no need for her appeal. I had no intention of being removed, like a bundle of laundry, to a safe spot behind the lines of battle.

"The suggestion is well meant, but I cannot accept it," I said briskly. "Either we all go, or all of us remain."

Emerson now turned his full attention to me. He drew a deep breath; the buttons of his shirt strained across his broad chest. They were all loose, and I reminded myself to fetch my sewing kit as soon as the argument was over.

"Ah, Miss Peabody," he said, in a low growl. "My dear Miss Peabody. May I take the liberty of inquiring how the devil——" His voice rose to a roar; a gesture from Walter stopped him, and he continued in a moderate voice that shook with the strain of control. "How on earth did you come to be mixed up in my affairs? I am a patient man; I seldom complain. But my life was calm and peaceful until you came into it. Now you behave as if you were the leader of the expedition! I quite agree with Walter; the women must go. Now don't argue with me, Peabody! Do you realize that I could have you bundled up and carried off to your boat? Michael and Abdullah would be delighted to do the job."

I glanced down at Michael, who was listening in openmouthed interest.

"No, Michael would not obey you. He would prefer to see me out of here, I'm sure, but he would not disregard my wishes. Now, Emerson, don't waste time arguing. I can see that you intend to remain here, and I must admit that I am reluctant to abandon the work—to see the British lion skulk away with its tail between its legs . . ."

"Oh, God," said Emerson. He rolled his eyes until the whites showed. I felt that the remark was not intended as a prayer, but decided not to make an issue of it. I continued.

"Having decided to remain, we must consider the next step. You cannot obtain workmen here. Unless my crew . . ."

I glanced at Michael, who shook his head, and went on, "No, I thought they would not. And I fear any workers you might import might be subject to the same harassment. I suggest, then, that today we all work at finishing up the pavement. Evelyn must complete her sketch; I will apply the rest of the tapioca. Tonight we will proceed to the obvious course of action. We must catch the Mummy, and unmask him!"

Walter sat upright and clapped his hands.

"Miss Amelia, you are a wonder. Of course! With four of us on guard——"

"Six of us," I said. "I think that is sufficient; there is no need to bring the boat crew into this. I suggest that one of us watch the village. Mohammed must slip out in his disguise if he wants to haunt us, and since he is determined to get rid of us, he will probably pay us a visit tonight. The rest of us will lie in wait for him. Have you firearms?"

Evelyn let out a little cry of alarm.

Emerson's face underwent a series of silent convulsions. He said in a muffled voice, "I do not have firearms. They are dangerous and unnecessary."

"Then we will have to use clubs," I said.

Emerson's lips writhed. "I can't stand this," he muttered, and sprang to his feet. As he walked away, I saw that his shoulders were shaking uncontrollably, and I realized he must be weaker than I had thought.

"Have a good rest," I called out after his retreating form. "We should all sleep this afternoon, in order to be alert tonight."

Emerson's only response was a sort of muted roar. He disappeared into his tomb, and I turned to Walter, who was staring after his brother.

"He is weak with exhaustion, Walter. You had better—"

"No," said Walter. "I don't think so."

"What is wrong with him, then?"

Walter shook his head dazedly. "It is impossible . . . But if I did not know better, I would swear he was laughing."

II

The rest of the day proceeded according to plan—*my* plan. Evelyn finished her sketch of the pavement. It was a lovely thing; she had caught perfectly the muted pastel shades of the original. I then sent her back to rest while I finished applying the protective coating. It was early evening before I was done, and when I returned to camp I found dinner underway. Thanks to my efforts, there was a new spirit about the place. We were a small, reduced force, but we were united. Even Michael and Abdullah seemed cheerful and alert. Over dinner we made the rest of our plans.

Walter and Abdullah were to watch the village, with special attention to the mayor's house. Like all primitive groups, the village retired as soon as the sun went down. We did not expect any activity much before midnight, but the watchers were to take their places as soon as it was completely dark. Should Mohammed emerge, they were to follow him. He probably did not keep his mummy disguise in the house; Emerson felt sure that his father was not one of the plotters. The old man's fear had seemed genuine. Mohammed, then, would go to the spot—of which there were many in the crumbling cliffs—where he had concealed his costume, and assume it there. The watchers were not to interfere with him until they saw him actually in his disguise. They would then apprehend him; one would hold him captive while the other ran to give us the news. In a body we would haul the miscreant back to the village and expose his trickery.

On the remote chance that Mohammed was able to elude our gallant watchers, the rest of us prepared a second line of defense. Evelyn, with Michael to guard her, would retire to her chamber, though not to her bed, of course. From the doorway Michael would keep watch. Meanwhile, Emerson and I would take up our positions in his tomb chamber, which was some distance down the ledge from the one we ladies occupied. Any visitor would have to pass this door in order to reach Evelyn, who would thus be doubly protected. I must confess I felt a trifle uneasy on Evelyn's behalf. Mohammed's vile remark fit only too neatly with the mute evidence of the crumbled wrappings outside the door of the chamber where Evelyn slept.

As soon as it was dark, Walter and Abdullah slipped away. I settled Evelyn, with Michael standing by; he was holding a long cudgel, and although he began to show signs of uneasiness as the mysterious dusk gathered. I felt sure he would use the club if anything threatened Evelyn. I did not expect such a necessity would arise. If the Mummy eluded the watchers at the village, Emerson and I would take care of him.

After assuming a suitable costume, I crept along the ledge to Emerson's tomb. He was seated at the packing case that served as a desk, writing by the light of a lamp. When I slid stealthily into the chamber, he dropped his pen and stared.

"Is this a masquerade party, Peabody? The Mummy will win first prize in any case; your old gypsy lady will not compete."

"Obviously dark clothing is necessary if I wish to be unseen," I replied, in some annoyance. "The black head scarf keeps my hair from flying about, and the dirt is necessary to darken the comparative pallor of my face and hands. I was about to suggest the same precautions for you. And put out the lamp, if you please."

"I will put out the lamp at the usual time," Emerson said coldly. "If someone is watching, we do not wish to alarm him by any deviation from our routine. I suggest you squat there in the corner, Peabody, where you will not be visible from the doorway. No one would ever believe, seeing you as you look just now, that I had invited you here for—er—amorous purposes."

I did not think it worthwhile to dignify this remark with a reply. Giving him a haughty look, I went to my corner.

The ensuing hours dragged tediously. At first I amused myself by watching Emerson, who continued to write as if I had not been there. He needed a haircut. Despite his illness his hair was healthy-looking—thick and black and a little wavy where it curled over his collar. The movement of the muscles of his back, under his thin shirt, was interesting to a student of anatomy.

After a time this occupation palled. I crawled across to the packing-case table, this maneuver winning an irritable growl from Emerson, and took one of the books that were scattered on its surface. It was a volume on the pyramids of Gizeh, by a certain Mr. Petrie. I remembered hearing Emerson mention this young scholar, if not with approval—for Emerson did not speak of anyone with approval—at least without the invective he directed toward most other archaeologists, so I began to read with considerable interest. I could see why Emerson approved of Mr. Petrie. The meticulous care with which his measurements were carried out, checked, and rechecked was most impressive. He had totally disproved the mystical theories of the people who think the Great Pyramid to be a great prophecy in stone; and his description of the methods used by the ancients in cutting and shaping stones with the most primitive tools was convincing and interesting. So I read on, in the dim light, the silence broken only by the whisper as I turned a page, and by the scratch of Emerson's pen. I suppose I must have presented a curious figure as I squatted there in my dusty black skirt and cloak, with my dirty face bent over the tome.

Finally Emerson laid down his pen and rose. He yawned and stretched ostentatiously. Then, without so much as a glance in my direction, he blew out the lamp. Darkness obliterated every object. As my eyes gradually adjusted, I made out the open entrance, a square of sky glittering with stars.

Placing the book carefully on the table, I crawled to the doorway. A whisper from Emerson told me of his position; I took up my post on the other side of the door.

An even more boring period of time followed. I had no book with which to beguile my time, and Emerson did not seem inclined for conversation. I believed it was safe to whisper; we could see some distance, and would have seen an intruder long before he could have heard low voices. Nor did I really believe Mohammed would get this far. He had no reason to expect an ambush, and would be trapped by Abdullah and Walter as soon as he betrayed himself by assuming his mummy attire.

But Emerson squelched my first attempt to discuss the theories of Mr. Petrie, so I did not try again.

The beauty of the night was unbelievable. I have never seen stars so thickly clustered as those that bestrew the night sky of Egypt; they blazed like a pharaoh's treasure against the dark. The cool, sweet air was as refreshing as water after a long thirst, and the silence was infinitely soothing. Even the distant howls of the jackals seemed fitting, a lonely cry that mourned the loss of past splendor.

I confess I was half asleep, leaning against the wall, when another sound broke the silence. I really did not expect it; I was so surprised and so stupid with sleep that I moved, and the brush of my sleeve against the stone sounded like an alarm. Emerson's arm moved in an abrupt warning gesture. My eyes were accustomed to the dark and the light from without helped me to see his movements; I was aware of the moment when his whole body stiffened and his head shifted forward as he stared.

From his side of the doorway he could see the far end of the ledge and the lower slope where the cooking tent, and the tent Abdullah occupied, were located. I saw the other end of the ledge, where it passed Evelyn's tomb. There was nothing to be seen there, although I thought the curtain before the doorway was pulled back just a little, where Michael stood watch.

Emerson put out his hand. We understood one another that night without the need of words. I grasped his hand and took two slow, silent steps to his side.

The thing was there. Pale in the moonlight, it stood motionless, not on the ledge, but on the lower slope. This time the moon shone full upon it, and there could be no mistake as to its nature. I could almost make out the pattern of the bandaging across its breast. The featureless head was wrapped all around with cloth. It was bad enough to see this monstrosity when it stood motionless; but as I watched, the head turned. Its slow, weaving movement was appalling, like that of an eyeless creature of the abyss blindly seeking some source of attraction even more alluring than light.

Emerson's hand closed over my mouth. I let it remain; I had been about to gasp aloud, and he had heard the inspiration of breath that warned him of my intent. Insanely, the Mummy seemed to hear it too, although I knew that was impossible. The blind head turned up, as if looking toward the ledge.

Emerson's fingers were ice cold; he was not so impervious as he pretended. And as the creature's right arm lifted, in a threatening gesture, Emerson's self-control broke. Releasing me so abruptly that I staggered, he bounded out onto the ledge.

I was at his heels. Secrecy was useless now. I called out a warning as Emerson, disdaining the ledge path, plunged over the edge and slithered down the slope amid an avalanche of sliding pebbles. It was an imprudent thing to do, in the poor light, and it received the usual consequences of imprudence. Emerson lost his footing, slipped, and fell headlong.

The Mummy was in full flight. I watched it for a moment; its lumbering, stiff-kneed stride attained unexpected speed. I knew I should not be able to catch it up; nor, to be honest, was I anxious to do so. I followed the path down and picked my way through the fallen rocks to where Emerson was struggling to sit up. Evelyn and Michael were both on the ledge, calling out to me, and I shouted a brief synopsis as I went along.

"It was here; it has gone. Michael, don't come down. Don't stir from Miss Evelyn's side."

For, by this time, I was ready to grant the nocturnal horror any degree of slyness. This might be a diversion, to draw us away from its intended victim.

Why did I believe the creature meant to do more than frighten us? Emerson asked this very question, when we had all calmed down and were seated in his tomb discussing the event.

"I can't say for sure," I answered, in a tentative manner that was uncharacteristic of me. "In part, it is simply logic; for if we fail to be frightened by the mere appearance of the thing, it must resort to more drastic measures. Then there is Mohammed's statement—you recall, Emerson, when we went to the village—"

I had not told Evelyn of this, and I did not intend to. Emerson understood my reference, and nodded. He was looking very grim; the bloodstained bandages around his brow and hands added to the warlike atmosphere of our council meeting.

"Yes, I recall. I think that was an empty threat, however; not even Mohammed would dare . . . Well, this has been a useless night. I will have something to say to young Walter when he wanders in; Mohammed diddled him and Abdullah very neatly."

"Should we not go out and look for them?" Evelyn asked anxiously. "Some accident may have befallen them."

"Not to both of them; that was why I sent two men, so that one might assist the other in case of misadventure. No, my two incapable friends are probably still hovering around the village waiting for Mohammed to come out. They may see him when he returns; but unless he has his disguise actually on his body, there is no use in apprehending him. No, Miss Evelyn, don't try to make me change my mind. Walter is perfectly safe, and we should only wander aimlessly in the dark if we went to search for him."

So far had the strangeness of our situation broken down formality that he actually addressed Evelyn by her first name. But then, I reflected in some surprise, we had all been informal, shockingly so. Several times, in the stress of emotion, I had so forgotten myself as to address Walter by his given name. I felt a genuine warmth toward the lad; it seemed as if I had known him a long time. Emerson, of course, could be called by no other name. His impertinence toward me did not allow me to address him respectfully, and I had no inclination to call him by his first name.

There was no sleep for us the rest of the night, although Emerson persuaded Evelyn to lie down on his cot. We had a long wait; the first streaks of dawn were red in the sky when the wanderers returned; and their astonishment, when they heard what had transpired, was equal to ours when we heard their report. Both were willing to swear that no one had left the village that night. Walter himself had watched the mayor's house, from an uncomfortable perch in a tree nearby. There was no possible way in which Mohammed could have been the Mummy.

Chapter Seven

I remember standing on the ledge, oblivious to the slow beauty of sunrise on the cliffs, as the impact of Walter's statement sank into my mind. None of us tried to argue with him; to believe that Mohammed had tricked both watchers, being unaware of surveillance, was really beyond the bounds of credibility.

Suddenly Emerson rose from his chair and ran off along the ledge. I knew where he was going. How I knew I cannot explain, but I did know; and I also knew what he would find. I followed him more slowly, my steps slowed by dread of the discovery. When I came up to him he was standing by the wooden shelter that had covered the painted pavement. The painting was no longer there. Only a broad expanse of broken shards covered the sand. The destruction had been vicious; some sections had been ground into powder.

So my work had gone for naught and the sacrifice of my skinned fingers had been in vain. This was not my first thought, however. The senseless, wanton loss of beauty miraculously preserved hurt like a physical blow.

Without conscious premeditation my hand reached out to Emerson's; his fingers closed bruisingly over mine and we stood for a moment with hands locked. After a moment Emerson seemed to realize what he was doing, and flung my hand away. The cut on his forehead was still oozing blood, but I knew his drawn, haggard expression was not caused by physical pain. I did not even resent his gesture.

"A vindictive apparition, our Mummy," I said.

"All part and parcel of the ridiculous story Mohammed is promulgating," Emerson said. "The priest of Amon wreaking his vengeance on Khuenaten's city. Peabody, has it occurred to you that this plot is too complex for a man of Mohammed's limited intelligence?"

"Perhaps you underestimate his intelligence"

"I think not. His motive is equally obscure to me. Why should he go to so much trouble for a petty revenge? Our presence brings income to the village—money these people badly need, however small it may seem to us."

"But if Walter is correct in claiming that Mohammed never left the village—"

"I cannot accept that. Who else could the Mummy be?"

"Then you think we must search for some power behind Mohammed. Who could *that* be?"

"That is equally difficult to understand. Unless some wealthy amateur excavator covets the site—"

"Oh, don't be ridiculous!" I exclaimed. "Next you will be accusing M. Maspero of planning this, in order to discredit you."

This injudicious remark ended the discussion. Emerson shot me a hateful look and started back toward camp.

Our spirits were at very low ebb that morning; if it had not been for Emerson's stubbornness, I think we would have taken our leave of Amarna. Only Evelyn's intervention prevented a full-scale battle at breakfast, and it was she who insisted that we all get some sleep before discussing the matter again. All our tempers were strained by fatigue, she said; we could not think clearly. This was, of course, Evelyn's tact; her temper was never strained, and I am rational under all circumstances. It was Emerson who needed rest in order to be sensible, although I doubted that sleep would improve his disposition very much.

We were all sleeping, then, when a shout from Abdullah, on guard below, roused us to the realization that some new factor had entered the scene. Stumbling out of the tomb and blinking against the brilliant sunlight, I made out a procession approaching us from the direction of the river. The leading figure was mounted on a donkey. It was soon clearly indentifiable.

I turned to Evelyn, who stood shading her eyes with her hand. "Reinforcements have arrived," I remarked. "It will be interesting to see what Lord Ellesmere makes of our little mystery."

"Lucas!" Evelyn exclaimed.

Walter, followed by his brother, came out in time to hear our exchange. At Evelyn's exclamation he gave her a piercing look. The surprise in her voice might well have been taken for another emotion; and Walter turned to view the newcomer with a frown. Lucas had seen us; he raised his arm and waved vigorously. We could see the flash of his white teeth against a face that was now tanned almost as deeply as the skin of the natives. Walter's frown became a scowl.

"So you are acquainted with this infernal intruder?" Emerson inquired. "I might have expected he would be a friend of yours, Peabody."

"After all, Emerson, this site is not your private property," I replied spiritedly. "It is surprising that we have not had more visitors."

This reasonable comment seemed to strike Emerson; he nodded thoughtfully. I went on to give the explanations I felt were his due.

"Lord Ellesmere is a distant relative of Evelyn's. We met him in Cairo just as we were about to sail, and he told us of his intention to take the same trip. We were expecting to meet in Luxor. No doubt he recognized the *Philae* at her moorings, and inquired as to our whereabouts."

I was rather pleased with this account, which seemed to me to convey the necessary information without adding any extraneous facts. I intended to caution Lucas not to betray his real relationship with Evelyn, or hers with the late Lord Ellesmere. Neither of the Emersons were interested in scandal, unless it concerned the love affairs of ancient Egyptian pharaohs, so it was unlikely that they should have heard of the escapade of the late Lord Ellesmere's young heiress; but there was no point in taking chances.

Then I looked at Evelyn; and my heart sank down into my scuffed boots. How could I try to shield her, when she was fully determined to expose the whole affair if it became necessary? She had paled a trifle as she watched her cousin's advance; her lips were set in an expression I had come to know very well. Young Walter's face, as he looked from Evelyn to the newcomer, gave his own feelings away more clearly than speech.

I experienced a revelation in that moment. I wanted Walter for Evelyn. They were ideally suited; he was an honorable, lovable young fellow, who would treat her well. If I had to give her up, I would not repine seeing her in the tender care of a man like Walter. I determined, in that instant, that it should come to pass. But I foresaw that it would take some effort, even for me.

Lucas was now close. Waving and laughing and shouting greetings, he came on. Walter turned to Evelyn.

"Will you not go down to meet this relative of yours?"

His tone was positively spiteful. I smiled to myself.

Evelyn started. "Yes, of course," she said.

"I will meet him," I said, taking her by the arm. "Stay here; I will have Michael bring tea."

Lucas fell on me with shouts of joy. The fellow would have embraced me if I had not fended him off with a well-placed shove. I interrupted his babble with the caution I had intended to give; and he shot me a reproachful look.

"No, such warning was necessary, Miss Amelia, I assure you. But tell me, what are you doing here? Your reis informed me that you have been here almost a week. Who are your friends, and why—"

Explanations and introductions followed, slowly, since Lucas kept interrupting. The interruptions ceased, however, when I—for of course it was I who was telling the story—reached the part of the narrative involving the Mummy. Lucas listened in silence. A grin spread slowly over his face, and when I concluded my story he burst into a shout of mirth.

"Excellent! Splendid! Little did I think when I set out for Egypt that I would have such luck. This is like one of Rider Haggard's tales; or the novels of Herr Ebers. How I look forward to meeting the Mummy!"

"I don't know that such an encounter will ever take place, Lord Ellesmere," Walter said. "There is no reason why you should concern yourself with our problems. If you will escort the ladies into safety, we—"

Lucas leaned forward; impetuously he placed a hand on the other young man's arm.

"But, my dear fellow, you would not deprive me of a part in this adventure? I don't claim any noble intentions; I'm sure you can manage quite well without me. My motives are purely selfish, and therefore you must give way to me!"

Watching his beaming face, hearing his jovial tones, I could understand why Mr. Dickens' Scrooge found his jolly nephew so irritating. I was also struck by the contrast between the two young men. They were almost of an age, I thought. Walter's slim height looked boyish next to Lucas' breadth of chest and shoulders. His tumbled dark hair and thin cheeks made him appear even younger. Lucas was dressed with his usual elegance; his pith helmet shone like snow in the sun, his light suit was tailored like a uniform and fit him like a glove. Walter's shirt was open at the throat, displaying reddened, peeling skin. His boots were shabby and dusty, his hands callused from hard labor.

At that, he looked relatively respectable next to his brother, whose bandaged brow and hand added to his look of a battered warrior just come off the battlefield. Emerson was contemplating Lucas with an expression that made me think we might become allies in this, if in nothing else. When he spoke, it was in the rasping growl that was more dangerous than his shouts.

"You should appeal to me, my lord, for permission to join our group. I confess I cannot think of any means of preventing you from pitching a tent anywhere you choose."

From Emerson this was positively a gracious speech. Lucas seemed to realize it; he turned his considerable charm on Emerson, who continued to study him with all the enthusiasm of a gruff old mastiff watching the gambols of a puppy. When Lucas expressed interest in the antiquities of the area, he unbent a trifle and offered to show Lucas some of the tombs.

"We have uncovered very little of the city," he explained. "The ruins that remain are not interesting to a layman. The carvings in the tombs have a certain appeal, however."

"I regret that I have not had time to examine them more closely," I interrupted. "I meant to ask you, Emerson, whether there might not be more tombs to be discovered. What of the king's own tomb, for instance? He of all people must have had a sepulcher here."

"That is one of the projects I had hoped to undertake this season," Emerson replied. "The royal tomb has never been properly cleared out, although these villainous villagers removed anything of salable value some time ago. There was not much; the reliefs in the tomb were never finished, and I question whether Khuenaten was ever buried there, although fragments of a sarcophagus may still be seen in the burial chamber. Hmmm. Yes, Peabody, I would like to have another look at it. Suppose we go this afternoon."

"The royal tomb is not to my taste today," Lucas said, stretching out his booted feet lazily. "It is quite a distance, I am told, and the path is rugged."

"It would mar the finish of your boots," Emerson agreed gravely. "You seem to know something about Amarna, Lord Ellesmere. The royal tomb is not on the ordinary traveler's list of sights."

"Oh, I have become an interested student of all things Egyptian. Already I have made a splendid collection of antiquities, and I hope to acquire more along the way. I intend to set up an Egyptian gallery at Ellesmere Castle."

Emerson had been keeping himself under tight rein—for what reason I could not imagine—but this was too much for him.

"Another amateur collection, ignorantly displayed and isolated from scholars," he burst out. "Of course you are collecting your antiquities from the dealers, my lord—which means that they have been wantonly pilfered from the original places, with no records kept—"

"I seem to have struck inadvertently at a tender spot," Lucas said, smiling at Evelyn.

She did not return the smile; instead she said seriously, "Mr. Emerson's feelings are more than justified, Lucas. It is vital that excavations should be carried out only by trained archaeologists. Some objects are fragile and can be damaged by unskilled hands. More important, the provenance of an object can sometimes tell us a great deal—where it was found, with what other objects, and so on. If visitors would not buy from dealers and peasants, they would stop their illicit digging."

"Dear me, you are becoming quite an enthusiast yourself," Lucas exclaimed. "That is what I shall need for my Egyptian gallery—an expert who will tend and classify my collection. Then perhaps Mr. Emerson will not despise me."

Evelyn's eyes fell under his meaningful regard.

"Emerson will despise you in any case," I said. "The only steps you can take to redeem yourself are, one, to cease buying antiquities, and two, to present the ones you have to the British Museum. The scholars there will take proper care of them."

Emerson muttered something which, though indistinct, was clearly uncomplimentary to the British Museum.

Lucas laughed. "No, I cannot give up my collection. But perhaps Mr. Emerson will read my papyrus for me."

"You have a papyrus?" I inquired interestedly.

"Yes, quite a good one—brown with age, crumbling, covered with those strange little scratches which were, I am told, developed from the hieroglyphic picture writing. When I unrolled it—"

An ominous moaning sound emerged from Emerson.

"You unrolled it," he repeated.

"Only the first section," said Lucas cheerfully. "It began to break apart then, so I thought. . . . Why, Mr. Emerson, you look quite pale. I gather I have done something reprehensible."

"You might as well confess to a murder," Emerson exclaimed. "There are too many people in the world as it is, but the supply of ancient manuscripts is severely limited."

Lucas seemed subdued by the reproof.

"I will give it to you, then, if you feel so strongly. Perhaps it will count as my payment of admission to this charming group," he added more cheerfully. "I must send back to my dahabeeyah for supplies, if I am to spend the night. Let us just have a look around, shall we? I can hardly wait to see the scenes of the Mummy's appearance, and select a tomb for myself."

Emerson acquiesced with no more than a mumble. I was at a loss to account for his amiability at first. Then two explanations occurred to me. I was ready to believe either or both, since neither reflected any credit on Emerson.

Money for excavation was hard to come by; a wealthy patron could relieve Emerson's anxieties in this area. Furthermore, it was as clear as print that Lucas was interested in Evelyn. His eyes seldom left her face, and he made no attempt to conceal his tender concern. Emerson must realize that Walter also loved the girl. He would not be pleased to lose his devoted acolyte; perhaps he meant Walter to marry well, in order to supply more funds for the gaping maw of his research. By encouraging a rival to his brother, he kept that brother under his callused thumb.

My suspicions were confirmed when Emerson waxed positively jovial as he showed Lucas the camp. As for Lucas, he bubbled with enthusiasm and admiration. Nothing could be more charming! He could not imagine anything more delightful than camping out in an ancient tomb! The scenery was magnificent, the air was like wine, and—in short, you would have thought our meticulous lordship was rhapsodizing over a modern luxury hotel and a vista of wooded grandeur. He plied Emerson with questions; shook his head over the perfidy of Mohammed and the superstitions of the visitors; insisted on pressing the hand of the faithful Abdullah, who looked askance at this demonstration. The only thing he expressed doubt about was Michael.

"Are you certain you can trust him?" he asked in a low voice, as we walked past the cook tent where Michael was preparing a simple lunch. The devoted fellow had taken over menial duties that would ordinarily have been below his dignity, since the villagers had abandoned us. We had decided not to involve any of our servants from the boat; there was no telling how they would react to the story, much less the sight, of the Mummy.

"I trust him implicitly," Evelyn replied firmly. "Amelia saved the life of his child; he would die for her, I think."

"Then there is no more to be said," said Lucas. But he did say more—a good deal more. Michael was, after all, a native. Was he not just as superstitious as the villagers? Could he be trusted to risk, not only his life, but his immortal soul, as he believed, with a demon of the night?

"I have considered that," Emerson replied shortly. "You need not concern yourself about it, your lordship."

His tone brooked no argument. Even Lucas recognized this, and he abandoned the subject.

Of the tombs in our immediate vicinity only a few were habitable; some were blocked by rock falls or heaps of debris. They were similar in plan, having a large hall with columns beyond the entrance corridor, from which another corridor led on to more rooms, including the burial chamber.

Evelyn and I occupied a tomb that had once belonged to a royal craftsman who bore the engaging title Washer of Hands of his Majesty. The title delighted me because it was a reminder of the constancy of human nature; I could not help recalling our own Tudor and Stuart monarchs, who were served by high noblemen who considered it an honor to be the official holders of the royal trousers.

But I digress.

Lucas was with difficulty dissuaded from moving into the most grandiose of the nearby tombs, that of one Mahu, who had been chief of police of the city. Clearing it out would have taken days. So Lucas's servants were set to work on another, smaller tomb, and one of them was sent back to the dahabeeyah with a long list of Lucas's requirements for the next day or two.

After luncheon we separated, Evelyn to rest, Walter to work at recording some pottery fragments which had been found on the last day of digging, and Lucas to explore. He went jogging off on his little donkey, looking sufficiently ridiculous with his long legs trailing. When he was out of sight, Emerson turned to me.

"Come along, Peabody."

"Where to?"

"You said you wanted to see the royal tomb."

"What, now?"

"Now is as good a time as any."

I looked up at the broiling sun, now near the zenith; then I shrugged. If Emerson thought to subdue me by such tactics, he would soon find out that I could keep up with any project he proposed. I went to my tomb to assume my rationals. They were dreadfully creased and dusty, and I wished I had purchased several similar costumes.

When I emerged, Emerson was pacing up and down and glaring at his watch.

"Will Walter come?" I inquired, deliberately dawdling.

"Walter had better remain here. There must be someone on guard; I have told Abdullah to go after his lordship, in case the fool breaks a leg trying to climb the cliffs or tumbles off his donkey. Come, come, Peabody; if you don't hurry I will go alone."

I went—not because he had ordered me to do so, but because I suspected he wanted a private discussion with me.

However, no such development ensued. The walk was too difficult for leisurely conversation. We turned into a long rocky wadi, or canyon, and followed its course for several miles. It was the most desolate area I had seen yet. The steep, barren walls of the wadi were streaked and cracking; not a single blade of grass or hardy weed found sustenance in the sunbaked soil. The floor of the valley was covered with rocks of all sizes, from enormous boulders to pebbles, which had fallen from the cliffs. The silence was absolute. It was like being in another world; a world in which life was an intrusion.

After about three miles the rock walls closed in and smaller wadis opened up to left and right. We turned to the northeast and picked our way through a narrow valley. As we stumbled along, Emerson began to ask questions, but they were not the questions I had expected. Instead he interrogated me about Lucas. I answered as shortly as I could. The drift of Emerson's curiosity convinced me that I had been correct in both my assumptions; he was immensely curious about the extent of Lord Ellesmere's fortune and the degree of his interest in Evelyn. I found it increasingly difficult to avoid his inquiries and finally put an end to them by picking a quarrel. That was never difficult with Emerson. He stalked along in offended silence until we reached the isolated tomb which had been prepared for the heretic king and his family.

In an effort to protect it from thieves seeking the rich treasures buried with the dead, the royal tomb had been situated in a remote part of the cliffs. The attempt at security had failed; the tomb had been robbed again and again. If Khuenaten had ever been buried there, the royal mummy had vanished centuries ago.

I shivered, even in the breathless heat, as I looked up the slope at the high dark hole that marked the entrance to the tomb. An air of brooding desolation hung over the spot. Disappointment and failure haunted it. Toward the end of his life, the royal reformer must have known that his religious revolution would not succeed. After his death his very name had been obliterated. I thought I would not like to come here after dark; it would be too easy to hear, in the jackals' howls, the lament of a starving, nameless ghost.

Emerson, unaffected by the aura of the place, was already scrambling up toward the entrance. Before it was a little plateau, about fifteen feet off the ground. I followed him, unassisted. He had brought candles; we lighted two of them and went in.

The tombs of Egyptian royalty were not the simple structures their subjects built. This one had long corridors, steep stairs, turns and curves designed to frustrate the cupidity of thieves. These devices had succeeded as well as such devices usually do—that is to say, not at all. The royal tomb had been roughly cleared, probably by the experienced thieves of Haggi Qandil. Otherwise we would not have been able to penetrate its interior at all, and even so, it was a breathless, dusty, uncomfortable trip. We were unable to reach the burial chamber, because a deep pit, like the one in the other tomb I had seen, cut straight across the corridor. There was nothing to bridge it with. Emerson's suggestion that we run and jump was probably not to be taken seriously. *I* certainly did not take it seriously.

We retraced our steps to the top of the second flight of stairs, where three small rooms were located off the main corridor. Here crumbling reliefs showed the death and burial of a princess, one of Khuenaten's daughters. She had died young, and had been laid to rest in her father's tomb. The little body, stretched out stiffly on its bed, looked very pathetic, and the grief of the parents, holding one another's hands for comfort, was strangely moving. Almost one could hear a thin moan of anguish echoing down the deserted corridors. . . .

And then there was a moan—or at least, a faint sound of some kind. The reader can only faintly imagine the horrific effect of such a sound—of sound of any sort—in those dark, musty rooms that had never been inhabited except by the dead. Before my scalp had time to prickle, the fainter sound was followed by another, less ghostly, but even more alarming. It was a loud crash of falling rock. Whatever the sound lost by reason of distance was regained by the rolling echoes. I started and dropped my candle.

Using language no lady could possibly remember, much less reproduce, Emerson scrabbled around in the debris that littered the floor until he found the candle. He relighted it from his own. Then he looked directly at me and spoke in the quiet voice he employed in moments of emergency.

"You are no fool, Peabody, if you are a woman. You know what that sound may mean. Are you prepared? You will not swoon, or scream, or become hysterical?"

I gave him a look of withering scorn, and in silence started out of the room.

With Emerson breathing heavily behind me, I made my way along the corridor. I did not expect that we would meet with any obstruction there. The walls and floors were carved from the living stone of the mountains. No; the difficulty would be at the entrance, and long before we reached that spot I knew that my surmise was unhappily correct. From the foot of the final stair I saw that the light which should have been apparent at the entrance was—not apparent.

We made our way up the stairs, not without difficulty, for rocks littered the steps, and stood at last before the entrance. The narrow opening was closed by stones—some as small as pebbles, some as large as boulders.

I blew out my candle. It was obvious that we had better conserve what little light we had. I was stooping to pluck at the rocks when Emerson turned to stick his candle onto a ledge in a pool of its own grease.

"Take care," he said curtly. "You may start another landslide that will sweep both of us down the stairs."

We dug for a long time; not as long as it seemed, perhaps, but the first candle was almost burned out when there came a sound from without. It was, to say the least, a welcome event. At first the words were indistinguishable. Then I realized that the person was speaking Arabic. I recognized the voice and, in the stress of the moment, understood what was being said. The voice was Abdullah's. He demanded to know if we were within.

"Of course we are within," shouted Emerson angrily. "Oh, son of a blind, bowlegged mule, where else should we be?"

A howl, which I took to be one of delight, followed this question. The howl was followed by a shout in quite another voice: "Hold on, Miss Amelia! Lucas is on the job!"

All at once Emerson threw his arms against me and pushed me against the wall, pressing his body close to mine.

Although I am now alone as I write, my Critic having gone off on an errand, I hesitate to express the thoughts that flashed through my mind at that moment. I knew Emerson was no weakling, but I had not fully realized his strength until I felt the rigid muscles of his breast against mine and felt my bones give under the strength of his grasp. I thought . . . I expected. . . . Well, why not admit it? I thought he was embracing me—relief at our unexpected rescue having weakened his mind.

Luckily these absurd notions had no time to burgeon in my brain. A horrible rattling crash followed, as the barricade gave way, and great rocks bounded down the stairs and banged against the walls. I felt Emerson flinch and knew he had been struck by at least one rock, from whose impact his quick action had saved me; for my body was shielded by his and his big hand pressed my face into the shelter of his shoulder.

I was quite out of breath when he released me, and gulped air for several seconds before I realized it was the clean, hot air of the outer world I breathed, and that sunlight was streaming into the vault.

The sunlight was too bright for my dazzled eyes, accustomed to darkness. I could just make out the silhouettes of the heads and shoulders of two men above the heap of rock that still lay on the threshold.

Emerson leaned back against the wall, his left arm hanging at an odd angle. As Abdullah and Lucas came scrambling in over the rocks, Emerson turned his head toward his foreman. Rivulets of perspiration were streaming down his face, turning the dust that covered it into a muddy mask.

"You d—— fool," he said.

"You are hurt," said Abdullah intelligently.

"Words fail me," said Emerson.

But of course they did not; he went on, though he spoke in gasps. "An experienced foreman . . . knows better . . . shoving like a battering ram. . . ."

"I tried to tell him to go slowly," Lucas broke in. "Unfortunately my Arabic is nonexistent."

He looked so guilty, and Abdullah so particularly enigmatic, that I realized who was probably responsible for the accident. There was no point in pressing the matter, however.

"He was anxious to get us out," I said. "Let us eschew recriminations and act. Is your arm broken?"

"Dislocated," said Emerson, between his teeth. "I must get back . . . Walter knows how. . . ."

"You cannot walk so far," I said.

This was patently true, and anyone but Emerson would have admitted the fact at once. His knees were buckling, and only the wall at his back kept him upright.

"I can do . . . what I must," he replied.

"No doubt; but there is no need. I saw our local surgeon perform this operation once, on a farmer whose shoulder had been put out of place. If you will direct me—"

The idea seemed to revive Emerson. His eyes rolled toward me; I swear, I saw a flash of enjoyment.

"You won't like it," said Emerson.

"Neither will you," I replied.

I think I prefer not to describe the procedure that followed. Emerson was not in any mood to make jokes when it was over, but I was the one who had to sit down on the ground and put my head between my knees. Fortunately Abdullah had brought water; we both had been thirsty from the heat and dust even before the accident. A long drink revived me and helped Emerson. I then tore up my petticoat in order to fasten his arm to his body so that it would not be jarred unnecessarily. He had his wicked temper back by then, and made a rude remark.

"As you would say, my lord, it is just like one of Mr. Haggard's romances. The heroine always sacrifices a petticoat at some point in the proceedings. No doubt that is why females wear such ridiculous garments; they do come in useful in emergencies."

The way to the royal tomb had seemed long; the road back was interminable. Lucas's strength was of great assistance, and Emerson did not disdain the help of his arm. As we walked along, Lucas explained how he had happened to find us.

He had had a little adventure of his own. Riding not far from the village, he had been accosted by the owner of his donkey, who had abandoned animal and rider when they first approached the camp. Now the donkey owner demanded his animal back.

"It occurred to me," Lucas explained, "that you had probably been deprived of donkeys as well as workers, so I determined to keep that one, if I could. If the villagers had realized I was acquainted with you, I never should have gotten it in the first place. I offered to buy the wretched little beast—thinking of Evelyn's using it, of course. But it was no use; when I insisted, I was set upon by a howling horde of villagers and forcibly removed from my steed. They offered me no violence, but I was shaken up and very angry. I was on my way back to camp when I met Abdullah. He said you had gone to the royal tomb; and after my adventure, I was somewhat concerned about you. So we came here—fortunately!"

"You did not see the rockfall, then?" Emerson asked.

"No."

"It couldn't have been an accident," Emerson grunted. "Too fortuitous. Why that one spot, while we happened to be inside the tomb?"

"We were fortunate that it was not a more extensive landslide," I said, stumbling into a thornbush.

"Hmmph," said Emerson, trying not to groan.

A mile or two from camp we were met by Walter and Evelyn, who, alarmed at our prolonged absence, had set out to look for us. Walter went quite pale when he saw Emerson's faltering steps and bandaged body, but he knew better than to commiserate.

"It is most unfortunate," he said thoughtfully. "Another accident, just now, will merely confirm the villagers' superstitions."

"We need not tell them, surely," said Lucas.

"They will know," I said. "I suspect one of them has good reason to know what has occurred."

"Aha!" Lucas exclaimed. "You think it was no accident?"

He was altogether too pleased about the whole affair. I knew it was unfair of me to blame him for enjoying the adventure; his acquaintance with Emerson and Walter was of the slightest, so he could not be expected to feel for them as Evelyn and I did. And certainly the wild events of those days would have appealed to the adventurous spirit of any young gentleman. Nevertheless, his grin annoyed me.

"It was no accident," I said curtly. "This was a foolish expedition. From now on we must stay in the camp and close to one another. Perhaps no real harm was intended—"

"We cannot know that," Walter interrupted. "If the rock had struck my brother's head instead of his shoulder—"

"But his injury *was* an unfortunate accident. It was incurred during our release, not during the rockfall, which could hardly have been designed to murder us. You knew our destination; you would have searched for us if we had not returned, so that even if Abdullah had not happened to go after us, we would not have been incarcerated long. No; the attempt could not have been at murder. I believe it was only another harassment."

"And if Peabody says so," remarked Emerson, "that is the Word of the Prophet."

We finished the journey in cool silence.

However, we had much to be thankful for. Evelyn pointed this out as we prepared for dinner in our homey tomb. She was not looking well that evening; I noticed her pallor and sober looks all the more because it contrasted so strikingly with her appearance during the preceding week. She had been frightened, weary, and uncomfortable, as we all were; but under the strain there had been a quiet happiness, a kind of bloom. The bloom was now gone. And of course I knew the reason.

"Has Lucas been annoying you?" I inquired, with my usual tact.

Evelyn was doing her hair in front of the mirror. Her hands faltered; a bright lock of golden hair tumbled down her back.

"He asked me again to marry him."

"And you said . . . ?"

Evelyn turned. The disordered masses of her hair flowed out with the force of her movement and fell about her shoulders. She had never looked lovelier, for the nobility of her purpose and the strength of her emotion transformed her face.

"Amelia, how can you ask? You know my feelings; I have never tried to conceal them from you, my cherished friend. I cannot marry the man I love; but I will never be the bride of another."

"You are wrong," I said forcefully. "Walter loves you. I know it; you must know it. You are being grossly unjust to him, not to give him the chance—"

"To know my shame—my folly? Never fear, Amelia; if he *should* ask me to marry him, I will tell him the truth."

"And why do you assume he will recoil? Oh, I agree; you must be candid, he would hear the story sooner or later, and he would have cause for resentment at hearing it from another than yourself. But he is a splendid lad, Evelyn; I like him more with every day that passes. He would not—"

"He is a man," said Evelyn, in a tone of weary wisdom that would have made me laugh, had I not been so distressed for her. "What man could forget or forgive such a thing in his wife?"

"Bah," I said.

"If I had anything to offer him," Evelyn went on passionately. "The fortune I once despised would be a godsend to him and his brother. If only—"

"You don't suppose that splendid boy would refuse you for your misstep and forgive you for a fortune, do you?" I demanded indignantly.

Evelyn's eyes narrowed.

"Amelia, why do you speak as if you were a hundred years old? Walter is only a few years younger than you, and you are still in your prime. In the last week you seem to have drunk from the fountain of youth; you are looking younger and more attractive every day."

I stared at her in astonishment.

"Come, now, Evelyn, don't let your fondness for me destroy your aesthetic sense. I have been scoured by windblown sand, dried out and burned by the sun, and I have ruined every decent dress I own. Forget me, and let us settle your problem once and for all. If you would only listen to me—"

"I honor and love you," she interrupted, in a low voice "But in this matter I cannot follow anything but my own conscience."

"But it is such a waste," I lamented. "You love this life. Your seeming fragility conceals a will of iron; you could be a helpmate as well as a wife to Walter."

"You are the one who loves this life," Evelyn said, watching me curiously. "What an archaeologist you would make, Amelia!"

"Hmmm," I said. "That is true. It is most unfortunate that I was not born a man. Emerson would accept me then as a colleague; my money would support his work; what a splendid time we would have, working and quarreling together. Oh, it is a pity that I am a woman. Emerson would agree."

"I am not so sure," said Evelyn. There was a faint smile on her lips.

"You are distracting me again," I complained. "You cannot avoid the issue, Evelyn. Suppose I were to finance—"

"No, Amelia," Evelyn said. I knew that gentle tone. It was as final as Emerson's growl.

"Then accept Lucas's offer. No, no, I mean his offer of money. Half of your grandfather's fortune is yours, morally. If you really believe Walter would accept—"

"Amelia, that is not worthy of you. Could I accept Lucas's generosity and use it to buy the affection of Lucas's rival?"

"You put things in such a cold-blooded way," I muttered.

"It is the honest way." Evelyn's animation had faded; she was pale and sad. "No, Amelia. I cannot—will not—marry Lucas, nor will I accept a penny from him. Are you so anxious to rid yourself of me? I had dared to let myself envision a life together. . . . Growing old with you, winding wool and keeping cats and tending a garden somewhere in the country. We could be content, could we not? Oh, Amelia, don't cry! I have never seen you weep; don't do it on my account. . . ."

She threw her arms around me and we clung together, both sobbing violently. I did not often cry, it is true; I don't know why I was crying then, but I found it soothing to do so. So I let myself go, wallowing in the luxuriance of openly expressed emotion, and Evelyn made me cry even harder by the fond expressions she choked out.

"I do love you, Amelia; you are dearer to me than any sister. Your kindness, your sense of humor, your saintly temper . . ."

The last phrase appealed too strongly to the sense of humor she had just mentioned; I stopped crying and began to laugh feebly.

"Deerest Evelyn, I have a temper like a fiend's, and the disposition of a balky mule. How beautiful is friendship, that it blinds one to the friend's true nature! Well, child, don't cry anymore; I know why you weep, and it is not because of my saintly nature. I suppose the Almighty will order our lives as He sees fit, and there is no reason for us to worry. I have not altogether decided to accept His decrees; but whatever happens, you and I will not part until I can give you up to a man who deserves you. Here, wipe your eyes, and then give me the handkerchief so I can wipe mine. I did not expect to need more than one handkerchief this evening."

We mopped our wet faces and went on with our dressing. Evelyn had one more comment to make.

"You speak as if I would be the one to leave you. Will you keep me on, Amelia, to wind wool and wash lapdogs, after *you* are married?"

"That is the most ridiculous remark you have made as yet," I said. "And many of your remarks have been extremely silly."

Chapter Eight

 WHEN we came out of the tomb, wearing fresh garments and rather red eyes, we found the men assembled. Lucas had brought enough articles to stock a shop; there were flowers on the table, and a glittering array of silverware and crystal. The look on Emerson's face as he contemplated the elegantly set table was almost enough to compensate for the absurdity of the business.

Lucas was attired in a fresh suit, spotless and expensively tailored. He sprang to his feet when we appeared and held a chair for Evelyn. Walter held one for me. Lucas offered us sherry. He behaved as if he were the host. Emerson, who was now staring at the toes of his deplorable boots, said nothing. His arm was still strapped to his side, and I concluded that he felt too ill to be as objectionable as he usually was.

"Such elegance," I commented, as Lucas handed me a delicate goblet. "We are not accustomed to luxury here, your lordship."

"I see no reason for depriving oneself of the amenities," Lucas replied, smiling. "If asceticism is necessary, I venture to say that you will find me ready to accept the most stringent measures; but while Amontillado and crystal are available, I will make use of them."

He lifted his own glass in a mock salute. It did not contain Amontillado, although the liquid was almost as dark a shade of amber. My father never drank spirits, but my brothers were not so abstemious. I looked critically at the glass, and remarked, "Do you think it wise to imbibe? We must be on the *qui vive* tonight. Or have you abandoned your intention of lying in wait for our visitor?"

"Not at all! I have a strong head, Miss Amelia, and a little whiskey only makes my senses more acute."

"That is the common delusion of the drinker," said Walter. His tone was offensive. Lucas smiled at him.

"We are appreciative of your luxuries, Lucas," Evelyn said. "But they really are not necessary. How heavily laden your dahabeeyah must be!"

"It would have been more heavily laden if I had had my way," Lucas replied. "Your boxes have arrived in Cairo, Evelyn. I intended to bring them along; but that old curmudgeon, Baring, refused to hand them over."

"Indeed?" I said. "He was an acquaintance of my father's."

"I am well aware of that. You should be complimented, Miss Amelia, that the new master of Egypt has taken the trouble to look after your affairs personally. The boxes were sent to you, since it was your address the Roman consul had for Evelyn. Baring took charge of them in Cairo and guards them like the dictator he is. I explained my relationship to Evelyn, but he was an adamant."

"Perhaps your reputation has preceded you," I said mildly.

It was impossible to offend Lucas. He laughed heartily.

"Oh, it has. I went to university with a young relative of Baring's. I am afraid certain—er—escapades reached the distinguished gentleman's ears."

"It does not matter," Evelyn said. "I am grateful for your efforts, Lucas, but I need nothing more than I have."

"You need nothing except yourself," Lucas said warmly. "That is treasure enough. But your needs and your desserts are two different things. One day, Evelyn, you will be persuaded to accept what you deserve; although all the treasure houses of the pharaohs could not hold its real value."

Evelyn flushed and was silent; she was too gentle to reproach him for his remarks, which were, to say the least, out of place at that time and in that company. I felt quite exasperated with the girl; could she not see that her response to Lucas's florid compliments only inflamed poor Walter's jealousy? With a lover's excessive sensibility he misinterpreted every blush, every glance.

Emerson removed his gaze from the toes of his boots and glowered at me. "Are we to sit here all evening exchanging compliments? No doubt you have planned the evening's entertainment, Peabody; enlighten us as to what we must do."

"I had not given the matter much thought."

"Really? And why not?"

I had found that the surest way of annoying Emerson was to ignore his provocative remarks and reply as if he had spoken in ordinary courteous exchange.

"I was thinking of the royal tomb," I explained. "Of the relief of the little princess and her grieving parents. Evelyn should copy it. She would do it beautifully."

"I am surprised at the suggestion," Lucas exclaimed. "After what happened today—"

"Oh, I don't mean she should do it now; but one day, when the situation has been cleared up. Since your connection with Evelyn has been so distant, Lucas, you may not know that she is a splendid artist. She has already done a painting of the pavement that was destroyed."

Lucas insisted on seeing this painting and exclaimed over it quite excessively. The conversation having turned to matters archaeological, he was reminded of the papyrus scroll he had mentioned.

"I had the bearers fetch it," he said, reaching into the box at his side. "Here you are, Mr. Emerson. I said I would hand it over, and I keep my word."

The papyrus was enclosed in a carved and colored wooden case, except for a single section—the one Lucas had unrolled.

"I put it between two squares of glass," he explained. "That seemed the best method of keeping it from crumbling any further."

"At least you had that much sense," Emerson grumbled. "Hand it to Walter, if you please, your lordship. I might drop it, having only one good hand."

Walter took the framed section, as gently as if it had been a baby, on the palms of his two hands. The sun was setting, but there was still ample light. As Walter bent over the sheet of papyrus, a lock of hair tumbled down over his brow. His lips moved as if in silent prayer. He seemed to have forgotten our presence.

I leaned forward to see better. The papyrus seemed to me to be in fairly good condition, compared with others I had seen in antiquities shops. It was brown with age and the edges were crumbling, but the black, inky writing stood out clearly on the whole. An occasional word was written in red, which had not fared so well; it had faded to a rusty brown. Of course I had no notion whatsoever what the writing said. It resembled the hieroglyphic writing; one could distinguish the shape of an occasional bird or squatting figure, each of which represented a letter in the ancient picture alphabet of the Egyptians. But the majority of the letters were abbreviated forms and resembled a written script such as Arabic more than it resembled hieroglyphic writing.

"It is splendid hieratic," said Emerson, who was leaning over his brother's shoulder. "Much closer to the hieroglyphs than some I have seen. Can you make it out, Walter?"

"You don't mean that Master Walter can read that scribble?" Lucas exclaimed.

"Master Walter," said his brother drily, "is one of the world's leading experts on the ancient language. I know a bit, but I am primarily an excavator. Walter has specialized in philology. Well, Walter?"

"Your partiality makes you praise me too highly," Walter said, his eyes greedily devouring the crabbed script. "I must show this to Frank Griffith; he is with Petrie at Naucratis this season, and unless I miss my guess, he is going to be one of our leading scholars. However, I believe I can make out a few lines. You are right, Radcliffe; it is splendid hieratic. That," he explained to the rest of us, "was the cursive script used on documents and records. The hieroglyphic signs were too ornate and cumbersome for the scribes of a busy kingdom. The hieratic was developed from the hieroglyphic, and if you look closely, you will see how the signs resemble the original pictures."

"I see!" Evelyn burst out. We were all bending over the papyrus now, except Lucas, who sipped his whiskey and watched us all with his patronizing smile. "Surely that is an owl—the letter 'm.' And the following word much resembles the seated man, which is the pronoun 'I.' "

"Quite right, quite right." Walter was delighted. "Here is the word for 'sister.' In ancient Egyptian that might mean. . . ." His voice faltered. Evelyn, sensitive to the slightest change in his feelings, quietly returned to her chair.

"Sister and brother were terms of endearment," said Emerson, finishing the sentence his brother had begun. "A lover spoke of his sweetheart as his sister."

"And this," said Walter in a low voice, "is a love poem."

"Splendid," exclaimed Lucas. "Read it to us, Master Walter, if you please."

Lucas had insisted that we be informal; but his address of Walter by the childish title was certainly meant to provoke. On this occasion it had no effect; Walter was too absorbed in his studies.

"I can only make out a few lines," he said. "You ought not to have unrolled it, Lord Ellesmere; the break goes through part of the text. However, this section reads:

I go down with thee into the water
And come forth to thee again
With a red fish, which is—beautiful on my fingers.

"There is a break here. The lovers are by the water; a pond, or the Nile. They—they disport themselves in the cool water."

"It doesn't have the ring of a love poem to me," Lucas said skeptically. "If I offered a fish, red or white, to a lady of my acquaintance as a love offering, she would not receive it graciously. A diamond necklace would be more welcome."

Evelyn moved slightly in her chair. Walter went on, "This is certainly a lover speaking. He is on one side of the river—

The love of the sister is upon yonder side;
A stretch of water is between
And a crocodile waiteth upon the sandbank.

But I go down into the water, I walk upon the flood;
My heart is brave upon the water
It is the love of her that makes me strong."

There was a brief silence when he stopped speaking. I don't know which impressed me more—the quaint charm of the lines or the expertness with which the modest young man had deciphered them.

"Brilliant, Walter," I cried, forgetting propriety in my enthusiasm. "How inspiring it is to realize that noble human emotions are as ancient as man himself."

"It seems to me not so much noble as foolhardy," said Lucas lazily. "Any man who jumps into a river inhabited by crocodiles deserves to be eaten up."

"The crocodile is a symbol," I said scornfully. "A symbol of the dangers and difficulties any true lover would risk to win his sweetheart."

"That is very clever, Miss Amelia," Walter said, smiling at me.

"Too clever," growled Emerson. "Attempting to read the minds of the ancient Egyptians is a chancy business, Peabody. It is more likely that the crocodile is a typical lover's extravagance—a boast that sounds well, but that no man of sense would carry out."

I was about to reply when Evelyn fell into a fit of coughing.

"Well, well," Lucas said. "How happy I am that my little offering has proved to be so interesting! But don't you think we ought to make plans for tonight? The sun is almost down."

It was one of the most stunning sunsets I had ever beheld. The fine dust in the atmosphere produces amazing conditions of light, such as our hazy English air does not allow. There was something almost threatening about the sunset that evening; great bands of blood-red and royal purple, translucent blue like the glaze on ancient pottery, gold and amber and copper streaks.

I asked Lucas whether his crew might not help us guard the camp, but he shook his head.

"Evidently they met some of the villagers today. Your crew has also been infected, Miss Amelia. I would not be surprised if all of them fled."

"They cannot do that," I exclaimed. "I am paying them! Nor do I believe that Reis Hassan would abandon his trust."

"He would have some excellent excuse," Lucas said cynically. "Adverse winds, threatening weather—any excuse for mooring elsewhere."

I was aware, then, of someone beside me. Turning, I beheld Michael, whom I had not seen all day.

"Sitt Hakim"—for so he always addressed me—"I must speak to you alone."

"Certainly," I said, although I was surprised at his request and at his interruption of our conversation.

"After dinner," Lucas said, giving the poor fellow a sharp look. Michael shrank back, and Lucas added, "Michael, or whatever your name is, you are not needed. My men will serve the meal. I promised them they might return before dark. Miss Peabody will speak with you later."

Michael obeyed, with a last pleading glance at me. As soon as he was out of earshot I said, "Lucas, I really cannot have you reprimanding my servants!"

"My first name!" Lucas exclaimed, with a broad smile. "You have broken down at last, Miss Amelia; you have done me the honor of addressing me as a friend. We must drink to that." And he refilled his wine glass.

"We—to use the word loosely—have drunk too much already," I retorted. "As for Michael—"

"Good heavens, such a fuss over a servant," Lucas said contemptuously. "I think I know what he wants to speak to you about, Miss Amelia, and if I were you I should not be in a hurry to hear it."

He held up his glass as if admiring the sparkle of the liquid in the fading light.

"What do you mean?" I asked.

Lucas shrugged.

"Why, the fellow means to be off. My men tell me that he is in a complete funk. It is to his babbling, in no small measure, that I attribute their cowardice. No doubt he will have some specious excuse for leaving you, but leave you he will."

"I cannot believe it," Evelyn said firmly. "Michael is a fine man. Loyal, devoted—"

"But a native," Lucas finished. "With a native's weaknesses."

"And you are quite familiar with the weaknesses of the—er—natives," Emerson put in. He had not spoken much; for once his grating purr, like the throaty emanation of a very large, angry cat, did not offend my ears.

"Human beings are much the same the world over," Lucas replied negligently. "The ignorant always have their superstitions and their fondness for money."

"I bow to your superior knowledge," Emerson said. "I had been under the impression that it was not only the ignorant who are corrupted by money."

"I cannot believe Michael will desert us," I said, putting an end to the bickering. "I will speak to him later."

But later I was forced to admit, little as I liked it, that Lucas had been right. Michael was nowhere to be found. At first, when he did not seek me out, I assumed he had changed his mind about wanting to speak to me. It was not until we began thinking of our plans for the night that we realized he was missing. A search produced no trace of him. Lucas's servants—a shabby-looking group if I had ever seen one—had long since departed, so we could not ask if they had seen him.

"He had not even the courage to make his excuses to you," Lucas said, "Depend upon it, he has crept away."

Michael's defection left us in rather serious condition, I thought, but when I expressed the idea, Lucas pooh-poohed my concern.

"We ought to get to our posts," he continued. "With all due respect to your measures, I do not believe you went about the business very sensibly."

"Let us hear your plans," said Emerson humbly.

I could not imagine what ailed the man. Except for brief outbursts of irony he adopted an attitude of subservient meekness toward Lucas, a man considerably his junior in age and certainly his inferior in experience. Nor could I believe that it was physical weakness that curbed his tongue. Emerson would criticize Old Nick himself when that individual came to bear him away as he lay dying.

"Very well," said Lucas, expanding visibly. "I see no reason to watch the village. If your villain means to frighten you away he will come here, and it is here that we must concentrate our forces. But we must not show force. You frightened him away the other night—"

"Oh, do you think that is what happened?" Emerson asked seriously.

"Only look at the sequence. The first time he came he ventured as far as the entrance to the ladies' residence and stood there for some time, if Miss Amelia's evidence is to be believed—"

"It is," I said, snapping my teeth together.

"Certainly, I did not mean. . . . Very well, then; on the next night, when Evelyn saw him, we do not know how far he progressed. He may have come no farther than the spot, down below, where she saw him. But on the third occasion he was definitely wary; he never came onto the ledge at all, and it was as if he knew you were awake and waiting for him."

Even in the dark I could sense Walter's increasing anger. The tone Lucas adopted was really quite insufferable. I was not surprised when the lad interrupted Lucas's lecture in a voice that shook with his efforts at self-control.

"You mean to imply, Lord Ellesmere, that the miscreant saw Abdullah and myself. I assure you—"

"No, no, my dear fellow," Lucas exclaimed. "I mean to imply that your friend Mohammed was warned in advance!"

There was a muffled exclamation from Emerson. It sounded to me as if he were strangling on an oath he did not dare speak aloud. Lucas took it for an expression of chagrin, and he nodded graciously at the older man.

"Yes; Michael. I am convinced that he has been in league with the villagers. No doubt they promised him part of the loot."

"Loot!" Evelyn exclaimed, with unusual heat. "What reward could they offer, when they are so poor they cannot clothe their own children?"

"I see you have not reasoned it out," Lucas said complacently. "Perhaps I can see more clearly because I am removed from the terror that has haunted you in recent days."

"Enlighten us," said Emerson, through his teeth. I saw them gleaming in the dark, like the fangs of a wolf.

Lucas leaned back in his chair. He stretched out his long legs and gazed admiringly at his boots.

"I asked myself," he began, "what motive these people could have for driving you away. Malice is not a sufficient explanation; they need the money you were paying them. Does not the answer seem obvious to you? For generations these fellahin have been robbing the tombs of their remote ancestors. Their discoveries fill the antika shops of Cairo and Luxor, and you archaeologists are always complaining that whenever you find a tomb, the natives have been there before you. I suggest that the villagers have recently discovered such a tomb—a rich one, or they would not be so anxious to drive you away before you can find it."

The explanation had occurred to me, of course. I had discarded it, however, and now I voiced the objections aloud.

"That would mean that all the villagers are in league with Mohammed. I do not believe that. If you had seen the trembling fear of the old mayor—"

"You ladies always trust people," Lucas said. "These villagers are congenital liars, Miss Amelia, and expert at dissimulation."

"If I really believed such a tomb existed, it would require an earthquake to make me leave," said Emerson.

"Naturally," Lucas said cheerfully. "I feel the same. All the more reason for catching our Mummy before he can do any serious damage."

"If your explanation is correct, my lord, catching the Mummy will not solve the problem." It was Walter who spoke. "According to you, the entire village knows that the Mummy is a fraud. Exposing him will not change their intention of forcing us to leave."

"But it will give us a hostage," Lucas explained tolerantly. "The mayor's own son. We will force him to lead us to the tomb and then dispatch a message back to Cairo for reinforcements. Also, once we have exposed the supposed curse we may be able to enlist the crews of our boats to help guard the tomb. They consider the villagers savages; the only thing they have in common is their superstitious terror of the dead."

"Another objection," I said. "If Michael is a traitor—though I still find it hard to believe—he will have warned the village of our plans for tonight. The Mummy again will be on his guard."

"What a splendidly logical mind you have," Lucas exclaimed. "That is quite true; and it prompts my next suggestion. We must appear to be off *our* guard, and we must offer the Mummy a lure, in order to entice it into our clutches."

"What sort of lure?" Walter asked suspiciously.

"I had not thought," Lucas said negligently. "I have appeared to drink more than I really have, in order to give the impression that I will sleep heavily. I wish you two gentlemen had done the same, but evidently you failed to follow my reasoning. Have you any suggestions, along the lines I have indicated?"

Several suggestions were made. Walter offered to take up his post at some distance, and then pretend to fall asleep. Emerson proposed to stand out in the open and consume an entire bottle of wine, and then collapse upon the sand as if overcome by intoxication. This last idea was received with the silent contempt it deserved, and no one spoke for a time. Then Evelyn stirred.

"I think there is only one object that may attract the creature to venture close enough to be seized," she said. "I shall steal out for a stroll after midnight. If I am far enough from the camp—"

The remainder of her sentence was drowned out by our cries of protest. Lucas alone remained silent; when Walter's voice had died, he said thoughtfully.

"But why not? There can be no danger; the villain only wants to catch one of us alone in order to play some silly trick."

"Do you call this a silly trick?" Emerson asked, indicating his bandaged shoulder. "You are mad, my lord, to consider such a thing. Walter," he added sternly, "be quiet. Do not speak if you cannot speak calmly."

"How can anyone speak calmly of such a thing?" Walter bellowed, in a fair imitation of his brother's best roar. "Under any circumstances it is an appalling idea; but remembering what that swine Mohammed said, when we were in the village . . ."

He broke off, with a glance at Evelyn.

"Lucas does not know that, Walter," she said steadily. "But I do. I overheard Amelia and Mr. Emerson speaking of it. Surely that makes my plan more practical."

Walter sputtered speechlessly. Lucas of course demanded to know what we were talking about. Seeing that Evelyn already knew the worst, I saw no reason not to repeat the statement to Lucas, and I did so, adding, "After all, Evelyn, you are being vain in assuming that the Mummy is only interested in you. Mohammed looked at *me* when he spoke; and I think if you are going to take a stroll, I will make myself available also. We will give him his choice of prey. Who knows, he may prefer a more mature type of lady."

This time the outcry was dominated by Emerson's bull-like voice.

"Why, Emerson," I said. "Do you mean to suggest that the Mummy will not be intrigued by me? You must not insult me."

"You are a fool, Peabody," said Emerson furiously. "And if you suppose

I am going to allow any such idiotic, imbecilic, stupid—"

The plot was arranged as I had suggested. As we discussed it, it became more complex. By 'we,' I refer to Evelyn, Lucas, and myself. Emerson's contribution took the form of a low rumble rather like the sound of a volcano about to erupt. Walter's tense silence was almost as threatening. He took Evelyn's behavior as evidence of an understanding between her and Lucas, and reacted accordingly; it was not at all difficult to feign a quarrel, which was part of our plan, in case any spy should be watching. We parted acrimoniously. Walter tried to make a last protest, and Lucas responded by producing a pistol.

"I shall be within ten feet of Evelyn the entire time," he said in a thrilling whisper, holding the gun so that no one outside our group could see it. "I think our bandaged friend will be deterred by the mere sight of this. If not, I have no scruples about using it."

"And what about me?" I asked.

Emerson was unable to ignore the opportunity.

"God help the poor mummy who encounters you, Peabody," he said bitterly. "We ought to supply *it* with a pistol, to even the odds."

So saying, he stalked away. He was followed by Walter. Lucas chuckled and rubbed his hands together.

"What an adventure! I can hardly wait!"

"Nor I," said Evelyn. "Amelia, will you not reconsider?"

"Certainly not," I said in a loud voice, and walked off with my head held stiffly. I did not like leaving them alone together, but I felt it wise to add to the impression of ill will. It would be helpful later, when Evelyn and I staged our quarrel.

It was a one-sided argument, for Evelyn could not even pretend to shout at me. I made up the deficiency, and ended the argument by storming out of our tomb with my pillow and counterpane under my arm. I carried them down the ledge and into the little tent Michael had been occupying. Any watcher might readily assume that Evelyn and I had had a falling out, and that I had refused to share our sleeping quarters.

I could not strike a light, since it would have been visible through the canvas walls of the tent. It was not an honest English tent, only a low shelter of canvas; I could not stand erect in it. Squatting on the sand which was the floor of the shelter, I thought seriously of the man who had been its occupant. I was not at all convinced that Michael had left of his own free will. Men are frail creatures, of course; one does not expect them to exhibit the steadfastness of women. All the same, I did not like having my judgment of Michael disproved, and I determined to search the tent in the hope of finding some clue.

There was just enough light from without to show me that Michael's scanty possessions had been removed; but as I wriggled around, my fingers touched an object buried in the sand. I dug it out. I did not need to see the moonlight sparkling off its metallic surface to comprehend what it was. A crucifix. Part of the chain was still there, but only part. It had been snapped, not unfastened in the usual way.

My fingers closed tightly over the small object. Michael would never have left it; it was the only thing of value he owned, as well as an amulet against evil. The breaking of the chain confirmed my dread. It must have been snapped during a struggle.

Heedless of possible watchers, I crawled around the confined space searching for further clues, but found nothing. I was relieved; I had feared to find bloodstains.

So absorbed was I in the conjectures and suspicions which followed my discovery that time passed swiftly. A sound from without brought me back to myself. Stretching out flat, I lifted one edge of the canvas and peered out.

There was nothing to be seen—literally nothing. I had miscalculated, and I cursed my stupidity. The tent was behind a low ridge of tumbled stones that extended out from the cliff; I could not see the ledge, or the tomb entrances. This would never do. I must be in a position to assist Evelyn if the Mummy pursued her; and, in spite of my boasts, I did not really think it was after me. Squirming out from under the tent, I began to crawl forward. Before long I had reached the end of the rocky ridge and, rising to my knees, peered cautiously around it.

I pride myself on my self-possession; but I confess I almost let out a cry when I saw what stood beyond the ridge, only a few feet away. I had never seen it so close before. We claim to be rational, but there is a layer of primitive savagery in all of us. My brain sturdily denied superstition, but some deeply hidden weakness inside whimpered and cowered at the sight of the thing.

It was a grisly sight in the cold moonlight. In that clear, dry air the moon gives a queer, deceptive light; small details are visible in it, but shadows distort and deceive the eyes; the pallid glow robs objects of their real color and gives them a sickly grayish-green shade. The Mummy stood out as if faintly luminescent. The bandaged hands resembled a leper's stumps. The hands were raised as if in invocation; the creature stood not twenty feet away, with its back toward me. It faced the ledge, and the blind head was tilted back as if the eyeless sockets could see.

If Evelyn carried out our plan, she would shortly emerge from the tomb and start along the ledge. I expected her; I knew that there were four strong, alert men hidden nearby. But when the slight white form appeared in the dark mouth of the tomb, I started as violently as if I had seen an actual spirit.

Evelyn stood for a moment staring up at the stars. I knew she was trying to gather her courage to leave the security of the ledge, and my heart went out to her. She could not see the Mummy. At the moment she emerged it had moved with horrid swiftness, sinking down behind a rock at the cliff's foot.

I have written that there were four defenders close at hand; but I was not absolutely certain of that fact. Despite Emerson's sneers, I am not a stupid woman. I had already considered an idea that must have occurred to my more intelligent readers, and as Evelyn turned and slowly began to descend, my brain rapidly reviewed this reasoning.

I had been impressed by Walter's insistence that Mohammed had not left the village on one occasion when we were visited by the Mummy. Moreover, much as I disliked agreeing with Emerson on any subject, I felt as he did, that the plot was un-Egyptian—if I may use that term. Not only was it too sophisticated for the crafty but uneducated mind of Mohammed, but it smacked quite strongly of European romanticism. It might have been invented by a reader of gothic novels, inspired by *An Egyptian Princess* and other fictional horrors.

If Mohammed was not the Mummy, who was? It is no wonder that a certain name came immediately to mind; for he had the shallow but fertile intelligence, the bizarre sense of humor that suited the plot.

I was fully aware of the objections to my theory. The greatest was the question of motive. Why should Lucas, Lord Ellesmere, go to such absurd extremes in order to frighten his cousin? Or was it I he was trying to frighten? However, I was not worried about this; Lucas's motives were beyond my comprehension, and I thought it possible that he had some insane notion of terrifying Evelyn into leaving Egypt and accepting his protection. He would never succeed, but he might not have sense enough to know that.

The other objections were more difficult. Lucas might possibly have caught us up in time to play his role; we had dawdled and stopped along the way. But he could not have anticipated our stay at Amarna. It had been purely fortuitous, not known to him in advance.

Despite the objections, I clung to the notion of Lucas's villainy. The truth is, I wanted him to be a villain—a veritable crocodile, like the one in the ancient poem, that lay in wait for the lover seeking to win his sweetheart. A woman's instinct, I always feel, supersedes logic. So you may believe that I waited with considerable interest to see whether Lucas would appear to rescue Evelyn.

My heart beat in sympathy with the girl as she advanced along the path that led away from safety. She put on a good act of indifference; only once, as she passed the quarters of Walter and his brother, did she falter and glance aside. But she squared her shoulders and went on. She reached the bottom of the ledge and started out across the sand.

If she continued on the route she had chosen, she would pass too close to the Mummy for comfort. I wondered if I was the only one who knew the creature's precise location. I was not sure where the men lay concealed; perhaps they had not seen the thing. If so, it was incumbent on me to interfere before Evelyn went much farther. I did not know the creature's intentions. It would be shock enough if it merely jumped out and began moaning and waving its arms. But suppose it tried to touch her? The horror of that, to a girl of Evelyn's sensitive temperament, would be dreadful. And yet if I moved too precipitately I might frighten the thing away before the men could seize it. I hesitated, in an agony of doubt.

Evelyn was walking straight toward the boulder behind which the Mummy lay concealed. But—wait! It had been concealed there; it was there no longer. While my attention had been fixed on Evelyn it must have slid away. Where was it now? What was happening? And where were our stalwart defenders? Except for Evelyn's slim white figure, not a living soul moved in the moonlight. The silence was so intense I could hear the pounding of my heart.

A flash of pale color among the rocks at the foot of the path! How silently the creature had moved! It was between Evelyn and the ledge now; she could not retreat to that point of safety. I could endure the suspense no longer. I started to rise. At the same moment the Mummy stepped out into the open, emitting a low, moaning growl that brought Evelyn spinning around to confront it.

Thirty paces—not more—separated the grisly monster from its intended prey. Evelyn's hands went to her throat. She swayed. I tried to get to my feet—stepped on the folds of my dressing gown—tripped—fell prostrate, my limbs entangled—and saw, from that position, the next act of the drama.

With slow, measured steps the Mummy advanced on Evelyn, who did not move. Either she was paralyzed by terror or she was carrying out her part of the plot with what seemed to me excessive devotion. I would have been in flight by then, and I am not ashamed to admit it. The blank, featureless face of the thing was more frightening than any possible distortion or scarred countenance. Two dark hollows, under the ridges of the brows, were the only sign of eyes.

Scratching at the sand, kicking ineffectually, I shouted. Evelyn did not even turn her head. She stood as if mesmerized, her hands clasped on her breast, watching the thing advance. Then—just as I was about to explode with horror and frustration—rescue came! Walter was the first to appear. In a single great bound he burst out of the tomb and reached the edge of the cliff. He flung himself down, preparatory to sliding down the slope. At the same moment Lucas stepped out from behind the concealment of a heap of rocks. I was not even disappointed at the collapse of my theory, I was so relieved to see him—and to see the firearm he held. He shouted and pointed the pistol.

The Mummy stopped. It stood still for a moment, its head turning from side to side, as if it were considering its next move. Its appearance of cool deliberation was maddening to me. I finally managed to struggle free of my encumbering skirts and stagger to my feet. Another shout from Lucas stopped me as I was about to run to Evelyn. His meaning was plain; he did not want me to get into the line of fire. The pistol was aimed straight at the Mummy's bandaged breast, but Lucas did not shoot; he meant only to threaten, and I could not help but admire his calm in that tense moment.

Lucas stepped slowly forward, his gun at the ready. The eyeless head turned toward him; from the creature came a horrible mewing cry. It was too much for Evelyn, whose nerves were already strained to the breaking point. She swayed and collapsed into a heap on the ground. With another ghastly moan, the Mummy lumbered toward her.

I felt sure then that the mummy wrappings did not conceal the form of Mohammed. These people knew firearms and had a healthy respect for them. Even as the thought passed through my mind, Lucas fired.

The explosion thundered through the silent night. The Mummy stopped and jerked back. One bandaged paw went to its breast. Holding my breath, I waited to see it fall. It did not! It came on, more slowly, emitting that low mewing growl. Lucas took careful aim and fired again. No more than a dozen yards separated the two; this time I could have sworn I saw the missile strike, full in the center of the creature's rotting body. Again it pawed at the place where the bullet had struck; again it came on.

Lucas stepped back a few paces. His face shone with sweaty pallor; his open mouth looked like a black wound. He fumbled in his jacket pocket. I deduced that his weapon held only two bullets and that he now had to refill it.

Walter had paused, poised on the edge of the drop, to see what would ensue. Needless to say, the actions which have taken so long to describe only occupied a few moments of real time. Now, with a shout of warning, Walter let himself drop. His booted feet struck the sloping heap of rocky detritus with a force that started a miniature landslide, but he did not lose his balance. Slipping, sliding, running, he reached the bottom and rushed on without a halt.

Lucas was shouting too, but I could not hear him because of the crash of falling rock. I would not have known he was speaking if I had not seen his lips move. He had finished loading the gun; he raised it. I cried out—but too late. Carried on by the impetus of his leap, Walter flung himself at the menace just as Lucas fired for the third time. And this time his bullet found a vulnerable target. Walter stood stock still. His head turned toward Lucas. His expression was one of utter astonishment. Then his head fell on his breast; his knees gave way; and he collapsed face down onto the sand.

For the space of a single heartbeat there was not a sound. Lucas stood frozen, the pistol dangling from his lax hand; his face was a mask of horror. Then, from the Mummy, came a sound that froze the blood in my veins. The creature was laughing—howling, rather, with a hideous mirth that resembled the shrieks of a lost soul. Still laughing, it retreated, and none of the horrified watchers moved to prevent it. Even after the thing had vanished from sight around the curve of the cliff, I could hear its ghastly laughter reverberating from the rocky walls.

Chapter Nine

WHEN I reached Walter's side I found Emerson there before me. Where he had been, or how he had come, I did not know; brain and organs of sight were hazy with horror. Kneeling by his young brother, Emerson ripped the bloodstained shirt away from the body. Then he looked up at Lucas, who had joined us and was staring down at the fallen man.

"Shot in the back," said Emerson, in a voice like none I had heard from him heretofore. "Your hunting colleagues in England would not approve, Lord Ellesmere."

"My God," stammered Lucas, finding his voice at last. "Oh, God—I did not mean. . . . I warned him to keep away, he rushed in, I could not help. . . . For the love of heaven, Mr. Emerson, don't say he is—he is—"

"He is not dead," said Emerson. "Do you think I would be sitting here, discussing the matter, if you had killed him?"

My knees gave way. I sat down hard on the warm sand.

"Thank God," I whispered.

Emerson gave me a critical look.

"Pull yourself together, Peabody, this is no time for a fit of the vapors. You had better see to the other victim; I think she has merely fainted. Walter is not badly hurt. The wound is high and clean. Fortunately his lordship's weapon uses small-caliber bullets."

Lucas let out his breath. Some of the color had returned to his face.

"I know you don't like me, Mr. Emerson," he said, with a new and becoming humility. "But will you believe me when I say that the news you have just given us is the best I have heard for a long, long time?"

"Hmm," said Emerson, studying him. "Yes, your lordship; if it is any consolation to you, I do believe you. Now go and give Amelia a hand with Evelyn."

Evelyn was stirring feebly when we reached her, and when she learned what had happened to Walter she was too concerned about him to think of herself. It is wonderful what strength love can lend; rising up from a faint of terror, she walked at Walter's side as his brother carried him to his bed, and insisted on helping me clean and dress the wound.

I was relieved to find that Emerson's assessment was correct. I had not had any experience with gunshot wounds, but a common-sense knowledge of anatomy assured me that the bullet had gone through the fleshy part of the right shoulder, without striking a bone.

I had not the heart to send Evelyn away, but really she was more of a handicap than a help; whenever I reached for a cloth or a bandage she was supposed to hand me, I would find her staring bemusedly at the unconscious lad, tears in her eyes and her feelings writ plain on her face for all the world to see. I could hardly blame her; Walter reminded me of the beautiful Greek youth Adonis, dying among the river reeds. He was slight, but his muscular development was admirable; the long lashes that shadowed his cheek, the tumbled curls on his brow, and the boyish droop of his mouth made a picture that must appeal to any woman who is sensitive to beauty and pathos.

Walter was conscious by the time I finished bandaging the wound. He did not speak at first, only watched me steadily, and when I had finished he thanked me with a pallid smile. His first look, however, had been for Evelyn; and having assured himself that she was safe, he did not look at her again. As she turned away with her bowl of water, I saw her lips tremble.

Emerson had produced a new atrocity—a dreadful pipe that smelled like a hot summer afternoon on a poultry farm—and was sitting in a corner puffing out clouds of foul smoke. When I had finished with Walter, Emerson rose to his feet and stretched.

"The evening's entertainment is over, it seems," he remarked. "We may as well get some sleep for what is left of the night."

"How can you talk of sleeping?" I demanded. "I am so full of questions and comments—"

"More of the latter than the former, I fancy," said Emerson, puffing away at his pipe. "I don't think Walter is up to your conversation, Peabody. It takes a well man, in his full strength, to—"

"Now, Radcliffe, that will do," Walter interrupted. His voice was weak, but the smile he gave me was his old sweet smile. "I am not feeling too bad; and I agree with Miss Amelia that we have much to discuss."

"I, too, agree," said Lucas, breaking a long—for him—silence. "But first—may I suggest a restorative, all around? A little brandy might ease Walter's pain—"

"I do not approve of spirits for such injuries," I said firmly.

Emerson snorted through his pipe, producing a great puff of smoke.

"I am not in much pain," Walter said. "But perhaps brandy might help—the ladies. They—they have undergone a considerable shock."

So we had our brandy. Emerson seemed to enjoy his very much. Although

I do not ordinarily approve of spirits, they are of use in some situations; I felt the need of stimulants myself, and the liquor lessened Evelyn's pallor. She was still wearing her nightclothes and dressing gown, not having had time to dress. They were embroidered lawn, of a pale blue, and I could see that Lucas admired them.

"Well, Peabody," said Emerson. "What is your first question?"

"Now that is not easy to say. The entire episode has been so bewildering. . . . First, though, I should like to know what has happened to Abdullah."

"Good heavens," exclaimed Lucas. "I had quite forgotten him. Where is the fellow?"

"Don't waste your suspicions on Abdullah," said Emerson. "He is probably following the Mummy. I told him to do so if we fail to apprehend it. But I fancy he will be returning soon. . . . Ah, yes, I believe I hear him now."

He beamed as complacently as if he had arranged Abdullah's opportune arrival. The tall, stately form of the foreman now appeared at the entrance to the tomb. His eyes widened as he beheld Walter, and sometime was wasted on explanations before Abdullah told us his story. Again, I translate into ordinary English.

He had been stationed by Emerson some distance from the camp. He had heard the shots but of course had not known what they betokened. They had, however, alerted him, and thus he was able to catch sight of the Mummy when it left us. Its speed amazed him; he kept repeating, "It ran like a swift young man." He had tried to interfere with the creature. Indeed, I think he was afraid to do so. But he had summoned up enough courage to follow it, at a safe distance.

"Where did it go?" I demanded. "To the village?"

Abdullah shook his head.

"Not village. Into the wadi, to the royal tomb. I did not follow; I thought you need me, I come here."

Emerson laughed shortly.

"So it is the ghost of Khuenaten we have with us? Come, now, Abdullah, that does not make sense. Our ghost is an avenging Amonist priest, if you remember, not a follower of the heretic king."

"Oh, stop it," I said impatiently. "I cannot blame Abdullah for not following the thing. We agreed, did we not, that the villain, whoever he is, must conceal his grisly costume in some remote place. He was on his way there. Perhaps he went to the village later."

Emerson was about to reply when Evelyn's quiet voice broke in.

"I think we should end the discussion. Walter ought to rest."

Walter opened his eyes when she spoke, but I had seen the signs of fatigue too.

"Evelyn is right," I said, rising. "She, too, has had a nasty experience."

"I am all right," Walter muttered.

"Of course you are," I said, with a cheer I did not feel. Fever commonly follows such wounds, and infection is rampant in Egypt. But there was no point in anticipating trouble. "All you need is rest. Come along, Evelyn—Lucas—"

"I must say one thing first." Lucas bent over the pallet where the sick man lay. "Walter, please tell me you forgive my clumsiness. I had no intention—"

"It was very stupid, all the same," said Emerson, as Walter made a feeble gesture of conciliation.

"You are right," Lucas muttered. "But if you had been in my place—you saw, I know, but you did not feel the recoil of the pistol, and then see that ghastly thing come on and on. . . ." With a sudden movement he pulled the gun from his pocket. "I shall never use this again. There is one bullet left. . . ."

His arm straightened, pointing the gun out the mouth of the tomb. His finger was actually tightening on the trigger when Emerson moved. The man was constantly surprising me; his leap had a tigerish swiftness I would not have expected. His fingers clasped around Lucas's wrist with a force that made the younger man cry out.

"You fool," Emerson mumbled around the stem of the pipe. Snatching the gun from Lucas's palsied hand, he put it in his belt. "The echoes from a shot in this confined place would deafen us. Not to mention the danger of a ricochet. . . . I will take charge of your weapon. Lord Ellesmere. Now go to bed."

Lucas left without another word. I felt an unexpected stab of pity as I watched him go, his shoulders bowed and his steps dragging. Evelyn and I followed. As soon as she had dropped off to sleep I went back onto the ledge, and somehow I was not surprised to see Emerson sitting there. His feet dangling over empty space, he was smoking his pipe and staring out at the serene vista of star-strewn sky with apparent enjoyment.

"Sit down, Peabody," he said, gesturing at the ledge beside him. "That discussion was getting nowhere, but I think you and I might profit from a quiet chat."

I sat down.

"You called me Amelia, earlier," I said, somewhat to my own surprise.

"Did I?" Emerson did not look at me. "A moment of aberration, no doubt."

"You were entitled to be distracted," I admitted. "Seeing your brother struck down. . . . It was not entirely Lucas's fault, Emerson. Walter rushed into the path of the bullet."

"In view of the fact that his lordship had already fired twice without result, I would have supposed he would have sensed enough to stop."

I shivered.

"Get a shawl, if you are cold," said Emerson, smoking.

"I am not cold. I am frightened. Are none of us willing to admit the consequences of what we say? Emerson, the bullet struck that thing. I saw them strike."

"Did you?"

"Yes! Where were you, that you did not see?"

"I saw its hands, or paws, clutch at its breast," Emerson admitted. "Peabody, I expected better of you. Are you becoming a spiritualist?"

"I hope I am reasonable enough not to deny an idea simply because it is unorthodox," I retorted. "One by one our rational explanations are failing."

"I can think of at least two rational explanations for the failure of the bullets to harm the creature," Emerson said. "A weapon of that type is extremely inaccurate, even in the hands of an expert, which I believe his lordship is not. He may have fired two clean misses, and the Mummy put on a performance of being hit in order to increase our mystification."

"That is possible," I admitted. "However, if I stood in the Mummy's shoes—or sandals, rather—I should hate to depend on Lucas's bad marksmanship. What is your other explanation?"

"Some form of armor," Emerson replied promptly. "I don't suppose you read novels, Peabody? A gentleman named Rider Haggard is gaining popularity with his adventurous tales; his most recent book, *King Solomon's Mines,* concerns the fantastic experiences of three English explorers who seek the lost diamond mines of that biblical monarch. At one point in the tale he mentioned chain mail, and its usefulness in deflecting the swords and spears of primitive tribes. I believe it would also stop a small-caliber bullet. Have we not all heard of men being saved from bullet wounds by a book—it is usually a Bible—carried in their breast pocket? I have often thought it a pity that our troops in the Sudan are not equipped with armor. Even a padded leather jerkin, such as the old English foot soldiers wore, would save many a life."

"Yes," I admitted. "The wrappings could cover some such protective padding. And I have read of Crusaders' armor being found in this mysterious continent, even in Cairo antique shops. But would such an ingenious idea occur to a man like Mohammed?"

"Let us abandon that idea once and for all. Mohammed was not the Mummy."

"How can you be so sure?"

"Its height," Emerson replied calmly. "For a moment Walter was close enough so that I could measure their comparative height. It was as tall as he, or taller. Mohammed and the other villagers are small people. Bad diet and poor living conditions. . . ."

"How can you be so cool? Discussing diet, at such a time. . . ."

"Why," said Emerson, puffing away, "I am beginning to enjoy myself. Lord Ellesmere's sporting instincts have infected me; he reminds me that an Englishman's duty is to preserve icy detachment under any and all circumstances. Even if he were being boiled to provide a cannibal's dinner it would be incumbent upon him to—"

"I would expect that you would be taking notes on the dietary habits of aborigines as the water bubbled around your neck," I admitted. "But I cannot believe you are really so calm about Walter's injury."

"That is perceptive of you. In fact, I mean to catch the person who is responsible for injuring him."

I believed that. Emerson's voice was even, but it held a note that made me glad I was not the person he referred to:

"You have left off your bandages," I said suddenly.

"You are absolutely brilliant tonight, Peabody."

"I am sure you should not—"

"I cannot afford to pamper myself. Matters are approaching a climax."

"Then what shall we do?"

"You, asking for advice? Let me feel your brow, Peabody, I am sure you must be fevered."

"Really, your manners are atrocious," I exclaimed angrily.

Emerson raised one hand in a command for silence.

"We had better take a stroll," he said. "Unless you want to waken Miss Evelyn. I don't know why you can't carry on reasonable discussion without raising your voice."

He offered me a hand to help me rise; but the jerk with which he lifted me to my feet was not gentle; for a moment my weight dangled from his arm in an undignified manner. He set me on my feet and walked off. I followed, and caught him up at the bottom of the cliff. We strolled along in silence for a time. Even Emerson was moved by the beauty of the night.

Before us, the moonlight lay upon the tumbled desolation of sand that had once been the brilliant capital of a pharaoh. For a moment I had a vision; I seemed to see the ruined walls rise up again, the stately villas in their green groves and gardens, the white walls of the temples, adorned with brilliantly painted reliefs, the flash of gold-tipped flagstaffs, with crimson pennants flying the breeze. The wide, tree-lined avenues were filled with a laughing throng of white-clad worshipers, going to the temple, and before them all raced the golden chariot of the king, drawn by matched pair of snow-white horses. . . . Gone. All gone, into the dust to which we must all descend when our hour comes.

"Well?" I said, shaking off my melancholy mood. "You promised me the benefit of your advice. I await it breathlessly."

"What would you say to striking camp tomorrow?"

"Give up? Never!"

"Just what I would have expected an Englishwoman to say. Are you willing to risk Miss Evelyn?"

"You think the Mummy has designs on her?"

"I am unwilling to commit myself as to its original intentions," said Emerson pedantically. "But it seems clear that the Mummy is now interested in her. I am afraid it is not attracted by your charms, Peabody. It must have known you were in the tent; I was watching, and I thought for a time, seeing the walls bulge and vibrate, that you would have the whole structure down about your ears. What were you doing—physical knee jerks?"

I decided to ignore his childish malice.

"I was looking for evidence of what had happened to Michael," I explained. "I found this."

I showed him the crucifix, pointing out the break in the chain. He looked grave.

"Careless of the attacker, to leave such a clue."

"You believe Michael was forcibly abducted?"

"I am inclined to think so."

"And you do nothing? A faithful follower—a helper we badly need—"

"What can I do?" Emerson inquired, reasonably enough. "One result of these activities has been to keep us fully occupied; we have not had time, or personnel, for retaliation; we can barely enact defensive measures. I think Michael has not been harmed."

"I wish I could be so confident. Well, we can hardly march into the village and demand that he be delivered up to us. What a pity we could not apprehend the Mummy. We might have effected an exchange of prisoners."

"We could do a great deal more than that if we had the Mummy," Emerson replied. He tapped out his pipe and put it in his pocket. "It does seem as if the stars are against us. Twice now we ought to have had our hands on it. But let us not waste time in vain regrets. I am concerned for Miss Evelyn—"

"Do you suppose I am not? I think I must take her away. She might at least sleep on the dahabeeyah, with the crew to guard her."

"The boat is only a few miles from here. Our mummified friend seems to have excellent powers of locomotion."

I felt as if a bucket of cold water had been dashed over me.

"It surely would not venture there! If its primary aim is to convince you to quit the site—"

"I am not in a position to state, unequivocally, what the aim of an animated mummy might be. But if that is its purpose, a serious threat to Miss Evelyn might accomplish it. Do you suppose Walter would remain here if he believed she was in danger?"

"Ah," I said. "So you have observed that."

"I am not blind, nor deaf, nor wholly insensible. I sense also that she is not indifferent to him."

"And, of course, you disapprove."

"Why, Peabody, you know my mercenary nature. I need money for my excavations. The aim is noble—to rescue knowledge from the vandalism of man and time. Walter might make an advantageous marriage; he is a handsome fellow, don't you think? You could hardly suppose I would allow him to throw himself away on a penniless girl. Miss Evelyn *is* penniless, is she not?"

As he spoke, in an insufferably sarcastic tone, I thought I detected a faint smell of singeing cloth.

"She is penniless," I replied shortly.

"A pity," Emerson mused. "Well, but if she is not good enough for Walter, she is too nice a child to be handed over to the Mummy. I propose that we test our theory. Let her sleep tomorrow night on the dehabeeyah, and—we will see what happens. You will have to use trickery, Peabody, to induce her to stay there; she does not lack courage, and will not willingly leave Walter. I suggest we propose an expedition to the boat tomorrow, to fetch various necessities. I will leave Abdullah to guard Walter—"

"Why not carry Walter with us? He would be better on the boat."

"I don't think we should risk moving him."

"Perhaps not. But to leave him here alone, with only Abdullah. . . . He is not the most reliable of guards. I think he is increasingly fearful."

"Walter will only be alone for a few hours, in daylight. I will return as soon as I have escorted you to the dahabeeyah. You must conterfeit illness, or something, to keep Miss Evelyn there overnight."

"Yes, sir," I said. "And then?"

"Then you must remain on guard. I may be wrong; the Mummy may not come. But if it does, you and you alone will be responsible for Miss Evelyn's safety. Can you take on such a task?"

The smell of singeing cloth grew stronger. I have a very keen sense of smell.

"Certainly I can."

"You had better take this," he said, and to my consternation, produced the revolver he had taken from Lucas. I shrank back as he offered it.

"No, don't be absurd! I have never handled firearms; I might injure someone. I can manage without a gun, you may be sure."

"So you do admit to some weaknesses."

There was definitely a small curl of smoke issuing from the pocket in which Emerson had placed his pipe. I had been about to point this out. Instead I remarked, "I have said that I can manage without a weapon. How many men can claim as much? Good night, Emerson. I accept your plan. You need have no fear of my failing in my role."

Emerson did not reply. A most peculiar expression had come over his face. I watched him for a moment, relishing the situation with, I fear, a malice most unbecoming a Christian woman.

"Your pocket is on fire," I added. "I thought when you put your pipe away that it was not quite out, but you dislike advice so much. . . . Good night."

I went away, leaving Emerson dancing up and down in the moonlight, beating at his pocket with both hands.

II

To my infinite relief, Walter was better next morning. The dreaded fever of infection had not appeared, and I was optimistic about his prospects, so long as he did not aggravate the wound. I had only time for a quick exchange with Emerson that morning. We agreed that Walter should not attempt the trip to the dahabeeyah.

So the scheme we had arranged was carried out. We had great difficulty in persuading Evelyn to go, but finally she agreed, as she thought, to a quick journey to and from the river. Glancing back, as our caravan set forth, I saw Abdullah squatting on the ledge, his knees up and his turbaned head bowed. He looked like the spirit of an ancient scribe brooding over the desolate site of his former home.

The walk, through sand and under a broiling sun, was not an easy one. It was with considerable relief that I made out the mast and furled sails of the *Philae,* bobbing gently at anchor. Beyond, I saw Lucas's boat. It was called the *Cleopatra.* If that famous queen was as fatally lovely as history claims, her namesake did not live up to its model; the *Cleopatra* was smaller than the *Philae* and not nearly so neat. As we drew nearer I saw some members of the crew lounging about the deck; they were as dirty and unkempt as their boat, and the sullen indifference with which they watched us contrasted eloquently with the enthusiastic welcome of my men. You would have thought we had returned from the jaws of death instead of a place only four miles away. Reis Hassan seemed to recognize Emerson; his white teeth gleamed in a smile as their hands met, and the two fell into animated conversation.

I did not need to follow the rapid Arabic to know that Emerson's first questions concerned our missing Michael; it had been my intention to investigate that matter immediately if he had not. The reis's response was equally intelligible—a firm negative.

And yet, despite my ignorance of the language, I felt there was something hidden behind the captain's steady look and quick reply—some reservation he did not care to state. I was ready, by that time, to believe that everyone around me was party to the plot, but I knew Hassan might be quite innocent and yet not quite candid. He might be concealing a shamed, fugitive Michael; he might have heard the tales of the villagers and be reluctant to confess his own fears.

Emerson's flashing glance at me indicated that he had similar doubts. He turned back to the reis with a barrage of questions, but got little satisfaction. Michael had not been seen. No doubt he had become bored, or lonely for his family, as "these Christians" were wont to do, and had deserted.

Emerson stamped impatiently as Hassan took his departure. He really did behave like a spoiled child at times; but now I could hardly blame him. He was on fire to return to Walter, and could not waste more time in interrogation; when an Egyptian decides not to speak, it requires a Grand Inquisitor to get a word out of him. Evelyn had gone below to pack the articles that were our ostensible reason for coming. Lucas had gone to his own dahabeeyah. Emerson and I stood alone on the upper deck.

"I must get back," he muttered. "Peabody, all is not well. The crewmen have been talking with the villagers. One of them has already run away, and I think Hassan is doubtful of his ability to control the others. Not that he would admit it—"

"I felt something was wrong. But you ought not to wait; I too am apprehensive about Walter. Go."

"You will not forget what I have told you?"

"No."

"And you will act as I have directed?"

"Yes."

The sun on the upper deck was burning hot, with the awning rolled back. Streaks of perspiration trickled down Emerson's face.

"The situation is intolerable," he exclaimed. "Amelia, swear to me that you will do precisely what I said; you will not take foolish chances, or expose yourself—"

"I have said I would. Don't you understand English?"

"Good God! You are the one who fails to understand; don't you realize there is not another woman living whom I would—"

He broke off. From the far end of the deck Lucas approached, his hands in his pockets, his lips pursed in a whistle. The strains of "Rule, Britannia" floated to my ears.

Emerson gave me a long, piercing look—a look that burned itself into my brain. Without another word he turned and vanished down the ladder to the lower deck.

I could not face Lucas just then. I followed Emerson. He was out of sight by the time I reached the lower deck, so I went on down, into the area where the cabins were located. My cheeks were tingling; I felt a foolish desire to imitate Lucas's whistling. It had been very hot on the upper deck; even those few moments had burned my face so that it felt warm and flushed.

In a narrow, dark corridor I ran full tilt into Evelyn.

"Amelia," she cried, clutching my arm. "I have just seen Mr. Emerson from my window. He is leaving—he is on his way back, without us. Stop him, pray do; I must go back—"

With a start of repugnance I remembered the role I must play.

Evelyn was trying to brush past me. I put my hands on her arms and leaned heavily against her.

"I am feeling ill," I muttered. "I really think I must lie down . . ."

Evelyn responded as I had known she would. She assisted me to my cabin and helped me loosen my dress. I pretended to be faint; I am afraid I did not do a convincing job of it, what with shame at betraying her trust and the odd exhilaration that bubbled inside me; but poor Evelyn never suspected me of false dealing. She worked assiduously to restore me; indeed, she waved the smelling salts so ardently under my nose that I went into a fit of sneezing.

"Leave off, do," I exclaimed between paroxysms. "My head will fly off in a moment!"

"You are better," Evelyn said eagerly. "That was your old strong voice. *Are* you better, Amelia? Dare I leave you for a moment? I will run after Mr. Emerson and tell him to wait—"

I fell back on the pillow with a heartrending groan.

"I cannot walk, Evelyn. I think—I think I must stay here tonight. Of course," I added craftily, "if you feel you must go—and leave me here alone—I will not try to keep you . . ."

I closed my eyes, but I watched Evelyn through my lashes. The struggle on the girl's face made me feel like Judas. Almost I weakened. Then I remembered Emerson's look, and his words. "There is not another woman alive whom I would—" What had he meant to say? "Whom I would trust, as I am trusting in your strength and courage?" Would the sentence, interrupted by Lucas, have ended in some such wise? If so—and there could hardly be any other meaning—it was an accolade I could not fail to deserve. The triumph of converting that arrogant misogynist into an admission that Woman, as represented by my humble self, had admirable qualities. . . . No, I thought, if I must choose between Evelyn or Emerson—or rather, between Evelyn and my own principles—I must betray Evelyn. It was for her own good.

Still, I felt rather uncomfortable, as I watched her fight her silent battle. Her hands were pressed so tightly together that the knuckles showed white, but when she spoke her voice was resigned.

"Of course I will stay with you, Amelia. How could you suppose I would do otherwise? Perhaps a quiet night's sleep will restore you."

"I am sure it will," I mumbled, unable to deny the girl that much comfort. Little did she know what sort of night I half expected!

I ought to have stayed in my bed, refusing food, to carry out my performance; but as the day went on, I began to be perfectly ravenous. Darkness fell, and I felt I was safe; not even Evelyn would insist that we make the journey by night. So I admitted to feeling a little better, and agreed that nourishment would do me good. I had a frightful time trying to prick at the food and not bolt it down like a laborer. The cook had outdone himself, as if in celebration of our return, and Lucas had fetched several bottles of champagne from his dahabeeyah.

He was attired in evening dress; the austere black and white became his sturdy body and handsome face very well. He had become exceedingly tanned. I felt as if he ought to be wearing the crimson sashes and orders of some exotic foreign emissary, or even the gold-embroidered robes of a Beduin sheik.

We dined on the upper deck. The canopy had been rolled back, and the great vault of heaven, spangled with stars, formed a roof finer than any oriental palace could boast. As we sipped our soup, a feeling of unreality swept over me. It was as if the preceding week had never happened. This was a night like the first nights on the dahabeeyah, surrounded by the sights and sounds and olfactory sensations that had so quickly become dear and familiar. The soft lapping of the water against the prow and the gentle sway of the boat; the liquid voices of the crewmen down below, as mellow and wordless as music to our untrained ears; the balmy night breeze, carrying the homely scents of burning charcoal and pitch and unwashed Egyptian; and under them all the indefinable, austere perfume of the desert itself. I knew I would never be free of its enchantment, never cease to desire it after it was gone. And although the strange events of past days seemed remote and dreamlike, I knew that in some indefinable way they had heightened the enjoyment of the journey, given it a sharp tang of danger and adventure.

Lucas was drinking too much. I must admit he held his wine like a gentleman; his speech did not become slurred nor his movements unsteady. Only his eyes showed the effect, becoming larger and more brilliant as the evening wore on; and his conversation became, if possible, quicker and more fantastical. One moment he declared his intention of returning to the camp, for fear of missing another encounter with the Mummy; the next moment he was ridiculing the whole affair—the Emerson brothers, their shabby way of life, the absurdity of spending the years of youth grubbing for broken pots—and declaring his intention to move on to the luxuries of Luxor and the glories of Thebes.

Evelyn sat like a pale statue, unresponsive to the jeers or to the increasingly soft glances her cousin directed at her. She had not dressed for dinner, but was wearing a simple morning frock, a faded pink lawn sprigged with tiny rosebuds.

Lucas kept looking at the gown; finally he burst out, "I don't mean to criticize your choice of costume, Cousin, but I yearn to see you in something becoming your beauty and your station. Since that first night in Cairo I have not seen you wear a gown that suited you. What a pity I could not bring your boxes with me!"

"You are too conscientious, Lucas," Evelyn replied. "It may relieve you to know that I am not looking forward to unpacking those boxes. I shall never wear the gowns again; their elegance would remind me too painfully of Grandfather's generosity."

"When we return to Cairo we will burn them unopened," Lucas declared extravagantly. "A grand auto-da-fé of the past! I want to supply you with a wardrobe fitting your station, my dear Evelyn—with garments that will have no painful memories associated with them."

Evelyn smiled, but her eyes were sad.

"I *have* the wardrobe befitting my station," she replied, with a loving glance at me. "But we cannot destroy the past, Lucas, nor yield to weakness. No; fortified by my faith as a Christian, I will look over Grandfather's gifts in solitude. There are trinkets, mementos I cannot part with; I will keep them to remind me of my errors. Not in any spirit of self-flagellation," she added, with another affectionate look at me. "I have too much to be thankful for to indulge in that error."

"Spoken like an Englishwoman and a Christian," I exclaimed. "But indeed, I have difficulty in hearing you speak, Evelyn; what is going on down below? The men are making a great deal of noise."

I spoke in part to change a subject that was clearly painful to Evelyn, but I was right; for some time the soft murmur of voices from the deck below had been gradually increasing in volume. The sound was not angry or alarming, there was considerable laughter and some unorganized singing.

Lucas smiled. "They are celebrating your return. I ordered a ration of whiskey to be served out. A few of them refused, on religious grounds; but the majority seem willing to forget the admonitions of the Prophet for one night. Moslems are very much like Christians in some ways."

"You ought not to have done that," I said severely. "We ought to strengthen the principles of these poor people, not corrupt them with our civilized vices."

"There is nothing vicious about a glass of wine," Lucas protested.

"Well, you have had enough," I said, removing the bottle as he reached for it. "Kindly recall, my lord, that our friends at the camp are still in danger. If we should receive a distress signal in the night—"

Evelyn let out a cry of alarm, and Lucas glared at me.

"Your friend Emerson would not call for help if he were being burned at the stake," he said, with a sneer that robbed the statement of any complimentary effect. "Why do you frighten Evelyn unnecessarily?"

"I am not frightened," Evelyn said. "And I agree with Amelia. Please, Lucas, don't drink any more."

"Your slightest wish is my command," said Lucas softly.

But I feared the request had come too late. Lucas had already taken more than was good for him.

Soon after this Evelyn pleaded fatigue and suggested that I too retire, in order to build up my strength. The reminder came at an opportune time, for I had forgotten I was supposed to be ailing. I sent her to her cabin and then called the reis; the noise from below was now so great that I was afraid Evelyn would not be able to sleep. Hassan, at least, showed no signs of inebriation, but I had a hard time communicating with him, for, of course, he spoke very little English. How I missed our devoted Michael! Eventually I got the reis to understand that we were retiring, and we wished the noise kept down. He bowed and retired; shortly thereafter the voices did drop in tone.

Lucas had been sitting in sullen silence, staring at the wine bottle, which was at my elbow. I was of two minds as to whether to carry it with me when I retired. I decided against it. Lucas probably had plenty more.

As I rose, he jumped up and held my chair.

"Excuse my bad manners, Miss Amelia," he said quietly. "But indeed, I am not at all drunk. I merely wanted to convey that impression."

"It seems to be a favorite plan of yours," I said drily, walking toward the stairs. Lucas followed me.

"I am sleeping in one of the cabins below," he said, in the same soft voice. "I will be awake and ready in case I am needed."

Now I had said nothing to Lucas of my conversation with Emerson the preceding night. Emerson had not needed to caution me against it; I had no particular confidence in Lucas myself. His comment meant that, independently, he had arrived at the same conclusion we had reached, and this fact both alarmed and interested me.

"I trust I will not need you," I replied.

We descended the narrow stairs and went into the cabin area. Lucas took my arm and brought me to a halt.

"This is the cabin I am occupying," he whispered. "Will you wait a moment, Miss Amelia? I want to show you something."

I waited in the dark corridor while he stepped into the cabin. He was back in a moment, carrying a long object, like a stick. I peered through the gloom before I was able to identify it; and then I started to expostulate.

"Never fear," said Lucas, holding up the rifle—for such it was. "It is not loaded. I would not make that mistake again."

"Then why carry it?"

"Sssh!" Lucas put a finger to his lips. "Only you and I know it is not loaded. Perhaps the Mummy has reason not to fear a small-caliber handgun, he will not be so nonchalant about a shell from an express that can bring down a charging elephant. And if all else fails, it makes an admirable club!"

He raised the rifle above his head.

"I think it is a foolish, idea," I snapped. "But if you are determined on it. . . . Good night, Lucas."

I left him brandishing the weapon, an idiotic grin on his face.

Ordinarily Evelyn and I occupied separate cabins, but I had no intention of leaving her alone that night. I feigned a return of weakness, in order to persuade her to share my room without alarming her, and she helped me into bed with sweet solicitude. She soon joined me. Darkness fell as she blew out the lamp, and before long her soft, regular breathing told me that fatigue had overcome the anxieties that still distressed her.

I did not sleep, but I found it more difficult than I had expected to overcome Morpheus. I had taken only a single glass of wine, despite Lucas's attempts to induce me to drink more. Ordinarily such a small amount does not affect me in the slightest, but as the minutes went on and the voices of the crewmen faded into silence, I fought sleep as if it had been a bitter enemy. Finally I arose—with care, so as not to waken Evelyn—and went into the adjoining cubicle, which served as our bathroom, where I splashed water on my face and even slapped it as vigorously as I dared. I was finally driven to pinching myself; and a foolish figure I would have made, if anyone had been there to see—standing bolt upright in the center of the room, applying my nails to the flesh of my arm at regular intervals.

The night was very silent. The men were asleep, I assumed. The soft night sounds of the Nile were as soothing as a lullaby. My knees kept bending, and I kept jerking myself erect. I had no idea how much time had passed. It seemed like hours.

At last, feeling slightly more alert, I went back into the sleeping chamber and approached the window. It was not the porthole sort of window one finds on regular sailing ships, but a wide aperture, open to the air but covered by a curtain in order to keep out the light. It opened onto the lower deck, not quite level with the flooring, but easily reached for it. I knew that if danger should approach, it must come this way. Our door was locked and bolted securely, but there was no way of locking the window without shutting out the air and making the room too stifling for comfortable sleep.

My hand went to the window frame all the same. After some internal debate I decided to leave it open. The increasingly stuffy air might waken Evelyn, and the window creaked, as I remembered from before. Instead I drew the curtain back just enough to see out, and remained standing, my elbows on the sill, my hands propping my drowsy head.

I could see a section of the deck from where I stood, and beyond it the silvered reaches of the river, with the night sky overhead. The moon's rays were so bright I could make out details like the nails in the planking. Nothing moved, except the rippling silver of the water.

How long I stood there I cannot calculate. I fell into a kind of waking doze, erect, but not wholly conscious. Finally I became aware of something moving along the deck to my right.

Lucas's cabin was in that direction, but I knew it was not Lucas. I knew what it was. Had I not expected it?

It kept to the shadows, but I made out the now familiar pale shape of it easily enough. I cannot explain why, but on this occasion I felt none of the superstitious terror that had paralyzed me on its earlier visits. Perhaps it was the skulking surreptitious movement of the thing; perhaps it was the familiarity of the surroundings. In any case, I began to feel enormous exasperation. Really, the Mummy was becoming ridiculous! Its repertoire was so limited; why didn't it do something different, instead of creeping around waving its arms?

I was no longer sleepy, and I calculated, quite coolly, what I should do. How I would crow over Emerson if, single-handedly, I could capture our mysterious adversary! I quite forgot his admonitions. I would not be satisfied with driving the Mummy away, as we had planned; no, I must catch it!

The only question was: Should I call for help, or should I attack the creature myself? I was reluctant to follow the former course. The crewmen were at the far end of the deck and were, no doubt, sleeping off their unaccustomed debauch so heavily that a cry would not waken them in time to prevent the creature's escape. As for Lucas, I did not doubt that he was snoring heavily. No, I thought; I would wait, to see what the Mummy did. If it tried to enter our room through the window—then I had it! My right hand already clasped the handle of the pitcher which, filled with water, stood beside the bed. It was a heavy earthenware jug and would raise a good lump on the head of anything it struck.

As I debated with myself, the Mummy stepped out into the moonlight. It had to do so, in order to reach our room; and as it did, my feelings underwent a sudden alteration. It was so large! It seemed bigger than a grown man, and although I told myself that the appearance of gigantism was the result of the bulky bandaging, my nerves were not quite convinced. Would the jug be sufficient to render the thing unconscious? I had forgotten that its head was padded. Suppose I struck and failed? I have considerable faith in my powers, but I was not mad enough to suppose that I could engage in hand-to-hand struggle with a creature of that size and come out victorious. Even if it were a mere man, and not a monster endowed with supernatural strength, it could overcome me; and then. . . . Evelyn lay sleeping and helpless in the bed. No—no, I could not risk that. I must wake her; better that she should be frightened than—the unspeakable alternative. I must call; better that the thing should escape than . . .

I drew a deep breath.

"Lucas! Lucas!" I shrieked. "*À moi,* Lucas! Help!"

I cannot imagine why I shouted in French. It was a dramatic moment.

To my taut nerves the results of my cry seemed long in coming. The Mummy stopped its stealthy advance. I had the decided impression that it was surprised to hear my voice. Behind me, Evelyn stirred and began to mutter sleepily. And then, with a loud thump and crash, Lucas jumped through the window of the next cabin onto the deck.

Even in that moment of danger I was glad Evelyn could not see him as he rushed to her rescue. He was fully dressed, but his shirt collar was open and his sleeves were rolled up, displaying muscular, rather hairy arms. His face was set in an expression of grim resolve; his right hand clasped the rifle. He was a sight to thrill any romantic girl; I felt a mild thrill myself as he threw the rifle to his shoulder and aimed it at the gruesome form that confronted him.

"Stop," he ordered, in a low but compelling voice. "Do not take another step, or I fire! D—it," he added vexedly, "does the monstrosity understand English? How absurd this is!"

"It understands the gesture, at least," I called, thrusting head and shoulders through the window. "Lucas, for pity's sake, seize it! Don't stand there deriding its linguistic inadequacies!"

The Mummy's head swung around until the featureless face looked directly at me. Oh, yes, it could see; I swear I caught a flash of eyes amid the darkness under its brows. It raised its arms and began to emit the mewing, growling cry that seemed to characterize its angry moods.

Evelyn was awake and calling out. I heard the bedsprings creak as she tried to rise.

"Stay where you are, Evelyn," I ordered. "Don't move. Lucas"—I disliked giving him the credit, but honesty demanded I should—"Lucas and I have the situation under control."

"What do I do now?" Lucas asked, addressing me. "It does not seem to understand me; and you know, Miss Amelia—"

"Strike it on the head," I shouted. "Rush at it and strike! Good Gad, why are you standing there? I will do it myself!"

I started to climb through the window. Evelyn had disregarded my orders; she was standing behind me, and as I essayed to move she caught me around the waist, crying out in alarm. Lucas was grinning broadly; the man had no sense of the proprieties. His smile did not endure, however. As I struggled with Evelyn, the Mummy moved. It lowered its arms; then one, the right arm, shot out with the force of a man throwing some object. Nothing left its hand. It did not step forward. But Lucas's body jerked violently. The rifle fell, as if his arms had suddenly lost their strength; it struck the deck with a metallic clatter, and Lucas fell upon it, face downward.

I stopped struggling. Evelyn and I stood with our arms wrapped around one another, frozen with horror. The Mummy's hideous laughter resounded through the quiet night. It turned to face our window.

Then, at long last, from the deck to the left came the sound of voices. The crewmen were awake. The Mummy heard. It raised one bandaged arm and shook a paw menacingly in the direction of the approaching men. I could not see them, but I knew they had seen the Mummy; they had probably seen the entire incredible performance, which had been played out on the open deck.

With a series of acrobatic bounds, the bandaged figure left. Evelyn was limp in my grasp. I shook her, none too gently.

"Lie down," I ordered. "You are safe, Evelyn; I must go to Lucas."

She slumped down onto the floor, and I scrambled through the window—no easy task in my voluminous night garments. I am afraid I displayed some part of my limbs as I crawled out onto the deck, but I was past worrying about that, and the crewmen were in no condition to notice my lack of dignity. I saw them as I got to my feet; they were clustered in a dark mass at the end of the deck, huddling together like silly sheep afraid of a wolf.

Lucas was still motionless.

I turned him over, not without difficulty; he was a heavy man, and would one day be fat if he continued to indulge himself. He did not appear to be injured; his pulse was strong, if a little too quick, and his color was good. But his breath came and went in the oddest whistling gasps and from time to time his whole body quivered in a kind of muscular spasm.

At first the men would not approach, and when they finally crept forward they refused to touch Lucas, even to carry him to a cabin. Reis Hassan finally came; his whiplash voice roused the men. I fancied they were almost as afraid of him as they were of the supernatural—but not quite. As soon as they had placed Lucas on his bed, they fled.

Hassan remained, standing just within the doorway, with his arms folded across his broad chest.

Never had I so regretted that I had not learned Arabic instead of Latin, Greek, and Hebrew. Hassan was not anxious to explain himself, and my incoherent questions were probably as unintelligible to him as his answers were to me. I thought he was rather ashamed of himself, but the cause of his shame was not easy to ascertain. He had slept too soundly, that much I was able to understand. All the crew had slept. It was not a natural sleep. It was like a spell—like magic. Otherwise they would, of course, have rushed to answer my call for help.

That much I grasped, or thought I grasped. It did not reassure me. I dismissed Hassan, after ordering him, as well as I could, to keep a man on watch for the remainder of the night. Lucas demanded my attention; and I was uneasily aware of the fact that I could no longer rely on my crew, not even my captain. If they had not already been frightened by tales of the Mummy, the night's adventure would have done the job.

Lucas was still unconscious. I did not dare consider the nature of the force that had struck him down so mysteriously; after examining him for a wound, and finding none, I decided to treat his condition as I would an ordinary faint. But none of my measures succeeded. His eyes remained closed; his broad chest rose and fell in the strange, stentorious breathing.

I began to be frightened. If this was a faint, it was an unnatural one. I rubbed his hands, slapped cold cloths on face and breast, elevated his feet—to no avail. Finally I turned to Evelyn, who was standing in the open doorway watching me.

"He is not . . ." She could not finish the sentence.

"No, nor in any danger of dying," I replied quickly. "I don't understand what is wrong with him."

"I can't bear it," Evelyn whispered; and then, as I started to speak, she added, "No, Amelia, it is not what you think; I admire, I like Lucas; after his courage tonight, I can hardly help but respect him. But my grief at his illness is that of a friend and cousin. Only—I am beginning to feel as if I brought disaster on all those who love me. Am I somehow accursed? Must I leave those I love, lest

I infect them, as my coming brought harm to Walter—and now to poor Lucas? Must I leave you, Amelia?"

"Don't talk nonsense," I replied brusquely. Harshness was the only proper response to the rising hysteria in the child's voice. "Go and fetch my smelling salts. If they are as strong as I remember, they ought to bring Lucas to his senses. They almost deprived me of mine."

Evelyn nodded. I could always command her by appealing to her sense of duty. As she turned, I was electrified by the first sign of life I had seen in my patient. His lips parted. In a low, sighing voice, he enunciated a single word.

"He calls your name," I said to Evelyn, who had paused. "Come quickly; answer him."

Evelyn knelt down by the bed. "Lucas," she said. "Lucas, I am here. Speak to me."

Lucas's hand moved. It groped feebly. Evelyn put her hand on his; the fingers closed around hers and clung.

"Evelyn," Lucas repeated. "My darling . . ."

"I am here," Evelyn repeated. "Can you hear me, Lucas?"

The sick man's head moved slightly. "So far away," he murmured, in a failing voice. "Where are you, Evelyn? Don't leave me. I am all alone in the dark. . . ."

Evelyn leaned over him. "I won't leave you, Lucas. Wake up, I implore you. Speak to us."

"Take my hand. Don't let me wander away. . . . I am lost without you. . . ."

This banal exchange continued for some time, with Lucas's weak voice pleading and Evelyn reassuring him. I shifted impatiently from one foot to the other. I suspected that Lucas was now fully conscious. He was certainly not delirious in the ordinary sense of the word. Only congenital stupidity could have produced such inane dialogue. Finally Lucas got to the point. His eyes were still closed.

"Don't leave me," he moaned. "Never leave me, my love, my hope. Promise you will never leave me."

Evelyn was bending so close that her unbound hair brushed his cheek. Her face was transformed by pity, and I rather hated to disillusion her, but I was not sure what she might promise in the heat of her innocent enthusiasm. If she made a promise, she would keep it. And I was determined that matters should proceed according to the plan I had conceived. So I said briskly, "He is coming around now, Evelyn. Are you going to promise to marry him, or shall we try the smelling salts first?"

Evelyn sat back on her heels. Her face was flushed. Lucas opened his eyes.

"Evelyn," he said slowly—but in his normal, deep tones, not the moaning whisper he had been using. "It is really you? I dreamed. God preserve me from any more such dreams!"

"Thank God," Evelyn said sincerely. "How do you feel, Lucas? We were so frightened for you."

"A little weak; otherwise, quite all right. It was your voice that brought me back, Evelyn; I seemed to be disembodied, lost and alone in a dark without a single spark of light. Then I heard you arrive and followed it as I would follow a beacon."

"I am glad I could help you, Lucas."

"You saved my life. Henceforth it is yours."

Evelyn shook her head shyly. She was trying to free her hand; and after a moment Lucas let it go.

"Enough of this," I interposed. "I am not so much interested in your dreams, Lucas, as I am in what produced them. What happened? I saw you stumble and fall, but I could swear the creature did not throw any missile."

"Nothing struck me," Lucas answered. "Nothing physical. . . . You found no bruise, no mark, I suppose?"

He glanced down at his bared chest. Blushing still more deeply, Evelyn got to her feet and retreated from the bed.

"There was no mark I could see," I replied. "What did you feel?"

"Impossible to describe it! I can only imagine that a man struck by a bolt of lightning might have a similar sensation. First a shocking thrill, electrical in intensity; then utter weakness and unconsciousness. I felt myself falling, but did not feel my body strike the deck."

"Splendid," I said sarcastically. "We now have a creature with the power to hurl thunderbolts. Emerson will be delighted to hear it."

"Emerson's opinions are of no interest to me," Lucas snapped.

III

I slept soundly for what remained of the night. I believe Evelyn did not sleep at all. When I awoke it was to see the exquisite pink flush of dawn staining the sky, and Evelyn silhouetted against it. She was standing at the window; she was fully dressed, in a businesslike serge skirt and blouse. The moment I moved, she spoke.

"I am going to camp," she announced firmly. "You need not come, Amelia; I will be back soon, I will hurry. I hope to persuade Mr. Emerson to bring his brother here, and to set sail at once for Luxor. But if they will not come, then—then I think we should go. I know you will not want to leave, Amelia; I have seen how interested you are in—in archaeology. But I think Lucas will go, if I ask him; and I shall leave, with him, if you want to remain here."

The sight of her pale, resolute face checked the remonstrance that had risen to my lips. I saw that I must speak with careful consideration. The girl believed the awful idea that had come to her the previous night! It was both pitiful and amusing to note that she had no qualms about burdening Lucas with her deadly presence, as she thought it, when it came to a choice between endangering Lucas or Walter.

"Well," I said, getting out of bed, "you will not go without breakfast, I hope. It would be silly to faint, from inanition, in the middle of the desert."

Evelyn unwillingly consented to partake of breakfast. As she restlessly paced the upper deck, I sent a servant to summon Lucas. It was easy to see how the events of the night had affected the crew. Young Habib, our smiling waiter, was not smiling that morning; and the usual cheerful babble of voices from the lower deck was not to be heard.

Lucas joined us while we were drinking our tea. He looked perfectly fit, and said he felt the same. Evelyn immediately told him of her plan. Lucas was not fool enough to fail to understand her agitation. His eyebrows climbed alarmingly as she spoke. In case he should miss the point I kicked him under the table. And when he turned to me indignantly, I semaphored warning as well as I could. He took the hint.

"My dearest," he said gently, "if you wish to leave this place, you shall leave. I told you that your slightest wish was my command. But I must make one small reservation. You can ask me for my life, but not for my honor as a gentleman and an Englishman! You cannot ask me to abandon our friends. No, do not speak; I will order the crew to be prepared to leave at a moment's notice, and to carry you and Miss Amelia to Luxor, or wherever you wish to go. But I will remain. You would not respect me if I fled now."

Evelyn sat in silence, her head bowed. I decided to intervene. I could hardly take exception to Lucas's sentiments but he managed to create an atmosphere of sticky sentimentality that disgusted me.

"I have no intention of leaving unless the Emersons join us," I said firmly. "And I will deal with my own crew, if you please, Lucas. You may give yours whatever orders you like."

"I will," Lucas replied huffily.

And he went off to do so, while I summoned Reis Hassan and made another effort to break through the language barrier. I had thought of asking Lucas for the loan of his dragoman as interpreter; but what I had seen of that shifty-eyed personage did not impress me, and if Emerson had not been able to induce Hassan to speak openly, I thought no one could.

Hassan managed to convey one concept unequivocally. He kept repeating the word "go," and pointing upstream.

"Emerson?" I asked, and gestured toward the camp.

Hassan nodded vigorously. We were all to go. Today.

That was one Arabic word I understood, although the word for "tomorrow" is even more commonly used. I repeated it now.

Hassan's face fell. Then he gave the queer Arab shrug.

"Tomorrow," he said soberly. *"In 'shallah."*

I knew that word too. It means, "God willing."

Chapter Ten

 SOON after breakfast we set out. The sun was well up; the sands shone palely gold, and the glare, even at that early hour, was hard on the eyes. There was little conversation during the walk. Evelyn had not spoken at all since she made her declaration; I was worried about her, and—which is not usual for me—uncertain as how I might best relieve her strange fears. Not that I blamed her for being distracted; most girls of her protected station in life would have been prostrate after the experiences she had undergone.

The first person to greet us was no other than Walter. He wore a sling, to support the injured arm, but otherwise he seemed well enough, and I was delighted to see him on his feet. He came to meet us, not quite running, and grasped my hand. But he looked at Evelyn.

"You cannot conceive how relieved I am to see you," he exclaimed. "I was furious with Radcliffe when he told me you had gone."

"I don't know why you should have been worried," I replied, returning his hearty handclasp. "It was you we worried about. How do you feel? And where is your brother?"

"You won't believe it," Walter said, smiling. "Guess."

"I don't need to guess," I replied. "Emerson has taken advantage of my absence to continue his excavations. He is totally without conscience! I suppose he has made another discovery. What is it? Another fragment of painting?"

Walter's eyes were wide with surprise.

"Miss Amelia, you astound me! You seem to read minds. How did you know?"

"I know your brother very well," I replied angrily. "He is capable of any stupidity where his precious antiquities are concerned. At such a time as this, to waste his time and energy. . . . Where is he? I want to speak to him."

"The pavement is not far from the other one that was destroyed," Walter replied. "But—"

"But me no buts," I said. "The rest of you return to camp. I will fetch Emerson."

I set off without another word, not waiting to see whether they obeyed me. By the time I found Emerson I had worked myself up into quite a state of anger. He was squatting on the ground, his tan clothing and dusty helmet blending so well with the hue of the sand that I did not distinguish his form until I was almost upon him. He was so preoccupied that he failed to hear my approach. I struck him, not lightly, on the shoulder with my parasol.

"Oh," he said, glancing at me. "So it's you, Peabody. Of course. Who else would greet a man by beating him over the head?"

I squatted down beside him. This posture, so difficult at first, had become easier. My knees no longer cracked when I knelt.

He had cleared a patch of pavement some three feet square. I saw the blue undersurface which denoted water, and upon it three exquisitely shaped lotus flowers, with green leaves framing the pure-white petals.

"So this is the explanation of your plot," I remarked. "Sending me off with Evelyn in order to distract the Mummy, so that you could work in peace. Thank you, Emerson, for your concern! You are the most despicable, selfish. . . . That is a great waste of time, you know, scooping at the sand with your bare hands. You will never clear the pavement that way. The sand trickles down as fast as you pull it away."

Emerson grinned unpleasantly at me over his shoulder.

"Tsk, tsk, Peabody, you are losing track of what you were saying. I am despicable, selfish—"

"Aren't you even curious?" I demanded angrily. "Don't you want to know what happened last night?"

"I know what happened." Emerson sat back on his haunches. "I went to the boat just before dawn this morning and had a talk with Hassan."

Now that I looked at him, I realized he appeared weary. There were dark circles under his eyes, and new lines around the firm mouth. I was momentarily deflated by this, and by his calm statement. But only momentarily.

"You did, did you? And what do you make of it all?"

"Why, matters transpired as I expected. The Mummy appeared, and was duly routed by you—"

"By Lucas," I interrupted.

"His lordship does not appear to have been particularly useful. His collapse threw the crew into a complete panic. Even Reis Hassan—who is far from being a coward, I assure you—is afraid. I trust his lordship is fully recovered this morning from what Hassan described as a personally delivered curse?"

"I don't know what was wrong with him," I admitted. "If he were not such an intrepid fellow, I would suspect he simply fainted."

"Ha," said Emerson.

"Jeer as much as you like, you cannot deny the man's courage. He is no coward."

Emerson shrugged and began to scoop away more sand.

"Have you taken leave of your senses?" I asked. "You have had one painting destroyed; uncover this, and it will meet the same fate. Its only safety now lies in obscurity."

"Perhaps its survival is not my chief concern," Emerson replied, still scooping. "We must have some lure for our mysterious visitor; better to lose this than Miss Evelyn."

I studied him in silence for several minutes.

"I cannot believe you mean that," I said finally.

"No, I am sure you have the lowest possible opinion of me and all my works. It is true, nevertheless."

There was a new note in his voice, one I had not heard before. Anger he had displayed, contempt, disgust; but never such weary bitterness. I felt peculiarly affected.

"I do not have a low opinion of you," I said—mumbled, rather.

Emerson turned.

"What did you say?"

We presented a ridiculous picture. Half kneeling, half squatting, Emerson was leaning forward to peer into my face. His hands rested on the ground, and his posture rather suggested that of an inquisitive orangutang. My own position, squatting on my heels with my skirts bunched up around me, was no less ludicrous. I was not conscious of absurdity or incongruity, however, I was only conscious of his eyes, blue and glittering as sapphires, holding my gaze with a strange intensity. Their look was too much to endure; my eyes fell, and my face felt uncomfortably warm.

And then the sound of a voice shattered the spell. Looking up, I saw Walter coming toward us. Emerson sat back.

"Radcliffe," Walter began, "what do you suppose has—"

He stopped speaking and looked from one of us to the other. "Is something wrong? Have I interrupted—"

"Nothing," Emerson said coldly. "You have not interrupted. What is it, Walter? You appear agitated."

"Agitated? I am, indeed! And so will you be, when you hear what transpired last night."

"I know what transpired," Emerson said, in the same cool voice.

I looked at him from under my lashes. His face was as impassive as one of the stone pharaohs in the Boulaq Museum. I decided I must have imagined the fleeting look of passionate inquiry. I was tired, after a sleepless night, and subject to fancies.

"Then Miss Amelia has told you," Walter said innocently. "Radcliffe, something must be done, this is frightful! You must persuade the ladies to leave—now—today! Come back to camp, I beg, and use your powers of persuasion. I cannot seem to prevail with either Miss Evelyn or his lordship."

"Oh, very well," Emerson grumbled, rising to his feet.

Walter extended his hand to me. His brother stalked away and we followed. When we caught him up, Walter continued to express his horror and alarm. Finally Emerson interrupted.

"Walter, you are babbling, and I don't believe you have thought the matter through. Suppose we do succeed in sending Miss Evelyn away; will that solve the difficulty? If the Mummy is a supernatural agent, which all you fools seem to believe, it can follow her wherever she goes. It can equally well follow her if it is not supernatural! Since you seem to be more concerned with her safety than with the success of our work here, perhaps you would agree that we ought to bend all our efforts on ascertaining the creature's motives, and apprehending it."

Walter looked distressed. The reasoning made some impression on his intellect, but all his protective instincts were at war with his brain; he wanted to see Evelyn out of danger.

"Indeed," I put in, "we really have no reason to suppose that the creature means Evelyn any harm. Both of you, and Lucas as well, have taken injury, but Evelyn has not been touched. She is the only one who has not been harmed—except for me."

"Ah," said Emerson, giving me a long, thoughtful look. "I assure you, Peabody, that point has not escaped me."

We finished the trip in silence. Walter was too worried, and I was too furious, to speak. I understood Emerson's implication. Could he really suspect *me* of being behind the diabolical plot? Surely not even Emerson was capable. . . . But, I told myself—he was! Such a cynic, who has never had an altruistic thought in his life, is always projecting his own failings onto other people.

Evelyn and Lucas were waiting for us, and we sat down for a discussion which at first proved fruitless. The fault was mine; ordinarily I have no difficulty in making up my mind, nor in convincing others of the correctness of my decision. On this occasion I could not come to a decision.

The safest course would have been for all of us to pack up and abandon the site. This I knew Emerson would never consider, and I had a certain sympathy for his point of view. Equally impossible to me was the idea of abandoning the Emersons and sailing away. Neither of them was in perfect health; they would be helpless if the villagers should turn from passive resistance to active hostility. They had no means of summoning help. Even in busy years the remote ruins of Amarna attract relatively few visitors, and the unsettled condition in the Sudan had frightened away many travelers.

An alternative was for me to remain with my dahabeeyah, in case of emergency, while Lucas and Evelyn returned to Cairo for assistance. It would be improper for them to travel unchaperoned; but by that time I was ready to consign the proprieties to perdition, where they belonged. However, the plan had a number of difficulties. Evelyn would refuse to leave me, and Emerson would howl like a jackal at the idea of my remaining to protect him. He had the lowest possible opinion of Maspero and the Antiquities Department; the notion of appealing to them for help would offend his masculine pride.

Nevertheless, I thought it my duty to propose the scheme. It was received with the unanimous, negative outcry I had expected. Did I say unanimous? I am incorrect. The only one who did not object was the one I had expected to be most vehement. Emerson sat with his lips pressed tightly together.

Lucas was the most outspoken.

"Abandon our friends?" he exclaimed. "And you, Miss Amelia? It is not to be thought of! Furthermore, I cannot possibly agree to allowing Evelyn to risk her reputation traveling alone with me. There is only one circumstance under which such a scheme would be feasible. . . ."

And he looked significantly at Evelyn, who flushed and turned her head away.

His meaning was clear. If Evelyn traveled as his affianced bride, the ceremony to be performed immediately upon their arrival in Cairo. . . . In our conventional times the proprieties might be shaken by such an arrangement, but they would not be unalterably shattered.

Walter caught the meaning as soon as I did. His ingenuous young countenance fell. Emerson had produced his pipe and was puffing away with every appearance of enjoyment; his eyes gleamed maliciously as he looked from one of us to the other.

"Oh, this is absurd," I said, jumping to my feet. "We must make some decision. The day is passing, and I am worn out."

"Of course you are," Evelyn exclaimed, immediately concerned. "You must have rest, that is more important than anything else. Go and lie down, Amelia."

"We have not yet made a decision," I began.

Emerson took his pipe from his mouth.

"Really, Peabody, this strange indecisiveness is not like you. Indeed, I am surprised at all of you. You are acting like impulsive children, ready to run from a shadow."

"A shadow!" I exclaimed indignantly. "It was a shadow, I suppose, that struck you down with a rock; a shadow that wounded Walter!"

"To be precise, it was an avalanche that injured me," Emerson replied coolly. "An equally unfortunate accident"—he stressed the word, glancing at Lucas as he did so—"an accident caused Walter's wound. Come, come, Peabody, use your head. To date, there is nothing to suggest that any of these mishaps were the result of deliberate malice. As for his lordship's strange collapse last night—the body is subject to inexplicable weaknesses. Fatigue, excitement—a trifle too much wine. . . ."

He paused, cocking his head and peering at Lucas with quizzical blue eyes. Lucas flushed angrily.

"I deny the allegation!"

"The only alternative is to believe in the supernatural powers of the Mummy," Emerson replied drily. "That I refuse to do. I will continue to seek a rational explanation until reason leaves me altogether; and unless one of you can suggest a motive, unknown to me, why any of us should be in danger. . . ."

Again he paused, raking us in turn with his cool stare. No one spoke.

"No vendettas, nor feuds?" Emerson asked mockingly. "No desperate lovers, or enemies burning for revenge? Very well, then; we return to the only sensible explanation for all this; it was suggested, I believe, by his lordship. The villagers wish to drive us away from here because they have made a valuable discovery. I will not be driven away. It is as simple as that."

I could not hope but be impressed by the man's irrefutable logic. And yet in my innermost soul a strange uneasiness lingered.

"Then what do you propose that we do?" I asked.

"I propose that we take the aggressive," Emerson replied. "So far we have not done so; we have been preoccupied with defending ourselves against fancied dangers. And that, I believe, is precisely what our opponents wish us to do. If the villagers can find a tomb, we can find it. Tomorrow I will begin searching. We will enlist the assistance of your crews. It will not be easy to do that; the men have been told by the villagers that we are under a curse. Yet I fancy that a judicious blend of flattery, appeal, and bribery will win them over. We must have sufficient manpower to protect the ladies and to conduct a thorough search. Well? What do you say? Is the scheme a good one?"

I had nothing to say. The scheme was a good one, but I would rather have died than admit it aloud. The others were clearly impressed. Evelyn's somber face had brightened.

"Then you really believe that the Mummy is only trying to frighten us? That no one is in danger?"

"My dear girl, I am convinced of it. If it will make you feel safer, we will damn the conventions and spend the night huddled together in a single room. But I feel sure no such discomfort is necessary. Are we all agreed? Excellent. Then Peabody had better retire to her bed; she is clearly in need of recuperative sleep; she has not made a sarcastic remark for fully ten minutes."

II

I thought I would not sleep. My mind was in a state of confusion such as I seldom permit in that organ; but on this occasion the methods I normally apply to resolve it were not effective. Something kept me from ratiocination. Mental fatigue, as well as physical exhaustion, finally sent me into heavy slumber, filled with bewildering fragments of dreams. The common theme of them all seemed to be light—bright beams of illumination that flashed on and then went out, leaving me in deeper darkness than before. I groped in the dark, seeking I knew not what.

It was such a beam of light that finally woke me. When the curtain at the mouth of the tomb was lifted, the rays of the setting sun struck straight into the shadowy gloom. I lay motionless, struggling against the bonds of sleep that still clung to me; my uneasy slumber had twisted the bedclothes about my limbs and loosened my hair from its net. Damp with perspiration, the thick coils weighted my heavy head.

Then I heard the voice. I did not recognize it at first; it was a harsh whisper, tremulous with fear and warning.

"Don't move! For your life, remain motionless!"

The tones woke me like a dash of cold water. I opened my drowsy eyes. The first object to meet my gaze was a coil of what appeared to be thick brown rope, resting on the foot of my couch. As I stared, the coil moved. A flat head lifted from the mass; two narrow orbs, sparkling with life, fixed themselves on mine.

The whisper came again.

"Be still. Not a breath, not a movement. . . ."

I did not need that injunction. I could not have moved, even if waking intelligence had not warned me that the slightest movement might rouse the serpent to strike. The small obsidian eyes held me. I had read that snakes paralyze their intended prey thus; and I knew how the trembling rabbit must feel when its murderer glides toward it.

With a desperate effort I wrenched my eyes from the hypnotic glare of the snake. I rolled them toward the door. I dared move no farther.

Emerson's face was streaked with rivulets of perspiration. He did not look at me. His eyes were fixed on the flat reptilian head, which was now weaving slowly back and forth. His hand, half lifted, shook with strain. It moved slowly, inch by inch. It touched his pocket and, with the same agonizing deliberation, reached inside.

Before and after that time I have made efforts that were not easy to make, but never have I done anything more difficult than remaining motionless. Lively terror had replaced my paralysis; every nerve in my body shook with the desire for action. I wanted to scream aloud, to fling myself from the deadly couch. Every ounce of my will was occupied in fighting this instinct. The strain was too much. A fog descended over my staring eyes. I knew that in another moment I must move.

When it finally came, the act was too quick for my failing eyes to see it. Emerson's arm flashed in a blur of motion. Simultaneously, or so it seemed, the heavens fell. Blinding light, a crash of sound that rolled like thunder. . . . Merciful oblivion overcame me.

I was not unconscious for long. When I awoke I could not remember, at first, what had happened. My head rested against a hard, warm surface that vibrated erratically. My ears still rang with the echoes of that final thunderclap. I decided, drowsily, that the rapid beating sound was that of my own blood rushing through my veins with the rapidity of terror; for a normal heartbeat was never so fast. I felt surprisingly comfortable—limp and boneless as a baby in its mother's arms. Then something began to touch my face—lips, closed eyes, cheeks—with a light pressure like the brush of fingers, only warmer and softer. That odd, fleeting touch had the strangest effect on me. I had been about to open my eyes. Instead, I closed them tighter. I decided I must be dreaming. Similar sensations had occurred, occasionally, in dreams; why should I dismiss such pleasurable experiences for a reality which would not be so enjoyable? I remembered everything now. The snake must have struck its fangs into me. I was poisoned—delirious—dreaming.

I genuinely resented the sounds that finally broke the spell. Voices crying out in alarm, running footsteps, streaks of light that irritated my closed eyes—yes, the dream was over. I felt myself being lowered to a flat surface, being shaken, and—crowning indignity—slapped smartly across the cheek. I opened my eyes, and then narrowed them in a frown as I recognized Emerson's face hovering over me like a nightmarish mask. It was he who had slapped me, of course. Beyond, I saw Evelyn, her face as white as her dress. She pushed Emerson away, with a strength and rudeness quite foreign to her nature, and flung herself down on the cot beside me.

"Amelia! Oh, my dear, dear Amelia—we heard the shot and came running—what has happened? Are you wounded? are you dying?"

"Not wounded, not dying, merely enjoying a ladylike swoon," said Emerson's familiar, detestable voice. "Allow me to congratulate you, Peabody; it is the first time I have seen you behave as a lady is supposed to do. I must make a note of it in my journal."

I tried to think of something sufficiently cutting to say in reply, but was too unstrung to do so; I simply glared at him. He had stepped back and was standing beside the cot, his hands in his pockets. A low cry from Walter interrupted Evelyn's agitated questions. He rose from the foot of the bed, holding the limp body of the serpent in his hand.

"Good God," he exclaimed, his voice shaking. "It is a hooded cobra—

one of the deadliest serpents in Egypt. Radcliffe—it was you who fired the shot? Are you certain it did not strike before you killed it?"

I thought for a moment Evelyn was going to faint. She roused herself and began to fumble around in the bedclothes, trying to examine my lower limbs. I pulled them away. I felt perfectly well now; Emerson's rudeness had the effect of rousing me.

"Don't fuss, Evelyn," I said irritably. "The snake did not touch me, it is a slow-witted creature and took so long making up its mind whether to bite me that Emerson had ample time to shoot it. He took plenty of time, too, I must say; I could have dealt with ten snakes during the interval he required to take out his pistol."

"You know better, Miss Amelia," Walter exclaimed. "It was necessary to move with deliberation; a rapid movement might have startled the snake into striking. To think that it was just here, at the foot of your bed! It turns me quite cold to think of it. Thank God you had a weapon, Radcliffe."

"My weapon, I suppose," said Lucas from the doorway. He came slowly into the room. "What a fortunate chance that you were carrying it with you."

"There was one bullet left," Emerson said. His lips curled in a frightful grimace; abruptly he turned his back.

"It was an extraordinary shot," Lucas said, his eyes on the other man's rigid shoulders. "A lucky shot, I should say. You might have struck Miss Amelia."

"It had to be attempted, whatever the risk," Walter exclaimed. The implied criticism of his brother brought a flush of anger to his face.

"Of course," cried Evelyn.

She was still pale with agitation, but she arose with her usual grace and, going to Emerson, placed her hand timidly on his arm.

"God bless you, Mr. Emerson. Your quick wits and keen eye saved Amelia's life. How can I ever thank you?"

Emerson's stiff, haughty pose relaxed. He turned and looked down at the girl. Some of the color returned to her face under his steady regard. Then he smiled faintly.

"I will let you know," he replied enigmatically.

"In the meantime, perhaps Master Walter might consider getting rid of his souvenir," said Lucas. "It cannot be a pleasant sight for the ladies."

Walter started. He was still holding the snake's body at arms' length. He crossed the room, brushing past Lucas, and went out the door.

"And," Lucas continued, "let us all leave this room, which reeks of gunpowder and holds unpleasant associations. Come, Miss Amelia, let me offer you my arm."

"Thank you," I replied. "I need no assistance. Perhaps a cup of tea . . ."

Evelyn and I had tea. The gentlemen had something stronger. Lucas was the only one who seemed normal; he kept speculating as to how the serpent got into the tomb.

"No doubt it crawled within during the night," he said.

"I wonder why I didn't see it earlier," I said. "I must have disturbed it when I flung myself down to sleep."

"Because it was not on the cot then," Lucas replied. "It was curled in a corner, and crept onto your bed later. It was fortunate that Emerson came in when he did; if you had awakened and moved about—"

"Enough of this," I interrupted. "The thing is over and done with. In the meantime, the sun is setting. We have yet to decide what we are going to do tonight."

"I have decided." It was Evelyn who spoke. We all turned to look at her as she rose slowly from her chair. Her face was as white and set as that of a marble statue; but unconquerable resolution shone in her eyes.

"I accept Lord Ellesmere's proposal of marriage," she went on. "He and I will leave here now—this moment. Tomorrow at dawn we will sail for Cairo."

Utter silence followed. It was broken by Walter. He leaped to his feet with an unintelligible cry; dark, dusky color stained his cheeks. Lucas also rose. His slow, deliberate moments and the smile that spread across his face had an insolent triumph that infuriated me.

"I am, of course, the happiest man in the world," he said coolly. "Although I could have wished, my darling, that you had not chosen to accept me quite so publicly. However, if that is what you prefer . . ."

Before any of us suspected what he meant to do, he had caught Evelyn's hands and pulled her roughly to him. I honestly believe the rascal would have embraced her, there before us all, if Walter had not intervened. With another wordless cry, he struck his rival's hands away. For a moment the two young men stood facing one another in open enmity. Walter's breast rose and fell with his agitated breathing; the sling supporting his wounded arm rose and fell with it.

Lucas's eyes narrowed. I saw, as never before, the hot Latin blood of his sire.

"So," he said softly. "You dare. . . . You will answer for this, Emerson, I promise you."

Evelyn stepped between them.

"Lucas—Walter—for shame! I have said what I must do. I *will* do it. Nothing can change my mind."

"Evelyn!" Walter turned to her, ignoring the other man. "You cannot do this! You don't love him—you are sacrificing yourself because of some absurd notion that you are the cause of our troubles—"

"She could not possibly be so stupid." Emerson's calm voice broke in. He had not moved during the little scene; sitting at ease, his legs stretched out, he was smoking his pipe and watching like a spectator at a play.

"Sit down, all of you," he went on, his voice taking on a sharp tone that forced obedience. "Now let us talk like reasonable human beings. If Miss Evelyn decides to become Lady Ellesmere, that is her right; but I cannot allow her to take that step under a misapprehension."

He turned to Evelyn, who had dropped into a chair, where she sat with one trembling hand over her eyes.

"Young woman, do you really believe that you are the jinx, the Jonah, who brings evil upon us? That is unbecoming a sensible woman."

"Amelia, today," said Evelyn in a faint voice. "It was the final warning. Danger to all those I love—"

"Nonsense!" The word burst from Emerson's lips. "Simple nonsense, my girl. Have you forgotten what we decided, at the beginning of this obscene charade? The only possible motive for it all is the desire of some unknown to force us away from this site. How will your departure accomplish this, if Walter and I remain? While you sail safely down the river toward Cairo, in the arms of your betrothed—"

There was a wordless protest from Walter at this. Emerson gave him a sardonic look before proceeding, in a tone that seemed designed to provoke the young fellow even more.

"As you sail along in soft dalliance under the moon, we may be beleaguered here. No; if your motive truly is to benefit us, your flight cannot accomplish that. If, on the other hand, you yearn to be alone with his lordship—"

It was Lucas's turn to protest.

"Emerson, how dare you take that tone? You insult a lady—"

"Quite the contrary," said Emerson, maddeningly cool. "I pay the lady the compliment of assuming that she has a brain and is capable of using it. Well, Evelyn?"

Evelyn sat motionless, her hand still shading her eyes.

I don't know what had kept me silent so long. Emerson's motive eluded me; that he had some ulterior purpose, however, I did not doubt. I decided it was time to add my opinion.

"Emerson states the facts with his usual boorishness, yet he is basically correct. We are still in the dark as to the motive for this charade, as he rightly terms it. Precipitate action maybe fatal. You may ignorantly do precisely what our unknown adversary wants you to do."

Lucas turned to look at me, and I knew that if I had not been a woman he would have threatened me as he had Walter. I cared not at all for his opinion. Anxiously I watched Evelyn.

"I don't know what to do," she whispered. "I must be alone—let me think. Don't follow me, please."

Slowly, her face averted, she passed along the ledge and began to descend. Lucas started to follow.

"Your lordship!" Emerson's voice cracked like a whip.

"Don't interfere with me, Emerson," Lucas said tightly. "You are not my master."

"Interfere?" Emerson's eyes widened in honest indignation. "I never interfere. You are, of course, too much of a gentlemen to lay hands on the young lady again; I need not caution you as to that. I was merely about to remind you not to wander out of sight."

"Very well," Lucas said shortly.

Evelyn had reached the bottom of the path and was walking slowly across the sand, away from camp. The poor child looked infinitely weary and sad as she proceeded with dragging steps and bowed head. The setting sun struck off her golden head like a flame.

Lucas's pace was quicker; he soon caught her up and they walked on together. Naturally I could not hear what they said, but I felt sure he was pressing his suit. The weary shake of her head gave me some hope, but not enough.

I turned to Walter, who was sitting beside me. His eyes were fixed on the distant couple. He looked ten years older than his real age.

"They make a pretty pair," said Emerson, who was outdoing himself in obnoxiousness that afternoon. "My lord and my lady, it will be an excellent match."

"Oh, do be still," I snapped.

"Why, I thought ladies enjoyed matchmaking. You may be proud if you bring this off. He is rich, titled, handsome; she is poor. A brilliant match for a girl like that."

My self-control, ordinarily excellent, suddenly snapped. I was utterly disgusted with the lot of them—with Evelyn and her morbid love of martyrdom, with Lucas and his arrogance, with Walter's hang-dog suffering acceptance—and most of all with Emerson. He thought he had won, and I feared he had; by handing Evelyn over to Lucas he kept his brother bound to his selfish wishes and now he was twisting the knife in the wound, convincing Walter that the girl was marrying Lucas out of the desire for wealth and worldly position. His smile maddened me; I could no longer hold my tongue.

"Bring it off!" I cried. "I would rather see Evelyn in a—in a monastery than married to that wretch. She does not love him. She loves—someone else, and thinks she will save him by accepting Lucas. Perhaps she is right after all. The man she loves is a poor-spirited wretch, who will not even take the trouble to declare himself!"

Walter grasped my hands. His face was transfigured.

"You can't mean it," he whispered. "You can't mean that I—"

"Yes, you young fool." I gave him a shove that sent him staggering. "She loves you; why, I cannot imagine, but she does. Now go and stop her!"

Walter gave me a look that made me tremble. He bounded off down the ledge; and I turned to face his brother, throwing my shoulders back defiantly. I had done a foolhardy thing; I did not know what would come of it. But at that moment I was prepared to face a whole horde of Mummies, much less Emerson, to defend my act.

He was rocking back and forth in his chair, shaken by silent spasms of laughter.

"My dear Peabody," he gasped. "You amaze me. Can it be that you are a secret romantic after all?"

He was impossible. I turned my back on him and watched the tableau down below.

Walter ran like a deer; he soon reached the others, and the three stood talking. It was only too easy to follow the conversation; Walter's impassioned gestures, Evelyn's startled response, and Lucas's angry interruption.

"I am going down," I said uneasily. "I may have acted a trifle precipitately. . . ."

"Intervention might be advisable," Emerson agreed calmly. "His noble lordship is not above striking a wounded man; and Walter is no match for him with only one arm. Damnation! I have waited too long!"

He *had* waited too long; and he had been correct in his assessment of Lucas's character. He struck; Walter went staggering back. Emerson was already halfway down the path, leaping along like a mountain goat. I followed; I dared not go quickly, for I could not remove my eyes from the little drama below.

Evelyn tried to intervene; Lucas shook her off. Walter had been shaken but not felled; he returned to the fray. Ducking his head under the other man's flailing blows, he returned them with interest; and I could scarcely repress a cheer when his clenched fist struck Lucas's outthrust jaw with a solid smack. Lucas fell just as Emerson came running up. He seized his brother's arm—unnecessarily, for Walter was not the man to take advantage of a fallen opponent. Running as fast as I could with the handicaps of full skirts and drifted sand, I came up to them as Lucas was rising to his feet.

He stood swaying unsteadily, his hand rubbing his chin. The fall had scarcely rumpled his elegant attire, but there was little of the English gentleman about him as he glared at Walter, his liquid black eyes hot with Latin rage.

"Two against one?" he inquired with a sneer. "Very sporting, gentlemen!"

"You are a fine one to talk of sportsmanship," I exclaimed. "To strike an injured man—"

"He used terms I allow no man to use to me," Lucas interrupted.

"I regret the terms," Walter said in a low voice. "But not the emotion that prompted them. Miss Amelia—Radcliffe—if you had heard the things he said of Evelyn—the implications he was vile enough to make—"

"They were true," Evelyn said.

All eyes turned toward Evelyn.

White as the lace at her throat, straight as a young birch tree, she faced the staring eyes without flinching. She stepped back—not in retreat, but in a deliberate movement that separated her from support. She waved me back with an irresistible gesture of command as I started toward her, expostulations rising to my lips.

"No, Amelia," she said, in the same quiet voice. "I had, for a time, the cowardly hope of avoiding this. But in justice to Lucas—and to all of you—I cannot remain silent. In the heat of anger Lucas spoke the truth. Not only have I lost a woman's most priceless jewel, I gave it up to a profligate, a wastrel, and a ruffian. I acted of my own free will. I abandoned an old man who loved me, and was only saved from the ultimate sin of taking my own life by Amelia's charity. Now that you know the worst, you will no longer seek to detain me. And you will accept my thanks for saving me, in the nick of time, from the despicable act I was about to commit. I see now that I cannot injure Lucas by taking advantage of his noble offer of marriage. That would be a fine way to repay his kindness, would it not?"

"Evelyn, my dearest," Lucas began.

She shook her head. It was a mild enough gesture, but even Lucas was convinced by the unalterable firmness of her expression. His outstretched hand fell to his side.

"I shall never marry. By devoting my life to good works and charitable undertakings I may one day partially redeem my ruined character."

She had intended to say more; she was proceeding in fine dramatic style, poor young thing, carried away by the tragedy of it all, as the young are. But her emotions were too genuine, too painful; her voice broke in a sob. She continued to stand pilloried under the astonished gaze of—Walter. She had spoken as if to all of us; but it was Walter she had really addressed.

He looked like a man who has received a mortal wound and does not yet realize that he ought to fall down. Emerson's countenance was as blank as the rock cliff behind him. Only his eyes were alive. They moved from Evelyn's ashen face to the equally corpselike countenance of his brother; but that was the only movement he made; he did not speak.

Suddenly the color rushed back into Walter's face, so hecticly that he looked fevered. His dull, blank eyes came alive. Stepping forward, he dropped to his knees before Evelyn.

I thought that the long-expected collapse was about to occur. It was with an indescribable thrill of emotion that I realized he had grasped Evelyn's limp hand in his and was pressing his lips against it. I did not need to hear his words to know he had risen to heights I never really expected a man to reach.

"You are the noblest girl I have ever met," he cried, raising his eyes to Evelyn's astonished face. "The truest, the most courageous, the loveliest. . . . I don't know many men who would have the strength to do what you have just done! But my dearest, sweetest girl. . . ." he rose, still holding her hand and looking down at her with tender reproach. "Do you think so little of me that you suppose I would not understand your tragic story? Evelyn, you might have trusted me!"

For a moment she returned his gaze, her eyes wide, wondering, unbelieving. Then, with a tired little sigh, she closed her eyes and let her golden head fall upon his breast. His arm around her waist, Walter held her close.

I watched them with the most thorough satisfaction I had ever felt in my life. I did not even wipe away the tears that rained down my face—although I began to think it was just as well Evelyn was leaving me. A few more weeks with her, and I should have turned into a rampageous sentimentalist.

"Thank goodness that is settled," said Emerson. "It took long enough, heaven knows, and became sickeningly maudlin toward the end. Come, Walter, kiss your fiancée, and let us all go back to camp. I am hungry; I want my dinner."

I don't think Walter heard a word of this speech. It struck just the right note for me; I needed some vent for my overflowing emotions.

"No one would ever accuse you of being sentimental," I said angrily. "Are you trying to suggest, you dreadful man, that you expected this development? Will you allow your brother to throw himself away on a penniless girl?"

"Not only penniless," said Emerson cheerfully, "but ruined. Although why 'ruined,' I cannot make out; she seems to be quite undamaged in all meaningful respects. A capable artist will be a useful addition to the staff. And I shan't have to pay her a salary—just think of the saving!"

"This is a trick."

The voice spoke just behind me. I started, and turned. Incredible as it seems, I had quite forgotten Lucas.

His passions were under control; only the intense glitter of his eyes betrayed his feelings as, ignoring me, he walked up to Emerson.

"A trick," he repeated. "You cannot mean to encourage this, Emerson. You don't mean it."

"Your lordship fails to understand my character," said Emerson smoothly. "Who am I to stand in the path of true love? I honestly believe," he added, looking intently at Lucas, "that this is the best of all possible arrangements for all of us. Don't you agree, my lord?"

Lucas did not reply immediately. I felt a faint stir of pity for him as he struggled with his emotions. They were intense; I wondered if, after all, he did love Evelyn, as much as a man of his limited capacity was capable of love. And when he finally spoke, I had to admire his attitude.

"Perhaps you are right. Perhaps this is how it was meant to be. 'There is a fatality that shapes our ends,' as Shakespeare has put it. . . ."

"If not precisely in those words," Emerson agreed. "May I congratulate you, my lord, on behaving like a true British nobleman. Will you heap coals of fire on our heads by joining us in a toast to the engaged couple? Walter—come, Walter, wake up, Walter—"

He joggled his brother's elbow. Walter raised his face from where it had been resting on Evelyn's bowed head; he looked like a man waking from an ecstatic dream to find that the dream is reality.

Lucas hesitated for a moment, looking at Evelyn. She didn't see him; she was gazing up into Walter's face like an acolyte adoring a saint. Lucas shrugged, or perhaps he shivered; the movement rippled through his body and was gone.

"I am not so noble as that," he said, with a faint smile. "Excuse me. I think I want to be alone for a while."

"Off into the sunset," said Emerson, as Lucas's retreating form was silhouetted against the west. "How theatrical these young persons are! Thank God for our sober, middle-aged common sense, eh, Peabody?"

I watched Evelyn and Walter walk away. His arm was about her waist; her head still rested on his shoulder, and if he felt pain, where it pressed against the bullet wound, he showed no signs of it.

"Yes, indeed," I replied sourly. "Thank God for it."

Chapter Eleven

 I never expected I would be concerned about Lucas, but as the hours passed and he did not return, I began to worry.

We had eaten one of the vilest dinners imaginable. It had been cooked by Abdullah; he explained that Lucas's cook and the waiter who had accompanied us to camp that morning were not to be found. I found this alarming, but Emerson, who was in an inexplicably good mood, shrugged it away.

We were all sitting on the ledge together, watching the moon rise; but Emerson and I might as well have been alone, for all the conversation we got out of the other two. They didn't hear a word anyone said to them. I was therefore forced to confide my worries about Lucas to Emerson, although I did not expect to find much concern in that quarter. In this assumption I was correct.

"He has probably gone with his men," Emerson said calmly. "I think, Peabody, that we have seen the last of his lordship."

"You mean—he has deserted us? He would not be so cowardly!"

"I fancy he might. But let me do him justice; he has not abandoned us to danger. Indeed, I think it possible that we have also seen the last of the Mummy."

"Nonsense," I said irritably. "Lucas could not have been the Mummy. We saw them together on more than one occasion."

"I may be wrong," said Emerson—in a tone that contradicted the false modesty of his words. "His suggestion—which had also occurred to me—may be the correct one: that there is an unrobbed tomb back in the hills which the villagers hope to exploit. In any case, it must be obvious even to you, Peabody, that the instigator of the plot is not an Egyptian; it contains too many features that could have been invented only by a European or an Englishman. Or perhaps an American; they have their share of unscrupulous collectors. . . ."

"What are you talking about?"

"Professional jealousy, Peabody. No doubt it seems incredible to you that any reasonable man would act so, but I assure you, there are colleagues in my field who would go to any extreme to exploit a sensational discovery such as a royal tomb. I have the concession at Amarna; I had a devil of a time wringing it out of Maspero, but not even he would dare take it away now. The man is quite capable of employing such tricks to make me abandon my excavation and leave the field open to him. Another feather in his cap! Not that Maspero is the only one—"

"Of all the absurd ideas!"

"What is the alternative? If not the place, it is a person who is under attack. I have no enemies—"

"Ha," I said.

"A few individuals may resent my justified criticism," Emerson said meditatively. "Yes; I daresay there are some individuals so degraded that they might respond to my well-intended suggestions with rancor—"

"If anyone murders you," I interrupted, "which seems quite likely, it will be in the heat of anger, with a club or some other convenient blunt instrument. I am only surprised it has not happened before this."

"My enemies are professional, not personal," Emerson insisted. "Walter has none, of either kind. His character is regrettably mild. Are you sure there are no discarded lovers pursuing you?"

The question did not deserve an answer.

After a moment, Emerson went on, "Then it must be Miss Evelyn who inspires such agitated activity on the part of our unknown enemy. If that is the case, the events of this evening must settle the question. His lordship, having received his *congé*, has departed—"

The rattle of pebbles on the path below disproved his words as soon as they were spoken. I knew the step.

The moon ws a spectacular silver orb, almost at the full, shedding a silvery radiance over the silent desert, the river, the cliffs. The light was not quite bright enough for me to distinguish Emerson's expression. I much regretted that.

"Lucas," I said, turning to welcome the newcomer with a warmth I had not heretofore displayed. "I am relieved you are back. I was worried about you."

"How kind of you." Lucas looked, betrayingly, into the shadows behind us, where Evelyn and Walter were sitting. Receiving no greeting from that quarter, his eyes returned to me. "I felt the need of a walk. I have walked; I have accomplished my purpose. You did not suppose I would desert you?"

"I felt sure you would not," I said.

From Emerson, beside me, came no comment.

"Of course not. Tomorrow I will endeavor to forget certain . . . personal griefs in hard work; it will be delightful to explore the cliffs for buried treasure. In the meantime, I remembered Emerson's suggestion; I have brought a bottle of wine, in which to drink to my cousin."

I could not help shooting a triumphant glance at Emerson. He sat in glum silence, his face in shadow; only his hand was visible, clenched whitely on the arm of his chair. I don't know why I should have been so pleased to see Lucas behaving like a gentleman for a change. I never liked the man. . . . But of course I do know why. I would have defended Satan himself if he had been in disfavor with Emerson.

Lucas was as good as his word; it was as if he had determined to humble himself as thoroughly as possible. He carried a tray with glasses and a bottle; putting this down, with a flourish that struck me as rather pathetic, he began to work at the cork.

"Won't you persuade Evelyn to join us?" he asked in a low voice. "I dare not; to be candid, I am ashamed of myself for my behavior this afternoon. I am of a passionate nature; I suppose dear old Grandfather would say it was my Latin blood."

So I called Evelyn, and she came out of the deep shadow where she had been sitting, holding Walter by the hand and smiling shyly at her cousin. I found his excuses inadequate. Nothing could possibly excuse his reference to her misfortune in front of Walter. But, on the other hand, this very reference had brought about the present happy state of affairs, and I must say that Lucas made his apologies like a man and a Briton. Walter received them in the same spirit; to see the two young fellows clasp hands, there in the moonlight, was a touching sight.

Then Lucas handed us each a glass and raised his own.

"To Evelyn's future!" he cried. "May it bring all that her closest kinsman could desire!"

We drank. Even Emerson took a sip. He made a face, like a nasty little boy taking medicine. He had moved his chair out near the table, and I could see him quite well; his expression of sour disapproval pleased me to no end. Seeing that he was in no mood to do the proper thing, and realizing that it was a little too much to expect of Lucas, I proposed the next toast.

"To Walter! May he make Evelyn as happy as she deserves—or I will deal with him!"

"Spoken with characteristic tact," said Emerson under his breath.

Walter leaned forward and put his hand on mine.

"You may deal with me as you see fit, Miss Amelia," he said warmly. "Don't think I shall ever forget that it is to your encouragement, in large measure, that I owe my present happiness. I hope you will be often with us; you may keep your eye on me that way and make sure I measure up to your expectations."

Emerson rolled his eyes heavenward.

"I may take advantage of your invitation," I said cheerfully. "I have developed quite a taste for archaeology."

I suppose it was the wine that made me feel so giddy. We all waxed cheerful under its benign influence—all but Emerson, who sat brooding like a hard stone statue. Finally, when the bottle was empty, Lucas concluded the fete.

"If all goes well, we shall have a busy day tomorrow. Rest is advisable. I suggest, gentlemen, that we stand watch tonight. Tomorrow may bring an end to the mysteries that surround us; let us make sure no mishap occurs tonight."

"Just what I was about to suggest," muttered Emerson, shooting a piercing glance at Lucas. "Which watch would you prefer, my lord?"

Lucas replied with a shrug. It was arranged that he should remain on guard for the first three hours of the night, Emerson for the second watch, and Walter for the remainder. I carried Evelyn off to our sleeping chamber; she was in such a fog her feet seemed not to touch the ground, and after a few incoherent exclamations of gratitude and joy, she quickly fell asleep.

I was drowsy myself, unusually so, for the hour was still early; yet my drooping eyelids obstinately refused to remain shut. Some indefinable nagging discomfort kept forcing them open. The discomfort was purely mental; I had become inured by then to the hard mattress and the other rugged accompaniments to camping out. There is nothing more abominable than being in a state of bodily exhaustion and mental irritation; I was too lethargic to get up and seek some means of occupying my mind, but I was too uneasy to fall asleep. Try as I might, I could not pin down the cause of my uneasiness. We were, of course, in danger of a nocturnal visit from a singularly unpleasant apparition, but that was not what bothered me; I was becoming accustomed to that worry, it was like a familiar ache in a particular tooth. I thought if it continued much longer I should probably become quite accustomed to it. No, this was another sort of twinge; I could not locate it. I ought to have been in a state of peaceful triumph; I had won out over Emerson and attained what I most desired for the girl who was so dear to me. . . .

Had I won out, though?

The more I recalled Emerson's behavior and speech that day, the more I wondered. It was almost as if he had been working to attain the same end; everything he had said was a spur, a prick, a goad, to urge his brother on to a declaration.

I ground my teeth together. If Emerson wanted Evelyn for his brother, he must have some ulterior motive that escaped me.

There came a sound, at the entrance to the tomb chamber. The curtain was lifted.

I rolled over. The rough mattress crackled.

"Who is it?" I whispered. "Lucas, is that you?"

"Yes. What is wrong, Miss Amelia? Can't you sleep?"

With a gigantic effort I dragged myself from bed and assumed my dressing gown. Evelyn was still sleeping sweetly. I tiptoed to the doorway.

"I can't sleep," I said softly. "Perhaps I am too tired. And you, Lucas? Did you have some reason for looking in just now?"

"I don't know. . . . I am strangely uneasy tonight. I heard you stirring, and was afraid. . . ."

"I am uneasy too."

I joined him on the ledge. The night was perfect. The world dreamed peacefully under the moon. The air felt cool; I shivered, and drew my dressing gown close around my throat.

"You ought to sleep," Lucas said. "Perhaps another glass of wine is what you need."

"Lucas, you are not drinking more wine? Surely that is unwise."

"I am not made of iron," Lucas said; his voice was so savage I recoiled. "I will do what must be done; but allow me something with which to fortify myself. Come; I insist that you join me."

Fool that I was! I felt sorry for him. His genuine emotion seemed more pathetic to me than the theatrics he had shown earlier. He was pouring the wine when Emerson came out of his chamber and advanced upon us.

"A party, and you did not invite me?" he said. "Or am I interrupting a more personal meeting?"

"Don't be any more foolish than you can help," I said. My last words were muffled in a huge yawn. "Oh, dear, I am so tired. I don't know why I can't sleep."

"Evelyn seems to be the only one with a clear conscience," said Lucas, snapping his teeth together. "Or is the lucky man sleeping too?"

"Yes," Emerson said. "Walter is asleep."

"And why not you? It is too early for you to relieve me."

"Still, you may as well retire now that I am here. There is no point in all of us being awake. Sometimes I never go to bed at all. This seems to be one of those nights. I don't know why they happen," said Emerson musingly. "It is unaccountable. But I feel just now as if I should never want to sleep again."

I knew then that something was badly wrong; and that Emerson was aware of it. His idiotic speech was an unconvincing lie; his lids were half closed, his shoulders drooped; and now that I looked at him more closely, I saw that his thick black hair was damp, as if he had been pouring water on it . . . to keep awake?

I had employed a similar trick myself, the preceding night. All my senses prickled in alarm.

"Oh, very well," Lucas said sulkily. "Since I am of no use, I may as well remove myself and finish my bottle in private—unless I can persuade you two to join me in a glass? No? Good night, then. I have no desire to go into that stifling hole of a tomb; I shall sleep in the tent down below, and you, my gallant Emerson, can waken me with a shout if we have unexpected visitors."

Cradling the wine bottle in his arms, he staggered down the path. I had not realized he was so intoxicated. Was that what Emerson feared—that Lucas would fail as a guard because of his drinking?

The moment he was out of sight, Emerson turned on me and dragged me up out of the chair into which I had slumped. He shook me till my head rolled and my hair came loose from the net.

"Wake up, Peabody! If you fall asleep, I shall slap you till you howl. Curse it, don't you understand that we have been drugged?"

"Drugged?" I repeated stupidly.

"I have been fighting sleep myself for an hour, and a hard fight it was. Have you nothing in that medicine box of yours to counteract the effects of laudanum?"

I tried to think. Something was certainly dulling my mind.

"My smelling salts," I said, with an effort. "They are extremely strong. . . ."

"Oh, damnation," said Emerson. "A pretty picture that will be! Well, it's better than nothing. Go fetch them. Hurry."

To hurry was impossible. I could barely drag myself along. But I found the smelling salts, and then had a look at Evelyn. A single glance told me Emerson was right. She was sleeping too soundly. I shook her, without effect. Either she had received a larger dose of the drug, or her delicate constitution was more susceptible to it than mine. It would be difficult to awaken her.

I applied the bottle to my own nose. It was certainly effective. Feeling much more alert, I hastened back to Emerson, who was leaning up against the cliff with his arms and legs at strange angles and his eyes slightly crossed. I thrust the bottle at him. He started back, banging his head against the rock, and made several profane remarks.

"Now tell me what is wrong," I said, recapping the bottle. "What is it you fear will happen? If your reasoning is correct—"

"My reasoning was damnably, stupidly, fatally wrong," Emerson replied forcibly. "I am missing a vital clue—a piece of information that would make sense of the whole business. I suspect you hold that clue, Peabody. You must tell me—"

He stopped speaking; I suppose the expression on my face struck him dumb. I felt the hairs on the back of my neck rising. I was facing the lower end of the path; and there, barely visible, around the corner of the cliff, something moved. A low moan echoed through the air.

Emerson spun around. The moaning cry came again.

It was a frightening sound, but I knew, after the first moment, that it did not come from the throat of the Mummy. This cry held human anguish and pain; I could not have resisted its appeal if a thousand gibbering, gesticulating Mummies had stood in my way.

Quickly as I moved, Emerson was before me. He went more cautiously than I would have done, his arm holding me back, and when we reached the bottom of the path he thrust me away while he went on to investigate. The object I had seen, whatever it was, had disappeared from sight; Emerson followed it into invisibility, and for a moment I held my breath. Then I heard his low exclamation—not of fear, but of horror and distress. Rounding the rock corner, I saw him kneeling on the ground beside the prostrate body of a man. I knew the man, although, God forgive me, I had almost forgotten him. It was our vanished servant—the dragoman, Michael.

"Oh, heavens," I cried, flinging myself down beside the recumbent form. "Is he dead?"

"Not yet. But I fear . . ."

Emerson raised his hand, which had been resting on the back of Michael's head. The stains on his fingers looked like ink in the moonlight.

Michael was wearing the same faded blue-and-white-striped robe that he had worn the day of his disappearance. It was now torn and crumpled. I reached for his wrist, to feel his pulse, but a closer sight of his outflung arm made me exclaim aloud. The bared wrist was swollen and bloody.

"He has been a prisoner," I said, forcing my fingers to touch the torn flesh. "These are the marks of ropes."

"They are. How is his pulse?"

"Steady, but feeble. He must have medical attention at once. I will do what I can, but my skill is so small. . . . Can we carry him up to the tomb? Perhaps Lucas will help."

"I can manage."

Emerson turned Michael over; with a single heave of his broad shoulders he lifted the dragoman's slight form into his arms, and rose.

And then—dear Heaven, I can scarcely write of it now without a reminiscent shudder. Screams—the high, agonized shriek of a woman in the extremity of terror! They died in a long, wailing moan.

Emerson bounded forward, carrying the unconscious man as if he weighed no more than a feather. I followed; and as we came around the corner of the cliff, the whole hideous tableau burst upon our eyes, like a scene from the worst conceptions of Madame Tussaud.

On the ledge above us stood the Mummy. The blind, bandaged head was turned toward us; one stubby leg was lifted, as if our sudden appearance had stopped it in midstep. To the crumbling, rotting bandages of its breast, the horror clasped the unconscious form of Evelyn.

Her tumbled golden curls hung down over its arm; her little white feet peeped pathetically out of the folds of her nightdress. After the first scream of terror she had fainted dead away, as any girl might, finding herself in the arms of such a suitor.

I began pounding on Emerson's back. He was barring the entrance to the narrow path, and I was frantic to pass him and attack the thing. I remembered poor Evelyn's exclamation on that far-off day, when a ghoulish peddler had tried to sell us a mummified hand. She would die, she said, if the withered flesh should touch her. . . . Well, we had it trapped now. If it had supernatural powers, it would need them all to escape *me.*

The passage of time seemed to halt; I felt like one trapped in quicksand, or the slow, floating motion of a dream, where enormous effort is required to make the slightest movement. Then all sorts of things happened at once.

Lucas came out of the tent, which was not far from us. I assumed he had been asleep, had been wakened by Evelyn's screams, and, his senses dulled by wine, had been slow to respond. He took in the situation at a glance, and moved more quickly than I would have expected. In his haste, he collided with us. Emerson kept his feet with difficulty, falling back against the cliff face with the body of the dying man still in his arms; I was thrown to the ground. While we were tumbling about, the Mummy took advantage of our confusion. Flexing its stiff knees, the creature jumped—actually leaped from the ledge. Such was my state of mind, I half expected to see it take wing and soar through the air like a giant bat. Alighting, still erect, amid the tumble of rocks at the base of the cliff, it scrambled down the slope and ran. Evelyn's fair hair streamed out behind.

"Pursue it!" I shrieked. "Do not let it escape!"

At least that is what I believe I shrieked. Emerson informs me that my language was less coherent, and so inflammatory that he positively blushed, despite the urgency of the moment. He, of course, was in a dreadful predicament; encumbered by the injured man, he could hardly fling him to the ground. I was so entangled in the abominable garments forced on women by the decrees of fashion that I could not arise. It all depended on Lucas; and after the first confused moments, he rose to the occasion.

"Never fear," he cried, leaping up. "It will not escape me! Remain here—we must not all abandon the camp—I will rescue Evelyn—"

Running fleetly, he was already several yards away as his last words reached my ears.

An echoing cry came from above. Looking up, I saw Walter, who had just emerged from his sleeping chamber. If he had been drugged, the vision before his eyes woke him with a vengeance; with another shout of mingled rage and horror, he flung himself down the slope and followed Lucas.

As I started after them, Emerson kicked me in the shin. I must confess he could not have stopped me in any other way, since his arms were occupied.

"This is madness," he groaned. "Keep your head, Peabody; someone must act sensibly—follow me, you must remain with Michael."

The advice was excellent; the difficulty was in following it. The folly of pursuit was manifest; if the young men could not catch up with the mummified miscreant, it was futile for a woman, hampered by her skirts, to try and do so. I could still see the pale shape of the Mummy, as it flitted in and out among the rocks. Walter stumbled along behind, waving his arms and shouting. All this happened, of course, in far less time than it takes to write it down.

I ran after Emerson, who was ascending the path in great leaps. If I was not wringing my hands, it was because I needed them to keep my balance. Emerson was correct; it was necessary for one of us to tend Michael's wounds, but I really did not see how I could bear to remain there, in ignorance and forced inactivity.

Emerson laid his burden gently upon his couch. To do him justice, he had not wasted a moment, nor did he waste time now in unnecessary directions to me. Instantly he turned back to the entrance. I reached for the lamp, meaning to light it. As I did so, there came a crack and a whine from without. Emerson's tall form, silhouetted in the doorway, staggered and fell.

Chapter Twelve

 IT is vain to attempt to describe my sensations at that moment. I had recognized the sound as that of a bullet. I dropped the lamp; I forgot my injured servant; for an instant I even forgot Evelyn and her deadly peril. I started toward the spot where I had seen Emerson fall.

My heart had not missed more than a few beats, however, when a hand caught my ankle and brought me crashing to the ground. I fell on top of Emerson, and heard him grunt with pain. My hands, fumbling at his face, encountered a wet, sticky flow.

"You are wounded," I exclaimed. "My God, Emerson—"

Emerson sneezed.

"I beg that you will leave off tickling me," he said irritably. "The region around the chin and jaw is particularly sensitive. For God's sake, Peabody, stop sniveling; it is only a cut from a bit of flying rock."

"Oh," I said. "But the shot was aimed at you! In heaven's name, what are you doing now? Don't go out there—"

He was crawling toward the entrance.

"The shot was meant as a warning," he said over his shoulder. "We are safe enough—for the moment—unless we try to leave the tomb. Hand me that shirt of Walter's, if you please—it is lying across his bed—and my walking stick. Thank you. Now let us see—"

A second shot rewarded his demonstration when he draped the shirt over the stick and extended it out the doorway. Emerson withdrew it.

"He is there, among the rocks," he said calmly.

"He? Who?"

"You sound like one of the villagers' donkeys," said Emerson. "Who else could it be? You must have deduced his identity by now. I have known it for some time; but his motive still eludes me. What the devil ails the fellow, to seek to win a wife by such means? I would not have thought him capable of the insane passion that prompts such acts."

Once—even a few hours earlier—his calm, drawling voice would have driven me wild. Now I was seized by the same icy calm. We had already delayed too long; even if we could escape from this ambush uninjured, Evelyn and her abductor would be out of sight. It was up to Walter now. At least he had only one enemy to face. The other was below, with rifle in his hands.

"There is motive," I said. "I am only now beginning to see. . . . No, no, it is impossible. From the first I too suspected Lucas. But he was not here. He did not arrive until long after we did, long after the Mummy made its first appearance. He did not know we would stop here—"

"I think it is high time we compared notes," said Emerson, recumbent before the entrance. "You might give Michael a little water, Peabody; I fear that is all we can do for the poor fellow now, since we dare not strike a light, and your medical supplies are in your sleeping chamber. Then come here and join me."

I did what I could for Michael. It was little enough. He was still breathing, but that was about all I could say. I then crawled to the entrance and lay down flat, next to Emerson, who was peering out across the moonlit plain, his chin propped on his folded arms.

"You and I have been at cross purposes since we met, Peabody," he said. "It is a pity; for we might have prevented this unfortunate business if we had taken the trouble to be civil to one another. You see, I have known for some days that his lordship has been lying. Reis Hassan talked to the reis of the *Cleopatra*, and passed some of the gossip on to me. His lordship's payments to his crew have been princely. By means of exorbitant bribes, he got underway the very day after you left. He was moored downriver, at Minieh, the day you landed here.

"But that is not the important thing. His lordship has a confederate—not a hired native, but a man as dedicated to evil as he is. That confederate is the man who is playing the role of the Mummy. This man's whereabouts, prior to his public appearance here, are unknown. I believe he came here some time ago and set the scene for the drama—bribing Mohammed, introducing the mummy Walter found into an empty tomb. His costume, his role were planned well in advance—probably in Cairo, where, I imagine, young Lord Ellesmere arrived earlier than he led you to believe. Do you have an idea who this confederate might be?"

"No. Lucas must have bribed him well. Of course it could be a friend of Lucas's—one of his companions in vice. I do not know them. But, Emerson, there is one great flaw in your argument. How could they know where to set the scene? We did not plan to stop here—"

"Then Reis Hassan is a liar. He informs me that you laid out your itinerary while still in Cairo, and that he tried several times to dissuade you from it."

"Oh, that. I did mention the possibility of visiting Amarna—along with a number of other sites. But how could Lucas know?"

"From Michael, I imagine. Did he have an opportunity to speak with him before you left Cairo?"

"He did indeed," I said grimly. "And to think that we introduced them, so that Michael might assist Lucas in the selection of a dragoman. . . . Good God, what a fool I was!"

"You had no reason to suspect any danger. Nor did Michael. His lordship was your friend, Evelyn's relation. It was not until developments here became serious that Michael began to wonder about his harmless indiscretion. He is an intelligent man, and devoted to you body and soul; on the day of his disappearance he asked to speak to you alone—"

"And Lucas heard him! He struck him down and spirited him away."

"Not Lucas, but one of his men. He kept the poor fellow prisoner in one of the caves that are so common in these cliffs, and when we obstinately refused to succumb to the laudanum he had placed in our wine, he carried Michael here to distract us while his confederate reached Evelyn.

"I must admit that the fellow has imagination; he acts brilliantly and unhesitatingly in emergencies, and makes good use of any fortuitous circumstances that can be turned to account. My illness was one such lucky accident—lucky for him—but I feel sure he and his confederate had planned some means of detaining you here—damage to the dahabeeyah, or to one of us. At that point in time, his lordship had not determined to commit murder. He hoped to attain his ends by less drastic means, although it seems clear he prepared for the worst, in case it should become necessary. And I was misled. Not until you were attacked this afternoon did I fully realize that Evelyn was the real object of the attentions we have been receiving, and even then I was fool enough to suppose that once she had accepted Walter, his lordship would give up his idiotic and dangerous games."

Emerson extended his stick once again out the entrance. Another shot rang out, followed by the splintering of rock.

"Still there," he said. "I wonder how long he means to keep us here. We are safe so long as we do not confront him. He will have some specious excuse to explain why he failed to rescue Evelyn; I think the fellow is actually vain enough to suppose he can get away with it. Shall we save our skins, Peabody, and sit still?"

"While Evelyn is in the clutches of that monster?" I demanded. "Don't bait me, Emerson; you have no more intention of accepting this than I do. Do you think Walter—"

"I am extremely concerned about Walter," said Emerson; I knew him well enough now to hear the controlled agony under his calm tones. "But at the moment we can do nothing to help him or Evelyn until we understand what is behind this affair. There is some more desperate motive behind his lordship's acts than frustrated love. Think, Peabody; if you have ever used your brain, now is the time."

"I have a faint inkling of the truth," I said, in a stifled voice. "I hate to contemplate it; for if I am right. . . . Emerson, you and I have behaved like fools. If I had known what you knew about Lucas's movements; and if you had known what I am about to tell you—"

"Speak, then. That is the trouble with women, even the best of them," Emerson added. "They *will* indulge in vain cries of 'if only' and 'had I but known.' "

"The criticism is justified," I said; my pride was thoroughly leveled by the magnitude of the disaster. "Listen, then, while I narrate Evelyn's story."

He listened. Only his eyes moved, so intent was he on what I had to say.

"Yes," he said, when I finished. "The clue is there, somewhere. A vast amount of money may be an inducement to violence. But how? I cannot see it, even now. Is it possible that his lordship lied to you about the old man's death? If he still lives, and contemplates restoring Evelyn as his heiress—"

"No, he is dead; one of my acquaintances in Cairo knew of it."

Emerson struck his fist against the floor.

"The conclusion is inescapable, Peabody; in some way we do not comprehend, Evelyn must have control of the fortune his lordship so ardently desires. He has done everything a man could do to induce her to become his wife. I believed his sole motive was passionate love of his cousin. But in this day and age an English girl cannot be forced into marriage, and a forced marriage is the only kind that could come out of this night's work. Nothing the wretch could do now would induce Evelyn to marry him of her own free will. No; it is the lady's money that is being sought, not the lady's person. If we only knew how—"

"I believe I do know," I interrupted. "I told you that before the late Lord Ellesmere died he gathered all Evelyn's belongings and sent them to her. Lucas told me—good heavens, he actually boasted of it—that he was in full control at Ellesmere Castle while the old gentleman lay ill. If Ellesmere had softened toward Evelyn and wished to restore her to favor, Lucas would make certain he did not reach his lawyers in order to make a new will. But he might write a new will—a holograph will, I believe it is called. Knowing Lucas as he did, the poor old man saw only one way to ensure that such a document would survive. He could send it to Evelyn—packed in with her other possessions. He hoped to escape arousing Lucas's suspicions that way."

"By Gad, Peabody, I think you've got it!" Emerson exclaimed.

"I think so too. Lucas has tried every possible means of getting to those boxes of Evelyn's, or of having them destroyed unopened. He must have missed them in Rome; and when they arrived in Egypt they went into the safekeeping of Baring, who is the most powerful man in the government. He was a friend of Father's, and he knows of Lucas's unsavory reputation; from such a man Lucas had no chance of extracting the precious boxes. Alas; for if he had—"

"Evelyn would not now be in danger," Emerson's quick wits supplied the conclusion. "He may not be certain that such a will exists, but he must have reason to suspect that it does. If he could destroy it he would be safe. Failing that, he pursued Evelyn. As her husband he would have control of her fortune in any case, and he would have a good excuse to take charge of her baggage. But the marriage plan failed as well; thanks to our strenuous efforts, his lordship has now only one means left of gaining his ends. . . . Peabody, you must not blame yourself. How could you possibly have suspected this?"

"I don't blame myself," I said, wiping away the tears that were stealing down my face. "As you say, I could not have suspected. It is the most farfetched scheme I have ever encountered; only a frivolous, amoral man, who had been reading too many wild romances, would think of such a thing. And vain regret is useless. I will not indulge in it. I will get out of here and go after Evelyn, and I will kill his lordship if he has harmed her."

I rose to my knees. Emerson put his hand in the center of my back and pushed me down again.

"I am in complete agreement with your program. But let us try to think of some safer way to do it."

"Can we expect no help from anyone? What of Abdullah? And the crewmen on the boat—surely they heard the shots."

"I have grave suspicions of Abdullah," Emerson said grimly. "You forget, Peabody, that these people are desperately poor."

"And Reis Hassan too? I thought he looked strange the other day when you were questioning him."

"Hassan is one of the few honest men I know. Unfortunately he is also superstitious. He was ashamed to admit to me that he had been terrorized by Mohammed's tales of ghosts and curses. No; he will come, I believe, if he can overcome his fears and persuade his crew. But we cannot count on that. Then there is the crew of his lordship's dahabeeyah to be considered. What if they have been paid to prevent a rescue attempt? No, Peabody, if we are to get out of here in time, it must be by ourselves. And I think we had better set about it."

"But how . . . ?"

"There are pebbles and rocks on the threshold. When I give the signal, begin rolling them down. Meanwhile, I will creep along the path in the other direction and try to get behind him."

"It is a foolhardy scheme," I said. "He will surely see or hear you."

"From below he has a poor chance of hitting me if I keep low. You must cover any sounds I make by the exuberance of your performance and, if possible, induce him to empty the magazine of his repeater. Come, come, Peabody; if you have any more practical suggestion, I will be happy to hear it. I have never had the inclination to be a hero. But we must do something, and soon."

I had nothing to say—nothing practical, that is. There were many things I wanted to say. I wanted to say them so badly that I had to bury my teeth in my lower lip to keep it from forming the words. I turned my head away.

Emerson took me by the shoulders and rolled me over. He had lifted himself upon his elbows; I lay between them, like an unfortunate mouse under a cat's paws. His face was so close I could see the bristles of his whiskers.

"It seems possible that we shall not live through the night," he remarked. "I would hate to die without having. . . . Damnation! I *will* do it, even at the risk of surviving to face the consequences!"

Whereupon he bent his head and kissed me full on the mouth.

At first I was too stupefied by surprise to do anything. Afterward, I was simply too stupefied to do anything. It was not the first time I had been kissed. Several of the suitors who appeared after I inherited Papa's money had presumed. . . . Well, let us be honest. I had encouraged them to kiss me. I was immensely curious about the process. In all cases it proved to be a deadly bore. It occurred to me, very soon after Emerson began kissing me, that previous experience in this field is not always a dependable guide.

At some point I must have closed my eyes, although I was not aware of doing so. I kept them closed after he raised his head. Thus I did not see him go. He was, I think, somewhat stupefied himself, or he would have waited for me to begin the divertissement he had suggested. The first intimation of his departure I received was a shot that struck the entrance above my head and sprayed my upturned face with little stinging pellets of stone.

I rolled over, snatched up a handful of pebbles, and pitched them down the path. They made considerable racket, but to my straining ears, Emerson's progress along the path made even more noise. I began throwing out everything I could lay my hands on. Boxes, books, bottles and Emerson's boots went tumbling down, followed by tins of peas and peaches, the mirror, and someone's shaving mug. What Lucas thought of this performance I cannot imagine; he must have concluded that we had lost our wits. Such a cacophony of different sounds was never heard. The mirror made a particularly effective crash.

The action accomplished what we had hoped. Lucas was nervous; he let off a perfect fusillade of shots. None of them came anywhere near the mouth of the tomb, so I concluded he was shooting at the mirror, the tins, and the boots.

A period of silence ensued. I had meant to count the shots, and had forgotten to do so. It would not have been much use in any case, since I had not the slightest idea of how many bullets the gun held. I could only hope that the cessation of shooting meant that he had emptied the weapon and was now reloading, or refilling, or whatever the term is; and that Emerson had succeeded in descending the cliff unharmed.

He had! Shouts, thuds, the sounds of a furious struggle told me that so far our plan had miraculously succeeded. I leaped to my feet and ran to join the fray, hoping to get in a blow or two on my own account. I had an urge to pound something, preferably Lucas, with my clenched fists.

As I neared the scene of battle I found Emerson engaged, or so it appeared, with two adversaries. The agitation of long white skirts identified one of them as the missing Abdullah.

In the struggle Emerson was flung to the ground. Stepping back, Lucas lifted the rifle to his shoulder and aimed at Emerson's defenseless breast.

I was several yards away, too far to do anything except shout, which of course I did. The sensation was nightmarish; I felt as if I were on a treadmill that ran backward as fast as I ran forward, so that I made no progress at all. I screamed again and ran faster, knowing I would be too late. . . .

And then Abdullah sprang forward and wrenched the weapon from Lucas's hands. The villain's finger had been on the trigger; the bullet exploded harmlessly into the air.

I did not pause to speculate on Abdullah's change of heart; I flew straight at Lucas. I shudder to think what damage I might have inflicted if Emerson had not anticipated me. Rising, he seized the wretch by the throat and shook him till he hung limp.

"Calm yourself," he gasped, fending me off with his elbow. "We can't murder the rascal until he has told us what we want to know." Then, turning to his erstwhile foreman, he said, "You will have to decide whose side you are on, Abdullah; vacillation is bad for the character. I am willing to forget your recent indescretions in return for cooperation."

"But I did not know," Abdullah muttered, holding the rifle as if it were burning his fingers. "He say, he want only his woman; she is his. What is a woman, to make such trouble for us?"

"A true Moslem philosophy," said Emerson drily. "As you see, Abdullah, he lied. He was ready to kill—and you, I think, would have been among the victims. He could not leave witnesses against him. Now . . ."

He was still holding Lucas, whose face had turned an unbecoming shade of lavender. He gave him an extra shake for good measure.

"Now, your lordship, speak up. Where have they gone? I beg, don't tell me you don't know; for the expectation of that information is the only thing that keeps me from throttling you here and now."

His tone was almost genial; his lips were curved in a slight smile. But Lucas was not deceived.

"Very well," he muttered. "The royal tomb. I told him to take her there—"

"If you are lying . . ." Emerson squeezed.

Lucas gurgled horribly. When he had gotten his breath back, he gasped.

"No, no, it is the truth! And now you will let me go? I can do you no more harm. . . ."

"You insult my intelligence," Emerson said, and flung him down on the ground. With one foot planted in the middle of Lucas's back, he turned to me. "You must sacrifice another petticoat, Peabody. Only be quick; we have lost too much time already."

We left Lucas bound hand and foot where he had fallen—not with my petticoat, for of course I was not wearing one. Using Abdullah's knife, which he politely offered me, I ripped up the full skirts of my dressing gown, slit them fore and aft, and bound them to my nether limbs. It was wonderful what a feeling of freedom this brought! I swore I would have trousers made as soon as possible.

Abdullah remained to guard Lucas. Emerson seemed to have regained all his former confidence in his foreman; he explained that Abdullah had not been fighting him, but had been trying to separate the two Englishmen. I suppose the Egyptian's attitude was understandable, considering his sex and his nationality.

If it had not been for the gnawing anxiety that drove us, I would have found the moonlight hike a thrilling experience. With what ease did I glide across the sand in my makeshift trousers! How lovely the contrast of shadow and silver light among the tumbled rocks of the wadi! There was food for meditation, too, in the events of the evening; our brilliant triumph just when disaster seemed imminent was a subject for modest congratulation. Hope began to raise a cautious head. Surely, if the mummified villain had carried Evelyn so far, her immediate demise was not meditated. We might yet be in time to save her.

The pace Emerson set left me no breath for conversation; and I do not think I would have spoken if it had. Let my reader not suppose that I had forgotten the effrontery—the bold action—in short, the kiss. I could not decide whether to bury the subject forever in icy silence, or to annihilate Emerson—at a more appropriate time, naturally—with a well-chosen, scathing comment. I occupied myself, when I was not picturing Evelyn in a variety of unpleasant positions, by composing scathing comments.

With such thoughts to distract me, the journey was accomplished in less time than I had expected, but it was a tiring, uncomfortable walk—or run—and I was breathless by the time we reached that part of the narrow canyon in which the royal tomb was located.

Emerson spoke then for the first time. It was only a curt order for silence and caution. We crept up to the entrance on all fours. The precaution was not necessary. Expecting Lucas's triumph, the foolish Mummy had not kept guard at the entrance. When I peered into the opening I saw a tiny pinprick of light, far down in the black depths.

Now that we were almost at our goal, feverish impatience replaced the exhilaration that had carried me to the spot. I was on fire to rush in. I feared, not only for Evelyn, but for Walter; either he had lost himself in the desert, or he had met some disastrous fate, for if he had succeeded in wresting Evelyn from her necromantic admirer we would have met him returning. Emerson's anxiety was as great as mine, but he held me back with an arm of iron when I would have rushed impetuously into the tomb. He did not speak; he merely shook his head and pantomimed a slow, exaggeratedly careful stride. So, like stage conspirators, we edged around the fallen rocks still remaining from the avalanche, and set off down the long, steep corridor.

It was impossible to move in utter silence, the path was too encumbered underfoot. Fortunately there were other things in the tomb that made noise. I say 'fortunately,' but I am a liar; I would rather have taken the chance of being overheard than walk through a curtain of bats. The tomb was full of them, and night had roused them to their nocturnal life.

The light grew stronger as we advanced, and before long I could hear a voice rambling on in a soliloquy or monologue, which was a great help in covering the small sounds we inadvertently made. The voice was a man's, and the tones were oddly familiar; but it was not Walter's voice. As we advanced I began to distinguish words; the words, and the smug, self-satisfied tones filled me with amazement. Who could it be who was chatting so unconcernedly in a tomb in the Egyptian desert?

Emerson was in the lead; he stopped me, at the entrance to the side chamber from which the light proceeded. We crouched there, listening; and gradually realization dawned. What a fool I had been. The plot now seemed so obvious I felt a child ought to have detected it.

". . . and so you see, my heart, that cousin Luigi and I are a pair of clever fellows, eh? You say 'luck,' that I won your heart; but no, it was no luck, it was my charm, my handsome face—and that the fool old grandfather not let you see men, any men. When we run away, then Luigi comes to the old grandfather. If grandfather not be good fellow and make Luigi rich, then Luigi make new will himself! Luigi can write like anyone; he writes many fine checks at the university before they catch him and tell him, go home. Luigi is smart fellow, almost as smart as me. When bad old grandfather make new will, hide it in box and send away, then Luigi come to me with new plàn. I search your room in Cairo, dressed up like old Egyptian fellow; but the box is not there. We must make another plan. Was I not fine mummy? I am fine actor; I make you all much afraid. And it is I who tell Luigi of this young fool—I was Arab in museum that day, when you meet Master Walter; you look at him as you look once at me, and I know. . . ."

An indignant exclamation from Evelyn interrupted this long-drawn-out piece of braggadocio. The relief of hearing her voice, weak as it was, almost made me collapse.

"If he had not been wounded, and drugged as well, you would never have overcome him," she cried. "What have you done to him? He lies so still. . . . Please let me see how he is injured. Unless—oh, heaven!—he is not—he cannot be—"

Emerson's shoulder, pressed against mine, jerked convulsively, but he did not move.

"No, no," Evelyn's tormentor replied, in a horrid parody of sympathy. "The brave young hero is not dead. But why you sorry? Soon you both be dead. You die together, like Aida and Radames in the beautiful opera of Signor Verdi. I thank my genius compatriot for this idea—so romantic. Together, in the tomb, in the arms of each other." His voice changed; he sounded like a sulky boy as he added, "Luigi say, kill you. Me, to kill? Always the bad job for me; Luigi too much gentleman to make hands dirty. So, I leave you here. I am gentleman too; I do not kill woman. At least I not do it often. Not woman who once I held in my—"

This was too much for Emerson, who was quivering like a boiler about to blow up. With a roar, he erupted into the lighted chamber. I need not say that I was close on his heels.

The first thing I saw was Evelyn's pallid face, streaked with dust and tears, her eyes fairly bulging out of her head as she saw me. The first sound I heard was her cry of "Amelia!" as she collapsed in a swoon of relief and joy.

The poor child was huddled on the littered floor, her hands bound behind her, her pretty hair all tangled and dusty. I lifted her up, and watched complacently as Emerson finished choking Alberto. Yes; the Mummy, the confederate of Lucas-Luigi, the abductor of Evelyn, was none other than her erstwhile lover, whose relationship to her scheming cousin had been made plain by his own boasts. I think that of the two he was the worst; I didn't feel the slightest inclination to interfere as his face turned purple and his flailing hands dropped limply.

Emerson dropped him with a thud and turned to his brother. Walter was lying in the opposite corner, bound hand and foot; he was unconscious, and a darkening bruise on his brow showed how the villain had struck him down. Evelyn came back to consciousness in time to hear Emerson proclaim, in ringing tones, "He is alive! He is not seriously injured!" Whereupon she fainted again, and I had quite a time bringing her around.

The journey back was long and arduous, but it did not seem so to us; our hearts were overflowing with happiness, increased by the knowledge that we had left Alberto bound and gagged in the tomb where he had intended to entomb Evelyn and Walter. The last thing I remember seeing as we left was the mummy costume lying limp and harmless on the floor. It seemed absurd when I looked at it closely that it could have frightened anyone. The head mask was made in a separate piece, the joint being covered by strips of bandaging. And the suit itself buttoned neatly up the front.

II

Two years have passed since the events of which I have written—two years full of thrilling events, both personal and historic. Emerson's fears for the gallant Gordon were, alas, justified; he was horribly murdered in January, before the expeditionary force arrived. But the cause for which he died was not lost; the mad Mahdi himself died the same year, and our forces are beating back the insurgents. My friend Maspero has left the Antiquities Department, which is now under the charge of M. Grebaut, whom Emerson detests even more than he did Maspero. As for Emerson himself . . .

I sit, writing this, on the ledge above the familiar and beloved plain of Amarna; and when I lift my eyes from the page I see the busy groups of workmen scattered about like black ants on the pale sand, as they bring the ruins of Khuenaten's city back to the light of day. My self-appointed Critic has left me in order to supervise the clearing of what appears to have been a sculptor's workshop; several splendid busts have already been found. Emerson pushes himself unnecessarily, for Abdullah is an excellent foreman, reliable and skilled. As Emerson says, there is nothing like a spot of blackmail to make a man perform to the best of his ability. Abdullah never refers to the events of that winter two years ago.

They are surprisingly clear and present to my mind, as if they had happened only yesterday. I never had such a good time in all my life. Oh, certainly, at the time there were moments of extreme discomfort; but the adventure, the danger, the exhilaration of doubt and peril are in retrospect something I rather regret having lost.

We had to interrupt the excavations for a few weeks. To Emerson's deep disgust, it was necessary to carry our captives to Cairo and explain to the authorities there what had happened. I had suggested leaving Alberto in the tomb; it seemed a fitting punishment. But I was dissuaded by Evelyn's horrified protests.

So, at sunrise, we returned to the dahabeeyah, and Emerson made a fine speech to the assembled crew, who squatted on the deck staring at him with round black eyes while he explained that the Mummy had been a hoax, the curse imaginary, and that an ordinary human being had been behind the whole thing. He produced his downcast, shivering captive at the appropriate moment, and I think the sight of an Englishman, one of the Master Race, in bonds and held up to scorn as a common criminal did as much as anything to win their wholehearted allegiance. Lucas's crew gave us no difficulty; their loyalty had been won with money, and as soon as the source of funds dried up, their devotion withered. An expedition set out immediately for the camp and brought back a very thirsty Alberto, together with our luggage and equipment. I myself supervised the removal of poor Michael, on a litter. We set sail at once for Cairo.

It was an enjoyable trip. With the great sail furled and lowered onto blocks on the deck, we let the current bear us downstream. There were occasional misadventures—grounding on sandbars, an encounter with another dehabeeyah that lost the latter its bowsprit and won us the collective curses of the exuberant American passengers; but these are only the normal accidents of Nile travel. In every other way matters could not have been more satisfactory. Michael began to make a good recovery, which relieved my worst fears. The crew outdid itself to please us. The cook produced magnificent meals, we were waited upon like princes, and Reis Hassan obeyed my slightest command. The full moon shone down upon us, the river rolled sweetly by. . . . And Emerson said not a word.

I had waited for him to make some reference, if not an apology, for his outrageous behavior in—for his daring to—for, in short, the kiss. Not only did he remain silent, but he avoided me with a consistency that was little short of marvelous. In such close quarters we ought to have been much together; but whenever I entered the saloon it seemed that Emerson was just leaving, and when I strolled on the deck, admiring the silvery ripples of moonlight on the water, Emerson vanished below. Walter was of no use. He spent all his time with Evelyn. They did not talk, they just sat holding hands and staring stupidly into one another's eyes. Walter was a sensible chap. Evelyn's fortune would not keep him from happiness. Was it possible that Emerson . . . ?

After two days I decided I could wait no longer. I hope I number patience among my virtues, but shilly-shallying, when nothing is to be gained by delay, is not a virtue. So I cornered Emerson on deck one night, literally backing him into a corner. He stood pressed up against the rail that enclosed the upper deck as I advanced upon him, and from the look on his face you would have thought I were a crocodile intent on devouring him, boots, bones, and all.

We had dined formally; I was wearing my crimson gown and I had taken some pains with my hair. I thought, when I looked at myself in the mirror that evening, that I did look well; perhaps Evelyn's flattery had not all been false. As I approached Emerson I was pleasantly aware of the rustle of my full skirts and the movement of the ruffles at my throat.

"No," I said, as Emerson made a sideways movement, like a crab. "Don't try to run away, Emerson, it won't do you a particle of good, for I mean to have my say if I have to shout it after you as we run about the boat. Sit or stand, don't mind me. I shall stand. I think better on my feet."

Emerson squared his shoulders.

"I shall stand. I feel safer on my feet. Proceed, then, Peabody; I know better than to interfere with you when you are in this mood."

"I mean to make you a business proposition," I said. "It is simply this. I have some means; I am not rich, like Evelyn, but I have more than I need, and no dependents. I had meant to leave my money to the British Museum. Now it seems to me that I may as well employ it for an equally useful purpose while I live, and enjoy myself in the bargain, thus killing two birds with one stone. Miss Amelia B. Edwards has formed a society for the exploration of Egyptian antiquities; I shall do the same. I wish to hire you as my archaeological expert. There is only one condition. . . ."

I had to stop for breath. This was more difficult than I had anticipated.

"Yes?" said Emerson in a strange voice. "What condition?"

I drew a deep breath.

"I insist upon being allowed to participate in the excavations. After all, why should men have all the fun?"

"Fun?" Emerson repeated. "To be burned by the sun, rubbed raw by sand, live on rations no self-respecting beggar would eat; to be bitten by snakes and mashed by falling rocks? Your definition of pleasure, Peabody, is extremely peculiar."

"Peculiar or not, it *is* my idea of pleasure. Why, why else do you lead this life if you don't enjoy it? Don't talk of duty to me; you men always have some high-sounding excuse for indulging yourselves. You go gallivanting over the earth, climbing mountains, looking for the sources of the Nile; and expect women to sit dully at home embroidering. I embroider very badly. I think I would excavate rather well. If you like, I will list my qualifications—"

"No," said Emerson, in a strangled voice. "I am only too well aware of your qualifications."

And he caught me in an embrace that bruised my ribs.

"Stop it," I said, pushing at him. "That was not at all what I had in mind. Stop it, Emerson, you are confusing me. I don't want—"

"Don't you?" said Emerson, taking my chin in his hand and turning my face toward his.

"Yes!" I cried, and flung my arms around his neck.

A good while later, Emerson remarked.

"You realize, Peabody, that I accept your offer of marriage because it is the only practical way of getting at your money? You couldn't join me in an excavation unless we were married; every European in Egypt, from Baring to Maspero, would be outraged, and Mme. Maspero would force her husband to cancel my concession."

"I fully understand that," I said. "Now if you will stop squeezing me quite so hard. . . . I cannot breathe."

"Breathing is unnecessary," said Emerson.

After another interval, it was my turn to comment.

"And you," I said, "understand that *I* accept *your* proposal of marriage because it is the only way in which I can gain my ends. It is so unfair—another example of how women are discriminated against. What a pity I was not born a hundred years from now! Then I would not have to marry a loud, arrogant, rude man in order to be allowed to excavate."

Emerson squeezed my ribs again and I had to stop for lack of breath.

"I have found the perfect way of silencing you," he said.

But then the laughter fled from his face and his eyes took on an expression that made me feel very odd—as if my interior organs had dissolved into a shapeless, sticky mass.

"Peabody, you may as well hear the truth. I am mad about you! Since the day you walked into my tomb and started ordering us all about, I have known you were the only woman for me. Why do you suppose I have sulked and avoided you since we left Amarna? I was contemplating a life without you—a bleak, gray existence, without your voice scolding me and your big bright eyes scowling at me, and your magnificent figure—has no one told you about your figure, Peabody?—striding up and down prying into all sorts of places where you had no business to be. . . . I knew I couldn't endure it! If you hadn't spoken tonight, I should have borrowed Alberto's mummy costume and carried you off into the desert! There, I have said it. You have stripped away my defenses. Are you satisfied with your victory?"

I did not reply in words, but I think my answer was satisfactory. When Emerson had regained his breath he let out a great hearty laugh.

"Archaeology is a fascinating pursuit, but, after all, one cannot work day and night. . . . Peabody, my darling Peabody—what a perfectly splendid time we are going to have!"

Emerson was right—as he usually is. We *have* had a splendid time. We mean to work at Gizeh next year. There is a good deal to be done here yet, but for certain practical reasons we prefer to be nearer Cairo. I understand that Petrie wants to work here, and he is one of the few excavators to whom Emerson would consider yielding. Not that the two of them get along; when we met Mr. Petrie in London last year, he and Emerson started out mutually abusing the Antiquities Department and ended up abusing one another over pottery fragments. Petrie is a nice-looking young fellow, but he really has no idea of what to do with pottery.

The practical reasons that demand we work near Cairo are the same reasons that keep me here, in my chair, instead of being down below supervising the workers as I usually do. Emerson is being overly cautious; I feel perfectly well. They say that for a woman of my age to have her first child is not always easy, and Emerson is in a perfect jitter of apprehension about the whole thing, but I have no qualms whatever. I do not intend that anything shall go amiss. I planned it carefully, not wanting to interrupt the winter excavation season. I can fit the child in quite nicely between seasons, and be back in Cairo ready for work in November.

We are now awaiting news from Evelyn of the birth of her second child, which is due at any moment. She is already the mother of a fair-haired male child, quite a charming infant, with a propensity for rooting in mud puddles which I am sure he inherited from his archaeological relatives. I am his godmother, so perhaps I am biased about his beauty, intelligence, and charm. But I think I am not.

Walter is not with us this season; he is studying hieroglyphics in England, and promises to be one of the finest scholars of our time. His library at Ellesmere Castle is filled with books and manuscripts, and when we join the younger Emersons there for the summer and early fall each year, he and Emerson spend hours arguing over translations.

Lucas? His present whereabouts are unknown to us. Without the money to support his title he could not live respectably in England. I wanted to prosecute the rascal as he deserved; but Baring dissuaded me. He was very helpful to us when we reached Cairo with our boatload of criminals; and he was present on the momentous occasion when Evelyn opened her boxes and found, among the diaries and books, an envelope containing her grandfather's last, holograph will. This was the final proof of Lucas's villainy; but, as Baring pointed out, a trial would bring unwished-for notoriety on all of us, particularly Evelyn, and Lucas was no longer a danger. He lives precariously, I believe, somewhere on the Continent, and if he does not soon drink himself to death, some outraged husband or father will certainly shoot him.

I see Alberto whenever we pass through Cairo. I make a point of doing so. As I warned him once, Egyptian prisons are particularly uncomfortable, and the life does not seem to agree with him at all.

Michael has just rung the bell for lunch, and I see Emerson coming toward me. I have a bone to pick with him; I do not believe he is correct in his identification of one of the sculptured busts as the head of the heretic pharaoh. It seems to me to be a representation of young Tutankhamon, Khuenaten's son-in-law.

I must add one more thing. Often I find myself remembering that blustery day in Rome, when I went to the rescue of a young English girl who had fainted in the Forum. Little did I realize how strangely our destinies would be intertwined; that that act of simple charity would reward me beyond my wildest dreams, winning for me a friend and sister, a life of busy, fascinating work, and. . . .

Evelyn was right. With the right person, under the right circumstances—it is perfectly splendid!

The Curse
of the
Pharaohs

To Phyllis Whitney

Chapter One

 THE events I am about to relate began on a December afternoon, when I had invited Lady Harold Carrington and certain of her friends to tea. Do not, gentle reader, be misled by this introductory statement. It is accurate (as my statements always are); but if you expect the tale that follows to be one of pastoral domesticity, enlivened only by gossip about the county gentry, you will be sadly mistaken. Bucolic peace is not my ambience, and the giving of tea parties is by no means my favorite amusement. In fact, I would prefer to be pursued across the desert by a band of savage Dervishes brandishing spears and howling for my blood. I would rather be chased up a tree by a mad dog, or face a mummy risen from its grave. I would rather be threatened by knives, pistols, poisonous snakes, and the curse of a long-dead king.

Lest I be accused of exaggeration, let me point out that I have had all those experiences, save one. However, Emerson once remarked that if I *should* encounter a band of Dervishes, five minutes of my nagging would unquestionably inspire even the mildest of them to massacre me.

Emerson considers this sort of remark humorous. Five years of marriage have taught me that even if one is unamused by the (presumed) wit of one's spouse, one does not say so. Some concessions to temperament are necessary if the marital state is to flourish. And I must confess that in most respects the state agrees with me. Emerson is a remarkable person, considering that he is a man. Which is not saying a great deal.

The state of wedlock has its disadvantages, however, and an accumulation of these, together with certain other factors, added to my restlessness on the afternoon of the tea party. The weather was dreadful—dreary and drizzling, with occasional intervals of sleety snow. I had not been able to go out for my customary five-mile walk; the dogs *had* been out, and had returned coated with mud, which they promptly transferred to the drawing-room rug; and Ramses . . .

But I will come to the subject of Ramses at the proper time.

Though we had lived in Kent for five years, I had never entertained my neighbors to tea. None of them has the faintest idea of decent conversation. They cannot tell a Kamares pot from a piece of prehistoric painted ware, and they have no idea who Seti the First was. On this occasion, however, I was forced into an exercise of civility which I would ordinarily abhor. Emerson had designs on a barrow on the property of Sir Harold, and—as he elegantly expressed it—it was necessary for us to "butter up" Sir Harold before asking permission to excavate.

It was Emerson's own fault that Sir Harold required buttering. I share my husband's views on the idiocy of fox hunting, and I do not blame him for personally escorting the fox off the field when it was about to be trapped, or run to earth, or whatever the phrase may be. I blame Emerson for pulling Sir Harold out of his saddle and thrashing him with his own riding crop. A brief, forceful lecture, together with the removal of the fox, would have gotten the point across. The thrashing was superfluous.

Initially Sir Harold had threatened to take Emerson to law. He was prevented by some notion that this would be unsportsmanlike. (Seemingly no such stigma applied to the pursuit of a single fox by a troop of men on horseback and a pack of dogs.) He was restrained from physically attacking Emerson by Emerson's size and reputation (not undeserved) for bellicosity. Therefore he had contented himself with cutting Emerson dead whenever they chanced to meet. Emerson never noticed when he was being cut dead, so matters had progressed peacefully enough until my husband got the notion of excavating Sir Harold's barrow.

It was quite a nice barrow, as barrows go—a hundred feet long and some thirty wide. These monuments are the tombs of antique Viking warriors, and Emerson hoped to discover the burial regalia of a chieftain, with perhaps evidences of barbaric sacrifice. Since I am above all things a fair-minded person, I will candidly confess that it was, in part, my own eagerness to rip into the barrow that prompted me to be civil to Lady Harold. But I was also moved by concern for Emerson.

He was bored. Oh, he tried to hide it! As I have said, and will continue to say, Emerson has his faults, but unfair recrimination is not one of them. He did not blame *me* for the tragedy that had ruined his life.

When I first met him, he was carrying on archaeological excavations in Egypt. Some unimaginative people might not consider this occupation pleasurable. Disease, extreme heat, inadequate or nonexistent sanitary conditions, and a quite excessive amount of sand do mar to some extent the joys of discovering the treasures of a vanished civilization. However, Emerson adored the life, and so did I, after we joined forces, maritally, professionally, and financially. Even after our son was born we managed to get in one long season at Sakkara. We returned to England that spring with every intention of going out again the following autumn. Then our doom came upon us, as the Lady of Shalott might have said (indeed, I believe she actually did say so) in the form of our son, "Ramses" Walter Peabody Emerson.

I promised that I would return to the subject of Ramses. He cannot be dismissed in a few lines.

The child had been barely three months old when we left him for the winter with my dear friend Evelyn, who had married Emerson's younger brother Walter. From her grandfather, the irascible old Duke of Chalfont, Evelyn had inherited Chalfont Castle, and a great deal of money. Her husband—one of the few men whose company I can tolerate for more than an hour at a time—was a distinguished Egyptologist in his own right. Unlike Emerson, who prefers excavation, Walter is a philologist, specializing in the decipherment of the varied forms of the ancient Egyptian language. He had happily settled down with his beautiful wife at her family home, spending his days reading crabbed, crumbling texts and his evenings playing with his ever-increasing family.

Evelyn, who is the dearest girl, was delighted to take Ramses for the winter. Nature had just interfered with her hopes of becoming a mother for the fourth time, so a new baby was quite to her taste. At three months Ramses was personable enough, with a mop of dark hair, wide blue eyes, and a nose which even then showed signs of developing from an infantile button into a feature of character. He slept a great deal. (As Emerson said later, he was probably saving his strength.)

I left the child more reluctantly than I had expected would be the case, but after all he had not been around long enough to make much of an impression, and I was particularly looking forward to the dig at Sakkara. It was a most productive season, and I will candidly admit that the thought of my abandoned child seldom passed through my mind. Yet as we prepared to return to England the following spring, I found myself rather looking forward to seeing him again, and I fancied Emerson felt the same; we went straight to Chalfont Castle from Dover, without stopping over in London.

How well I remember that day! April in England, the most delightful of seasons! For once it was not raining. The hoary old castle, splashed with the fresh new green of Virginia creeper and ivy, sat in its beautifully tended grounds like a gracious dowager basking in the sunlight. As our carriage came to a stop the doors opened and Evelyn ran out, her arms extended. Walter was close behind; he wrung his brother's hand and then crushed me in a fraternal embrace. After the first greetings had been exchanged, Evelyn said, "But of course, you will want to see young Walter."

"If it is not inconvenient," I said.

Evelyn laughed and squeezed my hand. "Amelia, don't pretend with me. I know you too well. You are dying to see your baby."

Chalfont Castle is a large establishment. Though extensively modernized, its walls are ancient and fully six feet thick. Sound does not readily travel through such a medium, but as we proceeded along the upper corridor of the south wing, I began to hear a strange noise, a kind of roaring. Muted as it was, it conveyed a quality of ferocity that made me ask, "Evelyn, have you taken to keeping a menagerie?"

"One might call it that," Evelyn said, her voice choked with laughter.

The sound increased in volume as we went on. We stopped before a closed door. Evelyn opened it; the sound burst forth in all its fury. I actually fell back a pace, stepping heavily on the instep of my husband, who was immediately behind me.

The room was a day nursery, fitted up with all the comfort wealth and tender love can provide. Long windows flooded the chamber with light; a bright fire, guarded by a fender and screen, mitigated the cold of the old stone walls. These had been covered by paneling hung with pretty pictures and draped with bright fabric. On the floor was a thick carpet strewn with toys of all kinds. Before the fire, rocking placidly, sat the very picture of a sweet old nanny, her cap and apron snowy white, her rosy face calm, her hands busy with her knitting. Around the walls, in various postures of defense, were three children. Though they had grown considerably, I recognized these as the offspring of Evelyn and Walter. Sitting bolt upright in the center of the floor was a baby.

It was impossible to make out his features. All one could see was a great wide cavern of a mouth, framed in black hair. However, I had no doubt as to his identity.

"There he is," Evelyn shouted, over the bellowing of this infantile volcano. "Only see how he has grown!"

Emerson gasped. "What the devil is the matter with him?"

Hearing—how, I cannot imagine—a new voice, the infant stopped shrieking. The cessation of sound was so abrupt it left the ears ringing.

"Nothing," Evelyn said calmly. "He is cutting teeth, and is sometimes a little cross."

"Cross?" Emerson repeated incredulously.

I stepped into the room, followed by the others. The child stared at us. It sat foursquare on its bottom, its legs extended before it, and I was struck at once by its shape, which was virtually rectangular. Most babies, I had observed, tend to be spherical. This one had wide shoulders and a straight spine, no visible neck, and a face whose angularity not even baby fat could disguise. The eyes were not the pale ambiguous blue of a normal infant's, but a dark, intense sapphire; they met mine with an almost adult calculation.

Emerson had begun circling cautiously to the left, rather as one approaches a growling dog. The child's eyes swiveled suddenly in his direction. Emerson stopped. His face took on an imbecilic simper. He squatted. "Baby," he crooned. "Wawa. Papa's widdle Wawa. Come to nice papa."

"For God's sake, Emerson!" I exclaimed.

The baby's intense blue eyes turned to me. "I am your mother, Walter," I said, speaking slowly and distinctly. "Your mama. I don't suppose you can say Mama."

Without warning the child toppled forward. Emerson let out a cry of alarm, but his concern was unnecessary; the infant deftly got its four limbs under it and began crawling at an incredible speed, straight to me. It came to a stop at my feet, rocked back onto its haunches, and lifted its arms.

"Mama," it said. Its ample mouth split into a smile that produced dimples in both cheeks and displayed three small white teeth. "Mama. Up. Up, up, up, UP!"

Its voice rose in volume; the final UP made the windows rattle. I stopped hastily and seized the creature. It was surprisingly heavy. It flung its arms around my neck and buried its face against my shoulder. "Mama," it said, in a muffled voice.

For some reason, probably because the child's grip was so tight, I was unable to speak for a few moments.

"He is very precocious," Evelyn said, as proudly as if the child had been her own. "Most children don't speak properly until they are a year old, but this young man already has quite a vocabulary. I have shown him your photographs every day and told him whom they represented."

Emerson stood by me staring, with a singularly hangdog look. The infant released its stranglehold, glanced at its father, and—with what I can only regard, in the light of later experience, as cold-blooded calculation—tore itself from my arms and launched itself through the air toward my husband.

"Papa," it said.

Emerson caught it. For a moment they regarded one another with virtually identical foolish grins. Then he flung it into the air. It shrieked with delight, so he tossed it up again. Evelyn remonstrated as, in the exuberance of its father's greeting, the child's head grazed the ceiling. I said nothing. I knew, with a strange sense of foreboding, that a war had begun—a lifelong battle, in which I was doomed to be the loser.

It was Emerson who gave the baby its nickname. He said that in its belligerent appearance and imperious disposition it strongly resembled the Egyptian pharaoh, the second of that name, who had scattered enormous statues of himself all along the Nile. I had to admit the resemblance. Certainly the child was not at all like its namesake, Emerson's brother, who is a gentle, soft-spoken man.

Though Evelyn and Walter both pressed us to stay with them, we decided to take a house of our own for the summer. It was apparent that the younger Emersons' children went in terror of their cousin. They were no match for the tempestuous temper and violent demonstrations of affection to which Ramses was prone. As we discovered, he was extremely intelligent. His physical abilities matched his mental powers. He could crawl at an astonishing speed at eight months. When, at ten months, he decided to learn to walk, he was unsteady on his feet for a few days; and at one time he had bruises on the end of his nose, his forehead, and his chin, for Ramses did nothing by halves—he fell and rose to fall again. He soon mastered the skill, however, and after that he was never still except when someone was holding him. By this time he was talking quite fluently, except for an annoying tendency to lisp, which I attributed to the unusual size of his front teeth, an inheritance from his father. He inherited from the same source a quality which I hesitated to characterize, there being no word in the English language strong enough to do it justice. "Bullheaded" is short of the mark by quite a distance.

Emerson was, from the first, quite besotted with the creature. He took it for long walks and read to it by the hour, not only from *Peter Rabbit* and other childhood tales, but from excavation reports and his own *History of Ancient Egypt,* which he was composing. To see Ramses, at fourteen months, wrinkling his brows over a sentence like "The theology of the Egyptians was a compound of fetishism, totemism and syncretism" was a sight as terrifying as it was comical. Even more terrifying was the occasional thoughtful nod the child would give.

After a time I stopped thinking of Ramses as "it." His masculinity was only too apparent. As the summer drew to a close I went, one day, to the estate agents and told them we would keep the house for another year. Shortly thereafter Emerson informed me that he had accepted a position as lecturer at the University of London.

There was never any need to discuss the subject. It was evident that we could not take a young child into the unhealthy climate of an archaeological camp; and it was equally obvious that Emerson could not bear to be parted from the boy. My own feelings? They are quite irrelevant. The decision was the only sensible solution, and I am always sensible.

So, four years later, we were still vegetating in Kent. We had decided to buy the house. It was a pleasant old place, Georgian in style, with ample grounds nicely planted—except for the areas where the dogs and Ramses excavated. I had no trouble keeping ahead of the dogs, but it was a running battle to plant things faster than Ramses dug them up. I believe many children enjoy digging in the mud, but Ramses' preoccupation with holes in the ground became absolutely ridiculous. It was all Emerson's fault. Mistaking a love of dirt for a budding talent for excavation, he encouraged the child.

Emerson never admitted that he missed the old life. He had made a successful career lecturing and writing; but now and then I would detect a wistful note in his voice as he read from the *Times* or the *Illustrated London News* about new discoveries in the Middle East. To such had we fallen—reading the ILN over tea, and bickering about trivia with county neighbors—we, who had camped in a cave in the Egyptian hills and restored the capital city of a pharaoh!

On that fateful afternoon—whose significance I was not to appreciate until much later—I prepared myself for the sacrifice. I wore my best gray silk. It was a gown Emerson detested because he said it made me look like a respectable English matron—one of the worst insults in his vocabulary. I decided that if Emerson disapproved, Lady Harold would probably consider the gown suitable.

I even allowed Smythe, my maid, to arrange my hair. The ridiculous woman was always trying to fuss over my personal appearance. I seldom allowed her to do more than was absolutely necessary, having neither the time nor the patience for prolonged primping. On this occasion Smythe took full advantage. If I had not had a newspaper to read while she pulled and tugged at my hair and ran pins into my head, I would have screamed with boredom.

Finally she said sharply, "With all respect, madam, I cannot do this properly while you are waving that paper about. Will it please you to put it down?"

It did not please me. But time was getting on, and the newspaper story I had been reading—of which more in due course—only made me more discontented with the prospect before me. I therefore abandoned the *Times* and meekly submitted to Smythe's torture.

When she had finished the two of us stared at my reflection in the mirror with countenances that displayed our feelings—Smythe's beaming with triumph, mine the gloomy mask of one who had learned to accept the inevitable gracefully.

My stays were too tight and my new shoes pinched. I creaked downstairs to inspect the drawing room.

The room was so neat and tidy it made me feel quite depressed. The newspapers and books and periodicals that normally covered most of the flat surfaces had been cleared away. Emerson's prehistoric pots had been removed from the mantel and the what-not. A gleaming silver tea service had replaced Ramses' toys on the tea cart. A bright fire on the hearth helped to dispel the gloom of the gray skies without, but it did very little for the inner gloom that filled me. I do not allow myself to repine about what cannot be helped; but I remembered earlier Decembers, under the cloudless blue skies and brilliant sun of Egypt.

As I stood morosely contemplating the destruction of our cheerful domestic clutter, and recalling better days, I heard the sound of wheels on the gravel of the drive. The first guest had arrived. Gathering the robes of my martyrdom about me, I made ready to receive her.

There is no point in describing the tea party. It is not a memory I enjoy recalling and, thank heaven, subsequent events made Lady Harold's attitude quite unimportant. She is not the most stupid person I have ever met; that distinction must go to her husband; but she combines malice and stupidity to a degree I had not encountered until that time.

Remarks such as, "My dear, what a charming frock! I remember admiring that style when it first came out, two years ago," were wasted on me, for I am unmoved by insult. What did move me, to considerable vexation, was Lady Harold's assumption that my invitation to tea signified apology and capitulation. This assumption was apparent in every condescending word she said and in every expression that passed across her fat, coarse, common face.

But I perceive, with surprise, that I am becoming angry all over again. How foolish, and what a waste of time! Let me say no more—except to admit that

I derived an unworthy satisfaction in beholding Lady Harold's ill-concealed envy of the neatness of the room, the excellence of the food, and the smart efficiency with which butler, footman, and parlormaid served us. Rose, my parlormaid, is always efficient, but on this occasion she outdid herself. Her apron was so starched it could have stood by itself, her cap ribbons fairly snapped as she moved. I recalled having heard that Lady Harold had a hard time keeping servants because of her parsimony and vicious tongue. Rose's younger sister had been employed by her . . . briefly.

Except for that minor triumph, for which I can claim no credit, the meeting was an unmitigated bore. The other ladies whom I had invited, in order to conceal my true motives, were all followers of Lady Harold; they did nothing but titter and nod at her idiotic remarks. An hour passed with stupefying slowness. It was clear that my mission was doomed to failure; Lady Harold would do nothing to accommodate me. I was beginning to wonder what would happen if I simply rose and left the room, when an interruption occurred to save me from that expedient.

I had—I fondly believed—convinced Ramses to remain quietly in the nursery that afternoon. I had accomplished this by bribery and corruption, promising him a visit to the sweetshop in the village on the following day. Ramses could consume enormous quantities of sweets without the slightest inconvenience to his appetite or digestive apparatus. Unfortunately his desire for sweets was not as strong as his lust for learning—or mud, as the case may be. As I watched Lady Harold devour the last of the frosted cakes I heard stifled outcries from the hall. They were followed by a crash—my favorite Ming vase, as I later learned. Then the drawing-room doors burst open and a dripping, muddy, miniature scarecrow rushed in.

It cannot be said that the child's feet left muddy prints. No; an unbroken stream of liquid filth marked his path, pouring from his person, his garments, and the unspeakable object he was flourishing. He slid to a stop before me and deposited this object in my lap. The stench that arose from it made its origin only too clear. Ramses had been rooting in the compost heap again.

I am actually rather fond of my son. Without displaying the fatuous adoration characteristic of his father, I may say that I have a certain affection for the boy. At that moment I wanted to take the little monster by the collar and shake him until his face turned blue.

Constrained, by the presence of the ladies, from this natural maternal impulse, I said quietly, "Ramses, take the bone from Mama's good frock and return it to the compost heap."

Ramses put his head on one side and studied his bone with a thoughtful frown. "I fink," he said, "It is a femuw. A femuw of a winocowus."

"There are no rhinoceroses in England," I pointed out.

"A a-stinct winocowus," said Ramses.

A peculiar wheezing sound from the direction of the doorway made me look in that direction in time to see Wilkins clap his hands to his mouth and turn suddenly away. Wilkins is a most dignified man, a butler among butlers, but I had once or twice observed that there were traces of a sense of humor beneath his stately exterior. On this occasion I was forced to share his amusement.

"The word is not ill chosen," I said, pinching my nostrils together with my fingers, and wondering how I could remove the boy without further damage to my drawing room. Summoning a footman to take him away was out of the question; he was an agile child, and his coating of mud made him as slippery as a frog. In his efforts to elude pursuit he would leave tracks across the carpet, the furniture, the walls, the ladies' frocks. . . .

"A splendid bone," I said, without even trying to resist the temptation. "You must wash it before you show it to Papa. But first, perhaps Lady Harold would like to see it."

With a sweeping gesture, I indicated the lady.

If she had not been so stupid, she might have thought of a way of diverting Ramses. If she had not been so fat, she might have moved out of the way. As it was, all she could do was billow and shriek and sputter. Her efforts to dislodge the nasty thing (it *was* very nasty, I must admit) were in vain; it lodged in a fold of her voluminous skirt and stayed there.

Ramses was highly affronted at this unappreciative reception of his treasure.

"You will drop it and bweak it," he exclaimed. "Give it back to me."

In his efforts to retrieve the bone he dragged it across several more square yards of Lady Harold's enormous lap. Clutching it to his small bosom, he gave her a look of hurt reproach before trotting out of the room.

I will draw a veil over the events that followed. I derive an unworthy satisfaction from the memory, even now; it is not proper to encourage such thoughts.

I stood by the window watching the carriages splash away and humming quietly to myself while Rose dealt with the tea-things and the trail of mud left by Ramses.

"You had better bring fresh tea, Rose," I said. "Professor Emerson will be here shortly."

"Yes, madam. I hope, madam, that all was satisfactory."

"Oh, yes indeed. It could not have been more satisfactory."

"I am glad to hear it, madam."

"I am sure you are. Now, Rose, you are not to give Master Ramses any extra treats."

"Certainly not, madam." Rose looked shocked.

I meant to change my frock before Emerson got home, but he was early that evening. As usual, he carried an armful of books and papers, which he flung helter-skelter onto the sofa. Turning to the fire, he rubbed his hands briskly together.

"Frightful climate," he grumbled. "Wretched day. Why are you wearing that hideous dress?"

Emerson has never learned to wipe his feet at the door. I looked at the prints his boots had left on the freshly cleaned floor. Then I looked at him, and the reproaches I had meant to utter died on my lips.

He had not changed physically in the years since we were wed. His hair was as thick and black and unruly as ever, his shoulders as broad, his body as straight. When I had first met him, he had worn a beard. He was now clean-shaven, at my request, and this was a considerable concession on his part, for Emerson particularly dislikes the deep cleft, or dimple, in his prominent chin. I myself approve of this little flaw; it is the only whimsical touch in an otherwise forbiddingly rugged physiognomy.

On that day his looks, manners, and speech were as usual. Yet there was something in his eyes. . . . I had seen the look before; it was more noticeable now. So I said nothing about his muddy feet.

"I entertained Lady Harold this afternoon," I said in answer to his question. "Hence the dress. Have you had a pleasant day?"

"No."

"Neither have I."

"Serves you right," said my husband. "I told you not to do it. Where the devil is Rose? I want my tea."

Rose duly appeared, with the tea tray. I meditated, sadly, on the tragedy of Emerson, querulously demanding tea and complaining about the weather, like any ordinary Englishman. As soon as the door had closed behind the parlormaid, Emerson came to me and took me in his arms.

After an interval he held me out at arm's length and looked at me questioningly. His nose wrinkled.

I was about to explain the smell when he said, in a low, hoarse voice, "You are particularly attractive tonight, Peabody, in spite of that frightful frock. Don't you want to change? I will go up with you, and—"

"What is the matter with you?" I demanded, as he . . . Never mind what he did, it prevented him from speaking and made it rather difficult for me to speak evenly. "I certainly don't feel attractive, and I smell like moldy bone. Ramses has been excavating in the compost heap again."

"Mmmm," said Emerson. "My darling Peabody . . ."

Peabody is my maiden name. When Emerson and I first met, we did not hit it off. He took to calling me Peabody, as he would have addressed another man, as a sign of annoyance. It had now become a sign of something else, recalling those first wonderful days of our acquaintance when we had bickered and sneered at one another.

Yielding with pleasure to his embraces. I nevertheless felt sad, for I knew why he was so demonstrative. The smell of Ramses' bone had taken him back to our romantic courtship, in the unsanitary tombs of El Amarna.

I left off feeling sad before long and was about to accede to his request that we adjourn to our room; but we had delayed too long. The evening routine was set and established; we were always given a decent interval alone after Emerson arrived, then Ramses was permitted to come in to greet his papa and take tea with us. On that evening the child was anxious to show off his bone, so perhaps he came early, It certainly seemed too early to me, and even Emerson, his arm still around my waist, greeted the boy with less than his usual enthusiasm.

A pretty domestic scene ensued. Emerson took his son, and the bone, onto his knee, and I seated myself behind the teapot. After dispensing a cup of the genial beverage to my husband and a handful of cakes to my son, I reached for the newspapers, while Emerson and Ramses argued about the bone. It *was* a femur—Ramses was uncannily accurate about such things—but Emerson claimed that the bone had once belonged to a horse. Ramses differed. Rhinoceroses having been eliminated, he suggested a dragon or a giraffe.

The newspaper story for which I searched was no longer on the front page, though it had occupied this position for some time. I think I can do no better than relate what I then knew of the case, as if I were beginning a work of fiction; for indeed, if the story had not appeared in the respectable pages of the *Times,* I would have thought it one of the ingenious inventions of Herr Ebers or Mr. Rider Haggard—to whose romances, I must confess, I was addicted. Therefore, be patient, dear reader, if we begin with a sober narrative of facts. They are necessary to your understanding of later developments; and I promise you we will have sensations enough in due course.

Sir Henry Baskerville (of the Norfolk Baskervilles, not the Devonshire branch of the family), having suffered a severe illness, had been advised by his physician to spend a winter in the salubrious climate of Egypt. Neither the excellent man of medicine nor his wealthy patient could have anticipated the far-reaching consequences of this advice; for Sir Henry's first glimpse of the majestic features of the Sphinx inspired in his bosom a passionate interest in Egyptian antiquities, which was to rule him for the remainder of his life.

After excavating at Abydos and Denderah, Sir Henry finally obtained a firman to excavate in what is perhaps the most romantic of all Egyptian archaeological sites—the Valley of the Kings at Thebes. Here the god-kings of imperial Egypt were laid to rest with the pomp and majesty befitting their high estate. Their mummies enclosed in golden coffins and adorned with jewel-encrusted amulets, they hoped in the secrecy of their rock-cut tombs, deep in the bowels of the Theban hills, to escape the dreadful fate that had befallen their ancestors. For by the time of the Empire the pyramids of earlier rulers already gaped open and desolate, the royal bodies destroyed and their treasures dispersed. Alas for human vanity! The mighty pharaohs of the later period were no more immune to the depredations of tomb robbers than their ancestors had been. Every royal tomb found in the Valley had been despoiled. Treasures, jewels, and kingly mummies had vanished. It was assumed that the ancient tomb robbers had destroyed what they could not steal, until that astonishing day in July of 1881, when a group of modern thieves led Emil Brugsch, of the Cairo Museum, to a remote valley in the Theban mountains. The thieves, men from the village of Gurneh, had discovered what archaeologists had missed—the last resting place of Egypt's mightiest kings, queens, and royal children, hidden away in the days of the nation's decline by a group of loyal priests.

Not all the kings of the Empire were found in the thieves' cache, nor had all their tombs been identified. Lord Baskerville believed that the barren cliffs of the Valley still hid kingly tombs—even, perhaps, a tomb that had never been robbed. One frustration followed another, but he never abandoned his quest. Determined to dedicate his life to it, he built a house on the West Bank, half winter home, half working quarters for his archaeological staff. To this lovely spot he brought his bride, a beautiful young woman who had nursed him through a bout of pneumonia brought on by his return to England's damp spring climate.

The story of this romantic courtship and marriage, with its Cinderella aspect—for the new Lady Baskerville was a young lady of no fortune and insignificant family—had been prominently featured in the newspapers at the time. This event occurred before my own interest in Egypt developed, but naturally I had heard of Sir Henry; his name was known to every Egyptologist. Emerson had nothing good to say about him, but then Emerson did not approve of any other archaeologists, amateur or professional. In accusing Sir Henry of being an amateur he did the gentleman less than justice, for his lordship never attempted to direct the excavations; he always employed a professional scholar for that work.

In September of this year Sir Henry had gone to Luxor as usual, accompanied by Lady Baskerville and Mr. Alan Armadale, the archaeologist in charge. Their purpose during this season was to begin work on an area in the center of the Valley, near the tombs of Ramses II and Merenptah, which had been cleared by Lepsius in 1844. Sir Henry thought that the rubbish dumps thrown up by that expedition had perhaps covered the hidden entrances to other tombs. It was his intention to clear the ground down to bedrock to make sure nothing had been overlooked. And indeed, scarcely had the men been at work for three days when their spades uncovered the first of a series of steps cut into the rock.

(Are you yawning, gentle reader? If you are, it is because you know nothing of archaeology. Rock-cut steps in the Valley of the Kings could signify only one thing—the entrance to a tomb.)

The stairway went down into the rock at a steep angle. It had been completely filled with rock and rubble. By the following afternoon the men had cleared this away, exposing the upper portion of a doorway blocked with heavy stone slabs. Stamped into the mortar were the unbroken seals of the royal necropolis. Note that word, oh, reader—that word so simple and yet so fraught with meaning. Unbroken seals implied that the tomb had not been opened since the day when it was solemnly closed by the priests of the funerary cult.

Sir Henry, as his intimates were to testify, was a man of singularly phlegmatic temperament, even for a British nobleman. The only sign of excitement he displayed was a muttered, "By Jove," as he stroked his wispy beard. Others were not so blasé. The news reached the press and was duly published.

In accordance with the terms of his firman, Sir Henry notified the Department of Antiquities of his find; when he descended the dusty steps a second time he was accompanied by a distinguished group of archaeologists and officials. A fence had been hastily erected to hold back the crowd of sightseers, journalists, and natives, the latter picturesque in their long flapping robes and white turbans. Among the latter group one face stood out—that of Mohammed Abd er Rasul, one of the discoverers of the cache of royal mummies, who had betrayed the find (and his brothers) to the authorities and had been rewarded by a position in the Antiquities Department. Onlookers remarked on the profound chagrin of his expression and the gloomy looks of other members of the family. For once, the foreigners had stolen a march on them and deprived them of a potential source of income.

Though he had recovered from the illness that had brought him to Egypt and was (as his physician was later to report) in perfect health, Sir Henry's physique was not impressive. A photograph taken of him on that eventful day portrays a tall, stoop-shouldered man whose hair appears to have slid down off his head and adhered somewhat erratically to his cheeks and chin. Of manual dexterity he had none; and those who knew him well moved unobtrusively to the rear as he placed a chisel in position against the stone barricade and raised his hammer. The British consul did not know him well. The first chip of rock hit this unlucky gentleman full on the nose. Apologies and first aid followed. Now surrounded by a wide empty space, Sir Henry prepared to strike again. Scarcely had he raised the hammer when, from among the crowd of watching Egyptians, came a long ululating howl.

The import of the cry was understood by all who heard it. In such fashion do the followers of Mohammed mourn their dead.

There was a moment's pause. Then the voice rose again. It cried (I translate, of course): "Desecration! Desecration! May the curse of the gods fall on him who disturbs the king's eternal rest!"

Startled by this remark, Sir Henry missed the chisel and hit himself on the thumb. Such misadventures do not improve the temper. Sir Henry may be excused for losing his. In a savage voice he instructed Armadale, standing behind him, to capture the prophet of doom and give him a good thrashing. Armadale was willing; but as he approached the milling crowd the orator wisely ceased his cries and thereby became anonymous, for his friends all denied any knowledge of his identity.

It was a trivial incident, soon forgotten by everyone except Sir Henry, whose thumb was badly bruised. At least the injury gave him an excuse to surrender his tools to someone who was able to use them more effectively. Mr. Alan Armadale, a young, vigorous man, seized the implements. A few skillful blows opened an aperture wide enough to admit a light. Armadale then respectfully stepped back, allowing his patron the honor of the first look.

It was a day of misadventures for poor Sir Henry. Seizing a candle, he eagerly thrust his arm through the gaping hole. His fist encountered a hard surface with such force that he dropped the candle and withdrew a hand from which a considerable amount of skin had been scraped.

Investigation showed that the space beyond the door was completely filled with rubble. This was not surprising, since the Egyptians commonly used such devices to discourage tomb robbers; but the effect was distinctly anticlimactic, and the audience dispersed with disappointed murmurs, leaving Sir Henry to nurse his barked knuckles and contemplate a long, tedious job. If this tomb followed the plans of those already known, a passageway of unknown length would have to be cleared before the burial chamber was reached. Some tombs had entrance passages over a hundred feet long.

Yet the fact that the corridor was blocked made the discovery appear even more promising than before. The *Times* gave the story a full column, on page three. The next dispatch to come from Luxor, however, rated front-page headlines.

Sir Henry Baskerville was dead. He had retired in perfect health (except for his thumb and his knuckles). He was found next morning stiff and stark in his bed. On his face was a look of ghastly horror. On his high brow, inscribed in what appeared to be dried blood, was a crudely drawn uraeus serpent, the symbol of the divine pharaoh.

The "blood" turned out to be red paint. Even so, the news was sensational, and it became even more sensational after a medical examination failed to discover the cause of Sir Henry's death.

Cases of seemingly healthy persons who succumb to the sudden failure of a vital organ are certainly not unknown, nor, contrary to writers of thrillers, are they always due to the administration of mysterious poisons. If Sir Henry had died in his bed at Baskerville Hall, the physicians would have stroked their beards and concealed their ignorance in meaningless medical mumbo-jumbo. Even under these circumstances the story would have died a natural death (as Sir Henry was presumed to have done) had not an enterprising reporter from one of our less reputable newspapers remembered the unknown prophet's curse. The story in the *Times* was what one might expect of that dignified journal, but the other newspapers were less restrained. Their columns bristled with references to avenging spirits, cryptic antique curses, and unholy rites. But this sensation paled into insignificance two days later, when it was discovered that Mr. Alan Armadale, Sir Henry's assistant, had disappeared—vanished, as the *Daily Yell* put it, off the face of the earth!

By this time I was snatching the newspapers from Emerson each evening when he came home. Naturally I did not believe for an instant in the absurd tales of curses or supernatural doom, and when the news of young Armadale's disappearance became known I felt sure I had the answer to the mystery.

"Armadale is the murderer," I exclaimed to Emerson, who was on his hands and knees playing horsie with Ramses.

Emerson let out a grunt as his son's heels dug into his ribs. When he got his breath back he said irritably, "What do you mean, talking about 'the murderer' in that self-assured way? No murder was committed. Baskerville died of a heart condition or some such thing; he was always a feeble sort of fellow. Armadale is probably forgetting his troubles in a tavern. He has lost his position and will not easily find another patron so late in the season."

I made no reply to this ridiculous suggestion. Time, I knew, would prove me right, and until it did I saw no sense in wasting my breath arguing with Emerson, who is the stubbornest of men.

During the following week one of the gentlemen who had been present at the official opening of the tomb came down with a bad attack of fever, and a workman fell off a pylon at Karnak, breaking his neck. "The Curse is still operating," exclaimed the *Daily Yell*. "Who will be next?"

After the demise of the man who tumbled off the pylon (where he had been chiseling out a section of carving to sell to the illicit antiquities dealers), his fellows refused to go near the tomb. Work had come to a standstill after Sir Henry's death; now there seemed no prospect of renewing it. So matters stood on that cold, rainy evening after my disastrous tea party. For the past few days the Baskerville story had more or less subsided, despite the efforts of the *Daily Yell* to keep it alive by attributing every hangnail and stubbed toe in Luxor to the operation of the curse. No trace of the unfortunate (or guilty) Armadale had been found; Sir Henry Baskerville had been laid to rest among his forebears; and the tomb remained locked and barred.

I confess the tomb was my chief concern. Locks and bars were all very well, but neither would avail for long against the master thieves of Gurneh. The discovery of the sepulcher had been a blow to the professional pride of these gentlemen, who fancied themselves far more adept at locating the treasures of their ancestors than the foreign excavators; and indeed, over the centuries they had proved to be exceedingly skillful at their dubious trade, whether by practice or by heredity I would hesitate to say. Now that the tomb had been located they would soon be at work.

So, while Emerson argued zoology with Ramses, and the sleety rain hissed against the windows, I opened the newspaper. Since the beginning of *l'affaire Baskerville,* Emerson had been buying the *Yell* as well as the *Times,* remarking that the contrast in journalistic styles was a fascinating study in human nature. This was only an excuse; the *Yell* was much more entertaining to read. I therefore turned at once to this newspaper, noting that, to judge by certain creases and folds, I was not the first to peruse that particular article. It bore the title "Lady Baskerville vows the work must go on."

The journalist—"Our Correspondent in Luxor"—wrote with considerable feeling and many adjectives about the lady's "delicate lips, curved like a Cupid's bow, which quivered with emotion as she spoke" and "her tinted face which bore stamped upon it a deep acquaintance with grief."

"Bah," I said, after several paragraphs of this. "What drivel. I must say, Emerson, Lady Baskerville sounds like a perfect idiot. Listen to this. 'I can think of no more fitting monument to my lost darling than the pursuit of that great cause for which he gave his life.' Lost darling, indeed!"

Emerson did not reply. Squatting on the floor, with Ramses between his knees, he was turning the pages of a large illustrated volume on zoology, trying to convince the boy that his bone did not match that of a zebra—for Ramses had retreated from giraffes to that slightly less exotic beast. Unfortunately a zebra is rather like a horse, and the example Emerson found bore a striking resemblance to the bone Ramses was flourishing. The child let out a malevolent chuckle and remarked, "I was wight, you see. It is a zebwa."

"Have another cake," said his father.

"Armadale is still missing," I continued. "I told you he was the murderer."

"Bah," said Emerson. "He will turn up eventually. There has been no murder."

"You can hardly believe he has been drunk for a fortnight," I said.

"I have known men to remain drunk for considerably longer periods," said Emerson.

"If Armadale had met with an accident he, or his remains, would have been found by now. The Theban area has been combed—"

"It is impossible to search the western mountains thoroughly," Emerson snapped. "You know what they are like—jagged cliffs cut by hundreds of gullies and ravines."

"Then you believe he is out there somewhere?"

"I do. It would be a tragic coincidence, certainly, if he met with a fatal accident so soon after Sir Henry's death; the newspapers would certainly set up a renewed howl about curses. But such coincidences do happen, especially if a man is distracted by—"

"He is probably in Algeria by now," I said.

"Algeria! Why there, for heaven's sake?"

"The Foreign Legion. They say it is full of murderers and criminals attempting to escape justice."

Emerson got to his feet. I was pleased to observe that his eyes had lost their melancholy look and were blazing with temper. I noted, as well, that four years of relative inactivity had not robbed his form of its strength and vigor. He had removed his coat and starched collar preparatory to playing with the boy, and his disheveled appearance irresistibly recalled the unkempt individual who had first captured my heart. I decided that if we went straight upstairs there might be time, before we changed for dinner—

"It is time for bed, Ramses; Nurse will be waiting," I said. "You may take the last cake with you."

Ramses gave me a long, considering look. He then turned to his father, who said cravenly, "Run along, my boy. Papa will read you an extra chapter from his *History of Egypt* when you are tucked in your cot."

"Vewy well," said Ramses. He nodded at me in a manner reminiscent of the regal condescension of his namesake. "You will come and say good night, Mama?"

"I always do," I said.

When he had left the room, taking not only the last cake but the book on zoology, Emerson began pacing up and down.

"I suppose you want another cup of tea," I said.

When I really supposed was that since I had suggested the tea, he would say he did not want it. Like all men, Emerson is very susceptible to the cruder forms of manipulation. Instead he said gruffly, "I want a whiskey and soda."

Emerson seldom imbibes. Trying to conceal my concern, I inquired, "Is something wrong?"

"Not something. Everything. You know, Amelia."

"Were your students unusually dense today?"

"Not at all. It would be impossible for them to be duller than they normally are. I suppose it is all this talk in the newspapers about Luxor that makes me restless."

"I understand."

"Of course you do. You suffer from the same malaise—suffer even more than I, who am at least allowed to hover on the fringes of the profession we both love. I am like a child pressing its nose against the window of the toy shop, but you are not even permitted to walk by the place."

This flight of fancy was so pathetic, and so unlike Emerson's usual style of speaking, that it was with difficulty that I prevented myself from flinging my arms about him. However, he did not want sympathy. He wanted an alleviation of his boredom, and that I could not provide. In some bitterness of spirit I said, "And I have failed to obtain even a poor substitute for your beloved excavations.

After today, Lady Harold will take the greatest pleasure in thwarting any request we might make. It is my fault; I lost my temper."

"Don't be a fool, Peabody," Emerson growled. "No one could make an impression on the solid stupidity of that woman and her husband. I told you not to attempt it."

This touching and magnanimous speech brought tears to my eyes. Seeing my emotion, Emerson added, "You had better join me in a little spirituous consolation. As a general rule I do not approve of drowning one's sorrows, but today has been a trial for both of us."

As I took the glass he handed me I thought how shocked Lady Harold would have been at this further evidence of unwomanly habits. The fact is, I abominate sherry, and I like whiskey and soda.

Emerson raised his glass. The corners of his mouth lifted in a valiant and sardonic smile. "Cheers, Peabody. We'll weather this, as we have weathered other troubles."

"Certainly. Cheers, my dear Emerson."

Solemnly, almost ritually, we drank.

"Another year or two," I said, "and we might consider taking Ramses out with us. He is appallingly healthy; sometimes I feel that to match our son against the fleas and mosquitoes and fevers of Egypt is to place the country under an unfair disadvantage."

This attempt at humor did not win a smile from my husband. He shook his head. "We cannot risk it."

"Well, but the boy must go away to school eventually," I argued.

"I don't see why. He is getting a better education from us than he could hope to obtain in one of those pestilential purgatories called preparatory schools. You know how I feel about them."

"There must be a few decent schools in the country."

"Bah." Emerson swallowed the remainder of his whiskey. "Enough of this depressing subject. What do you say we go upstairs and—"

He stretched out his hand to me. I was about to take it when the door opened and Wilkins made his appearance. Emerson reacts very poorly to being interrupted when he is in a romantic mood. He turned to the butler and shouted, "Curse it, Wilkins, how dare you barge in here? What is it you want?"

None of our servants is at all intimidated by Emerson. Those who survive the first few weeks of his bellowing and temper tantrums learn that he is the kindest of men. Wilkins said calmly, "I beg your pardon, sir. A lady is here to see you and Mrs. Emerson."

"A lady?" As is his habit when perplexed, Emerson fingered the dent in his chin. "Who the devil can that be?"

A wild thought flashed through my mind. Had Lady Harold returned, on vengeance bent? Was she even now in the hall carrying a basket of rotten eggs or a bowl of mud? But that was absurd, she would not have the imagination to think of such a thing.

"Where is the lady?" I inquired.

"Waiting in the hall, madam. I attempted to show her into the small parlor, but—"

Wilkins' slight shrug and raised eyebrow finished the story. The lady had refused to be shown into the parlor. This suggested that she was in some urgency, and it also removed my hope of slipping upstairs to change.

"Show her in, then, Wilkins, if you please," I said.

The lady's urgency was even greater than I had supposed. Wilkins had barely time to step back out of the way before she entered; she was advancing toward us when he made the belated announcement: "Lady Baskerville."

Chapter Two

THE words fell on my ears with almost supernatural force. To see this unexpected visitor, when I had just been thinking and talking about her (and in no kindly terms) made me feel as if the figure now before us was no real woman, but the vision of a distracted mind.

And I must confess that most people would have considered her a vision indeed, a vision of Beauty posing for a portrait of Grief. From the crown of her head to her tiny slippers she was garbed in unrelieved black. How she had passed through the filthy weather without so much as a mud stain I could not imagine, but her shimmering satin skirts and filmy veils were spotless. A profusion of jet beads, sullenly gleaming, covered her bodice and trailed down the folds of her full skirt. The veils fell almost to her feet. The one designed to cover her face had been thrown back so that her pale, oval countenance was framed by the filmy puffs and folds. Her eyes were black; the brows lifted in a high curve that gave her a look of perpetual and innocent surprise. There was no color in her cheeks, but her mouth was a full rich scarlet. The effect of this was startling in the extreme; one could not help thinking of the damnably lovely lamias and vampires of legend.

Also, one could not help thinking of one's mud-stained, unbecoming gown, and wonder whether the aroma of whiskey covered the smell of moldy bone, or the reverse. Even I, who am not easily daunted, felt a pang of self-consciousness. I realized that I was trying to hide my glass, which was still half full, under a sofa cushion.

Though the pause of surprise—for Emerson, like myself, was gaping—
seemed to last forever, I believe it was only a second or two before I regained my
self-possession. Rising to my feet, I greeted our visitor, dismissed Wilkins, offered
a chair and a cup of tea. The lady accepted the chair and refused the tea. I then
expressed my condolences on her recent bereavement, adding that Sir Henry's
death was a great loss to our profession.

This statement jarred Emerson out of his stupor, as I had thought it
might, but for once he showed a modicum of tact, instead of making a rude remark
about Sir Henry's inadequacies as an Egyptologist. Emerson saw no reason why
anything, up to and including death, should excuse a man from poor scholarship.

However, he was not so tactful as to agree with my compliment or add
one of his own. "Er—humph," he said. "Most unfortunate. Sorry to hear of it.
What the deuce do you suppose has become of Armadale?"

"Emerson," I exclaimed. "This is not the time—"

"Pray don't apologize." The lady lifted a delicate white hand, adorned
with a huge mourning ring made of braided hair—that of the late Sir Henry, I
presumed. She turned a charming smile on my husband. "I know Radcliffe's good
heart too well to be deceived by his gruff manner."

Radcliffe indeed! I particularly dislike my husband's first name. I was under
the impression that he did also. Instead of expressing disapproval he simpered like
a schoolboy.

"I was unaware that you two were previously acquainted," I said, finally
managing to dispose of my glass of whiskey behind a bowl of potpourri.

"Oh, yes," said Lady Baskerville, while Emerson continued to grin foolishly at her. "We have not met for several years; but in the early days, when we
were all young and ardent—ardent about Egypt, I mean—we were well acquainted. I was hardly more than a bride—too young, I fear, but my dear Henry
quite swept me off my feet."

She dabbed at her eyes with a black-bordered kerchief.

"There, there," said Emerson, in the voice he sometimes uses with
Ramses. "You must not give way. Time will heal your grief."

This from a man who curled up like a hedgehog when forced into what
he called society, and who never in his life had been known to utter a polite cliché!
He began sidling toward her. In another moment he would pat her on the
shoulder.

"How true," I said. "Lady Baskerville, the weather is inclement, and you
seem very tired. I hope you will join us for dinner, which will be served shortly."

"You are very kind." Lady Baskerville removed her handkerchief from her
eyes, which appeared to be perfectly dry, and bared her teeth at me. "I would not
dream of such an intrusion. I am staying with friends in the neighborhood, who
are expecting me back this evening. Indeed, I would not have come so unceremoniously, unexpected and uninvited, if I had not had an urgent matter to put
before you. I am here on business."

"Indeed," I said.

"Indeed?" Emerson's echo held a questioning note; but in fact I had already deduced the nature of the lady's business. Emerson calls this jumping to conclusions. I call it simple logic.

"Yes," said Lady Baskerville. "And I will come to the point at once, rather than keep you any longer from your domestic comforts. I gather, from your question about poor Alan, that you are au courant about the situation in Luxor?"

"We have followed it with interest," Emerson said.

"We?" The lady's glowing black eyes turned to me with an expression of curiosity. "Ah, yes, I believe I did hear that Mrs. Emerson takes an interest in archaeology. So much the better; I will not bore her if I introduce the subject."

I retrieved my glass of whiskey from behind the potpourri. "No, you will not bore me," I said.

"You are too good. To answer your question, then, Radcliffe: no trace has been found of poor Alan. The situation is swathed in darkness and in mystery. When I think of it I am overcome."

Again the dainty handkerchief came into play. Emerson made clucking noises. I said nothing, but drank my whiskey in ladylike silence.

At last Lady Baskerville resumed. "I can do nothing about the mystery surrounding Alan's disappearance; but I am in hopes of accomplishing something else, which may seem unimportant compared with the loss of human life, but which was vital to the interests of my poor lost husband. The tomb, Radcliffe—the tomb!"

Leaning forward, with clasped hands and parted lips, her bosom heaving, she fixed him with her great black eyes; and Emerson stared back, apparently mesmerized.

"Yes, indeed," I said. "The tomb. We gather, Lady Baskerville, that work has come to a standstill. You know, of course, that sooner or later it will be robbed, and all your husband's efforts wasted."

"Precisely!" The lady turned the clasped hands, the lips, the bosom, et cetera, et cetera, on me. "How I do admire your logical, almost masculine, mind, Mrs. Emerson. That is just what I was trying to express, in my poor silly way."

"I thought you were," I said. "What is it you want my husband to do?"

Thus directed, Lady Baskerville had to get to the point. How long she would have taken if she had been allowed to ramble on, heaven only knows.

"Why, to take over the direction of the excavation," she said. "It must be carried on, and without delay. I honestly believe my darling Henry will not rest quietly in the tomb while this work, possibly the culmination of his splendid career, is in peril. It will be a fitting memorial to one of the finest—"

"Yes, you said that in your interview in the *Yell*," I interrupted. "But why come to us? Is there no scholar in Egypt who could take on the task?"

"But I came first to you," she exclaimed. "I know Radcliffe would have been Henry's first choice, as he is mine."

She had not fallen into my trap. Nothing would have enraged Emerson so much as the admission that she had approached him only as a last resort. And, of course, she was quite correct; Emerson *is* the best.

"Well, Emerson?" I said. I confess, my heart was beating fast as I awaited his answer. A variety of emotions struggled for mastery within my breast. My feelings about Lady Baskerville have, I trust, been made plain; the notion of my husband spending the remainder of the winter with the lady was not pleasing to me. Yet, having beheld his anguish that very evening, I could not stand in his way if he decided to go.

Emerson stood staring at Lady Baskerville, his own feelings writ plainly across his face. His expression was that of a prisoner who had suddenly been offered a pardon after years of confinement. Then his shoulders sagged.

"It is impossible," he said.

"But why?" Lady Baskerville asked. "My dear husband's will specifically provides for the completion of any project that might have been in progress at the time of his demise. The staff—with the exception of Alan—is in Luxor, ready to continue. I confess that the workers have shown a singular reluctance to return to the tomb; they are poor, superstitious things, as you know—"

"That would present no problem," Emerson said, with a sweeping gesture. "No, Lady Baskerville; the difficulty is not in Egypt. It is here. We have a young child. We could not risk taking him to Luxor."

There was a pause. Lady Baskerville's arched brows rose still higher; she turned to me with a look that expressed the question she was too well bred to voice aloud. For really, the objection was, on the face of it, utterly trivial. Most men, given an opportunity such as the one she had offered, would coolly have disposed of half a dozen children, and the same number of wives, in order to accept. It was because this idea had, obviously, not even passed through Emerson's mind that I was nerved to make the noblest gesture of my life.

"Do not consider that, Emerson," I said. I had to pause, to clear my throat; but I went on with a firmness that, if I may say so, did me infinite credit. "Ramses and I will do very well here. We will write every day—"

"Write!" Emerson spun around to face me, his blue eyes blazing, his brow deeply furrowed. An unwitting observer might have thought he was enraged. "What are you talking about? You know I won't go without you."

"But—" I began, my heart overflowing.

"Don't talk nonsense, Peabody. It is out of the question."

If I had not had other sources of deep satisfaction at that moment, the look on Lady Baskerville's face would have been sufficient cause for rejoicing. Emerson's response had taken her completely by surprise; and the astonishment with which she regarded me, as she tried to find some trace of the charms that made a man unwilling to be parted from me, was indeed delightful to behold.

Recovering, she said hesitantly, "If there is any question of a proper establishment for the child—"

"No, no," said Emerson. "That is not the question. I am sorry, Lady Baskerville. What about Petrie?"

"That dreadful man?" Lady Baskerville shuddered. "Henry could not abide him—so rude, so opinionated, so vulgar."

"Naville, then."

"Henry had such a poor opinion of his abilities. Besides, I believe he is under obligation to the Egypt Exploration Fund."

Emerson proposed a few more names. Each was unacceptable. Yet the lady continued to sit, and I wondered what new approach she was contemplating. I wished she would get on with it, or take her leave; I was very hungry, having had no appetite for tea.

Once again my aggravating but useful child rescued me from an unwelcome guest. Our good-night visits to Ramses were an invariable custom. Emerson read to him, and I had my part as well. We were late in coming, and patience is not a conspicuous virtue of Ramses. Having waited, as he thought, long enough, he came in search of us. How he eluded his nurse and the other servants on that particular occasion I do not know, but he had raised evasion to a fine art. The drawing-room doors burst open with such emphasis that one looked for a Herculean form in the doorway. Yet the sight of Ramses in his little white nightgown, his hair curling damply around his beaming face, was not anticlimactic; he looked positively angelic, requiring only wings to resemble one of Raphael's swarthier cherubs.

He was carrying a large folder, clasping it to his infantile bosom with both arms. It was the manuscript of *The History of Egypt*. With his usual single-minded determination he gave the visitor only a glance before trotting over to his father.

"You pwomised to wead to me," he said.

"So I did, so I did." Emerson took the folder. "I will come soon, Ramses. Go back to Nurse."

"No," said Ramses calmly.

"What a little angel," exclaimed Lady Baskerville.

I was about to counter this description with another, more accurate, when Ramses said sweetly, "And you are a pitty lady."

Little did the lady know, as she smiled and blushed, that the apparent compliment was no more than a simple statement of fact, implying nothing of Ramses' feelings of approval or disapproval. In fact, the slight curl of his juvenile lip as he looked at her, and the choice of the word "pretty" rather than "beautiful" (a distinction which Ramses understood perfectly well) made me suspect that, with that fine perception so surprising in a child of his age, which he has inherited from me, he held certain reservations about Lady Baskerville and would, if properly prompted, express them with his customary candor.

Unfortunately, before I could frame an appropriate cue, his father spoke, ordering him again to his nurse, and Ramses, with that chilling calculation that is such an integral part of his character, decided to make use of the visitor for his own purposes. Trotting quickly to her side, he put his finger in his mouth (a habit I broke him of early in his life) and stared at her.

"Vewy pitty lady. Wamses stay wif you."

"Dreadful hypocrite," I said. "Begone."

"He is adorable," murmured Lady Baskerville. "Dear little one, the pretty lady must go away. She would stay if she could. Give me a kiss before I go."

She made no attempt to lift him onto her lap, but bent over and offered a smooth white cheek. Ramses, visibly annoyed at his failure to win a reprieve from bed, planted a loud smacking kiss upon it, leaving a damp patch where once pearl powder had smoothly rested.

"I will go now," Ramses announced, radiating offended dignity. "You come soon, Papa. You too, Mama. Give me my book."

Meekly Emerson surrendered his manuscript and Ramses departed. Lady Baskerville rose.

"I too must go to my proper place," she said, with a smile. "My heartfelt apologies for disturbing you."

"Not at all, not at all," said Emerson. "I am only sorry I was unable to be of help."

"I too. But I understand now. Having seen your darling child and met your charming wife—" Here she grinned at me, and I grinned back—"I comprehend why a man with such affable domestic ties would not wish to leave them for the danger and discomfort of Egypt. My dear Radcliffe, how thoroughly domesticated you have become! It is delightful! You are quite the family man! I am happy to see you settled down at last after those adventurous bachelor years. I don't blame you in the least for refusing. Of course none of us believes in curses, or anything so foolish, but there is certainly something strange going on in Luxor, and only a reckless, bold, free spirit would face such dangers. Good-bye, Radcliffe—Mrs. Emerson—such a pleasure to have met you—no, don't see me out, I beg. I have troubled you enough."

The change in her manner during this speech was remarkable. The soft murmuring voice became brisk and emphatic. She did not pause for breath, but shot out the sharp sentences like bullets. Emerson's face reddened; he tried to speak, but was not given the opportunity. The lady glided from the room, her black veils billowing out like storm clouds.

"Damn!" said Emerson. He stamped his foot.

"She was very impertinent," I agreed.

"Impertinent? On the contrary, she tried to state the unpalatable facts as nicely as possible. 'Quite the family man! Settled down at last!' Good Gad!"

"Now you are talking just like a man," I began angrily.

"How surprising! I am not a man, I am a domesticated old fogy, without the courage or the daring—"

"You are responding precisely as she hoped you would," I exclaimed.

"Can't you see that she chose every word with malicious deliberation? The only one she did not employ was—"

"Henpecked. True, very true. She was too courteous to say it."

"Oh, so you think you are henpecked, do you?"

"Certainly not," said Emerson, with the complete lack of consistency the male sex usually exhibits during an argument. "Not that you don't try—"

"And you try to bully me. If I were not such a strong character—"

The drawing-room doors opened. "Dinner is served," said Wilkins.

"Tell Cook to put it back a quarter of an hour," I said. "We had better tuck Ramses in first, Emerson."

"Yes, yes. I will read to him while you change that abominable frock. I refuse to dine with a woman who looks like an English matron and smells like a compost heap. How dare you say that I bully you?"

"I said you tried. Neither you nor any other man will ever succeed."

Wilkins stepped back as we approached the door.

"Thank you, Wilkins," I said.

"Certainly, madam."

"As for the charge of henpecking—"

"I beg your pardon, madam?"

"I was speaking to Professor Emerson."

"Yes, madam."

"Henpecking was the word I used," snarled Emerson, allowed me to precede him up the stairs. "And henpecking was the word I meant."

"Then why don't you accept the lady's offer? I could see you were panting to do so. What a charming time you two could have, night after night, under the soft Egyptian moon—"

"Oh, don't talk like a fool, Amelia. The poor woman won't go back to Luxor; her memories would be too much to bear."

"Ha!" I laughed sharply. "The naivety of men constantly astonishes me. Of course she will be back. Especially if you are there."

"I have no intention of going."

"No one is preventing you."

We reached the top of the stairs. Emerson turned to the right, to continue up to the nursery. I wheeled left, toward our rooms.

"You will be up shortly, then?" he inquired.

"Ten minutes."

"Very well, my dear."

It required even less than ten minutes to rip the gray gown off and replace it with another. When I reached the night nursery the room was dark except for one lamp, by whose light Emerson sat reading. Ramses, in his crib, contemplated the ceiling with rapt attention. It made a pretty little family scene, until one heard what was being said.

". . . the anatomical details of the wounds, which included a large gash in the frontal bone, a broken malar bone and orbit, and a spear thrust which smashed off the mastoid process and struck the atlas vertebra, allow us to reconstruct the death scene of the king."

"Ah, the mummy of Seqenenre," I said. "Have you got as far as that?"

From the small figure on the cot came a reflective voice. "It appeaws to me that he was muwduwed."

"What?" said Emerson, baffled by the last word.

"Murdered," I interpreted. "I would have to agree, Ramses; a man whose skull has been smashed by repeated blows did not die a natural death."

Sarcasm is wasted on Ramses. "I mean," he insisted, "that it was a domestic cwime."

"Out of the question," Emerson exclaimed. "Petrie has also put forth that absurd idea; it is impossible because—"

"Enough," I said. "It is late and Ramses should be asleep. Cook will be furious if we do not go down at once."

"Oh, very well." Emerson bent over the cot. "Good night, my boy."

"Good night, Papa. One of the ladies of the hawem did it, I think."

I seized Emerson by the arm and pushed him toward the door, before he could pursue this interesting suggestion. After carrying out my part of the nightly ritual (a description of which would serve no useful purpose in the present narrative), I followed Emerson out.

"Really," I said, as we went arm in arm along the corridor, "I wonder if Ramses is not too precocious. Does he know what a harem is, I wonder? And some people might feel that reading such a catalog of horrors to a child at bedtime will not be good for his nerves."

"Ramses has nerves of steel. Rest assured he will sleep the sleep of the just and by breakfast time he will have his theory fully developed."

"Evelyn would be delighted to take him for the winter."

"Oh, so we are back to that, are we? What sort of unnatural mother are you, that you can contemplate abandoning your child?"

"I must choose, it appears, between abandoning my child or my husband."

"False, utterly false. No one is going to abandon anyone."

We took our places at the table. The footman, watched critically by Wilkins, brought on the first course.

"Excellent soup," Emerson said, in a pleased voice. "Tell Cook, will you please, Wilkins?"

Wilkins inclined his head.

"We are going to settle this once and for all," Emerson went on. "I refuse to have you nagging me for days to come."

"I never nag."

"No, because I don't permit it. Get this straight, Amelia: I am not going to Egypt. I have refused Lady Baskerville's offer, and do not mean to reconsider. Is that plain enough?"

"You are making a grave mistake," I said. "I think you should go."

"I am well aware of your opinion. You express it often enough. Why can't you allow me to make up my own mind?"

"Because you are wrong."

There is no need to repeat the remainder of the discussion. It continued throughout the meal, with Emerson appealing from time to time to Wilkins, or to John, the footman, to support a point he was trying to make. This made John, who had been with us only a few weeks, very nervous at first. Gradually, however, he became interested in the discussion and added comments of his own, ignoring the winks and frowns of Wilkins, who had long since learned how to deal with Emerson's unconventional manners. To spare the butler's feelings I said we would have coffee in the drawing room, and John was dismissed, though not before he had said earnestly, "You had better stay here, sir; them natives is strange people, and I'm sure, sir, we would all miss you if you was to go."

Dismissing John did not dismiss the subject, for I stuck to it with my usual determination, despite Emerson's efforts to introduce other topics of conversation. He finally flung his coffee cup into the fireplace with a shout of rage and stormed out of the drawing room. I followed.

When I reached our bedchamber, Emerson was undressing. Coat, tie, and collar were draped inappropriately over various articles of furniture, and buttons flew around the room like projectiles as he removed his shirt.

"You had better purchase another dozen shirts the next time you are in Regent Street," I said, ducking as a button whizzed past my face. "You will need them if you are going abroad."

Emerson whirled. For so burly and broad-chested a man he is surprisingly quick in his movements. In one stride he bridged the space between us. Taking me by the shoulders, he . . .

But here I must pause for a brief comment. Not an apologia—no, indeed! I have always felt that the present-day sanctimonious primness concerning the affection between the sexes, even between husband and wife—an affection sanctified by the Church and legalized by the Nation—is totally absurd. Why should a respectable, interesting activity be passed over by novelists who pretend to portray "real life"? Even more despicable, to my mind, are the circumlocutions practiced by writers on this subject. Not for me the slippery suavity of French or the multi-syllabled pretentiousness of Latin. The good old Anglo-Saxon tongue, the speech of our ancestors, is good enough for me. Let the hypocrites among you, readers, skip the following paragraphs. Despite my reticence on the subject the more discerning will have realized that my feelings for my husband, and his for me, are of the warmest nature. I see no reason to be ashamed of this.

To return to the main stream of the argument, then:

Taking me by the shoulders, Emerson gave me a hearty shake.

"By Gad," he shouted. "I will be master in my own house! Must I teach you again who makes decisions here?"

"I thought we made them together, after discussing problems calmly and courteously."

Emerson's shaking had loosened my hair, which is thick and coarse and does not yield easily to restraint. Still holding me by one shoulder, he passed the fingers of his other hand into the heavy knot at the back of my neck. Combs and hairpins went flying. The hair tumbled down over my shoulders.

I do not recall precisely what he said next. The comment was brief. He kissed me. I was determined not to kiss him back; but Emerson kisses very well. It was some time before I was able to speak. My suggestion that I call my maid to help me out of my frock was not well received. Emerson offered his services. I pointed out that his method of removing a garment often rendered that garment unserviceable thereafter. This comment was greeted with a wordless snort of derision and a vigorous attack upon the hooks and eyes.

After all, much as I commend frankness in such matters, there are areas in which an individual is entitled to privacy. I find myself forced to resort to a typographical euphemism.

By midnight the sleet had stopped falling, and a brisk east wind shook the icy branches of the trees outside our window. They creaked and cracked like spirits of darkness, protesting attack. My cheek rested against my husband's breast; I could hear the steady rhythmic beat of his heart.

"When do we leave?" I inquired softly.

Emerson yawned. "There is a boat on Saturday."

"Good night, Emerson."

"Good night, my darling Peabody."

Chapter Three

 READER, do you believe in magic—in the flying carpets of the old Eastern romances? Of course you don't; but suspend your disbelief for a moment and allow the magic of the printed word to transport you across thousands of miles of space and many hours of time to a scene so different from wet, cold, dismal England that it might be on another planet. Picture yourself sitting with me on the terrace of Shepheard's

Hotel in Cairo. The sky is a brilliant porcelain blue. The sun casts its benevolent rays impartially on rich merchants and ragged beggars, on turbaned imams and tailored European tourists—on all the infinitely varied persons who compose the bustling crowds that traverse the broad thoroughfare before us. A bridal procession passes, preceded by musicians raising cacophonous celebration with flutes and drums. The bride is hidden from curious eyes by a rose silk canopy carried by four of her male relations. Poor girl, she goes from one owner to another, like a bale of merchandise; but at that moment even my indignant contemplation of that most iniquitous of Turkish customs is mellowed by my joy in being where I am. I am filled with the deepest satisfaction. In a few moments Emerson will join me and we will set out for the Museum.

Only one ripple mars the smooth surface of my content. Is it concern for my little son, so far from his mother's tender care? No, dear reader, it is not. The thought that several thousands of miles separate me from Ramses inspired a sense of profound peace such as I have not known for years. I wonder that it never before occurred to me to take a holiday from Ramses.

I knew he would receive from his doting aunt care as tender and devoted as he could expect at home. Walter, who had followed Ramses' developing interest in archeology with profound amusement, had promised to give him lessons in hieroglyphs. I did feel a trifle guilty about Evelyn's children, who were, as Emerson put it, "in for a long, hard winter." But after all, the experience would probably be good for their characters.

It had, of course, proved impossible to leave as soon as Emerson optimistically expected. For one thing, the holidays were almost upon us, and it would have been impossible to leave Ramses only a few days before Christmas. So we spent the festal season with Walter and Evelyn, and by the time we took our departure, on Boxing Day, even Emerson's grief at parting from his son was mitigated by the effects of a week of juvenile excitement and overindulgence. All the children except Ramses had been sick at least once, and Ramses had set the Christmas tree on fire, frightened the nursery maid into fits by displaying his collection of engravings of mummies (some in an advanced state of decrepitude), and . . . But it would require an entire volume to describe all Ramses' activities. On the morning of our departure his infantile features presented a horrific appearance, for he had been badly scratched by little Amelia's kitten while trying to show the animal how to stir the plum pudding with its paw. As the kitchen echoed to the outraged shrieks of the cook and the growls of the cat, he had explained that, since every other member of the household was entitled to stir the pudding for luck in the coming year, he had felt it only fair that the pets should share in the ceremony.

With such memories, is it any wonder that I contemplated a few months away from Ramses with placid satisfaction?

We took the fastest possible route: train to Marseilles, steamer to Alexandria, and train to Cairo. By the time we reached our destination my husband had shed ten years, and as we made our way through the chaos of the Cairo train station he was the old Emerson, shouting orders and expletives in fluent Arabic. His bull-like voice made heads turn and eyes open wide, and we were soon surrounded by old acquaintances, grinning and calling out greetings. White and green turbans bobbed up and down like animated cabbages, and brown hands reached out to grasp our hands. The most touching welcome came from a wizened old beggar, who flung himself on the ground and wrapped his arms around Emerson's dirty boot, crying, "Oh, Father of Curses, you have returned! Now I can die in peace!"

"Bah," said Emerson, trying not to smile. Gently disengaging his foot, he dropped a handful of coins onto the old man's turban.

I had cabled Shepheard's to book rooms as soon as we decided to accept Lady Baskerville's offer, for the hotel is always crowded during the winter season. A magnificent new structure had replaced the rambling old building we had stayed in so often. Italianite in style, it was an imposing edifice with its own generating plant—the first hotel in the East to have electric lights. Emerson grumbled at all the unnecessary luxury. I myself have no objection to comfort so long as it does not interfere with more important activities.

We found messages awaiting us from friends who had heard of Emerson's appointment. There was also a note from Lady Baskerville, who had preceded us by a few days, welcoming us back to Egypt and urging us to proceed as soon as possible to Luxor. Conspicuous by its absence was any word from the Director of Antiquities. I was not surprised. Monsieur Grebaut and Emerson had never admired one another. It would be necessary for us to see him, and Grebaut was making certain we would have to sue humbly for an audience, like any ordinary tourists.

Emerson's comments were profane. When he had calmed down a little, I remarked, "All the same, we had better call on him at once. He can, if he wishes, make difficulties for us."

This sensible suggestion brought on another spell of ranting, in the course of which Emerson predicted Grebaut's future residence in a warm and uncomfortable corner of the universe, and declared that he himself would rather join the rascal in that place than make the slightest concession to rude officiousness. I therefore abandoned the subject for the time being and agreed to Emerson's proposal that we go first to Aziyeh, a village near Cairo from which he had in the past recruited his workmen. If we could take with us to Luxor a skeleton crew of men who were not infected with the local superstitions, we could begin work at once and hope to recruit other workers after success had proved their fears to be vain.

This concession put Emerson in a better mood, so that I was able to persuade him to dine downstairs instead of going to a native eating place in the bazaar. Emerson prefers such places, and so do I; but as I pointed out, we had been a long time away and our resistance to the local diseases had probably decreased. We dared not risk illness, for the slightest malaise would be interpreted as further evidence of the pharaoh's curse.

Emerson was forced to agree with my reasoning. Grumbling and swearing, he got into his boiled shirt and black evening suit. I tied his tie for him and stood back to observe him with pardonable pride. I knew better than to tell him he looked handsome, but indeed he did; his sturdy, upright frame and square shoulders, his thick black hair and his blue eyes blazing with temper formed a splendid picture of an English gentleman.

I had another reason for wishing to dine at the hotel. Shepheard's is the social center for the European colony, and I hoped to meet acquaintances who could bring us up to date on the news of the Luxor expedition.

Nor was I disappointed. When we entered the gilded dining hall the first person I saw was Mr. Wilbour, whom the Arabs call Abd er Dign because of his magnificent beard. White as the finest cotton, it sweeps down to the center of his waistcoat and frames a face both benevolent and highly intelligent. Wilbour had wintered in Egypt for many years. Rude gossip whispered of a political peccadillo in his native New York City, which made it expedient for him to avoid his homeland; but we knew him as an enthusiastic student of Egyptology and a patron of young archeologists. Seeing us, he came at once to greet us and ask us to join his party, which included several other old friends.

I took care to seat myself between Emerson and the Reverend Mr. Sayce; there had been an acrimonious exchange of letters the previous winter on the subject of certain cuneiform tablets. The precaution proved useless. Leaning across me, his elbow planted firmly on the table, Emerson called loudly, "You know, Sayce, that the people at Berlin have confirmed my date for the tablets from Amarna? I told you you were off by eight hundred years."

The Reverend's gentle countenance hardened; and Wilbour quickly intervened. "There was a rather amusing story about that, Emerson; did you hear how Budge managed to trick Grebaut out of those tablets?"

Emerson disliked Mr. Budge of the British Museum almost as much as he did Grebaut, but that evening, with the Director's discourtesy fresh in his mind, he was pleased to hear of anything to Grebaut's discredit. Distracted from his attack on the Reverend, he replied that we had heard rumors of the event but would be glad of a first-hand account.

"It was really a most reprehensible affair in every way," Wilbour said, shaking his head. "Grebaut had already warned Budge that he would be arrested if he continued to purchase and export antiquities illegally. Quite unperturbed, Budge went straight to Luxor and bought not only eighty of the famous tablets but a number of other fine objects. The police promptly moved in, but Grebaut had neglected to provide them with a warrant, so they could only surround the house and wait for our popular Director of Antiquities to arrive with the requisite authority. In the meantime they saw no harm in accepting a fine meal of rice and lamb from the manager of the Luxor Hotel—next to which establishment Budge's house happened to be located. While the honest gendarmes gorged themselves, the hotel gardeners dug a tunnel into the basement of Budge's house and removed the antiquities. By a strange coincidence Grebaut's boat had run aground twenty miles north of Luxor, and he was still there when Budge set out for Cairo with his purchases, leaving the police to guard his empty house."

"Shocking," I said.

"Budge is a scoundrel," Emerson said. "And Grebaut is an idiot."

"Have you seen our dear Director yet?" Sayre inquired.

Emerson made rumbling noises. Sayce smiled. "I quite agree with you. All the same, you will have to see him. The situation is bad enough without incurring Grebaut's enmity. Are you not afraid of the curse of the pharaohs?"

"Bah," said Emerson.

"Quite! All the same, my dear chap, you won't find it easy to hire workers."

"We have our methods," I said, kicking Emerson in the shin to prevent him from explaining those methods. Not that there was anything underhanded in what we planned; no, indeed. I would never be a party to stealing skilled workmen from other archaeologists. If our men from Aziyeh preferred to come with us, that was their choice. I simply saw no point in discussing the possibility before we had made our arrangements. I think Mr. Wilbour suspected something, however; there was an amused gleam in his eyes as he looked at me, but he said nothing, only stroked his beard in a contemplative fashion.

"So what is happening in Luxor?" I asked. "I take it the curse is still alive and well?"

"Good heavens, yes," Mr. Insinger, the Dutch archaeologist, answered. "Marvels and portents abound. Hassan ibn Daoud's pet goat gave birth to a two-headed kid, and ancient Egyptian ghosts haunt the Gurneh hills."

He laughed as he spoke, but Mr. Sayce shook his head sadly.

"Such are the superstitions of paganism. Poor ignorant people!"

Emerson could not let such a statement pass. "I can show you equal ignorance in any modern English village," he snapped. "And you can hardly call the creed of Mohammed paganism, Sayce; it worships the same God and the same prophets you do."

Before the Reverend, flushing angrily, could reply, I said quickly, "It is a pity Mr. Armadale is still missing. His disappearance only adds fuel to the fire."

"It would scarcely improve matters if he were found, I fear," Mr. Wilbour said. "Another death, following that of Lord Baskerville—"

"You believe he is dead, then?" Emerson asked, giving me a sly look.

"He must have perished or he would have turned up by now," Wilbour replied. "No doubt he met with a fatal accident while wandering the hills in a state of distraction. It is a pity; he was a fine archaeologist."

"At any rate, their fears may keep the Gurnawis from trying to break into the tomb," I said.

"You know better than that, my dear Mrs. Emerson," said Insinger. "At any rate, with you and Mr. Emerson on the job, we need not worry about the tomb."

Nothing of further consequence was said that evening, only speculations as to what marvels the tomb might contain. We therefore bid our friends good night as soon as the meal was concluded.

The hour was still early, and the lobby was crowded with people. As we approached the staircase someone darted out from among the throng and caught my arm.

"Mr. and Mrs. Emerson, I presume? Sure, and I've been looking forward to a chat with you. Perhaps you will do me the honor of joining me for coffee or a glass of brandy."

So confident was the tone, so assured the manner, that I had to look twice before I realized that the man was a total stranger. His boyish figure and candid smile made him appear, at first, far too young to be smoking the cigar that protruded at a jaunty angle from his lips. Bright-red hair and a liberal sprinkling of freckles across a decidedly snub nose completed the picture of brash young Ireland, for his accent had been unmistakably of that nation. Seeing me stare at his cigar, he immediately flung it into a nearby container.

"Your pardon, ma'am. In the pleasure of seeing you I forgot my manners."

"Who the devil are you?" Emerson demanded.

The young man's smile broadened. "Kevin O'Connell, of the *Daily Yell,* at your service. Mrs. Emerson, how do you feel about seeing your husband brave the pharaoh's curse? Did you attempt to dissuade him, or do you—"

I caught my husband's arm with both hands and managed to deflect the blow he had aimed at Mr. O'Connell's prominent chin.

"For pity's sake, Emerson—he is half your size!"

This admonition, as I expected, had the effect that an appeal to reason, social decorum, or Christian meekness would not have had. Emerson's arm relaxed and his cheeks turned red—though, I fear, with rising anger rather than shame. Seizing my hand, he proceeded at a brisk pace up the stairs. Mr. O'Connell trotted after us, spouting questions.

"Would you care to venture an opinion as to what has become of Mr. Armadale? Mrs. Emerson, will you take an active part in the excavation? Mr. Emerson, were you previously acquainted with Lady Baskerville? Was it, perhaps, old friendship that prompted you to accept such a perilous position?"

It is impossible to describe the tone of voice in which he uttered the word "friendship," or the indelicate overtone with which he invested that harmless word. I felt my own face grow warm with annoyance. Emerson let out a muted roar. His foot lashed out, and with a startled yelp Mr. O'Connell fell backward and rolled down the stairs.

As we reached the turn of the stair I glanced back and saw, to my relief, that Mr. O'Connell had taken no serious injury. He had already regained his feet and, surrounded by a staring crowd, was engaged in brushing off the seat of his trousers. Meeting my eye, he had the effrontery to wink at me.

Emerson had his coat, tie, and half the buttons of his shirt off before I closed the door of our room.

"Hang it up," I said, as he was about to toss his coat onto a chair. "I declare, Emerson, that is the third shirt you have ruined since we left. Can you never learn—"

But I never finished the admonition. Obeying my order, Emerson had flung open the doors of the wardrobe. There was a flash of light and a thud; Emerson leaped back, one arm held at an unnatural angle. A bright line of red leaped up across his shirt sleeve. Crimson drops rained onto the floor, spattering the handle of the dagger that stood upright between Emerson's feet. Its haft still quivered with the force of its fall.

II

Emerson's hand clamped down on his forearm. The rush of blood slowed and stopped. A pain in the region of my chest reminded me that I was holding my breath. I let it out.

"That shirt was ruined in any case," I said. "Do, pray, hold your arm out so that you do not drip onto your good trousers."

I make it a rule always to remain calm. Nevertheless, it was with considerable speed that I crossed the room, snatching a towel from the washstand as I passed it. I had brought medical supplies with me, as is my custom; in a few moments I had cleaned and bandaged the wound which, fortunately, was not deep. I did not even mention a physician. I was confident that Emerson shared my own feelings on that matter. The news of an accident to the newly appointed director of the Luxor expedition could have disastrous consequences.

When I had finished I leaned back against the divan; and I confess I was unable to repress a sigh. Emerson looked at me seriously. Then a slight smile curved the corners of his mouth.

"You are a trifle pale, Peabody. I trust we are not going to have a display of female vapors?"

"I fail to see any humor in the situation."

"I am surprised at you. For my part, I am struck by the ludicrous ineptitude of the whole business. As nearly as I can make out, the knife was simply placed on the top shelf of the wardrobe, which rests somewhat insecurely on wooden pegs. The vigor of my movement in opening the door caused the weapon to topple out; it was pure accident that it struck me instead of falling harmlessly to the floor. Nor could the unknown have been sure that I would be the one to. . . ." As realization dawned, anger replaced the amusement on his face, and he cried out, "Good Gad, Peabody, you might have been seriously injured if you had been the one to open that wardrobe!"

"I thought you had concluded that no serious injury was contemplated," I reminded him. "No masculine vapors, Emerson, if you please. It was meant as a warning, nothing more."

"Or as an additional demonstration of the effectiveness of the pharaoh's curse. That seems more likely. No one who knows us would expect that we would be deterred from our plans by such a childish trick. Yet unless the incident becomes public knowledge it will be wasted effort."

Our eyes met. I nodded. "You are thinking of Mr. O'Connell. Would he really go to such lengths in order to get a story?"

"These fellows will stop at nothing," Emerson said with gloomy conviction.

He was certainly in a position to know, for during his active career he had featured prominently in sensational newspaper stories. As one reporter had explained to me, "He makes such splendid copy, Mrs. Emerson—always shouting and striking people."

There was some truth in this statement, and Emerson's performance that evening would undoubtedly make equally splendid copy. I could almost see the headlines: "Attack on our reporter by famous archaeologist! Frenzied Emerson reacts violently to question about his intimacy with dead man's widow!"

No wonder Mr. O'Connell had looked so pleased after being kicked down the stairs. He would consider a few bruises a small price to pay for a good story. I remembered his name now. He had been the first to break the story about the curse—or rather, to invent it.

There was no question about Mr. O'Connell's scruples, or lack thereof. Certainly he would have had no difficulty in gaining access to our room. The locks were flimsy, and the servants were amenable to bribery. But was he capable of planning a trick that might have ended in injury, however slight? I found that hard to believe. Brash, rude, and unscrupulous he might be, but I am an excellent judge of character, and I had seen no trace of viciousness in his freckled countenance.

We examined the knife but learned nothing from it; it was a common type, of the sort that can be bought in any bazaar. There was no point in questioning the servants. As Emerson said, the less publicity, the better. So we retired to our bed, with its canopy of fine white mosquito netting. In the ensuing hour I was reassured as to the negligibility of Emerson's wound. It did not seem to inconvenience him in the slightest.

III

We set out for Aziyeh early next morning. Though we had sent no message ahead, the news of our coming had spread, by that mysterious unseen means of communication common to primitive people, so that when our hired carriage stopped in the dusty village square, most of the population was assembled to greet us. Towering over the other heads was a snowy turban surmounting a familiar bearded face. Abdullah had been our reis, or foreman, in the past. His beard was now almost as white as his turban, but his giant frame looked as strong as ever, and a smile of welcome struggled with his instinctive patriarchal dignity as he pushed forward to shake our hands.

We retired to the house of the sheikh, where half the male population crowded into the small parlor. There we sat drinking sweet black tea and exchanging compliments, while the temperature steadily rose. Long periods of courteous silence were broken by repeated comments of "May God preserve you" and "You have honored us." This ceremony can take several hours, but Emerson's audience knew him well, and they exchanged amused glances when, after a mere twenty minutes, he broached the reason for our visit.

"I go to Luxor to carry on the work of the lord who died. Who will come with me?"

The question was followed by soft exclamations and well-feigned looks of surprise. That the surprise was false I had no doubt. Abdullah's was not the only familiar face in the room; many of our other men were there as well. The workers Emerson had trained were always in demand, and I did not doubt that these people had left other positions in order to come to us. Obviously they had anticipated the request and had, in all probability, already decided what they would do.

However, it is not the nature of Egyptians to agree to anything without a good deal of debate and discussion. After an interval Abdullah rose to his feet, his turban brushing the low ceiling.

"Emerson's friendship for us is known," he said. "But why does he not employ the men of Luxor who worked for the dead lord?"

"I prefer to work with my friends," Emerson replied. "Men I can trust in danger and difficulty."

"Ah, yes." Abdullah stroked his beard. "Emerson speaks of danger. It is known that he never lies. Will he tell us what danger he means?"

"Scorpions, snakes, landslides," Emerson shot back. "The same dangers we men have always faced together."

"And the dead who will not die, but walk abroad under the moon?"

This was a much more direct question than I had anticipated. Emerson, too, was caught off guard. He did not answer immediately. Every man in the room sat with his eyes fixed unwinkingly on my husband.

At last he said quietly, "You of all men, Abdullah, know that there is no such thing. Have you forgotten the mummy that was no mummy, but only an evil man?"

"I remember well, Emerson, but who is to say that such things cannot exist? They say that the lord who is dead disturbed the sleep of the pharaoh. They say—"

"They are fools who say so," Emerson interrupted. "Has not God promised the faithful protection against evil spirits? I go to carry on the work. I look for *men* to come with me, not fools and cowards."

The issue had never really been in doubt. When we left the village we had our crew, but thanks to Abdullah's piously expressed doubts we had to agree to a wage considerably higher than was customary. Superstition has its practical uses.

IV

On the following morning I sat, as I have described, on the terrace of Shepheard's and reviewed the events of the past two days. You will now comprehend, reader, why a single small cloud cast a faint shadow on the brightness of my pleasure. The cut on Emerson's arm was healing nicely, but the doubts that incident had raised were not so easily cured. I had taken it for granted that the death of Lord Baskerville and the disappearance of his assistant were parts of a single, isolated tragedy, and that the so-called curse was no more than the invention of an enterprising journalist. The strange case of the knife in the wardrobe raised another and more alarming possibility.

It is foolish to brood about matters one cannot control, so I dismissed the problem for the moment and enjoyed the constantly changing panorama unrolling before me until Emerson finally joined me. I had sent a messenger to Monsieur Grebaut earlier, informing him that we planned to call on him that morning. We were going to be late, thanks to Emerson's procrastination, but when I saw his scowl and his tight-set lips I realized I was fortunate to persuade him to go at all.

Since we were last in Egypt the Museum had been moved from its overcrowded quarters at Boulaq to the Palace of Gizeh. The result was an improvement in the amount of space only; the crumbling, overly ornate decorations of the palace were poorly suited for purposes of display, and the antiquities were in wretched condition. This increased Emerson's bad temper; he was red with annoyance by the time we reached the office, and when a supercilious secretary informed us that we must come back another day, since the Director was too busy to see us, he pushed the young man rudely aside and hurled himself at the door of the inner office.

I was not surprised when it failed to yield, for I had heard a sound like that of a key being turned in a lock. Locks do not hinder Emerson when he wishes to proceed; a second, more vigorous assault burst the door open. With a consoling smile at the cowering secretary I followed my impetuous husband into Grebaut's sanctum.

The room was crowded to the bursting point with open boxes containing antiquities, all awaiting examination and classification. Pots of baked clay, scraps of wood from furniture and coffins, alabaster jars, ushabtis, and dozens of other items overflowed the packing cases onto tables and desk.

Emerson let out a cry of outrage. "It is worse than it was in Maspero's day! Curse the rascal, where is he? I want to give him a piece of my mind!"

When antiquities are visible, Emerson is blind to all else. He did not observe the toes of a pair of rather large boots protruding from under a drapery that covered one side of the room.

"He appears to have stepped out," I replied, watching the boots. "I wonder if there is a door behind those draperies."

The polished toes shrank until only a bare inch remained visible. I assumed Grebaut was pressed up against a wall or a closed window and could retreat no further. He is a rather stout man.

"I have no intention of searching for the wretch," Emerson announced loudly. "I will leave him a note." He began to scrabble in the litter atop the Director's desk. Grebaut's papers and correspondence went flying.

"Calm yourself, Emerson," I said. "Monsieur Grebaut won't thank you for making a mess of his desk."

"I could not make it worse than it is." Emerson tossed away papers with both hands. "Just let me come face to face with that imbecile! He is totally incompetent. I intend to demand his resignation."

"I am thankful he is not here," I said, glancing casually at the drapery. "You have such a temper, Emerson; you are really not accountable for your actions at times like this, and I would hate for you to injure the poor man."

"I would like to injure him. I would like to break both his arms. A man who would allow such neglect—"

"Why don't you leave a message with the secretary?" I suggested. "He must have pen and paper on his desk. You will never find it there."

With a final gesture that sent the remaining papers sailing around the room, Emerson stamped out. The secretary had fled. Emerson seized his pen and began scribbling furiously on a sheet of paper. I stood in the open doorway, one eye on Emerson, one eye on the boots; and I said loudly, "You might suggest, Emerson, that Monsieur Grebaut send the firman giving you charge of the expedition to our hotel. That will save you another trip."

"Good idea," Emerson grunted. "If I have to come again I *will* murder that moron."

Gently I closed the door of Grebaut's office.

We took our departure. Three hours later a messenger delivered the firman to our room.

Chapter Four

ON my first trip to Egypt I had traveled by dahabeeyah. The elegance and charm of that mode of travel can only be dimly imagined by those who have not experienced it. My boat had been equipped with every comfort, including a grand piano in the salon and an outdoor sitting room on the upper deck. How many blissful hours did I spend there, under the billowing sails, drinking tea and listening to the songs of the sailors while the magnificent panorama of Egyptian life glided by on either side—villages and temples, palm trees, camels, and holy hermits perched precariously on pillars. How fond were my memories of that journey, which had culminated in my betrothal to my spouse! How gladly would I have repeated that glorious experience!

Alas, on this occasion we could not spare the time. The railroad had been extended as far south as Assiût, and since it was by far the fastest means of travel, we endured eleven hours of heat, jolting, and dust. From Assiut we took a steamer for the remaining distance. Though less uncomfortable than the train, it was a far cry from my dear dahabeeyah.

On the day we were to dock at Luxor I was on deck at dawn, hanging over the rail and gaping like any ignorant Cook's tourist. The Luxor temple had been cleared of the shacks and huts that had so long marred its beauty; its columns and pylons glowed rosy pink in the morning light as the steamer glided in to the dock.

Here the peaceful visions of the past were replaced by noisy modern bustle, as porters and guides converged on the disembarking passengers. The dragomen of the Luxor hotels shouted out the advantages of their various hostelries and attempted to drag bewildered tourists into the waiting carriages. No one bothered us.

Emerson went off to collect our luggage and locate our workmen, who had traveled in the same boat. Leaning on my parasol, I gazed complacently at the scene and took deep breaths of the soft air. Then a hand touched my arm, and I turned to meet the intense gaze of a stout young man wearing gold-rimmed spectacles and the most enormous pair of mustaches I had ever seen. The ends of them curled up and around like the horns of a mountain goat.

Heels together, body stiff, he bent himself at the waist and said, "Frau Professor Emerson? Karl von Bork, the epigrapher of the ill-fated Baskerville expedition. To Luxor I give you greeting. By Lady Baskerville was I sent. Where is the Professor? Long have I to the honor of meeting him looked forward. The brother of the so distinguished Walter Emerson—"

This rapid spate of conversation was all the more remarkable because the young man's face remained utterly expressionless throughout. Only his lips and the gigantic mustache above them moved. As I was to learn, Karl von Bork spoke seldom, but once he began to talk, it was virtually impossible to stop him except by the means I adopted on that occasion.

"How do you do," I said loudly, drowning out his last words. "I am pleased to meet you. My husband is just . . . Where is he? Ah, Emerson; allow me to present Herr von Bork."

Emerson grasped the young man's hand. "The epigrapher? Good. I trust you have a boat ready—one of sufficient size. I have brought twenty men with me from Cairo."

Von Bork bowed again. "An excellent idea, Herr Professor. A stroke of genius! But I had expected nothing less from the brother of the distinguished—"

I interrupted this speech, as I had interrupted the first; and we found that when Herr von Bork was not talking he was efficient enough to please even my demanding husband. The felucca he had hired was commodious enough to hold us all. Our men gathered in the bow, looking loftily at the boatmen and making comments about the stupidity of Luxor men. The great sails swelled, the prow dipped and swung about; we turned our backs on the ancient temples and modern houses of Luxor and moved out onto the broad bosom of the Nile.

I could not help but be keenly sensitive to the implications of this westward journey, the same one made by generations of Thebans when, the troubles of life behind them, they set sail on the road to heaven. The rugged western cliffs, gilded by the morning sun, had for thousands of years been honeycombed by tombs of noble, pharaoh, and humble peasant. The ruined remains of once-great mortuary temples began to take shape as we drew near the shore: the curving white colonnades of Deir el Bahri, the frowning walls of the Ramesseum, and, towering above the plain, those colossal statues that alone remained of Amenhotep the Third's magnificent temple. Even more evocative were the wonders we could not see—the hidden, rock-cut sepulchers of the dead. As I looked, my heart swelled within me, and the last four years in England seemed but a horrid dream.

The sound of von Bork's voice roused me from my blissful contemplation of that gigantic cemetery. I hoped the young man would not continue to refer to Emerson as the brother of the distinguished Walter. Emerson has the highest regard for Walter's abilities, but one could hardly blame him for taking umbrage at being regarded only as an appendage to his brother. Von Bork's specialty was the study of the ancient language, so it was not surprising that he should venerate Walter's contributions to that field.

However, von Bork was merely telling Emerson the latest news.

"I have, at Lady Baskerville's orders, a heavy steel door at the entrance to the tomb erected. In the Valley reside two guards under the authority of a sub-inspector of the Antiquities Department—"

"Useless!" Emerson exclaimed. "Many of the guards are related to the tomb robbers of Gurneh, or are so woefully superstitious that they will not leave their huts after dark. You ought to have guarded the tomb yourself, von Bork."

"*Sie haben recht,* Herr Professor," the young German murmured submissively. "But difficult it was; only Milverton and myself remain, and he of a fever has been ill. He—"

"Mr. Milverton is the photographer?" I asked.

"Quite correct, Frau Professor. The expedition staff of the finest was; now that you and the Professor have come, only an artist is lacking. Mr. Armadale that task performed, and I do not—"

"But that is a serious lack," Emerson remarked. "Where are we to find an artist? If only Evelyn had not abandoned a promising career. She had a nice touch. She might have amounted to something."

Considering that Evelyn was one of the wealthiest women in England, the devoted mother of three lovely children and the adoring wife of a man who doted on her every movement, I could not see that she had lost a great deal. However, I knew there was no sense in pointing this out to Emerson. I therefore contented myself with remarking, "She has promised to come out with us again after the children are in school."

"Yes, but when will that be? She keeps on producing the creatures in endless succession and shows no sign of stopping. I am fond of my brother and his wife, but a continual progression of miniature Evelyns and Walters is a bit too much. The human race—"

When the human race entered the discussion I stopped listening. Emerson is capable of ranting on that subject for hours.

"If I may suggest," von Bork said hesitantly.

I looked at him in surprise. The tentative tone was quite unlike his usual confident voice, and although his countenance remained impassive, his sunburned cheeks had turned a trifle pink.

"Yes, certainly," said Emerson, as surprised as I.

Von Bork cleared his throat self-consciously. "There is a young lady—an English lady—in Luxor village who is an accomplished painter. In an emergency she might be persuaded . . ."

Emerson's face fell. I sympathized; I shared his opinion of young lady artists of the amateur persuasion.

"It is early days yet," I said tactfully. "When we have uncovered something worth copying, we can worry about a painter. But I thank you for the suggestion, Herr von Bork. I believe I will call you Karl. It is easier and more friendly. You do not object, I hope?"

By the time he had finished assuring me that he did not, we were docking on the west bank.

Thanks to Karl's efficiency and Emerson's curses, we soon found ourselves mounted on donkeyback and ready to proceed. Leaving Abdullah to arrange for the transport of the men and the baggage, we set out across the fields, now green with crops. The pace of a donkey is leisurely in the extreme, so we were able to converse as we rode along; and as we came near to the place where the fertile black soil left by the annual inundation gives way to the red desert sands, Emerson said abruptly, "We will go by way of Gurneh."

Karl was more relaxed now that he had performed his task of greeting and transporting us without mishap; I observed that when he was calm he was able to keep his verbs straight instead of relapsing into tortuous German sentence structure.

"It is not the direct path," he objected. "I had thought you and Mrs. Emerson would wish to rest and refresh yourselves after—"

"I have my reasons for suggesting it," Emerson replied.

"*Aber natürlich!* Whatever the Professor wishes."

Our donkeys crossed into the desert, a line so distinct that their front feet pressed the hot sands while their back feet were still on the cultivated land. The village of Gurneh is several hundred yards beyond the cultivation, in the rocky foothills of the mountains. The huts of sun-dried brick blend into the pale-brown rock of the hillside. One might wonder why the residents, who have lived in this place for hundreds of years, do not seek a more comfortable locale. They have solid economic reasons for remaining, for they make their livelihood on that spot. Between the huts and under their very floors lie the ancient tombs whose treasures form the inhabitants' source of income. In the hills behind the village, a convenient half-hour's walk away, are the narrow valleys where the kings and queens of the Empire were buried.

We heard the sounds of the village before we could make out its dwellings—the voices of children, the barking of dogs, and the bleating of goats. The cupola of the old village mosque could be seen on the desert slope, and a few palms and sycamores half concealed a row of antique columns. Emerson headed toward these, and before long I realized why he had chosen that route. A precious spring of water was there, with a broken sarcophagus serving as a cattle trough. The village well is always a scene of much activity, with women filling their jars and men watering their beasts. Silence descended upon the group as we approached, and all movement was suspended. The jars remained poised in the arms of the women; the men stopped smoking and gossiping as they stared at our little caravan.

Emerson called out a greeting in sonorous Arabic. He did not pause or wait for a reply. At as stately a pace as a small donkey could command he rode past, with Karl and me following. Not until we had left the well far behind did I hear the sounds of renewed activity.

As our patient beasts plodded across the sand, I allowed Emerson to remain a few feet ahead, a position he much enjoys and seldom obtains. I could see by the arrogant set of his shoulders that he fancied himself in the role of gallant commander, leading his troops; and I saw no reason to point out that no man can possibly look impressive on donkeyback, particularly when his legs are so long he must hold them out at a forty-five-degree angle to keep his feet from dragging on the ground. (Emerson is not unusually tall; the donkeys are unusually small.)

"For what was this?" Karl asked in a low voice, as we rode side by side. "I understand it not. To ask the Professor I do not dare; but you, his companion and—"

"I have not the least objection to explaining," I replied. "Emerson has flung down the gauntlet to that pack of thieves. In effect he has said: 'I am here. I do not fear you. You know who I am; interfere with me at your peril.' It was well done, Karl; one of Emerson's better performances, if I may say so."

Unlike Karl, I had not troubled to moderate my voice. Emerson's shoulders twitched irritably, but he did not turn around. After an interval we rounded a rocky spur and saw before us the curving bay that shelters the ruined temples of Deir el Bahri, near which the house was situated.

Most readers, I imagine, are familiar with the appearance of the now-famous Baskerville Expedition House, since photographs and engravings of it have been featured in numerous periodicals. I had never happened to see the place myself, since it was still under construction on the occasion of our last visit to Luxor, and though I had seen reproductions and plans, my first sight of the place impressed me considerably. Like most Eastern houses it was built around a courtyard, with rooms on all four sides. A wide gate in the center of one side admitted visitors to the courtyard, onto which the chambers opened. The material was the usual mud brick, neatly plastered and whitewashed, but the size was enormous, and it had suited Lord Baskerville's fancy to decorate it in ancient Egyptian style. The gate and the windows were capped by wooden lintels painted with Egyptian motifs in bright colors. Along one side a row of columns with gilded lotus capitals supported a pleasant shady loggia, where orange and lemon trees grew in earthenware pots and green vines twined around the columns. A nearby spring provided water for palm and fig trees; and in the brilliant sunlight the white walls and archaic decoration reminded us of what the ancient palaces must have looked like before time reduced them to heaps of mud.

My husband has no appreciation of architecture unless it is three thousand years old. "The devil!" he exclaimed. "What a frightful waste of money!"

We had slowed our animals to a walk, the better to appreciate our first view of our new home. My donkey misinterpreted this gesture. It came to a complete standstill. I refused Karl's offer of a stick—I do not believe in beating animals—and spoke sternly to the donkey. It gave me a startled look and then proceeded. I promised myself that as soon as I had time I would examine the animal and any others hired by Lord Baskerville. These poor beasts were wretchedly treated and often ·suffered from saddle sores and infections caused by inadequate cleanliness. I never permitted that sort of thing in my other expeditions and did not intend to allow it here.

The wooden gates swung open as we approached, and we rode directly into the courtyard. Pillars supported a cloister-like walkway, roofed with red tiles, which ran along three sides. All the rooms opened onto this open-sided corridor, and at my request Karl took us on a brief tour of inspection. I could not help but be impressed at the forethought that had gone into the arrangement of the house; if I had not known better, I would have thought a woman had planned it. A number of bedchambers, small but comfortable, had been designed for the use of the staff and for visitors. Larger chambers, as well as a small room which served as a bath, had been reserved for Lord and Lady Baskerville. Karl informed us that his lordship's room was now ours and I found the arrangements all I could wish. One section of the room had been fitted out as a study, with a long table and a row of bookshelves containing an Egyptological library.

Today such accommodations are not unique, and archaeological staffs are often large; but at that time, when an expedition sometimes consisted of one harassed scholar directing the diggers, keeping his own records and accounts, cooking his own meals and washing his own stockings—if he bothered to wear them—Baskerville House was a phenomenon. One entire wing contained a large dining room and a sizable parlor or common room, which opened onto the columned loggia. The furnishings of this latter chamber were a curious blend of the ancient and modern. Woven mattings covered the floor, and filmy white curtains at the long French doors helped to keep out insects. Chairs and couches were of royal-blue plush; the picture frames and mirrors were heavily carved and gilded. There was even a Gramophone with a large collection of operatic recordings, the late Sir Henry having been a devotee of that form of music.

As we entered, a man rose from the sofa on which he had been reclining. His pallor, and the unsteadiness of his gait as he advanced to meet us, rendered Karl's introduction unnecessary; this was the ailing Mr. Milverton. I immediately led him back to the sofa and placed my hand on his brow.

"Your fever is gone," I said. "But you are still suffering from the debility produced by the illness and should not have left your bed."

"For heaven's sake, Amelia, restrain yourself," Emerson grumbled. "I had hoped that on this expedition you would not succumb to your delusion that you are a qualified physician."

I knew the cause of his ill temper. Mr. Milverton was an extremely handsome young fellow. The slow smile that spread across his face as he glanced from me to my husband showed even white teeth and well-cut lips. His golden locks fell in becoming disarray over a high white brow. Yet his good looks were entirely masculine and his constitution had not been seriously impaired by his illness; the breadth of his chest and shoulders were those of a young athlete.

"You are more than kind, Mrs. Emerson," he said. "I assure you, I am quite recovered and have been looking forward to meeting you and your famous husband."

"Humph," said Emerson, in a slightly more genial tone. "Very well; we will begin tomorrow morning—"

"Mr. Milverton should not risk the noonday sun for several days," I said.

"Again I remind you," said Emerson, "that you are not a physician."

"And I remind you of what happened to you on one occasion when you disregarded my medical advice."

A singularly evil look spread over Emerson's features. Deliberately he turned from me to Karl. "And where is Lady Baskerville?" he inquired. "A delightful woman!"

"She is," said Karl. "And I have for you, Professor, a particular message from that most distinguished lady. She stays at the Luxor Hotel; it would not be proper, you understand, for her to inhabit this place without another lady to companion her, now that her esteemed husband—"

"Yes, yes," Emerson said impatiently. "What is the message?"

"She wishes you—and Mrs. Emerson, of course—to dine with her this evening at the hotel."

"Splendid, splendid," Emerson exclaimed vivaciously. "How I look forward to the meeting!"

Needless to say, I was quite amused at Emerson's transparent attempt to annoy me by professing admiration for Lady Baskerville. I said calmly, "If we are dining at the hotel you had better unpack, Emerson; your evening clothes will be sadly wrinkled. You, Mr. Milverton, must go back to bed at once. I will visit you shortly to make sure you have everything you need. First I will inspect the kitchen and speak to the cook. Karl, you had better introduce me to the domestic staff. Have you had difficulty in keeping servants?"

Taking Karl firmly by the arm, I left the room before Emerson could think of a reply.

The kitchen was in a separate building behind the main house, a most sensible arrangement in a hot climate. As we approached, a variety of delicious aromas told me that luncheon was being prepared. Karl explained that most of the house servants were still at their jobs. Apparently they felt there was no danger in serving the foreigners so long as they did not actively participate in the desecration of the tomb.

I was pleased to recognize an old acquaintance in Ahmed the chef, who had once been employed at Shepheard's. He seemed equally happy to see me.

After we had exchanged compliments and inquiries concerning the health of our families I took my leave, happy to find that in this area at least I would not have to exercise constant supervision.

I found Emerson in our room going through his books and papers. The suitcases containing his clothes had not been opened. The young servant whose task it was to unpack them squatted on the floor, talking animatedly with Emerson.

"Mohammed has been telling me the news," Emerson said cheerfully. "He is the son of Ahmed the chef—you remember—"

"Yes, I have just spoken to Ahmed. Luncheon will be ready shortly." As I spoke I extracted the keys from Emerson's pocket; he continued to sort his papers. I handed the keys to Mohammed, a slender stripling with the luminous eyes and delicate beauty these lads often exhibit; with my assistance he soon completed his task and departed. I observed with pleasure that he had filled the water jar and laid out towels.

"Alone at last," I said humorously, unbuttoning my dress. "How refreshing that water looks! I am sadly in need of a wash and change, after last night."

I hung my dress in the wardrobe and was about to turn when Emerson's arms came round my waist and pressed me close.

"Last night was certainly unsatisfactory," he murmured (or at least he thought he was murmuring; Emerson's best attempt at this sound is a growling roar, exceedingly painful to the ear). "What with the hardness of the bunks and their extreme narrowness, and the motion of the ship—"

"Now, Emerson, there is no time for that now," I said, attempting to free myself. "We have a great deal to do. Have you made arrangements for our men?"

"Yes, yes, it is all taken care of. Peabody, have I ever told you how much I admire the shape of your—"

"You have." I removed his hand from the area in question, though I confess it required some willpower for me to do so. "There is no time for that now. I would like to walk across to the Valley this afternoon and have a look at the tomb."

It is no insult to me to admit that the prospect of archaeological investigation is the one thing that can distract Emerson from what he was doing at that moment.

"Hmmm, yes," he said thoughtfully. "It will be hot as the hinges of Hades, you know."

"All the better; the Cook's people will have gone and we will enjoy a little peace and quiet. We must leave immediately after luncheon if we are to dine with Lady Baskerville this evening."

So it was agreed, and for the first time in many years we assumed our working attire. A thrill permeated my being to its very depths when I beheld my dear Emerson in the garments in which he had first won my heart. (I speak figuratively, of course; those original garments had long since been turned into rags.) His rolled-up sleeves bared his brawny arms, his open collar displayed his strong brown throat. With an effort I conquered my emotion and led the way to the dining room.

Karl was waiting for us. I was not surprised to find him prompt at his meals; his contours indicated that a poor appetite was not one of his difficulties. A look of faint surprise crossed his features when he saw me.

In my early days in Egypt I had been vexed by the convention that restricted women to long, inconveniently trailing skirts. These garments are wholly unsuited to climbing, running, and the active aspects of archaeological excavation. I had progressed from skirts to Rationals, from Rationals to a form of bloomer; in my last season I had taken the bull by the horns and ordered a costume that seemed to me to combine utility with womanly modesty. In a land where snakes and scorpions abound, stout boots are a necessity. Mine reached to the knees and there met my breeches, cut with considerable fullness, and tucked into the boot tops in order to avoid any possibility of accidental disarrangement. Over the breeches I wore a knee-length tunic, open at the sides to allow for the stretching of the lower limbs to their widest extent, in case rapid locomotion, of pursuit or of flight, became desirable. The costume was completed by a broad-brimmed hat and a stout belt equipped with hooks for knife, pistol, and other implements.

A similar costume became popular for hunting a year or two later, and although I never received any credit for my innovation, I do not doubt that it was my example that broke the ice.

When he heard of our plans for that afternoon, Karl offered to accompany us, but we declined, wishing to be alone on this first occasion. There is a carriage road, of sorts, leading through a cleft in the cliffs to the Valley where the royal dead of Egypt were entombed; but we took the more direct path, over the high plateau behind Deir el Bahri. Once we left the shady grove and the gardens the sun beat down upon us; but I could not repine, as I remembered the dreary winter weather and tedious routine we had left behind.

A brisk scramble up a rocky, steep incline brought us to the top of the plateau. There we paused for a moment to catch our breath and enjoy the view. Ahead lay a rough waste of barren stone; behind and below, the width of the Nile Valley lay spread out like a master painting. The temple of Queen Hatasu, cleared by Maspero, looked like a child's model. Beyond the desert the fields bordered the river like an emerald-green ribbon. The air was so clear that we could make out the miniature shapes of the pylons and columns of the eastern temples. To the south rose the great pyramid-shaped peak known as the Goddess of the West, she who guards the ancient sepulchers.

Emerson began to hum. He has a perfectly appalling singing voice and no idea whatever of pitch, but I made no objection, even when words emerged from his drone.

> . . . from Coffee and from
> supper rooms, from Poplar to Pall Mall,
> The girls on seeing me exclaim, "O what a
> champagne swell!"

I joined in.

> Champagne Charlie is my name, good for any
> game
> at night, boys, who'll come and join me in a spree?

Emerson's hand reached for mine. In perfect harmony of soul (if not voice) we proceeded; and I did not feel that our melodies profaned that solemn spot since they arose from joyful anticipation of a noble work.

At the end of our stroll we found ourselves on the edge of a cliff looking down into a canyon. Rocky walls and barren floor were of the same unrelieved drab brown, bleached by the sunlight to the color of a pale and unpalatable pudding. A few small patches of shadow, abbreviated by the height of the sun, were the only breaks in the monotony—except for the rectangular black openings that had given the Valley of the Kings its name. They were the doorways of royal tombs.

I was gratified to observe that my hope of relative privacy had been correct. The tourists had departed to their hotels, and the only living objects to be seen were shapeless bundles of rags that covered the sleeping forms of the Egyptian guides and guards whose work lay in the Valley. But no!—with chagrin I revised my first impression when I beheld a moving figure. It was too far away for me to see more than its general outline, which was that of a tall male person in European clothing. It appeared to be engaged in rapt contemplation of the surrounding cliffs.

Though we had never visited the tomb which was the object of our present quest, I have no doubt that Emerson could have drawn an accurate map of its precise location. I know I could have. Our eyes were drawn to it as if by a magnet.

It lay below, on the opposite side of the Valley from where we stood. The steep, almost vertical configuration of the cliffs framed it like a theatrical backdrop. At the foot of the cliff was a long slope of rock and gravel, broken by heaps of rubble from earlier excavations, and by a few modern huts and storage buildings. A triangular cut into the gravel framed the doorway of the tomb of Ramses VI. Below this, and to the left, I saw the stout iron gate to which Karl had referred. Two dusty bundles—the alert guards Grebaut had appointed to guard the tomb— lay near the gate.

Emerson's hand tightened on mine. "Only think," he said softly, "what wonders that bare rock still hides! The tombs of Thutmose the Great, of Amenhotep the Second and Queen Hatasu. . . . Even another cache of royal mummies like the one found in 1881. Which of them awaits our labor?"

I shared his sentiments, but his fingers were crushing my hand. I pointed this out. With a deep sigh Emerson returned to practicality. Together we scrambled down the path to the floor of the Valley.

The sleeping guards did not stir even when we stood over them. Emerson prodded one bundle with his toe. It quivered; a malevolent black eye appeared among the rags, and from a concealed mouth a spate of vulgar Arabic curses assailed us. Emerson replied in kind. The bundle sprang to its feet and the rags parted to reveal one of the evilest faces I have ever beheld, seamed by lines and scars. One eye was a milky-white, sightless blank. The other eye glared widely at Emerson.

"Ah," said my husband, in Arabic, "it is thou, Habib. I thought the police had locked thee up forever. What madman gave to thee a task proper to an honest man?"

They say the eyes are the mirror of the soul. In this case Habib's one serviceable orb displayed, for a moment, the intensity of his real feelings. Only for a moment; then he groveled in a deep obeisance, mumbling greetings, apologies, explanations—and assurances that he had given over his evil ways and merited the trust of the Antiquities Department.

"Humph," said Emerson, unimpressed. "Allah knows thy true heart, Habib; I have not his all-seeing eye, but I have my doubts. I am going into the tomb. Get out of the way."

The other guard had roused himself by this time and was also bowing and babbling. His countenance was not quite as villainous as Habib's, probably because he was somewhat younger.

"Alas, great lord, I have no key," said Habib.

"But I have," said Emerson, producing it.

The gate had been cemented into place across the doorway. The bars were stout, the padlock massive; yet I knew they would prove no lasting impediment to men who have been known to tunnel through solid rock in order to rob the dead. When the grille swung open we were confronted with the sealed doorway that had frustrated Lord Baskerville on the last day of his life. Nothing had been touched since that hour. The small hole opened by Armadale still gaped, the only break in the wall of stones.

Lighting a candle, Emerson held it to the opening and we both looked in, bumping heads in our eagerness. I had known what to expect, and yet it was dampening to the spirits to behold a heap of rocky rubble that completely concealed whatever lay beyond.

"So far, so good," Emerson remarked. "No one has attempted to enter since Baskerville's death. Frankly, I expected that our friends from Gurneh would have tried to break in long before this."

"The fact that they have not makes me suspect that we have a long job ahead of us," I said. "Perhaps they are waiting for us to clear the passageway so they can get at the burial chamber without having to engage in boring manual labor."

"You may be right. Though I hope you are wrong about the extent of clearance necessary; as a rule the rubble fill does not extend beyond the stairwell."

"Belzoni mentions climbing over heaps of rubble when he entered Seti's tomb, in 1844," I reminded him.

"The cases are hardly parallel. That tomb had been robbed and re-used for later burials. The debris Belzoni described . . ."

We were engaged in a delightfully animated archaeological discussion when there was an interruption. "Hello, down there," called a loud, cheery voice. "May I join you, or will you come up?"

Turning, I beheld a form silhouetted against the bright rectangle of the opening at the head of the stairs. It was that of the tall personage I had noticed earlier, but I could not see it clearly until we had ascended the stairs—for Emerson promptly replied that we would come up. He was not anxious to have any stranger approach his new toy.

The form revealed itself to be that of a very tall, very thin gentleman with a lean, humorous face and hair of that indeterminate shade which may be either fair or gray. His accent had already betrayed his nationality, and as soon as we emerged from the stairway he continued in the exuberant strain typical of the natives of our erstwhile colony. (I flatter myself that I reproduce the peculiarities of the American dialect quite accurately.)

"Well, now, I declare, this is a real sure-enough pleasure. I don't need to ask who you are, do I? Let me introduce myself—Cyrus Vandergelt, New York, U.S.A.—at your service, ma'am, and yours, Professor Emerson."

I recognized the name, as anyone familiar with Egyptology must have done. Mr. Vandergelt was the American equivalent of Lord Baskerville—enthusiastic amateur, wealthy patron of archaeology.

"I knew you were in Luxor," Emerson remarked unenthusiastically, taking the hand Mr. Vandergelt had thrust at him. "But I did not expect to meet you so soon."

"You probably wonder what I am doing here at this goldurned hour," Vandergelt replied with a chuckle. "Well, folks, I am just like you—we are birds of a feather. It would take more than a little heat to keep me from what I mean to do."

"And what is that?" I inquired.

"Why, to meet you, sure enough. I figured you would get out here just the minute you arrived. And, ma'am, if you will permit me to say so, the sight of you would make any effort worthwhile. I am—I make no bones about it, ma'am, indeed I say it with pride—I am a most assiduous admirer of the ladies and a connoisseur, in the most respectable sense, of female loveliness."

It was impossible to take offense at his words, they displayed such irrepressible trans-Atlantic good humor and such excellent taste. I allowed my lips to relax into a smile.

"Bah," said Emerson. "I know you by reputation, Vandergelt, and I know why you are here. You want to steal my tomb."

Mr. Vandergelt grinned broadly. "I sure would if I could. Not just the tomb, but you and Mrs. Emerson to dig it out for me. But"—and here he became quite serious—"Lady Baskerville has set her heart on doing this as a memorial to the dear departed, and I am not the man to stand in a lady's way, particularly when her aim is so fraught with touching sentiment. No, sir; Cyrus Vandergelt is not the man to try low tricks. I only want to help. Call on me for any assistance you may require."

As he spoke, he straightened to his full height—which was well over six feet—and raised his hand as if taking an oath. It was an impressive sight; one almost expected to see the Stars and Bars waving in the breeze and hearing the stirring strains of "Oh Beautiful America."

"You mean," Emerson retorted, "that you want to get in on the fun."

"Ha, ha," said Vandergelt cheerfully. He gave Emerson a slap on the back. "I said we were alike, didn't I? There's no fooling a sharp lad like you. Sure I do. If you don't let me play, I'll drive you crazy thinking of excuses to drop in. No, but seriously, folks, you're going to need all the help you can get. Those Gurneh crooks are going to be on you like a hornets' nest, and the local imam is stirring up the congregation in a fancy way. If I can't do anything else, I can at least help guard the tomb, and the ladies. But look, why are we standing here jawing in the hot sun? I've got my carriage down at the other end of the Valley; let me give you a lift home and we can talk some more."

We declined this offer, and Mr. Vandergelt took his leave, remarking, "You haven't seen the last of me, folks. You're dining with Lady Baskerville tonight? Me, too. I'll see you then."

I fully expected a diatribe from Emerson on Mr. Vandergelt's manners and motives, but he was uncharacteristically silent on the subject. After a further examination of what little could be seen we prepared to go; and then I realized Habib was no longer with us. The other guard burst into a garbled explanation, which Emerson cut short.

"I was about to dismiss him anyway," he remarked, addressing me but speaking in Arabic for the benefit of anyone who might be listening. "Good riddance."

The shadows were lengthening when we started the climb up the cliff, and I urged Emerson, who was preceding me, to greater haste. I wanted ample time to prepare for the evening's encounter. We had almost reached the top when a sound made me glance up. I then seized Emerson by the ankles and pulled him down. The boulder which I had seen teetering on the brink missed him by less than a foot, sending splinters of rock flying in every direction when it struck.

Slowly Emerson rose to his feet. "I do wish, Peabody, that you could be a little less abrupt in your methods," he remarked, using his sleeve to wipe away the blood that was dripping from his nose. "A calm 'Watch out, there,' or a tug at my shirttail would have proved just as effective, and less painful."

This was a ridiculous statement, of course; but I was given no time to reply to it, for as soon as Emerson had ascertained, with one quick glance, that I was unharmed, he turned and began to climb with considerable speed, vanishing at last over the rim of the cliff. I followed. When I reached the top he was nowhere in sight, so I sat down on a rock to wait for him, and—to be candid—to compose my nerves, which were somewhat shaken.

The tentative theory I had briefly considered in Cairo was now strengthened. Someone was determined to prevent Emerson from continuing the work Lord Baskerville had begun. Whether the latter's death had formed part of this plan, or whether the unknown miscreant had made use of a tragic accident in order to further his scheme I could not then make out, but I felt sure we had not seen the last of attempts aimed at my husband. How glad I was that I had yielded to what had seemed a selfish impulse and come with him. The apparent conflict between my duty to my husband and my duty to my child had been no conflict. Ramses was safe and happy; Emerson was in deadly danger, and my place was at his side, guarding him from peril.

As I mused I saw Emerson reappear from behind a heap of boulders some distance from the path. His face was smeared with blood, and his eyes bulged with rage, so that he presented quite a formidable sight.

"He got away, did he?" I said.

"Not a trace. I would not have left you," he added apologetically, "but that I felt sure the rascal had taken to his heels the moment the rock fell."

"Nonsense. The attempt was aimed at you, not at me—although the perpetrator does not seem to care whom he endangers. The knife—"

"I don't believe the two incidents can be related, Amelia. The hands that pushed this rock were surely the filthy hands of Habib."

This suggestion made a certain amount of sense. "But why does he hate you so much?" I asked. "I could see you were on bad terms, but attempted murder. . . ."

"I was responsible for his being apprehended on the criminal charge I spoke of." Emerson accepted the handkerchief I gave him and attempted to clean his face while we walked on.

"What was his crime? Stealing antiquities?"

"That, of course. Most of the Gurneh men are involved in the antiquities game. But the case that brought him to justice, through me, was of a different and very distressing nature. Habib once had a daughter. Her name was Aziza. When she was a small child she worked for me as a basket girl. As she matured she turned into an unusually pretty young woman, slight and graceful as a gazelle, with big dark eyes that would melt any man's heart."

The tale Emerson proceeded to unfold would indeed have melted the hardest heart—even that of a man. The girl's beauty made her a valuable property, and her father hoped to sell her to a wealthy landowner. Alas, her beauty attracted other admirers, and her innocence rendered her vulnerable to their wiles. When her shame became known the rich and repulsive buyer rejected her, and her father, enraged at losing his money, determined to destroy a now-valueless object. Such things are done more often than the British authorities like to admit; in the name of "family honor" many a poor woman has met a ghastly fate at the hands of those who should have been her protectors. But in this case the girl managed to escape before the murderer had completed his vile act. Beaten and bleeding, she staggered to the tent of Emerson, who had been kind to her.

"Both her arms were broken," said Emerson, in a soft, cold voice quite unlike his usual tones. "She had tried to shield her head from the blows of her father's club. How she eluded him, or walked so far in her condition, I cannot imagine. She collapsed at my feet. I made her as comfortable as I could and ran to get help. In the few moments I was gone, Habib, who must have been close behind her, entered my tent and crushed her skull with a single blow.

"I returned in time to see him running away. One glance told me I could do no more for poor Aziza, so I went in pursuit. I gave him a good beating before I turned him over to the police. He got off much more lightly than he deserved, for of course the native courts found his motive entirely reasonable. If I had not threatened the sheikh with various unpleasant things he would probably have set Habib free."

I pressed his arm sympathetically. I understood why he had not mentioned the story; even now the memory affected him deeply. The softer side of Emerson's character is not known to many people, but those who are in trouble instinctively sense his real nature and seek him out, as the unhappy girl had done.

After a moment of thoughtful silence he shook himself and said, in his usual careless tone, "So take care with Mr. Vandergelt, Amelia. He was not exaggerating when he called himself an admirer of the fair sex, and if I learn that you have yielded to his advances I will beat you."

"I will take care that you don't catch me, never fear. But, Emerson, we are going to have a hard time solving this case if we hope to do it by using you as bait. There are too many people in Egypt who would like to kill you."

Chapter Five

A magnificent sunset turned the reflecting water to a shimmering scarf of crimson and gold as we set sail for the east bank and our appointment with Lady Baskerville. Emerson was sulking because I had insisted we take a carriage from the house to the quay. No man but Emerson would have considered walking across the fields in full evening kit, much less expected me to trail my red satin skirts and lace ruffles through the dirt; but Emerson is unique. When he behaves irrationally it is necessary to be firm with him.

He cheered up, however, when we embarked, and indeed few people could fail to be moved to enjoyment at such sensations. The cool evening breeze bathed our faces, the felucca slid smoothly across the water, and before us unrolled the glorious panorama of Luxor—the vivid green of palms and gardens, the statues and pillars and pylons of the Theban temples. A carriage was waiting for us and it bore us swiftly through the streets to the Luxor Hotel, where Lady Baskerville was staying.

As we entered the lobby the lady came gliding to meet us, her hands outstretched. Although she wore black I did not consider the gown suitable for a recently bereaved widow. The abominable bustle, which had so vexed me in the past, was on its way out. Lady Baskerville's gown was of the latest style, with only a small drapery behind. The layers of black net forming the skirts were so full and the puffs of fabric at her shoulders so exaggerated that her waist looked ridiculously small. She was tightly corseted, and the extent of shoulder and throat exposed was, in my opinion, almost indecent. The waxy white flowers crowning her upswept hair were also inappropriate.

(I do not apologize for this digression into fashion. Not only is it intrinsically interesting, but it shows something of the woman's character.)

Lady Baskerville gave me her fingertips and clasped Emerson's hand warmly. She then turned to introduce us to her companion.

"We met earlier," said Cyrus Vandergelt, beaming down at us. "It sure is nice to see you folks again. Mrs. Emerson, may I say your dress is right pretty. That red color suits you."

"Let us go in to dinner," Lady Baskerville said, with a slight frown.

"I thought Miss Mary and her friend were joining us," Vandergelt said.

"Mary said she would come if she were able. But you know her mother."

"I sure enough do!" Vandergelt rolled his eyes heavenward. "Have you met Madame Berengeria, Mrs. Emerson?"

I indicated that I had not had the pleasure. Vandergelt went on, "She claims she came here to study ancient Egyptian religion, but I opine it's because living is cheap. I don't like to speak ill of any member of the fair sex, but Madame Berengeria is an awful woman."

"Now, Cyrus, you must not be unkind," said Lady Baskerville, who had listened with a faint pleased smile. She enjoyed hearing other women criticized as much as she disliked hearing them complimented. "The poor thing cannot help it," she went on, turning to Emerson. "I believe her mind is deficient. We are all very fond of Mary, so we tolerate her mother; but the poor child is kept dancing attendance on the old . . . on the unfortunate creature, and can seldom get away."

Emerson shifted restlessly from one foot to the other and inserted a finger under his collar, as he does when he is uncomfortable or bored. Reading these signs correctly—as any married woman would—Lady Baskerville was turning toward the dining salon when Mr. Vandergelt let out a muffled exclamation.

"Holy shucks!" (At least I believe that was the phrase.) "How the dickens—look who's here. You didn't invite her, did you?"

"Certainly not." Lady Baskerville's voice had a distinct rasp as her eyes lit on the person who had prompted Vandergelt's remark. "That would not prevent her from coming, though. The woman has the manners of a peasant."

Coming toward us was a singular pair. One was a young lady dressed modestly in a somewhat out-of-date evening frock of pale-yellow voile. Ordinarily she would have captured anyone's attention, for she was the possessor of an unusually exotic style of beauty; her olive skin and dark, long-lashed eyes, her delicate features and slender frame were so like those of the aristocratic Egyptian ladies depicted in the tomb paintings that her modern dress looked out of place, like a riding habit on an antique statue of Diana. One expected to see diaphanous linen robes, collars of turquoise and carnelian, anklets and bracelets of gold adorning her limbs.

All these, and more, bedecked the woman who was with her, and whose extraordinary appearance drew the eye from the girl's pretty face. She was an extremely large woman, standing several inches taller than her daughter and being correspondingly broad. The linen robe she wore was no longer pure white, but a dingy gray. The beaded collar that attempted in vain to cover her ample bosom was a cheap imitation of the jewels worn by pharaohs and their ladies. On her very large feet were skimpy sandals; around the imprecise region of her waist a brightly embroidered sash had been knotted. Her hair was a huge black beehive surmounted by a bizarre headdress consisting of feathers, flowers, and cheap copper ornaments.

I pinched Emerson. "If you say just one of the words that are in your mind . . ." I hissed, leaving the threat unspecified.

"I'll keep quiet if you will," Emerson replied. His shoulders were shaking and his voice quivered.

"And try not to laugh," I added.

A stifled whoop was the only answer.

Madame Berengeria swept toward us, towing her daughter along in her wake. A closer examination confirmed what I had suspected—that the unnaturally black hair was a wig, like those worn by the ancients. The contrast between this dreadful object, which appeared to be constructed of horsehair, and Miss Mary's soft, shining locks would have been amusing if it had not been so horrid.

"I came," Madame Berengeria announced dramatically. "The messages were favorable. I was given the strength to endure a meeting devoid of spiritual comfort."

"How nice," said Lady Baskerville, baring her long white teeth as if she thirsted to sink them in the other woman's throat. "Mary, my child, I am delighted to see you. Let me present you to Professor and Mrs. Emerson."

The girl acknowledged the introduction with a shy smile. She had very pretty, old-fashioned manners—which she had certainly not learned from her mother. Emerson, his amusement forgotten, studied the girl with a blend of pity and admiration, and I wondered if her lovely face, so Egyptian in character, had reminded him of the murdered Aziza.

Without waiting to be introduced, Madame thrust herself forward, catching Emerson's hand and holding it, with odious familiarity, in both of hers. Her fingers were stained with henna and quite dirty.

"We need no formal presentation, Professor," she boomed, in a voice so loud that the few heads that had not turned to mark her entrance now swiveled in our direction. "Or may I call you . . . Set-nakhte?"

"I don't see why the devil you should," Emerson replied in astonishment.

"You don't remember." They were almost of a height, and she had come so close to him that when she let out a gusty sigh Emerson's hair waved wildly. "It is not given to all of us to remember former lives," she went on. "But I had hoped . . . I was Ta-weseret, the Queen, and you were my lover."

"Good Gad," Emerson exclaimed. He tried to free his hand, but the lady hung on. Her grip must have been as strong as a man's, for Emerson's fingers turned white as hers tightened.

"Together we ruled in ancient Waset," Madame Berengeria continued raptly. "That was after we had murdered my wretched husband, Ramses."

Emerson was distracted by this inaccuracy. "But," he protested, "Ramses was not the husband of Ta-weseret, and it is not at all certain that Set-nakhte—"

"Murdered!" Madame Berengeria shouted, causing Emerson to flinch back. "Murdered! We suffered for that sin in other lives, but the grandeur of our passion . . . Ah, Setnakhte, how could you forget?"

Emerson's expression, as he contemplated the self-proclaimed partner of his passion, was one I will long remember with enjoyment. However, the woman was beginning to wear on me, and when my husband cast a look of piteous appeal in my direction, I decided to intervene.

I always carry a parasol. I find it invaluable in many different ways. My working parasol is of stout black bombazine with a steel shaft. Naturally the one I carried that evening matched my frock and was eminently suitable for formal occasions. I brought it down smartly on Madame Berengeria's wrist. She yelped and let go of Emerson.

"Dear me, how careless of me," I said.

For the first time the lady looked directly at me.

Black kohl, lavishly smeared around her eyes, made her look as if she had suffered a severe beating. The orbs themselves were unusual. The irises were of an indeterminate shade between blue and gray, and so pale that they blended with the muddy white of the eye. The pupils were dilated to an unusual degree. Altogether it was a most unpleasant set of optics, and the concentrated and venomous intelligence with which they regarded me assured me of two things: one, that I had made an enemy; two, that Madame's eccentricities were not entirely without calculation.

Lady Baskerville seized Mr. Vandergelt's arm; I took possession of my poor gaping Emerson; and leaving Madame and her unfortunate daughter to bring up the rear, we proceeded to the dining salon. A table had been prepared for us, and it was there that the next difficulty arose, caused, as one might have expected, by Madame Berengeria.

"There are only six places," she exclaimed, settling herself at once into the nearest chair. "Did not Mary tell you, Lady Baskerville, that my young admirer will also be dining?"

The effrontery of this was so enormous as to leave the hearers with nothing to say. Shaking with fury, Lady Baskerville summoned the maitre d'hôtel and requested that an additional place be set. In defiance of custom I placed Emerson firmly between myself and our hostess, which left Mr. Vandergelt to partner Madame Berengeria. Her appearance had thrown the arrangements out in every conceivable way, for there was now an uneven number of ladies and gentlemen. The empty chair awaiting Madame Berengeria's "admirer" chanced to be between me and Miss Mary. So preoccupied was I with other matters that it did not occur to me to wonder who this person might be. I was taken completely by surprise when a familiar freckled face surmounted by an equally well-known shock of flaming red hair made its appearance.

"Heartfelt apologies for my tardiness, Lady Baskerville," said Mr. O'Connell, bowing. "'Twas unavoidable, I assure you. What a pleasure to see so many friends! Is this my place? Sure an' I couldn't want a better one."

As he spoke he inserted himself neatly into the vacant chair and bestowed an inclusive hearty smile upon the party.

Seeing, by the intensifying livid hue of his countenance, that Emerson was on the verge of an explosive comment, I trod heavily upon his foot.

"I did not expect to meet you here, Mr. O'Connell," I said. "I trust you have recovered from your unfortunate accident."

"Accident?" Mary exclaimed, her soft dark eyes widening. "Mr. O'Connell, you did not tell me—"

"It was nothing," O'Connell assured her. "I clumsily lost my footing and fell down a few stairs." He looked at me, his eyes narrowed with amusement. "'Tis kind you are, Mrs. Emerson, to be remembering such a trivial incident."

"I am relieved to hear that you considered it trivial," I said, maintaining my pressure on Emerson's foot, which twitched and writhed under the sole of my shoe.

Mr. O'Connell's eyes were as innocent as limpid pools of water. "To be sure I did. I only hope my editors feel the same."

"I see," I said.

Waiters bustled up carrying bowls of clear soup, and the meal began. Conversation also began, each person turning to his dinner partner. Thanks to Madame, this comfortable social custom was confused by the presence of an extra person, and I found myself with no one to talk to. I did not object; sipping my soup, I was able to eavesdrop on the other conversations in turn, to my edification and entertainment.

The two young people seemed on friendly terms. Indeed, I suspected Mr. O'Connell's feelings were somewhat warmer; his eyes never left the girl's face and his voice took on the soft, caressing tones that are typical of the Irish. Though Mary evidently enjoyed his admiration, I was not sure that her affections were seriously engaged. I also observed that though Madame Berengeria was regaling Mr. Vandergelt with a description of her romance with Setnakhte, she kept a close eye on the young people. Before long she turned abruptly and interrupted O'Connell in the middle of a compliment. This freed Vandergelt; catching my eye, he pantomimed a sigh of relief and joined in the discussion between Emerson and Lady Baskerville.

Thanks to Emerson, this had taken a strictly archaeological turn, despite Lady Baskerville's sighs and fluttering lashes and repeated thanks for his gallantry in coming to the rescue of a poor lonely widow. Happily impervious to these hints, Emerson continued to explain his plans for excavating the tomb.

Do not believe for an instant, reader, that I had lost sight of what had now become my main object. To discover the murderer of Lord Baskerville was no longer a matter of purely intellectual interest. Mr. O'Connell might have been responsible for the injury to Emerson in Cairo (though I doubted this); the villainous Habib might have been the motive power behind the boulder that had so narrowly missed him that very day. *Might*, I say; for I felt sure that two attempts in such a short space of time had a deeper and more sinister significance. The person who had murdered Baskerville now had designs on the life of my husband, and the sooner I discovered his identity, the sooner Emerson would be safe.

I use the masculine pronoun for reasons of grammatical simplicity, but I could not dismiss the possibility that a woman's hand had wielded the death weapon (whatever that might have been). Indeed, as I looked around the table I felt I had never beheld such a suspicious-looking group of persons.

That Lady Baskerville was capable of murder, I did not doubt. Why she should want to kill her husband I did not know at that time, but I felt sure that a brief investigation would provide a motive and also explain how she had managed the two attacks on Emerson.

As for Mr. Vandergelt, amiable as he appeared to be, I had to consider him a suspect. We all know how ruthlessly these American millionaires crush their rivals as they climb to power. Vandergelt had lusted after Lord Baskerville's tomb. Some might consider that an inadequate motive for murder, but I knew the archaeological temperament too well to dismiss it.

As if she felt my speculative glance move to her, Madame Berengeria looked up from the roast mutton she was stuffing into her mouth. Once again her pallid eyes glowed with hate. No need to ask myself if she was capable of committing murder! She was certainly mad, and the actions of a madwoman are unaccountable. She might have hailed Lord Baskerville as a long-lost lover and killed him when he rejected her, as any normal man must.

Madame Berengeria continued to wolf her food and I turned my attention to her daughter, who was listening in silence to Mr. O'Connell's low-voiced remarks. She was smiling, but it was a sad smile; the bright lights of the salon showed the shabbiness of her frock and the weary lines in her young face. I immediately removed her from my list of suspects. The fact that she had not yet exterminated her mother proved that she was incapable of violence.

Mr. O'Connell? Without a doubt he must be on my list. He was on good terms with all three of the ladies, which indicated a sly and hypocritical turn of character. To win Mary's regard would not be difficult; the child would respond to any show of kindness or affection. In order to facilitate his acquaintance with the girl, O'Connell had ingratiated himself with her mother, by sheer duplicity and falsehood (for no one could honestly admire, or even tolerate, the woman). The same slippery slyness probably accounted for his acceptance by Lady Baskerville. He had written about her in the most disgustingly sentimental terms, and she was vain enough to be deceived by empty flattery. In short, his was not a character to be trusted.

Of course those present did not exhaust all the possible suspects. The missing Armadale was high on my list, and Karl von Bork and Milverton might have motives as yet unknown to me. I did not doubt that as soon as I applied myself seriously to the problem, the answer would be easily discovered; and, to be truthful, the prospect of a little detective work was not at all displeasing.

In such entertaining speculations the meal passed, and we prepared to retire to the lounge. Madame Berengeria had eaten everything she could get her hands on, and her round face shone greasily. So must ancient Egyptian diners have looked, at the end of a formal party, when the cone of scented fat atop their wigs had melted and run down their faces. She had also drunk vast quantities of wine. When we rose from the table she caught her daughter's arm and leaned heavily against her. Mary's knees buckled under the weight. Mr. O'Connell promptly came to her rescue, or rather, he tried to, for when he took Madame's other arm she pulled away from him.

"Mary will help me," she muttered. "Dear daughter—help Mother— good daughter never leaves Mother. . . ."

Mary turned pale. Supporting Madame, she said in a low voice, "Perhaps you would call a carriage, Mr. O'Connell. We had better not stay. Mother, you are unwell."

"Never felt better," Madame Berengeria declared. "Have a little coffee. Must talk to old lover—Amenhotep—I called him the Magnificent—he was, too—you remember your darling queenie, don't you, Amen?"

Releasing her daughter's arm, she lunged at Emerson.

But this time she had underestimated my husband. On the first occasion he had been caught off guard; now he acted, and Emerson is seldom, if ever, restrained from action by any remote notion of what is socially acceptable. Catching the lady in a paralyzing grip, he frogmarched her toward the door, calling out, "A carriage here! Madame Berengeria's carriage, if you please!"

The hotel porter leaped to assist him. Mary started after them. O'Connell caught her hand.

"Can you not stay? I haven't had a chance to talk to you—"

"You know I cannot. Good night, everyone. Lady Baskerville, my thanks—and apologies—"

Slim and graceful in her shabby frock, her head bowed, she followed the porters who were dragging her mother out the door.

Mr. O'Connell's countenance plainly displayed his chagrin and his affectionate concern. I began to warm to the young man; but then he gave himself a sort of shake and remarked, "Well, Mrs. Emerson, have you changed your mind about that interview? Your thoughts on arriving in Luxor would interest my readers enormously."

The transformation of his face was extraordinary. His eyes sparkled with malice, his mouth curved in a tight-lipped half-moon grin. This expression, which I thought of as his journalist's face, reminded me of the leprechauns and mischievous elves which are said to abound in the Emerald Isle.

Not wishing to dignify the suggestion with a reply, I ignored it. Fortunately Emerson had not heard the question. Leaning on the back of Lady Baskerville's chair, he was explaining his plans for the next day. "And," he added, glancing at me, "since we must be out at the first light, we had better be getting back, eh, Amelia?"

I promptly rose. To my surprise, so did Lady Baskerville.

"I am packed and ready. If you will summon the porter, Radcliffe?" Seeing my expression, she smiled sweetly at me. "Had I not explained that I mean to go with you, Mrs. Emerson? Now that you are here, I need not fear scandal if I resume my old place, hallowed by so many fond memories."

I need not say that my response was perfectly calm and courteous.

II

I had feared the presence of Lady Baskerville in the adjoining room might inhibit Emerson to some extent. It did, in the beginning. Casting an irritated glance at the closed portal, which I had promptly bolted, he muttered, "Curse it, Amelia, this is going to be a nuisance; I shan't be able to say a thing for fear of being overheard." However, as time went on he became so involved in what he was doing that all reserve fled and all external distractions were forgotten. My own contributions toward achieving this end were not inconsiderable.

Lying at peace in my husband's arms, I drifted off to sleep. But we were not destined for a quiet rest that night. Scarcely, it seemed, had my eyelids closed when I was reft of slumber by an outrageous howl, so penetrating that it seemed to come from within our very chamber.

I pride myself on being able to arise from meditation or sleep fully alert and ready for whatever action seems required. Rising up, I prepared to bound out of bed. Unfortunately I had not completely readjusted to the sleeping arrangements necessary in that clime; and, as I had done on another memorable occasion, I plunged headlong into the mosquito netting draped around the bed. My efforts to free myself only wound the fabric more tightly around me. The howling continued. It had now been joined by cries of alarm from elsewhere in the house.

"Help me, Emerson," I cried irritably. "I am entangled in the netting. Why do you not arise?"

"Because," said a faint voice from the bed, "you stepped onto my stomach when you stood up. I have just now recovered my breath."

"Then employ it, if you please, in action rather than words. Unloose me."

Emerson obeyed. It is not necessary to reproduce the comments he made while doing so. Once he had freed me he ran to the door. As his form crossed the band of moonlight from the open window I let out a shriek.

"Emerson, your trousers—your dressing gown—something—"

With a violent oath Emerson snatched up the first garment that came to hand. It proved to be the one I had discarded upon retiring, a nightgown of thin white linen trimmed with wide bands of lace. Tossing this at me, with an even more violent oath, he began searching for his clothes. By the time we reached the courtyard the shrieks had stopped, but the excitement had not subsided. All the members of the expedition were gathered around a servant who sat on the ground with his arms over his head, rocking back and forth and moaning. I recognized Hassan, one of Lord Baskerville's men, who was employed as a night watchman.

"What has happened?" I demanded of the person nearest me. This happened to be Karl, who was standing with his arms folded and every hair in his mustache neatly in place. He was fully dressed. Bowing, in his formal German fashion, he replied calmly, "The foolish person claims he saw a ghost. You know how superstitious these people are; and at the present time—"

"How ridiculous," I said, in considerable disappointment. I had hoped the disturbance might have been caused by the murderer of Lord Baskerville, returning to the scene of the crime.

Emerson seized Hassan by the neck and hoisted him up off the ground. "Enough!" he shouted. "Art thou a man, or a dribbling infant? Speak; tell me what sight brought our valiant watchman to this pass."

Emerson's methods, though unconventional, are usually effective. Hassan's sobs died away. He began kicking his feet, and Emerson lowered him till his dusty bare soles rested on the beaten earth of the courtyard.

"Oh, Father of Curses," he gulped. "Wilt thou protect thy servant?"

"Certainly, certainly. Speak."

"It was an efreet, an evil spirit," Hassan whispered, rolling his eyes. "The spirit of the one with the face of a woman and the heart of a man."

"Armadale!" Mr. Milverton exclaimed.

He and Lady Baskerville were standing side by side. Her delicate white hands clutched his sleeve, but it would be hard to say which of them was supporting the other, for he was as pale as she.

Hassan nodded vigorously, or at least he tried to do so; Emerson was still holding him by the throat.

"The hand of the Father of Curses renders speech difficult," he complained.

"Oh, sorry," Emerson said, releasing him.

Hassan rubbed his bony neck. He had recovered from his initial fright, and there was a crafty gleam in his eyes that made me suspect he was beginning to enjoy being the center of attention.

"I saw it clearly in the moonlight, as I made my rounds," he said. "The very form and image of the one with the face—"

"Yes, yes," Emerson interrupted. "What was he doing?"

"Creeping through the shadows like a serpent or a scorpion or an evil djinn! He wore the long linen robe of a corpse, and his face was thin and drawn, with staring eyes and—"

"Stop that!" Emerson roared. Hassan subsided, with another roll of his eyes, as if he were judging the effect of the ghost story on his audience.

"The superstitious fellow was dreaming," Emerson said, addressing Lady Baskerville. "Return to bed. I will see to it that he—"

Like many of the men, Hassan understood English much better than he spoke it. "No!" he exclaimed. "It was no dream, I swear; I heard the jackals howling in the hills, I saw the grass blades bend under his feet. He went to one of the windows, oh, Father of Curses—one of the windows there."

He gestured toward the side of the house in which all our rooms were located.

Karl let out a grunt. Lady Baskerville's face turned muddy gray. But Milverton's reaction was the most dramatic. With a queer soft sigh he folded at the knees and fell to the ground in a dead faint.

III

"It means nothing," I said, some time later, as Emerson and I again prepared to retire. "I told you the young man was not fully recovered; the shock and excitement were too much for him."

Emerson was standing on a chair trying to get the mosquito netting back in place. He had irritably refused my suggestion that I call one of the servants to do the job.

"I am surprised at you, Amelia," he grunted. "I made sure you would take that faint as a sign of guilt."

"Don't be absurd. Armadale is the murderer; I have insisted on that all along. Now we know he is still alive, and in the area."

"We know nothing of the kind. Hassan is perfectly capable of imagining the spirits of Ramses One through Twelve, simultaneously. Forget it and come to bed."

He descended from the chair. To my astonishment I saw that he had the netting in place. Emerson is constantly displaying talents I never knew he had. So I did as he suggested.

Chapter Six

DESPITE our disturbed night we were awake before daylight. It was a glorious morning. To breathe the air was like drinking chilled white wine. When the sun lifted in majesty over the horizon the western cliffs blushed rosy red in welcome. Larks rose singing to greet the dawn, and all objects shone with a luster that made them appear newly washed—a most deceptive appearance, I might add, since cleanliness is not a conspicuous characteristic of the inhabitants of Upper Egypt or their belongings.

By sunrise we were riding across the plain, through fields of waving barley and ripening vegetables. It was necessary to carry a certain amount of gear with us, so we took this route rather than the shorter, more difficult path over the cliffs. Following us in a ragged but cheerful procession were our loyal men from Aziyeh. I felt quite like a general of a small army; when my rising spirits demanded an outlet I turned in my saddle and raised my arm with a shout of "Huzzah!" to which our troop responded with a cheer and Emerson with a snarl of "Don't make an ass of yourself, Amelia."

Abdullah marched at the head of his men, his vigorous stride and keen brown face belying his years. We encountered the usual morning crowd—women in long brown gulabeeyahs carrying naked children, donkeys almost hidden under their loads of brushwood, haughty camels and their drivers, peasants with rakes and hoes setting out for the fields. Abdullah, who has a fine voice, struck up a song. The men joined in the chorus, and I heard a note of defiance in the way they sang. The watchers muttered and nudged one another. Though no one offered a hostile gesture, I was glad when we left the cultivated land and entered the narrow opening in the cliffs. The towering rocks that guard the entrance had been shaped by wind and water into weird suggestions of watchful statues, though the very idea of water in that now desolate place seems fantastic. The pale limestone walls and chalky ground are as lifeless as the icy wastes of the north.

As we entered the Valley proper we saw that a large crowd had assembled near our tomb. My eye was caught by one man, conspicuous by his unusual height and heavy farageeyeh, the outer robe worn chiefly by men of the learned professions. His arms folded, his wiry black beard jutting out, he stood alone; the others, jostling and shoving one another, had left a respectful space around him. His green turban proclaimed him a descendant of the Prophet; his stern face and fixed, deep-set eyes gave the impression of a forceful and commanding personality.

"That is the local holy man," Karl said. "I feel I must warn you, Professor, that he has been hostile to—"

"Unnecessary," Emerson replied. "Be silent and keep out of the way."

Dismounting, he turned to face the imam. For a moment the two confronted one another in silence. I confess I had seldom seen two more impressive men. They seemed to transcend individuality and become symbols of two ways of life: the past and the future, the old superstition and the new rationalism.

But I digress.

Solemnly the imam raised his hand. His bearded lips parted.

Before he could utter a word, Emerson said loudly, *"Sabâhkum bilkheir,* Holy One. Have you come to bless the work? *Marhaba*—welcome."

Emerson maintains, justly or unjustly, that all religious leaders are showmen at heart. This man reacted to being "upstaged" as any skilled actor would, conquering the anger that flared in his eyes and replying, with scarcely a pause, "I bring no blessing but a warning. Will you risk the curse of the Almighty? Will you profane the dead?"

"I come to save the dead, not profane their tombs," Emerson replied. "For centuries the men of Gurneh have strewn the sands with their pitiful bones. As for curses, I do not fear efreets and demons, for the God we both worship has promised us protection against evil. I invoke His blessing on our work of rescue! *Allâhu akbar; lâ ilâha illa'llâh!"* Sweeping off his hat, he turned toward Mecca and raised his hands to each side of his face in the gesture prescribed for the recitation of the *takbir.*

I could hardly repress a shout of "bravo!" A murmur of surprise and approval rippled through the watchers. Emerson held his theatrical pose just long enough. Clapping his hat back on his head before his surprised adversary could think of a fitting reply, he said briskly, "Now then, Holy One, you will excuse me if I get to work."

Without further ado he started down the steps. The imam, recognizing defeat with the dignity his office demanded, turned on his heel and walked away, followed by part of the audience. The rest squatted down on their haunches and prepared to watch us work—hoping, no doubt, for a catastrophe of some kind.

I was about to follow Emerson when I realized that the dispersal of the crowd had revealed a form thus far concealed in their ranks. Mr. O'Connell's fiery-red hair was hidden by an inordinately large solar kepi. He was scribbling busily in a notebook. Feeling my eyes upon him, he looked up and raised his hat.

"Top of the morning to you, Mrs. Emerson. I hope you are not tired after your disturbed night?"

"How did you know about that?" I demanded. "And what the—that is, what are you doing here?"

"Why, this is a public place, to be sure. The opening of the tomb is important news. Your husband has already given me a first-rate lead. What an actor he is!"

He had not answered my first question. Obviously he had sources of information within our very household and was not inclined to betray them. As for the second point, he was quite correct; we might prevent him from entering the tomb, but we could not keep him from watching. As I stared angrily at him he coolly produced a folding stool, opened it, and seated himself. Then he poised his pencil over his notebook and regarded me expectantly.

I felt a new sympathy for the imam. Like him, I had been left with nothing to say. So, following his example, I retreated with as much dignity as I could command.

Descending the stairs, I found that Emerson had unlocked the iron gate and was conversing with the guards—not the ill-favored Habib and his friend, but two of our own men. Being unaware that Emerson had taken this step, I remarked upon it.

"You must think me a fool if you believe I would neglect such an elementary precaution," Emerson replied. "I am not at all sure that such measures will suffice, however. Once we have the passage cleared, it may be necessary for one of us to spend the night here. When Milverton is healthy enough to satisfy you, there will be three of us—"

"Four," I corrected, taking a firm hold of my parasol.

There was a certain amount of grumbling from the men when they realized they would have to carry away the baskets of debris. This menial chore was usually delegated to children, but Emerson had determined not to ask for any help from the villagers. Once they saw that the work was proceeding without incident, they would come to us. At least we had counted on that; but events like our "ghost" of the night before would not help matters. If only we could catch the elusive Armadale!

When the men saw that Karl, Emerson, and I pitched in with the work they stopped complaining. Indeed, Abdullah was horrified when I raised the first basket of rock in my arms and prepared to carry it off.

"Obviously you have forgotten my habits, Abdullah," I said. "You have seen me do ruder labor than this."

The old man smiled. "I have not forgotten your temper, at least, Sitt Hakim. It would take a graver man than Abdullah to prevent you from acting as you choose."

"There is no such man," I retorted. I was pleased with this remark, for it conveyed a delicate compliment as well as being a simple statement of fact. I then asked my husband where he wished to form the refuse dump, since my basket would have the honor of being the first to be deposited there.

Emerson looked up over the rim of the staircase and stroked his chin thoughtfully. "There," he said, pointing to a spot to the southwest, near the entrance to Ramses the Sixth's tomb. "There can be nothing of interest in that area; the ruins are only the remains of ancient workmen's huts."

As I trudged back and forth with my basket I was, at first, a strifle self-conscious under Mr. O'Connell's steady regard and unfailing smile, for I knew he was drawing a verbal portrait of me for the benefit of his readers. Gradually, however, I forgot him in the pressure of work. The pile of debris mounted with what seemed painful slowness. Since I did not enter the tomb, but received my loaded basket from the man who had filled it, I had no way of measuring the progress being made, and I found it devilish discouraging, as Emerson might have said.

I also developed a considerable respect for the humble basket children. How they could run merrily back and forth, singing and making jokes, I did not know; I was dripping with perspiration and conscious of unfamiliar aches in various portions of my anatomy. The tourists gathered as the morning went on, and in addition to the fence around the tomb itself, it became necessary to string ropes along the path between the entrance and the rubbish dump. The more impertinent tourists ignored these, and I was constantly having to shove gaping idiots aside. Half blinded by sun, dust, and perspiration, I paid no more attention to these forms than was necessary to propel them out of my way, so that when I encountered a very elaborate pale-gray walking gown trimmed with black lace, in the exact center of the path, I gave it a little nudge with my elbow in passing. A shriek, echoed by a masculine exclamation, made me pause. Wiping my sleeve across my brow to clear my vision, I recognized Lady Baskerville. No doubt it was her corsets that prevented her from bending at the waist; her entire body was tilted backward, as stiff as a tree trunk, her heels resting on the ground and her shoulders supported by Mr. Vandergelt. She glowered at me from under the flower-trimmed bonnet, which had fallen over her brow.

"Good morning, Mrs. Emerson," said Mr. Vandergelt. "I sure hope you'll excuse me for not removing my hat."

"Certainly. Good morning, Lady Baskerville; I did not see you. Excuse *me* while I empty this basket."

When I returned Lady Baskerville was standing upright, adjusting her hat and her temper. The sight of me, unkempt, dusty and damp, restored her equanimity. She gave me a pitying smile.

"My dear Mrs. Emerson, I never expected to see you engaged in menial labor."

"It is necessary," I replied briefly. "We could do with a few more workers." I inspected her from head to toe and saw her face go rigid with indignation before I added, "I hope Mr. Milverton is better?"

"You saw him yourself earlier, I am told," Lady Baskerville replied, following after me, for of course I did not pause in my work any longer than was absolutely necessary.

"Yes, I told him to stay indoors today."

I was about to continue when a shout from the tomb made me drop my basket and break into a trot. The watching crowd also realized the significance of that cry; they pressed so close around the entrance that I had to shove through them to reach the steps, and only Emerson's outraged gestures kept several of them from following me down.

The men were working close enough to the entrance to render artificial lighting unnecessary, but at first my eyes were dazzled by the abrupt transition from bright sunlight to gloom. Then I saw what had caused the excitement. On one wall, now cleared to a depth of several feet, was part of a painting. Greater than life size, it showed the upper portion of the body of a male figure, one hand lifted in benediction. The colors shone as brightly as they had on that far-off day when the artist had applied them: the red-brown of the skin, the corals and greens and lapis blues of the beaded collar, the gold of the tall plumes crowning the black head.

"Amon," I exclaimed, recognizing the insignia of that god. "Emerson, how splendid!"

"The workmanship is as fine as the tomb of Seti the First," Emerson said. "We will have to go slowly to avoid damaging the paint."

Vandergelt had followed us down the stairs. "You are going to remove all the debris? Why not tunnel through it, to reach the burial chamber sooner?"

"Because I am not interested in providing a journalistic sensation, or making it easier for the Gurnawis to rob the tomb."

"You've got me there," Vandergelt said, with a smile. "Much as I'd like to stay, Professor, I reckon I had better get Lady Baskerville back home."

We kept at it until early in the evening. By the time we stopped, several yards of the tunnel lay open, and two splendid paintings had been brought to light, one on either wall. They formed part of a procession of gods. Not only Amon but Osiris and Mut and Isis had made their appearance. There were inscriptions, which Karl was eagerly copying, but to our disappointment the name of the tomb owner had not appeared.

After locking the iron grille and the door of the little shed that had been built to hold our equipment, we started back to Baskerville House. Darkness stretched long blue velvet arms toward us as we proceeding eastward; but behind us, toward the west, the last sullen streaks of sunset scarred the sky, like bleeding wounds.

II

Emerson may—and does—sneer at unnecessary luxuries; but I noticed that he did not scruple to avail himself of the comforts of the pleasant little bathroom next to our bedchamber. I heard the servants refilling the great earthenware jars as I completed my own ablutions; and very enjoyable the cool water was, I must say, after a day in the sun and dust. Emerson followed me; and I smiled to myself as his voice rose in song. It had to do, I believe, with a young man on a trapeze.

A late tea was set out when we went to the elegant drawing room. The windows opened onto the vine-shaded loggia, and the scent of jasmine pervaded the chamber.

We were the first to come, but scarcely had I taken my seat behind the tea tray when Karl and Mr. Milverton made their appearance, and a moment later we were joined by Mr. Vandergelt, who strolled in through the French doors with the familiarity of an old friend.

"I was invited," he assured me, as he bowed over my hand. "But I'm bound to admit I'd have butted in anyhow, I am so anxious to hear what you found today. Where is Lady Baskerville?"

Even as he inquired the lady swept in, trailing ruffles and laces, and carrying a spray of sweet white jasmine. After a (I hardly need add) courteous discussion as to which of us should dispense the genial beverage, I filled the cups. Emerson then condescended to give a brief but pithy lecture on the day's discoveries.

He began, generous creature that he is, by mentioning my own not inconsiderable contributions. I had spent the last hours of the afternoon sifting through the debris removed from the passageway. Few excavators bother with this task when they are in quest of greater goals, but Emerson has always insisted on examining every square inch of the fill, and in this case our efforts had been rewarded. With some pride I displayed my finds, which had been set out on a tray: a heap of pottery shards (common buff ware), a handful of bones (rodent), and a copper knife.

Lady Baskerville let out a gasp of laughter.

"My poor dear Mrs. Emerson: All that effort for a handful of rubbish."

Mr. Vandergelt stroked his goatee. "I'm not so sure about that, ma'am. They may not look like much, but I'll be doggoned surprised if they don't mean something—something not too good. Eh, Professor?"

Emerson nodded grudgingly. He does not like to have his brilliant deductions anticipated. "You are sharp, Vandergelt. Those bits of broken pottery came from a jar that was used to hold scented oil. I very much fear, Lady Baskerville, that we are not the first to disturb the pharaoh's rest."

"I don't understand." Lady Baskerville turned to Emerson with a pretty little gesture of bewilderment.

"But it is only too clear," Karl exclaimed. "Such perfumed oil was buried with the dead man for his use in the next world, as were foodstuffs, clothing, furniture, and other necessities. We know this from the tomb reliefs and from the papyrus that—"

"Very well, very well," Emerson interrupted. "What Karl means, Lady Baskerville, is that such shards could be found in the outer corridor only if a thief had dropped one of the jars as he was carrying it out."

"Perhaps it was dropped on the way in," suggested Milverton cheerfully. "My servants are always breaking things."

"In that case the broken jar would have been swept up," said Emerson. "No; I am almost certain that the tomb was entered after the burial. A difference in the consistency of the filling material indicates that a tunnel had been dug through it."

"And re-filled," said Vandergelt. He shook his finger playfully at Emerson. "Now, Professor, you're trying to get us all het up. But I'm on to you. The thieves' tunnel wouldn't have been filled up, and the necropolis seals re-applied, if the tomb had been empty."

"Then you believe there are treasures yet to be found?" Lady Baskerville asked.

"If we found nothing more than painted reliefs of the quality we have uncovered thus far, the tomb would be a treasure," Emerson replied. "But, in fact, Vandergelt is right again." He gave the American a malignant look. "I do believe there is a chance the thieves never reached the burial chamber."

Lady Baskerville exclaimed with delight. I turned to Milverton, who was seated beside me, his expression one of poorly concealed amusement.

"Why do you smile, Mr. Milverton?"

"I confess, Mrs. Emerson, that I find all this fuss over a few bits of broken pottery somewhat bewildering."

"That is a strange thing for an archaeologist to say."

"But I am no archaeologist, only a photographer, and this is my first venture into Egyptology." His eyes shifted; they continued to avoid mine as he continued rapidly. "In fact, I had begun to have doubts about my usefulness even before Lord Baskerville's unfortunate death. Now that he is gone I don't believe . . . that is, I feel I can do better. . . ."

"What?" Lady Baskerville had overheard, despite the fact that Milverton's voice had been scarcely louder than a murmur. "What are you saying, Mr. Milverton? You cannot be thinking of leaving us?"

The wretched young man turned all colors of the rainbow. "I was telling Mrs. Emerson that I don't believe I can be of use here. My state of health—"

"Nonsense!" Lady Baskerville exclaimed. "Dr. Dubois assured me you are making a splendid recovery, and that you are better off here than alone in a hotel. You mustn't run away."

"We need you," Emerson added. "We are desperately understaffed, Milverton, as you know."

"But I have no experience—"

"Not in archaeology, perhaps. But what we need are guards and supervisors. Besides, I assure you, your special skills will be required as soon as you are able to come out with us."

Under my husband's keen regard the young man squirmed like a schoolboy being quizzed by a stern master. The analogy was irresistible; Milverton was the very model of a young English gentleman of the finest type, and it was difficult to see in his fresh, candid face anything except normal embarrassment. I flatter myself, however, that I can see beyond the obvious. Milverton's behavior was highly suspicious.

He was saved from answering by Karl, who had been eagerly examining the pottery fragments in the hope of finding writing on them. Now the young German looked up and said, "Excuse me, Herr Professor, but have you considered my suggestion regarding an artist? Now that paintings have been found—"

"Quite, quite," Emerson said. "An artist would certainly be useful."

"Especially," Vandergelt added, "since there is so much antagonism toward your work. I wouldn't put it past the local hoodlums to destroy the paintings out of spite."

"They will have to get to them first," Emerson said grimly.

"I am sure your guards are trustworthy. All the same—"

"You need not belabor the point. I'll give the girl a try."

Milverton had relaxed as the attention of the others was directed away from him. Now he sat up with a start.

"Is it Miss Mary of whom you speak? You cannot be serious. Karl, how can you suggest—"

"But she is a fine artist," Karl said.

"Granted. But it is out of the question for her to risk herself."

Karl turned beet red. "Risk? *Was ist's? Was haben Sie gesagt? Niemals würde ich* . . . Excuse me, I forget myself; but that I would endanger—"

"Nonsense, nonsense," shouted Emerson, who had apparently decided never to let the young German complete a sentence. "What do you mean, Milverton?"

Milverton got to his feet. Despite the grave doubts his peculiar behavior had raised in my mind, I could not help but admire him at that moment: pale as linen, his handsome blue eyes burning, his manly figure erect, he halted the general outcry with a dramatic gesture.

"How can you all be so blind? Of course there is risk. Lord Baskerville's mysterious death, Armadale missing, the villagers threatening. . . . Am I the only one among you who is willing to face the truth? Be it so! And be assured I will not shirk my duty as an Englishman and a gentleman! Never will I abandon Miss Mary—or you, Lady Baskerville—or Mrs. Emerson—"

Seeing that he was losing the superb emotional import of his speech, I rose and seized him by the arm.

"You are overexcited, Mr. Milverton. I suspect you are not fully recovered. What you need is a good dinner and a quiet night. Once you have regained your health, these fancies will no longer trouble you."

The young man gazed at me with troubled eyes, his sensitive lips quivering, and I felt constrained to add, "The natives call me 'Sitt Hakim,' the lady doctor, you know; I assure you that I know what is best for you. Your own mother would advise you as I have done."

"Now that makes good sense," Vandergelt exclaimed heartily. "You listen to the lady, young fellow; she's a sharp one."

Dominated by a stronger personality (I refer to my own, of course), Mr. Milverton nodded submissively and said no more.

However, the effects of his outburst could not be dismissed so easily. Karl was silent and sullen for the remainder of the evening; it was clear, from the angry looks he shot at the other young man, that he had not forgotten or forgiven Milverton for his accusation. Lady Baskerville also seemed upset. After dinner, when Mr. Vandergelt prepared to return to the hotel, he urged her to come with him. She refused with a laugh; but in my opinion the laughter was hollow.

Vandergelt took his departure, bearing with him a note that he had promised to deliver to Mary, and the rest of us retired to the drawing room. I allowed Lady Baskerville to dispense the coffee, thinking that domesticity and soothing activity would calm her nerves, which it undoubtedly would have done if the others had cooperated with me in behaving normally. But Karl sulked, Emerson relapsed into the blank-faced silence that is indicative of his more contemplative moods, and Milverton was so nervous he could hardly sit still. It was with considerable relief that I heard Emerson declare we must all retire early, in view of the hard day's work ahead of us.

Lady Baskerville accompanied us as we crossed the courtyard. I noticed that she stayed close to us, and I wondered if she was afraid to be alone with one or another of the young men. Had there been a veiled threat in Milverton's speech? Had Karl's sudden display of anger suggested to her that he was not incapable of violence?

Milverton was not far behind us. I was relieved to see him leave the room, not only because he needed his rest, but because it seemed inadvisable for the two men to be left alone, in view of the antagonism between them. His hands in his pockets, his head bowed, he strolled slowly along, and he was still in the courtyard when we reached our doors. Lady Baskerville's was next to ours; we paused to bid her a courteous good night. Scarcely had she stepped into the room, however, when an appalling shriek burst from her lips and she staggered back, her arms outthrust as if to ward off an attacker.

I reached the lady first and supported her swaying frame while Emerson snatched a lantern and ran into the room to see what had caused such alarm. As usual, Lady Baskerville was rudely unappreciative of my attentions. She wrenched herself from me and flung herself into the arms of Milverton, who had rushed to her side.

"Help me, Charles, help me!" she cried. "Save me from—from—"

I itched to slap her, but could not do so because her face was buried against Milverton's shoulder. At that moment an incongruous sound reached my ears. It was the sound of my husband's hearty laugh.

"Come and see, Amelia," he called.

Pushing Lady Baskerville and Milverton out of the way, I entered the room.

Though smaller than the chamber formerly occupied by his lordship, it was of ample size and decorated with feminine delicacy. Soft matting covered the floor; the china vessels were of fine porcelain, painted with flowers. Under the window stood a dressing table equipped with crystal lamps and polished mirrors. Emerson stood by the table, holding the lantern high.

Firmly planted in the center of the tabletop, surrounded by the little pots and jars that contained Lady Baskerville's beauty aids, was a huge brindled cat. Its shape and its pose were startlingly similar to the statues of felines that have come down to us in great number from ancient Egypt, and the color of its fur was like that shown in the paintings—a ticked brownish and fawn pattern. The triple mirror behind the animal reflected its form, so that it seemed as if not one but an entire pride of ancient Egyptian cats confronted us. Unsympathetic as I am with female vapors in any form, I could not entirely blame Lady Baskerville for behaving as she had; the lantern light turned the creature's eyes to great luminous pools of gold, and they seemed to stare directly into mine with a cold intelligence.

Emerson is insensitive to subtler nuances. Putting out his hand, he tickled the descendant of Bastet, the cat goddess, under its lean chin.

"Nice kitty," he said, smiling. "Whose pet is it, I wonder? It is not wild; see how sleek and fat it is."

"Why, it is Armadale's cat," Milverton exclaimed. Supporting Lady Baskerville, he advanced into the room. The cat closed its eyes and turned its head so that Emerson's fingers could reach the spot under its ears. With its glowing orbs hidden and its purr resounding through the room, it lost its uncanny appearance. Now I could not imagine what Lady Baskerville had made such a fuss about, especially since the cat was known to her personally.

"I wonder where it has been all this time?" Milverton went on. "I haven't seen it since Armadale disappeared. We called it his, and he made himself responsible for its care, but in fact it was something of a house mascot, and we were all fond of it."

"I was not fond of it," Lady Baskerville exclaimed. "Horrid, slinking beast, always leaving dead mice and insects on my bed—"

"That is the nature of cats," I replied, studying the beast with more favor. I had never been particularly fond of cats. Dogs are more English, I believe. I now began to realize that felines may be excellent judges of character, and this belief was confirmed when the cat rolled over and embraced Emerson's hand with its paws.

"Precisely," Milverton said, helping Lady Baskerville to a chair. "I remember hearing his lordship explain that. The ancient Egyptians domesticated cats because of their ability to control rodents—a useful talent in an agricultural society. When Bastet brought her mice to you, Lady Baskerville, she was paying you a delicate attention."

"Ugh," said Lady Baskerville, fanning herself with her handkerchief. "Get the dreadful creature out of here. And do make certain, Mr. Milverton, that it has not left me any other 'attentions.' Where is my maid? If she had been here, as was her duty—"

The door opened, and the apprehensive visage of a middle-aged Egyptian woman appeared.

"Oh, there you are, Atiyah," Lady Baskerville said angrily. "Why weren't you here? What do you mean, allowing this animal to get in?"

From the bewilderment on the woman's face I could see that she understood very little English. Her mistress's anger was only too apparent from her tone, however; Atiyah began to babble in Arabic, explaining that the cat had come in through the window and she had been unable to put it out. Lady Baskerville continued to berate her in English and Atiyah continued to wail in Arabic until Emerson put an end to the performance by scooping the cat up in his arms and marching to the door.

"Pull your curtains and go to bed, Lady Baskerville. Come along, Amelia. Go to your room, Mr. Milverton. Ridiculous business," he added, and strode out. The cat peered at us from over his shoulder.

When we reached our room Emerson put the animal on the floor. It immediately jumped onto the bed and began washing itself. I advanced toward it, somewhat tentatively—not through fear, but because I had never been intimately acquainted with cats. As I put out my hand it rolled over and began to purr.

"Interesting," said Emerson. "That is a position of submission, Amelia; by exposing its soft and vulnerable underbelly it demonstrates that it trusts you. It is unusually tame. I am surprised that it has managed to fend for itself so long."

This aspect of the matter had not occurred to me. Scratching the cat's stomach (a surprisingly pleasant sensation, I confess), I considered the point.

"Emerson," I cried. "It has been with Armadale! Do you suppose it could lead us to him?"

"You know nothing of the nature of cats," Emerson replied, unbuttoning his shirt.

As if to prove him correct, the cat wound all its limbs around my arm and sank its teeth into my hand. I gazed at it in shocked surprise.

"Release your grip at once," I said severely. "You may mean this as another delicate attention, but I assure you it is not appreciated by the recipient."

The cat at once obeyed and licked my fingers apologetically. It then stretched. Its body elongated to a perfectly astonishing degree, as if its muscles were made of India rubber. In a series of agile bounds it passed through the window and disappeared into the night.

I examined my hand. The cat's teeth had left dents in the skin, but had not drawn blood.

"A curious way of demonstrating affection," I remarked. "But it seems a most intelligent creature. Should we not go in search of it?"

"It is a nocturnal animal," Emerson replied. "Now don't get into one of your fits of enthusiasm, Amelia, the way you always do when some new subject captures your agile imagination. Leave the cat to do what cats do in the night-time—an activity, let me add, that we might emulate."

However, we did not do so. Overcome by the fatigues of the day, we were swiftly overcome by slumber so profound that no sound from without disturbed our rest. Yet at some time in the dark hours before the dawn, not far from our open window, Hassan the watchman met the jackal god of cemeteries and set out on the road to the West.

III

Unfortunately we had no chance of hiding this latest evidence of "the curse of the pharaoh." Hassan's body was discovered by a fellow servant, whose woeful ululations roused us from sleep. Departing unceremoniously by way of our bedroom window, Emerson was the first on the scene. I need not say that I was close behind him. We were in time to see the shirttails of the discoverer vanish into the grove. Attributing this disappearance to the horror primitive people feel for a dead body, Emerson did not attempt to call him back, but knelt and turned the dusty bundle of cotton over onto its back.

The blank staring eyes and livid face confronted me almost with a look of accusation. I had not found Hassan a prepossessing character; but a wave of pity and indignation washed over me, and I vowed on the spot that his murderer would not go unpunished.

I said as much to Emerson. Intent on the limp form, which he was examining with some care, he remarked acrimoniously, "There you go again, Amelia, jumping to conclusions. What makes you think the man was murdered?"

"What makes you think he was not?"

"I don't know how the devil he died." Emerson rose to his feet, slapping absently at the cloud of small insects that swarmed around him. "There is a bump on the back of his head, but it was certainly not enough to kill him. Other than that, there is not a mark on him. But there are plenty of fleas. . . . Curse it, I am going to be late for work."

The pace of life in Egypt is slow, and death is commonplace. Ordinarily the authorities would have taken their time in responding to a summons such as ours. But our case was different. If I had required any demonstration of the passionate interest in our affairs that possessed all of Luxor, I would have found it in the speed with which the police appeared on the scene.

Emerson had already left for the Valley, at my suggestion. I had pointed out that it was unnecessary for both of us to waste working hours, for he could add nothing to what I knew of the matter; and since this accorded with his own inclinations, he did not object. I saw no reason to mention my chief reason for wanting him away. I anticipated that the press would soon descend on the house and felt that we were providing enough of a journalistic thrill without any additional contributions from my husband.

Eventually the body of poor Hassan was removed, though not without considerable discussion as to its disposition; for the constable wished to restore it to the family, whereas I insisted on a postmortem. I won my point, naturally, but it was obvious, from the way the men shook their heads and murmured, that they considered such investigation unnecessary. Hassan had been killed by an efreet, the ghost of the pharaoh; why look for further evidence?

Chapter Seven

EAGER as I was to depart at once, I felt obliged to inquire after Lady Baskerville. She was in bed, with her Egyptian maid in attendance. The dark circles under her eyes and the pallor of her cheeks assured me that her complaints of being quite overcome were not entirely fictitious.

"When will this horror end?" she demanded, wringing her hands.

"I am sure I have no idea," I replied. "Is there anything I can do for you, Lady Baskerville, before I go?"

"No. No, I believe I will try to sleep. I had the most dreadful dreams."

I took my departure, before she could tell me about her dreams. It was a pleasure to assume my working garb and set out in the fresh morning air.

Yet dark forebodings haunted me during my walk, for I well knew that once word of Hassan's death got out, even our dedicated workmen might throw down their tools and refuse to enter the accursed tomb. Emerson was not the man to stand meekly aside and let his orders be defied. He would resist—the men would turn on him—attack him. . . . My affectionate imagination presented me with a ghastly image. I could see my husband's life blood soaking into the white dust, and the men trampling his fallen body as they fled. By the time I reached the cliff overlooking the Valley, I was running.

One glance told me that the tragedy I had envisioned had not occurred, though it was clear that news of the latest disaster had spread. The crowd of the previous day had multiplied tenfold. Among the watchers I saw three of our men reinforcing the fence around the work area. They had not rebelled; they were loyal. I do not scruple to admit that a tear of relief dampened my eye. Brushing it resolutely aside, I descended.

Once again my trusty parasol proved its usefulness. By poking it at the backs of the crowd, I won a path through to the stairs. One of the basket men was just coming up. I greeted him effusively. He mumbled something and would not meet my eye. Again my apprehensions rose. Before they could flower into hysteria I heard the sound I yearned to hear—Emerson's voice raised in a blistering Arabic swear word.

It was echoed, bizarrely, by a girl's soft laugh. Squinting into the shadows below, I saw Miss Mary perched on a stool at the bottom of the stairs. Her position must have been uncomfortable, for she was pressed against the wall in order to leave a path for the basket men. But she appeared quite cheerful; greeting me with a shy smile, she said softly, "The Professor does not realize, I am sure, that my Arabic is quite fluent. Pray don't tell him; he needs some outlet for his feelings."

I did not doubt that she found her cramped, hot position a pleasant change from her usual morning's occupation, for any activity that did not include her mother must be pleasurable. However, I found her cheerfulness somewhat frivolous under the circumstances, and I was about to utter a kindly reproof when her pretty face grew sober and she went on, "I am so sorry you had such a distressing experience this morning. I did not learn of it until I arrived here; but I assure you, Mrs. Emerson, that I want to help in any way I can."

This speech convinced me that my initial appraisal of the girl's character had not been at fault. Her cheerfulness was simply an effort to keep her chin up, in the best British tradition. I replied warmly, "You must call me Amelia; we will be working together, I hope, for a long time."

She was about to reply when Emerson came storming out and told me to get to work. I drew him aside. "Emerson," I said in a soft voice, "it is time we took action to end this nonsense about the curse, instead of simply ignoring it. We can only lose that way; every incident will be interpreted as a new instance of supernatural hostility unless—"

"For the love of heaven, Amelia, don't make a speech," Emerson snapped.

"I see the point you are attempting to make; proceed, if you are able, to a specific suggestion."

"I was about to do so when you so rudely interrupted me," I replied spiritedly. "The men seem perturbed by last night's accident. Give them a day or two away from the tomb; set them to work searching for Armadale. If we can find him and prove he was responsible for Lord Baskerville's death—"

"How the devil can we hope to find him when weeks of search produced nothing?"

"But we know he was here, on our very doorstep (so to speak) less than twelve hours ago! Hassan saw the man himself, not his ghost; Armadale must have returned last night and murdered Hassan in order to escape discovery. Or Hassan may have attempted to blackmail him—"

"Good Gad, Amelia, will you attempt to control your rampageous imagination? I admit that what you have suggested is possible. It had, of course, already occurred to me as one explanation among many—"

"You never thought of it until this moment," I said indignantly. "It is just like you to claim the credit for my—"

"Why should I wish to claim credit for such a wild, farfetched—"

"Kindly lower your voice."

"I never raise my voice," Emerson bellowed. A ghostly echo came rolling back from the depths of the tomb, as if the king's spirit were objecting to being awakened.

"Then you will not do as I suggest?"

Emerson's voice dropped to a thunderous growl. "I came here to excavate, Amelia, not to play Sherlock Holmes, a role, let me point out, for which you are no better equipped than I. If you wish to assist me, get to work. If you do not, return to the house and drink tea with Lady Baskerville."

Whereupon he charged back into the tomb. Turning, I met the wide, apprehensive gaze of Mary. I smiled at her.

"Pay no attention to the Professor, Mary. His bark is worse than his bite."

"Oh, I know that. I . . ." The girl raised a trembling hand to brush a lock of hair from her brow. "I am not at all afraid of the Professor."

"You aren't afraid of me, I hope," I said, laughing.

"Oh, no," Mary replied quickly.

"I should hope not. My temper is always mild—though at times Emerson would try the patience of a saint. That is one of the small difficulties of the married state, my dear, as you will discover."

"It is most unlikely that I will," Mary replied bitterly. Before I could pursue this interesting comment, she went on, "I could not help overhearing, Mrs. Emerson. Do you really believe poor Alan is still alive?"

"What other explanation can there be?"

"I don't know. I cannot explain the mystery, but I am sure Alan would never have harmed Lord Baskerville. He was the gentlest of men."

"You knew him well?"

Mary blushed and lowered his eyes. "He . . . he had done me the honor to ask me to be his wife."

"My dear child." I placed a sympathetic hand on her shoulder. "I did not know you were engaged to Mr. Armadale, or I would not have spoken so critically of him."

"No, no, we were not engaged. I was obliged to tell him his hopes could never be realized."

"You did not love him?"

The girl gave me a strange look, in which surprise and amusement were blended with a fatalism unexpected in one of her tender years. "How often does love come in question, Mrs. Emerson?"

"It is—it should be—the only possible basis for marriage," I exclaimed.

Mary continued to study me curiously. "You really believe that! Oh, do forgive me; I did not intend—"

"Why, there is nothing to forgive, my dear. I am always pleased to pass on the benefit of my age and experience to the young, and at the risk of hubris I must say that I consider my marriage a sterling example of what that condition can and should be. My feelings for Emerson, and his for me, are too deep to be concealed. I am the most fortunate of women. And he considers himself the most fortunate of men. I am sure he would say so, if he ever discussed such matters."

Mary was overtaken with a sudden fit of coughing. Struggling heroically to control it, she covered her face with her hands. I administered a brisk slap on the back, remarking, "You had better come up out of the dust for a while."

"No, thank you; I am quite all right now. It was . . . something caught in my throat. Mrs. Emerson—"

"Amelia. I insist."

"You are too kind. I would like, if I may, to return to the subject of Alan Armadale."

"By all means. I am not so narrow-minded, I hope, to refuse to entertain other hypotheses."

"I certainly cannot blame you for suspecting poor Alan," Mary said ruefully. "You are not the first to do so. But if you had been acquainted with him, you would know he could not be guilty of such a vile act. Lord Baskerville was his patron, his benefactor. Alan was devoted to him."

"Then what do you think has become of Mr. Armadale?"

"I fear he has met with a fatal accident," Mary said. Her voice was grave but composed; it assured me that her feelings for the missing man, though affectionate, were not of that degree of tenderness that made it impossible for me to discuss his guilt or innocence freely. She went on, "He had been in a strange mood for several weeks preceding Lord Baskerville's death: wildly gay one moment, gloomy and silent the next. I wondered if my refusal of his offer of marriage was preying on his mind—"

"That hardly seems likely," I interrupted, attempting to reassure her.

"Believe me, I do not assess my charms so highly," Mary replied, with a faint smile. "He took it well at the time; it was not until a week or so later that he began to exhibit the characteristics I speak of, and he did not renew his offer. Something was certainly amiss with him—whether physical or spiritual, I cannot say. Naturally we were all shocked by Lord Baskerville's mysterious death, but Alan's reaction . . . He was like the man in the poem—perhaps you know the one I am thinking of—fearful to turn his head lest he see some foul fiend close behind. I am convinced that his mind gave way and that he wandered into the mountains, where he met with an untimely end."

"Humph," I muttered. "That is conceivable. Though I find it hard to believe that Lord Baskerville's death could affect him so strongly. His lordship was not, I believe, the sort of man who was capable of winning the devoted love of his subordinates."

"Really," Mary said hesitantly, "I would not like—"

"Your discretion does you credit. *Nil nisi bonum,* and all that; but remember, Mary, we are investigating the poor man's death, and this is no time—"

"This is no time for gossip," shouted a voice behind me. Mary started and dropped her pencil. I turned to behold Emerson, his pose one of extreme belligerence, his face flushed with heat and anger. "You are not investigating anything," he went on. "Get that clear in your mind, Amelia, if you can. Stop interfering with my artist and return to your rubbish heap, or I will put you over my shoulder and carry you back to the house."

Without waiting for an answer he vanished into the interior of the tomb.

"Men are such cowards," I said indignantly. "He knew I had more to say. Well, I will deal with him later; it would make a bad impression on the men if I were to follow him and point out the weakness of his argument. I am glad we had this little talk, Mary."

With a reassuring pat on the shoulder, I left the girl to her work. Not that I was at all intimidated by Emerson's anger—no, indeed. I wanted to think over what the girl had told me. She had given me much food for thought. I was particularly struck by her description of Armadale's strange behavior preceding the death of Lord Baskerville. What she failed to see, being fond of the young man, was that this phenomenon only strengthened the theory that Armadale had murdered his patron. The absence of a motive had been one of the things in Armadale's favor; but a maniac needs no motive, as we know from our studies of criminal behavior.

II

Upon returning to the house that evening, tired and hot and out of sorts, it was no pleasure to be told that Lady Baskerville wanted to see us immediately. Emerson replied with a single vehement word and went stamping off to our room. I delayed a moment in order to reassure the messenger, who had turned quite green with terror.

Atiyah, Lady Baskerville's attendant, was a Cairene and a Copt, and therefore was not popular with the Moslem servants. A shy, timid creature of indeterminate age—as are most Egyptian women, once they pass the brief bloom of youth—she spent most of her time in Lady Baskerville's chamber attending to her duties or in the small room in the servants' wing that had been assigned to her use. Lady Baskerville was constantly reprimanding her. Once, after overhearing such a lecture, I asked the lady why she did not employ an English maid, since Atiyah seemed so inadequate. The lady replied, with a curl of her handsome lip, that Lord Baskerville had preferred not to incur the expense. That accorded with what I had heard of his lordship's peculiar blend of professional extravagance and personal parsimony—he had, for instance, never employed a manservant while in Egypt—but I suspected the true reason was that Lady Baskerville could not have bullied and berated a free-born Englishwoman as she did the humble native.

I therefore made it a point to speak gently to the woman, whose hands were fumbling with a string of carved wooden beads, which I took to be a kind of rosary.

"Tell Lady Baskerville we will come as soon as we have changed our clothing, Atiyah." Atiyah continued to stare blankly and finger her beads, so I added, "There is nothing to be afraid of."

These consoling words had precisely the opposite effect from what I had intended. Atiyah started violently and began to speak. Her voice was so low and her discourse so poorly organized that I was obliged to shake her—gently, of course—before I could make any sense of what she said. I then dismissed her, with appropriate reassurances, and hastened to find Emerson.

He had finished bathing and was in the process of putting on his boots. "Hurry up," he said. "I want my tea."

"I assure you, I want it too. Emerson, I have just had a most interesting conversation with Atiyah. She tells me that last night, about the time Hassan was murdered, she saw the figure of a woman, robed and veiled in filmy white, flitting through the palm grove. She is in a state of pitiable terror, poor thing; I was obliged to—"

Emerson had paused in the act of putting on his second boot. Now he flung it across the room. It struck a china vessel, which fell to the floor and smashed into bits. Mingled with the crash was Emerson's roar. I bowdlerize the comment, which concluded with a request that I spare him further examples of local superstition, a subject with which he was only too well acquainted.

As he spoke I began my ablutions. When he finally ran out of breath I said calmly, "I assure you, Emerson, that the woman's story was replete with a wealth of detail that gave it an air of convincing verisimilitude. She saw something, there is no doubt of that. Has it not struck you that not a thousand miles from here dwells a lady who is in the habit of wearing ancient Egyptian dress?"

Emerson's apoplectic countenance relaxed. He let out a snort of laughter. " 'Flit' is hardly the word I would use to describe Madame Berengeria's movements."

"Nor was it the word Atiyah used. I resorted to some permissible poetic license. Help me with these buttons, Emerson, we are late."

I fully expected that we would be even later, for the process of fastening buttons has the effect of arousing Emerson's amative instincts. On this occasion he simply did as he was asked before retrieving his boot and finishing his toilette. I confess—since I have determined to be completely candid about such matters—that I was a trifle put out.

When we reached the drawing room Lady Baskerville was pacing up and down, clearly annoyed at our tardiness, so—as is my invariable custom—I attempted to cast oil on the troubled waters.

"I hope we did not keep you waiting, Lady Baskerville. Had you paused to consider the matter, I am sure you would have realized we required time to freshen up after our arduous labors."

My graceful apology was received with a malignant look, but when the lady turned to Emerson, she was all charm. Mr. Milverton and Karl were also present. The latter still wore his crumpled work clothes. By contrast, Mr. Cyrus Vandergelt was the picture of sartorial elegance in a white linen suit of snowy freshness. A diamond the size of a cherry sparkled in his cravat.

"Here I am again," he remarked cheerfully, as he took my hand. "Hope you aren't tired of seeing my weather-beaten old face, Mrs. Emerson."

"Not at all," I replied.

"Glad to hear it. To tell you the truth, I've been pestering Lady Baskerville for an invitation. Do you think you could persuade her to offer a bed to a poor homeless Yankee?"

His eyes twinkled and the creases in his cheeks deepened as they always did when he was amused; but I had the impression that there was something serious beneath his seemingly humorous suggestion.

"There is something serious beneath your seemingly humorous suggestion," I said. "What are you driving at?"

"Amazing acumen!" Mr. Vandergelt exclaimed. "As always, Mrs. Emerson, you are one hundred percent correct. I'm downright unhappy about the way things are going. You folks haven't spent much time in Luxor, but take my word for it, the town is humming like a beehive. Somebody broke into Madame Berengeria's room this afternoon while she was taking her siesta, and made off with her jewelry—"

"That cannot have been a great loss," Lady Baskerville murmured.

"Maybe not, but it scared the poor woman half to death when she woke up and found the place all topsy-turvy. I happened to be at the hotel when the servants pelted in yelling. Poor little Miss Mary is in for a hard time when she gets home; Madame was raving about ungrateful daughters who abandon their mothers, and so on." Mr. Vandergelt took a handkerchief from his pocket and mopped his brow as he relived the painful interview. "I know as well as you do that sneak thieves aren't unusual," he went on. "But I can't remember any thief being quite as bold as this one; it's a sign of rising feelings against foreigners, especially the ones connected with this expedition. I'm proposing to move in to help protect you ladies in case of trouble. That's what it amounts to."

"Humph," said Emerson. "I assure you, Vandergelt, I am perfectly capable of protecting not only Amelia and Lady Baskerville but any indeterminate number of helpless females."

I opened my mouth, an indignant comment trembling on my lips; but I was not allowed to make it. With rising heat Emerson went on, "Curse it, Vandergelt, there are three able-bodied men here, not to mention my men from Aziyeh, who are completely reliable and who would defend Amelia and myself to the death. What are you up to?"

"The Professor has it correct," said Karl, in his Germanic way. "We can defend the ladies; never will they be in danger when here I am."

There was a faint murmur of agreement from Mr. Milverton. I found the murmur and the young man's troubled countenance far from reassuring, but Karl was the picture of manly devotion as he rose to his feet, his muscular frame (and his mustache) vibrant with emotion and his gold-rimmed spectacles gleaming. He added, "I only wish, ladies and sirs, that Miss Mary could be here. It is not right that she should be alone in Luxor with her aging and peculiar maternal parent."

"We can't ask her to come here unless we invite her mother," said Mr. Vandergelt.

There was a brief pause while everyone considered the idea. Karl was the first to break the silence. "If it must be—"

"Certainly not," Lady Baskerville exclaimed. "I will not tolerate that woman's presence. But if you wish to join us, Cyrus, you know you are always welcome. Not that I feel there is any real danger."

"Wait until the townspeople hear about the white lady," I said ruefully.

Lady Baskerville let out an exclamation and gazed on me with burning eyes. "Have you had . . ." She checked herself for a moment and then went on, ". . . a conversation with my foolish Atiyah?"

I had the distinct impression that this was not what she had meant to say.

"She mentioned seeing a figure in white robes last night, about the time Hassan was killed," I replied. "To be sure, it might have been imagination."

"What else could it have been?" Lady Baskerville demanded. "The woman is hopelessly superstitious."

"It doesn't matter." Vandergelt shook his head. "That's the kind of talk you folks don't need."

"It is perfectly ridiculous," Lady Baskerville exclaimed angrily. She walked toward the windows. The swift desert night had fallen; the evening breeze set the flimsy curtains billowing and carried the sweet, cloying scent of jasmine into the room. With one white hand holding the curtains, Lady Baskerville stood with her back to us, looking out into the night. I had to admit she made a handsome picture in her softly draped black gown, her queenly head with its crown of shining hair poised on her slender throat.

The discussion continued. Emerson could hardly refuse to receive Mr. Vandergelt when the mistress of the house had made him welcome, but he did not attempt to conceal his displeasure. Vandergelt replied with perfect good humor, but I rather thought he enjoyed Emerson's discomfiture and, in numerous sly ways, added to it.

Suddenly Lady Baskerville gave a sharp cry and stepped away from the window. The warning was too late. With the celerity of a speeding bullet (though of considerably larger dimensions), a missile hurtled through the open window and crossed the room, landing with a crash on the tea table and sending broken china flying in all directions. Before it reached its final destination, however, it achieved its aim. With a violent (and, I am sorry to report, profane) exclamation, Emerson clapped his hand to his head, staggered, and fell full length upon the floor. The impact of his body toppled several small fragile objects from the tables and shelves where they stood, so that the collapse of the colossus (if I may be permitted a literary metaphor) was accompanied by a perfect symphony of breaking glass.

As one man (speaking figuratively, in my case) we rushed to Emerson's side. The only exception was Lady Baskerville, who stood frozen to the spot like Lot's wife. Needless to say, I was the first to reach my husband; but before I could clasp him to my bosom he sat up, his hand still pressed to his temple. From beneath his fingers, already horribly stained with his gore, a crimson stream flowed down his brown cheek.

"Curse it," he said; and would have said more, no doubt, but dizziness overcame him; his eyes rolled up, his head fell back, and he would have collapsed again had I not flung my arms about him and cradled his head on my breast.

"How many times have I told you that you must not move suddenly after receiving a blow on the head?" I demanded.

"I hope you have not had occasion to offer that advice frequently," said Mr. Vandergelt. He proffered his handkerchief.

Believe me, reader, I did not mistake his coolness for callousness. Like myself, he had observed that the missile had only grazed Emerson's cranium in passing. I admire a man of that temperament; I gave him a quick, approving smile before I accepted the handkerchief and applied it to Emerson's head. The stubborn man was beginning to struggle, attempting to rise.

"Lie still," I said sharply, "or I will have Mr. Milverton sit on your legs."

Mr. Milverton gave me a startled look. Fortunately the expedient I had proposed was not necessary. Emerson relaxed, and I was able to lower his head onto my lap. At this point, as things were calming down, Lady Baskerville created a new sensation.

"The woman in white!" she shrieked. "I saw her—there—"

Mr. Vandergelt reached her just in time to catch her as she fainted. If I were an evil-minded woman, I would have suspected she delayed her collapse long enough to give him time.

"I will go for a doctor," Mr. Milverton exclaimed.

"There is no need," I replied, pressing the handkerchief against the gash on Emerson's temple. "The cut is superficial. There is a possibility of a mild concussion, but I can deal with that."

Emerson's eyes opened. "Amelia," he croaked, "remind me to tell you, when I am feeling a little stronger, what I think of your—"

I covered his lips with my hand. "I know, my dear," I said soothingly. "You need not thank me."

Now at ease with regard to Emerson's condition, I could turn my attention to Lady Baskerville, who was draped becomingly over Mr. Vandergelt's arm. Her eyes were closed; her long black hair had broken free of its pins and hung in a dark, shining waterfall, almost touching the floor. For the first time since we had met, Mr. Vandergelt looked mildly disconcerted, though he held the lady's limp form to his breast with considerable fervor.

"Put her on the couch," I said. "It is only a faint."

"Mrs. Emerson, just look at this," said Karl.

In his outstretched hand he held the projectile that had inflicted so much damage. At first I thought it was only a rough-hewn rock, approximately eight inches in diameter. A shudder passed through my body as I contemplated what might have occurred if it had struck its target squarely. Then Karl turned the rock over, and I found myself staring into a human face.

The eyes were deep-set, the chin unnaturally long, the lips curved in a strange, enigmatic smile. Traces of blue paint still marked the helmet-shaped headdress—the Battle Crown of an Egyptian pharaoh. I had seen that peculiar physiognomy before. It was, in fact, as familiar to me as the face of an old friend.

"Khuenaton!" I exclaimed.

In my excitement I had forgotten that this—among other archaeological terms—would have aroused Emerson from a deep coma, much less a bump on the head. Casting off my hand, which I had kept absentmindedly pressed to his lips, he sat up and snatched the carved head from Karl's hand.

"That is wrong, Amelia," he said. "You know Walter believes the name should be read Akhenaton, not Khuenaton."

"He will always be Khuenaton to me," I replied, giving him a meaningful look as I recalled the days of our first acquaintance in the derelict city of the heretic pharaoh.

My tender reference was wasted on Emerson, who continued to study the object that had nearly crushed his skull.

"Amazing," he muttered. "It is genuine—not a copy. Where on earth—"

"This is no time for archaeologizing," I said severely. "You must get to bed at once, Emerson, and as for Lady Baskerville—"

"Bed? Nonsense." Emerson got to his feet, assisted by the assiduous Karl. Dazedly his eyes scanned the room and finally focused on the limp body of Lady Baskerville. "What is wrong with her?" he demanded.

As if on cue, Lady Baskerville opened her eyes.

"The woman in white!" she cried.

Vandergelt dropped to one knee beside the couch and took her hand. "You are perfectly safe, my dear. Don't be alarmed. What did you see?"

"A woman in white, obviously," I said, before the lady could reply. "Who was it, Lady Baskerville? Did she hurl the missile?"

"I don't know." Lady Baskerville passed her hand over her brow. "I caught a glimpse of her—a dim white figure, ghostly, with a gleam as of gold on her arms and brow. Then something came rushing at me, and involuntarily I recoiled. Oh! Oh, Radcliffe, you are covered with blood! How ghastly!"

"I am perfectly well," Emerson replied, oblivious of the crimson stains that disfigured his face. "Where the devil do you suppose the fellow found this carved head?"

This sort of thing might have gone on indefinitely—Emerson speculating about the origin of the head, and Lady Baskerville keening about blood like a banshee—if someone had not intervened. To my surprise, it was Mr. Milverton. An amazing transformation had passed over him. His step was elastic, his color good, his tone firm yet respectful.

"Forgive me, Professor, but we really must have an interlude for rest and reflection. You took quite a crack on the head, you know, and we can't risk anything going wrong with you. Lady Baskerville ought to rest too, she has had a frightful shock. If you will allow me."

With a smiling, conspiratorial glance at me, he took Emerson's arm. My husband allowed himself to be led from the room. He was still crooning over the lethal little head, which he held cupped in his hands.

Lady Baskerville followed, leaning weakly on Mr. Vandergelt's arm. After escorting Emerson to our room, Mr. Milverton drew me aside.

"I will go and tidy up the drawing room," he said. "We don't want the servants to know of this."

"I fear it is already too late," I replied. "But it is a good thought, Mr. Milverton; thank you."

The young fellow went out, whistling under his breath. I looked at my husband, who was staring as if mesmerized into the strange carved eyes of the heretic pharaoh. But as I tended Emerson's wound and thanked the Almighty for his miraculous escape, I realized that there was an explanation for Mr. Milverton's sudden access of good spirits. He could not be suspected of hurling the deadly missile. Was he relieved because a second party—a confederate, perhaps—had cleared him of suspicion?

Chapter Eight

WHEN I attempted to lead my wounded spouse to his bed I discovered that he was determined to go out.

"I must talk to the men," he insisted. "They will have heard of this latest incident, you may be sure, and if I am not completely honest with them—"

"I see your point," I said coldly. "At least change your shirt, will you, please? That one is ruined. I told you you should have ordered another dozen before we left England; you are the most destructive man—"

At this point Emerson precipitately left the room. Of course I followed him.

The men were housed in a building that had been meant to be a storeroom. It was a little distance from the house, and we had had it fitted up with all the necessary comforts. When we reached the place I saw that Emerson had been right. The men *had* heard the news, and were talking it over.

They stared at Emerson as if he were a ghost. Then Abdullah, who had been squatting by the fire, rose to his impressive height.

"You live, then," he said, the glow of repressed emotion in his eyes belying his calm tone. "We had heard—"

"Lies," Emerson said. "An enemy threw a stone at me. It struck a glancing blow."

He swept the thick waving locks from his brow, baring the ugly wound. The red glow of the fire illumined his stalwart frame. The bloodstains on his shirt looked black. He stood unmoving, his brown hand raised to his brow, his countenance as proudly calm as that of a sculptured pharaoh. Shadows deepened the cleft in his chin and framed his firm lips in dark outline.

After he had given them time to look their fill, he lowered his hand, allowing his black locks to fall back in place.

"The spirits of the dead do not throw stones," he said. "What man of Gurneh hates me enough to wish me dead?"

At that the men nodded and exchanged meaningful glances. It was Abdullah who replied, a humorous gleam warming his austere bearded face.

"Emerson, there are many men in Gurneh and elsewhere who hate you so much. The guilty man hates the judge, and the chidden child resents a stern father."

"You are not guilty men, or children," Emerson replied. "You are my friends. I came at once to you, to tell you what happened. *Allah yimmessikum bilkheir.*"

II

Of course if I had really felt Emerson should stay in bed I would have seen that he stayed there, by one means or another. It was apparent, however, that he was in the rudest possible health; he bounded out of bed next morning with all the panache of d'Artagnan preparing to storm La Rochelle. Disdaining my offer of assistance, he affixed a huge square of sticking plaster to his forehead, as if scorning to conceal his injury.

I was out of temper with him. The primeval drama of the confrontation with our men had aroused correspondingly primeval emotions in me; but when I expressed them to Emerson he replied that he had a headache. This was certainly a reasonable excuse, but I could not help being vexed.

Naturally I concealed my feelings with my customary dignity, and as we set out for the Valley my spirits rose. It was a typically glorious Upper Egyptian morning. The rising orb of the sun lifted majestically over the eastern mountains, and its golden rays seemed to caress us with loving arms, as the arms of the god Aten embraced the divine king who was his son.

Yet the day, which began so auspiciously, turned out to be replete with disasters. No sooner had we arrived at the tomb than we came face to face with the imam. Brandishing a long staff, he burst into an impassioned harangue, threatening us with death and damnation and pointing dramatically to Emerson's bandaged brow as evidence of the latest demonstration of the pharaoh's curse.

Emerson may deny it, but I am convinced he enjoys these encounters. His arms folded, he listened with an air of courteous boredom. Once he even yawned. Instead of interrupting, he let the man go on and on and on; and eventually the inevitable happened. The listeners also showed signs of boredom as the imam started to repeat himself, and the hoped-for battle of words degenerated into a monologue. Eventually the imam ran out of imprecations, as even the most fanatical man must. When he had stopped ranting, Emerson waited a little longer, his head tilted at an expectant angle. Then he said politely, "Is that all? Thank you,

Holy One, for your interest," and, circling respectfully around the infuriated religious person, he descended into the tomb.

Scarcely an hour later there was another disturbance. Hearing angry voices from the tomb, I went to see what was the matter and found Karl and Mr. Milverton facing one another in combative attitudes. Milverton stood with his feet apart and his fists raised; Karl, restrained by Emerson, was struggling and demanding to be let loose so he could administer some unspecified punishment. A rising lump on Karl's jaw showed that the struggle had gone beyond words.

"He insulted Miss Mary," Milverton cried, without abandoning his pugilistic stance.

Karl burst into impassioned German. He had not insulted the lady; Milverton had. When he had objected, Milverton had struck him.

Milverton's normally pale countenance turned red, and the fight would have broken out again if Emerson had not clamped an iron hand over one young man's bicep and throttled the other by catching hold of his collar.

"How ridiculous!" Mary, who had been standing quietly to one side, now came forward. Her cheeks were flushed and her eyes sparkled. She looked amazingly pretty; and for a moment all the men, including my husband, stopped arguing and stared at her in open admiration.

"No one insulted me," she declared. "I appreciate your efforts to defend me; but you are being very silly, and I insist you shake hands and make up, like good boys."

This speech—accompanied by a languishing glance from under her thick black lashes, impartially divided between Milverton and Karl—did not do much to improve relations between the two, but it forced them to make a pretense at reconciliation. Coldly they touched fingertips. Mary smiled. Emerson threw up his hands. I returned to my rubbish heap.

Early in the afternoon Emerson came up to join me.

"How is it going?" he inquired genially, fanning himself with his hat.

We were talking quietly, about one thing and another, when Emerson's eyes wandered from my face and his own countenance underwent such a dreadful alteration that I turned in alarm.

A fantastic cortege was approaching. Leading it were six men whose bowed shoulders supported two long poles on which was balanced a boxlike structure completely enclosed by curtains. This object swayed dangerously as the bearers staggered along under what was clearly a considerable weight. A straggling crowd of natives in turbans and long robes accompanied the apparition.

The procession made its laborious way to where we stood staring. I then saw a man in European garb walking behind the palanquin. His hat was drawn down over his brows, but a few locks of red hair had escaped to betray an identity he seemed not eager to proclaim.

The panting, sweating bearers came to a halt and lowered the carrying poles. Unfortunately they did not move in unison; the palanquin tilted and spilled a stout form out onto the ground, where it lay emitting cries of pain and alarm. I had already surmised who the occupant of the weird structure must be. No one else in Luxor would have attempted to travel in such a way.

Madame Berengeria was wearing her linen robe, a clumsy copy of the exquisite pleated gowns noble ladies were accustomed to wear in pharaonic times. Her fall had disarranged this garment to betray a truly appalling extent of fat, pallid flesh. Her black wig, which was surrounded by a cloud of small insects, had tumbled over her eyes.

Emerson stood with his hands on his hips, staring down at the writhing form of the lady. "Well, help her up, O'Connell," he said. "And if you want to avert a nasty scene, shove her back into that ridiculous contraption and take her away."

"Mr. O'Connell has no desire to avoid a scene," I said. "He promotes them."

My acerbic comment restored the young man's composure. He smiled and pushed his hat back so that it rested at a jaunty angle.

"How unkind, Mrs. Emerson. Will one of you give me a hand? I can't manage the job alone, and that's the truth."

The bearers had collapsed onto the ground, panting and cursing. It was clear that we would get no help from them. Seeing that Emerson had no intention of touching the prostrate form—and indeed, I could not blame him—I joined Mr. O'Connell in his attempt to hoist Madame Berengeria to her feet. We succeeded, though I think I strained several muscles in my back.

Hearing the altercation, the others emerged from the tomb. I distinctly heard Mary pronounce a word I never expected a well-bred English girl to say.

"Mother, what in heaven's name are you doing here? You should not have come. The sun—the exertion—"

"I was called!" Madame Berengeria flung off the hand her daughter had placed on her shoulder. "I was told to come. The warning must be passed on. My child, come away!"

"Curse it," Emerson said. "Clap your hand over her mouth, Amelia, quickly."

Of course I did nothing of the sort. The damage was done. The watching tourists, the natives who had followed the palanquin—all were listening avidly. Striking an imposing attitude, Madame went on.

"It came to me as I meditated before the shrine of Amon and Serapis, lord of the underworld. Danger! Disaster! It was my duty to come, at whatever effort, to warn those who profane the tomb. A mother's heart gave a dying woman strength to fly to the aid of her child—"

"Mother!" Mary stamped her foot. So might the divine Cleopatra have looked as she defied Caesar—if one could picture Cleopatra in a shirtwaist and walking skirt, with tears of embarrassment flooding her eyes.

Madame Berengeria stopped speaking, but only because she had finished what she wanted to say. Her mean little mouth was set in a self-satisfied smirk.

"I am sorry, Mother," Mary said. "I didn't mean to be impertinent, but—"

"I forgive you," Madame said.

"But you must not talk like this. You must go home at once."

One of the bearers understood English. He let out a howl and addressed Mary in impassioned Arabic. Though embroidered with expletives and complaints, the gist of his speech was simple enough. His back was broken, the backs of his friends were broken; they could not carry the lady another step.

Emerson settled the difficulty with a combination of threats and bribery. When the price had gone high enough the men discovered that their backs were not broken after all. We bundled Madame Berengeria unceremoniously into her palanquin, resisting her efforts to embrace Emerson, whom she addressed affectionately as Ramses the Great, her lover and husband. Groaning piteously, the men were preparing to lift the palanquin when Madame's disheveled head once more appeared between the curtains. Thrusting out an arm, she prodded the nearest bearer.

"To the house of Lord Baskerville," she said.

"No, Mother," Mary exclaimed. "Lady Baskerville does not want . . . It would be rude to call on her without an invitation."

"An errand of mercy requires no invitation," was the reply. "I go to cast the mantle of my protection over that house of blood. By prayer and meditation I will avert the danger." Then, with a sudden descent from her lofty tone, she added, "I have brought your things too, Mary; there is no need for you to return to Luxor tonight."

"You mean—you mean you are planning to stay?" Mary gasped. "Mother, you cannot—"

"I certainly don't intend to spend another night in that house where I was almost murdered in my bed yesterday."

"Why don't you avert the danger by prayer and meditation?" I inquired.

Madame Berengeria glowered at me. "You are not the mistress of Baskerville House. Let her ladyship deny me, if she can." Again she prodded the bearer. "Go—now—Baskerville House."

"It may be just as well," I said to Emerson in a low voice. "We can keep her under observation if she is actually living in the house."

"What an appalling idea," said Emerson. "Really, Amelia, I don't think Lady Baskerville—"

"Then stop her. I don't see how you can do it, short of binding and gagging her. But if that is your desire—"

"Oh, bah!" Emerson folded his arms. "I wash my hands of the entire affair."

Mary, overcome by shame, had also withdrawn from the discussion.

Seeing she had won, Madame Berengeria's face split into a narrow toadlike grin. The procession set out, leaving Mr. O'Connell behind like a small dapper whale stranded on a sandy beach.

Emerson's chest swelled as he turned on the young man, but before he could speak Mary anticipated him.

"How dare you, Kevin? How could you encourage her to do this?"

"Ah, my dear, but I did my best to stop her, and that's the truth. What else could I do but come along to protect her in case of trouble? You do believe me, don't you, Mary?"

He attempted to take her hand. She snatched it away with a gesture of ineffable disdain. Tears of distress sparkled in her eyes. Quickly she turned and walked back toward the tomb.

Mr. O'Connell's freckled face fell. The faces of Karl and Milverton took on identical expressions of smug pleasure. As one man they wheeled and followed Mary.

O'Connell caught my eye. He shrugged and tried to smile. "Spare me your comments, Mrs. Emerson. I'll be back in her good graces soon, never fear."

"If one word of this incident gets into the newspapers," I began.

"But what can I do?" O'Connell's china-blue eyes widened. "Every journalist in Luxor will know of the affair by dinnertime, if they don't know of it already. I would lose my position if I let personal feelings interfere with my duty to my readers."

"You had better take yourself off," I said, seeing that Emerson was beginning to shuffle his feet and growl, like a bull preparing to charge. Mr. O'Connell grinned broadly at me. With the assistance of Mr. Vandergelt I managed to remove my husband; and after an interval of profound cogitation he remarked glumly, "Vandergelt, I believe I will have to accept your offer after all—not to protect the ladies, but to protect *me* from *them.*"

"I'm tickled to death," the American said promptly.

Returning to my rubbish heap, I saw that Mr. O'Connell had taken himself off. As I proceeded with the methodical and monotonous chore of sifting the debris I considered an idea that had come to me during my conversation with the young journalist. It was clear that he would cheerfully endure personal violence in his pursuit of a story, and sooner or later Emerson, if goaded, would oblige him. Since we could not rid ourselves of his attentions, why not turn them to our own advantage and control his comments by offering him the exclusive rights to our story? In order to maintain this advantageous position he would be obliged to defer to our wishes and refrain from baiting my excitable husband.

The more I thought about this scheme, the more brilliant it seemed to me. I was tempted to propose it to Emerson at once; but since his immediate reaction to my suggestions is usually an emphatic negative, I decided to wait till later, when he had, hopefully, recovered from the ill temper induced by the latest encounter with Madame Berengeria.

An alarming development occurred later that afternoon, when a section of the exposed ceiling of the passageway collapsed, narrowly missing one of the men. The rumbling crash and cloud of dust emerging from the stairwell caused a flutter of excitement among the watchers and brought me rushing to the spot. Through the fog of dust I saw Emerson, dimly visible like a demon in a pantomime, wiping his face with his sleeve and cursing nobly.

"We will have to shore up the ceiling and walls as we proceed," he declared. "I saw that the rock was in bad condition, but hoped it would improve as we proceeded. Unhappily the reverse seems to be the case. Abdullah, send Daoud and his brother back to the house to fetch wood and a bag of nails. Curse it, this will slow the work even more."

"But it must be done," I said. "A serious accident now would convince the men that we are indeed under a curse."

"Thank you for your tender concern," Emerson snarled. "What are you doing down here anyway? Get back to work."

Obviously the time was not ripe for me to discuss my scheme regarding Mr. O'Connell.

No one can accuse me of being an uncritically doting wife. I am fully cognizant of Emerson's many faults. In this case, however, I recognized his evil temper as a manifestation of that well-nigh supernatural force of character which drove the men to efforts exceeding their natural powers. The ill-omened words of Madame Berengeria, closely followed by the rockfall, had rendered even more uneasy temperaments not wholly unaffected by earlier uncanny events. With a lesser man than my husband at the helm, they might have walked off the job that very day.

Unfortunately Emerson's mood of majestic authority is accompanied, in the domestic sphere, by an arrogance that any woman less understanding than I would refuse to tolerate for an instant. I put up with it only because I was as anxious as he to see the work proceed apace.

Only with the imminence of night did Emerson dismiss the exhausted men. It was a weary group that started back along the rocky path. I had attempted to persuade Mary to go the long way around, on donkeyback, but she insisted on accompanying us, and of course the two young men followed her like sheep. Vandergelt had left earlier, assuring us he would meet us at the house after he had collected his luggage from the hotel.

I was still pleased with my idea of enlisting Mr. O'Connell, but I knew better than to mention it to Emerson. Hands in his pockets, head bowed, he tramped along in grim silence. In addition to the other disasters of the day, the final hours of work had brought to light some ominous evidence. The men had cleared almost ten metres of the corridor and had finally exposed the figure of a royal personage, probably the owner of the tomb; but, alas, the head of this figure had been savagely mutilated, and the royal name in the inscription above it had been similarly defaced. This proof that the tomb had been violated depressed us all. After moving mountains of stone, would we find only an empty sarcophagus? This fear would have been enough in itself to justify my husband's gloomy silence. The prospect of facing Madame Berengeria and Lady Baskerville, whose mood would undoubtedly be unpleasant, further depressed him.

If Mary was concerned about the social embarrassment awaiting her she showed no signs of it. She had endured the long day's labor far better than her fragile appearance had led me to expect. She and the young men were ahead of us, for Emerson was not in any hurry, and I heard her chatting merrily and even laughing. I observed that she had accepted Karl's arm and was addressing most of her comments to him. Milverton, on her other side, attempted without success to attract her attention. After a time Milverton stopped and let the others draw ahead. As Emerson and I came up to him, I saw that he was watching the girl's slim figure with a look of poignant distress.

Emerson plodded on without so much as a glance at the disconsolate young man, but I did not feel it right to neglect such obvious signs of mental perturbation. I therefore let my husband go ahead and, taking Milverton's arm, requested his assistance. I do not scruple to employ mendacity and a fictitious appearance of female incompetence when the occasion demands it.

Milverton responded like a gentleman. We walked in silence for a time and then, as I had expected, his wounded heart sought the relief of conversation.

"What can she see in him?" he burst out. "He is plain, pedantic, and poor!"

I was tempted to laugh at this damning and alliterative catalog of deficiencies. Instead I sighed and shook my head.

"I fear she is a heartless flirt, Mr. Milverton."

"I beg to differ," Mr. Milverton said warmly. "She is an angel."

"She is certainly as beautiful as an angel," I agreed amiably.

"She is; she is! She reminds me of that Egyptian queen, don't you know?—I forget the name—"

"Nefertiti?"

"Yes, that's the one. And her figure. . . . Look how gracefully she walks."

This was not easy to do, for dusk was far advanced, and as I realized this a new uneasiness shadowed my mind even as twilight shadowed the scene. The path was difficult enough in daylight; the rocky descent would not be easy in the dark. Also, night would serve as a cloak to enemies. I only hoped that Emerson's stubbornness had not exposed us to accident or worse. I took a firmer hold of Milverton's arm and quickened my pace. We had fallen far behind the others, and Emerson's form, some distance ahead, was now no more than a shadowy outline against the blossoming stars.

Milverton was still alternately rhapsodizing and reproaching Mary. Conquering my apprehension, I attempted to make him see the situation in the calm light of reason.

"Perhaps she doubts your intentions, Mr. Milverton. They are, I assume, those of an honorable gentleman?"

"You wound me inexpressibly, Mrs. Emerson," the young man exclaimed. "My feelings are so profound, so respectful—"

"Then why don't you express them to their object? Have you proposed to her?"

Milverton sighed. "How can I? What have I to offer her, in my situation—"

He stopped speaking with a sharp intake of breath.

I verily believe that my own respiration halted for an instant as the import of that betraying pause dawned on me. If he had ended his sentence with that word, or allowed it to trail off into the mournful silence of indecision, I would have assumed he was referring to his subordinate position, his youth, and his lack of financial security. My detective instincts—the result of natural aptitude and of a certain not inconsiderable experience—immediately showed me the true meaning of his gasp. The comfortable cloak of darkness and the seductive influence of womanly sympathy had lowered his guard. He had been on the verge of confessing!

The detective instinct, when in full bloom, ruthlessly suppresses softer feelings. I am ashamed to admit that my next speech was dictated, not by sympathy, but by guile. I was determined to break through his guard, to trick him into an admission.

"Your situation is difficult," I said. "But I know Mary will stand by you, if she loves you. Any true woman would."

"Would she? Would you?" Before I could reply he turned and caught me by the shoulders.

I confess that a slight qualm dampened my detective ardor. The darkness was now complete, and the tall form of Milverton hovered over me like a creature of night, no longer entirely human. I felt his hot breath on my face and felt his fingers pressing painfully into my flesh. It occurred to me that possibly I might have been guilty of a slight error in judgment.

Before I was stampeded into committing some foolish act, such as calling for help or striking Mr. Milverton with my parasol, a silvery light illumined the darkness as the moon, almost at the full, rose over the cliffs. I had forgotten that this phenomenon must inevitably occur; for almost never are there cloudy skies in Luxor. So pure, so limpid is the lunar illumination in that southern clime that it is possible to read a book by its rays; but who would dream of turning his eyes to a sterile page of print when a magical landscape of shadow and silver lies before him? Moonlight in ancient Thebes! How often and how understandably has this theme formed the subject of literary masterpieces!

My feeble pen, moved by a mind more susceptible to cold reason than to poetry (though not untouched by its influence, never think that) . . . my feeble pen, as I say, will not attempt to rival the effusions of more gifted writers. More to the point, the light enabled me to see Mr. Milverton's face which, in his extremity, he had pressed close to mine. I saw, with considerable relief, that his handsome features bore a look of anxiety and distress, with no trace of the mania I had feared to see.

The same light allowed him to see *my* face, which must have betrayed discomfort. Immediately he loosened his grasp.

"Forgive me. I—I am not myself, Mrs. Emerson, indeed I am not. I think I have been half mad these past weeks. I can endure it no longer. I must speak. May I confide in you? May I trust you?"

"You may!" I cried.

The young man took a deep breath and drew himself up to his full height, his broad shoulders squared. His lips parted.

At that precise moment a long-drawn-out shriek echoed across the wilderness of tumbled stone. For a moment I thought Mr. Milverton was howling like a werewolf. But he was as startled as I; and almost at once I realized that the peculiar acoustical qualities of the area had made a sound whose origin was some distance away sound mysteriously close at hand. The moon was fully up by then, and as I scanned the terrain, seeking the source of the eerie cry, I beheld an alarming sight.

Bounding across the plateau came Emerson, leaping boulders and soaring over crevasses. His speeding form was followed by a silvery cloud of dust, and his unearthly cries, combined with this ectoplasmic accompaniment, would have struck terror into a superstitious heart. He was moving in our direction, but at an angle to the path. Waving my parasol, I immediately set off on a course that would cross his.

I was able to intercept him, for I had calculated the intersecting angles accurately. Knowing him well, I did not attempt to stop him by touching him or grasping him lightly; instead I threw the whole weight of my body against his, and we both went tumbling to the ground. As I had planned, Emerson was underneath.

Once he had gotten his breath back, the moonlit scene again echoed to the fervor of his cries, now entirely profane and almost entirely directed at me. Taking a seat on a convenient boulder, I waited until he had calmed himself.

"This is too much," he remarked, raising himself to a sitting position. "Not only am I under attack by every malcontent and religious maniac in Luxor, but my own wife turns against me. I was in pursuit, Amelia—hot pursuit! I would have caught the rascal if you had not interfered."

"I assure you, you would not," I said. "There was no one else in sight. He undoubtedly crept away among the rocks while you were rushing around and howling. Who was it?"

"Habib, I suppose," Emerson replied. "I caught only a glimpse of a turban and a fluttering robe. Curse it, Amelia, I was just about—"

"And I was just about to become the repository of a confidence from Mr. Milverton," I said, in considerable bitterness of spirit. "He was on the verge of confessing to the crime. I do wish you could learn to control that juvenile joie de vivre which leads you to act before you—"

"That is certainly a case of the pot reprimanding the kettle," Emerson cried. "Joie de vivre is too kind a word for the inveterate conceit that leads you to believe yourself—"

Before he could finish this insulting comment we were joined by the others. Agitated questions and explanations followed. We then proceeded, Emerson conceding reluctantly that there was no sense in continuing a pursuit of someone who had long since vanished. Rubbing his hip and limping ostentatiously, he headed the procession.

Once again I found myself with Mr. Milverton. As he offered me his arm I saw that he was struggling to repress a smile.

"I could not help overhearing part of your conversation," he began.

I tried to recall what I had said. I knew I had made some references to a confession. But when Milverton continued I was relieved to learn that he had not heard that part of my speech.

"I don't mean to be impertinent, Mrs. Emerson, but I am intrigued by the relationship between you and the Professor. Was it really necessary for you to knock him flat?"

"Of course it was. Nothing short of physical violence can stop Emerson when he is in a rage, and if I had not stopped him he would have gone on running until he tumbled over the cliffs or caught his foot in a hole."

"I see. He did not seem to—er—appreciate your concern for his safety."

"Oh, that is just his manner," I said. Emerson, still limping in a vulgar and unconvincing fashion, was not far ahead, but I did not trouble to lower my voice. "Like all Englishmen, he does not care to display his true emotions in public. In private, I assure you, he is the tenderest and most affectionate—"

This was too much for Emerson, who turned and shouted, "Hurry up, you two; what are you doing, dawdling along back there?"

So, with considerable vexation, I abandoned hope of regaining Milverton's confidence. As we made our way down the winding and dangerous descent, there was no opportunity for a private conversation. We had gone only a short distance toward the house, whose lights we could see gleaming through the palm fronds, when we were met by Mr. Vandergelt, who, anxious at our tardiness, had come out in search of us.

As we entered the courtyard Milverton caught my hand.

"Did you mean it?" he whispered. "You assured me—"

A flame of exultation soared from the dying embers of hope.

"Every word," I whispered back. "Trust me."

"Amelia, what are you muttering about?" Emerson demanded pettishly. "Hurry up, can't you?"

I took a firm grip on my parasol and managed not to hit him with it. "I am coming," I replied. "Do you go on."

We were almost at the door. I heard a voice in my ear murmur, "Midnight; on the loggia."

III

As soon as we stepped into the house Emerson fled toward our room like a man pursued by demons, and, indeed, the distant echo of a resounding voice which could only be that of Madame Berengeria gave him some excuse for flight. When I entered our room he began to groan and wince. Displaying a large area of scraped, reddened skin, he accused me of being responsible for it.

I paid no attention to this childish exhibition.

"Emerson," I cried eagerly, "you will never guess what has happened. Despite your stupid interference . . ." Here he began to expostulate. I raised my voice and went on, "I have won Mr. Milverton's confidence. He is going to confess!"

"Well, do shout a little louder," Emerson said. "There must be a few people in the house who haven't heard you."

The reproof was justified, if rudely expressed. I dropped my voice to a whisper. "He is deeply disturbed, Emerson. I am sure the murder was unpremeditated; no doubt he was driven to it."

"Humph." Standing on a mat, Emerson pulled off his shirt and began to sponge himself off. "What precisely did he say?"

"You are very calm," I exclaimed. I took the sponge from his hand and washed the sand and dust from his back. "He was unable to give me any details. That will come later. I am to meet him at midnight, in—"

"You have lost your wits," said Emerson. His voice was calmer, however, and as I continued to move the sponge rhythmically over the hard muscles of his back, he let out an absurd purring murmur of pleasure. "Do you really suppose, my dear Peabody, that I will let you go out to meet a murderer in the middle of the night?"

"I have it all planned," I said, replacing the sponge with a towel. "You will be in hiding nearby."

"No, I won't," said Emerson. He took the towel from me and hastily finished drying himself. "I am spending the night at the tomb, and you are going to lock yourself in this room and stay in it."

"What are you talking about?"

"We are getting near the end of the passageway. Another day or two should see it cleared. A couple of determined thieves, working in haste, can dig a tunnel through in a few hours."

I did not ask how he knew the end of the corridor was near. In professional matters Emerson is the greatest archaeologist of this, and perhaps any, age. It is only in the routine aspects of life that he displays a normal degree of masculine incompetence.

"But our men are on guard, are they not?" I asked.

"Two men, who are, by this time, in such a state of nerves that a howling jackal could send them scampering for cover. And two men could not hold out against an assault in force. The Gurnawis have attacked archaeologists before."

"So you are proposing yourself as one of the victims?"

"They won't dare attack an Englishman," Emerson said sublimely.

"Ha," I said. "I see your real motive for wishing to absent yourself. You are afraid of Madame Berengeria."

"Ridiculous." Emerson let out a hollow laugh. "Let us not argue, Peabody. Why don't you get out of that dusty costume? You must be hot and uncomfortable."

I skipped agilely back as he put out his hands. "That device will not work, Emerson. And do put on some clothes. If you think the sight of your admittedly muscular and well-developed frame will seduce me from my plain duty—"

This time it was not Emerson who interrupted me, though he was advancing in a manner indicative of intentions along those lines. A knock at the door caused him to fumble for his trousers; and a voice announced that we were summoned by Lady Baskerville.

By the time I had washed and changed, the others had assembled in the drawing room. The atmosphere was not that of a social gathering, but a council of war. I was pleased to see that Madame Berengeria had relapsed into a state of semi-stupor, and the strong smell of brandy that surrounded her did not surprise me in the least. She simpered sleepily at Emerson, but was otherwise incapable of speech or movement.

Relieved of his greatest fear by Madame's collapse, Emerson expressed his intentions and plans with his usual forcefulness. Lady Baskerville let out a cry of distress.

"No, Radcliffe, indeed you must not think of risking yourself. I would rather have the entire tomb vandalized than see one hair of your head injured."

This idiotic statement, which would have won me a blistering reproof, brought a look of fatuous pleasure to Emerson's face. He patted the white hand that clung to his sleeve.

"There is not the slightest danger, I promise you."

"You're probably right about that," said Vandergelt, who had not appreciated this display of concern by the lady. "Howsoever, I think, I'll just mosey along with you, Professor. Two six-shooters are better than one, and a fellow is safer with a pal to watch his back."

But at this Lady Baskerville cried out in greater alarm. Would they abandon her to the mercies of the ghostly form that had already killed one man and attempted a murderous assault on Emerson? Vandergelt, to whom she was now clinging, showed himself just as susceptible to amateur theatrics as my husband.

"She's right, I reckon," he said in a worried voice. "We can't leave the ladies unprotected."

At this both Milverton and Karl expressed their willingness to be of service. It was finally decided that Karl would join Emerson in guarding the tomb. So impatient was Emerson to be gone that he would not even wait to dine, so a picnic basket was prepared, and he and Karl made ready to depart. Despite Emerson's efforts to avoid me, I managed to draw him aside for a moment.

"Emerson, it is absolutely necessary that I speak with Mr. Milverton while his mood is chastened. By tomorrow he may have decided to brazen it out."

"Amelia, there is not the slightest possibility that Milverton intends to confess. Either the meeting is meant as a trap—in which case it would be infinitely stupid of you to fall into it—or, as I suspect, it is solely the product of your rampageous imagination. In either case I forbid you to leave the house tonight."

His grave, quiet tone made a deep impression on me. Nevertheless, I should have replied to his arguments had he not suddenly caught me in his arms and pressed me close, oblivious of Mary, who was passing through the courtyard toward her room.

"For once in your life, Peabody, do as I ask! If anything happens to you, I will murder you!"

With an emphatic squeeze that completely robbed me of breath, he was gone. A moment later I heard him shouting for Karl to hurry.

I leaned against the wall, holding my bruised ribs and struggling to control the emotion induced by this tender parting. A gentle hand touched my shoulder, and I beheld Mary beside me.

"Don't worry about him, Mrs. Emerson. Karl will watch over him; he is devoted to the Professor."

"I am not at all worried, thank you." Unobtrusively I applied my handkerchief to my face. "Heavens, how I am perspiring. It is very hot here."

The girl put her arm around me. "It is *very* warm," she agreed. "Come, let us go back to the drawing room."

The evening was one of the most uncomfortable I have ever passed. Lady Baskerville concentrated her undeniable charms on Mr. Vandergelt. Milverton was silent and moody, avoiding my attempts to catch his eye. Madame Berengeria had been removed to her room, but her presence seemed to hover over us like a squat, threatening shadow. Above all else, coloring every word that was spoken and spoiling the taste of every bite that went into my mouth was the thought of

Emerson on guard at the tomb, vulnerable to that malice that had already displayed itself as intent on his life. If there had been no other enemy—and I felt sure there was—the malevolent Habib had a double motive to inspire an attack, greed and revenge.

The party broke up early. It was only ten o'clock when I got into bed and tucked the netting in place. So softened was I by the thought of my husband's peril that I had almost decided to obey his last command. However, I was unable to sleep. I watched the mystic path of moonlight glide across the floor, and after a time its lure was as irresistible as the charm of a road leading into strange, unknown lands. I had to follow.

I rose. Cautiously I opened my door.

The dreaming silence of the night was broken only by the buzzing of nocturnal insects and the mournful howls of jackals far back in the hills. The household had succumbed to slumber. I continued to wait and watch; and after a while I saw the dark form of a man pass silently through the courtyard. After Hassan's death Emerson had assigned one of our own people to the watchman's post.

Not a whit discouraged, for I had never intended to go that way, I softly closed my door and put on my clothing. Another peep out the door assured me that the house was quiet and that the watchman was still in the courtyard. I then went to the window.

I had one knee on the sill and was preparing to draw the other foot up when a dark bulk loomed up, and a familiar voice murmured in Arabic, "The Sitt desires something? Her servant will bring it."

If I had not had a firm grip on the sill, I would have tumbled over backward. Recovering myself, I climbed up into the embrasure.

"The Sitt desires to climb out the window, Abdullah," I replied. "Give me a hand or get out of my way."

The tall form of the reis did not move. "Efreets and evildoers haunt the darkness," he remarked. "The Sitt will be better in her bed."

Seeing that discussion could not be avoided, I sat down, with my feet dangling. "Why did you not go with Emerson, to protect him?"

"Emerson left me here, to guard the treasure dearer to him than the gold of the pharaoh."

I doubted that Emerson had put it quite that way—though he was florid enough when he spoke Arabic. My compunctions at ignoring his request quite vanished. He had not trusted me!

"Help me down," I said, holding out my hands.

Abdullah let out a groan. "Sit Hakim, please do not do this. Emerson will have my head on a pole if harm comes to you."

"How can harm come to me if you are guarding me? I am not going far, Abdullah. I want you to follow, making sure you are not seen, and conceal yourself behind a bush or a tree when I have reached the loggia."

I lowered myself to the ground. Abdullah shook his head despairingly, but he knew better than to try and prevent me. As I stole through the shrubbery, trying to avoid the bright patches of moonlight, I knew he was following, though I did not hear a sound. For all his size Abdullah could move like a bodiless spirit when he had to.

Turning the corner of the house I saw the loggia before me, the bright paint of its pillars strangely altered by the eerie light. Its interior was deep in shadow. I made out the shapes of the white wicker chairs and tables, but saw no sign of a human form. Pausing, I spoke softly.

"Wait here, Abdullah. Do not make a sound, or intervene unless I call for help."

I crept on. Emerson may accuse me of lack of caution, but I knew better than to approach the place openly. I meant to survey the scene from the shelter of a pillar before venturing in.

Emerson's suggestion that the midnight rendezvous was solely the product of my imagination was of course ridiculous. However, cool reflection had reminded me that I could not be absolutely sure Milverton intended to confess to Lord Baskerville's murder. He might have other, less interesting information, or—disconcerting thought—he might only wish to avail himself of my sympathy while he talked about Mary. Young men commonly suffer from the delusion that the rest of the world is absorbed in their love affairs.

I felt a thrill pass through me when I saw the round red tip of a cigar at the far end of the loggia. Abandoning my place of concealment, I glided toward it.

"Mrs. Emerson!" Milverton rose and crushed out his cigar. "You did come. God bless you."

"You must have eyes like a cat's," I said, chagrined because I had not been able to reach him unobserved.

I spoke in a low murmur, as did he. "My hearing is preternaturally sharp," he replied. "I heard you approach."

I groped for a chair and sat down. Milverton followed my example, selecting a chair next to mine. The cool breeze rustled the vines that wound green arms around the pillars.

For a few moments neither of us spoke. Realizing that the situation was delicate, fearing I would say the wrong thing, I said nothing. Milverton was wrestling with his fears and his awareness of guilt. At least I hoped that was what he was doing, rather than planning the quickest method of dispatching me. If he grasped me by the throat I would not be able to call Abdullah. I wished I had brought my parasol.

Milverton's first remark did nothing to calm my apprehension. "You are a courageous woman, Mrs. Emerson," said he, in a sinister voice. "To come here alone, in the middle of the night, after a mysterious death and a series of strange accidents."

"It was rather stupid of me," I admitted. "I fear that overconfidence is one of my failings. Emerson often accuses me of that."

"I had no intention of suggesting anything so insulting," Milverton exclaimed. "I would rather believe that your decision was based on a profound knowledge of human nature and on that womanly compassion for the unfortunate which is so conspicuous in your conduct."

"Well, since you put it that way . . . ."

"And you were right," Milverton continued. "Your appraisal of my character was correct. I am weak and foolish, but not vicious, Mrs. Emerson. You are in no danger from me. I am incapable of harming a woman—or, indeed, of harming anyone; and your confidence in me has raised you to a lofty place in my esteem. I would die to defend you."

"Let us hope the necessity for that does not arise," I said. Though reassured, I felt a certain flatness. This speech did not sound like the prelude to a confession of murder.

"But," I went on, "I appreciate the offer, Mr. Milverton. The hour is late; may I request that you tell me . . . whatever it was you wanted to tell me?"

From the man beside me, no more than a dim outline in the darkness, came an odd stifled sound that might have been a laugh. "You have hit on the essence of my confession, Mrs. Emerson. You have addressed me by a name that is not my own."

"Who are you, then?" I demanded in surprise.

"I am Lord Baskerville," was the astonishing reply.

Chapter Nine

MILVERTON had gone out of his mind. That was my first thought. Guilt and remorse take strange forms; wishing to deny the vile deed, his conscience had persuaded the young man that Lord Baskerville yet lived—and that he was he (Lord Baskerville, to be precise).

"I am glad to make your acquaintance," I said. "Obviously the reports of your death were greatly exaggerated."

"Please don't joke," Milverton said with a groan.

"I was not joking."

"But . . . Oh, I see." Again came the stifled laugh that was more like a cry of pain. "I cannot blame you for thinking me mad, Mrs. Emerson. I am not—not yet—though I am not far from it at times. Let me make myself plain."

"Please do," I said emphatically.

"I call myself Lord Baskerville because that is now my title. I am the nephew of his late lordship, and his heir."

The explanation was as unexpected as my original idea. Even *my* agile brain required several seconds to assimilate the fact and its sinister connotations.

"Then what on earth are you doing here under an assumed name?" I asked. "Did Lord Baskerville—the late Lord Baskerville—know your true identity? Good Gad, young man, don't you realize what a suspicious position you have placed yourself in?"

"Of course I do. I have been in such distress since my uncle died that I verily believe it added to the severity of the fever I caught. Indeed, but for that I would have taken to my heels long ago."

"But, Mr. Milverton . . . What am I to call you, then?"

"My name is Arthur. I would be honored to have you use it."

"Then, Arthur—it is just as well you could not flee. That would have been tantamount to an admission of guilt. And your claim, if I understand you, that you had nothing to do with your uncle's death."

"On my honor as a British nobleman," came the tense, thrilling whisper from the darkness.

It was hard to doubt that impressive oath, but my reservations lingered. "Tell me," I said.

"My father was his late lordship's younger brother," Arthur began. "When only a boy he incurred the displeasure of his stern parent because of some youthful peccadillo. From what I have heard, the old gentleman was a tartar, who would have been more at home in the Puritan Commonwealth than in the present century. Following the precepts of the Old Testament, he promptly cut off the right hand that had offended him and cast the prodigal son out in the cold. My poor father was dispatched to Africa with a small monthly stipend, to live or die as Fate decreed."

"Did not his brother intercede for him?"

Arthur hesitated for a moment. "I will hide nothing from you, Mrs. Emerson. The late Lord Baskerville was in complete agreement with his father's cruel behavior. He came to the title only a year after his brother had been sent into exile, and one of his first acts was to write Pater informing him that he need not waste time applying for assistance, for both personal conviction and filial respect compelled him to cast his brother off as he had been cast off by their parent."

"How unfeeling," I said.

"I was brought up to consider him a veritable fiend," Arthur said.

A shudder passed through my body when I heard this damning admission. Did not the young man realize that every word deepened the pit he was digging for himself? Did he believe I would keep silent about his identity—or did he count on other means of rendering himself safe from detection?

Arthur went on with his story. "I heard my father curse him nightly, when he was . . . Well, not to put too fine a face upon it, when he had taken too much to drink. This happened, I regret to say, with increasing frequency as time went on. Yet when he was himself, my father was the most delightful of men. His engaging character won the heart of my mother, who was the daughter of a gentleman of Nairobi and, despite her parents' objections, they were wed. My mother had a small income of her own, and on this we lived.

"She loved him devotedly, I know. Never did I hear a word of complaint or accusation from her lips. But six months ago, after he had succumbed to the inevitable consequences of his indulgence, it was my mother who persuaded me that my hatred of my uncle might be unjust. She did this, mark you, without the slightest criticism of my father—"

"Which must have been no small feat," I interrupted. I had formed a clear mental picture of Arthur's father and I felt great sympathy for his wife.

Ignoring my comment, Arthur continued. "She also pointed out that since Lord Baskerville was childless, I was his heir. He had made no attempt to communicate with me, even though she had, in duty bound, notified him of his brother's death. But as she said, omissions and unfairness on his part did not justify my behaving badly. I owed it to myself and to my family to present myself to the man whom in the course of time I must succeed.

"She convinced me; but I never admitted to her that she had, for I had formed a foolish, thoughtless scheme of my own. When I left Kenya I told her only that I meant to seek my fortune in the wide world, by means of the photography which had been my youthful hobby. I am sure she has read of the mystery surrounding my uncle's death, but she does not dream that the Charles Milverton of the newspapers is her miserable son."

"But she must be beside herself with worry about you," I exclaimed. "She has no idea where you are?"

"She believes I am on my way to America," the young man confessed in a low voice. "I told her I would send an address when I was settled."

I could only shake my head and sigh. But there was no point in urging Arthur to communicate at once with his mother; the truth would be far more painful than any uncertainty she presently felt, and though I had only the most dismal forebodings as to his future, there was always a possibility, however remote, that I might be wrong.

"My scheme was to present myself to my uncle as a stranger and win his regard and confidence before proclaiming my true identity," Arthur said. "You needn't comment, Mrs. Emerson; it was a naive idea, worthy of a sensational novel. But it was harmless. I swear to you, I had no intention of doing anything except proving myself, by hard work and devotion. Naturally I knew of my uncle's plans to winter in Egypt—most of the English-speaking population of the globe must have known. I journeyed to Cairo and applied to him as soon as he arrived. My credentials—"

"Forged?" I inquired.

"I could hardly offer him genuine recommendations, now could I? The ones I produced were impressive, I assure you. He hired me on the spot. And that is how matters stood when he died. He did not know my identity, although . . ."

He hesitated. Feeling sure I knew what he was about to say, I finished the sentence for him. "You think he suspected? Well, that does not matter now. My dear Arthur, you must make a clean breast of this to the authorities. Admittedly it places you under grave suspicion of murder—"

"But there is no evidence of murder," Arthur interrupted. "The police were satisfied that his lordship died a natural death."

He was correct; and his quickness to point out this minor flaw in my reasoning did not augur well for his innocence. However, unless I could prove *how* Lord Baskerville was murdered, there was no sense in asking *who* had murdered him.

"All the more reason for you to tell the truth," I insisted. "You must proclaim yourself in order to claim your inheritance—"

"Sssh!" Arthur clapped his hand over my mouth. The fear for my own safety, which had been forgotten in the interest of his narrative, now came back to me; but before I had time to experience more than a momentary alarm he went on in a whisper, "There is someone out there in the shrubbery. I saw movement—"

I pulled his hand from my mouth. "It is only Abdullah. I was not so foolish as to come alone. But he did not overhear—"

"No, no." Arthur rose to his feet and I thought he was about to rush out into the shrubbery. After a moment he relaxed. "It is gone now. But it was not Abdullah, Mrs. Emerson. It was slighter, and shorter—dressed in gauzy robes of snowy pallor."

I caught my breath. "The Woman in White," I gasped.

II

Before we parted I asked Arthur's permission to tell his story to Emerson. He agreed, probably because he realized I meant to do so with or without his approval. My suggestion that he go next day to Luxor to confess his true identity was rejected, and after some argument I had to admit that his reasoning had validity. The proper persons to receive this intelligence were, of course, the British authorities, and there was no one in Luxor of sufficient rank to deal with the matter, the consular agent being an Italian whose primary occupation was to supply Budge of the British Museum with stolen antiquities. Arthur promised he would accept Emerson's judgment as to what action he ought to take, and I promised I would assist him in any way I could.

They say confession is good for the soul. It had certainly improved Arthur's peace of mind. He went off with a springy step, whistling softly.

But oh, my own heart was heavy as I went to reassure my faithful Abdullah of my safety. I liked the young man—not, as Emerson claims, because he was a handsome specimen of English manhood, but because he was kind and amiable. However, I was unfavorably impressed with certain aspects of his character, which reminded me of his description of the charming ne'er-do-well who had sired him. The levity he had displayed concerning his forged credentials, the immature folly of his romantic scheme of gaining his uncle's regard, and other things he had said indicated that his good mother's influence had not overcome the shallowness he had inherited from the paternal side. I wished him well; but I was afraid his plausible story was only an attempt to win my goodwill before the truth came out, as it inevitably would when he claimed his title.

I found Abdullah concealed (more or less) behind a palm tree. When I questioned him about the apparition in white, he denied having seen anything. "But," he added, "I was watching you, or rather the dark place into which you went; never did I take my eyes away. Sitt Hakim, there is no need to tell Emerson of this."

"Don't be such a coward, Abdullah," I replied. "I will explain that you did your best to stop me."

"Then will you strike me hard on the head so I may have a bruise to show him?"

I would have thought he was joking, but although Abdullah does have quite a sense of humor, this was not the sort of joke he would be likely to make.

"Don't be ridiculous," I said.

Abdullah groaned.

III

I could hardly wait to tell Emerson I had solved the murder of Lord Baskerville. Of course there were a few small details to be worked out, but I felt sure that if I applied myself seriously to the matter I would soon discover the answers. I meant to begin working on it that very night, but unfortunately I fell asleep before I could arrive at any conclusions.

My first thought on awakening was a renewal of concern over Emerson's safety. Reason assured me that the household would have been roused if there had been a disturbance; but affection, never susceptible to logic, hastened my preparations to proceed to the Valley.

Early as I was, Cyrus Vandergelt was already in the courtyard when I emerged from my room. For the first time I saw him in his working costume, instead of one of the snowy linen suits he habitually wore. His tweed jacket was as beautifully tailored as his other clothes; it bore little resemblance to the shabby garments in which Emerson was wont to attire himself. On his head the American wore a military-looking solar kepi with a band of red, white, and blue ribbon. He doffed this with a flourish when he saw me and offered his arm to escort me to the breakfast table.

Lady Baskerville seldom joined us at this meal. I had heard the men speculating on her need for prolonged rest; but of course I knew she spent the time on her toilette, for the artificial perfection of her appearance was obviously the result of hours of work.

Imagine my surprise, therefore, when we found the lady already at her place. She had not taken the time that morning to make up her face, and consequently she looked her age. Shadows circled her heavy-lidded eyes, and there were lines of strain around her mouth. Vandergelt was so struck by her appearance that he exclaimed with concern. She admitted that her night's sleep had been disturbed and would have elaborated had not Milverton—or rather, Arthur Baskerville—rushed in full of apologies for having overslept.

Of all the persons in the room he, the guilty man, alone appeared to have had a refreshing, dreamless rest. The looks of smiling gratitude he kept shooting at me assured me he had quite cast off his melancholy. It was another demonstration of the immaturity that had already struck me; having confessed to an older, wiser individual, he now felt completely relieved of responsibility.

"Where is Miss Mary?" he asked. "We ought not linger; I am sure Mrs. Emerson is anxious to see her husband."

"Attending on her mother, I suppose," Lady Baskerville replied, in the sharp tone she always employed when referring to Madame Berengeria. "I cannot imagine what you were thinking of, to allow that dreadful woman to come here. Since the damage is done, I must accept it, but I absolutely refuse to be left alone in the house with her."

"Come with us," Vandergelt suggested. "We'll fix you up a nice little place in the shade."

"Thank you, my friend, but I am too tired. After what I saw last night . . ."

Vandergelt rose to the bait, expressing concern and demanding details. I summarize the lady's reply, for it was replete with gasps and sighs and theatrical descriptions. Stripped of these meaningless appendages, it was simple enough. Unable to sleep, she had gone to the window and seen the now notorious white-clad apparition gliding through the trees. It had disappeared in the direction of the cliffs.

I looked at Arthur and read his intentions in his ingenuous countenance. The young idiot was on the verge of exclaiming that we had also seen the White

Lady—which would have brought out the whole story of our midnight meeting. It was necessary to stop him before he could speak. I kicked out under the table. In my haste I missed my object and administered a sharp blow on Mr. Vandergelt's calf. This served the purpose, however; his shout of pain and the ensuing apologies gave Arthur time to recollect himself.

Vandergelt continued to beg Lady Baskerville to join us, and, when she refused, offered to stay with her.

"My dear Cyrus," she said, with an affectionate smile, "you are burning to get to your nasty, dirty tomb. Not for the world would I deprive you of this opportunity."

A prolonged and foolish discussion ensued; it was finally decided that Arthur would stay with the ladies. So Vandergelt and I started out and at the last minute Mary joined us, breathless and apologetic. Made even more anxious by the delay, I set a pace that even the long-legged American was hard pressed to match.

"Whoa, there, Mrs. Amelia" (or perhaps it was "Gee"—some American cattle term, at any rate). "Poor little Miss Mary is going to be all tuckered out before she starts working. There's no cause for alarm, you know; we'd have heard by this time if some early bird had found the Professor weltering in his gore."

Though the thought was meant to be comforting, I did not think it particularly well expressed.

After a night spent apart I expected that Emerson would greet me with some degree of enthusiasm. Instead he stared at me blankly for a moment, as if he could not remember who I was. When recognition dawned, it was immediately followed by a scowl.

"You are late," he said accusingly. "You had better get to work at once; we are far ahead of you, and the men have already turned up a considerable number of small objects in the rubble."

"Have they?" Vandergelt drawled, stroking his goatee. "Doesn't look too salubrious, does it, Professor?"

"I said before that I suspected the tomb had been entered by robbers in antiquity," Emerson snapped. "That does not necessarily mean—"

"I get you. How about letting me have a gander at what has been done? Then I promise I'll get to work. I'll even tote baskets if you want."

"Oh, very well," Emerson said in his most disagreeable manner. "But be quick."

No one but the most fanatical enthusiast would have found the effort of inspection worthwhile, for the interior of the passage, now cleared to a length of about fifteen metres, had reached an unbelievable degree of discomfort. It sloped sharply down into abysmal and stifling darkness lighted only by the wan glow of lanterns. The air was foul with the staleness of millennia, and so hot that the men had stripped off all their garments except those required by decency. Every movement, however slight, stirred up the fine white dust left by the limestone chips with which the corridor had been filled. This crystalline powder, clinging to the men's perspiring bodies, gave them a singularly uncanny appearance; the pallid, leprous forms moving through the foggy gloom resembled nothing so much as reanimated mummies, preparing to menace the invaders of their sleep.

Partially concealed by the rough scaffolding, the procession of painted gods marched solemnly down into the darkness. Ibis-headed Thoth, patron of learning, Maat, goddess of truth, Isis and her falcon-headed son Horus. But what caught my attention and made me forget the extreme discomfort of heat and stifling air was the pile of rubble. In the beginning this had entirely closed the passageway. Now it had shrunk to a height barely shoulder high, leaving a gap between its top and the ceiling.

After a quick glance at the paintings, Vandergelt caught up a lantern and went straight to the pile of rubble. Standing on tiptoe, I peered over his arm as he moved the light forward, over the top of the pile.

The debris sloped sharply downward from that point on. In the shadows beyond the lantern rays loomed a solid mass—the end of the passageway, blocked, as the entrance had been, by a barrier of stone.

Before either of us could comment, Emerson made a commanding gesture and we followed him out into the vestibule at the foot of the stairs. Wiping dust from my streaming brow, I gazed reproachfully at my husband.

"So this is the true explanation for your decision to remain on guard last night! How could you, Emerson? Have we not always shared the thrill of discovery? I am cut to the quick by your duplicity!"

Emerson's fingers nervously stroked his chin. "Peabody, I owe you an apology; but honestly, I had no intention of stealing a march on you. What I said was true; from now on the tomb is in imminent peril of being robbed."

"And when have I shrunk from the prospect of peril?" I demanded. "When have you sunk to the contemptible practice of attempting to shield me?"

"Quite often, actually," Emerson replied. "Not that I often succeed; but really, Peabody, your inclination to rush headlong where angels fear to tread—"

"Hold on," Vandergelt interrupted. He had removed his hat and was methodically wiping the sticky dust from his face. He seemed unaware of the fact that this substance, which, when mixed with perspiration, took on the consistency of liquid cement, was running down into his goatee and dripping off the end.

"Don't get into one of your arguments," he went on. "I don't have the patience to wait till you finish fighting. What the hades is down there, Professor?"

"The end of the passageway," Emerson answered. "And a well or shaft. I couldn't cross it. There were a few scraps of rotten wood, the remains of a bridge or covering—"

"Brought by thieves?" Vandergelt asked, his blue eyes alert.

"Possibly. They would have come prepared for such pitfalls, which were common in tombs of the period. However, if they did find a door at the far end, there is no sign of it now—only a blank wall surface painted with a figure of Anubis."

"Humph." Vandergelt stroked his goatee. This action produced a stream of mud that ran down the front of his once-neat coat. "Either the door is hidden behind the plaster and paint, or the wall is a blind alley and the burial chamber lies elsewhere—perhaps at the bottom of the shaft."

"Correct. As you see, we have quite a few more hours' work ahead of us. We must test every foot of the floor and ceiling carefully. The closer we get to the burial chamber, the greater the chance of encountering a trap."

"Then let us get to work," I cried excitedly.

"Precisely what I have been suggesting," Emerson replied.

His tone was decidedly sarcastic, but I decided to overlook it, for there was some excuse for his behavior. My brain teemed with golden visions. For the moment archaelogical fever supplanted detective fever. I was actually at work, sifting the first portion of rubble, before I remembered I had not told Emerson of Arthur's confession.

I assured myself that there was no need for haste. Emerson would undoubtedly insist on finishing the day's work before returning to the house, and Arthur had agreed to take no action until we had had a chance to confer. I decided to wait until the noon break before confiding in Emerson.

Jealous persons might claim, in the light of later events, that this was an error of judgment on my part. I cannot see it this way. Only another Cassandra, gifted or cursed with the ability to foresee the future, could have predicted what transpired; and if I *had* had a premonition, I could not possibly have convinced Emerson to act on it.

Proof positive of this assertion is given by his reaction when I did tell him about my conversation with Arthur. We had gone to eat our frugal meal and rest for a while under the canvas canopy that had been erected to shelter me from the sun's rays while I worked. Mary was below, attempting to trace the most recently uncovered paintings. The only time she could work was while the men were resting, for the clouds of dust their feet stirred up made vision, much less breathing, virtually impossible. Needless to say, Karl was in attendance upon her. Vandergelt had wolfed down his food and returned at once to the tomb, which exerted a powerful fascination over him. Emerson would have followed had I not restrained him.

"I must tell you of my conversation with Arthur last night," I said.

Emerson was grumbling and trying to free his sleeve from my grasp. This statement had the effect of catching his attention.

"Curse it, Amelia, I ordered you not to leave our room. I ought to have known Abdullah wasn't man enough to stop you. Just wait till I get my hands on him!"

"It was not his fault."

"I am well aware of that."

"Then stop fussing and listen to me. I assure you, you will find the story interesting. Arthur confessed—"

"Arthur? How friendly you have become with a murderer! Wait a moment—I thought his name was Charles."

"I call him Arthur because if I were to use his last name and title it would be confusing. His name is not Milverton."

Emerson flung himself down on the ground with a look of bored patience, but when I reached the climax of my story he abandoned his efforts to appear disinterested.

"Good Gad," he exclaimed. "If he is telling the truth—"

"I am sure he is. There would be no reason for him to lie."

"No—not when the facts can be checked. Doesn't he realize what an extremely awkward position this places him in?"

"He certainly does. But I have persuaded him to make a clean breast of it. The question is, to whom should he tell his story?"

"Hmmm." Emerson drew his feet up and rested his forearms on his knees while he considered the question. "He must show proof of his identity if he wants to establish his claim to the title and estate. We had better communicate directly with Cairo. They will certainly be surprised."

"To find him here, yes. Though I feel sure his existence, as the next heir, is known to whatever government persons concern themselves with such matters. I wonder I did not think of that myself. For, of course, Lord Baskerville's heir would be the most logical suspect."

Emerson's heavy brows drew together. "He would be, if Lord Baskerville's death *was* murder. I thought you had concluded that Armadale was the criminal."

"That was before I knew Milverton's—I mean Arthur's—real identity," I explained patiently. "Naturally he denies having killed his uncle—"

"Oh, he does?"

"You would hardly expect him to admit it."

"*I* would not; *you* did, if you recall. Ah, well; I will talk with the young fool tonight—or tomorrow—and we will see what steps ought to be taken. Now we have wasted enough time. Back to work."

"I feel we ought to act on this matter without delay," I said.

"I don't. The tomb is the matter that will not brook delay."

Her copy of the paintings completed, Mary returned to the house, and the rest of us resumed work. As the afternoon wore on, I found increasing numbers of objects in the rubble—potsherds and bits of blue faience, and many beads molded of the same glasslike substance. The beads were a nuisance, for they were very small, and I had to sift every cubic centimeter to make sure I had not missed any.

The sun declined westward, and its rays crept under my canvas canopy. I was still looking for beads when a shadow fell across my basket; looking up, I saw Mr. O'Connell. He doffed his hat with a flourish and squatted down beside me.

"Sure and it's a pity to see a lovely lady spoiling her hands and her complexion with such work," he said winsomely.

"Don't waste your Hibernian charm on me," I said. "I am beginning to think of you as a bird of ill omen, Mr. O'Connell. Whenever you appear, some disaster follows."

"Ah, don't be hard on a poor fellow. I'm not my usual cheery self today, Mrs. Emerson, and that's the truth."

He sighed heavily. I remembered my scheme to enlist this presumptuous young person in our cause, and moderated my sharp voice. "You have not managed to regain your place in Miss Mary's affections, then?"

"You're a canny lady, Mrs. E. Indeed she's still vexed with me, God bless her for a darling little tyrant."

"She has other admirers, you know. They leave her little time to miss an impertinent red-haired journalist."

"That's what I'm afraid of," O'Connell replied gloomily. "I have just come from the house. Mary refused even to see me. She sent a message telling me to take myself off or she would have the servants throw me out. I'm beaten, Mrs. E., and that's the truth. I want a truce. I'll accept any reasonable terms if you will help me make my peace with Mary."

I bowed my head, pretending to concentrate on my work, in order to hide my smile of satisfaction. Having been about to propose a compromise, I was now in the happy position of being able to dictate terms.

"What are you suggesting?" I asked.

O'Connell appeared to hesitate; but when he spoke the words poured forth so glibly that it was obvious he had already formulated his plan.

"It's the most charming of fellows I am," he said modestly. "But if I never see the girl, my charm is not of much use. If I were to be invited to stay at the house, now . . ."

"Oh, dear me, I don't see how I could possibly arrange that," I said in a shocked voice.

"There would be no difficulty with Lady Baskerville. She thinks the world of me."

"Oh, I've no doubt you can get round Lady Baskerville. Unfortunately Emerson is not so susceptible."

"I can win him over," O'Connell insisted.

"How?" I demanded bluntly.

"If, for instance, I promised to submit all my stories to him for approval before sending them to my editor."

"Would you really agree to that?"

"I hate like the very devil—excuse me, ma'am, my feelings got the better of me—I hate the idea. But I would do it to gain my ends."

"Ah, love," I said satirically. "How true it is, that the tender emotion can reform a wicked man."

"Say rather that it can soften the brain of a clever man," O'Connell replied morosely. He caught my eye; and after a moment the corners of his mouth curved in a rueful smile, devoid of the mockery that so often marred his expression. "You've got a bit of charm yourself, Mrs. E. I think you have a great deal of sentiment in your nature, though you try to hide it."

"Absurd," I said. "Take yourself off now, before Emerson discovers you. I will discuss your proposal with him this evening."

"Why not now? I am on fire to begin my wooing."

"Don't press your luck, Mr. O'Connell. If you come by the dig tomorrow at about this time, I may have good news for you."

"I knew it!" O'Connell exclaimed. "I knew a lady with a face and figure like yours could not be cruel to a lover!" Seizing me around the waist he planted a kiss on my cheek. I immediately seized my parasol and aimed a blow at him, but he skipped back out of reach. Grinning broadly and blowing me a kiss, the impertinent young man sauntered off.

He did not go far away, however; whenever I looked up from my work I saw him among the staring tourists. When his eyes met mine he would either sigh and press his hand to his heart or wink and smile and tip his hat. Though I did not show it, I could not help being amused. After an hour or so he evidently felt that his point had been made; he vanished from the scene and I saw him no more.

The molten orb of the sun was low in the west and the blue gray shadows of evening were cool on the ground when a cessation in the monotonous flow of loaded baskets made me sense that something had occurred. I looked up to see the crew file out of the tomb. Surely, I thought, Emerson cannot have dismissed them for the day; there is still an hour of daylight left. I went at once to see what had happened.

The heap of rubble had been considerably reduced. No longer did it consist solely of moderate-sized stones and pebbles. One end of a massive stone block was now visible. Emerson and Vandergelt stood by it, looking down at something on the floor.

"Come here, Peabody," said Emerson. "What do you think of this?"

His pointing finger indicated a brown, brittle object covered with limestone dust, which Vandergelt began to remove with a small brush.

Experienced in such matters, I realized immediately that the strange object was a mummified human arm—or rather the tattered remains of one, for a great deal of the skin was missing. The bared bones were brown and brittle with age. The patches of skin had been tanned to a hard leathery shell. By some strange quirk of chance the delicate fingerbones had been undisturbed; they seemed to reach out as if in a desperate appeal for air—for safety—for life.

Chapter Ten

 I was peculiarly moved by the gesture, though I realized it was only a fortuitous arrangement of skeletal material. However, sangfroid is necessary to an archaeologist, so I did not voice my sentiments aloud.

"Where is the rest of him?" I inquired.

"Under the slab," replied Vandergelt. "We seem to have here a case of poetic justice, Mrs. Amelia—a thief who was caught in the act in the most literal sense."

I looked up at the ceiling. The rectangular gap in the surface formed a pocket of deeper darkness. "Could it have been an accident?" I asked.

"Hardly," Emerson replied. "As we have learned to our sorrow, the rock here is dangerously brittle. However, the symmetrical shape of this block shows that it was deliberately freed from the matrix and balanced so that it would fall if a thief inadvertently disturbed the triggering mechanism. Fascinating! We have seen other such devices, Peabody, but never one so effective."

"Looks as if the slab is a couple of feet thick," Vandergelt remarked. "I opine there won't be much left of the poor rascal."

"Quite enough, however, to rattle our workmen," Emerson replied.

"But why?" I asked. "They have excavated hundreds of mummies and skeletons."

"Not under these particular circumstances. Could there possibly be a more convincing demonstration of the effectiveness of the pharaoh's curse?"

His last word echoed from the depths beyond: "Curse . . . curse . . ." and yet again the faintest murmured "curse . . ." before the final sibilant faded into silence.

"Hey, cut it out, Professor," Vandergelt said uneasily. "You'll have *me* gibbering about demons in a minute. What do you say we quit for the night? It's getting late, and this appears to be a sizable job."

"Quit? Stop, you mean?" Emerson stared at him in surprise. "No, no, I must see what is under the slab. Peabody, fetch Karl and Abdullah."

I found Karl sitting with his back against the fence, making a fair copy of an inscription. Urgent as Emerson's summons had been, I could not help pausing for a moment to admire the rapidity with which his hand traced the complex shapes of the hieroglyphic signs: tiny birds and animals and figures of men and women, and the more abstruse symbols derived from flowers, architectural shapes, and so on. So absorbed was the young man in his task that he did not notice my presence until I touched him on the shoulder.

With the aid of Karl and the reis we managed to lift the slab, though it was a delicate and dangerous procedure. By means of levers and wedges it was gradually raised and at last tipped back onto its side, exposing the remains of the long-dead thief. It was hard to think of those brittle scraps as having once been human. Even the skull had been crushed to fragments.

"Curse it, this is when we need our photographer," Emerson muttered. "Peabody, go back to the house and—"

"Be reasonable, Professor," Vandergelt exclaimed. "This can wait till morning. You don't want the missus wandering around the plateau at night."

"Is it night?" Emerson inquired.

"Permit that I make a sketch, Herr Professor," Karl said. "I do not draw with the grace and facility of Miss Mary, but—"

"Yes, yes, that is a good idea." Emerson squatted. Taking out a little brush, he began to clean the muffling dust from the bones.

"I don't know what you expect to find," Vandergelt grunted, wiping his perspiring brow. "This poor fellow was a peasant; there won't be any precious objects on his body."

But even as he spoke a brilliant spark sprang to life in the dust Emerson's brush had shifted. "Wax," Emerson snapped. "Hurry, Peabody. I need wax."

I moved at once to obey—not the imperious dictates of a tyrannical husband, but the imperative need of a fellow professional. Paraffin wax was among the supplies we commonly kept on hand; it was used to hold broken objects together until a more permanent adhesive could be applied. I melted a considerable quantity over my small spirit lamp and hastened back to the tomb to find that Emerson had finished clearing the object whose first glitter had told us of the presence of gold.

He snatched the pan from me, careless of the heat, and poured the liquid in a slow stream onto the ground. I saw only flashes of color—blue and reddish orange and cobalt—before the hardening wax hid the object.

Emerson transferred the mass to a box and, with his prize in his hand, was persuaded to stop work for the night. Abdullah and Karl were to remain on guard.

As we neared the house, Emerson broke a long silence. "Not a word of this, Vandergelt, even to Lady Baskerville."

"But—"

"I will inform her in due course and with the proper precautions. Curse it, Vandergelt, most of the servants have relatives in the villages. If they hear that we have found gold—"

"I get you, Professor," the American replied. "Hey—where are you going?" For Emerson, instead of following the path to the front gate, had started toward the back of the house.

"To our room, of course," was the reply. "Tell Lady Baskerville we will be with her as soon as we have bathed and changed."

We left the American scratching his disheveled head. As we climbed in through our window, I reflected complacently on the convenience of this entrance—and, less complacently, on its vulnerability to unauthorized persons.

Emerson lighted the lamps. "Bolt the door, Peabody."

I did so, and drew the curtains across the window. Meanwhile Emerson cleared the table and placed a clean white handkerchief on its surface. Opening the box, he carefully slid the contents out onto the kerchief.

His wisdom in using wax to fasten the broken pieces together was immediately manifest. Crushed and dispersed as they were, they yet retained traces of the original pattern. Had he plucked them out of the dust one by one, any hope of restoring the object would have been lost.

It was a pectoral, or pendant, in the shape of a winged scarab. The central element was cut from lapis, and this hard stone had survived almost intact. The delicate wings, formed of thin gold set with small pieces of turquoise and carnelian, were so badly battered that their shape could only be surmised by an expert—which, of course, I am. Enclosing the scarab was a framework of gold which had held, among other elements, a pair of cartouches containing the names of a pharaoh. The tiny hieroglyphic signs were not incised in the gold, but inlaid, each small shape being cut out of a chip of precious stone. These were now scattered at random, but my trained eye immediately fell on an "ankh" sign shaped from lapis and a tiny turquoise chick, which represented the sound "u" or "w."

"Good Gad," I said. "I am surprised it was not crushed to powder."

"It was under the thief's body," Emerson replied. "His flesh cushioned and protected the jewel. When the flesh decayed the stone settled and the gold was flattened, but not smashed to bits as it would have been had the slab fallen directly onto it."

It was not difficult for my trained imagination to reconstruct the ancient drama, and its setting: the burial chamber, lighted only by the smoky flame of a cheap clay lamp, the lid of the great stone sarcophagus flung aside, and the carved face of the dead man staring enigmatically at the furtive figures that darted hither and thither, scooping up handfuls of jewelry, stuffing golden statues and bowls into the sacks they had brought for that purpose. Hardened men, these thieves of ancient Gurneh; but they could not have been entirely immune to terror, for one of them had flung the dead king's amulet over his head so that the scarab rested on his wildly beating heart. Fleeing with his loot, he had been caught by the trap, whose thunderous fall must surely have roused the cemetery guards. The priests, coming to restore the damage, had left the fallen monolith as a warning to future thieves; and indeed, as Emerson had said, no better proof of the disfavor of the gods could have been found.

With a sigh I returned to the present, and to Emerson, who was carefully restoring the object to the box.

"If we could only read the cartouche," I said. "The ornament must belong to the owner of our tomb."

"Ah, you missed that, did you?" Emerson grinned maliciously at me.

"Do you mean—"

"Of course I do. You are letting your feminine weakness for gold cloud your wits, Peabody. Use your brain. Unless you would like me to enlighten you—"

"That will not be necessary," I replied, thinking rapidly. "From the fact that the name and figure of the tomb owner have been hacked out, we may suppose that he was one of the heretic pharaohs—possibly even Akhenaton himself, if the tomb was begun in the early days of his reign before he left Thebes and forbade the worship of the old gods. However, the fragments of the remaining hieroglyphs do not fit his name. There is only one name that does fit. . . ." I hesitated, hastily searching my memory. "The name of Tutankhamon," I concluded triumphantly.

"Humph," said Emerson.

"We know," I went on, "that the royal personages of—"

"Enough," Emerson said rudely. "I know more about the subject than you do, so don't lecture me. Please hurry and change. I have a great deal to do, and I want to get at it."

Ordinarily Emerson is as free of professional jealousy as any man can be, but occasionally he reacts badly when my wits prove to be sharper than his. So I let him sulk, and as I dressed I tried to remember what I knew of the pharaoh Tutankhamon.

Not much was known of him. He had married one of Akhenaton's daughters, but had not followed the heretical religious view of his father-in-law after he returned to Thebes. Though it would be an unparalleled thrill to discover any royal tomb, I could not help but wish we had found someone other than this ephemeral and short-reigned king. One of the great Amenhoteps or Thutmosids would have been much more exciting.

We found the others awaiting us in the drawing room. I really believe Emerson had forgotten about Madame Berengeria in the delight of his discovery. A stricken expression crossed his face when he beheld the lady's ample form, decked in its usual bizarre costume. But the others paid us little heed; even Madame was listening openmouthed to Vandergelt's dramatic description of the thief's remains. (He did not mention the gold.)

"Poor fellow," Mary said gently. "To think of him lying there all these thousands of years, mourned by wife and mother and children, forgotten by the world."

"He was a thief and criminal who deserved his fate," said Lady Baskerville.

"His accursed soul writhes in the fiery pits of Amenti," remarked Madame Berengeria in sepulchral tones. "Eternal punishment . . . doom and destruction. . . . Er, since you insist, Mr. Vandergelt, I believe I will take another drop of sherry."

Vandergelt rose obediently. Mary's lips tightened but she said nothing; no doubt she had long since learned that any attempt to control her mother only resulted in a strident argument. So far as I was concerned, the sooner the lady drank herself into a stupor, the better.

Lady Baskerville's black eyes flashed contemptuously as she gazed at the other woman. Rising, as if she were too restless to sit still, she strolled to the window. It was her favorite position; the whitewashed walls set off the grace of her black-clad figure. "So you believe we are nearing our goal, Professor?" she asked.

"Possibly. I want to get back to the Valley at first light tomorrow. From now on, our photographer's aid will be essential. Milverton, I want . . . But where the devil is he?"

How well I remember the premonitory chill that froze the blood in my veins at that moment. Emerson may scoff; but I knew instantly that something dreadful had happened. I ought to have observed at once that the young man was not with the others. My only excuse is that my archaeological fever was still in the ascendency.

"He is in his room, I suppose," Lady Baskerville said casually. "I thought this afternoon that he looked feverish and suggested that he rest."

Across the width of the room Emerson's eyes sought mine. In his grave countenance I read a concern that matched my own. Some wave of mental vibration must have touched Lady Baskerville. She paled visibly and exclaimed, "Radcliffe, why do you look so strange? What is wrong?"

"Nothing, nothing," Emerson replied. "I will just look in on the young man and remind him we are waiting. The rest of you stay here."

I knew the order did not apply to me. However, Emerson's longer legs gave him an advantage; he was the first to reach the door of Milverton's room. Without pausing to knock he flung it wide. The room was in darkness, but I knew at once, by means of that sixth sense that warns us of another human presence—or its absence—that no one was there.

"He has fled," I exclaimed. "I knew he was weak; I ought to have anticipated this."

"Wait a moment, Amelia, before you jump to conclusions," Emerson replied, striking a match and lighting the lamp. "He may have gone for a walk, or . . ." But as the lamp flared up, the sight of the room put an end to this and every other innocent explanation.

Though not equipped with the degree of luxury that marked the quarters of Lord Baskerville and his lady, the staff rooms were comfortable enough; Lord

Baskerville held, quite correctly in my opinion, that people could work more effectively when they were not distracted by physical discomfort. This chamber contained an iron bedstead, a table and chair, a wardrobe and chest of drawers, and the usual portable offices, chastely concealed behind a screen. It was in a state of shocking disarray. The wardrobe doors stood open, the drawers of the dresser spilled garments out in utter confusion. In contrast, the bed was made with almost military precision, the corners of the spread tucked in and the folds falling neatly to the floor.

"I knew it," I groaned. "I had a feeling of . . ."

"Don't say it, Peabody!"

". . . of impending doom!"

"I asked you not to say that."

"But perhaps," I went on, more cheerfully, "perhaps he has not fled. Perhaps the disorder is the result of a frantic search—"

"For what, in God's name? No, no; I am afraid your original idea is correct. Curse the young rascal, he has a ridiculously large wardrobe, doesn't he? We shall never be able to determine whether anything is missing. I wonder . . ."

He had been rummaging through the strewn garments as he spoke. Now he kicked the screen away and examined the washbasin. "His shaving tackle is still here. Of course he may have had an extra set, or planned to purchase replacements. I confess it begins to look bad for the new Lord Baskerville."

A sharp cry from the doorway betokened the presence of Lady Baskerville. Her eyes wide with alarm, she leaned on the arm of Mr. Vandergelt.

"Where is Mr. Milverton?" she cried shrilly. "And what did you mean, Radcliffe, by your reference to . . . to . . ."

"As you see, Milverton is not here," Emerson replied. "But he is not . . . that is to say, his real name is Arthur Baskerville. He is your late husband's nephew. He promised to go to the authorities today, but it looks as if he— Here—look out, Vandergelt—"

He jumped to assist the American; for on hearing the news Lady Baskerville had promptly fainted, in the most graceful manner imaginable. I watched in aloof silence as the two men tugged at the lady's limp form; finally Vandergelt won out, and lifted her into his arms.

"By Jimminy, Professor, tact is not your strong point," he exclaimed. "Was that the truth, though, about Milverton—Baskerville—whoever he is?"

"Certainly," Emerson replied haughtily.

"Well, this has sure been a day of surprises all around. I'll just take the poor lady to her room. Then maybe we'd better have a little council of war, to decide what to do next."

"I know what we ought to do next," Emerson said. "And I mean to do it."

Scowling in magisterial fashion, he strode to the door. Vandergelt vanished with his burden. I lingered, scanning the room in hopes of seeing a hitherto unnoticed clue. Though Arthur's cowardly flight had confirmed my suspicions of his guilt, I felt no triumph, only chagrin and distress.

Yet—why should he flee? That very morning he had seemed cheerful, relieved of his anxiety. What had happened in the intervening hours to make him a fugitive?

I do not claim, nor have I ever claimed, any powers of spiritual awareness. Yet I will assert to this day that a cold wind seemed to touch my shrinking flesh. Something was amiss. I sensed it, even though none of the conventional senses confirmed my feeling of disaster. Again my eyes scanned the room. The wardrobe doors were open, the screen had been flung aside. But there was one place we had not searched. I wondered that I had not thought of it, since it was usually the first place I looked. Dropping to my knees beside the bed, I lifted the edge of the coverlet.

Emerson claims that I shrieked out his name. I have no recollection of doing so, but I must admit he was instantly at my side, panting from the speed with which he had returned.

"Peabody, my dear girl, what is it? Are you injured?" For he assumed, as he afterward told me, that I had collapsed or been struck to the floor.

"No, no, not I—it is he. He is here, under the bed. . . ." Again I raised the coverlet, which in my shock I had let fall.

"Good Gad!" Emerson exclaimed. He grasped the limp hand that had been my first intimation of young Arthur's presence.

"Don't," I cried. "He is still alive, but in dire straits; we dare not move him until we can ascertain the nature of his injury. Can we lift the bed, do you think?"

In a crisis Emerson and I act as one. He went to the head of the bed, I to the foot; carefully we lifted the bed and set it to one side.

Arthur Baskerville lay on his back. His lower limbs were stiffly extended, his arms pressed close to his sides; the position was unnatural, and horribly reminiscent of the pose in which the Egyptians were wont to arrange their mummified dead. I wondered if my appraisal had been too optimistic, for if he was breathing, there was no sign of it. Nor was there any sign of a wound.

Emerson slipped his hand under the young man's head. "No mystery about this," he said quietly. "He has been struck a vicious blow on the head. I fear his skull is fractured. Thank God you stopped me when I was about to drag him out from under the bed."

"I will send for a doctor," I said.

"Sit down for a moment, my love; you are as white as paper."

"Don't worry about me; send at once, Emerson, time may be of the essence."

"You will stay with him?"

"I will not leave his side."

Emerson nodded. Briefly his strong brown hand rested on my shoulder—the touch of a comrade and a friend. He had no need to say more. Again our minds were as one. The person who had struck Arthur Baskerville down had intended to commit murder. He (or she) had failed on this occasion. We must make sure he had no chance to try again.

II

It was past midnight before Emerson and I were able to retire to our room, and my first act was to collapse across the bed with a long sigh.

"What a night!"

"An eventful night indeed," Emerson agreed. "I believe it is the first time I ever heard you admit you had encountered a case that was beyond your skill."

But as he spoke he sat down beside me and began loosening my tight gown with hands as gentle as his voice had been sarcastic. Stretching luxuriously, I allowed my husband to remove my shoes and stockings. When he brought a damp cloth and began to wipe my face, I sat up and took it from his hand.

"Poor man, you deserve consideration too," I said. "After a sleepless night on a rocky bed you worked all day in that inferno; lie down and let me take care of you. I am better, indeed I am; there was no reason for you to treat me like a child."

"But you enjoyed it," Emerson said, smiling. I gave him a quick, tactile demonstration of my appreciation. "I did. But now it is your turn. Get into bed and try to snatch a few hours' sleep. I know that in spite of everything you will be up at daybreak."

Emerson kissed the hand with which I was wiping his brow (as I have had occasion to remark, he is amazingly sentimental in private), but slipped away from me and began pacing up and down the room.

"I am too keyed up to sleep, Peabody. Don't fuss over me; you know I can go for days without rest if need be."

In his rumpled white shirt, open down the front to display his muscular chest, he was again the man I had first adored in the desert wilds, and I watched him for a time in tender silence. I sometimes compare Emerson's physique to that of a bull, for his massive head and disproportionately wide shoulders do resemble that animal in form, as his fits of temper resemble it in disposition. But he has a surprisingly light and agile walk; when in motion, as on this occasion, one is rather reminded of a great cat, a stalking panther or tiger.

I was in no mood for sleep either. I arranged a pillow behind me and sat up.

"You have done all you could for Arthur," I reminded him. "The doctor has agreed to spend the night, and I fancy Mary will not leave him either. Her concern was very touching. It would be quite a romantic situation if it were not so sad. I am more sanguine than Dr. Dubois, though. The young fellow has a strong constitution. I believe he has a chance of recovery."

"But he will not be able to speak for days, if ever," Emerson replied, in a tone that told me romance and tragedy alike were wasted on him. "This is getting out of hand, Peabody. How can I concentrate on my tomb with all this nonsense going on? I see I must settle the matter or I will have no peace."

"Ah." I sat up alertly. "So you agree with the suggestion I made some time ago—that we must find Armadale and force him to confess."

"We must certainly do something," Emerson said gloomily. "And I admit that with Milverton-Baskerville out of the picture, Mr. Armadale is the leading suspect. Curse the fellow! I was prepared to let him escape justice if he would leave me alone, but if he persists in interfering with my work, he will force me to take action."

"What do you propose?" I asked. Of course I knew quite well what ought to be done, but I had decided it would be more tactful to let Emerson work it out for himself, assisted by occasional questions and comments from me.

"We will have to look for the rascal, I suppose. It will be necessary to enlist some of the Gurneh men for that job. Our people are not familiar with the terrain. I know some of these sly devils quite well; in fact, there are a few old debts owing me which I now intend to call in. I had been saving them for an emergency. Now, I believe, the emergency has come."

"Splendid," I said sincerely. Emerson is always surprising me. I had no idea he was so unscrupulous, or that his acquaintance with the criminal element of Luxor was so extensive—for his reference to old debts, I felt sure, must refer to the trade in forgeries and stolen antiquities which is always going on in this region. What he was proposing, in short, was a form of blackmail. I approved heartily.

"It will take me all morning to arrange it," Emerson went on, continuing to pace. "These people are so cursed leisurely. You will have to take charge of the dig, Amelia."

"Of course."

"Don't sound so blasé. You will have to proceed with extreme caution, for fear of rockfalls and traps; and if you do find the burial chamber and enter it without me, I will divorce you."

"Naturally."

Emerson caught my eye. His frown turned to a sheepish smile, and then to a hearty laugh. "We don't make such a bad team, do we, Peabody? By the way, that costume you are wearing is singularly becoming; I am surprised that ladies haven't adopted it for daytime wear."

"A pair of drawers and a camisole, lace-trimmed though they are, would hardly constitute fitting daytime wear," I retorted. "Now don't try to change the subject, Emerson; we still have a great deal to talk about."

"True." Emerson sat down on the foot of the bed. Taking my bare feet in his hands, he pressed his lips to them in turn. My attempts to free myself were in vain; and, to be honest, I did not try very hard.

Chapter Eleven

 THE following morning Arthur's condition was unchanged. He lay in a deep coma, barely breathing. But the mere fact that he had lived through the night was a hopeful sign. I finally forced the physician to admit this. He was a fussy little Frenchman with ridiculous waxed mustaches and a large stomach, but he had quite a reputation among the European colony of Luxor, and after I had questioned him I was forced to admit that he seemed to know the rudiments of his trade. We agreed, he and I, that a surgical operation was not called for at that time; the bone of the skull, though cracked, did not appear to be pressing on the brain. I was, of course, relieved at this, but it would have been most interesting to assist at such an operation, which was successfully performed by several ancient cultures, including the Egyptian.

In short, there was nothing we could do for Arthur but wait until nature performed her task, and since there was no good hospital closer than Cairo, it would have been folly to move him.

Lady Baskerville offered to do the nursing. She would have been the logical person to assume the responsibility, but Mary was equally determined to tend the young man, and the argument became rather heated. Lady Baskerville's eyes began to flash and her voice took on the rasping quality indicative of rising temper. When summoned to settle the dispute, Emerson aggravated both ladies by announcing that he had already asked for professional assistance. The professional, a nun from a nursing order in Luxor, duly arrived; and although I have no sympathy with the idolatrous practices of Popery, the sight of the calm, smiling figure in its severe black robes had an amazingly comforting effect.

Emerson and I then set out for the Valley; for he could not bear to carry out his business with the Gurnawis without at least looking in on his beloved tomb. I had a hard time keeping up with him; he went loping along the path as if a few seconds' delay could be disastrous. I finally persuaded him to slow down because there were several questions I wanted to ask him. But before I could speak, he burst out, "We are so cursedly shorthanded! Mary won't be worth much today, she will be mooning over that worthless young man."

This seemed an auspicious time to introduce the proposal I had formed concerning Mr. O'Connell. Emerson responded more calmly than I had hoped.

"If that young —— comes within six feet of me, I will kick him in the rear," he remarked.

"You will have to abandon that attitude. We need him."

"No, we don't."

"Yes, we do. In the first place, giving him the exclusive rights to report on our activities means that we can exercise control over what he writes. Moreover, we are increasingly short of able-bodied men. I include myself in that category, of course—"

"Of course," Emerson agreed.

"Even so, we are shorthanded. Someone ought to be at the house, with the women. The rest of us are needed at the dig. O'Connell knows nothing about excavation, but he is a sharp young fellow, and it would relieve my mind to know that a capable person was watching over the household. Mary is not incapable, I don't mean to imply that, but between her work at the tomb and her duties to her mother, she will have more than enough to do."

"True," Emerson admitted.

"I am glad you agree. After all, Armadale may strike again. You may think me fanciful, Emerson—"

"I do, Amelia, I do."

"—but I am worried about Mary. Armadale once proposed to her; he may yet cherish an illicit passion. Suppose he decides to carry her off?"

"Across the desert on his fleet white camel?" Emerson inquired with a grin.

"Your levity is disgusting."

"Amelia, you must overcome your ridiculous weakness for young lovers," Emerson exclaimed. "If Armadale is skulking in the mountains, he has a great deal more on his mind than making love to some chit of a girl. But I agree with your earlier remark. Why do you suppose I called in a professional nurse? The blow aimed at Milverton-Baskerville (curse these people who travel under assumed names) was meant to silence him forever. The attacker may try again."

"So that occurred to you, did it?"

"Naturally. I am not senile yet."

"It is not kind of you to expose the poor nun to the attentions of a murderer."

"I don't believe there is any danger until Milverton shows signs of returning consciousness—if he ever does. All the same, your proposal about O'Connell has some merit, and I am willing to consider it. However, I refuse to speak to that fiend of a journalist myself. You will have to make the arrangements."

"I will gladly do so. But I think you are a little hard on him."

"Bah," said Emerson. "The Egyptians knew what they were about when they made Set, the ancient equivalent of Old Nick, a redheaded man."

Our workmen had already arrived at the tomb. All of them, as well as Abdullah and Karl, were gathered around Feisal, the second in command, who was telling them about the attack on Arthur. Feisal was the best raconteur in the group, and he was going at it in great style, with furious gestures and grimaces. Our two guards, who of course had known nothing of the event until now, had forgotten their dignity and were listening as avidly as the men. Arabs greatly enjoy a well-told story and will listen over and over to a tale they know by heart, especially if it is narrated by a skilled storyteller. I suspected that Feisal had added a few embellishments of his own.

Emerson erupted onto the scene and the group hastily dispersed, except for Abdullah and Karl. The former turned to Emerson, stroking his beard in obvious agitation. "Is this true, Emerson? That liar"—with a contemptuous gesture at Feisal, who was pretending not to listen—"will say anything to get attention."

Emerson responded with an accurate description of what had happened. The widening of Abdullah's eyes and his increasingly rapid manipulation of his beard indicated that the bare facts were distressing enough.

"But this is terrible," Karl said. "I must to the house go. Miss Mary is alone—"

I tried to reassure him. The mention of Mr. O'Connell as the prospective protector of the ladies did not soothe the young German at all, and he would have continued to expostulate if Emerson had not cut the discussion short.

"Mrs. Emerson will be in charge today," he announced. "I will return as soon as I can; in the meantime you will, of course, obey her as you would me." And, with a forlorn glance into the depths of the tomb—the sort of a look a lover might have cast on his beloved as he took leave of her before a battle—he strode away, followed, I was distressed to observe, by a little tail of curiosity seekers and journalists, all shouting questions. My beleaguered husband finally snatched the bridle of a donkey from a surprised Egyptian, leaped onto the beast, and urged it into a trot. The cavalcade disappeared in a cloud of dust, with the infuriated owner of the beast leading the pursuit.

I looked in vain for the fiery-red head of Mr. O'Connell. I was surprised at his absence, for I felt sure that with his sources of information he had already heard of the latest catastrophe and would be eager to rush to Mary's side. The mystery was explained shortly thereafter when a ragged child handed me a note. I gave the messenger some baksheesh and opened the note.

"I hope you have been able to convince the Professor," it began abruptly. "If you haven't, he will have to evict me personally and by force. I have gone to the house to be with Mary."

Much as I deplored the young man's impetuosity, I could not but respect the depth of his devotion to the girl he loved. And it was certainly a relief to know that the able-bodied man we needed was on duty. With my mind at ease on this point—if on few others—I could turn my attention to the tomb.

The first order of business was to photograph the area we had uncovered the previous evening. I had caused Arthur's camera to be fetched to the tomb, since I felt perfectly confident that with a little study I could operate it. With the help of Karl I set up the apparatus. Mr. Vandergelt, who arrived at about that time, was also useful. We took several exposures. Then the men were set to removing the remains, which included a number of beads and bits of stone that had been overlooked. It was then necessary to remove the massive stone from the passageway. Its appearance outside caused a great buzzing and shoving among the sightseers. Two of them actually fell over the edge of the excavation into the stairwell and had to be removed, bruised and threatening legal action.

Now the way was clear for the removal of the remaining fill, but when I was about to direct the men to carry out this task, Abdullah pointed out that it was time for the noon rest. I was not averse to stopping; for I was becoming increasingly anxious about Emerson.

Do not suppose, reader, that because I have not expressed my fears they did not exist. To say that my husband was unpopular with the thieves' guild of Gurneh is to express a laughable understatement. Certain other archaeologists tacitly cooperate with these gentry in order to have first chance at the illicit antiquities they dig up, but to Emerson an object ripped from its location lost much of its historical value, and it was often damaged by ignorant handling. Emerson insisted that if people would not buy illicit antiquities, the thieves would have no reason to dig. He was therefore anathema to the entrepreneurs of the trade on economic grounds, and personally—I think I have made it clear that tact is not his strong point. I was fully cognizant of the risk he ran in approaching the Gurnawis. They might decide not to pay blackmail but to remove the blackmailer.

It was therefore with profound relief that I beheld the familiar form striding vigorously toward me, brushing away tourists as one might swat at gnats. The journalists followed at a respectful distance. I observed that the man from the *Times* was limping, and hoped devoutly that Emerson had not been responsible for his injury.

"Where is the donkey?" I inquired.

"How is the work going?" Emerson asked simultaneously.

I had to answer his question first or he would never have answered mine, so I gave him a summary of the morning's activities while he seated himself beside me and accepted a cup of tea. When his speech was temporarily impeded by the medium of a sandwich, I repeated my question.

Emerson stared blankly around him. "What donkey? Oh—that donkey. I suppose the owner retrieved it."

"What happened at Gurneh? Did you succeed in your mission?"

"We ought to be able to remove the rest of the fill today," Emerson said musingly. "Curse it, I knew I had forgotten something—all that hullaballoo last night distracted me. Planks. We need more—"

"Emerson!"

"There is no need to shout, Amelia. I am sitting next to you, in case you failed to observe that."

"What happened?"

"What happened where? Oh," Emerson said, as I reached for my parasol. "You mean at Gurneh. Why, just what I had planned, of course. Ali Hassan Abd er Rasul—he is a cousin of Mohammed—was quite cooperative. He and his friends have already begun searching for Armadale."

"As simple as that? Come now, Emerson, don't assume that air of lofty competence, you know how it enrages me. I have been sick with worry."

"Then you weren't thinking clearly," Emerson retorted, holding out his cup to be refilled. "Ali Hassan and the rest have every incentive to do what I asked, quite aside from the—er—private matters we discussed to our mutual satisfaction. I offered a sizable reward for Armadale. Also, this search gives them a legitimate reason to do what they habitually do on the sly—prowl around the mountains looking for hidden tombs."

"Naturally I had thought of that."

"Naturally." Emerson smiled at me. He finished his tea, dropped the cup (he is almost as hard on crockery as he is on shirts) and rose to his feet. "Back to work. Where is everyone?"

"Karl is sleeping. Now, Emerson," I added, as his brows drew together in a scowl, "you can hardly expect the young man to watch all night and work all day. Vandergelt returned to the house for luncheon. He wanted to make sure everyone was all right and get the latest news about Arthur."

"He wanted to lunch in comfort and bask in Lady Baskerville's smiles," Emerson snapped. "The man is a dilettante. I suspect him of desiring to steal my tomb."

"You suspect everyone of that," I replied, picking up the pieces of the broken cup and packing away the remainder of the food.

"Come along, Amelia, you have wasted enough time," Emerson said and, shouting for Abdullah, he bounded away.

I was about to resume my labors when I saw Vandergelt approaching. He had taken advantage of the opportunity to change his clothes and was wearing another immaculately tailored set of tweeds, of which he seemed to have an endless number. Leaning on my parasol, I watched him stride toward me, and wondered what his real age might be. In spite of his graying hair and lined, leathery face he walked like a young man, and the strength of his hands and arms was remarkable.

Seeing me, he raised his hat with his usual courtesy. "I am glad to report that all is well," he said.

"You mean that Lady Baskerville has not yet murdered Madame Berengeria?"

The American looked at me quizzically and then smiled. "That British sense of humor! To tell you the truth, Mrs. Amelia, when I got there the two ladies were squaring off like prizefighters. I had to play peacemaker, and I flatter myself I did it neatly. I suggested that Madame intercede with the gods of Egypt and beg them to spare young Arthur's life. She jumped on that like a duck on a June bug. When I left she was squatting in the middle of the parlor crooning to herself and making mystical gestures. It was sure a horrible sight."

"There is no change in Arthur's condition?" I asked.

"No. But he is holding his own. Say, Mrs. Amelia, I have to ask you—did you really tell that young rapscallion O'Connell he could move in? He was buttering up to Lady Baskerville for all he was worth, and when I asked him why he was there, he told me you had given him permission."

"That will not please Lady Baskerville. I assure you, Mr. Vandergelt, I had no intention of impinging on her prerogatives. Emerson and I felt that under the circumstances—"

"I get you. And I've got to admit I felt easier leaving the ladies there with him. He's a scoundrel, but I think he would be a good man in a fight."

"Let us hope it does not come to that," I said.

"Sure. . . . All right, ma'am, let's get to work before the Professor comes out and accuses me of making eyes at you. I have to confess that I'm torn between my duty to Lady Baskerville and my interest in the tomb. I'd sure hate to miss the opening of the burial chamber."

In this latter hope he was doomed to disappointment, for that day at least. By late afternoon the men had carried out the last of the limestone fill and the corridor lay clear before us. They then withdrew, to enable the dust to settle, and the four of us gathered at the edge of the well.

Emerson held a lantern whose dust-fogged light cast eerie shadows across the faces of the men—Vandergelt, considerably more disheveled but no less excited than he had been four hours earlier; Karl, showing the signs of sleeplessness in his sunken eyes and weary face; Emerson, alert and energetic as ever. I was conscious of not looking my best.

"It's not so wide," Vandergelt remarked, appraising the width of the shaft. "I reckon I could jump it."

"I reckon you won't," said Emerson, with a scornful look at the speaker. "You might clear the gap, but where would you land? The space is less than a foot wide and it is backed by a sheer wall."

Advancing to the rim of the pit he lay flat, with his head and shoulders protruding over emptiness, and lowered the lantern as far as his arm would reach. The dim flame burned bluer. The air in those deep recesses was still bad, for there was no circulation, and in the depths of the shaft it was even worse. Though I had immediately followed Emerson's example, I could make out very few details. Far below, at the utmost extremity of the light, was a pale amorphous glimmer—more of the omnipresent limestone chips, so many tons of which he had already removed from the tomb.

"Yes," Emerson said, when I had voiced this observation. "The shaft is partially filled. The upper part was left open in the hope that a thief would tumble into it and break his bones." Rising, he directed the light toward the far wall. There, in ominous dignity, the jackal-headed guide of the dead raised his hands in greeting.

"You see, Amelia, and gentlemen, the options open to us," Emerson said. "The continuance of the passageway is concealed. Either it lies behind that figure of Anubis, on the far wall, or it is on a lower level, opening out from the depths of the shaft. Obviously we must investigate both possibilities. We can do neither tonight. I must have a clear copy of the figure of Anubis before we bring in planks to bridge the gap and begin chopping away at the wall. To investigate the shaft we will need ropes, and it would be advisable for us to wait for the air to clear a little more. You saw how blue the lamp burned."

"Shucks," Vandergelt exclaimed. "Listen here, Professor, I'll take my chances down there; you've got some ropes here, just you lower me down and I'll—"

"*Aber nein,* it is the younger and stronger who will descend," Karl exclaimed. "Herr Professor, let me—"

"The first person to descend will be myself," Emerson said, in a tone that silenced further comment. "And that will be tomorrow morning." He looked hard at me. I smiled, but did not speak. It was obvious that the lightest person in the group should be the one to make the descent, but there would be time to discuss that later.

After a moment Emerson cleared his throat. "Very well, we are agreed. I propose that we stop for the day and make an early start tomorrow. I am anxious to learn how matters are going at the house."

"And who will be on guard tonight?" Vandergelt asked.

"Peabody and I."

"Peabody? Who is—oh, I see. Now look here, Professor, you wouldn't cheat on me, would you? No fair you and Mrs. Amelia going ahead with the work tonight."

"May I remind you that I am the director of this expedition?" Emerson said.

When he speaks in that tone it is seldom necessary for him to speak twice. Vandergelt, a man of strong personality, recognized a stronger, and fell silent.

However, he dogged our footsteps all the way back, and it was impossible for me to speak privately to my husband, as I had hoped to do. My heart had leaped with exultation at hearing him name me the partner of his watch, and the decision had confirmed my hunch that he meant to do more than watch. Whom else could he trust as he trusted me, his life and professional partner? His decision to stop work early made excellent sense; so long as there was light, of sun or moon, the tomb was safe. The ghouls of Gurneh, like other evil creatures of the night, worked only in darkness. When the moon set behind the hills the danger began; and by then, perhaps, we would have penetrated the secret of the pharaoh.

Although this thought roused me to the highest pitch of archaeological excitement, never believe I neglected my duties. I went first to the chamber where Arthur lay. The silent, black-garbed figure of the nun might not have moved since morning. Only the faint clack of the beads that slipped through her fingers showed she was a living woman and not a statue. She did not speak when I asked about the patient, only shook her head to indicate there had been no change.

Madame Berengeria was next on my agenda. I decided it would be more convenient for everyone if she were safely tucked away for the night before I left. I assumed she was still in the parlor communing with the gods, and as I walked in that direction I pondered how my aim might best be achieved. A wholly contemptible and unworthy idea occurred to me. Dare I confess it? I have vowed to be completely honest, so, at the risk of incurring the censure of my readers, let me admit that I contemplated making use of Madame's weakness for drink to render her inebriated and unconscious. If those who would condemn me had faced the situation that confronted me, and had seen the dreadful woman in action, they would, I daresay, be more tolerant of this admittedly reprehensible plan.

I was spared the necessity of acting, however. When I reached the room in question, I found that Berengeria had anticipated me. The sound of her rasping snores was audible at some distance; even before I saw her sprawled in an ungainly and indecent heap on the carpet, I knew what had happened. An empty brandy bottle lay by her right hand.

Lady Baskerville was standing over her, and I trust I may not be accused of malice if I remark that one of the lady's dainty slippers was lifted as if in preparation for a kick. Seeing me, she hastily lowered her foot.

"Abominable!" she exclaimed, her eyes flashing. "Mrs. Emerson, I insist that you remove this dreadful woman from my house. It was an act of extreme cruelty to bring her here when I am in such a state of nerves, worn by grief—"

"Let me point out, Lady Baskerville, that the decision was not mine," I broke in. "I fully sympathize with your viewpoint; but we can hardly send her back to Luxor in this condition. How did she get at the brandy? I thought you kept the liquor cabinet locked."

"I do. I suppose she managed to get at the keys; drunkards are amazingly cunning when it comes to feeding their weakness. But good heavens, what does it matter?" She raised her white hands to her breast and wrung them vigorously. "I am going mad, I tell you!"

Her theatrics assured me that she had a new audience, for she knew I was impervious to that approach; I was therefore not surprised to see Vandergelt enter.

"Holy Jehoshaphat," he said, with a horrified look at the snoring mound on the floor. "How long has she been like that? My poor girl." Here he clasped the hand Lady Baskerville had extended, and pressed it tenderly in his.

"We must take her to her room and lock her in," I said. "Do you take her head, Mr. Vandergelt; Lady Baskerville and I will take—"

The lady let out a plaintive scream. "You jest, Mrs. Emerson; surely you jest!"

"Mrs. Emerson never jokes about such things," said Vandergelt, with a smile. "If you and I refuse to help, she will do it alone—dragging the woman by her feet. Mrs. Emerson, I suggest we call one—or two, or three—of the servants. There is no hope of concealing the poor creature's condition, or preserving her reputation."

This procedure was duly carried out; and I went next to the kitchen to tell Ahmed that Emerson and I would be dining out. As I strode along, deep in thought, out of the corner of my eyes I caught a glimpse of something moving among the trees. A corner of pale fabric, like the blue zaaboots worn by Egyptian men, fluttered and disappeared.

It might have been one of our own people. But there had been something hasty and surreptitious about the darting movement. I therefore took a firm grip of my parasol and went in pursuit.

Since the night on the loggia with poor Arthur I had determined never to go abroad without this useful instrument. To be sure, I had not needed it then; but one never knew when an emergency might arise. I had therefore attached the parasol to my belt, by means of one of the hooks with which this article of clothing was supplied. This was occasionally inconvenient, for the shaft had a tendency to slip between my legs and trip me up; but better to bruise one's knees than be left defenseless in case of attack.

I moved quietly over the soft grass, taking cover when I could. Peeping out from behind a thorny bush, I beheld the form of a man in native garb behind another bush. After glancing around in a furtive manner that assured me he was up to no good, he glided serpentlike across the turf and passed through the doorway of a small building, one of the mud-brick auxiliary structures used for storage of tools. I caught a glimpse of his face as he glanced slyly over his shoulder, and a villainous countenance it was. A livid scar twisted his cheek and ran down into his heavy grizzled beard.

Normally the door of the storage shed was padlocked. Theft, or worse, was obviously the man's aim. I was about to raise the alarm when I realized that an outcry would warn the felon and enable him to escape. I decided I would capture him myself.

Dropping flat, in Red Indian style, I slid forward. I did not rise to my feet until I had reached the shelter of the wall, where I pressed myself flat. I heard voices within, and marveled at the effrontery of the thieves. There were at least two of them—unless the original miscreant was talking to himself. They were speaking Arabic, but I could only make out an occasional word.

I took a deep breath and rushed into the hut, striking out with my parasol. I heard a grunt of pain as the iron shaft thudded against a soft surface. Hands seized me. Struggling, I struck again. The parasol was wrenched from my grasp. Undaunted, I kicked my attacker heavily on the shin, and was about to call out when a voice bade me cease. I knew that voice.

"What are you doing here?" I demanded somewhat breathlessly.

"I might echo that question," replied Emerson, in the same style. "But why ask? I know you are ubiquitous. I don't mind that, it is your impetuosity that distresses me. I believe you have broken my leg."

"Nonsense," I said, retrieving my parasol. "If you would condescend to inform me of your plans, these tiring encounters might be avoided, to our mutual benefit. Who is with you?"

"Allow me to present Ali Hassan Abd er Rasul," said Emerson. He finished the introduction in Arabic, referring to me as his learned and high-born chief wife—which would have been very flattering if his tone had not been so sarcastic. Ali Hassan, whom I now saw huddled in the corner, rolled his eyes till the whites showed, and made an extremely insulting remark.

"Son of a one-eyed camel and offspring of a deceased goat," I said (or words to that effect; the original Arabic is far too emphatic for decent English), "keep your infected tongue from comments about your betters."

Emerson amplified this statement at some length, and Ali Hassan cowered. "I had forgotten that the honored Sitt has our language," he remarked. "Give me my reward and I will go."

"Reward!" I exclaimed. "Emerson, do you mean—"

"Yes, my honored chief wife, I do," Emerson replied. "Ali Hassan sent a message by one of the servants to meet him here. Why he won't come to the house I do not know and frankly I do not care; but he claims he has found Armadale. Of course I have no intention of paying him until I am sure."

"Where is Armadale?"

"In a cave in the hills."

I waited for him to go on, but he said no more; and as the silence lengthened, a shiver of comprehension ran through me.

"He is dead."

"Yes. And," Emerson said gravely, "according to Ali Hassan, he has been dead for quite some time."

Chapter Twelve

THE declining sun thrust a long red-gold arm through the open doorway, lighting the shadowy corner where Ali Hassan crouched. I saw that Emerson was watching me quizzically.

"Throws your theories off a bit, doesn't it?" he inquired.

"I can hardly say at present," I replied. " 'Quite a long time' is a rather indefinite term. But if it should prove that after all Armadale was already dead when the latest attack took place . . . No, that would really not surprise me; the alternative theory I had formulated—"

"Curse it, Amelia, have you the infernal gall to pretend . . ." Emerson cut the comment short. After a few moments of heavy breathing he bared his teeth at me. The expression was evidently meant to be a smile, for when he continued his voice was sickeningly sweet. "I will say no more; I don't want Ali Hassan to think we are at odds with one another."

"These Arabs do not understand Western means of expressing affection," I agreed, somewhat absently. "Emerson, we must act at once. We face a dilemma of considerable proportions."

"True. Armadale's body must be brought back here. And someone must go to the tomb. It has never been more vulnerable than at this moment."

"Obviously we must divide forces. Shall I go after Armadale or guard the tomb?"

"Armadale," was the prompt reply. "Though I don't like to ask you, Peabody."

"You are giving me the less dangerous task," I said, much moved by the expression on Emerson's face as he looked at me. But there was no time for sentiment. With every passing moment the sun sank lower in the west.

Ali Hassan grunted and got to his feet. "I go now. You give me—"

"Not until you have taken us to the body of Armadale," Emerson answered. "The Sitt will go with you."

An avaricious gleam brightened Ali Hassan's eyes. He began to whine about his advanced age and state of exhaustion. After some bargaining he accepted

Emerson's offer of an additional fifty piasters to lead me to the cave. "And," Emerson added, in a soft, menacing growl, "you answer for the Sitt's safety with your life, Ali Hassan. Should she suffer so much as a scratch, should a single hair be missing from her head, I will tear out your liver. You know I speak truly."

Ali Hassan sighed. "I know," he said mournfully.

"You had better go at once, Peabody," Emerson said. "Take Abdullah and one or two other men; and perhaps Karl—"

"Won't I do instead?" a voice inquired.

The sun set O'Connell's hair ablaze. Only his head was visible around the doorjamb, and that gave the impression of being ready to disappear at the slightest sign of hostility. His smile was as broad and cocky as ever, though.

"Humph," said Emerson. "I looked for you earlier, Mr. O'Connell."

"I thought I had better keep out of your way at first," the journalist replied. Emerson's mild tone had reassured him; he stepped out from behind the shelter of the wall, his hands tucked in his pockets. "I couldn't help overhearing," he went on.

"Grrr," said Emerson. (I assure you, there is really no other way of reproducing this sound.)

"Honestly." O'Connell's blue eyes widened. "And it's as well I did, now isn't it, Professor? You don't want Mrs. E. wandering off into the hills without a man to protect her."

"I don't need a man to protect me," I said indignantly. "And if I did, Abdullah would be more than adequate."

"To be sure, to be sure. You'd be a match for Cormac himself, ma'am, and that's the truth. Just let me come along now, for my own sake, like the sweet lady you are; and I swear by the gods of old Ireland that after I've written my story I'll bring it straight to you."

Emerson and I exchanged glances.

"What about Mary?" I inquired. "Will you leave her here, with Karl? He admires her very much, you know."

"She's still not speaking to me," O'Connell admitted. "But, don't you see, this is the story of the year! 'New Victim of the Pharaoh's Curse! Our correspondent on the scene! The Courage of Mrs. Emerson, parasol in hand!' " Emerson growled again at this. I confess I found it rather amusing.

After a moment Emerson said grumpily, "Very well, O'Connell, fetch Abdullah. Ask him to bring the necessary equipment—ropes, lanterns—and meet us here in ten minutes, with two of his best men."

Grinning from ear to ear like an Irish Brownie, O'Connell rushed off. Heedless of the staring Ali Hassan, Emerson caught me in a fond embrace.

"I hope I shan't regret this," he muttered. "Peabody, take care."

"And you." I returned his embrace. "Go now, Emerson, before darkness falls to endanger us even more."

II

It was, of course, impossible to organize an expedition of that nature in ten minutes; but scarcely half an hour had passed before Abdullah arrived with the required supplies. His grave face was its usual copper mask, but I knew him well enough to sense a deep perturbation, and the behavior of the two men he had selected to accompany us was even more revealing. They looked like prisoners being led to execution.

"Do they know what we seek?" I whispered to Abdullah.

"I could not keep the redheaded man silent," Abdullah replied, with a hostile glance at O'Connell. "Sitt Hakim, I fear—"

"So do I. Let us go, quickly, before they have time to think and become more afraid."

We set out, with Ali Hassan slouching along ahead. O'Connell also seemed subdued; his eyes constantly darted from side to side, as if he were taking note of the surroundings for the story he would later write.

Ali Hassan led us directly to the cliffs behind Deir el Bahri. Instead of taking the path that led to the Valley of the Kings, he went south and soon began to climb, scrambling over the jagged rocks with the agility of a goat. I rejected O'Connell's attempts to assist me. Thanks to my parasol and my training I was in far better shape than he, and he was soon forced to use both hands in the climb. Abdullah came close behind me. I could hear him muttering, and although I could not make out the words I fancied I knew what was bothering him. Ali Hassan seemed to choose, deliberately, the most difficult path. At least twice I saw easier ways of ascent than the ones he selected.

At last, however, we reached the top of the plateau, and the going became easier. If we had had leisure to enjoy it, the view was spectacular. The broad reach of the river was stained crimson by the setting sun. The eastern cliffs were washed in soft shades of pink and lavender. Above them the sky had darkened to cobalt, with a few diamond points of starlight showing. But this view lay behind us. Ali Hassan headed toward the west, where the sun hung suspended, a swollen orb of fiery copper. Before long it would set and darkness would rush in like a black-winged bat; for there is little twilight in these climes. I tried to remember when the moon was due to rise. This part of the plateau was unfamiliar to me: an uninhabited wilderness of barren rock cut by innumerable cracks and fissures. It would make for dangerous walking after dark, even with the aid of the lanterns we had brought.

O'Connell was in some distress, having cut his hand rather badly during the climb. Since time was of the essence, I had not paused to attend him, except to wrap a handkerchief around the injured member. Abdullah was now close behind me, his quickened breathing betraying his agitation. He had ample cause for concern—the natural dangers of the terrain, the possibility of ambush, and the uneasiness of our own men, fearful of night demons and efreets.

Trotting along several feet ahead of me, Ali Hassan was singing, or keening, to himself. He showed no signs of fearing the supernatural terrors of the night; and indeed a man who practiced the sinister trade of robbing the dead might not be expected to be susceptible to superstition. His good spirits had precisely the opposite effect on me. Whatever pleased Ali Hassan was likely to prove unpleasant for me. I suspected he was deliberately leading us astray, but without proof I could hardly accuse him.

My eyes were fixed on the tattered robe of Ali Hassan, alert for the first sign of treachery; I did not see the creature until it brushed against my ankle. One's first thought, in that region, is of snakes; automatically I took a quick sideward step, catching Mr. O'Connell off balance, so that he went sprawling. Reaching for my parasol, I turned to confront the new danger.

The cat Bastet perched atop a nearby boulder. It had leaped out of my way, as I had leaped away from it, and its outraged expression showed how little it approved of my rude greeting.

"I beg your pardon," I said. "But it is your own fault; you ought to give notice of your approach. I trust I have not hurt you."

The cat only stared; but Ali Hassan, who had come back to see why we had stopped, invoked the name of Allah in a voice fraught with emotion.

"She speaks to the cat," he exclaimed. "It is a demon, a spirit; and she is its mistress." He turned so quickly that his robe ballooned out; but before he could flee I hooked him around the neck with the crook of my parasol.

"We have played this game long enough, Ali Hassan," I said. "You have been leading us in circles. The cat, who is indeed the spirit of the goddess Sekhmet, came to tell me of your treachery."

"I thought as much," Abdullah growled. He tried to seize hold of Ali Hassan. I waved him away.

"Ali Hassan knows what Emerson will do to him if I report this. Now, Ali, take us directly to the place—or I will send the cat goddess to tear you in your sleep."

I released the miscreant and Abdullah moved forward ready to seize him if he tried to run. But there was no need. Ali Hassan stared wild-eyed at the cat, who had leaped down from the rock and was standing by my side, its tail lashing ominously.

"She was there, when I found the dead man," he muttered. "I should have known then. I should not have tried to strike her with a stone. O Sekhmet, lady of terror, forgive this evildoer."

"She will if I ask her," I said pointedly. "Lead on, Ali Hassan."

"Why not?" Ali shrugged fatalistically. "She knows the way; if I do not lead, she will show you."

When we went on Abdullah accompanied Ali Hassan, his big hand firmly clamped over the Gurneh man's arm. Ali Hassan sang no more.

"How did you know?" O'Connell asked respectfully. "I had no suspicion at all."

"I simply acted on my suspicions, knowing the man's character; and he was stupid enough to confess."

"You are a wonder, ma'am, and that's the truth," O'Connell exclaimed.

I smiled in acknowledgment of the compliment, well deserved though it was. "Hurry, Ali Hassan," I called. "If darkness falls before we reach the cave . . ."

The cat had disappeared, almost as if, having completed her mission, she had no need to stay. Ali Hassan's pace increased. I was not at all surprised to see that our path now led eastward, in the direction from which we had come. The lower rim of the sun dipped below the horizon. Ali Hassan broke into an undignified trot, his blue robe flapping. Our shadows rushed along before us, elongated gray-blue shapes like the protective *kas* of the ancient Egyptians.

Though the lengthening shadows made it easier to see obstructions in the path, it was necessary to keep a sharp look-out to avoid falling. I was aware that our general direction was eastward, but because I had to watch my footing I did not realize where we were heading until Ali Hassan came to a stop.

"We are here, oh, Sitt Hakim," he said, between pants. "We have come to the place and the sun is not down; I have done what you asked. Tell this man to take his hands from me and assure the divine Sekhmet that I have obeyed her command."

He had spoken the literal truth. A last thin crescent of fiery red marked the place where the sun had sunk. Dusk was gathering fast. Not until I raised my eyes from the immediate surroundings did I realize that we were near the edge of the cliff, only a few hundred yards north of where we had ascended.

"Son of a rabid dog," snarled Abdullah, shaking Ali Hassan till his teeth rattled, "you have led us in a circle. There is no cave here. What trick are you playing?"

"It is here," Ali Hassan insisted. "I lost my way at first; anyone might lose his way; but we have come to the place. Give me my money and let me go."

Naturally we paid no attention to this ridiculous demand. I ordered the men to light the lanterns. By the time they had done so only a faint lingering afterglow relieved the black of the star-sprinkled heavens. In the lamplight Ali Hassan's malevolent countenance might have belonged to one of the night demons whose baleful influence he flouted so contemptuously. His open mouth was a cavern of darkness, ringed by rotting fangs of teeth.

Abdullah took a lantern and led the way, pushing our reluctant robber ahead of him. The path led down the cliff. It proved less hazardous than I had feared; but the descent was breathtaking enough, in almost total darkness and with an inexperienced companion. Poor Mr. O'Connell had lost his Gaelic joie de vivre; groaning and swearing under his breath he followed me down, and when the light shone on the bloodstained bandage that covered his hand I had to admire his courage, for I knew the injury must pain him considerably. We were close to the bottom of the cliff when Ali Hassan turned to one side and pointed.

"There. There. Now let me go."

Trained as I am, I would never have seen the opening without the aid of his pointing finger. The cliffs are so seamed by cracks and fissures, each one of which casts its own shadow, that only prolonged investigation can tell which leads to an opening. While Abdullah held the lantern—and Ali Hassan—I investigated the indicated crevice.

It was low and very narrow. My height is not much over five feet and I had to stoop in order to enter. Once under the rock lintel the space opened up; I could tell by the feel of the air that a cave lay before me, but it was as black as ink and I am not ashamed to admit that I had no intention of proceeding without light. I called to Abdullah to hand me the lantern. Advancing, I held it high.

Imagine a hollow sphere, some twenty feet in diameter. Bisect the sphere and close off the open section, leaving only a narrow slit for entrance. Such was the extent and the shape of the space I now beheld, though the interior was as jagged and rocky as a hollowed sphere would be smooth. These observations were made at a later moment; just then I had no eyes for anything but the object that lay crumpled on the floor at my feet.

It lay on its side, with its knees drawn up and its head back. The tendons in the bared throat looked like dried rope. One hand was so close to my shoe that I was almost treading on it. My hand was not as steady as it might have been; the tremor of the lantern I held made the shadows shift, so that the bent fingers seemed to clutch at my ankle.

I had seen photographs of Armadale, but if I had not known the body must be his I would not have recognized this ghastly face. In life the young man had been boyishly attractive rather than handsome, with a long, narrow face and delicate features that explained the Arabs' nickname for him. He had attempted to conceal the almost feminine structure of his face with a cavalry-style mustache. This facial adornment was now missing. A heavy lock of brown hair concealed the eyes, and I cannot say I was sorry for that.

As I stood attempting to control the uncharacteristic tremors that passed through my frame, an eerie event occurred. From the shadows at the back of the cave, pacing with slow dignity, came the cat Bastet. She walked to the head of the corpse and sat down, ears pricked, whiskers bristling.

Abdullah's increasingly agitated cries finally roused me from the paralysis that had taken hold of me. I called back a reassuring reply; and my voice, I think, was steady. But before summoning my faithful reis or the inquisitive young reporter, I knelt by the pitiful remains and made a brief examination.

The skull was intact and the visible parts of the corpse were without a wound. There was no blood. Finally I forced myself to brush the dry, lifeless hair from the forehead. No wound marred its tanned surface. But traced in flaking red paint was the rough sketch of a snake—the royal uraeus serpent of the pharaoh.

III

I cast a veil over the hour that followed, not, I assure you, because the memory is intolerable—I have had worse hours, many of them—but because so much happened in such a short time that a detailed description would be interminably long.

Removing Armadale's body was not difficult, since we were only fifteen minutes' walk from the house and our efficient reis had brought along materials with which to construct a makeshift litter. The difficulty arose from the reluctance of the men to touch the body. I knew both these persons well; in fact, I considered them friends of mine. Never before had I seen them daunted. Yet on this occasion it required all my eloquence to persuade them to do what was necessary; and as soon as the remains had been deposited in an empty storeroom the litter bearers fled as if pursued by fiends.

Ali Hassan watched them go with a cynical smile. "They will work no more in the accursed tomb," he said, as if to himself. "Fools they may be, but they are wise enough to fear the dead."

"A pity you don't feel the same," I said. "Here is your money, Ali Hassan; you do not deserve it, after playing us such a trick, but I always keep my word. Remember this: if you attempt to enter the tomb, or interfere with our work, I will call down the wrath of Sekhmet upon you."

Ali Hassan burst into loud protestations, which did not end until Abdullah started toward him with his fist clenched. After the Gurmeh man had left, Abdullah said gravely, "I go to talk to my men, Sitt. The robber is right; it will be hard to make them return to the tomb once this news gets out."

"A moment, Abdullah," I said. "I understand your reasoning, and agree with it; but I need you. I am going to the Valley. Emerson must know of this at once. It may be that Ali Hassan was delaying us in order to give his friends a chance to attack the tomb."

"I'll go with you," O'Connell said.

"Is it the journalist speaking, or the gentleman?" I inquired.

A flush spread over the young man's face. "I deserved that," he said, with unusual humility. "And I confess that my reporter's instincts yearn to observe the Professor's reaction when you tell him the latest news. But that is not my reason for wishing to be of service to you. Abdullah is needed here."

Under the cold moonlight the rocky cliffs might have been part of a lunar landscape, desolate of life for millions of years. We spoke little at first. Finally O'Connell let out a deep sigh.

"Is your hand paining you?" I inquired. "I apologize for not tending to your wound; concern for my husband must be my excuse."

"No, the wound, as you call it, is a mere scratch and does not trouble me. I am concerned about other things. Mrs. Emerson, this situation was only a journalistic sensation to me before—the greatest story of my life, perhaps. Now that I find myself acquainted with all of you, and increasingly attached to some of you, my viewpoint has changed."

"May I assume, then, that we have your wholehearted cooperation?"

"You may indeed! I only wish I could do more to relieve you. How did that poor chap meet his end? So far as I could tell there was not a mark on him—just like Lord Baskerville."

"He may have died a natural death from hunger and thirst," I said cautiously. I was inclined to believe O'Connell's protestations, but he had tricked me too often to deserve my full confidence. "Remember," I went on, "you have promised to show me your stories. No more speculations about curses, if you please."

"I feel like Dr. Frankenstein," O'Connell admitted with a rueful laugh. "I have created a monster which has come to life. The curse was my own invention, and a wholly cynical one; I have never believed in such things. But how are we to explain—"

He did not finish the sentence. Breaking into his speech came the sharp crack of a gunshot.

In the silence the sound carried and echoed, but I knew whence it had come. Logic would have told me as much even if domestic affection had not sharpened my senses. I broke into a run. Another round of firing followed. Loosening my revolver from its holster and removing my parasol from its hook in order to prevent it from tripping me, I plunged down the slope into the Valley at a speed that would have been unsafe even in daylight. Perhaps it was my very velocity that prevented me from falling. My parasol in my left hand, my revolver in my right, I rushed on, firing the latter as I went. I shot most often into the air, I believe, though I would not care to take my oath on it; my aim was to assure the attackers that assistance was rapidly approaching.

I heard no more shots. What did the deadly silence presage? Victory for us, the robbers wounded or in flight? Or . . . But I refused to consider an alternative theory. Running ever faster I saw before me, pallid in the moonlight, the pile of limestone chips we had removed from the tomb. The opening itself was just ahead. There was no sign of life.

Then a dark form loomed up before me. Leveling my revolver, I pulled the trigger.

A click sounded as the hammer struck the empty chamber. The voice of

Emerson remarked, "You had better reload, Peabody; you fired the last bullet some time ago."

"All the same," I said breathlessly, "it was very foolhardy of you to step out in front of me."

"I assure you I would not have done so had I not counted the shots. I know your reckless temperament too well."

I was unable to reply. A belated realization of what I had done robbed me of my remaining breath. Although I knew Emerson had spoken the truth when he said he would not have faced me without the knowledge that my revolver was empty, I was sick with remorse and distress. Sensing my emotion, Emerson put his arm around me.

"Are you all right, Peabody?"

"I am sick with remorse and distress. Indeed, in the future I must endeavor to act more calmly. I believe the situation is affecting my nerves. Ordinarily I would never behave so foolishly."

"Humph," said Emerson.

"Truly, my dear Emerson—"

"Never mind, my dear Peabody. The panache with which you plunge headlong into danger is what first drew me to you. But devil take it, you didn't come alone, did you?"

"No, Mr. O'Connell is with me or he was. Mr. O'Connell?"

"Is it safe to come out now?" inquired the young man's voice.

"You heard me say her revolver is empty," Emerson replied.

"Hers, yes," said O'Connell, still invisible. "What about yours, Professor?"

"Don't be a coward, man! The danger is over; I fired a few warning shots to keep the rascals off. Though," Emerson added, smiling at me, "I might not have gotten off so easily had not Mrs. Emerson arrived, masquerading as an entire squad of policemen. She made enough noise for a dozen men."

"That was what I planned," I said.

"Ha," said Emerson. "Well, well; sit down, both of you, and tell me what you found."

So we took seats on the blanket he had spread out before the entrance to the tomb and I narrated the events of the evening.

A lesser man than Emerson might have exclaimed in horror at the dreadful experiences I had undergone—but then a lesser man would never have allowed me to face them. When I had finished my story he simply nodded.

"Well done, Peabody. I have no doubt that it was Ali Hassan's band of burglars who attacked just now; if you had not caught on to his trick and forced him to move more quickly, you might not have arrived here in time to rescue me." I thought I detected a trace of amusement in the last words and looked at him suspiciously; but his face was quite serious, and so was his voice when he continued. "Never mind that; we have scared them off, for this evening at least. What interests me more is the news about Armadale. There was no indication of how he died?"

"None," I said.

"But there was the scarlet cobra on his brow," O'Connell said.

I gave the young man a hard stare. I had been careful to brush Armadale's hair back over his forehead before I allowed the others to enter the cave, and I had hoped this omen had escaped the reporter.

"Then," said Emerson, "we must face the probability that he was murdered, even though no signs of violence were visible. Furthermore, I cannot believe that the body would have reached the state you describe in less than three or four days. Who, then, was responsible for the attack on young Arthur?"

"Madame Berengeria," I said.

"What?" It was Emerson's turn to give me a hard stare. "Amelia, the question was rhetorical. You cannot possibly—"

"I assure you, I have been thinking of nothing else since I found Armadale. Who had an interest in his death? Who but the madwoman who clings like a leech to her daughter's youthful strength, and who would be loath to relinquish her to a husband? Mr. Armadale had proposed marriage to Mary—"

"The spalpeen!" Mr. O'Connell exclaimed. "Did he have the infernal gall to do that?"

"He was not the only one to find Miss Mary an object worthy of devotion," I retorted. "Is not jealousy one motive for murder, Mr. O'Connell? Would you commit the sin of Cain to win the woman you love?"

Mr. O'Connell's eyes popped. The moonlight drained all color from the scene; his face had the pallor of death—or guilt.

"Amelia," said my husband, grinding his teeth. "I beg you to control yourself."

"I have barely begun," I cried indignantly. "Karl von Bork is also a suspect. He also loves Mary. Don't forget that the other person who was murderously attacked is also an admirer of the young lady. But I consider Madame Berengeria the most likely person. She is mentally deranged, and only a mad person would commit murder for such a trivial reason."

Emerson clutched his hair with both hands and appeared to be trying to pull it out by the roots. "Amelia, you are arguing in circles!"

"Wait, now, Professor," O'Connell said thoughtfully. "I think Mrs. E. may be on to something. The only reason I've been allowed to be friends with Mary was because I pretended to admire her mother. The old—er—witch has frightened off a good many men, I can tell you."

"But murder!" Emerson exclaimed. "Curse it, Amelia, there are too many holes in your theory. The old—er—witch hasn't the figure or the stamina to go running around the Theban hills striking down strong young men."

"She may have hired assassins," I said. "I admit I have not worked out the idea in detail, but I hope to do so soon. There is no sense in discussing it further tonight; we all need rest."

"You always say that when I am winning an argument," grumbled Emerson.

I saw no reason to dignify this childish comment with a reply.

Chapter Thirteen

 AS soon as the first streaks of light blossomed in the eastern sky we were up and stirring. I had slept well, though of course I insisted on taking my turn to stand watch. Emerson was fairly twitching, he was so anxious to attack the tomb; but the presence of the journalist restrained him, and he reluctantly agreed that we had better return to the house and deal with the latest crisis before starting work. We left O'Connell on guard, promising to send a relief, and the last thing I saw as we climbed the path was his red head glowing with the rays of the rising sun. Emerson had locked the iron grille so that he would not be tempted to sneak into the tomb while we were gone.

Despite the grim tasks that awaited us I felt an upsurge of pleasure as we strode along hand in hand through the crisp morning air and watched the sky brighten to greet the rising majesty of the sun. The great god Amon Ra had survived another nightly journey through the perils of darkness, as he had done millions of times before and would continue to do long after we who watched this day's sunrise were dust and ashes. A humbling thought.

Such were my poetic and philosophical musings when Emerson, as is his habit, spoiled my mood with a rude remark.

"You know, Amelia, what you were saying last night was bloody nonsense."

"Don't swear."

"You drive me to it. Furthermore, it was irresponsible of you to discuss your suspicions in front of one of the major suspects."

"I only said that to shake him up a bit. I don't suspect Mr. O'Connell."

"Who is it this morning? Lady Baskerville?"

Ignoring the raillery in his voice, I replied seriously, "I cannot eliminate her from suspicion, Emerson. You seem to have forgotten that Lord Baskerville was the first to die."

"I seem to have forgotten? I?" Emerson sputtered for a few moments.

"You were the one who insisted last night that jealousy on Miss Mary's account was the motive."

"I presented it as one possibility. What we have here, Emerson, is a series of murders, designed to cover up the real motive. We must first determine the principal murderee, if you will permit me to use that expression."

"I do not see how I can prevent you from doing so. Offensive as the expression is, it offends me less than the theory you propose. Are you seriously suggesting that two of the murderous attacks—three, if you include Hassan— were no more than camouflage, and that a killer is slaughtering people at random in order to cover his tracks?"

"What is so ridiculous about that? Murders are solved by determining the motive. The principal suspects are those who have most to gain by the victim's death. Here we have four victims—for I certainly do include Hassan—and, consequently, a confusing plethora of motives."

"Humph," said Emerson in a milder tone. He stroked his chin thoughtfully. "But Lord Baskerville was the first."

"And if he had died under ordinary circumstances, without all this nonsense about a curse, who would have been the major suspects? His heirs, of course—young Arthur (when he arrived to claim his inheritance) and Lady Baskerville. However, if my ideas are right, Lord Baskerville's was not the primary murder. That would be too obvious. It is more likely that the killer committed the first murder to confuse us, and that the principal murderee was Armadale or Arthur."

"Heaven help the world if you ever take to crime," Emerson said feelingly. "Amelia, the idea is so mad that it has a sort of insane seductiveness. It charms me, but it fails to convince me. No"—as I started to speak—"while I agree that in most cases motive is of great importance in solving a crime, I do not believe it will help us here. There are too many motives. The ones you have suggested pertaining to Lord Baskerville are only two of many possibilities. The fact that these events began after the discovery of a new royal tomb is surely significant. The local thieves, led by Ali Hassan, may have hoped Baskerville's death would halt work long enough to allow them to rob the tomb. The imam may have been moved by religious fervor to destroy the desecrator of the dead. Vandergelt seems to have designs on Lord Baskerville's wife as well as his excavation firman. An examination of the personal life of his lordship might turn up half a dozen other motives."

"True enough. But how do you explain Armadale's death and the attack on Arthur?"

"Armadale may have witnessed the murder and attempted to blackmail the killer."

"Weak," I said, shaking my head. "Very weak, Emerson. Why would Armadale run away and remain in hiding so long?"

"Perhaps he has not been in hiding. Perhaps he has been dead all this time."

"I don't think he has been dead for over a month."

"Well, we won't know until the doctor has examined him. Let us abjure speculation until we have more facts."

"Once we have the facts, we will not need to speculate," I replied smartly. "We will know the truth."

"I wonder," Emerson said morosely.

II

I had hoped to have time to bathe and change before facing the uproar that would result when Armadale's death became known to the others. Though I am accustomed to "roughing it," I had not changed my attire for almost twenty-four hours, and it showed the effects of the strenuous activities I had engaged in since. However, as soon as we entered the courtyard I knew that indulgence must be postponed again. The first thing to strike me was the unnatural silence. The servants ought to have been up and about their labors long since. Then I saw Mary running toward us. Her hair was disheveled and her eyes stained with tears. "Thank God you are here," she exclaimed.

"Steady, my dear," I said gently. "Is it Arthur? Has he—"

"No, I thank heaven; if anything, he seems a little better. But, oh, Amelia, everything else is so terrible. . . ."

She seemed on the verge of breaking down, so I said firmly, "Well, my dear, we are here and you have nothing more to worry about. Come into the drawing room and have a cup of tea, while you tell us what has happened."

Mary's quivering lips shaped themselves into a valiant attempt at a smile. "That is part of the trouble. There is no tea—and no breakfast. The servants have gone on strike. One of them discovered poor Alan's body a few hours ago. The news spread rapidly, and when I went to the kitchen to order breakfast for the Sister, I found Ahmed packing his belongings. I felt I had to arouse Lady Baskerville, since she is his employer, and . . ."

"And Lady Baskerville promptly went into hysterics," I finished.

"She was not herself," Mary replied tactfully. "Mr. Vandergelt is talking with Ahmed, trying to persuade him to stay on. Karl has gone to the village to ascertain whether he can hire replacements—"

"Idiotic!" Emerson exclaimed. "He has no business going off like that without consulting me. Besides, it will prove a futile errand. Amelia, do you go and—er—persuade Ahmed to unpack. His decision will be an example to the others. I had planned to send Karl to relieve O'Connell; now I must send Feisal or Daoud. I will see them directly. First things first."

He started to stride away. Mary put out a timid hand. "Professor . . ." she began.

"Don't delay me, child, I have much to do."

"But, sir—your men are also on strike."

The words caught Emerson in midstride. His boot remained poised six inches off the ground. Then he lowered it, very slowly, as if he were treading on glass. His big hands clenched into fists and his teeth were bared. Mary gasped and shrank closer to me.

"Now calm yourself, Emerson, or one of these days you will have a stroke," I said. "We might have anticipated this; it would have happened days ago, if your charismatic personality had not influenced the men."

Emerson's mouth snapped shut. "Calm myself," he repeated. "Calm myself? I cannot imagine what leads you to suppose I am not calm. I hope you ladies will excuse me for a moment. I am going to speak calmly to my men and calmly point out to them that if they do not immediately turn out and prepare to go to work I will calmly knock them unconscious, one by one."

Whereupon he departed, walking with slow, stately strides. When I saw him open the door of our room I started to expostulate; then I realized he was taking the most direct route, through our room and out the window. I only hoped he would not step on the cat or smash my toilette articles as he proceeded on his single-minded path.

"It really astonishes me that the male sex is so completely devoid of a sense of logic," I said. "There is little danger of an attack on the tomb by daylight; Emerson might have waited until we had settled other, more pressing, matters. But, as usual, everything is left to me. Go back to Arthur's room, my dear. I will send someone to you with breakfast shortly."

"But," Mary began, her eyes widening. "But how—"

"Leave that to me," I said.

I found Mr. Vandergelt with Ahmed. The cook was squatting on the floor completely surrounded by the bundles that held his worldly possessions, including his prized cooking pots. His wrinkled face serene, he was staring pensively at the ceiling while Vandergelt waved fistfuls of American greenbacks at him.

When I left the kitchen, Ahmed was at work. I cannot claim all the credit; Ahmed's exaggerated disinterest had betrayed the fact that the sight of the money was beginning to affect him, and the salary he eventually agreed to accept was truly princely. But I flatter myself that my passionate appeals to honor, loyalty, and friendship had their effect.

Gracefully I disclaimed the compliments Mr. Vandergelt lavished on me, and asked him to carry the good news to Lady Baskerville. Then at last I was free to strip off my work-stained garments. I was relieved to find that the water jars in the bathroom were full. Much as I would have liked to prolong my immersion in the cool water, I made as much haste as I could, for although the immediate crisis had been resolved I felt sure other problems awaited me. I was half dressed when Emerson climbed in through the window and, without so much as a glance in my direction, walked into the bathroom and slammed the door.

I knew from his face that his mission had been unsuccessful. Though I yearned to comfort him I could not linger—nor, indeed, was he in any mood to accept condolences just then.

I went first to the dining room, where a waiter was arranging a tray of steaming dishes on the sideboard, and ordered him to prepare a tray and follow me to Arthur's room. When I entered, Mary rose from her chair with a cry of surprise.

"Have you convinced the servants to remain, then?"

"The strike is settled," I replied wittily. "Good morning, Sister."

The nun nodded benignly at me. Her round rosy face was as fresh as if she had had eight hours' sleep, and I observed there was not a drop of perspiration on her brow, despite her muffling garments. While she applied herself to her well-deserved breakfast, I examined my patient.

I saw at once that Mary's optimism was justified. The young man's face was still sunken, his eyes tightly closed; but his pulse was distinctly stronger. "He cannot continue without nourishment, however," I mused. "Perhaps some broth. I will have Ahmed boil a chicken. There is nothing as strengthening as chicken broth."

"The doctor suggested brandy," Mary said.

"The worst possible thing. Mary, go to your room and rest. If you go on this way you will fall ill yourself, and then what will I do?"

This argument halted the girl's objections. When she had gone, with a last lingering look at the still face of her lover, I sat down beside the bed. "Sister, I must speak frankly."

Again the nun nodded and beamed at me, but did not speak.

"Are you dumb?" I inquired sharply. "Answer, if you please."

The good woman's placid brow grew troubled. "*Quoi?*" she inquired.

"Oh, dear," I sighed. "I suppose you speak only French. A fine help you will be if Arthur awakens and tries to tell us what happened. Ah, well, we must do the best we can."

So, in the plainest possible terms, I explained the situation. From the startled look on the nun's face I saw that she had believed her patient to be the victim of an accident. No one had mentioned attempted murder, and alarm replaced her surprise as I pointed out that the murderer might return to try again.

"*Alors,*" I concluded, "*vous comprenez bien, ma soeur,* that the young man must not be left alone for a single instant. Guard yourself as well. I do not think you are in danger, but it is possible that the villain may try to drug you so he can reach his victim. Touch no food that I have not brought you with my own hands."

"*Ah, mon Dieu,*" the sister exclaimed, reaching for her rosary. "*Mais quel contretemps!*"

"I could not have put it better myself. But you will not abandon us in our need?"

After a moment of struggle, the nun bowed her head. "We are all in the hands of God," she remarked. "I will pray."

"An excellent idea, so far as it goes," I replied. "But I suggest you also keep your eyes open. Do not be alarmed, Sister, I am about to arrange for a guard. You can trust him completely."

On this errand I went, via my window, to the building where our men were housed. Several of them were lounging on the grass in carefree attitudes. At the sight of me they precipitately vanished inside the house. Abdullah alone remained, his back against a palm tree, a cigarette between his fingers.

"I am unworthy of your confidence, Sitt," he murmured, as I sat down beside him. "I have failed you."

"It is not your fault, Abdullah; the circumstances are extraordinary. I promise you, before many hours have passed Emerson and I will settle this case as we settled the other you know of, and will convince the men that these tragedies were also caused by human evil. I come now to ask a favor. Will the men help with the work at the house? I want someone to watch under the window of the sick man and protect him and the holy woman in black."

Abdullah assured me that the men would be glad to relieve their guilty consciences by assisting me in any way that did not directly involve the accursed tomb, and I found myself able to choose between a dozen volunteers. I selected Daoud, one of Abdullah's many nephews, and introduced him to the sister. With my mind at ease on that point, I could at last go to my breakfast.

Emerson was already at the table, attacking his bacon and eggs furiously. Karl had returned; sitting as far as possible from Emerson, he ate in timid little bites, his mustache drooping. I deduced that he had felt the sharp edge of Emerson's tongue, and felt sorry for him. Vandergelt, always the gentleman, rose to hold a chair for me.

"Things are sure in a mess," he said. "I don't know how much longer we can go on this way. How is the patient today, Mrs. Amelia?"

"No change," I replied, helping myself to tea and toast. "I doubt that he will ever speak again, poor fellow. Where is Lady Baskerville?"

Scarcely had I spoken when the lady swept into the room. She was in dishabille—gray chiffon ruffles, sweeping flounces, her hair flowing around her shoulders. Seeing my astonished gaze, she had the grace to blush.

"Forgive my attire; my stupid maid has run away and I am too nervous to be alone. What are we to do? The situation is dreadful."

"Not at all," I replied, eating my toast. "Sit down, Lady Baskerville, and have some breakfast. You will feel better when you have eaten."

"Impossible!" Lady Baskerville paced up and down wringing her hands. She required only an armful of weedy flowers to make a somewhat mature Ophelia.

Karl and Vandergelt followed her, trying to calm her. Finally she allowed herself to be helped to a chair.

"I cannot eat a mouthful," she declared. "How is poor Mr. Milverton— Lord Baskerville, I suppose I should say; I cannot take it all in. I tried to see him earlier, but was denied, most officiously. Mary had the effrontery to tell me, Radcliffe, that it was by your orders."

"I feared it would distress you," he replied coolly. "Rest assured that everything possible is being done. It is little enough, I am sorry to say. Don't you agree, Amelia?"

"He is dying," I said bluntly. "I doubt that he will ever regain consciousness."

"Another tragedy!" Lady Baskerville wrung her long white hands, a gesture that displayed their slender beauty. "I can endure no more. Radcliffe, much as I regret the decision, I must bow to fate. The expedition is canceled. I want the tomb closed, today."

I dropped my spoon. "You can't do that! Within a week it will be stripped by robbers."

"What do I care for robbers or tombs?" Lady Baskerville cried. "What are ancient relics compared with human life? Two men have died, one lies near death—"

"Three men," Emerson said quietly. "Or do you not consider Hassan the watchman a human being? He was not much of a man, to be sure, but if he were the only victim I would still feel obliged to bring his murderer to justice. I intend to do that, Lady Baskerville, and I also intend to finish excavating the tomb."

Lady Baskerville's jaw dropped. "You can't do that, Radcliffe. I hired you and I can—"

"I think not," Emerson replied. "You begged me to take on the job and told me, if I recall correctly, that his lordship left funds with which to carry on the work. Furthermore, I have Grebaut's order appointing me archaeologist in charge. Oh, it may involve a long, complex legal battle, when all is said and done, but"—and his eyes sparkled wickedly—"but I enjoy battles, legal or otherwise."

Lady Baskerville took a deep breath. Her bosom swelled to alarming proportions. Vandergelt leaped to his feet. "Goldurn you, Emerson, don't you talk to the lady like that."

"Keep out of this, Vandergelt," Emerson said. "It is none of your affair."

"You just bet it is." Vandergelt moved to Lady Baskerville's side. "I have asked the lady to be my wife, and she has done me the honor to accept."

"A bit sudden, is it not?" I inquired, spreading marmalade on another piece of toast (my busy day and night had given me quite an appetite). "With your husband dead less than a month—"

"Naturally we will not announce our engagement until the proper time," Vandergelt said in shocked tones. "I wouldn't have told you folks if the situation had not been so perilous. This poor lady needs a protector, and Cyrus Vandergelt, U.S.A., is privileged to take that part. My dear, I think you ought to leave this cursed place and move to the hotel."

"I will obey your slightest wish, Cyrus," the lady murmured submissively. "But you must come with me. I cannot flee, leaving you in danger."

"That's right, Vandergelt, desert the sinking ship," Emerson said.

A look of embarrassment spread over the American's rugged features. "Now you know I'm not about to do that. No, sir, Cyrus Vandergelt is no four-flusher."

"But Cyrus Vandergelt is a dedicated archaeology buff," said Emerson mockingly. "Admit it, Vandergelt; you cannot tear yourself away until you know what lies beyond that wall at the end of the passageway. What is it to be, wedded bliss or Egyptology?"

I smiled quietly to myself, seeing the agonized indecision that twisted the American's features. The hesitation did not flatter his promised bride (though I confess that, faced with a similar dilemma, Emerson might have hesitated too).

Lady Baskerville saw the signs of struggle on her fiancé's face and was too wise in the ways of the male sex to force him into a reluctant sacrifice. "If that is how you feel, Cyrus, of course you must stay on," she said. "Forgive me. I was distraught. I am better now."

She applied a dainty kerchief to her eyes. Vandergelt patted her shoulder distractedly. Then his face brightened.

"I have it! There is no need to make such a choice. At a time like this, convention must yield to necessity. What do you say, my dear girl—will you defy the world and be mine at once? We can be married in Luxor, and I will then have the right to be at your side day and—er—that is, at all times and in all places."

"Oh, Cyrus," Lady Baskerville exclaimed. "This is so sudden. I should not . . . and yet . . ."

"Congratulations," I said, seeing that she was about to yield. "I trust you will excuse us if we do not attend the ceremony. I expect to be occupied with a mummy at about that time."

With a sudden rush Lady Baskerville left her chair and flung herself at my feet. "Do not be harsh with me, Mrs. Emerson! Conventional minds may condemn me; but I had hoped that *you* would be the first to understand. I am so alone! Will you, a sister woman, abandon me because of an old-fashioned, senseless rule?"

Snatching my hands, toast and all, in hers, she bowed her head.

Either the woman was a consummate actress or she was genuinely distressed. Only a heart as hard as granite could be unmoved.

"Now, Lady Baskerville, you must not act this way," I said. "You are getting marmalade all over your sleeve."

"I will not rise until you say you understand and condone my decision," was the murmured response from my lap, where the lady's head had sunk.

"I do, I do. Please rise. I will be your matron of honor, or your flower girl, or I will give you away, whatever you wish; only stand up."

Vandergelt added his appeals, and Lady Baskerville consented to restore my hands and my crumbling toast. As she rose I caught the eye of Karl von Bork, who was watching in openmouthed astonishment. Shaking his head, he murmured low, *"Die Engländer! Niemals werde ich sie verstehen!"*

"Thank you," Lady Baskerville sighed. "You are a true woman, Mrs. Emerson."

"That's right," Vandergelt added. "You're a brick, Mrs. Amelia. I'd never have proposed this if matters weren't so doggoned desperate."

The door burst open and Madame Berengeria billowed in. Today she was enveloped in a tattered cotton wrapper and her wig was not in evidence. Her wispy hair, which I saw for the first time, was almost pure white. Swaying, she scanned the room with bloodshot eyes.

"A person could starve to death," she muttered. "Insolent servants—wretched household—where is the food? I require. . . . Ah, there you are!" Her eyes focused on my husband, who pushed his chair back from the table and sat poised, ready for retreat. "There you are, Tut—Thutmosis, my lover!"

She rushed at him. Emerson slid neatly out of his chair. Berengeria tripped and fell face- or rather, stomach-down across the seat. Even I, hardened as I am, felt constrained to avert my eyes from the appalling spectacle thus presented.

"Good Gad," said Emerson.

Berengeria slid to the floor, rolled over, and sat up. "Where is he?" she demanded, squinting at the table leg. "Where has he gone? Thutmosis, my lover and my husband—"

"I suppose her attendant has run away with the other servants," I said resignedly. "We had better get her back to her room. Where on earth did she get brandy at this hour of the morning?"

It was a rhetorical question, and no one tried to answer it. With some difficulty Karl and Vandergelt, assisted by me, lifted the lady to an upright position and steered her out of the room. I sent Karl to seek out Madame's missing attendant, or any reasonable facsimile thereof, and returned to the dining room. Lady Baskerville had left, and Emerson was coolly drinking tea and making notes on a pad of paper.

"Sit down, Peabody," he said. "It is time we had a council of war."

"Did you, then, succeed in convincing the men to return to work? You seem much more cheerful than you were earlier, and I am sure the admiration of Madame Berengeria is not the cause of your good humor."

Emerson ignored this quip. "I did not succeed," he replied, "but I have worked out a plan that may have the desired effect. I am going across to Luxor. I wish I could ask you to go with me, but I dare not leave the house unguarded by at least one of us. I can trust no one else. Too many matters hang on a sword's edge. Amelia, you must not leave young Baskerville unattended."

I told him what I had done, and he looked pleased. "Excellent. Daoud is dependable; but I hope you will keep a watchful eye out as well. Your description of the young man's worsening condition was designed to mislead, I hope?"

"Precisely. In actual fact he seems stronger."

"Excellent," Emerson repeated. "You must be on the qui vive, Peabody. Trust no one. I think I know the identity of the murderer, but—"

"What?" I cried. "You know—"

Emerson clapped a large hard hand over my mouth. "I will make the announcement myself, at the proper time," he growled.

I peeled his fingers from my lips. "That was unnecessary." I said. "I was only surprised at your statement, after you have consistently disclaimed any interest in the matter. In fact, I too have discovered the identity of the person in question."

"Oh, you have, have you?"

"Yes, I have."

We studied one another warily.

"Would you care to enlighten me?" Emerson inquired.

"No. I think I know; but if I am wrong you will never let me hear the end of it. Perhaps *you* will enlighten *me.*"

"No."

"Ha! You are not sure either."

"I said as much."

Again we exchanged measuring glances.

"You have no proof," I said.

"That is the difficulty. And you—"

"Not yet. I hope to obtain it."

"Humph," said Emerson. "Peabody, please refrain from any reckless actions while I am away. I wish you could bring yourself to confide in me."

"Truly, Emerson, I would if I had anything useful to suggest. At the present time my suspicions are based on intuition, and I know how scornful you are of that; you have mocked me often enough. I promise that the moment I obtain concrete evidence I will tell you."

"Very well."

"You might return the compliment," I said pointedly.

"I will tell you what I will do. Let us both write down the name of the person we suspect and put it in a sealed envelope. When this is over, the survivor, if there is one, can see who was right."

I found this attempt at humor not at all amusing, and said so. We proceeded to do as Emerson had suggested, placing the sealed envelopes in a table drawer in our room.

Emerson then departed. I had hoped to have a few moments to myself, in order to jot down a few notes about the case and consider methods of obtaining the evidence I had spoken of. I was not given time for reflection, for one duty succeeded the next. After sending Karl to the Valley to relieve Mr. O'Connell I interviewed Dr. Dubois, who had come to visit Arthur. When I suggested broth to strengthen the patient, his response was positively rude.

I then led the medical man to the building where Armadale's body had been placed. I was pleased to see that an attempt had been made to lend some dignity to the poor fellow's resting place. The body had been decently swathed in a clean white sheet and upon the breast of the still form lay a bouquet of flowers. I fancied that Mary must have supplied these, and regretted I had not been there to support the girl as she carried out this sad task.

Dubois was of no help whatever. His examination was cursory in the extreme; his conclusion was that Armadale had died of exposure—a perfectly ridiculous idea, as I pointed out. He was even more vague about the time of death. The atmospheric conditions that produced so many excellent mummies prevailed in the cave where Armadale had been found, so that desiccation rather than decay had affected the body. Dubois declared he had been dead no less than two days and no more than two weeks.

I then turned to the needs of the living, first ordering the chicken broth from Ahmed and then hastening to my room to carry out a task which had been too long delayed. Only the succession of unnerving incidents that had required all my attention had made me neglect this pressing duty. At least by waiting I had more hopeful news to send Arthur Baskerville's long-suffering mother. As I sat trying to compose a message that would be both peremptory and soothing, it occurred to me that I did not know Mrs. Baskerville's full name or address. After some thought I decided to send the message to the authorities in Nairobi; surely, with all the publicity attendant on Lord Baskerville's death, they would be able to locate his brother's widow.

Scarcely had I finished this task when I was summoned to the drawing room to assist Lady Baskerville in explaining to the police how Armadale's body had been discovered. After much fuss and bureaucratic delay the requisite documents were completed. Armadale had no living relatives, except for distant cousins in Australia. It was decided that he should be buried in the small European cemetery in Luxor, delay in this matter being both insanitary and unnecessary; and when Lady Baskerville showed signs of relapsing into sobs and sighs, I assured her I would make the necessary arrangements.

It was midafternoon before Emerson returned, and by then even my iron constitution was beginning to feel some strain, for in the meantime, in addition to the tasks I have described, I had visited the sick man and forced some broth down his throat, had interviewed Mr. O'Connell on his return from the Valley, dressed his injured hand and put him to bed, and had enjoyed an acrimonious argument with Madame Berengeria over the luncheon table. Like many drunkards, she had astonishing powers of recuperation; a few hours' rest completely restored her, and when she forced her way into the dining room she was again dressed in her appalling costume. The strong perfume she had poured over her frame did not entirely cover the unmistakable olfactory evidences of her lack of interest in the most rudimentary personal cleanliness. She had learned of Armadale's death, and her dire predictions of further disasters to come were interrupted only by intervals of munching and mumbling as she crammed food into her mouth. I did not blame Lady Baskerville for her precipitate departure from the table. Vandergelt followed, but I felt obliged to remain until Madame had eaten herself into a semistupor. My request that she return to her room revived her and was the cause of the argument, during the course of which she made a number of unwarranted personal remarks and asserted her intention of reclaiming her reincarnated lover, Thutmosis-Ramses-Amenhotep the Magnificent-Setnakhte.

When Emerson entered our room, by way of the window, he found me recumbent on the bed with the cat at my feet. He hastened to my side, dropping the armful of papers he was carrying.

"Peabody, my dear girl!"

"Everything is under control," I assured him. "I am a little tired, that is all."

Emerson sat down beside me and wiped the perspiration from his brow. "You cannot blame me for being alarmed, my love; I don't recall ever seeing you in bed during the daytime—to rest, that is. And," he added, with an amused glance at the sleeping cat, "you looked for all the world like a small Crusader on a tombstone with your faithful hound at your feet. What is the cause of this unusual weariness? Have the police been here?"

I gave him a succinct, well-organized summary of the events of the day.

"What a frightful time you have had," he exclaimed. "My poor girl, I only wish I could have been with you."

"Bah," I said. "You don't wish that at all. You are relieved to have missed all the fuss, particularly Madame."

Emerson smiled sheepishly. "I confess that the lady comes as close to throwing me off balance as any living creature—with the exception of yourself, my love."

"She is more appalling every day, Emerson. The ways of Providence are inscrutable, to be sure, and I would never dream of questioning its decree; but I cannot help but wonder why Madame Berengeria is allowed to flourish when good young men like Alan Armadale are cruelly cut off. It would be an act of positive benevolence to remove her from this world."

"Now, Amelia, be calm. I have something for you that will restore your equanimity; the first mail from home."

Shuffling through the envelopes I came upon a familiar hand and a sentiment long repressed, through stern necessity, would not be denied. "A letter from Ramses," I exclaimed. "Why did you not open it? It is addressed to both of us."

"I thought we could read it together," Emerson replied. He stretched out across the bed, his hands supporting his head, and I opened the envelope.

Ramses had learned to write at the age of three, disdaining the clumsy art of printing. His hand, though unformed, proclaimed the essentials of his character, being large and sprawling, with emphatic punctuation marks. He favored very black ink and broad-nibbed pens.

" 'Dearest mama and papa,' " I read. " 'I miss you very much.' "

Emerson let out a choked sound and turned his head away.

"Do not yield to emotion yet," I said, scanning the next lines. "Wait till you hear his reasons for missing us. 'Nurse is very cruel and will not give me any sweets. Aunt Evelyn would, but she is afraid of Nurse. So I have not been to a sweetshop since you left and I think you were cruel and vishus [I reproduce Ramses' spelling literally] to leave me. Uncle Walter spanked me yesterday—' "

"What?" Emerson sat up. The cat, disturbed by his violent movement, let out a grumble of protest. "The wretch! How dare he lay hands on Ramses! I never thought he had it in him."

"Neither did I," I said, pleased. "Pray let me continue, Emerson. 'Uncle Walter spanked me yesterday only because I tore some pages out of his dikshunary. I needed to use them. He spanks very hard. I will not tear any more pages out of his dikshunary. Afterwards he taught me how to write "I love you, mama and papa," in hieroglyphs. Here it is. Your son, Ramses.' "

Together Emerson and I contemplated the untidy little row of picture signs. The signs blurred a trifle as I looked at them; but, as always when Ramses was concerned, amusement and irritation tempered sentimentality.

"How typical of Ramses," I said, smiling. "He misspells dictionary and vicious, but misses not a letter of hieroglyphs."

"I fear we have bred a monster," Emerson agreed, with a laugh. He began to tickle the cat under the chin. The animal, annoyed at being awakened, promptly seized his hand and began to bite it.

"What Ramses needs is discipline," I said.

"Or an adversary worthy of his steel," Emerson suggested. He pried the cat's teeth and claws from his hand and studied the animal thoughtfully. "I have just had an inspiration, Amelia."

I did not ask what it was. I preferred not to know. Instead I turned to the rest of the mail, which included a long, loving letter from Evelyn reassuring me as to Ramses' health and happiness. Like the good aunt she was, she did not even mention the dictionary incident. Emerson opened his own mail. After a while he handed two items to me for perusal. One was a telegram from Grebaut, canceling Emerson's permission to excavate and demanding that he re-hire the guards he had dismissed. After I had read it Emerson crumpled it up and tossed it out the window.

The second item was a clipping from a newspaper, sent us by Mr. Wilbour. The story, under the byline of Kevin O'Connell, described in vivid detail not only the kicking of the reporter down the stairs of Shepheard's Hotel, but also the knife in the wardrobe. Mr. O'Connell's informant had played him false with the latter incident, however; the knife, "a bejeweled weapon worthy of being worn by a pharaoh," was said to have been found driven into the center of the bedside table.

"Wait till I get my hands on that young man," I muttered.

"At least he did not break his word," Emerson said with surprising tolerance. "This story was written some days ago, before we made our agreement. Do you want to change the name in that envelope, Amelia?"

It took me a moment to understand what he meant. When I did, I replied, "Certainly not. Though this does raise a point I cannot yet explain. What about you?"

"My opinion is unchanged."

A low growl from the cat warned us that someone was approaching. A moment later there was a knock at the door. I opened it and admitted Daoud.

"The holy woman calls you to come," he said. "The sick man is awake and speaking."

"Curse it," Emerson exclaimed, shaking his fist in the astonished man's face. "Keep your voice down, Daoud. No one must know of this. Now get back to your post and hold your tongue."

Daoud obeyed and we proceeded, posthaste, to Arthur's room.

The Sister was bending over the sick man, as was Mary. Worn by illness as he was, it required both women's strength to keep him from sitting up.

"He must not move his head!" I exclaimed in alarm.

Emerson went to the bed. His big brown hands, so strong and yet so gentle, took hold of the injured member, immobilizing it. Arthur immediately left off struggling. So intense is the degree of animal magnetism Emerson projects that it seemed to flow through his fingers into the injured brain. Arthur opened his eyes.

"He is awake," Mary cried. "Do you know me, Mr. . . . I mean, Lord Baskerville?"

But there was no awareness in the dazed blue orbs. If they focused at all, it was on some object high in midair, invisible to the rest of us.

I have always held that the various states of semiconsciousness, even deep coma, do not necessarily involve the complete cessation of sensation. The means of communication may be interrupted, but who is to say that the brain does not function or the ears do not hear? I therefore seated myself by the bed and approached my mouth close to the ear of the injured man.

"Arthur," I said. "It is Amelia Emerson who speaks to you. You have been struck down by an assailant as yet unknown. Have no fear; I am watching over you. But if you could possibly answer a question or two—"

"How the devil do you expect him to do that?" Emerson demanded, in the muted roar that passes, with him, for a whisper. "The poor chap has all he can do to continue breathing. Ignore her, Milverton—er—Baskerville."

Arthur paid no attention to either speech. He continued to stare raptly into space.

"He seems calmer now," I said to the nun, in French. "But I fear a repetition of this; should we tie him to the bed, do you think?"

The sister replied that Dr. Dubois had predicted the possibility of such a violent awakening and had given her medicine to administer should it occur. "I was taken by surprise," she added apologetically. "It happened so suddenly; but do not fear, madame, I can deal with him."

Mary had collapsed into a chair, pale as . . . I was about to say "snow" or "paper" or one of the common comparatives; however, in strict accuracy I must say that a complexion as brown as hers could never turn ashy white. Her pallor was in reality a delicate shade of coffee well laced with milk; three quarters milk to one quarter coffee, let us say.

Suddenly we were all electrified at hearing a strange voice. It was young Arthur's; but I identified it only because I knew it could belong to no one else. The soft, droning tone was totally unlike his normal speaking voice.

"The beautiful one has come. . . . Sweet of hands, beautiful of face; at hearing her voice one rejoices. . . ."

"Good Gad," Emerson exclaimed.

"Ssssh!" I said.

"Lady of joy, his beloved. . . . Bearing the two sistrums in her two beautiful hands. . . ."

We waited, after that, until my chest ached with holding my breath, but Arthur Baskerville spoke no more that day. His darkly stained lids closed over his staring eyes.

"He will sleep now," the nun said. "I give you felicitations, madame; the young man will live, I believe."

Her calm struck me as inhuman until I realized that she was the only one who had not understood a word. To her the patient had simply been babbling nonsense syllables, in his delirium.

Mary's reaction was inclined more toward confusion than the awestruck disbelief that had effected Emerson and me.

"What was he talking about?" she asked.

"Don't ask," Emerson said, with a groan.

"He was delirious," I said. "Mary, once again I am going to ask that you go to your room. It is ridiculous for you to sit here hour after hour. Touching, but ridiculous. Go and take a nap, or a walk, or talk to the cat."

"I second the motion," Emerson added. "Get some rest, Miss Mary; I may want you later this evening."

We escorted the girl to her room and then confronted one another with identical expressions of disbelief.

"You heard, Peabody," Emerson said. "At least I hope you did; if not, I was experiencing auditory hallucinations."

"I heard. They were the titles of Queen Nefertiti, were they not?"

"They were."

"Such tender phrases . . . I am convinced, Emerson, that they were the compliments of Khuenaten—excuse me, Akhenaton—to his adored wife."

"Amelia, you have an absolutely unparalleled talent for straying from the point. How the devil did that ignorant young man know those words? He told us himself that he was untrained in Egyptology."

"There must be a logical explanation."

"Of course there must. All the same—he sounded rather like Madame Berengeria in one of her fits, didn't he? Though his ravings were a great deal more accurate than hers."

"Curse it," I exclaimed, "he must have heard the titles from Lord Baskerville or Armadale at some time. They say the sleeping brain retains everything, though the waking mind cannot recall it."

"Who says?"

"I forget. I read it somewhere—one of those newfangled medical theories. However farfetched it may be, it makes more sense than . . ."

"Precisely," Emerson agreed. "All that aside, Peabody, has it struck you that the young man's ravings may have a bearing on who murdered Lord Baskerville?"

"Naturally that aspect of the matter had not escaped me."

Emerson let out a roar of laughter and flung his arms around me. "You are indestructible, Peabody. Thank God for your strength; I don't know what I would do without it, for I feel like an antique chariot driver trying to control half a dozen spirited steeds at once. Now I must be off again."

"Where?"

"Oh—here and there. I am arranging a little theatrical performance, my dear—a regular Egyptian *fantasia*. It will take place this evening."

"Indeed! And where is the performance to take place?"

"At the tomb."

"What do you want me to do? I don't promise," I added, "that I will do it; I simply ask."

Emerson chuckled and rubbed his hands together. "I rely on you, Peabody. Announce my intentions to Lady Baskerville and Vandergelt. If they wish to spend the night at the hotel, they may do so, but not until my performance is ended. I want everyone there."

"Including Madame Berengeria?"

"Humph," said Emerson. "As a matter of fact, yes; she might add a certain *je ne sais quoi*."

Alarm seized me. Emerson never speaks French unless he is up to something.

"You are up to something," I said.

"Certainly."

"And you expect me to submit tamely—"

"You have never submitted to anything tamely in your life! You will work with me, as I would with you, because we are as one. We know one another's minds. You suspect, I am sure, what I intend."

"I do."

"And you will assist me?"

"I will."

"I need not tell you what to do."

"I . . . No."

"Then *à bientôt*, my darling Peabody."

He embraced me so fervently that I had to sit down on a bench for a few moments to catch my breath.

In fact, I had not the slightest idea what he meant to do.

When he rises to heights of emotional intensity Emerson can carry all before him. Mesmerized by his burning eyes and fervent voice, I would have agreed to anything he proposed, up to and including self-immolation. (Naturally, I never let him know he has this effect on me; it would be bad for his character.) Once he had departed I was able to think more calmly, and then, indeed, a glimmer of an idea occurred to me.

Most men are reasonably useful in a crisis. The difficulty lies in convincing them that the situation has reached a critical point. Being superior to others of his sex, Emerson was more efficient than most—and harder to convince. He had finally admitted that there was a murderer at large; he had agreed that the responsibility of identifying the miscreant was ours.

But what, in fact, was Emerson's chief concern? Why, the tomb, of course. Let me be candid. Emerson would cheerfully consign the entire globe and its inhabitants (with a few exceptions) to the nethermost pits to save one dingy fragment of history from extinction. Therefore, I reasoned, his activities of that evening must be designed to attain his dearest wish, the resumption of work on the tomb.

I am sure, dear reader, that you can follow my reasoning to its logical conclusion. Remember Emerson's fondness for playacting; bear in mind the regrettable susceptibility of all segments of the human race to crass superstition; stretch your imagination—and I have no doubts you will forward as eagerly as I did to Emerson's *fantasia*.

Chapter Fourteen

THE moon was up when we set out on our journey to the Valley. It was on the wane, no longer a perfect silver globe; but it emitted enough light to flood the plain with silver and cast deep shadows across the road.

I would have preferred to lead our caravan over the lofty path behind Deir el Bahri, but such a walk would have been beyond Lady Baskerville's powers, and Madame Berengeria was also incapable of self-locomotion. Therefore I resigned myself to a prolonged and bumpy ride. I was the only one of the ladies who was sensibly dressed. Being unable to anticipate what might eventuate from Emerson's performance, I thought it best to be prepared for anything; so my working costume was complete, down to the knife, the revolver, and the parasol. Madame Berengeria was decked out in her decaying Egyptian costume; Lady Baskerville was a vision in black lace and jetty jewels; and Mary wore one of her shabby evening frocks. The poor child did not own a gown that was less than two years old. I wondered if she would be offended if I made her a present of the best Luxor had to offer. It would have to be done tactfully, of course.

Though I did not really believe Arthur was in any danger that evening, since all the suspects would be under my watchful eyes, I had taken the precaution of requesting Daoud to remain on guard at the window, with his cousin Mohammed at the door. They were not pleased at missing the *fantasia*, but I promised to make it up to them. I also told them the truth about Arthur's identity. I felt sure they already knew, since such news has a way of spreading, but they appreciated being taken into my confidence. As Daoud remarked, nodding sagely, "Yes, if he is rich, it is not surprising that someone should wish to kill him."

It was easier to arrange matters with my loyal men than to persuade the others to agree with my plans. Lady Baskerville at first refused to join the party; it had required all my persuasion, and that of Mr. Vandergelt, to convince her. The American was mightily intrigued and kept pestering me (as he put it) to give him a hint of what was going to transpire. I did not yield to his importunities, in order to maintain an air of mystery and suspense (and also because I was not sure myself).

Knowing that Emerson would appreciate any little dramatic touches I could add, I had mounted several of our men on donkeys and set them at the head of the procession with lighted torches in their hands. Any superstitious fears they may have had were overcome by anticipation, for Emerson had already spoken to them, promising them wonders and revelations. I suspected that Abdullah had some idea of what my husband meant to do, but when I asked him he only grinned and refused to answer.

As the carriages proceeded along the deserted road, the scene cast its spell on all our hearts; and when we turned into the narrow cleft in the cliffs I felt myself an intruder, pushing rudely into byways that rightfully belonged to the thronging ghosts of the past.

A great fire blazed before the entrance to the tomb. Emerson was there; and when he advanced to meet us I did not know whether to laugh or exclaim in astonishment. He wore a long flowing crimson gown and a most peculiar cap with a tassel on top. The cap and the shoulders of the robe were trimmed with fur; and although I had never seen this particular dress before, my familiarity with the academic world enabled me to deduce that it was the robe of a doctor of philosophy, probably from some obscure European university. It had obviously been designed for a much taller person, for as Emerson reached out to help me from the carriage, the full sleeves fell down and enveloped his hand. I assumed he had bought this amazing creation in one of the antiquities shops of Luxor, where a remarkable variety of objects is to be found; and although its effect on me, at least, was rather more productive of hilarity than awe, Emerson's complacent expression indicated that he was enormously pleased with the ensemble. Shaking back his sleeve, he took my hand and led me to one of the chairs that had been arranged in a semicircle facing the fire. Surrounding us on all sides was a sea of brown faces and turbans. Among the Gurnawis I saw two faces I recognized. One was that of the imam; the other was Ali Hassan, who had had the audacity to take up a position in the front row of the spectators.

The others took their chairs. No one spoke, though Vandergelt's lips were twitching suspiciously as he watched Emerson bustling about in his trailing finery. I had feared Madame Berengeria would be unable to resist the opportunity to make a spectacle of herself, but she sat down in silence and folded her arms across her breast like a pharaoh holding the twin scepters. The flames were beginning to die down, and in the growing gloom her bizarre costume was much more effective than it had been in the brightly lighted hotel. As I studied her somber and unattractive countenance I found a new source of uneasiness. Had I, after all, underestimated this woman?

With a loud "hem!" Emerson called us to attention. My heart swelled with affectionate pride as I looked on him, his hands tucked in his flowing sleeves like a Chinese mandarin, the silly cap perched on top of his thick black hair. Emerson's impressive presence invested even that absurd garb with dignity, and when he began to speak no one had the slightest inclination to laugh.

He spoke in English and in Arabic, translating phrase by phrase. Instead of making the audience impatient, this deliberate pace was all the more effective theatrically. He mocked the cowardice of the men of Gurneh and praised the courage and intelligence of his own men, tactfully omitting their recent lapse.

Then his voice rose to a shout that made his audience jump.

"I will tolerate this no longer! I am the Father of Curses, the man who goes where others fear to tread, the fighter of demons. You know me, you know my name! Do I speak the truth?"

He paused. A low murmur responded to this peculiar jumble of ancient formulas and modern Arabic boasting. Emerson went on.

"I know your hearts! I know the evildoers among you! Did you think you could escape the vengeance of the Father of Curses? No! My eye can see in the blackness of night, my ear can hear the words you think but do not utter!"

He strode quickly back and forth, moving his arms in mystic gestures. Whenever his steps took him toward the staring crowd, those in the front ranks drew back. Suddenly he came to a complete standstill. One arm lifted, the forefinger rigid and quivering. An almost visible current of force emanated from this extended digit; the awestruck watchers fell back before it. Emerson bounded forward and plunged into the crowd. The blue and white robes undulated like waves. When Emerson emerged from the human sea he was dragging a man with him—a man whose single eye glared wildly in the firelight.

"Here he is," Emerson bellowed. "My all-seeing eye has found him where he cowered among his betters."

The surrounding cliffs flung his words back in rumbling echoes. Then he turned to the man he held by the throat.

"Habib ibn Mohammed," he said. "Three times you have tried to kill me. Jackal, murderer of children, eater of dead man's bones—what madness seized you, that you dared to threaten me?"

I doubt that Habib could have produced a reply worthy of that eloquent demand even if he had been capable of speaking. Turning again to the circle of rapt faces, Emerson cried, "Brothers! What punishment does the Koran, the word of the Prophet, decree for a murderer?"

"Death!" came the answer, thundering among the echoing cliffs.

"Take him away," Emerson said and flung Habib into the waiting arms of Feisal.

A sigh of pure delight went up from a hundred throats. No one appreciates a good theatrical performance more than an Arab. An audience of Luxor men had sat enthralled through *Romeo and Juliet*—in English—a few years earlier. This was much more entertaining. Before they could turn to their friends and begin an animated critique of the show, Emerson spoke again.

"Habib was not the only evildoer among us," he called out.

Agitated eddies appeared here and there, as certain members of the audience hastily headed for the obscurity of darkness. Emerson made a contemptuous gesture.

"They are even smaller jackals than Habib; let them go. They did not cause the deaths of the English lord and his friend. They did not kill the watchman Hassan."

Vandergelt stirred uneasily. "What is he up to now?" he whispered. "That was a first-rate performance; he ought to let the curtain down."

I was myself a trifle apprehensive. Emerson has a tendency to overdo things. I hoped he knew what he was doing. His next sentence made me doubt that he did.

"Were they slain by the curse of the pharaoh? If so . . ." Emerson paused; and not one pair of eyes in that assemblage blinked or moved from his face. "If so, I take that curse on myself! Here and now I challenge the gods to strike me down or give me their blessing. O Anubis, the High, the Mighty, the Chief over the mysteries of those in the underworld, O Horus, son of Osiris, born of Isis, O Apet, mother of fire . . ."

He turned to face the fire, which had died to a bed of red coals, against which his form was darkly silhouetted. Arms raised, he invoked the gods of Egypt in a sonorous but rather oddly pronounced form of their own language. All at once the dying fire soared heavenward in a rainbow flame, blue and sea-green and ghastly lavender. A gasp went up from the crowd; for in the uncanny light they saw on the topmost step of the tomb entrance an object that had certainly not been there before.

It had the form of a giant black cat with glowing yellow eyes. The play of firelight along the lean flanks gave the illusion of tensed muscles, as if the weird beast were preparing to spring on its prey.

The cat shape was a hollow shell, covered with bituminous pitch, and had once contained, if it did not still, the mummified figure of a real cat. Emerson had presumably acquired this object in Luxor, from one of the dealers, and had undoubtedly paid a pretty penny for it. No doubt many of the watchers were as cognizant as I of the true nature of the feline mummy case; but its seemingly miraculous appearance had as dramatic effect as any showman could wish.

Emerson broke into a weird, stiff-kneed dance, waving his arms. Vandergelt chuckled. "Reminds me of an old Apache chief I used to know," he whispered. "Suffered terribly from rheumatism, but wouldn't give up the rain dance."

Fortunately the rest of the audience was less critical. Watching Emerson's hand, I saw the same movement that had preceded the burst of multicolored flame. This time the substance he tossed onto the fire produced a huge puff of lemon-colored smoke. It must have contained sulfur, or some similar chemical, for it was singularly odorous and the spectators who were on its fringes began to cough and flap their hands.

For a few seconds the tomb entrance was completely veiled in coiling smoke. As it began to disperse we saw that the cat coffin had split down the middle. The two sections had fallen, one to each side, and between them, in the exact pose of the coffin, sat a living cat. It wore a jeweled collar; the gleaming stones winked emerald and ruby-red in the firelight.

The cat Bastet was extremely annoyed. I sympathized with her feelings. Caged, boxed, or bagged, as the case might be, she had been kidnapped and then thrust into a cloud of evil-smelling smoke. She sneezed and rubbed her nose with her forepaw. Then her glowing golden eyes lit on Emerson.

I feared the worst. But then came the crowning wonder of that night of wonders, which would be the subject of folktales in the nearby villages for years to come. The cat walked slowly toward Emerson—who was invoking it as Sekhmet, goddess of war, death, and destruction. Rising on its hind feet, it clung to his trouser leg with its claws and rubbed its head against his hand.

Emerson flung his arms high. "Allah is merciful! Allah is great!" Another mighty puff of smoke burst from the fire, and the majestic invocation ended in a fit of violent coughing.

The performance was ended. Murmuring appreciatively, the audience drifted away. Emerson emerged from the fog and walked toward me.

"Not bad, eh?" he inquired, grinning demonically.

"Let me shake your hand, Professor," Vandergelt said. "You are as smooth a crook as I ever met, and that's saying something."

Emerson beamed. "Thank you. Lady Baskerville, I took the liberty of ordering a feast for our men once they get back to the house. Abdullah and Feisal particularly deserve an entire sheep apiece."

"Certainly." Lady Baskerville nodded. "Really, though, Radcliffe, I hardly know what to say about this—this peculiar business. Was it, by chance, my emerald-and-ruby bracelet around the beast's neck?"

"Ah—hem," said Emerson. He fingered the dent in his chin. "I must apologize for the liberty. Never fear, I will restore it."

"How? The cat has run away."

Emerson was still trying to think what to say when Karl joined us.

"Herr Professor, you were splendid. One little point, if you permit—the imperative form of the verb *iri* is not *iru*, as you said, but—"

"Never mind," I said quickly. Emerson had directed an outraged scowl at the earnest young German, rather like Amon Ra glowering at a priest who ventured to criticize his pronunciation. "Had we not better return to the house? I am sure everyone is tired out."

"There will be no sleep for the guilty tonight," said a sepulchral voice.

Madame Berengeria had risen from her chair. Her daughter and Mr. O'Connell, who flanked her on either side, made ineffectual attempts to keep her quiet and move her on. She waved them away.

"A fine show, Professor," she went on. "You remember more of your past lives than you admit. But not enough; you fool, you have mocked the gods, and now you must suffer. I would have saved you if you had let me."

"Oh, the devil," Emerson exclaimed. "Really, I can't tolerate much more of this. Amelia, do something."

The woman's bloodshot eyes moved to me. "You share his guilt and will share his fate. Remember the words of the sage: 'Be not proud and arrogant of speech, for the gods love those who are silent.' "

"Mother, please," Mary said, taking the woman by the arm.

"Ungrateful girl!" With a twist of her shoulder, Madame sent Mary staggering back. "You and your lovers . . . You think I don't see, but I know! Filth, uncleanliness . . . Fornication is a sin, and so is failure to revere your mother. 'It is an abomination to the gods, going into a strange woman to know her . . .' "

The last comment was apparently aimed at Karl and O'Connell, whom she indicated by a wild gesture. The journalist was ashen with rage. Karl's reaction seemed to be chiefly one of surprise. I half-expected to hear him repeat, "The English! Never will I understand them."

Yet neither spoke to deny the vile allegations. Even I was momentarily nonplussed. I realized that Berengeria's earlier exhibitions had contained a certain element of deliberate calculation. She was not acting now; beads of froth oozed from the corners of her mouth. She turned her burning gaze on Vandergelt, who had thrown a protective arm around his bride-to-be.

"Adultery and fornication!" shouted Madame. "Remember the two brothers, my fine American gentleman; by the wiles of a woman Anubis was driven to murder his younger brother. He put his heart in the cedar tree and the king's men chopped it down. The lock of hair perfumed the garments of pharaoh; the talking beasts warned him to beware . . ."

The narrow cord of sanity had finally snapped. This was madness and delirium. I suspected that not even a brisk slap, my usual remedy for hysteria, would avail in this case. Before I could decide what to do, Berengeria pressed her hand to her heart and slowly subsided onto the ground.

"My heart . . . I must have a stimulant . . . I have overtaxed my strength . . ."

Mr. Vandergelt produced an elegant silver flask of brandy, which I administered to the fallen woman. She lapped it greedily, and by holding it in front of her, like a carrot in front of a balky mule, I was able to get her into the carriage. Mary was weeping with embarrassment, but when I suggested she ride with us she shook her head.

"She is my mother. I cannot abandon her."

O'Connell and Karl offered to go with her, and so it was arranged. The first carriage set out on the return journey and the rest of us were about to follow when I remembered that Lady Baskerville had planned to spend the night at the hotel. I assured her that if she wanted to carry out her plan, Emerson and I could walk back.

"How can you suppose me capable of abandoning you?" was the heated reply. "If that wretched woman has suffered a heart attack you will have two sick persons on your hands, in addition to all your other responsibilities."

"That's my noble girl," said Mr. Vandergelt approvingly.

"Thank you," I said.

When we reached the house I rolled up my sleeves and went first to Arthur's room. He was deep in slumber, so I proceeded to see how Madame was getting on. The Egyptian woman who had been assigned to attend the lady was leaving her room as I approached. When I asked her where the devil she thought she was going she informed me that the Sitt Baskerville had sent her for fresh water. I therefore allowed her to proceed on her errand.

Lady Baskerville was bending over the gross shape that sprawled across the bed. In her elegant gown and delicate lace shawl she was an incongruous figure to be found in a sickroom, but her movements were quick and efficient as she straightened the sheets.

"Will you have a look at her, Mrs. Emerson? I don't believe her condition is serious, but if you feel we ought to call Dr. Dubois, I will send someone at once."

After taking Berengeria's pulse and heartbeat I nodded agreement. "It can wait till morning, I think. There is nothing wrong with her now, except that she is dead drunk."

Lady Baskerville's full red lips curved in a wry smile. "Blame me, if you wish, Mrs. Emerson. As soon as she had been placed on the bed she reached under the mattress and brought out a bottle. She did not even open her eyes! At first I was too surprised to interfere. Then . . . well, I told myself that to attempt to wrest the bottle from her would only lead to a struggle which I must lose; but to be honest I wanted to see her insensible. I am sure you must despise me."

In fact, I rather admired her. For once, she was being honest with me, and I could not blame her for carrying out a scheme which I had myself once contemplated.

After directing the servant, who had returned with the water, to keep a close watch and wake me if there was any change in Madame's condition, I went with Lady Baskerville to the drawing room, where the others were assembled. Emerson had commanded their presence, and as we entered we heard Kevin O'Connell berating my husband for his lack of consideration.

"Miss Mary is on the verge of collapse," he cried. "She ought to be in bed. Just look at her!"

The young lady's appearance did not support this diagnosis. Her cheeks were tear-stained and her costume somewhat the worse for wear, but she sat upright in her chair, and when she spoke her voice was calm.

"No, my friend, I do not require pity. I need to be reminded of my duty. My mother is a tormented, unhappy person. Whether she is ill or mad or simply evil-minded I do not know, but it does not matter. She is my cross and I will bear it. Lady Baskerville, we will leave you tomorrow. I am ashamed that I have allowed this to go on as long as it has."

"Very well, very well," Emerson burst out, before anyone else could speak. "I am sure we all sympathize with you, Miss Mary, but at the moment I have more pressing matters to discuss. I must have a copy of the painting of Anubis before I demolish the wall. You had better be at work early, before—"

"What the—" O'Connell sprang to his feet, red as a turkey cock. "You cannot be serious, Professor."

"Be still, Kevin," Mary said. "I made a promise and I will keep it. Work is the best medicine for a wounded heart."

"Humph," said Emerson, kneading his chin. "I agree with the sentiment, at least. You might think about it too, Mr. O'Connell; how long has it been since you sent off a story to your newspaper?"

O'Connell sank limply into a chair and shook his disheveled red head. "I will probably lose my position," he said gloomily. "When one is living the news, it is hard to find time to write about it."

"Cheer up," Emerson said. "In forty-eight hours—perhaps less—you will be able to steal a march on your colleagues with a story that will restore you to the good graces of your editor. You may even be able to demand a rise in pay."

"What do you mean?" Fatigue forgotten, O'Connell sat up alertly and reached for his notebook and pencil. "You hope to enter the tomb by then?"

"Of course. But that is not what I meant. You will be the one to announce to the world the identity of the murderer of Lord Baskerville."

Chapter Fifteen

THE listeners were galvanized by this announcement. Vandergelt let out a loud "by Jimminy!" Mary's eyes opened wide. Even the phlegmatic young German stared at Emerson in surprise.

"Murderer?" O'Connell repeated.

"He was murdered, of course," Emerson said impatiently. "Come now, Mr. O'Connell, you have always suspected as much, though you did not have the effrontery to suggest it in your newspaper stories. The succession of violent tragedies that has occurred here makes it impossible that

Lord Baskerville could have died a natural death. I have been working on the case and I will soon be in a position to announce results. I await one last piece of evidence. It will be here late tomorrow or the following morning. By the way, Amelia," he added, looking at me, "don't try to intercept my messenger; the news he carries has meaning only to me; you won't understand it."

"Indeed?" I said.

"Well, well," said O'Connell. He crossed his legs, put his notebook on his knees, and gazed at Emerson with the impish grin that betokened his professional mood. "You wouldn't care to drop a hint, would you, Professor?"

"Certainly not."

"There is nothing to prevent me from speculating a bit, is there?"

"At your own risk," Emerson replied.

"Never fear, I am no more anxious to commit myself prematurely than you are. Hmmm. Yes, this will require some rather delicate phrasing. Excuse me, please; I had better get to work."

"Don't forget your promise," I said.

"You may see the story before I send it off," O'Connell said. He departed with a springy step, whistling.

"The rest of us had better retire too," Emerson said. "Vandergelt, can I count on your assistance tomorrow morning when I reopen the tomb?"

"I wouldn't miss it for . . . That is, if you don't mind, my dear?"

"No," Lady Baskerville replied wearily. "Do as you like, Cyrus. This latest news has quite overwhelmed me."

When she had taken her departure, leaning on Vandergelt's arm, Emerson turned to me. Before he could speak I made a warning gesture.

"I believe Karl wishes to ask you something, Emerson. Either that, or he has fallen asleep there in the shadows."

Emerson looked startled. Karl had been so still; and the corner where he sat was so far distant from the nearest lamp, that he might have fallen into a doze; but I suspected another, more sinister explanation. Now he roused himself and came forward.

"Not to ask do I wish, Herr Professor, but to warn. An act very foolish it was, to say what you said. A gauntlet of defiance you have thrown down to a killer."

"Dear me," Emerson said. "That was careless of me."

Von Bork shook his head. He had lost considerable weight during the past week, and the lamplight emphasized the new hollows under his cheekbones and in his eye sockets.

"A stupid man you are not, Professor. I myself ask why you have so acted. But," he added, with a faint smile, "I do not an answer expect. *Gute Nacht,* Herr Professor, Frau Professor—*Schlafen Sie wohl.*"

Frowning, Emerson watched the young man go. "He is the most intelligent of the lot," he muttered. "I may have made a mistake there, Peabody. I ought to have handled him differently."

"You are tired," I said magnanimously. "No wonder, after all that shouting and jumping around. Come to bed."

Arm in arm, we sauntered across the courtyard, and as we went Emerson remarked, "I believe I detected a slight note of criticism in your comment, Amelia. To describe my masterful performance as 'shouting and jumping around' is hardly—"

"The dancing was an error."

"I was not dancing. I was performing a grave ritual march. The fact that the space was limited—"

"I understand. It was the only flaw in an otherwise superb performance. The men have agreed to return to work, I take it?"

"Yes. Abdullah will be on guard tonight, though I don't expect any trouble."

I opened our door. Emerson struck a match and lighted the lamp. The wick flared up and a hundred fiery sparks reflected the light from the neck of the cat Bastet, who sat on the table by the window. As soon as she caught sight of Emerson she let out an eager, throaty mew and trotted toward him.

"What did you use to attract the animal?" I inquired, watching Bastet claw at Emerson's coattails.

"Chicken," Emerson replied. He withdrew a greasy packet from his trouser pocket. I was pained to observe that it had left a nasty spot. Grease is so difficult to get out.

"I spent an hour training her earlier this afternoon," Emerson said, feeding the remainder of the chicken to the cat.

"You had better get Lady Baskerville's bracelet off her neck," I said. "She has probably knocked half the stones out already."

And indeed it proved that she had. Seeing Emerson's face fall, as he tried to calculate the weight and value of the rubies and emeralds he would be obliged to replace, I quite forgave him for being so puffed up about his performance.

II

When I went to see Arthur next morning the Sister gave me a smiling *"bon jour"* and informed me that the patient had spent a quiet night. His color was much better—which I attributed to the strengthening effect of the chicken broth—and when I placed my hand on his brow he smiled in his sleep and murmured something.

"He is calling for his mother," I said, brushing a tear from my eye with my sleeve.

"Vraiment?" the sister asked doubtfully. "He has spoken once or twice

before, but so softly I could not make out the word."

"I am sure he said *'Mother.'* And perhaps by the time he wakes he will see that good lady's face bending over him." I allowed myself the pleasure of picturing that exquisite scene. Mary would be there, of course (I really must do something about the child's clothes; a pretty white gown would be just the thing); and Arthur would hold her hand in his thin, wasted fingers as he told his mother to greet her new daughter.

To be sure, Mary had announced her intention of devoting the rest of her life to her mother, but that was just a young girl's romantic fancy. A fondness for martyrdom, especially of the verbal variety, is common to the young. I had dealt with this phenomenon before and did not doubt my ability to bring this love affair also to a happy conclusion.

However, time was passing, and if I expected to see Mary become the new Lady Baskerville, it was up to me to make sure her bridegroom survived to take that step. I repeated my caution to the nun, to give the sick man nothing except what was brought to her by myself or by Daoud.

I then went to my next patient. A peep into the room assured me that Madame was in no need of my attention. She slept the calm, deep-breathing sleep of the wicked. It is a misconception that the innocent sleep well. The worse a man is, the more profound his slumber; for if he had a conscience, he would not be a villain.

When I reached the dining room Emerson growled at me for being late. He and Mary had already finished breakfast.

"Where are the others?" I inquired, buttering a piece of toast and ignoring Emerson's demands that I bring it with me and eat as we walked.

"Karl has gone ahead," Mary said. "Kevin has crossed to Luxor, to the telegraph office—"

"Emerson!" I exclaimed.

"It is all right, he showed the story to me," Emerson replied. "You will enjoy reading it, Amelia; the young man has an imagination almost as uncontrolled as yours."

"Thank you. Mary, your mother seems better this morning."

"Yes, she has had these attacks before and made a remarkable recovery. As soon as I have finished the copy of the painting I will make arrangements to move her back to Luxor."

"There is no hurry," I said sympathetically. "Tomorrow morning will be soon enough; you will be worn out this evening after working in the heat."

"Well, if you really think so," Mary said doubtfully. Her morose expression lightened a little. One may be determined to embrace martyrdom gracefully, but a day of reprieve is not to be sneezed at. I am sure even the early Christian saints raised no objection if Caesar postponed feeding them to the lions until the next circus.

Tiring of Emerson's nagging, I finished my breakfast and we prepared to leave. "Where is Mr. Vandergelt?" I asked. "He wanted to be with us, I thought."

"He has taken Lady Baskerville over to Luxor," Emerson replied. "There were matters to arrange for their approaching nuptials; and I persuaded the lady to stay there and do a little shopping. That always cheers ladies, does it not?"

"Why, Professor," Mary said with a laugh. "I had no idea you were so well acquainted with the weaknesses of our sex."

I looked suspiciously at Emerson. He had turned his back and was attempting to whistle. "Well, well," he said, "Let us be off, shall we? Vandergelt will join us later; it will be some time before we can actually breach the wall."

III

It was, in fact, midmorning before our preparations were complete. The air in the depths of the tomb was still bad, and the heat was so unbelievable that I refused to let Mary work for more than ten minutes at a time. Impatient as Emerson was, he had to agree that this was reasonable. In the meantime he occupied himself with supervising the construction of a stout wooden cover for the well. Karl had taken over the operation of the camera. And I?

You know little of my character, dear reader, if you are unable to imagine the nature of the thoughts that occupied my mind. I sat under the shade of my awning, supposedly making scale drawings of pottery fragments, but the sound of Emerson's cheerful shouts and curses as he supervised the carpenter work roused the gravest suspicions. He seemed very sure of himself. Was it possible, after all, that he was right in his identification of Lord Baskerville's murderer, and that I was wrong? I could not believe it. However, I decided it might be advisable to go over my reasoning once more, in the light of the most recent developments. I could always think of a way of changing the name in my envelope if I had to.

Turning over a page of my sketching pad, I abandoned pots for plans. I would make a neat little chart, setting forth the various motives and means and so on.

So I began.

THE DEATH OF LORD BASKERVILLE

Suspect: Lady Baskerville.

Motive in the murder of:

Lord Baskerville. Inheritance. (How much Lady Baskerville would inherit I, of course, did not know yet; but I felt sure it was enough to account for her willingness to do away with her husband. By all accounts he had been a singularly boring man.)

Armadale. He witnessed the crime. The room he had occupied was next to Lady Baskerville's. (To be sure, this did not explain why Armadale had disappeared. Had he lost his mind from horror after seeing Lady B. massacre her husband? And how the devil—as Emerson might have said—did she massacre him? If some obscure and unidentifiable poison had been used, all Armadale could have seen was Lord Baskerville sipping a cup of tea or a glass of sherry.)

Hassan. Hassan had seen Armadale and observed something—perhaps the particular window to which the "ghost" had gone—that betrayed the identity of the murderer. Attempted blackmail; destruction of blackmailer.

I read over this last paragraph with satisfaction. It made sense. Indeed, the motive for Hassan's murder would apply to all the suspects.

The next section of my little chart was not so neat. Lady Baskerville's motives for bashing Arthur on the head were obscure, unless there was some clause in his lordship's will that allowed certain properties to revert to his wife in the event of the death of his heir. That seemed not only unlikely, but positively illegal.

I went doggedly on to the question of opportunity.

Lord Baskerville. His wife's opportunity of getting at him was excellent. But how the devil had she done it?

Armadale. No opportunity. How had Lady Baskerville known the location of the cave? If she had killed Armadale at or near the house, she would have had to transport his body to the cave—obviously impossible for a woman.

Weak, very weak! I could almost hear Emerson's jeer. The truth of the matter was I wanted Lady Baskerville to be the murderer. I never liked the woman.

I gazed disconsolately at my chart, which was not working as I had hoped. With a sigh I turned to a fresh page and tried another arrangement.

THE DEATH OF LORD BASKERVILLE

Suspect: Arthur Baskerville, alias Charles Milverton.

That had a fine, professional look to it. Emboldened, I went on:

Motive: inheritance and revenge. (So far, so good.)

In fact, Arthur's motive was particularly strong. It accounted for his imbecilic behavior in presenting himself to his uncle incognito. This was the act of a romantic young idiot. Arthur *was* a romantic young idiot; but if he had planned in advance to kill his uncle, he had a very good reason for taking a false name. Once Baskerville was dead (how? curse it, how?) Arthur could return to Kenya, and it was most unlikely that anyone would have connected Arthur, Lord Baskerville, with the former Charles Milverton. He would probably claim the title and estates without ever going to England, and if he did have to go, he could make excuses to avoid Lady Baskerville.

With a start I realized that my chart had taken to wandering all over the page. I took a firm grip on my wits and my pencil, and returned to the proper form.

THE DEATH OF LORD BASKERVILLE

Suspect: Cyrus Vandergelt. His motives were only too clear. Contrary to the stern warning of Scripture, he had coveted his neighbor's wife.

It was at that point I realized I had not discussed Arthur's means or opportunity, or explained who had struck him down if he was the original killer.

Gritting my teeth, I turned the page over and tried again.

THE MURDER OF ALAN ARMADALE

This approach was based on the assumption that Lord Baskerville's death was a red herring—or, to put it more elegantly, that his lordship had died a natural death; that the so-called mark on his brow was a meaningless stain, misinterpreted by sensation-seekers; and that the murderer had taken advantage of the furor following his lordship's death to commit a murder whose true motive would be obscured.

The obvious suspect here was Mr. O'Connell. He had not only taken advantage of the story of the curse, he had invented it. I did not suppose that he had murdered Armadale in cold blood; no, the killing had obviously resulted from a sudden rush of jealous passion. Once the deed was done, a clever man—which O'Connell undoubtedly was—might have seen how he could avert suspicion by making Armadale's death seem related to that of Lord Baskerville.

The same motive—love of Mary—could apply in the case of Karl von Bork. In my opinion he was not capable of the sort of grand passion that might drive a man to violence. But still waters run deep. And once or twice Karl had displayed hidden depths of feeling and of cunning.

By this time my chart had abandoned all pretense of form, and my random jottings, embodying the thoughts I have expressed in more developed form above, were sprawling all over the page. I studied it in some exasperation. My thought processes are always orderly. The case was simply not susceptible to this means of organization. It is all very well for writers of crime fiction; they invent the crime and the solution, so they can arrange things the way they like.

I decided to abandon the outline and let my thoughts stray where they would.

Solely on the basis of opportunity one would have to eliminate all the women from suspicion. Madame Berengeria's motive was excellent; she might not be mad in the medical sense, but she was mad enough to destroy anyone who might wish to interfere with her selfish hold on her daughter. However, she and Mary resided on the east bank. The bodies had all been discovered on the west bank. I could not visualize either Mary or her mother scampering through the dark streets of Luxor, hiring a boat and bribing the boatmen to silence, then running through the fields of the western shore. The idea that Madame could have done this not once but several times was ludicrous—unless she had hired accomplices to do the actual killing. And although Lady Baskerville had been on the scene, such activity on the part of a lady of elegant and languid habits seemed equally unlikely. The murder of Armadale presented particular difficulties, as I had indicated in my initial attempt at a chart.

At this point in my cogitations Mr. Vandergelt and Mr. O'Connell arrived, having met at the quay. I was glad to abandon my futile outlines; for I had decided I had been right all along.

Mr. Vandergelt's first question concerned the state of our operations on the tomb.

"You haven't broken through that wall yet, have you?" he demanded. "I'll never forgive you, Mrs. Amelia, if you didn't wait for me."

"I think you are just in time," I retorted, hastily hiding my notebook under a pile of chips. "I was about to go down myself to see how matters are progressing."

We met Mary on her way out. She was in an indescribable state of dampness and dirt, but her eyes shone triumphantly as she displayed a splendid drawing, the result of her uncomfortable labors. It was not, I thought, quite equal to Evelyn's efforts; but perhaps I am prejudiced. Certainly it was a fine piece of work, and I knew Emerson would be pleased with it.

Crooning in an exaggerated Irish brogue, Mr. O'Connell carried Mary off to rest, and Vandergelt and I descended the steps.

Already the newly constructed wooden structure was in place over the shaft, and the men were preparing to make a hole in the wall.

"Ah, there you are," Emerson remarked unnecessarily. "I was just about to go and fetch you."

"Like fun you were," said Vandergelt. "Never mind, Professor; if I were in your shoes I wouldn't want to wait either. What's the plan?"

I will spare the reader further technical details; they can be found in Emerson's superb report, which is to appear this fall in the *Zeitchrift für Aegyptische Sprache*. Suffice it to say that the hole was drilled and Emerson looked through it. Waiting with bated breath, Vandergelt and I heard him groan.

"What is it?" I cried. "A dead end? An empty sarcophagus? Tell us the worst, Emerson."

Silently Emerson made way for us. Vandergelt and I each put one eye to the opening.

Another corridor stretched down into darkness. It was half filled with debris—not the deliberate limestone fill of the first corridor, but fragments of a collapsed ceiling and wall, mingled with scraps of gilded wood and brown linen—the remains of mummy wrappings.

Withdrawing the candle from the hole, I held it up, and in its light we three contemplated one another's disappointed faces.

"That is surely not the burial chamber," Vandergelt exclaimed.

Emerson shook his untidy head, now gray with dust. "No. It appears that the tomb was used for later burials, and that the ceiling has collapsed. It is going to be a long, tedious job clearing that mess out and sifting the debris."

"Well, then, let's get to it," Vandergelt exclaimed, mopping his streaming brow.

Emerson's lips curved in a reluctant smile as he studied the American. Fifteen minutes in the heat of the corridor had changed Vandergelt from a dapper, handsome man of the world to a specimen that would have been denied entrance to the cheapest London hotel. His goatee dripped, his face was white with dust, and his suit sagged. But his face shone with enthusiasm.

"Quite right," Emerson said. "Let us get at it."

Vandergelt took off his coat and rolled up his shirt sleeves.

IV

The sun had passed the zenith and begun its westward journey before Emerson halted the work. I remained up above, having a comfortable woman-to-woman chat with Mary. She proved to be remarkably resistant to my efforts to ascertain which of her suitors she preferred. She kept insisting that since she did not intend to marry, her preference did not matter; but I think I was on the verge of winning her confidence when we were interrupted by the approach of two dusty, disheveled ragamuffins.

Vandergelt collapsed under the awning. "I sure hope you ladies will excuse me. I'm not in a fit state for the company of the gentler sex just now."

"You look like an archaeologist," I said approvingly. "Have a cup of tea and a little rest before we start back. What results, gentlemen?"

Again I refer the reader to the technical publications about to appear. We had an animated and extremely enjoyable discussion on professional matters. Mary seemed to enjoy it too; her timid questions were very sensible. It was with visible reluctance that she finally rose and declared she must get back.

"May I escort Miss Mary?" Karl asked. "It is not right that she should go alone—"

"I need you here," Emerson replied absently.

"I'll be escorting the lady," O'Connell announced, smirking triumphantly at his rival. "Unless, Professor, that matter of which we spoke last night is imminent?"

"What on earth is he talking about?" Emerson asked me.

"You remember," O'Connell insisted. "The message—the evidence that would—er—"

"Message? Oh, yes. Why can't you speak out, young man, instead of being so confoundedly mysterious? It must be the effect of your profession; always sneaking and spying. As I think I told you, the messenger will probably not arrive until tomorrow morning. Run along, now."

Emerson then drew me aside. "Amelia, I want you to go back to the house also."

"Why?"

"Matters are rapidly approaching the final crisis. Milverton—curse it, I mean young Baskerville—may not be out of danger. Watch him. And make sure everyone knows that I expect the fatal message tomorrow."

I folded my arms and looked at him steadily. "Are you going to confide your plans to me, Emerson?"

"Why, surely you know them already, Amelia."

"It is impossible for any rational mind to follow the peculiar mental convolutions that pass for logic among the male sex," I replied. "However, the course of action you have suggested happens to suit my own plans. I will therefore do as you ask."

"Thank you," said Emerson.

"You are quite welcome," I replied.

Mary and Mr. O'Connell had gone off in Vandergelt's carriage. I took the path over the hills, so was the first to arrive at the house. Though climbing in and out my bedroom window had now become a natural and convenient procedure, I decided on this occasion to make a formal entrance, by way of the gate. I wanted my presence to be noted.

As I entered the courtyard Lady Baskerville came out of her room. She greeted me with unusual warmth. "Ah, Mrs. Emerson. Another hard day's work accomplished? Is there any news?"

"Only of an archaeological variety," I replied. "That would not interest you, I suppose."

"Once it did. My husband's enthusiasms were my own. He spoke of them constantly. But can you blame me for now regarding the entire subject as darkly stained by unfortunate memories?"

"I suppose not. Let us hope, however, those memories will fade. It is unlikely that Mr. Vandergelt will ever abandon his absorption in Egyptology, and he will want his wife to share it."

"Naturally," said Lady Baskerville.

"Was your trip to Luxor a success?" I asked.

The lady's somber countenance brightened. "Yes, the arrangements are being made. And I found a few things that were not too bad, considering. Do come to my room and let me show you my purchases. Half the pleasure in new clothes is in showing them to another woman."

I was about to refuse, but Lady Baskerville's sudden fondness for my company struck me as highly suspicious. I decided to go along with her in order to ascertain her true motives.

I thought I understood one such motive when I saw the disorder of her room, every surface being strewn with garments that she had taken from their boxes. Automatically I began to shake them out and fold them neatly away.

"Where is Atiyah?" I asked. "She ought to be performing this service for you."

"Didn't you know? The wretched woman has run away," was the careless reply. "What do you think of this shirtwaist? It is not very pretty, but—"

The rest of her speech went unheard by me. I was seized by a grim foreboding. Had Atiyah become another victim?

"Some effort ought to be made to locate the woman," I said, interrupting Lady Baskerville's criticism of an embroidered combing mantle. "She may be in danger."

"What woman? Oh, Atiyah." Lady Baskerville laughed. "Mrs. Emerson, the poor creature was a drug addict; did you not realize that? She has probably spent her wages on opium and is in a stupor in some den in Luxor. I can manage without a maid for a few more days; thank heaven I will soon be back in civilization, where decent servants are to be found."

"Let us hope you will," I agreed politely.

"But I count on Radcliffe to free me. Did he not promise all our doubts and questions would be settled today? Cyrus—and I, of course—would be reluctant to leave you all unless we were sure you were no longer in danger."

"Apparently that longed-for moment will not occur until tomorrow," I said drily. "Emerson tells me his messenger has been delayed."

"Today, tomorrow, what matter? So long as it is soon." Lady Baskerville shrugged. "Now this, Mrs. Emerson, is to be my wedding hat. How do you like it?"

She placed the hat, a broad-brimmed straw trimmed with lavender ribbons and pink silk flowers, on her head and skewered it in place with a pair of jeweled pins. When I did not reply at once, she flushed and a spark of anger shone in her black eyes.

"You think me wrong to wear something so frivolous when I am supposed to be in mourning? Should I replace the ribbons with black and dye the flowers sable?"

I took the question as it was meant, a display of sarcasm rather than a request for information, and did not reply. I had other things on my mind. Lady Baskerville was visibly annoyed at my lack of interest, and when I rose to leave she did not press me to remain.

The carriage was just passing through the gate when I emerged from Lady Baskerville's room. The young people had had no reason to hurry. After greeting me, Mary asked if I had seen her mother.

"No, I have been with Lady Baskerville. If you can wait a few minutes, until I have visited Arthur, I will accompany you."

Mary was glad to agree to this.

The nun greeted us with shining eyes and a look of genuine happiness in the news she had to give. "He has shown signs of regaining consciousness. It is a miracle, madame. How great is prayer!"

How great is chicken soup, I thought to myself. But I did not say so; let the good creature enjoy her delusions.

Arthur was painfully thin—there are limits even to the powers of chicken broth—but his improvement in the past twenty-four hours had indeed been astonishing. As I leaned over the bed he stirred and murmured. I motioned to Mary.

"Speak to him, my dear. Let us see if we can rouse him. You may hold his hand, if you like."

Scarcely had Mary taken the wasted hand in her own and called the young man's name in a voice tremulous with emotion than his long golden lashes fluttered and his head turned toward her.

"Mary," he murmured. "Is it you, or a heavenly spirit?"

"It is I," the girl replied, tears of joy trickling down her cheeks. "How happy I am to see you better!"

I added a few appropriate words. Arthur's eyes moved to me. "Mrs. Emerson?"

"Yes. Now you know you have not died and gone to heaven." (I always feel that a little touch of humor relieves situations of this nature.) "I know you are still weak, Arthur," I went on, "but for your own safety I hope you can answer one question. Who struck you?"

"Struck me?" The sick man's pallid brow wrinkled. "Did someone . . . I cannot remember."

"What is the last thing you remember?"

"Lady . . . Lady Baskerville." Mary gasped and looked at me. I shook my head. Now, of all times, we could not leap to conclusions on the basis of a wounded man's confused recollections.

"What about Lady Baskerville?" I asked.

"Told me . . . rest." Arthur's voice grew even weaker. "Went to my room . . . lay down . . ."

"You remember nothing more?"

"Nothing."

"Very well, my dear Arthur, don't tire yourself any further. Rest. There is nothing to worry about; I am on the job."

A smile curved the young man's bearded lips. His weary lids drooped shut.

As we went toward Madame's room, Mary said with a sigh, "I can leave with a lighter heart. Our fears for his safety are now relieved."

"True," I said, half to myself. "If he was struck during his sleep, as seems to be the case, he never saw the villain's face, so there is no reason why he should be attacked again. However, I do not regret the precautions we took. We had to make sure."

Mary nodded, though I do not think she really heard what I was saying. The closer we came to that room which must seem to her like a goblin's foul lair, the more slowly she moved. A shudder passed through her frame as she reached for the knob.

The room was in shadow, the shades having been drawn to keep out the afternoon sun. The attendant lay huddled on a pallet at the foot of the bed. She looked like a corpse in her worn brown robes, but she was only asleep; I could hear her breathing.

Mary touched her mother gently on the arm. "Mother, wake up. I am back. Mother?"

Suddenly she reeled back, her hands clasped on her breast. I leaped to support her. "What is it?" I cried. She only shook her head dumbly.

After helping her into a chair I went to the bed. It required no great stretch of imagination to anticipate what I would find.

When we entered, Madame Berengeria had been lying on her side with her back to the door. Mary's touch, gentle as it was, had disturbed the balance of the body and caused it to roll onto its back. One glance at the staring eyes and lax mouth told the story. It was not even necessary for me to seek a nonexistent pulse, though I did so, as a matter of routine.

"My dear child, this could have happened at any time," I said, taking Mary by the shoulders and giving her a sympathetic shake. "Your mother was a sick woman, and you should regard this as a blessed release."

"You mean," Mary whispered. "You mean it was—her heart?"

"Yes," I said truthfully. "Her heart stopped. Now, child, go and lie down. I will do what needs to be done here."

Mary was visibly heartened by the false assumption I had allowed her to form. Time enough for her to learn the truth later. The Arab woman had awakened by this time; she cringed when I turned to her, as if expecting a blow.

I did not see how she could be blamed, so I spoke gently to her, instructing her to take care of Mary.

When they had gone, I went back to the bed. Madame's fixed stare and sagging jowls were not a pleasant sight, but I have seen worse things and done worse; my hands were quite steady as I went about my ghoulish but necessary tasks. The flesh was still warm. That proved little, since the temperature of the room was hot, but the eyes gave away the truth. They were so widely dilated as to appear black. Berengeria's heart had certainly stopped, but it had stopped as the result of a large dose of some narcotic poison.

Chapter Sixteen

I sent a message at once to Emerson, although I never supposed for a moment that he would allow the small matter of another murder to distract him from his work. In fact, it was not until teatime that he returned. I was waiting for him; and as he stripped off his work-stained garments I brought him up to date on the events of the day. He seemed more struck by what Arthur had told me.

"Very interesting," he said, stroking his chin. "Ve-ry interesting! That should relieve us of one concern; if he did not see the killer we may assume, may we not, that he is not liable to a second attack. I say, Amelia, did you think of summoning Dr. Dubois to look at Madame, or did you do the postmortem yourself?"

"I did call him, not because he could add anything to what I already knew, but because he had to sign the death certificate. He agreed with me that death was due to an overdose of laudanum or some similar poison; even he could not overlook the signs of that. He claims, however, that the drug was self-administered, by accident. Apparently all Luxor knew Madame's habits."

"Humph," said Emerson, rubbing his chin so hard it turned pink. "Ve-ry interest—"

"Do stop that," I said crossly. "You know as well as I do that it was murder."

"Are you sure you didn't do it? You said the other day that the world would be a better place if the lady were removed from it."

"I am still of that opinion. Apparently I was not the only one who thought so."

"I would say the viewpoint was virtually unanimous," Emerson agreed.

"Well, well, I must change. Do you go to the parlor, Amelia; I will be with you shortly."

"Don't you want to discuss the motives for Madame's murder? I have a theory."

"I felt sure you would."

"It has to do with her wild ravings last night."

"I prefer to defer discussion of that."

"You do, eh?" Absently I stroked my own chin, and we eyed one another suspiciously. "Very well, Emerson. You will find me ready for you."

I was the first one in the drawing room. By the time Emerson made his appearance the others had assembled. Mary, in a black dress borrowed from Lady Baskerville, was tenderly supported by Mr. O'Connell.

"I persuaded her to come," the young man explained in a proprietary manner.

"Quite right," I agreed. "After all, there is nothing like a nice hot cup of tea to comfort one."

"It will take more than a cup of tea to comfort me," Lady Baskerville announced. "Say what you will, Radcliffe, there is a curse on this place. Even though Madame's death was an unfortunate accident—"

"Ah, but are we sure of that?" Emerson inquired.

Vandergelt, who had taken his agitated fiancée in the shelter of his white linen arm, looked sharply at my husband.

"What do you mean, Professor? Why look for trouble? It's no secret that the poor woman was—er—"

He broke off, with an apologetic look at Mary. She was staring at Emerson in wide-eyed surprise. I quickly passed her a cup of tea.

"We may never know the truth," Emerson replied. "But it would have been easy to slip a dose of poison into the lady's favorite beverage. As for the motive . . ." He glanced at me, and I took up the narrative.

"Last night Madame made a number of wild accusations. Pure malice and hysteria, most of them; but now I wonder if there might not have been a grain of wheat in all that chaff. Do any of you know the ancient tale to which she referred?"

"Why sure," Vandergelt replied. "Anyone who knows the least little thing about Egyptology must be familiar with it. 'The Tale of the Two Brothers,' isn't that right?"

His reply was prompt. Too prompt, perhaps? A stupid man might have pretended ignorance of that potentially dangerous story. A clever man might know his ignorance would be suspect, and admit the truth at once.

"What are you talking about?" Mary asked pathetically. "I don't understand. These hints—"

"Let me explain," Karl said.

"As a student of the language you probably know the story best," Emerson said smoothly. "Go on, Karl."

The young man cleared his throat self-consciously. I noted, however, that when he spoke his verb forms were in perfect English alignment. That meant something.

"The tale concerns two brothers. Anubis the elder and Bata the younger. Their parents were dead, and Bata lived with his older brother and his wife. One day when they were working in the fields, Anubis sent Bata back to the house to fetch some grain. The wife of Anubis saw the young man's strength and desired— er—that is, she asked him—er—"

"She made advances to him," Emerson said impatiently.

"*Ja, Herr Professor!* The young man indignantly refused the woman. But, fearing that he would betray her to her husband, she told Anubis Bata had—er— made advances to *her.* So Anubis hid in the barn, meaning to kill his younger brother when he came in from the field.

"But," Karl continued, warming to the tale, "the cattle of Bata were enchanted; they could speak. As each entered the barn it warned Bata that his brother was hiding behind the door, intending to murder him. So Bata ran away, pursued by Anubis. The gods, who knew Bata was innocent, caused a river full of crocodiles to flow between them. And then Bata, across the river, called out to his brother, explaining what had really happened. As a sign of his innocence he cut off—er—that is—"

Karl turned fiery-red and stopped speaking. Vandergelt grinned broadly at the young man's discomfiture, and Emerson said thoughtfully, "There really is no acceptable euphemism for that action; omit it, Karl. In view of what happens later in the story, it does not make much sense anyway."

"*Ja, Herr Professor.* Bata told his brother he was going away to a place called the Valley of the Cedar, where he would put his heart in the top of a great cedar tree. Anubis would know his brother was in good health so long as his cup of beer was clear; but when the beer turned cloudy he would know Bata was in danger, and then he must search for Bata's heart and restore it to him."

Lady Baskerville could restrain herself no longer. "What is this nonsense?" she exclaimed. "Of all the stupid stories—"

"It is a fairy tale," I said. "Fairy tales are not sensible, Lady Baskerville. Go on, Karl. Anubis returned to the house and destroyed his faithless wife—"

For once—the first and last time—Karl interrupted me instead of the other way around.

"*Ja, Frau Professor.* Anubis regretted his injustice to his poor young brother. And the immortal gods, they also felt sorry for Bata. They determined to make a wife for him—the most beautiful woman in the world—to keep him company in his lonely exile. And Bata loved the woman and made her his wife."

"Pandora," Mr. O'Connell exclaimed. "I never heard this story, and

that's the truth; but it's just like the tale of Pandora, that the gods made for
. . . begorrah, but I can never remember the fellow's name."

No one enlightened him. I would never have taken the young man for a
student of comparative literature; it seemed much more likely that he was trying
to emphasize his ignorance of the story.

"The woman was like Pandora," Karl admitted. "She was a bringer of evil.
One day when she was bathing, the River stole a lock of her hair and carried it to
the court of pharaoh. The scent of the hair was so wonderfully sweet that pharaoh
sent soldiers to find the woman from whose head it had come. With the soldiers
went women who carried jewels and beautiful garments and all the things women
love; and when the woman saw the fine things she betrayed her husband. She told
the soldiers about the heart in the cedar tree; and the soldiers cut down the tree.
Bata fell dead, and the faithless woman went to the court of pharaoh."

"Bedad, but it's the Cinderella story," said Mr. O'Connell. "The lock of
hair, the glass slipper—"

"You have made your point, Mr. O'Connell," I said.

Unabashed, O'Connell grinned broadly. "It never hurts to make sure,"
he remarked.

"Go on, Karl," I said.

"One day the older brother Anubis saw that his cup of beer was clouded,
and he knew what it meant. He searched, and he found his brother, and he found
the heart of his brother in the fallen tree. He put the heart in a cup of beer and
Bata drank it and came back to life. But the woman—"

"Well, well," Emerson said, "that was splendidly told, Karl. Let me
synopsize the rest, it is just as long and even more illogical than the first part. Bata
eventually avenged himself on his treacherous wife and became pharaoh."

There was a pause.

"I have never heard anything so nonsensical in my life," said Lady Baskerville.

"Fairy tales are meant to be nonsensical," I said. "That is part of their
charm."

II

The general reaction to "The Tale of the Two Brothers" was approximately the same as Lady Baskerville's. All agreed that Madame's references to it
had been meaningless, the product of a deranged mind. Emerson seemed content
to let the subject drop, and it was not until we were almost finished with dinner
that he again electrified the company by introducing a controversial topic.

"I intend to spend the night at the tomb," he announced. "After tomorrow's revelations I will be able to procure all the workmen and guards I need; until
then, there is still some slight risk of robbery."

Vandergelt dropped his fork. "What the devil do you mean?"

"Language, language," Emerson said reproachfully. "There are ladies present. Why, you have not forgotten my messenger, have you? He will be here tomorrow. Then I will know the truth. A simple 'yes' or 'no'; the message will be no more than that; and if it is 'yes' . . . Who would suppose that one person's fate could hang on such a little word?"

"You are overdoing it," I said, out of the corner of my mouth. Emerson scowled at me, but took the hint.

"Are we all finished?" he inquired. "Good. Let us retire. I am sorry to rush you, but I want to get back to the Valley."

"Then perhaps you wish to be excused now," said Lady Baskerville, her raised eyebrows showing what she thought of this piece of rudeness.

"No, no. I want my coffee. It will help keep me awake."

As we left the room, Mary came up to me. "I don't understand, Mrs. Emerson. The story Karl told was so strange. How can it have any bearing on my mother's death?"

"It may have no bearing at all," I said soothingly. "We are still walking in a thick fog, Mary; we cannot even see what objects are hidden by the mist, much less know if they are landmarks to guide us on our quest."

"How literary we all are tonight," remarked the ubiquitous Mr. O'Connell, smiling. It was his professional, leprechaun's smile; but it seemed to me his eyes held a glint of something more serious and more sinister.

With a defiant glance at me Lady Baskerville took her place behind the coffee tray. I smiled tolerantly. If the lady chose to make this trivial activity a show of strength between us, let her. In a few more days I would be in charge officially, as I already was in actuality.

We were all extremely polite that evening. As I listened to the genteel murmurs of "black or white?" and "two lumps, if you please," I felt as if I were watching the commonplace, civilized scene through distorting glasses, like those in a fairy tale I had once read. Everyone in the room was acting a part. Everyone had something to conceal—emotions, actions, thoughts.

Lady Baskerville would have done better to let me serve the coffee. She was unusually clumsy; and after she had managed to spill half a cup onto the tray, she let out a little scream of exasperation and clapped her hands to her head.

"I am so nervous tonight I don't know what I am doing! Radcliffe, I wish you would reconsider. Stay here tonight. Don't risk yourself, I could not stand another . . ." Smiling, Emerson shook his head, and Lady Baskerville, summoning up a faint answering smile, said more calmly, "I ought to know better. At least you will take someone with you? You will not go alone?"

Stubborn creature that he is, Emerson was about to deny this reasonable request, but the others all joined in urging him to accept a companion. Vandergelt was the first to offer his services.

"No, no, you must stay and guard the ladies," Emerson said.

"As ever, Herr Professor, I would be honored to be of service to the most distinguished—"

"Thank you, no."

I said nothing. There was no need for me to speak; Emerson and I habitually communicate without words. It is a form of electrical vibration, I believe. He felt my unspoken message, for he avoided looking at me as he scanned the room in a maddeningly deliberate fashion.

"The chosen victim must be Mr. O'Connell, I believe," he said at last. "I hope we will have a restful night; he can work on his next dispatch."

"That suits me, Professor," said the young Irishman, taking his cup from Lady Baskerville.

Suddenly Emerson rose to his feet with a cry. "Look there!"

Every eye went to the window, where he was pointing. O'Connell rushed across the room and pulled back the curtains.

"What did you see, Professor?"

"A flutter of white," Emerson said. "I thought someone passed rapidly by the window."

"There is nothing there now," O'Connell said. He went back to his chair.

No one spoke for a time. I sat gripping the arms of my chair, trying to think; for a new and terrible idea had suddenly occurred to me. I had no idea what Emerson was up to, with his ridiculous suggestions of flutters of white and his dramatic cries; the matter that concerned me was of quite another nature. I might be wrong. But if I was not wrong, something had to be done, and without delay.

"Wait," I cried, rising in my turn.

"What is it?" Emerson demanded.

"Mary," I exclaimed. "Quickly—she is about to swoon—"

The gentlemen all converged on the astonished girl. I had hoped, but had not really expected, that she would have the wits to follow my lead. Evelyn would have done it instantly. But Evelyn is used to my methods. It did not matter; the distraction gave me the opportunity I needed. Emerson's coffee cup and mine were on a low table next to my chair. Quickly I exchanged them.

"Honestly, there is nothing wrong with me," Mary insisted. "I am a little tired, but I don't feel at all faint."

"You are very pale," I said sympathetically. "And you have had such a dreadful day, Mary; I think you ought to retire."

"So should you," Emerson said, looking at me suspiciously. "Drink your coffee, Amelia, and excuse yourself."

"Certainly," I said, and did so without hesitation.

The group dispersed soon thereafter. Emerson offered to escort me to our room; but I informed him I had other matters to take care of before I retired. The first and most imperative I will not describe in detail. It had to be done, and I did it; but the process was unpleasant to experience and distasteful to recount. If I had been able to anticipate Emerson's plans I would not have eaten quite so much at dinner.

I then felt obliged to look in on Mary. She was still in the state of false composure that often follows a shock, whether the shock be one of joy or sorrow—but sooner or later she must give way to the bewildering mixture of emotions that filled her heart. I treated her as I would a hurt or frightened child, tucking her into bed, and leaving a candle burning for comfort; and she seemed pathetically grateful for the attentions, which, I have no doubt, were new to her. I took the opportunity of speaking to her about Christian fortitude and British spunk in the face of adversity, adding that, with all due respect to her mother, the future could only appear bright. I might have said more; but at this point in the conversation she fell asleep. So I tucked the netting around her and tiptoed out.

Emerson was waiting outside the door. He was leaning against the wall with his arms folded and his look of "I would stamp and shout if I were not such an unusually patient man" on his face.

"What took you so cursed long?" he demanded. "I am in a hurry."

"I did not ask you to wait for me."

"I want to talk to you."

"We have nothing to talk about."

"Ah!" Emerson exclaimed, in the surprised tone of someone who has just made a discovery. "You are angry because I didn't ask you share the watch with me tonight."

"Ridiculous. If you wish to sit there like Patience on a monument waiting for a murderer to attack you, I will not interfere."

"Is that what you are thinking?" Emerson laughed loudly. "No, no, my dear Peabody. I was bluffing about the message, of course—"

"I know."

"Humph," said Emerson. "Do you suppose the others know?"

"Probably."

"Then what are you worried about?"

He had me there. The message was such a transparent subterfuge that only a fool would fail to see it for the trick it was.

"Humph," I said.

"I had hoped," Emerson admitted, "that the device would stimulate our suspect, not to murder me—I am no hero, my dear, as you may have observed— but to flee. Like you, I believe now that the trick has failed. However, just in case the killer is more nervous or more stupid than we believe, I want you here to observe whether anyone leaves the house."

We had been pacing slowly around the courtyard as we spoke. Now we reached the door of our room; Emerson opened it, shoved me in, and enveloped me in a bruising embrace.

"Sleep well, my darling Peabody. Dream of me."

I flung my arms around his neck. "My dearest husband, guard your precious life. I would not attempt to keep you from your duty, but remember that if you fall—"

Emerson pushed me away. "Curse it, Peabody, how dare you make fun of me? I hope you fall over a chair and sprain your ankle."

And with this tender farewell he left me, cursing under his breath.

I addressed the cat Bastet, whose sleek form I had seen outlined against the open window.

"He deserved that," I said. "I am inclined to agree with you, Bastet; cats are much more sensible than people."

III

Bastet and I kept watch together while the hands of my little pocket watch crept on toward midnight. I was flattered that the cat stayed with me; always before she had seemed to prefer Emerson. No doubt her keen intelligence told her that the truest friend is not always the one who offers chicken.

I had not been deceived for a moment by Emerson's glib excuses. He did hope the murderer would believe his lies about messages and decisive clues; he expected to be attacked that very night. The more I thought about it, the more uneasy I became. A sensible murderer (if there is such a thing) would not have been fooled for a moment by Emerson's playacting. But if my theory was correct the murderer was stupid enough, and desperate enough, to react as Emerson had planned.

After I put on my working costume I blackened my face and hands with soot from the lamp and removed every touch of white from my attire. Opening my door a crack, I ascertained that the watchman was on duty in the courtyard. I could not see anyone outside the window. When midnight finally came I left the cat sleeping quietly on my bed and slipped out the window.

The moon was gibbous, but it gave too strong a light for my purposes. I would rather have walked unseen under heavy clouds. Despite the cool of the night air I was perspiring by the time I reached the cliff that overlooked the Valley.

Below me the abode of the dead lay at peace under the light of Egypt's eternal moon. The fence around the tomb obstructed my view until I was quite near. I had not expected to hear sounds of revelry, so the dead silence that enveloped the place was not in itself alarming, nor was the fact that I saw no glow from the lantern Emerson usually kept burning. He might have left it unlit in the hope of luring the killer close. Yet the now only too familiar grue of apprehension chilled my limbs as I glided on.

I approached the barrier cautiously. I did not want to be mistaken for the criminal and knocked down by my own husband. My approach was certainly not noiseless, for the stony ground was littered with pebbles and gravel that crunched underfoot. Reaching the fence, I peered through the gap between two stakes.

"Emerson," I whispered. "Don't shoot; it is I."

No voice replied. Not the slightest sound broke the uncanny stillness. The enclosed space was like a badly focused photograph, crisscrossed by the shadows of the fence stakes and blurred by the shapes of boulders and miscellaneous objects. Instinct told me the truth even before my straining eyes made out a huddled, darker shape beside the stairwell. Abandoning caution, I ran forward and flung myself down beside it. My groping hands found creased fabric, thick tumbled hair, and features whose shape would have been familiar to me in the darkest night.

"Emerson," I gasped. "Speak to me! Oh, heavens, I am too late. Why did I wait so long? Why did—"

The motionless body was suddenly galvanized into life. I was seized—throttled—muffled—pulled down to the ground with a force that left me breathless—enclosed in an embrace that held the ferocity of a deadly enemy instead of the affection of a spouse.

"Curse you, Amelia," Emerson hissed. "If you have frightened my quarry away I will never speak to you again. What the devil are you doing here?"

Being unable to articulate, I gurgled as meaningfully as I could. Emerson freed my mouth. "Softly," he whispered.

"How dare you frighten me so?" I demanded.

"How did you . . . Never mind; get back out of sight, with O'Connell, while I resume my position. I was pretending to be asleep."

"You *were* asleep."

"I may have dozed off for a moment. . . . No more talk. Retire to the hut where O'Connell—"

"Emerson—where is Mr. O'Connell? This encounter has not been exactly silent; should he not have rushed to your assistance by this time?"

"Hmmm," said Emerson.

We found the journalist behind a boulder on the hillside. He was breathing deeply and regularly. He did not stir, even when Emerson shook him.

"Drugged," I said softly. "This is a most alarming development, Emerson."

"Alarming but hopeful," was the reply, in tones as soft as Emerson could make them. "It confirms my theory. Stay here out of sight, Peabody, and for heaven's sake don't give the alarm too soon. Wait till I actually have my hands on the wretch."

"But, Emerson—"

"No more. I only hope our animated discussion has gone unheard."

"Wait, Emerson—"

He was gone. I sat down beside the boulder. To pursue him and insist on being heard was to risk the failure of our scheme; and besides, the information I had meant to give him was no longer pertinent. Or was it? Chewing on my lip, I tried to sort out my thoughts. O'Connell had been drugged. No doubt Emerson's coffee, which I had drunk, had also been doctored. Fearing such an eventuality, I had drunk Emerson's coffee, and rid myself of it. Yet when I came upon him just now he had been sound asleep. I could not have mistaken pretense for reality. I had felt the limpness of his body, and if he had only been feigning sleep he would have heard my whispers. He had drunk *my* coffee. Or had someone else exchanged cups with him? I felt as if my head were spinning like a top.

A soft glow of artificial light roused me from my disquieting thoughts. Emerson had lit the lantern. I approved this decision; if my reasoning was correct, the murderer would expect to find him drugged and helpless, and the lamplight would enable this prostrate condition to be observed more readily. I only wished I could be certain he was free of the influence of some drug. I took a deep breath and clenched my hands. It did not matter. I was on the job. I had my knife, my gun, my parasol; I had the resolve of duty and affection to strengthen every sinew. I told myself that Emerson could not have been in better hands than mine.

I told myself that; but as time wore on I began to doubt my own assurances—not because I had lost faith in my abilities, but because I stood to lose so much if, by some unexpected mischance, I should fail to act in time. Emerson had seated himself on the ground by the stairs, his back against a rock, his pipe in his mouth. After smoking for a while he knocked out the pipe and sat motionless. Gradually his head drooped forward. The pipe fell from his lax hand. Shoulders bowed, chin on his breast, he slept—or was he pretending to sleep? A breeze ruffled his dark hair. I beheld his unmoving form with mounting apprehension. I was at least ten yards away. Could I reach him in time, if action proved necessary? Beside me, Mr. O'Connell rolled over and began to snore. I was tempted to kick him, even though I knew his comatose condition was not his fault.

The night was far advanced before the first betraying sound reached my ear. It was only the soft click of a pebble striking stone, and it might have been made by a wandering animal; but it brought me upright, with every sense alert. Yet I almost missed the first sign of movement. It came from behind the fence, outside the circle of light.

I had known what to expect; but as the shadowy shape emerged cautiously into view, I caught my breath. Muffled from head to foot in clinging muslin that covered even its face, it reminded me of the first appearance of Ayesha, the immortal woman or goddess, in Mr. Haggard's thrilling romance *She*. Ayesha veiled her face and form because her dazzling beauty drove men mad; this apparition's disguise had a darker purpose, but it conveyed the same sense of awe and terror. No wonder the persons who had seen it had taken it for a demon of the night or the spirit of an ancient queen.

It stood poised, as if prepared for instant flight. The night wind lifted its draperies like the wings of a great white moth. So strong was my desire to rush at it that I sank my teeth in my lower lip and tasted the saltiness of blood. I had to wait. There were too many hiding places in the nearby cliffs. If it escaped us now, we might never bring it to justice.

Almost I waited too long; for when the figure finally moved it did so with such speed that I was caught unawares. Rushing forward, it bent over Emerson, one hand raised.

It was apparent by this time that Emerson really had dozed off and was not mimicking sleep. Naturally I would have cried out if the danger had been imminent; but seeing the ghostly figure, I knew all. My theories had been right, from start to finish. Knowing the method of attack, I knew it required a certain delicacy and deliberation of execution. I had plenty of time. Triumph soared within me as I rose slowly to my feet.

As soon as I put my weight on it, my left ankle gave way, tingling with the pain of returning circulation. The crash of my fall, I am sorry to say, was quite loud.

By the time I had recovered myself, the white form was in rapid retreat. Emerson had tumbled over onto his side and was stirring feebly, like an overturned beetle. I heard his bewildered curses as I staggered past him, leaning on my parasol for support.

A woman in less excellent physical condition might have continued to stagger till all was lost; but my blood vessels and muscles are as well trained as the rest of me. Strength returned to my limbs as I progressed. The white apparition was still visible, some distance ahead, when I broke into my famous racing form, arms swinging, head high. Nor did I scruple to make the echoes ring with my demands for assistance from anyone who might be listening.

"Help! *Au secours! Zu Hilfe!* Stop thief," accompanied my progress, and I daresay these cries had an effect on the person I pursued. There was no escape for it, but it continued to run until I brought my parasol down on its head with all the strength I could muster. Even then, as it lay supine, it reached out with clawed hands for the object it had dropped in its fall. I put my foot firmly on the weapon—a long, sharp hatpin. With my parasol at the ready, I looked down on the haggard, no longer beautiful face that glared up at me with Gorgonlike ferocity.

"It is no use, Lady Baskerville," I said. "You are fairly caught. You should have known when we first met that you were no match for me."

Chapter Seventeen

EMERSON was unreasonably annoyed with me for what he called my unwarranted interference. I pointed out to him that if I had not interfered he would have moved on to a better, but probably less interesting, world. Unable to deny this, but reluctant to admit it, he changed the subject.

We made a little ceremony of opening the envelopes to which we had earlier committed our deductions as to the identity of the murderer. I suggested we do this publicly. Emerson agreed so readily that I knew he had either guessed correctly or been able to substitute a new envelope for the original.

We held our conference in Arthur's room. Though still very weak, he was out of danger, and I felt his recovery would be hastened if he knew he was no longer under suspicion of murder.

Everyone was there except Mr. Vandergelt, who had felt duty-bound to accompany Lady Baskerville to Luxor, where, I had no doubt, she was proving a considerable embarrassment to the authorities. They seldom had a criminal of such exalted social status, and a woman to boot. I only hoped they would not let her escape out of sheer embarrassment.

After Emerson and I had opened our envelopes and displayed the two slips of paper, each bearing the name of Lady Baskerville, Mary exclaimed, "You amaze me, Amelia—and you too, of course, Professor. Though I cannot say I admired her ladyship, it would never have occurred to me that she could be guilty."

"It was obvious to an analytical mind," I replied. "Lady Baskerville was shrewd and vicious but not really intelligent. She committed one error after another."

"Such as asking the Professor to take command of the expedition," Karl said. "She ought to have known a man so brilliant, so distinguished—"

"No, that was one of her more intelligent actions," Emerson said. "The work would have been carried on, with or without her approval. His late lordship's will specifically directed that it be done. She had a role as a devoted widow to play; and at the time she approached us she took it for granted that the matter was ended. Armadale, she hoped, would either die in the desert or flee the country.

She underestimated his stamina and the depth of his passion; but, though she was not very intelligent, she knew how to act promptly and decisively when action was necessary."

"And," I added, "the idea of disguising herself as a lady in white was one of her brighter notions. The veils were so voluminous that there was no way of identifying the figure; it might even have been that of a man. Also, its ghostly appearance made some of those who saw it reluctant to approach it. Lady Baskerville made good use of the white lady by pretending to see it herself the night Emerson was so nearly hit by the stone head. It was, of course, Habib who threw the stone. Other indications, such as Lady Baskerville's preference for an inefficient and timid Egyptian servant, were highly suspicious. I have no doubt that Atiyah observed a number of things that a sharper attendant would have understood, and perhaps reported to me."

I would have gone on had not O'Connell interrupted me.

"Just a minute, ma'am. All this is very interesting but, if you will pardon me, it is the sort of thing anyone might see, after the fact. I need more details, not only for my editor, but to satisfy my own curiosity."

"You already know the details of one incident in the case, though you may not care to describe them to your readers," I said meaningfully.

Mr. O'Connell blushed fiery red, so that his face almost matched his hair. He had confessed to me in private that he had been responsible for the knife in the wardrobe. He had bribed a hotel servant to place an elaborate, ornamented knife—of the sort that is made for the tourist trade—in a prominent place in our room. His inefficient and underpaid ally had replaced the expensive trinket with a cheaper weapon and put it in the wrong place.

Seeing the journalist's blushes, I said no more. In the last few days he had earned my goodwill, and besides, he was due for a comeuppance if my suspicions about Mary and Arthur were correct.

"Yes, well, let us proceed," said O'Connell, gazing intently at his notebook. "How did you—and Professor Emerson, of course—arrive at the truth?"

I had decided I had better hear what Emerson had to say before I committed myself. I therefore remained silent and allowed him to begin.

"It was evident from the first that Lady Baskerville had the best opportunity to dispose of her husband. It is a truism in police science—"

"I can only allow you ten minutes, Emerson," I interjected. "We must not tire Arthur."

"Humph," said Emerson. "You tell it, then, since you consider my narrative style too verbose."

"I'll just ask questions, if you permit," said Mr. O'Connell, looking amused. "That will save time. I am trained, you know, to a terse journalistic style."

"Terse" was not the word I would have used; but I saw no reason to interfere with the procedure he suggested.

"You have mentioned opportunity," he said. "What about motive? Professor?"

"It is a truism in police science," said Emerson stubbornly, "that a victim's heirs are the primary suspects. Though I was unaware of the stipulations of the late Lord Baskerville's will, I assumed his wife stood to inherit something. But I suspected an even stronger motive. The archaeological world is small. Like all small communities, it is prone to gossip. Lady Baskerville's reputation for—er—let me think how to put it . . ."

"Extramarital carrying on," I said. "I could have told you that."

"How?" Emerson demanded.

"I knew it the moment I set eyes on her. She was that sort of woman."

"So," Mr. O'Connell intervened, as Emerson's face reddened, "you inquired about the lady's reputation, Professor?"

"Precisely. I had been out of touch for several years. I spoke with acquaintances in Luxor and sent off a few telegrams to Cairo, to ascertain whether she had continued her old habits. The replies confirmed my suspicions. I concluded that Lord Baskerville had learned of her affairs—the husband is always the last to know—and had threatened her with divorce, disgrace, and destitution."

In reality, he had discovered these facts only that morning, when Lady Baskerville broke down and confessed all. I wondered how many other facets of that most interesting confession would turn up, in the form of deductions, as he went along.

"So she killed her husband in order to preserve her good name?" Mary asked incredulously.

"To preserve her luxurious style of living," I said, before Emerson could reply. "She had designs on Mr. Vandergelt. He would never have married a divorced woman—you know how puritanical these Americans are—but as an unhappy widow she did not doubt she could capture him."

"Good," said Mr. O'Connell, scribbling rapidly. "Now, Mrs. E., it is your turn. What clue gave away the murderer's identity to you?"

"Arthur's bed," I replied.

Mr. O'Connell chuckled. "Wonderful! It is almost as deliciously enigmatic as one of Mr. Sherlock Holmes's clues. Elucidate, please, ma'am."

"The evening we found our friend here so near his end," I said, with a nod at Arthur, "his room was in disorder. Lady Baskerville had tossed his belongings around in order to suggest a hasty flight. She had, however—"

"Forgotten to take his shaving tackle," Emerson interrupted. "I knew then that the murderer must be a woman. No man would overlook such an obvious—"

"And," I said, raising my voice, "no man could have made Arthur's bed so neatly. Remember, he was resting on it when he was attacked. The killer had to remake the bed so that the counterpane hung all the way down to the floor and concealed his unconscious form. The longer the delay, the more difficult it would have been for innocent persons to establish an alibi. Those neat hospital corners were a dead giveaway."

"Good, good," crooned Mr. O'Connell, scribbling. "But how did she commit the crime, Mrs. E.? That is the most baffling thing of all."

"With a hat pin," I replied.

Exclamations of astonishment followed. "Yes," I went on. "I confess that I puzzled over that for a long time. Not until yesterday afternoon, when Lady Baskerville was trying on her trousseau, did I realize how deadly a hat pin can be. Lady Baskerville had been a nurse, and she had known—er—been acquainted with—medical students and doctors. A sharpened steel needle inserted into the base of the brain will penetrate the spinal column and kill the victim instantly. A small puncture, hidden by the victim's hair, would not be observed; or, if it was, it would be taken for an insect bite. She killed Mr. Armadale the same way."

"But why Armadale?" O'Connell asked keenly, his pencil poised. "Did he suspect her?"

"Quite the contrary," I replied. (My breath control is much better than Emerson's; I could start speaking while he was still inhaling.) "Mr. Armadale thought *he* had killed Lord Baskerville."

A gratifying burst of surprised exclamations interrupted me.

"It is only conjecture, of course," I said modestly, "but it is the only explanation that fits all the facts. Lady Baskerville had cold-bloodedly seduced Mr. Armadale. Mary noticed that he was distracted and depressed for several weeks preceding Lord Baskerville's death. More significantly, he did not renew his offer of marriage. He had found another love, and the torment of knowing he had betrayed his patron was tearing him apart. Lady Baskerville pretended to feel the same. She informed Armadale that she intended to tell her husband the truth and, professing fear of his reaction, asked the young man to wait in her room while the confrontation took place. Not unnaturally her husband began to shout at her. She screamed; Armadale rushed in and struck the enraged husband, thinking he was protecting his mistress. As soon as Lord Baskerville fell, his wife bent over him and cried, 'You have killed him!' "

"And Armadale believed her?" O'Connell asked skeptically. "My readers are going to love this, Mrs. E., but it's a little hard to swallow."

"He loved her," Arthur said weakly. "You don't understand true love, Mr. O'Connell."

I reached for Arthur's wrist. "You are flushed," I said. "You are becoming overexcited. We had better adjourn."

"No, no." The sick man took hold of my hand. His golden beard had been neatly trimmed and his hair arranged. His pallor and emaciation made him handsomer than ever, like a young Keats (except, of course, that the poet was dark).

"You can't leave the story unfinished," Arthur went on. "Why did she attack me?"

"Yes, why?" Emerson said, catching me off guard this time. "I'll warrant even my omniscient wife does not know that."

"Do you?" I inquired.

"No. It makes no sense. Arthur never saw her; she entered his room while he was asleep, and why she did not use the handy hat pin on him—"

"She had to render him unconscious first," I explained. "The insertion of the needle into the pertinent spot requires some dexterity; it cannot be done while the victim is awake and capable of resistance. Once she had struck him, she believed him to be dead. Perhaps, also, she was afraid of being interrupted. In Arthur's case she had to act during the daylight hours. Something may have startled her, and she had only time to hide him under the bed. The question is, why did she feel it necessary to silence you, Arthur? If someone had become suspicious of how Lord Baskerville died, you were the obvious suspect. Your naive folly in telling no one of your identity—"

"But I did tell someone," Arthur said innocently. "I told Lady Baskerville, barely a week after I came here."

I exchanged glances with Emerson. He nodded. "So that was it," he said. "You did not mention that to my wife, when you bared your soul to her."

The young man flushed. "It hardly seemed cricket. Mrs. Emerson had told me in no uncertain terms what she thought of my stupidity. To admit that Lady Baskerville had encouraged me to retain my anonymity would be to accuse her . . ." He broke off, looking startled. Handsome Arthur Baskerville might be; wealthy and endowed with all the good things of this world. Outstandingly intelligent he was not.

"Hold on now." O'Connell's pencil had been racing across the page. He now looked up. "This is all good stuff, but you are not following the right order. Let's go back to the murder of Armadale. I presume that she persuaded the poor booby to flee after Baskerville collapsed and then did his lordship in with her hat pin. Hey—wait a minute. No one mentioned a bruise on Baskerville's face—"

"Dr. Dubois would not notice if the man's throat had been cut," I said. "But, to do him justice, he was looking for the cause of death, not a slight swelling on the jaw or chin. Lord Baskerville seems to have been astonishingly prone to self-mutilation. He probably had many bruises, cuts, and scrapes."

"Good." O'Connell wrote this down. "So Armadale ran away—disguised himself as a native, I suppose, and hid in the hills. I am surprised he didn't flee the country."

"And leave his mistress behind?" I countered. "I doubt that the young man's mental state was quite normal. The horror of what he thought he had done was enough to turn his brain and render him incapable of decisive action of any kind. If he *had* wanted to confess, he would have been deterred by the knowledge that by doing so he must incriminate the woman he loved, as an accessory after the fact. But when Lady Baskerville returned he could bear it no longer. He came to her window at night and was seen by Hassan. That foolish man tried to blackmail Lady Baskerville—for of course he had seen which window Armadale approached. She disposed of both of them the next night, Armadale at the cave, where he had told her to meet him, and Hassan on the way back, when he intercepted her. I am not surprised that she appeared so exhausted next day."

"But what about—"

"No more at the present time," I said, rising. "Arthur has had all the excitement he ought to have. Mary, will you stay with him and make sure he rests? As soon as the good Sister finishes her well-deserved nap, I will send her to relieve you."

As we left the room, I saw Arthur reach for Mary's hand. Mary blushed and lowered her lashes. I had arranged that matter as well as I could, they must do the rest. Avoiding Mr. O'Connell's reproachful glance, I led the way to the sitting room.

"There are a few more loose ends to tie up," I said, taking a chair. "I did not want Mary to hear us discuss her mother's death."

"Quite correct," said Karl approvingly. "I thank you, Frau Professor, for—"

"That is all right, Karl," I said, wondering why he was thanking me, but not really caring very much.

Before I could continue, the door opened to admit Mr. Vandergelt. He gave the impression of having shrunk several inches since the day before. No one knew what to say, until Emerson, rising to the sublime heights of which he is sometimes capable, uttered the mot juste.

"Vandergelt, have a drink!"

"You're a real pal, Professor," the American said with a long sigh. "I think maybe I will."

"Did she send you away, Mr. Vandergelt?" I inquired sympathetically.

"With language that would make a mule-skinner blush," was the reply. "She sure enough took me in. I guess you think I'm a blamed silly old fool."

"You were not the only one to be deceived," I assured him.

"*Aber nein,*" Karl exclaimed. "I had for her always the most respectful, most—"

"That is why I refused your offer to stand guard with me last night," said Emerson, from the table where he was pouring whiskey for the afflicted Vandergelt. "Your respect for the lady might have prevented you from acting, if only for a split second; and even that brief time could have meant the difference between life and death."

"And naturally you turned *me* down," said Vandergelt gloomily. "I tell you, Professor, I'd have been too flabbergasted to move if I had seen her."

Emerson handed him the glass and he nodded his thanks before continuing. "You know that confounded woman expected me to marry her after all? She
started cursing at me when I said I had to respectfully decline. I felt like a rat, but,
gee whiz, folks, marrying a woman who has already murdered one husband just
isn't sensible. A fellow would always be wondering if his morning coffee tasted
peculiar."

"It would also be impractical to wait twenty or thirty years before enjoying
the pleasures of connubial bliss," I said. "Cheer up, Mr. Vandergelt; time will heal
your wound, and I know happiness awaits you in the future."

My well-chosen words lifted a little of the gloom from the American's
countenance. He raised his glass in a graceful salute to me.

"I was just about to discuss the death of Madame Berengeria," I went on.
"Will it pain you too much to hear . . ."

"One more whiskey and it wouldn't pain me to hear that Amalgamated
Railroads had fallen twenty points," Mr. Vandergelt replied. He handed his empty
glass to Emerson. "Join me in the next round, won't you, Professor?"

"I believe I will," Emerson replied, with an evil look at me. "We will
drink, Vandergelt, to the perfidy of the female sex."

"I will join you both," I said gaily. "Emerson, your jests are sometimes
a bit ill-timed. Mr. O'Connell is sitting on the edge of his chair, his pencil poised;
explain in your own inimitable fashion the meaning of the little fairy tale we
discussed last evening, and why that seemingly harmless story caused a murder."

"Ahem," said Emerson. "Well, if you insist, Peabody."

"I do. In fact, I will be barmaid and wait on you both." I took Vandergelt's empty glass from his hand. Emerson gave me a sheepish smile. He is
pathetically easy to manage, poor man. The slightest kind gesture quite softens
him.

"May I impose on your good nature too, ma'am?" O'Connell asked.

"Certainly," I replied graciously. "But none of your brash Irish gestures
at the barmaid, Mr. O'Connell."

This little sally completed the atmosphere of good humor I was endeavoring to create. As I served the gentlemen—including Karl, who thanked me with
a smile—Emerson took the floor.

"Lady Berengeria's death was in its way a masterpiece of tragic irony, for
the poor stupid woman did not have the slightest intention of accusing Lady
Baskerville of murder. Like all the good ladies of Luxor, who, in their infinite
Christian charity spend most of their time dissecting their fellow women, she knew
Lady Baskerville's reputation. 'The Tale of the Two Brothers' was a slam at an
adulteress, not a murderess. And it could not have been more apt. The heart in the
cedar tree is the heart of a lover—vulnerable, exposed, trusting in the love of the
beloved. If the object of adoration proves false the lover has no defense. Lord
Baskerville trusted his wife. Even when he had ceased to love her he did not think
of defending himself against her. It is a tribute to some long-buried streak of

intelligence and sensitivity in Madame Berengeria that she sensed the meaning of the metaphor. Who knows what she might have been, if the vicissitudes of life had not proved too great for her will?"

I gazed at my husband with tears of affection dimming my sight. How often is Emerson misjudged by those who do not know him! How tender, how delicate are the feelings he conceals beneath a mask of ferocity!

Unaware of my sentiments, Emerson took a stiff drink of whiskey and resumed, in a more practical vein. "The first part of the story of the Two Brothers concerns a faithless wife who turns one man against another by her lies. Think of that story, gentlemen and Peabody, in terms of our tragic triangle. Again, the metaphor was apt; and Lady Baskerville's guilty conscience led her to choose the wrong reference. She thought herself in danger of exposure—and it was so easy to slip a fatal dose of opium into Madame Berengeria's bottle of brandy. What was one more murder? She had already committed three. And what was the death of one dreadful old woman? A blessing in disguise, really."

Silence followed the conclusion of his remarks. Then he addressed Mr. O'Connell, whose pencil had been racing across the page. "Any questions?" he said.

"Wait, just let me get the last part. 'What was the death of one dreadful . . .' "

"Old woman," Emerson supplied.

"Silly old fool," Mr. Vandergelt muttered, staring into his empty glass.

The door opened and Mary entered.

"He is asleep," she said, smiling at me. "I am so happy for him. He will so enjoy being Lord Baskerville."

"And I am happy for you," I replied, with a meaningful look.

"But how did you know?" Mary exclaimed, blushing prettily. "We have not told anyone yet."

"I always know these things," I began.

Fortunately I said no more; for even as I spoke Karl von Bork crossed to Mary's side. He put his arm around her and she leaned against him, her flush deepening into a rosy glow.

"We have you to thank, Frau Professor," he said, his mustaches positively curling in the ardor of his happiness. "It is not proper to speak of this so soon after the unhappy, the unfortunate occurrence we have been discussing; but my dear Mary is quite alone in the world now, and she needs me. I have confidence that you will be to her a true friend until comes the blissful time when I can take her to the place which is—"

"What?" Emerson exclaimed, staring.

"Begorrah!" cried Mr. O'Connell, flinging his pencil across the room.

"Silly old fool," said Mr. Vandergelt to his empty glass.

"My very best wishes to both of you," I said. "Of course I knew it all along."

II

"Has it occurred to you," Emerson inquired, "that you have quite a number of acquaintances in prisons around the world?"

I considered the question. "Why, really, I can only think of two—no, three, since Evelyn's cousin was apprehended last year in Budapest. That is not a great number."

Emerson chuckled. He was in an excellent mood, and with good reason. The surroundings, the state of his career, the prospects before us—all were conducive to the most unexampled good spirits.

Two and a half months had passed since the events I have narrated, and we were on our way home. We were sitting on the deck of the steamer *Rembrandt;* the sun shone down and the white-capped waves curled away from the prow as the boat plunged rapidly toward Marseilles. The rest of the passengers were huddled at the farthest end of the boat (I can never remember whether it is the poop or the stern). Whatever it was, they were there, leaving us strictly alone. I had no objection to the privacy thus obtained, though I failed to understand their objections to our mummies. The poor things were dead, after all.

They were also very damp. That is why Emerson carried them out on deck every day to let them dry out. They lay in their brightly painted coffins staring serenely up at the sun, and I have no doubt they felt quite comfortable; for was not the sun-god the supreme deity they once worshiped? Ra Harakhte was performing his last service for his devotees, enabling them to survive for a few more centuries in the solemn halls of a modern temple of learning—a museum.

Our tomb had proved a disappointment after all. It had once been a royal sepulcher, there was no doubt of that; the design and the decorations were too grand for a commoner. But the original inhabitant had been anathema to someone; his name and portrait had been viciously hacked to bits wherever they appeared, and his mummy and funerary equipment had long since vanished. Some enterprising priest of a later dynasty had used the tomb for his own familial burial ground. Still later, the ceiling had collapsed and water had gotten into the burial chamber. We had found the remains of no less than ten mummies, all more or less battered, all more or less equipped with jewelry and amulets. M. Grebaut had been generous in his division of the spoils, giving Emerson the nastiest and most water-logged of the mummies. So the Chantress of Amon, Sat-Hathor, and the First Prophet of Min, Ahmose, enjoyed a few last days in the sun.

Karl and Mary had spoken their vows the day before we left Luxor. I had been matron of honor, and Emerson had given the bride away, with Mr. Vandergelt acting as best man. Mr. O'Connell had not been present. I had no fear for his broken heart, however; he was too dedicated a newsman to make a good husband. His account of the wedding had appeared in the Cairo newspaper and had been more notable for sensationalism—the last chapter of the Curse of the Pharaoh—than for spite.

As I remarked to Emerson at the time, there is nothing like a hobby to take a person's mind off personal troubles. Mr. Vandergelt was a good example of this, although I did not think his attraction to Lady Baskerville had ever been more than superficial. He had applied to the Department of Antiquities for Lord Baskerville's concession and was eagerly planning a new season of digging.

"Are you going to accept Mr. Vandergelt's offer of a position as chief archaeologist next season?" I asked.

Emerson, lying back in his chair with his hat over his eyes, simply grunted. I tried a new approach. "Arthur—Lord Baskerville—has invited us to stay with him this summer. He will soon find a substitute for his lost love; a young man with his personal and financial attractions can take his pick of young ladies. But Mary was quite right not to accept him. Luxor is home to her, and she is deeply interested in Egyptology. She is far more intelligent than Arthur; such a match would never work out. I liked Arthur's mother, though. I was quite moved when she kissed my hand and wept and thanked me for saving her boy."

"Shows what a fool the woman is," Emerson said from under his hat. "Your carelessness almost killed the young man. If you had only thought to ask him—"

"What about you? I never asked you this before, Emerson, but confess, now that we are alone; you did not know the guilty party was Lady Baskerville until the last night. All that nonsense about clues and deductions was drawn from her confession. If you had known, you would not have been so careless as to allow her to drop laudanum into your cup of coffee."

Emerson sat up and pushed his hat back. "I admit that was an error in judgment. But how the devil was I to know that her maidservant was an opium addict and that her ladyship had obtained supplies of the drug from Atiyah? You say you knew; you might have warned me, you know."

"No one could possibly have anticipated that," I said, back-tracking with my usual skill. "It is ironic, is it not? If Atiyah had not been an addict, she would probably have made an addition to the long list of Lady Baskerville's victims. Though she saw the lady several times on her nocturnal journeys, she was too befuddled by the drug to realize what she was seeing. Nor would she have been a convincing witness."

"When it comes to that," said Emerson, now thoroughly aroused, and on the defensive, "how did you come to suspect Lady Baskerville? And don't tell me it was intuition."

"I told you before. It was Arthur's bed. Besides," I added, "it was not difficult for me to understand why a woman might be driven to murder her husband."

"Vice versa, Peabody, vice versa." Emerson slid down into a semirecumbent position and pushed his hat over his eyes.

"There is one other point I never raised with you," I said.

"And what is that?"

"You," I said, "were overcome with sleepiness that last night. Don't deny it; you were stumbling and muttering for hours afterward. If I had not tied Lady Baskerville up with her own veils, she would have escaped. What did you put in my coffee, Emerson?"

"I never heard such nonsense," Emerson mumbled.

"You drank my coffee," I continued remorselessly. "Unlike you, I suspected Lady Baskerville might take steps to ensure that you would be asleep and helpless that night. I therefore drank the poison myself, like . . . well, like a number of heroines I have read about. So, my dear Emerson—what was in *my* coffee, and who put it there?"

Emerson was silent. I waited, having discovered that cold forbearance is more effective than accusations in loosening a witness's tongue.

"It was your own fault," Emerson said at last.

"Oh?"

"If you would stay peacefully at home, like a sensible woman, when you are told to—"

"So you put opium in my coffee. Lady Baskerville put it in yours, and in Mr. O'Connell's, after you had chosen him to accompany you. Really," I said, in some vexation, "the affair is positively farcical. Emerson, your carelessness astonishes me. What if Lady Baskerville had wished to render *me* hors de combat too? Your little contribution, which I presume you obtained from my medical chest, added to hers, would have put an end to my nocturnal activities permanently."

Emerson leaped to his feet. His hat, lifted from his head by the vigor of his movement, floated around for a few seconds and then dropped onto the head of Sat Hathor, the Chantress of Amon. It was a rather amusing sight, but I had no impulse to laugh. Poor Emerson's face had gone white under his deep tan. Careless of the watchers on the lower deck he lifted me up out of my chair and crushed me to him.

"Peabody," he exclaimed, in a voice hoarse with emotion, "I am the stupidest idiot in creation. My blood runs cold when I think . . . Can you forgive me?"

I forgave him, with gestures instead of words. After a long embrace he released me.

"In fact," he said, "we should call it a draw. You tried to shoot me, I tried to poison you. As I said before, Peabody, we are well matched."

It was impossible to resist him. I began to laugh, and after a moment Emerson's deep-throated chuckle blended with mine.

"What do you say we go down to the cabin?" he inquired. "The mummies will do very well alone for a while."

"Not just yet. Bastet was just waking when we came up; you know she will prowl and howl for some time before she resigns herself."

"I should never have brought that cat," Emerson growled. Then he brightened up. "But just think, Peabody, what a pair she and Ramses will make. Never a dull moment, eh?"

"It will toughen him up for next season," I agreed.

"Do you really think—"

"I really do. Good heavens, Emerson, Luxor is becoming known as a health resort. The boy will be better off there than in that nasty damp winter climate of England."

"No doubt you are right, Peabody."

"I always am. Where do you think we should excavate next winter?"

Emerson retrieved his hat from the Chantress of Amon and clapped it onto the back of his head. His face had the look I loved to see—baked as brown as a Nubian's by the Egyptian sun, his eyes narrowed speculatively, a half-smile on his lips.

"I fear the Valley is exhausted," he replied, stroking his chin. "There will be no more royal tombs found. But the Western Valley has possibilities. I will tell Vandergelt we ought to work there next season. And yet, Peabody . . ."

"Yes, my dear Emerson?"

Emerson took a turn around the deck, his hands clasped behind his back. "Do you remember the pectoral we found on the crushed body of the thief?"

"How could I forget it?"

"We read the cartouche as that of Tutankhamon."

"And decided that our tomb must have belonged to him. It is the only possible conclusion, Emerson."

"No doubt, no doubt. But, Peabody, consider the dimensions of the tomb. Would such a short-lived and ephemeral king have time enough and wealth enough to construct such a sepulchre?"

"You discussed that in your *Zeitschrift* article," I reminded him.

"I know. But I cannot help wondering . . . You don't suppose a gang of thieves would rob two tombs in the same night?"

"Not unless the said tombs were practically side by side," I said, laughing.

"Ha, ha." Emerson echoed my mirth. "Impossible, of course. That part of the Valley cannot contain any other tombs. All the same, Peabody, I have a strange feeling that I have missed something."

"Impossible, my dear Emerson."

"Quite, my dear Peabody."

The
Mummy
Case

This volume of memoirs
is respectfully dedicated to
Mary Morman,
a lady whose estimable qualities
(we venture to assert)
strongly resemble those of the author and editor.

Foreword

AFTER the death of the author of these memoirs (of which this is the third volume to appear), her heirs felt that her animated (if biased) descriptions of the early days of excavation in Egypt should not be kept from historians of that period. Since certain episodes involve matters that might embarrass the descendants of the participants therein (and possibly render publisher and editor subject to legal action), it was agreed that the memoirs should appear in the guise of fiction. A certain amount of judicious editing was done, and many of the names were changed, including that of Mrs. "Emerson." However, in recent years rumors have circulated regarding the accuracy of these works and the identity of their author—originated, we suspect, by disaffected members of Mrs. "Emerson's" family, who resent their exclusion from the financial proceeds (modest though they are) of the works in question. The editor therefore wishes to disclaim all responsibility for, first, the opinions expressed herein, which are those of the late lamented Mrs. "Emerson"; and second, certain minor errors of fact, which are due in part to Mrs. "Emerson's" faulty memory and in even larger part to her personal eccentricities and prejudices.

The editor also wishes to apologize for the stylistic peculiarities of this foreword, which seems to have been unconsciously influenced by the literary style of Mrs. "Emerson." She would no doubt be pleased at such a demonstration of the influence she continues to exert on those who were affected by it during her long and vigorous life.

Chapter One

I never meant to marry. In my opinion, a woman born in the last half of the nineteenth century of the Christian era suffered from enough disadvantages without willfully embracing another. That is not to say that I did not occasionally indulge in daydreams of romantic encounters; for I was as sensible as any other female of the visible attractions of the opposite sex. But I never expected to meet a man who was my match, and I had no more desire to dominate a spouse than to be ruled by him. Marriage, in my view, should be a balanced stalemate between equal adversaries.

I had resigned myself to a life of spinsterhood when, at a somewhat advanced age, I met Radcliffe Emerson. Our first encounter was *not* romantic. Never will I forget my initial sight of Emerson, as we stood face to face in that dismal hall of the Boulaq Museum—his black beard bristling, his blue eyes blazing, his fists clenched, his deep baritone voice bellowing invectives at me for dusting off the antiquities. Yet even as I answered his criticism in kind, I knew in my heart that our lives would be intertwined.

I had several logical, sensible reasons for accepting Emerson's offer of marriage. Emerson was an Egyptologist; and my first visit to the realm of the pharaohs planted seeds of affection for that antique land that were soon to blossom into luxuriant flower. Emerson's keen intelligence and acerbic tongue—which had won him the title "Father of Curses" from his devoted Egyptian workmen—made him a foeman worthy of my steel. And yet, dear Reader, these were not my real reasons for yielding to Emerson's suit. I deplore clichés, but in this case I must resort to one. Emerson swept me off my feet. I am determined to be completely candid as I pen these pages, for I have made certain they will not be published, at least during my lifetime. They began as a personal Journal, perused only by a Critic whose intimate relationship gave him access to my private thoughts—so he claimed at any rate; as his remarks on the style and content of my writing became more critical, I decided to disallow the claim and lock up my Journals. They are therefore mine alone, and unless my heirs decide that the scholarly world should not be deprived of the insights contained therein (which may well occur), no eyes but mine will read these words.

Why, then, the gentle Reader will ask, do I infer his or her existence by addressing her, or him? The answer should be obvious. Art cannot exist in a vacuum. The creative spirit must possess an audience. It is impossible for a writer to do herself justice if she is only talking to herself.

Having established this important point, I return to my narrative.

Not only did Emerson sweep me off my feet, I swept him off his. (I speak figuratively, of course.) By current standards I am not beautiful. Fortunately for me, Emerson's tastes in this area, as in most others, are highly original. My complexion, which others find sallow and dark, he described (on one memorable occasion) as resembling the honey of Hymettus; my coarse, jet-black hair, which refuses to remain confined in braids, buns, or nets, arouses in him a peculiar variety of tactile enjoyment; and his remarks about my figure, which is unfashionably slender in some areas and overly endowed in others, cannot be reproduced, even here.

By any standards Emerson is a remarkably fine-looking man. He stands over six feet tall, and his stalwart frame possesses the elasticity and muscular development of youth, thanks to a vigorous outdoor life. Under the rays of the benevolent Egyptian sun his brawny arms and rugged face turn golden-brown, forming a striking setting for the sapphire brilliance of his eyes. The removal of his beard, at my urgent request, uncovered a particularly attractive dimple in his chin. Emerson prefers to call it a cleft, when he refers to the feature at all; but it is a dimple. His hair is sable, thick and soft, shining with Titian gleams in the sunlight. . . .

But enough of that. Suffice it to say that the wedded state proved highly agreeable, and the first years of our marriage were fully as pleasant as I had expected. We spent the winter in Egypt, excavating by day and sharing the delightful privacy of an (otherwise) unoccupied tomb by night; and the summer in England with Emerson's brother Walter, a distinguished philologist, and the husband of my dear friend Evelyn. It was a thoroughly satisfactory existence. I cannot imagine why I, who am normally as farsighted and practical as a woman can be, did not realize that the matrimonial state quite often leads to another, related state. I refer, of course, to motherhood.

When the possibility of this interesting condition first manifested itself I was not excessively put out. According to my calculations, the child would be born in the summer, enabling me to finish the season's work and get the business over and done with before returning to the dig in the autumn. This proved to be the case, and we left the infant—a boy, named after his uncle Walter—in the care of that gentleman and his wife when we set out for Egypt in October.

What ensued was not entirely the child's fault. I had not anticipated that Emerson's next view of his son the following spring would induce a doting idiocy that manifested itself in baby talk, and in a reluctance to be parted from the creature. Ramses, as the child came to be called, merited his nickname; he was as imperious in his demands and as pervasive in his presence as that most arrogant of ancient Egyptian god-kings must have been. He was also alarmingly precocious. A lady of my acquaintance used that term to me, after Ramses, aged four, had treated her to a lecture on the proper method of excavating a compost heap—hers, in point of fact. (Her gardener was extremely abusive.) When I replied that in my opinion the adjective was ill-chosen, she believed me to be offended. What I meant was that the word was inadequate. "Catastrophically precocious" would have been nearer the mark.

Despite his devotion to the child, Emerson pined in the dreary climate of England. I refer not only to its meteorological climate, but to the sterile monotony of academic life to which my husband had been doomed by his decision to forgo his Egyptian excavations. He would not go to Egypt without Ramses, and he would not risk the boy's health in that germ-infested part of the world. Only an appeal from a lady in distress (who turned out to be, as I suspected from the first, a thoroughgoing villainess) drew him from Ramses' side; and, seeing him glow and expand among his beloved antiquities, I determined that never again would I allow him to sacrifice himself for family commitments.

We decided to take Ramses with us the following year, but a series of distressing events allowed me to postpone that pleasure. My dear friend and sister-in-law, Evelyn, who had produced four healthy children without apparent effort, suffered two successive disappointments (as she called them). The second miscarriage threw her into a state of deep depression. For some reason (possibly related to her confused mental condition) she found Ramses' company comforting and burst into tears when we proposed to take him away. Walter added his appeals, claiming that the boy's merry little tricks kept Evelyn from brooding. I could well believe that, because it required the concentrated attention of every adult in the household to restrain Ramses from self-immolation and a widespread destruction of property. We therefore yielded to the pleas of Ramses' aunt and uncle, I with gracious forbearance, Emerson with grudging reluctance.

When we returned from Egypt the following spring, Ramses seemed nicely settled at Chalfont, and I saw no reason to alter the arrangement. I knew, however, that this excellent situation (excellent for Evelyn, I mean, of course) could not endure forever. But I decided not to worry about it. "Sufficient unto the day," as the Scripture says.

The day duly arrived. It was during the third week in June. I was at work in the library trying to get Emerson's notes in order before he returned from London with the next installment. Some dark premonition undoubtedly brushed my mind; for though I am not easily distracted, particularly from a subject that enthralls me as much as Eighteenth Dynasty rock-cut tombs, I found myself sitting with idle hands, staring out at the garden. It was at its best that lovely summer afternoon; the roses were in bloom and my perennial borders were looking their loveliest. None of the plants had been trampled or dug up; the blossoms had been culled with tender deliberation by the expert in that trade, not torn out, roots and all, to make bouquets for the servants and the dogs; the smooth green turf was unmarked by small booted feet or the holes of amateur excavation. Never before had I seen it in that pristine condition. Ramses had begun walking a month after we moved into the house. A gentle nostalgia suffused me and I brooded in quietude until my meditation was interrupted by a knock on the door.

Our servants are trained to knock before entering. This custom confirms the suspicions of our county neighbors that we are uncouth eccentrics, but I see no reason why the well-to-do should lack the privacy poor people enjoy. When Emerson and I are working or when we are alone in our bedchamber we do not appreciate being interrupted. One knock is allowed. If there is no response, the servant goes quietly away.

"Come in," I called.

"It is a telegram, madam," said Wilkins, tottering toward me with a tray. Wilkins is perfectly hale and hearty, but he makes a point of tottering, in order not to be asked to do anything he doesn't want to do. I took the telegram, and again the wings of shadowy foreboding brushed my spirit. Wilkins quavered (he quavers for the same reason he totters), "I hope it is not bad news, madam."

I perused the telegram. "No," I said. "On the contrary, it appears to be good news. We will be leaving for Chalfont tomorrow, Wilkins. Make the arrangements, if you please."

"Yes, madam. I beg your pardon, madam . . ."

"Yes, Wilkins?"

"Will Master Ramses be returning home with you?"

"Possibly."

A shadow of some passionate emotion passed rapidly over Wilkins' face. It did not linger; Wilkins knows what is proper.

"That will be all, Wilkins," I said sympathetically.

"Yes, madam. Thank you, madam." He weaved an erratic path to the door.

With a last wistful look at my beautiful garden I returned to my labors. Emerson found me so engaged when he returned. Instead of giving me the affectionate embrace to which I was accustomed, he mumbled a greeting, flung a handful of papers at me, and seated himself at his desk, next to mine.

An ordinary, selfish spouse might have made a playful comment on his preoccupation and demanded her due in the form of non-verbal greetings. I glanced at the new notes and remarked temperately, "Your date for the pottery checks with Petrie's chart, then? That should save time in the final—"

"Not enough time," Emerson grunted, his pen driving furiously across the page. "We are badly behind schedule, Peabody. From now on we work day and night. No more strolls in the garden, no more social engagements until the manuscript is completed."

I hesitated to break the news that in all probability we would soon have with us a distraction far more time-consuming than social engagements or strolls. And, since most archaeologists consider themselves prompt if they publish the results of their work within ten years, if at all, I knew something must have happened to inspire this fiend-ridden haste. It was not difficult to surmise what that something was.

"You saw Mr. Petrie today?" I asked.

"Mmmp," said Emerson, writing.

"I suppose he is preparing his own publication."

Emerson threw his pen across the room. His eyes blazed. "He has finished it! It goes to the printer this week. Can you imagine such a thing?"

Petrie, the brilliant young excavator, was Emerson's bête noire. They had a great deal in common—their insistence on order and method in archaeology, their contempt for the lack of order and method displayed by all other archaeologists, and their habit of expressing that contempt publicly. Instead of making them friends, this unanimity had made them rivals. The custom of publishing within a year was unique to the two of them, and it had developed into an absurd competition—a demonstration of masculine superiority on an intellectual level. It was not only absurd, it was inefficient, resulting, at least in Petrie's case, in rather slipshod work.

I said as much, hoping this would comfort my afflicted husband. "He can't have done a good job in such a short time, Emerson. What is more important, the quality of the work or the date on which it is published?"

This reasonable attitude unaccountably failed to console Emerson. "They are equally important," he bellowed. "Where the devil is my pen? I must not waste an instant."

"You threw it against the wall. I doubt that we will be able to get the ink off that bust. Socrates looks as if he has measles."

"Your humor—if it can be called that—is singularly misplaced, Peabody. There is nothing funny about the situation."

I abandoned my attempts to cheer him. The news might as well be told.

"I had a telegram from Evelyn this afternoon," I said. "We must go to Chalfont at once."

The flush of temper drained from Emerson's face, leaving it white to the lips. Remorsefully I realized the effect of my ill-considered speech on a man who is the most affectionate of brothers and uncles and the most fatuous of fathers. "All is well," I cried. "It is good news, not bad. That is what Evelyn says." I picked up the telegram and read it aloud. " 'Wonderful news. Come and share it with us. We have not seen you for too long.' There, you see?"

Emerson's lips writhed as he struggled to find words in which to express his relief. Finally he shouted, "Amelia, you are the most tactless woman in the universe. What the devil ails you? You did that deliberately."

I pointed out the injustice of the charge, and we had a refreshing little discussion. Then Emerson mopped his brow, gave himself a shake, and remarked calmly, "Good news, eh? An honorary degree for Walter, perhaps. Or someone has endowed a chair of Egyptology for him."

"Foolish man," I said with a smile. "You are off the mark. My guess is that Evelyn is expecting again."

"Now that is ridiculous, Peabody. I have no strong objection to my brother and his wife continuing to produce offspring, but to call it wonderful news—"

"My sentiments are in accord with yours, Emerson. But neither of us wrote this telegram. You know Evelyn's feelings about children."

"True." Emerson reflected, pensively, on the peculiar opinions of Evelyn. Then his face became radiant. "Peabody! Do you realize what this means? If Evelyn has recovered from her melancholia, she will no longer require Ramses to keep her company. We can bring our boy home!"

"I had arrived at the same conclusion."

Emerson leaped up. I rose to meet him; he caught me in his arms and spun me around, laughing exultantly. "How I have missed the sound of his voice, the patter of his little feet! Reading to him from my *History of Ancient Egypt,* admiring the bones he digs up from the rose garden. . . . I have not complained, Peabody— you know I never complain—but I have been lonely for Ramses. This year we will take him with us. Won't it be wonderful, Peabody—we three, working together in Egypt?"

"Kiss, me, Emerson," I said faintly.

II

Our neighbors are not interesting people. We have little to do with them. Emerson has antagonized most of the gentlemen, who consider him a radical of the most pernicious sort, and I have not cultivated their ladies. They talk of nothing but their children, their husbands' success, and the faults of their servants. One of the favorite sub-topics under the last head is the rapidity with which the servants' hall becomes acquainted with the private affairs of the master and mistress. As Lady Bassington once declared, in my presence, "They are frightful gossips, you know. I suppose they have nothing better to do. By the by, my dear, have you heard the latest about Miss Harris and the groom?"

Our servants unquestionably knew more about our affairs than I would have liked, but I attributed this to Emerson's habit of shouting those affairs aloud, without regard for who might be listening. One of the footmen may have over- heard his cries of rapture at the prospect of being reunited with his child, or perhaps Wilkins had allowed himself to theorize. In any event, the word spread quickly. When I went up to change for dinner, Rose knew all about it.

Rose is the housemaid, but since I do not employ a personal servant, she acts in that capacity when I require assistance with my toilette. I had not called her that evening; yet I found her in my room, ostensibly mending a skirt I could not recall having ripped. After asking what she should pack for the journey to Chalfont, she said, "And while you are away, ma'am, shall I see that Master Ramses' room is got in order?"

"His room is in order," I replied. "I see no reason to do anything more, since it won't remain in order for five minutes after he occupies it."

"Then Master Ramses will be coming home, ma'am?" Rose asked with a smile.

Rose's fondness for Ramses is absolutely unaccountable. I cannot calculate how many cubic feet of mud she has scraped off carpets and walls and furniture as a result of his activities, and mud is the least disgusting of the effluvia Ramses trails in his wake. I replied, rather shortly, that the day and hour of Ramses' return was as yet mere speculation, and that if any action on her part was necessary, she would be informed as soon as I knew myself.

Ramses had no nanny. We had naturally employed one when we took the house; she left after a week, and her successors passed in and out of the place so rapidly, Emerson complained that he never got to know what they looked like. (He had once taken the Honorable Miss Worth, whose religious beliefs demanded a puritanical simplicity of dress, for the new nanny, and before this assumption could be corrected, he had insulted the lady to such a degree that she never called on me again.) At the age of three Ramses had informed us that he did not need a nanny and would not have one. Emerson agreed with him. I did not agree with him. He needed something—a stout healthy woman who had trained as a prison wardress, perhaps—but it had become more and more difficult to find nannies for Ramses. Presumably the word had spread.

When we went in to dinner I saw that Ramses' imminent return had been accepted as fact. Wilkins' face bore the look of supercilious resignation that constitutes his version of sulking, and John, the footman, was beaming broadly. Like Rose, he is unaccountably devoted to Ramses.

I had long since resigned myself to the impossibility of teaching Emerson the proper subjects of conversation before the servants. Wilkins is not resigned; but there is nothing he can do about it. Not only does Emerson rant on and on about personal matters at the dinner table, but he often consults Wilkins and John. Wilkins has a single reply to all questions: "I really could not say, sir." John, who had never been in service before he came to us, had adapted very comfortably to Emerson's habits.

That evening, however, Emerson sipped his soup and made banal remarks about the weather and the beauty of the roses. I suspected he was up to something; and sure enough, as soon as John had retired to fetch the next course, he said casually, "We must make plans for our winter campaign, Peabody. Will you be taking your maid?"

Neither of us has ever taken a personal attendant on our expeditions. The very idea of Rose, in her neat black frock and ruffled cap, crawling in and out of a tent or pitching a camp cot in an abandoned tomb, was preposterous. I reminded Emerson of this, which he knew as well as I did.

"You may do as you like, of course," he replied. "But I believe that this year I may require the services of a valet. John—" for the young man had returned with the roast beef, "how would you like to go with us to Egypt this year?"

Wilkins rescued the platter before much of the juice had dripped onto the floor. John clasped his hands. "What, sir? Me, sir? Oh, sir, I would like it above all things. D'you really mean it, sir?"

"I never say anything I don't mean," Emerson shouted indignantly.

"Have you taken leave of your senses?" I demanded.

"Now, now, Mrs. Emerson—*pas devant les domestiques.*" Emerson grinned in a vulgar manner.

Naturally I paid no attention to this remark, which was only meant to annoy me. Emerson had introduced the subject; I was determined to thrash it out then and there.

"You, with a valet? You don't employ one here; what possible use could you have for an attendant in Luxor?"

"I had in mind—" Emerson began.

He was interrupted by John. "Oh, please, sir and madam—I'd be of use, truly I would. I could keep them tombs clean, and polish your boots—I'm sure they take a deal of polishing, with all that sand there—"

"Splendid, splendid," Emerson said. "That's settled, then. What the devil are you doing, Wilkins? Why don't you serve the food? I am ravenous."

There was no response from Wilkins, not even a blink. "Put the platter on the table, John," I said resignedly. "Then take Mr. Wilkins away."

"Yes, madam. Thank you, madam. Oh, madam—"

"That will do, John."

Though John is an extremely large person, he is only a boy, and his fair complexion reflects every shade of emotion. It had run the gamut from the flush of excitement to the pallor of apprehension; he was now a delicate shell-pink with pleasure as he led his unfortunate superior away.

Emerson attacked the beef with knife and fork. He avoided my eye, but the quirk at the corner of his mouth betokened a smug satisfaction I found maddening.

"If you believe the subject is closed, you are in error," I said. "Really, Emerson, you ought to be ashamed of yourself. Will you never learn? Your inconsiderate behavior has shocked Wilkins into a stupor and raised hopes in John that cannot be realized. It is too bad of you."

"I'll be cursed if I will apologize to Wilkins," Emerson mumbled. "Whose house is this, anyway? If I can't behave naturally in my own house—"

"He will recover; he is accustomed to your ways. It is John I am thinking of. He will be so disappointed—"

"I am surprised at *you*, Amelia," Emerson interrupted. "Do you suppose I really want John to act as my valet? I have another function in mind."

"Ramses," I said.

"Naturally. Devoted as I am to that adorable child, I know his ways. I cannot concentrate on my work if I must worry about him."

"I had, of course, planned to employ a woman to look after the boy when we arrive in Cairo—"

"A woman!" Emerson dropped the knife and planted both elbows on the table. "No native servant can deal with Ramses; Egyptians spoil their own children badly, and those who work for English people have been taught to indulge all members of the so-called superior race. Superior! It makes my blood boil when I hear such—"

"You are changing the subject," I warned, knowing his propensity to lecture on this topic. "We will find a man, then. A strong, healthy young man—"

"Like John. Do use your head, Amelia. Even if we could find a suitable person in Cairo—what about the journey out?"

"Oh," I said.

"It turns me cold with terror to think of Ramses running loose aboard ship," Emerson said—and indeed, his bronzed countenance paled visibly as he spoke. "Aside from the possibility that he might tumble overboard, there are the other passengers, the crew, and the ship's engines to be considered. We could go down with all hands, never to be heard of again. Only a life preserver, floating on the surface. . . ."

With an effort I shook off the dreadful vision. "That seems an exaggeration," I assured him.

"Perhaps." Emerson gave me a look I knew well. "But there are other difficulties, Amelia. If Ramses has no attendant, he will have to share our cabin. Curse it, my dear, the trip lasts two weeks! If you expect me to forgo—"

I raised a hand to silence him, for John had returned, carrying a bowl of brussels sprouts and beaming like the sun over the pyramids of Giza. "You have made your point, Emerson. I confess that problem had not occurred to me."

"Had it not?" The intensity of Emerson's gaze increased. "Perhaps I had better remind you, then."

And he did, later that evening, in a most effective manner.

III

We reached Chalfont on the next afternoon and were greeted by Evelyn herself. One look at her radiant face assured me of the correctness of my surmise, and as I gave her a sisterly embrace I murmured, "I am so happy for you, Evelyn."

Emerson's acknowledgment of the news was less conventional. "Amelia informs me you are at it again, Evelyn. I had hoped you were finished; you promised to come out with us once you had got this business of children over and done with; we haven't had a satisfactory artist on a dig since you abandoned the profession, and it does seem to me—"

Laughing, Walter interrupted him. "Now, Radcliffe, you ought to know that in these matters Evelyn is not solely responsible. Leave off abusing my wife, if you please, and come see my latest acquisition."

"The demotic papyrus?" Emerson can be distracted from almost any subject by an antiquity. He released his affectionate grasp of Evelyn and followed his brother.

Evelyn gave me an amused smile. The years had dealt kindly with her; her fair beauty was as serene as it had been when I first met her, and motherhood had scarcely enlarged her slim figure. Her blooming looks reassured me, but I could not help but feel a certain anxiety; as soon as the gentlemen were out of earshot, I inquired, "You are certain this time that all is well? Perhaps I ought to stay with you for the remainder of the summer. If I had been here last time—"

I had believed Emerson could not overhear, but his ears are abnormally keen on occasion. He turned. "Are you at it again, Amelia? The Egyptians may call you Sitt Hakim, but that does not qualify you to practice medicine. Evelyn will do much better without your dosing her."

Having made this pronouncement, he vanished into the corridor that led to the library.

"Ha," I exclaimed. "Now you know, Evelyn—"

"I know." Her arm stole round my waist. "I will never forget the day you restored me to life when I fainted in the Roman Forum. Your husband cannot spare you to nurse me, Amelia, and I assure you, there is no need. I am past the point where . . . That is, the dangerous period has . . ."

Evelyn is absurdly modest about these things. Since I consider motherhood a natural and interesting event, I see no reason for reticence. I said briskly, "Yes, the first three months were, for you, the period of risk. I conclude then that you will bear the child in December or January. Speaking of children . . ."

"Yes, of course. You will be eager to see Ramses."

She spoke in a hesitating manner, avoiding my eyes. I said coolly, "Has something happened to him?"

"No, no, of course not. At least . . . The truth is, he is missing."

Before I could pursue my inquiries, Emerson came bursting into the hallway where we stood. "Missing!" he bellowed. "Peabody—Ramses has disappeared! He has not been seen since breakfast. Curse it, why are you standing there? We must search for him immediately."

I caught hold of a marble pillar and managed to resist Emerson's efforts to drag me toward the door.

"Calm yourself, Emerson. I have no doubt a search is underway. You can do nothing that is not already being done. In fact, you would probably lose your way, and then everyone would have to look for you. It is not unheard of for Ramses to take himself off for long periods of time; he will return when he is ready."

The last part of this calm and reasonable speech was lost on Emerson. Finding himself unable to budge me, he released his hold and rushed out the door, leaving it open.

"There is no cause for concern," Evelyn assured me. "As you said, Ramses has done this before."

"Ra-a-amses!" Emerson's voice is notable for its carrying quality. "Papa is here, Ramses—where are you? Ram-ses . . ."

I said to Evelyn, "I believe I could fancy a cup of tea."

Tea is regarded, in these islands and elsewhere, as a restorative. It was in this light that Evelyn offered it, as she continued to reassure me as to Ramses' safety. I was glad of the tea, for the long train ride had made me thirsty. If I had wanted a restorative, I would have asked for whiskey and soda.

As I could have predicted, it was only a few minutes later that Emerson returned, with Ramses cradled in his arms. I studied the touching tableau with disfavor. Ramses was, as usual, incredibly dirty, and Emerson's suit had just been sponged and pressed.

Trotting behind them came the large brindled cat we had brought from Egypt on our last expedition but one. She was Ramses' constant companion, but unfortunately few of the admirable habits of the feline species had rubbed off onto her young owner. She threw herself down on the carpet and began cleaning herself. Ramses freed himself from his father's hold and rushed at me without so much as wiping his feet.

His small and sticky person was redolent of dog, chocolate, straw (used straw, from the stables) and stagnant water. Having embraced me, and left liberal traces of his presence on the skirt of my frock, he stood back and smiled. "Good afternoon, Mama."

Ramses has a rather prepossessing smile. He is not otherwise a handsome child. His features are too large for his juvenile countenance, especially his nose, which promises to be as commanding as that of his ancient Egyptian namesake. His chin, which is almost as oversized in proportion to the rest of his face, has the same cleft as his father's. I must confess that Ramses' chin softens me. I returned his smile. "Where have you been, you naughty boy?"

"Letting de animals out of de traps," Ramses replied. "I t'ought your train was not coming till later."

"What is this?" I frowned. "You are lisping again, Ramses. I told you—"

"It is not a lisp, Amelia." Evelyn hastened to defend the miscreant, who had turned to the tea table and was devouring sandwiches. "He pronounced his *s*'s perfectly."

"Some other speech defect, then," I replied. "He does it deliberately. He knows how it annoys me."

Leaning against his father's knee, Ramses stuffed an entire watercress sandwich into his mouth and regarded me enigmatically. I would have continued the lecture but for the arrival of Walter, breathless and perspiring. He let out a sigh of relief when he saw the boy.

"So there you are, you young rascal. How could you wander off when you knew your mama and papa would be here?"

"I t'ought . . ." Ramses glanced at me. Slowly and deliberately he repeated, "I t'ought de train would be later dan was de case. You must swear out a warrant against Will Baker, Uncle Walter. He is setting traps again. It was necessary for me to free de unfortunate captives dis afternoon."

"Indeed? I will see to it at once," said Walter.

"Good Gad," I exclaimed loudly. Walter had once spanked Ramses (for tearing pages out of his dictionary), and now he too had succumbed to the imperious dictates of the miniature tyrant.

"Language, Amelia, language," Emerson exclaimed. "Remember that young, innocent, impressionable ears are listening."

At my suggestion Ramses retired to bathe and change. When he returned after a short interval he was accompanied by his cousins. It would have been difficult to deduce the relationship. Ramses' cheeks of tan and mop of curly black hair resembled the coloring of residents of the eastern Mediterranean regions, while his cousins had inherited their mother's fair hair and the sweet regularity of countenance of both parents. They are handsome children, especially Emerson's namesake, young Radcliffe. Raddie, as we called him, was then nine years of age, but looked older. (A few months of Ramses' companionship has that effect on sensitive individuals.) The twins, Johnny and Willy, appeared to have suffered less, perhaps because there were two of them to share the tempestuous effect of Ramses' personality. They greeted us with identical gap-toothed smiles and shook hands like little gentlemen. Then Ramses came forward with the fourth and (as yet) youngest of Evelyn's children—a dear little cherub of four, with golden curls and wide blue eyes. The curls were somewhat disheveled and the eyes were bulging, since Ramses had her firmly about the neck. Thrusting her at me, he announced, "Here is 'Melia, Mama."

I freed the unoffending infant from his stranglehold. "I know my namesake well, Ramses. Give Aunt Amelia, a kiss, my dear."

The child obeyed with the grace all Evelyn's offspring possess, but when I suggested she sit beside me she shook her head shyly. "T'ank you, Auntie, but if I may I will sit wit' Ramses."

I sighed as I beheld the look she turned on my son. I have seen the same expression on the face of a mouse about to be devoured by a cobra.

Evelyn fussed over the children, stuffing them with cakes and encouraging them to chatter about their activities; but I joined in the discussion between the men, which had to do with our plans for the autumn campaign.

"You won't be returning to Thebes, then?" Walter asked.

This was news to me, and I was about to say so when Emerson exclaimed in exasperation, "Curse you, Walter, it was to be a surprise for Amelia."

"I don't like surprises," I replied. "Not in matters concerning our work, at any rate."

"You will like this one, my dear Peabody. Guess where we are to excavate this winter."

The beloved name halted the reproof hovering on my lips. Its use goes back to the early days of our acquaintance, when Emerson used my surname in an attempt to annoy me. Now hallowed by tender memories, it is a symbol of our uniquely satisfying relationship. Emerson prefers me to use his last name for the same touching reason.

So I said, humoring him, "I cannot possibly guess, my dear Emerson. There are dozens of sites in Egypt I am dying to dig up."

"But what do you yearn for most? What is your Egyptological passion, hitherto unsatisfied? What is it you crave?"

"Oh, Emerson!" I clasped my hands. In my enthusiasm I overlooked the fact that I was holding a tomato sandwich. Wiping the fragments from my hands, I went on in mounting rapture, "Pyramids! Have you found us a pyramid?"

"Not one, but five," Emerson replied, his sapphire orbs reflecting my delight. "Dahshoor, Peabody—the pyramid field of Dahshoor—that is where I mean to dig. I intended it as a treat for you, my dear."

"You mean to dig," I repeated, my first enthusiasm fading. "Do you have the firman for Dahshoor?"

"You know I never apply to the Department of Antiquities beforehand, my love. If certain other archaeologists learned where I wanted to excavate they would also apply, out of pure spite. I don't mention names, but you know whom I mean."

I waved this unwarranted slur upon Mr. Petrie aside. "But, Emerson, M. de Morgan dug at Dahshoor last spring. As head of the Department of Antiquities he has first choice; what makes you suppose he will yield the site to you?"

"I understand that M. de Morgan is more reasonable than his predecessor," said Walter, the peacemaker. "Grebaut was an unfortunate choice for the position."

"Grebaut was an idiot," Emerson agreed. "But he never interfered with ME."

"He was terrified of you," I exclaimed. "I recall at least one occasion upon which you threatened to murder him. De Morgan may not be so timid."

"I cannot imagine where you get such ideas," Emerson said in mild surprise. "I am a particularly even-tempered man, and to suggest that I would threaten the Director General of the Department of Antiquities with physical violence—even if he *was* the most consummate fool in the entire universe—really, Amelia, you astonish me."

"Never mind," said Walter, his eyes twinkling with amusement. "Let us hope there will be no violence of any kind this season. Especially murder!"

"I certainly hope not," said Emerson. "These distractions interfere with one's work. Amelia suffers from the delusion, derived I know not whence, that she has talents as a criminal investigator—"

"I, at least, have cause to thank her for those talents," said my dear Evelyn quietly. "You cannot blame Amelia, Radcliffe; I was the unwitting cause of your first encounter with crime."

"And," Walter added, "on the second occasion you were the guilty party, Radcliffe—taking on the direction of an expedition plagued with mysterious disappearances and ancient curses."

"She tricked me into it," Emerson grumbled, glancing at me.

"I don't know what you are complaining about," I retorted. "It was a most interesting experience, and we made some valuable discoveries that season in the Valley of the Kings."

"But you were wrong about de identification of de tomb," said Ramses, turning to his father. "I am of de opinion dat Tutankhamon's sepulcher is yet to be discovered."

Seeing that an argument was about to ensue—for Emerson brooks criticism of his Egyptological expertise from no one, not even his son—Walter hastened to change the subject.

"Radcliffe, have you heard anything more about the recent flood of illegal antiquities? Rumor has it that some remarkably fine objects have appeared on the market, including jewelry. Can it be that the tomb robbers of Thebes have found another cache of royal mummies?"

"Your uncle is referring to the cave at Deir el Bahri," Emerson explained to Ramses. "It contained mummies of royal persons hidden by devout priests after the original tombs had been robbed."

"T'ank you, Papa, but I am fully acquainted wit' de details of dat remarkable discovery. De cache was found by de tomb robbers of Gurneh near Thebes, who marketed de objects found on de mummies, enabling de den Head of de Antiquities Department, M. Maspero, to track dem down and locate de cleft in de cliffs where de—"

"Enough, Ramses," I said.

"Hmph," said Emerson. "To answer your question, Walter—it is possible that the objects you refer to come from such a collection of royal mummies. However, from what I have heard, they range widely in date; the most remarkable is a Twelfth Dynasty pectoral ornament in gold, lapis lazuli and turquoise, with the cartouche of Senusret the Second. It seems to me more likely that a new and more efficient gang of tomb robbers has taken up the trade, plundering a variety of sites. What vultures these wretches are! If I could lay my hands on them—"

"You have just now declared you will not play detective," said Walter with a smile. "No murders for Amelia and no burglaries for you, Radcliffe. Only an innocent excavation. Don't forget you promised to look out for papyri—demotic papyri, if you please. I need more examples of that form of the language if I am to succeed with my dictionary."

"And I," said Ramses, feeding the last of the sandwiches to the cat, "wish to dig up dead people. Human remains are de indicators of de racial affiliations of de ancient Egyptians. Furdermore, I feel a useful study might be made of techniques of mummification down de ages."

Emerson bent a tender look upon his son and heir. "Very well, Ramses; Papa will find you all the dead bodies you want."

Chapter Two

THE voyage from Brindisi to Alexandria was without incident. (I do not consider the halting of the ship, at Emerson's frenzied insistence, as truly an incident in Ramses' career; as I told Emerson at the time, there was almost no possibility that the boy could have fallen overboard. Indeed he was soon found, in the hold, examining the cargo—for reasons which I did not care then, or at a later time, to inquire into.)

Except for this single error—which for John could not be blamed, since Ramses had locked him in their cabin—the young man performed well. He followed Ramses' every step and scarcely took his eyes off the boy. He attended to the needs of Bastet, such as they were; the cat required far less attendance than a human child. (Which is one of the reasons why spinster ladies prefer felines to babies.) Ramses had not insisted on bringing the cat; he had simply taken it for granted that she would accompany him. The few occasions on which they had been parted had proved so horrendous for all concerned that I gave in with scarcely a struggle.

But to return to John. He proved to be one of Emerson's more brilliant inspirations, and with my characteristic graciousness I admitted as much to my husband.

"John," I said, "was one of your more brilliant inspirations, Emerson."

It was the night before we were to dock at Alexandria, and we reclined in harmonious marital accord on the narrow bunk in our stateroom. John and Ramses occupied the adjoining cabin. Knowing that the porthole had been nailed shut and the key to the locked cabin door was in Emerson's possession, I was at ease about Ramses' present location and therefore able to enjoy my own, in the embrace of my husband. His muscular arms tightened about me as he replied sleepily, "I told you so."

In my opinion this comment should be avoided, particularly by married persons. I refrained from replying, however. The night was balmy with the breezes of the Orient; moonlight made a silver path across the floor; and the close proximity of Emerson, necessitated by the narrowness of the couch on which we reclined, induced a mood of amiable forbearance.

"He has not succumbed to mal de mer," I continued. "He is learning Arabic with remarkable facility; he gets on well with the cat Bastet."

Emerson's reply had nothing to do with the subject under discussion, and succeeded in distracting me, accompanied as it was by certain non-verbal demonstrations. When I was able to speak, I went on, "I am beginning to believe I have underestimated the lad's intelligence. He may be of use to us on the dig: keeping the records of pay for the men, or even—"

"I cannot conceive," said Emerson, "why you insist on talking about the footman at such a moment as this."

I was forced to concede that once again Emerson was quite correct. It was not the time to be talking about the footman.

II

John proved a weak vessel after all. He was snuffling next morning, and by the time we reached Cairo he had a fully developed case of catarrh, with all the attendant internal unpleasantnesses. Upon being questioned he weakly admitted he had left off the flannel belt with which I had provided him, cautioning him to wear it day and night in order to prevent a chill.

"Madness!" I exclaimed, as I tucked him into bed and laid out the appropriate medications. "Absolute madness, young man! You disregarded my instructions and now you see the consequences. Why didn't you wear your belt? Where is it?"

John's face was crimson from the base of his sturdy throat to the roots of his hair, whether from remorse or the exertion of attempting to prevent me from putting him to bed I cannot say. Pouring out a dessert spoonful of the gentle aperient I commonly employ for this ailment, I seized him by the nose and, as his mouth opened in a quest for oxygen, I poured the medicine down his throat. A dose of bismuth succeeded the aperient, and then I repeated my question. "Where is your belt, John? You must wear it every instant."

John was incapable of speech. However, the briefest flicker of his eyes in the direction of Ramses gave the answer I expected. The boy stood at the foot of the bed, watching with a look of cool curiosity, and as I turned in his direction he answered readily, "It is my fault, Mama. I needed de flannel to make a lead for de cat Bastet."

The animal in question was perched on the footboard, studying the mosquito netting draped high above the couch with an expression that aroused my deepest suspicions. I had noted with approval the braided rope with which Bastet had been provided. It was one item I had not thought to bring, since the cat usually followed Ramses' steps as closely as a devoted dog; but in a strange city, under strange circumstances, it was certainly a sensible precaution. Not until that moment, however, had I recognized the rope as the remains of a flannel belt.

Addressing the most pressing problem first, I said sternly, "Bastet, you are not to climb the mosquito netting. It is too fragile to bear your weight and will collapse if you attempt the feat." The cat glanced at me and murmured low in its throat, and I went on, now addressing my son, "Why did you not use your own flannel belt?"

"Because you would have seen it was gone," said Ramses, with the candor that is one of his more admirable characteristics.

"Who needs the cursed belts anyway?" demanded Emerson, who had been ranging the room like a caged tiger. "I never wear one. See here, Amelia, you have wasted enough time playing physician. This is a temporary affliction; most tourists suffer from it, and John will get on better if you leave him alone. Come; we have a great deal to do, and I need your assistance."

So adjured, I could only acquiesce. We retired to our own room, which adjoined that of the sufferer, taking Ramses (and of course the cat) with us. But when I would have turned toward the trunk that contained our books and notes, Emerson grasped my arm and drew me to the window.

Our room was on the third floor of the hotel, with a small iron-railed balcony overlooking the gardens of Ezbekieh Square. The mimosa trees were in bloom; chrysanthemums and poinsettias mingled in riotous profusion; the famous roses formed velvety masses of crimson and gold and snowy white. But for once the flowers (of which I am exceedingly fond) did not hold my gaze. My eyes sought the upper air, where roofs and domes, minarets and spires swam in a misty splendor of light.

Emerson's broad breast swelled in a deep sigh, and a contented smile illumined his face. He drew Ramses into his other arm. I knew—I shared—the joy that filled his heart as for the first time he introduced his son to the life that was all in all to him. It was a moment fraught with emotion—or it would have been, had not Ramses, in an effort to get a better look, swarmed up onto the railing, whence he was plucked by the paternal arm as he teetered perilously.

"Don't do that, my boy," said Emerson. "It is not safe. Papa will hold you."

With a visible sneer of contempt for human frailty the cat Bastet took Ramses' place on the rail. The noises from the street below rose in pitch as travelers returning from the day's excursions dismounted from donkeys or carriages. Conjurers and snake charmers sought to attract the attention, and the baksheesh, of the hotel guests; vendors of flowers and trinkets raised their voices in discordant appeal. A military band marched down the street, preceded by a water carrier running backward as he poured from a huge jar in order to lay the dust. Ramses' juvenile countenance displayed little emotion. It seldom did. Only a gentle flush warmed his tanned cheek, which was, for Ramses, a display of great excitement and interest.

The cat Bastet attacked her sleek flank with bared teeth.

"She cannot have picked up a flea already," I exclaimed, carrying the animal to a chair.

But she had. I dealt with the offender, made certain it had been a solitary explorer, and then remarked, "Your notion of a lead was a good idea, Ramses, but this dirty rag will not do. Tomorrow we will purchase a proper leather collar and lead in the bazaar."

My husband and son remained at the window. Emerson was pointing out the sights of the city. I did not disturb them. Let Emerson enjoy the moment; disillusionment would come soon enough when he realized he was destined to enjoy several days—and nights—of his son's companionship. Ramses could not share the infected chamber where John reposed, and John was in no state to provide the proper degree of supervision. He was barely up to the job even when he was in the full bloom of health.

The burden would rest principally on me, of course. I was resigned. Clapping my hands to summon the hotel safragi, I directed him to help me unpack.

III

We were to dine that evening with an old friend, Sheikh Mohammed Bahsoor. He was of pure Bedouin stock, with the acquiline features and manly bearing of that splendid race. We had decided to take Ramses with us—to leave him in the hotel with only the feeble John to watch over him was not to be thought of for a moment—but my misgivings as to his behavior were happily unfulfilled. The good old man welcomed him with the gracious courtesy of a true son of the desert; and Ramses, uncharacteristically, sat still and spoke scarcely a word all evening.

I was the only female present. The sheikh's wives, of course, never left the harim, and although he always received European ladies courteously, he did not invite them to his intimate dinner parties, when the conversation dwelled upon subjects of political and scientific interest. "Women," he insisted, "cannot discuss serious matters." Needless to say, I was flattered that he did not include me in that denunciation, and I believe he enjoyed my spirited defense of the sex of which I have the honor to be a member.

The gathering was cosmopolitan. In addition to the Egyptians and Bedouins present, there was M. Naville, the Swiss archaeologist, Insinger, who was Dutch, and M. Naville's assistant, a pleasant young fellow named Howard Carter. Another gentleman was conspicuous by the magnificence of his dress. Diamonds blazed from his shirt front and his cuffs, and the broad crimson ribbon of some foreign order cut a swath across his breast. He was of medium height, but looked taller because of his extraordinary leanness of frame. He wore his black hair shorter than was the fashion; it glistened with pomade, as did his sleek little mustache. A monocle in his right eye enlarged that optic with sinister effect, giving his entire face a curiously lopsided appearance.

When he caught sight of this person, Emerson scowled and muttered something under his breath; but he was too fond of Sheikh Mohammed to make a scene. When the sheikh presented "Prince Kalenischeff," my husband forced an unconvincing smile and said only, "I have met the—er—hem—gentleman."

I had not met him, but I knew of him. As he bowed over my hand, holding it pressed to his lips longer than convention decreed, I remembered Emerson's critical comments. "He worked at Abydos with Amelineau; between them, they made a pretty mess of the place. He calls himself an archaeologist, but that designation is as inaccurate as his title is apocryphal. If he is a Russian prince, I am the Empress of China."

Since Emerson was critical of all archaeologists, I had taken this with a grain of salt; but I must admit the prince's bold dark eyes and sneering smile made a poor impression on me.

The conversation was largely confined that evening to archaeological subjects. I remember the main topic concerned the proposed dam at Philae, which in its original design would have drowned the Ptolemaic temples on the island. Emerson, who despises the monuments of this degenerate period, annoyed a number of his colleagues by saying the cursed temples were not worth preserving, even if they did retain their original coloring. In the end, of course, he added his name to the petition sent to the Foreign Office, and I do not doubt that the name of Emerson carried considerable weight in the final decision to lower the height of the dam and spare the temples.

His eyes twinkling merrily, the sheikh made his usual provocative remarks about the female sex. I countered, as usual, and treated the gentlemen to a lecture on women's rights. Only once did a ripple of potential strife disturb the calm of the evening, when Naville asked Emerson where he would be digging that season. The question was asked in all innocence, but Emerson replied with a dark scowl and a firm refusal to discuss his plans. It might have passed off had not Kalenischeff said, in a lazy drawl, "The most promising sites have been allocated, you know. You ought not delay so long in applying, Professor."

Emerson's response would certainly have been rude. I managed to prevent it by popping a chunk of lamb into his open mouth. We were eating Arab-style, sitting cross-legged around the low table and feeding one another choice bits, a manner of dining that proved particularly useful on this occasion.

Throughout the meal Ramses sat like a little statue, speaking only when spoken to and eating as neatly as was possible under the circumstances. When we were ready to take our departure he made an impeccable salaam and thanked the sheikh in flawless Arabic. The ingenuous old gentleman was delighted. Folding Ramses to the bosom of his spotless robes, he addressed him as "son" and proclaimed him an honorary member of his tribe.

When we were at last in the carriage, Emerson subsided with a groan and clasped his hands over his midsection. "The only fault I have to find with Arab hospitality is its extravagance. I have eaten too much, Amelia. I know I shan't sleep a wink tonight."

Since the main course had consisted of a whole roasted sheep stuffed with chickens, which were in turn stuffed with quail, I shared Emerson's sentiments. But of course it would have been the height of discourtesy to refuse a dish. Suppressing an unseemly sound of repletion, I said, "Ramses, you behaved very well. Mama was proud of you."

"I was testing my knowledge of de language," said Ramses. "It was reassuring to discover dat de purely academic training I have received from Uncle Walter was adequate for de purpose. I comprehended virtually everyt'ing dat was said."

"Did you indeed?" I said, somewhat uneasily. Ramses had been so subdued I had almost forgotten he was present, and I had expressed myself forcibly on certain of the sexual and marital customs that keep Egyptian women virtually slaves in their own homes. While I was trying to remember what I had said, Ramses went on, "Yes, I have no complaints regarding Uncle Walter's tuition. I am somewhat weak wit' regard to current slang and colloquialisms, but dat is only to be expected; one can best acquire dem from personal experience."

I murmured an abstracted agreement. I had certainly used some expressions I would have preferred Ramses not to hear. I consoled myself by hoping that Walter had not taught him words like "adultery" and "puberty."

When we reached the hotel Ramses flew to embrace the cat and Emerson flung open the shutters. The room was stifling, but we had been afraid to leave the windows open for fear Bastet would escape. She had resented her imprison-ment, and told Ramses so, in hoarse complaint, but I was pleased to see that she had taken my warning about the mosquito netting to heart. It hung in filmy, unmarred folds about our bed, and another netting enclosed the smaller cot which had been moved in from the next room.

Leaving Emerson to prepare Ramses for bed, I went to see how John was getting on. He assured me he was better and expressed himself as prepared to resume his duties at once; but my questioning brought out the fact that the internal disturbances were not yet reduced to a normal number (an interrogation that rendered John incoherent with embarrassment). So I told him to stay in bed, administered his medicine (he told me he had already taken it, but naturally I paid no attention), checked to make sure the new flannel belt I had given him was in place, and bade him good night.

Returning to my own chamber, I found Emerson, Ramses, and the cat lying in a tangled heap atop our bed, all sound asleep and, in Emerson's case, snoring. Contrary to his opinion, repletion does not affect Emerson's ability to sleep; it only makes him snore. I placed Ramses in his cot without waking him and tucked the netting securely in place. The cat wanted to get in with him—she always slept with Ramses at home—but after I had pointed out the problem of the netting and the hindrance it presented to her nocturnal prowling, she settled down on the foot of the bed. They made a picture to touch any mother's heart. The filmy fabric softened my son's rather large features, and in his little white nightgown, with his mop of sable curls, he resembled a small Semitic saint with a lion at his feet.

It may have been the charm of this sight that relaxed my internal guards, or it may have been that I was exhausted after a long tiring day. Whatever the cause of my negligence, I awoke after daylight to find Ramses' cot empty and the miscreant flown.

I was not surprised, but I was put out. Emerson was still snoring in blissful ignorance. I dressed quickly, not because I was alarmed about Ramses' safety but because I preferred to deal with the matter without my husband's agitated and vociferous assistance. Remembering one of Ramses' statements the previous night, to which I had not paid the attention it deserved, I was able to locate him almost immediately.

The street in front of the hotel teemed with the usual motley array of beggars, guides, donkeys and donkey boys, lying in wait for the tourists. Sure enough, Ramses was among them. Though I had expected to find him there, it took me several moments to recognize him. Barefoot and bareheaded, his white nightgown similar in design (and, by now, in filthiness) to the robes worn by the donkey boys, he blended admirably with the others, even to his tanned complexion and tousled black curls. I admit it gave me something of a shock. I was unable to move for an instant; and during that instant one of the bigger boys, finding Ramses blocking his path, addressed him in a flood of gutter slang. The shock I had experienced earlier paled by comparison to the sensation that seized me when I heard my offspring respond with a phrase of whose meaning even I was uncertain, though the general reference, to certain animals and their habits, was unfortunately only too clear.

I was not the only European standing on the terrace. Several other early birds had emerged, ready for touring. Though I am ordinarily unmoved by the uninformed opinions of others, I was not keen to admit an acquaintance with the dusty child in the dirty white robe; but, seeing that Ramses was about to be knocked unconscious by the infuriated young person he had just addressed as a misbegotten offspring of an Englishman and a camel, I thought I had better intervene.

"Ramses!" I shouted.

Everyone within earshot stopped and stared. I suppose it must have been startling to hear an aristocratic English person shout the name of an ancient Egyptian pharaoh at dawn on the terrace of Shepheard's Hotel.

Ramses, who had ducked behind a morose little donkey, started to his feet. His assailant halted, fist raised; and the cat Bastet, appearing out of nowhere, landed on the latter's back. The cat Bastet is a large cat, weighing approximately twelve pounds. The unlucky donkey boy fell flat upon the ground with a sound like that of a cannonball hitting a wall, this effect being further strengthened by the cloud of dust that billowed up. Emerging from the cloud, Bastet sneezed and fell in behind Ramses, who advanced toward me. I seized him by the collar. In silence we retreated into the hotel.

We found Emerson placidly drinking tea. "Good morning, my dears," he said, with a smile. "What have you been doing so bright and early?"

Bastet sat down and began to wash herself. This struck me as an excellent idea. I thrust Ramses into his father's arms. "Wash him," I said briefly.

As they went out I heard Ramses explain, "I was improving my command of de colloquial form of de language, Papa," to which Emerson replied, "Splendid, my boy, splendid."

IV

After breakfast we set out on our errands, Emerson to call on M. de Morgan, in order to obtain his firman for excavating at Dahshoor, I to do some necessary shopping. Normally I would have accompanied Emerson, but that would have meant taking Ramses along, and after hearing the latest additions to his Arabic vocabulary I felt it would be unwise to expose de Morgan to my linguistically unpredictable child—not to mention the cat, for Ramses refused to stir a step without her. I gave in to this request, since one of my errands was to buy a proper collar for Bastet.

The Muski, which is the main thoroughfare of old Cairo, had quite lost its former quaint oriental character; modern shops and buildings lined its broad expanse. We left our hired carriage at the entrance to the bazaars, for the narrow alleyways do not permit vehicular traffic. At my suggestion Ramses took the cat up lest she be stepped on. She assumed her favorite position, her head on one of Ramses' shoulders and her hindquarters on the other, with her tail hanging down in front.

We went first to the bazaar of the leathermakers, where we purchased not one but two collars for Bastet. One was plain and well constructed (my selection); the other was bright-red, adorned with fake scarabs and imitation turquoise. I was surprised to see Ramses exhibit such tawdry taste, but decided the issue was not worth arguing about. Ramses immediately decorated Bastet with the bejeweled collar and attached the matching crimson lead. They made a singular pair, Ramses in the tweed jacket and trousers his father had ordered to be made in imitation of his own working costume and the great feline, looking exactly like the hunting cats depicted in Egyptian tomb paintings. I was only relieved that Ramses had not suggested putting a gold earring in her ear, as had been done by the ancient pet owners.

I proceeded methodically with my shopping—medications, tools, ropes and other professional needs. The morning was well advanced by the time I finished, for even the simplest transaction cannot be completed without bargaining, coffee-drinking and an exchange of florid compliments. There was one other inquiry I wanted to pursue before returning to the hotel; turning to ask if Ramses was hungry, I saw the question was unnecessary. He had just stuffed into his mouth a piece of pastry dripping with honey and bristling with nuts. The honey had trickled down his chin and onto his jacket. Each spot was already black with flies.

"Where did you get that?" I demanded.

"De man gave it to me." Ramses indicated a vendor of sweetmeats who stood nearby, his large wooden tray balanced expertly on his head. Through the swarm of insects that surrounded him the vendor gave me a gap-toothed smile and a respectful salutation.

"Did I not tell you you were not to eat anything unless I gave you permission?" I asked.

"No," said Ramses.

"Oh. Well, I am telling you now."

"Very well," said Ramses. He wiped his sticky hands on his trousers. A wave of flies dived upon the new spots.

We proceeded in single file through a covered passageway into a small square with a public fountain. Women in ragged black robes clustered around the marble structure, filling their jars. The appearance of Ramses and Bastet distracted them; they pointed and giggled, and one boldly lifted her veil in order to see better.

"Where are we going?" Ramses asked.

"To the shop of an antiquities dealer. I promised your Uncle Walter I would look for papyri."

Ramses began, "Papa says antiquities dealers are cursed rascals who—"

"I know your papa's opinions concerning antiquities dealers. However, it is sometimes necessary to resort to these persons. You are not to repeat your papa's comments to the man we are about to meet. You are not to speak at all unless you are asked a direct question. Do not leave the shop. Do not touch anything in the shop. Do not allow the cat to wander off. And," I added, "do not eat anything unless I tell you you may."

"Yes, Mama," said Ramses.

The Khan el Khaleel, the bazaar of the metalworkers, is, if possible, even more crowded than the others. We threaded our way past the cupboard-sized shops and the narrow stone benches called mastabas in front of them. Many of the mastabas were occupied by customers; the merchant, just inside the shop, produced his glittering wares from the locked drawers within.

Abd el Atti's place of business was on the edge of the Khan el Khaleel. The small shop in front was only a blind; preferred customers were invited into a larger room at the rear of the shop, where the old rascal's collection of antiquities was displayed.

Ever since the days of M. Mariette, the distinguished founder of the Department of Antiquities, excavation in Egypt has been—in theory at least—strictly controlled. Firmans are awarded only to trained scholars. The results of their labors are studied by an official of the Department, who selects the choicest objects for the Museum. The excavator is allowed to keep the remainder. Anyone wishing to export antiquities must have a permit, but this is not hard to obtain when the object in question has no particular monetary or historical value.

The system would work well enough if the law were obeyed. Unfortunately it is impossible to supervise every square acre of the country, and illegal excavation is common. Working in haste and in fear of discovery, untrained diggers demolish the sites at which they work and of course keep no records of where the objects were found. The fellahin of Egypt have a keen nose for treasure; they have often located tombs unknown to archaeologists. The famous cache of royal mummies that Emerson had mentioned is a conspicuous example. But the peasants are not the only offenders. Wallis Budge of the British Museum took a positive delight in outwitting the antiquities officials. The Amarna tablets, the papyrus of Ani, and the great Greek manuscript of the Odes of Bacchylides are among the valuables smuggled out of Egypt by this so-called scholar.

In this ambiguous moral ambience the antiquities dealers flourished. Some were more unscrupulous than others, but scarcely any of them operated wholly within the law. The honest merchant had no chance against his dishonest colleagues, for the best wares were obtained from illegal excavations. Abd el Atti's reputation was middle-of-the-road—worse than some merchants, not so bad as others—which meant he might have the kind of papyrus I wanted for Walter.

The mastaba before the shop was unoccupied. I looked within. The room was dimly lit and crowded with merchandise. Most of the remaining space was filled by Abd el Atti himself. He was almost as short as I and almost as wide as he was tall. Before affluence got the better of his figure he must have been a handsome fellow, with soft brown eyes and regular features. He was still something of a dandy. His outer robe was of salmon-pink cashmere and he wore a huge green turban, perhaps in order to increase his stature. From behind, which was how I saw him, the effect was that of a large orange balloon surmounted by a cabbage.

His body very nearly concealed the other man, who stood just inside the curtained doorway at the rear of the shop. I saw only the latter's face, and a most sinister countenance it was—almost as dark as a Nubian's, shaped into lines and pouches of sagging flesh that suggested dissipation rather than age. When he saw me, his lips drew back in a snarl under his ragged black mustaches, and he interrupted Abd el Atti with a harsh warning. "*Gaft—ha'at iggaft . . .*"—followed by another comment of which I caught only a few words.

Turning with a serpentine swiftness surprising in a man of his bulk, Abd el Atti cut the other short with a peremptory gesture. His brown face shone greasily with perspiration. "It is the Sitt Hakim," he said. "Wife to Emerson. You honor my house, Sitt."

Since I knew who I was, and Abd el Atti knew who I was, I could only assume that the identifying statement was aimed at the other man. It was not an introduction, for upon hearing it the creature vanished, so suddenly and smoothly that the curtain scarcely swayed. A warning, then? I had no doubt of it. When he greeted me, Abd el Atti had spoken ordinary Arabic. The whispered remarks I had overheard had been in another kind of speech.

Abd el Atti bowed, or tried to; he did not bend easily. "Be welcome, honored lady. And this young nobleman—who can he be but the son of the great Emerson! How handsome he is, and how great the intelligence that shines in his eyes."

This was a deadly insult, for one does not praise a child for fear of attracting the envy of malicious demons. I knew Abd el Atti must be badly rattled to make such a mistake.

Ramses said not a word, only bowed in response. The cat—I observed with a touch of uneasiness—was nowhere to be seen.

"But come," Abd el Atti went on, "sit on the mastaba; we will drink coffee; you will tell me how I may serve you."

I let him nudge me out of the shop. He squatted beside me on the mastaba and clapped his hands to summon a servant. Under his salmon robe he wore a long vest of striped Syrian silk, bound with a sash stiff with pearls and gold thread. He paid no attention to Ramses, who remained inside the shop. Hands clasped ostentatiously behind his back in compliance with my instructions, Ramses appeared to be studying the merchandise on display. I decided to let him remain where he was. Even if he broke something, it would not matter; most of the objects were forgeries.

Abd el Atti and I drank coffee and exchanged insincere compliments for a while. Then he said, apropos of nothing in particular, "I hope the speech of that vile beggar did not offend you. He was trying to sell me some antiquities. However, I suspected they were stolen, and as you and my great good friend Emerson know, I do not deal with dishonest people."

I nodded agreeably. I knew he was lying and he knew I knew; we were playing the time-honored game of mercantile duplicity, in which both parties profess the most noble sentiments while each plans to cheat the other as thoroughly as possible.

Abd el Atti smiled. His countenance was trained in imperturbability, but I knew the old wretch well; his remark was not an apology, but an implicit question. He was desperately anxious to learn whether I had understood those whispered words.

Many trades and professions, especially criminal trades, develop private languages in order that the members may speak among themselves without being understood by outsiders. The thieves' cant of seventeenth-century London is one example of such an argot, as it is called. Abd el Atti and his companion had employed the *siim issaagha,* the argot of the gold- and silver-sellers of Cairo. It is based on ancient Hebrew, a language I had studied with my late father. In fact, they had spoken so rapidly and so softly, I had only comprehended a few words. Abd el Atti had said, "The Master will eat our hearts if . . ." Then the other man had warned him to watch what he said, since a stranger had entered.

I had no intention of admitting that I was familiar with the *siim issaagha.* Let the old man wonder and worry.

He was worried. Instead of *fahddling* (gossiping) for the prescribed length of time, he abruptly got down to business, asking what I wanted.

"It is for the brother of Emerson that I come," I explained. "He studies the ancient language of Egypt, and I promised I would bring him papyri."

Abd el Atti sat like a glittering statue, his hands rock-steady; but a strange livid hue overspread his face. The harmless word "papyri" had wrought that remarkable change; could it be, I wondered, that a cache of these objects had been found? I saw myself exposing the criminal ring, arresting the criminals, carrying back basketfuls of papyri to Walter.

Abd el Atti cleared his throat. "It grieves me that I cannot assist one whom I would wish to honor. Alas, alas, I have no papyri."

Well, I had expected that. Abd el Atti never had the object one wanted, and if my suspicions were correct (as I felt sure they were) he had pressing reasons for refusing to admit that he possessed those particular objects. I did not doubt, however, that cupidity would eventually overcome his caution. He had to market his loot to someone; why not to me?

So I proceeded to the next stage of the negotiations, which usually ended with Abd el Atti suddenly remembering that he had heard of such a thing—not that he made a habit of dealing with thieves, but as a favor to an old friend he might be willing to act as middleman. . . . But to my surprise Abd el Atti remained firm. He offered me other antiquities, but not papyri.

Finally I said, "It is a pity, my friend. I will have to go to another dealer. I regret this; I would rather have bought from you." And I made as if to rise.

This was the last stage in the maneuvering and usually brought the desired result. An expression of agony crossed Abd el Atti's rotund face, but he shook his head. "I also regret, honored Sitt. But I have no papyri."

His fat body filled the narrow doorway of the shop. Over his shoulder there appeared a strange appendage, like a third arm—a small, thin arm clothed in brown tweed. Ramses' voice piped, "Mama, may I speak now?"

Abd el Atti made a frantic grab for the object Ramses was holding. He missed. Before he could try again, a heavy weight landed on his shoulder, tipping him backward. He let out a shriek and began beating the air with ringed brown hands. Bastet leaped again, onto the mastaba next to me, and Ramses squeezed through the space the cat had cleared for him. He was still holding the scrap of papyrus.

I took it from him. "Where did you find this?" I asked, in English.

"In de room behind de curtain," said Ramses. He squatted beside me, crossing his legs in Egyptian style. Gesturing at Bastet, he added, "I was looking for de cat Bastet. You told me not to let her wander off."

Abd el Atti levered himself to an upright position. I expected he would be angry—and indeed he had some reason to be—but the look he gave the great brindled cat and the small boy held a touch of superstitious terror. I saw his hand move in a quick gesture—the old charm against the evil eye and the forces of darkness. "I know nothing of it," he said heavily. "I have never seen it before."

The scrap had been broken off a larger manuscript. It was roughly rectangular and about six inches by four in size. The papyrus was brown with age, but less brittle than such relics usually are, and the writing stood out black and firm. "It is not hieratic or demotic," I said. "These are Greek letters."

"It is as I said," Abd el Atti babbled. "You asked for Egyptian papyri, Sitt; this is not what you desire."

"I t'ink dat de writing is Coptic," said Ramses, legs crossed, arms folded. "It *is* Egyptian—de latest form of de language."

"I believe you are correct," I said, examining the fragment again. "I will take it, Abd el Atti, since you have nothing better. How much?"

The dealer made an odd, jerky gesture of resignation. "I ask nothing. But I warn you, Sitt—"

"Are you threatening me, Abd el Atti?"

"Allah forbid!" For once the dealer sounded wholly sincere. Again he glanced nervously at the cat, at Ramses, who contemplated him in unblinking silence, and at me. And behind me, I knew, he saw the shadow of Emerson, whom the Egyptians called Father of Curses. The combination would have daunted a braver man than poor, fat Abd el Atti. He swallowed. "I do not threaten, I warn. Give it to me. If you do, no harm will follow, I swear it."

As Emerson might have said, this was the wrong approach to take to me. (In fact, Emerson would have put it more emphatically, using terms like "red flag to a bull.") I tucked the fragment carefully into my bag. "Thank you for your warning, Abd el Atti. Now hear mine. If the possession of this scrap is dangerous to me, it is also dangerous to you. I suspect you are in over your turbaned head, old friend. Do you want help? Tell me the truth. Emerson and I will protect you—word of an Englishman."

Abd el Atti hesitated. At that moment Bastet rose upon her hind legs and planted her forefeet on Ramses' shoulder, butting her head against his. It was a habit of hers when she was restless and desirous of moving on, and it was sheer coincidence that she should have chosen that precise moment to move; but the sight seemed to strike terror into Abd el Atti's devious soul.

"It is the will of Allah," he whispered. "Come tonight, with Emerson— when the muezzin calls from the minaret at midnight."

He would say no more. As we retraced our steps I glanced over my shoulder and saw him squatting on the mastaba, still as a glittering life-sized statue. He was staring straight ahead.

We pressed against the wall to let a donkey squeeze by. Ramses said, "De old gentleman was lying, wasn't he, Mama?"

"What about, my boy?" I inquired absently.

"About everyt'ing, Mama."

"I rather think you are correct, Ramses."

V

I was afire with impatience to tell Emerson we had been given an opportunity to expose the ring of antiquities thieves. When we reached Shepheards I was surprised to find he had not yet returned. He was not so fond of de Morgan that he would have lingered, chatting. However, he had many friends in Cairo, and I supposed he had stopped to see one of them and, as he often did, lost track of the time.

After looking in on John and finding him sweetly sleeping, I ordered water to be brought. Ramses needed a bath. He needed a bath three or four times a day under normal circumstances, and the dust of the bazaars, not to mention the honey, had had dire effects. Ramses obediently retired behind the plaited screen that concealed the implements of ablution. For a time he splashed and sputtered in silence; then he began to hum, another annoying habit he had picked up while staying with his aunt and uncle. Like his father, Ramses is completely tone-deaf. The flat insistent drone of his voice was extremely trying to sensitive ears like mine, and it seemed now to have acquired a certain oriental quality—a quavering rise and fall, reminiscent of the Cairo street singers. I listened until I could bear it no longer and then requested that he desist.

He had finished bathing and was almost dressed before my senses, straining for the longed-for harbingers of his father's return, became aware of a sound like distant thunder. Ever louder and more furious the noise became as it neared our door. I looked at Ramses. He looked at me. The cat Bastet rose from the mat and retreated, with dignity but in haste, under the bed. The door quivered, shuddered, and flew open, striking the wall with a crash. Loosened plaster dribbled floorward..

Emerson stood in the opening. His face was brick-red. The veins in his throat stood out like ropes. He strove to speak, and failed; only a low growling noise emerged from his writhing lips. The growl rose to a roar and from the roar words finally took shape.

I covered my ears with my hands, then removed one hand to gesture imperatively at Ramses. Emerson was cursing in Arabic, and I felt sure the boy was making mental notes of "de colloquial speech."

Emerson's rolling eyes focused on his son's fascinated face. With a mighty effort he controlled his wrath. He allowed himself the final solace of kicking the door closed. A stream of plaster added itself to the heap already on the floor. Emerson took a long breath, his chest expanding to such an extent, I feared the buttons would pop off his shirt. "Er—hem," he said. "Hello, my boy. Amelia. Did you have a pleasant morning?"

"Let us eschew the amenities on this occasion," I exclaimed. "Get it off your chest, Emerson, before you explode. Only avoid profanity, if at all possible."

"It is not possible," Emerson cried in an anguished voice. "I cannot speak without expletives concerning that villain—that vile—that . . . that—de Morgan!"

"He has refused you the firman for Dahshoor."

Emerson kicked a stool, sending it flying across the room. The head of Bastet, which had cautiously protruded from under the bed, vanished again.

"He means to work at Dahshoor himself this season," said Emerson in a strangled voice. "He had the effrontery to tell me I was too late in applying."

My lips parted. Before I could speak, Emerson turned a hideous glare upon me. "If you say 'I told you so,' Peabody, I will—I will—kick the bed to splinters!"

"By all means do so, if it will relieve your feelings, Emerson. I am deeply wounded by your accusation, which I feel sure you would never have made had you been in control of your emotions. You know I abhor the phrase you mentioned and that I never in all the years of our marriage—"

"The devil you haven't," Emerson snarled.

"De devil you haven't," echoed Ramses. "Don't you remember, Mama, yesterday on de train from Alexandria, and de day before dat, when Papa forgot—"

"Ramses!" Emerson turned, more in sorrow than in wrath, to his offending heir. "You must not use such language, particularly to your dear mama. Apologize at once."

"I apologize," Ramses said. "I meant no offense, Mama, but I do not see what is wrong wit' dat expression. It has a quality of colorful emphasis dat appeals strongly—"

"Enough, my son."

"Yes, Papa."

The silence that ensued was like the hush after a tempest, when the leaves hang limp in the quiet air and nature seems to catch her breath. Emerson sat down on the bed and mopped his streaming brow. His complexion subsided to the handsome walnut shade that is its normal color in Egypt, and a tender, affectionate smile transformed his face. "Were you waiting for me before lunching? That was kind, my dears. Let us go down at once."

"We must discuss this, Emerson," I said.

"Certainly, Amelia. We will discuss it over luncheon."

"Not if you are going to lose your temper. Shepheard's is a respectable hotel. Guests who shout obscenities and throw china across the dining salon—"

"I cannot imagine where you get such notions, Amelia," Emerson said in a hurt voice. "I never lose my temper. Ah—there is Bastet. That is a very handsome collar she is wearing. What is she doing under the bed?"

Bastet declined Ramses' invitation to lunch—an invitation made, I hardly need say, without reference to me—so the three of us went down. I was not deceived by Emerson's apparent calm; the blow had been cruel, the disappointment grievous, and I felt it hardly less than he. Of course it was Emerson's fault for not doing as I had suggested, but I would not for all the world have reminded him of that. After we had taken our places and the waiters had been dispatched in quest of the sustenance we had ordered, I said, "Perhaps I might have a little chat with M. de Morgan. He is a Frenchman, after all, and young; his reputation for gallantry—"

"Is only too well deserved," Emerson growled. "You are not to go near him, Amelia. Do you suppose I have forgotten the abominable way he behaved the last time we met?"

M. de Morgan's abominable behavior had consisted of kissing my hand and paying me a few flowery French compliments. However, I was touched by Emerson's assumption that every man I met had amorous designs on me. It was a delusion of his, but a pleasant delusion.

"What did he do?" Ramses asked interestedly.

"Never mind, my boy," Emerson said. "He is a Frenchman, and Frenchmen are all alike. They are not to be trusted with ladies or with antiquities. I don't know a single Frenchman who has the slightest notion of how to conduct an excavation."

Knowing that Emerson was capable of lecturing on this subject interminably and that Ramses was about to request more specific information about the untrustworthiness of Frenchmen with ladies, I turned the conversation back to the subject that concerned me.

"Very well, Emerson, if you would prefer I did not talk with him I will not. But what are we going to do? I assume he offered you another site?"

Emerson's cheeks darkened. "Control yourself," I implored. "Speak slowly and breathe deeply, Emerson. It cannot be as bad as that."

"It is worse, Peabody. Do you know what site that bas—that wretch had the effrontery to offer me? 'You desire pyramids,' he said, with that French smirk of his, 'I give you pyramids, my dear cabbage. Mazghunah. What do you say to Mazghunah?' "

He gave the guttural a rolling sound that made the word resemble an oath in some exotic language. "Mazghunah," I echoed. "Emerson, I confess the name is wholly unfamiliar. Where is it?"

My admission of ignorance had the desired effect of soothing Emerson's wounded dignity. He seldom gets the chance to lecture me on Egyptology. However, in this case I was not just being tactful. I did not recognize the name, and when Emerson had explained, I knew why it meant nothing to me—and why my poor spouse had been so wroth.

Mazghunah is only a few kilometers south of Dahshoor, the site we had wanted. Dahshoor, Sakkara, Giza and Mazghunah itself are the ancient cemeteries of Memphis, the once-great capital of ancient Egypt, of which only a few mounds of ruins now remain. All are close to Cairo and all boast pyramid tombs; but the two "pyramids" of Mazghunah exist only as limestone chips on the level desert floor. No one had bothered to investigate them because there was hardly anything left to investigate.

"There are also late cemeteries," said Emerson with a sneer. "De Morgan made a point of that, as if it were an added inducement instead of a handicap."

He pronounced the word "late" as if it were an insult, which to Emerson it was. Emerson's interest in Egypt began about 4000 B.C. and stopped 2500 years later. Nothing after 1500 B.C. had the slightest attraction for him, and the late cemeteries were dated to Roman and Ptolemaic times—trash, so far as Emerson was concerned.

Though my own spirits were low, I sought to cheer my afflicted husband. "There may be papyri," I said brightly. "Remember the papyri Mr. Petrie found at Hawara."

Too late I realized that the name of Mr. Petrie was not designed to improve Emerson's mood. Scowling, he attacked the fish the waiter had set in front of him, as if his fork were a spear and the fish were Mr. Petrie, boiled, flayed and at his mercy.

"He lied to me," he grunted. "His publication was not ready. It was late this year. Did you know that, Amelia?"

I did know. He had told me approximately fifteen times. Emerson brooded darkly on the iniquities of Petrie and de Morgan. "He did it deliberately, Amelia. Mazghunah is close to Dahshoor; he will make sure I receive daily reports of his discoveries while I dig up Roman mummies and degenerate pottery."

"Then don't take Mazghunah. Demand another site."

Emerson ate in silence for a time. Gradually his countenance lightened and a smile curved his well-shaped lips. I knew that smile. It boded ill for someone— and I thought I knew for whom.

At last my husband said slowly, "I will accept Mazghunah. You don't mind, do you, Peabody? When I visited the site some years ago I determined to my own satisfaction that the remains were those of pyramids. The superstructures have entirely disappeared, but there are surely passageways and chambers underground. There is not a chance of anything better; Firth has Sakkara, and the Giza pyramids are so popular with tourists, one can't work there."

"I don't mind. 'Whither thou goest,' you know, Emerson; but I do hope you are not planning any ill-advised assaults on M. de Morgan."

"I cannot imagine what you mean," said Emerson. "Naturally I will offer the gentleman the benefit of my experience and superior knowledge whenever the opportunity presents itself. I am determined to turn the other cheek, and render good where . . ."

He broke off, catching my skeptical eye upon him; and after a moment his great hearty laugh boomed out across the dining salon, stopping conversation and making the crystal chime. Emerson's laugh is irresistible. I joined him, while Ramses watched with a faint smile, like an elderly philosopher tolerant of the antics of the young. It was not until after we had returned to our room that I discovered Ramses had taken advantage of our distraction to conceal his fish under his blouse as a present for Bastet. She enjoyed it very much.

Chapter Three

THOUGH I attempted to conceal my feelings, I was exceedingly put out. It seemed hard indeed that I should have to suffer from Emerson's blunder, for it was nothing less. De Morgan had dug at Dahshoor the year before. It would have required considerable tact and persuasion to convince him to yield the site to another excavator, and Emerson's methods of persuasion were not calculated to win over an opponent. Though I had not been present, I knew only too well what had transpired. Emerson had marched into de Morgan's office, unannounced and uninvited; rested his fists on the director's desk; and proclaimed his intent. "Good morning, monsieur. I will be working at Dahshoor this season."

De Morgan had stroked his luxuriant mustache. "*Mais, mon cher collègue, c'est impossible.* I will be working at Dahshoor this season."

Emerson's response would have been an indignant shout and a crash of his fist on the table; de Morgan would have continued to stroke his mustache and shake his head until Emerson stamped out of the door, annihilating small tables and miscellaneous chairs as he went.

I looked through the reference books we had brought with us in a vain attempt to find something about Mazghunah. Few of the authorities so much as mentioned it, and if there were pyramids at the site, that fact was not widely known. If Emerson had not confirmed their existence, I would have suspected de Morgan of inventing them, to taunt Emerson.

Emerson exaggerates, in his humorous fashion, when he says I have a passion for pyramids. However, I admit to a particular affection for these structures. On my first visit to Egypt as a tourist I had fallen victim to the charm of their dark, stifling passageways, carpeted with rubble and bat droppings. Yet, since taking up the practice of archaeology I had never been able to investigate a pyramid professionally. Our interests had taken us elsewhere. I had not realized how I yearned to explore a pyramid until I found I could not.

"Abusir," I said. "Emerson, what about Abusir? The pyramids there are much decayed, but they *are* pyramids."

"We will dig at Mazghunah," said Emerson. He said it very quietly, but his chin protruded in a manner I knew well. Emerson's chin is one of his most seductive features. When it jutted out in that particular fashion, however, I had to repress a desire to strike it smartly with my clenched fist.

"The remains of the pyramid at Zawaiet el 'Aryân," I persisted. "Maspero failed to enter it ten years ago. We might find the entrance he missed."

Emerson was visibly tempted. He would love to do Maspero or any other archaeologist one better. But after a moment he shook his head. "We will dig at Mazghunah," he repeated. "I have my reasons, Amelia."

"And I know what they are. They do you no credit, Emerson. If you intend—"

Crossing the room in a few long strides, he stopped my mouth with his. "I will make it up to you, Peabody," he murmured. "I promised you pyramids, and pyramids you will have. In the meantime, perhaps this . . ."

Being unable to articulate, I gestured wordlessly at the door connecting our room to the next. Ramses had retired thither, purportedly to give John an Arabic lesson. The murmur of their voices, broken now and again by a chuckle from John, bore out the claim.

With a hunted look at the door, my husband released me. "When will this torment end?" he cried, clutching his hair with both hands.

Ramses' voice broke off for a moment and then continued.

"John should be able to resume his duties tomorrow," I said.

"Why not tonight?" Emerson smiled meaningfully.

"Well . . . Good heavens," I exclaimed. "I had forgotten. We have a rendezvous this night, Emerson. The distressing news quite shook it out of my head."

Emerson sat down on the bed. "Not again," he said. "You promised me, Amelia. . . . What are you up to now?"

I told him what had transpired at the bazaar. Little gasps and cries escaped his lips as I proceeded, but I raised my voice and went on, determined to present him with a connected narrative. At the end I produced the scrap of papyrus.

"Obviously Abd el Atti was lying when he claimed he had no papyri," I said. "To be sure, this is Coptic, but—"

Emerson pushed the fragment aside. "Precisely. Walter is not interested in Coptic; that is the language of Christian Egypt."

"I am well aware of that, Emerson. This fragment proves—"

"You had no business going to that fat scoundrel. You know what I think of—"

"And you know that the dealers are likely to have the best manuscripts. I promised Walter—"

"But this is not—"

"Where there is one scrap there must be a papyrus. I—"

"I told you—"

"I am convinced—"

"You—"

"You—"

By this time we were both on our feet and our voices had risen considerably. I make no apologies for my exasperation. Emerson would try the patience of a saint. He loses his temper on the slightest provocation.

We broke off speaking at the same time, and Emerson began pacing rapidly up and down the room. In the silence the rise and fall of Ramses' voice went placidly on.

Finally Emerson left off pacing. Rapid movement generally calms him, and I will do him the justice to admit that although he is quick to explode, he is equally quick to regain his temper. I smoothed his ruffled locks. "I told Abd el Atti we would come to the shop tonight."

"So you said. What you failed to explain is why the devil I should put myself out for the old rascal. There are other things I would rather do tonight."

His eyes sparkled significantly as he looked at me, but I resisted the appeal. "He is desperately afraid of something or someone, Emerson. I believe he is involved in the illicit antiquities business."

"Well, of course he is, Peabody. All of them are."

"I am referring, Emerson, to the recent, unprecedented flood of stolen objects you and Walter were discussing. You yourself said that some new player must have entered the game—some unknown genius of crime, who has organized the independent thieves into one great conspiracy."

"I said no such thing! I only suggested—"

"Abd el Atti is a member of the gang. His reference to the Master eating his heart—"

"Picturesque, but hardly convincing," said Emerson. His tone was less vehement, however, and I saw that my arguments had made an impression. He went on, "Are you certain you understood correctly? I cannot believe he would make a damaging admission in your presence."

"He didn't know I was present. Besides—weren't you listening, Emerson?—he was speaking the *siim issaagha.*"

"Very well," Emerson said. "I agree that Abd el Atti may well be involved in something deeper and darker than his usual shady activities. But your notion that he is a member of some imaginary gang is pure surmise. You have an absolutely unique ability to construct a towering structure of theory on one single fact. Foundationless towers totter, my dear Peabody. Control your rampageous imagination and spare your afflicted spouse, I beg."

He was working himself into another fit of temper, so I only said mildly, "But supposing I am right, Emerson? We may have an opportunity to stop this vile traffic in antiquities, which we both abhor. Is not the chance of that, however remote, worth the trifling inconvenience I propose?"

"Humph," said Emerson.

I knew the grunt was as close to a concession as I was likely to get, so I did not pursue the discussion, which would have been ended in any case by the advent of our son, announcing that the Arabic lesson was over. I did not want Ramses to get wind of our plan. He would have insisted on accompanying us, and his father might have been foolish enough to agree.

I was about to put my scrap of papyrus away when Ramses asked if he might look at it. I handed it over, cautioning him to be careful, an admonition to which he replied with a look of mingled scorn and reproach.

"I know you will," I said. "But I don't see what you want with it. Your Uncle Walter has not taught you Coptic along with hieroglyphs, has he?"

"Uncle Walter does not know de Coptic," replied Ramses loftily. "I am only curious to see what I can make of dis from my acquaintance wit' de ancient language; for, as you may be aware, de Coptic language is a development of de Egyptian, t'ough written in Greek script."

I waved him away. Bad enough to be lectured on Egyptology by one's husband; the smug and dogmatic pronouncements of my juvenile son were sometimes extremely trying to my nerves. He settled down at the table with Bastet beside him. Both bent their attention upon the text, the cat appearing to be as interested as the boy.

The door of the adjoining room now responded to a series of blows— John's version of a knock. He has extremely large hands and no idea of his own strength. It was a pleasure to hear the sound, however, after the long silence from that direction, and I bade him enter. Emerson took one look at him and burst out laughing.

He wore the uniform of a footman, which he had presumably brought with him from England—knee breeches, brass buttons and all—and I must confess that he looked rather ridiculous in that setting. Emerson's mirth brought a faint blush to his boyish face, though it was apparent he had no idea what his master found so funny. "I am at your service, sir and madam," he announced. "With apologies for failing to carry out me duties in the past days and respectful thanks for the kind attentions received from madam."

"Very well, very well," Emerson said. "Sure you are fit, my boy?"

"Quite fit," I assured him. "Now, John, be sure never to leave off your flannel, and take care what you eat and drink."

I glanced at Ramses as I concluded my advice, remembering the sweet-meat he had consumed—an incident I had not thought worth mentioning to his father. He seemed quite all right. I had been sure he would. Poisonous leaves and berries, india rubbers, ink and quantities of sweets that would have felled an ox had all passed through Ramses' digestive tract without the slightest disturbance of that region.

Standing stiffly at attention, John asked for orders. I said, "There is nothing to do at present; why don't you go out for a bit? You have seen nothing of the city, or even the hotel."

"I will go wit' him," said Ramses, pushing his chair back.

"I don't know," I began.

"What of your work, my son?" inquired Emerson. This attempt, more subtle than my own, was equally fruitless. Ramses picked up his hat and started for the door. "De manuscript appears to have belonged to a person called Didymus Thomas," he said coolly. "Dat is all I can make out at present, but I will have anodder go at it after I have procured a Coptic dictionary. Come along, John."

"Stay in the hotel," I said quickly. "Or on the terrace. Do not eat anything. Do not speak to the donkey boys. Do not repeat to anyone the words you learned from the donkey boys. Do not go in the kitchen, or the bathrooms, or any of the bedrooms. Stay with John. If you mean to take Bastet with you, put her on the lead. Do not let her off the lead. Do not let her chase mice, dogs, other cats or ladies' skirts."

I paused for breath. Ramses pretended to take this for the end of the lecture. With an angelic smile he slipped out the door.

"Hurry," I implored John. "Don't let him out of your sight."

"You may count on me, madam," said John, squaring his shoulders. "I am ready and equal to the task. I—"

"Hurry!" I pushed him out the door. Then I turned to Emerson. "Did I cover all the contingencies?"

"Probably not," said my husband. He drew me into the room and closed the door.

"There is no way of locking it," I said, after an interval.

"Mmmm," said Emerson agreeably.

"They will not be gone long. . . ."

"Then we must make the best use of the time at our disposal," said Emerson.

II

I had neglected to forbid Ramses to climb the palm trees in the courtyard. He explained in an injured tone that he had only wanted to get a better look at the dates, of which he had heard; but he had not eaten a single one. In proof of this he presented me with a handful, removing them with some difficulty from the pocket of his little shirt.

I sent him off to be bathed by John and began laying out Emerson's evening clothes. He studied them with loathing.

"I told you, Amelia, I have no intention of wearing those garments. What torture have you planned now?"

"I have invited guests to dine with us tonight," I said, removing my wrapper. "Help me with my dress, will you please?"

Emerson is so easily distracted. He moved with alacrity to drop the gown over my head, and then bent his attention upon the buttons. "Who is it? Not Petrie; he never accepts invitations to dine. Sensible man. . . . Naville? Carter? Not . . ." The hands fumbling along my spine stopped, and Emerson's face loomed up over my shoulder, glaring like a gargoyle. "Not de Morgan! Peabody, if you have some underhanded scheme in mind—"

"Would I do such a thing?" De Morgan had refused the invitation, with polite regrets; he was engaged elsewhere. "No," I continued, as Emerson returned to the buttons—the frock had dozens of them, each about the size of a pea. "I was happy to learn the *Istar* and the *Seven Hathors* are in port."

"Oh. Sayce and Wilberforce." Emerson breathed heavily on the back of my neck. "I cannot imagine what you see in those two. A dilettante clergyman and a renegade politician"

"They are excellent scholars. The Reverend Sayce has just been appointed to the new chair of Assyriology at Oxford."

"Dilettantes," Emerson repeated. "Sailing up and down the Nile on their dahabeeyahs instead of working like honest men."

A wistful sigh escaped me and Emerson, the most sensitive of men, again interrupted his labors to look inquiringly over my shoulder. "Do you miss your dahabeeyah, Peabody? If it would please you—"

"No, no, my dear Emerson. I confess that season of sailing was utter bliss; but I would not exchange it for the pleasure of our work together."

This admission resulted in a longer interruption of the buttoning, but I finally persuaded Emerson to complete the task. Turning, I demanded his comment.

"I like that dress, Peabody. Crimson becomes you. It reminds me of the gown you wore the night you proposed marriage to me."

"You will have your little joke, Emerson." I inspected myself in the mirror. "Not too bright a shade for a matron and the mother of a growing boy? No? Well, I accept your judgment as always, my dear Emerson."

I too had fond memories of the gown to which he referred. I had worn it on the night *he* proposed to me, and I took care always to have in my wardrobe a frock of similar cut and color. One abomination of the past was gone, however—the bustle. I could have wished that some fashion arbiter would also do away with corsets. Mine were never as tight as fashion decreed, for I had grave suspicions about the effect of tight lacing on the internal organs. I did not wear them at all under my working clothes, but some concession was necessary with evening dress in order to attain the smooth flowing line then in style.

I clasped about my neck a gold chain bearing a scarab of Thutmose III—my husband's gift—and, my toilette completed, went to assist Emerson with his. John and Ramses returned in time to contribute their assistance, which was not unwelcome, for Emerson carried on in his usual fashion, losing collar buttons, studs and links because of the vehemence with which he attacked these accessories. Ramses had become particularly good at locating collar buttons; he was small enough to crawl under beds and other furniture.

Emerson looked so handsome in evening dress that the effort was all worthwhile. His heightened color and the brilliant blue of his eyes, flaming with rage, only added to his splendid appearance. Unlike most of the men of my acquaintance, he remained clean-shaven. I preferred him without hirsute adornment, but I suspected it was only another example of Emersonian perversity. If beards had gone out of style, Emerson would have grown one.

"You are very handsome, Papa," said Ramses admiringly. "But I would not like a suit like dat. It is too hard to keep clean."

Emerson brushed absently at the cat hairs adhering to his sleeve, and I sent Ramses off for another bath. It was apparent that no one ever dusted under the bed. We ordered supper to be sent up for John and Ramses and went downstairs to meet our guests.

Dinner was not wholly a success. But then dinner never was when Emerson was in a surly mood, and he was almost always in a surly mood when he was forced to dine out in public and in formal attire. I have seen him behave worse. He had a grudging respect for Mr. Wilberforce, but the Reverend Sayce brought out all his baser instincts. There could not have been a greater contrast between two men—Emerson, tall, broad-shouldered and hearty, Sayce small and spare, with sunken eyes behind his steel-rimmed spectacles. He wore clerical garb even when on an excavation, and looked like a magnified beetle in his long-tailed black coat and reversed collar.

Wilberforce, whom the Arabs called "Father of a Beard," was a more phlegmatic character, and Emerson had given up teasing him, since he only responded by smiling and stroking his magnificent white beard. They greeted us with their customary affability and expressed regret that they would not have the pleasure of meeting Ramses that evening.

"As usual you are au courant with all the news," I said in a spritely manner. "We only arrived yesterday, yet you are aware that our son is with us this season."

"The community of scholars and Egyptologists is small," said Wilberforce with a smile. "It is only natural we should take an interest in one another's activities."

"I don't see why," said Emerson, with the air of a man who has determined to be disagreeable. "The personal activities of others, scholars or not, are exceedingly dull. And the professional activities of most of the archaeologists of my acquaintance are not worth talking about."

I tried to turn the conversation by a courteous inquiry after Mrs. Wilberforce. I had, of course, included that lady in my invitation, but she had been forced to decline. She was always forced to decline. She appears to have been a rather sickly person.

My tactful efforts were unavailing, however. The Reverend Sayce, who had been needled by Emerson on only too many occasions, was not Christian enough to forgo a chance at revenge. "Speaking of professional activities," he said, "I understand our friend de Morgan has great hopes for his excavations at Dahshoor. Where is it that you will be working this season, Professor?"

Seeing by Emerson's expression that he was about to launch into a diatribe against de Morgan, I kicked him under the table. His expression changed to one of extreme anguish and he let out a cry of pain. "Mazghunah," I said, before Emerson could collect himself. "We are excavating at Mazghunah this season. The pyramids, you know."

"Pyramids?" Wilberforce was too courteous to contradict a lady, but he looked doubtful. "I confess I don't know the site, but I did think I was familiar with all the known pyramids."

"These," I said, "are unknown pyramids."

Conversation then became general. It was not until we had retired to the lounge for brandy and cigars (in the case of the gentlemen) that I produced my scrap of papyrus and handed it to the reverend.

"I procured this today from one of the antiquities dealers. Since you are the biblical authority among us, I thought you might make more of it than I have been able to do."

The reverend's deep-set eyes lit with the flame of inquiry. Adjusting his spectacles, he examined the writing, saying as he did so, "I am no authority on Coptic, Mrs. Emerson. I expect this is probably . . ." His voice trailed off as he bent his full attention to the text, and Wilberforce remarked, smiling, "I am surprised at you, Mrs. Amelia. I thought you and your husband refused to buy from dealers."

"I do refuse," said Emerson, his nose in the air. "Unfortunately, my wife's principles are more elastic than mine."

"We are looking for papyri for Walter," I explained.

"Ah, yes—Professor Emerson the younger. One of the finest students of the language. But I'm afraid you will find the competition keen, Mrs. Amelia. With so many of the younger men studying Egyptian, everyone wants new texts."

"Including yourself?" I asked, with a keen look at Mr. Wilberforce.

"To be sure. But," the American said, his eyes twinkling, "I'll play fair and square, ma'am. If you find something worthwhile, I won't try to steal it."

"Which is more than can be said for some of our associates," grumbled Emerson. "If you happen to meet Wallis Budge, tell him I carry a stout stick and will use it on anyone who tries to make off with my property."

I did not hear Mr. Wilberforce's reply. My attention was caught by two people who had just entered the lounge.

The young man had turned his head to address his companion. The profile thus displayed was pure Greek, with the spare and exquisite modeling of a fifth-century Apollo or Hermes. His hair, brushed back from his high, classical brow, shone like electrum, the blend of silver and gold used by the Egyptians in their most priceless ornaments. The extreme pallor of his skin— which led me to deduce that he had not been long in the sunny clime of Egypt—added to the impression of a carving in alabaster. Then he smiled, in response to some comment of his companion, and a remarkable transformation took place. Benevolence beamed from every aspect of his countenance. The marble statue came alive.

The lady with him . . . was no lady. Her gown of deep-purple satin in the latest and most extravagant style suggested not the world of fashion but the demi-monde. It was trimmed with sable and beads, ruffles and lace, bows, puffs and plumes, yet it managed to bare an improper amount of plump white bosom. Gems blazed from every part of her portly person, and cosmetics covered every square centimeter of her face. If the gentleman was a classic marble carving, his companion was a blowsy, painted carnival statue.

Emerson jogged my elbow. "What are you gaping at, Amelia? Mr. Wilberforce asked you a question."

"I beg your pardon," I said. "I confess I was staring at that extremely handsome young man."

"You and every other lady in the room," said Mr. Wilberforce. "It is a remarkable face, is it not? I was reminded when I first met him of the young horsemen on the Parthenon frieze."

The pair came toward us, the female clinging to her companion's arm, and I saw with a shock that the Greek hero wore a clerical collar. "A clergyman," I exclaimed.

"That accounts for the fascination of the ladies," said Emerson with a curling lip. "All weak-minded females dote on weedy curates. One of your colleagues, Sayce?"

The reverend looked up. A frown wrinkled his brow. "No," he said, rather curtly.

"He is an American," Wilberforce explained. "A member of one of those curious sects that proliferate in my great country. I believe they call themselves the Brethren of the Holy Jerusalem."

"And the—er—lady?" I inquired.

"I cannot imagine why you are interested in these persons," Emerson grumbled. "If there is anything more tedious than a pious hypocrite of a preacher, it is an empty-headed fashionable woman. I am thankful I have nothing to do with such people."

It was Mr. Wilberforce to whom I had addressed my inquiry, and as I expected he was able to satisfy my curiosity. "She is the Baroness von Hohensteinbauergrunewald. A Bavarian family, related to the Wittelsbachs, and almost as wealthy as that royal house."

"Ha," Emerson cried. "The young man is a fortune hunter. I knew it. A weedy, sanctimonious fortune hunter."

"Oh, do be quiet, Emerson," I said. "Are they engaged? She seems very friendly with the young man."

"I hardly think so," said Wilberforce, smothering a smile. "The baroness is a widow, but the disparity of their ages, to mention only one incongruity . . . And to call the young man a fortune hunter is unjust. All who know him speak of him with the greatest respect."

"I don't want to know him, or talk about him," said Emerson. "Well, Sayce, what do you make of Mrs. Emerson's fragment?"

"It is a difficult text," Sayce said slowly. "I can read the proper names—they are Greek—"

"Didymus Thomas," I said.

"I congratulate you on your understanding, Mrs. Emerson. I am sure you also noted this ligature, which is the abbreviation for the name of Jesus."

I smiled modestly. Emerson snorted. "A biblical text? That's all the Copts ever wrote, curse them—copies of Scripture and boring lies about the saints. Who was Didymus Thomas?"

"The apostle, one presumes," said the reverend.

"Doubting Thomas?" Emerson grinned. "The only apostle with an ounce of sense. I always liked old Thomas."

Sayce frowned. " 'Blessed are they who have not seen and who have believed,' " he quoted.

"Well, what else could the man say?" Emerson demanded. "I admit he knew how to turn a phrase—if he ever existed, which is questionable."

Sayce's wispy goatee quivered with outrage. "If that is your view, Professor, this scrap can be of little interest to you."

"Not at all." Emerson plucked it from the reverend's hand. "I shall keep it as a memento of my favorite apostle. Really, Sayce, you are no better than the other bandits in my profession, trying to steal my discoveries."

Mr. Wilberforce loudly announced that it was time to go. Emerson continued to talk, expressing a series of opinions calculated to infuriate the Reverend Sayce. They ranged from his doubts as to the historicity of Christ to his poor opinion of Christian missionaries. "The effrontery of the villains," he exclaimed, referring to the latter. "What business have they forcing their narrow-minded prejudices on Muslims? In its pure form the faith of Islam is as good as any other religion—which is to say, not very good, but . . ."

Wilberforce finally drew his affronted friend away, but not before the reverend got off a final shot. "I wish you luck with your 'pyramids,' Professor. And I am sure you will enjoy your neighbors at Mazghunah."

"What do you suppose he meant by that?" Emerson demanded as the two walked off, Wilberforce's tall form towering over that of his slighter friend.

"We will find out in due course, I suppose."

Those were my precise words. I recall them well. Had I but known under what hideous circumstances they would recur to me, like the slow tolling of a funeral bell, a premonitory shudder would have rippled through my limbs. But it did not.

After looking in on Ramses and finding him wrapped in innocent slumber, with the cat asleep at his feet, Emerson proposed that we seek our own couch.

"Have you forgotten our assignation?" I inquired.

"I hoped that you had," Emerson replied. "Abd el Atti is not expecting us, Amelia. He only said that to get rid of you."

"Nonsense, Emerson. When the muezzin calls from the minaret at midnight—"

"He will do no such thing. You ought to know better, Amelia. There is no midnight call to prayer. Daybreak, midday, midafternoon, sunset and nightfall—those are the prescribed times of *salah* for faithful Muslims."

He was quite correct. I cannot imagine why the fact had slipped my mind. Rallying from my momentary chagrin, I said, "But surely I have sometimes heard a muezzin call in the night."

"Oh yes, sometimes. Religious fervor is apt to seize the devout at odd times. But one cannot predict such occasions. Depend on it, Amelia, the old scoundrel won't be at his shop."

"We can't be certain of that."

Emerson stamped his foot. "Curse it, Amelia, you are the most stubborn woman of my acquaintance. Let us compromise—if that word is in your vocabulary."

I folded my arms. "Propose your compromise."

"We'll sit on the terrace for another hour or so. If we hear a call to prayer, from any mosque within earshot, we will go the Khan el Khaleel. If by half past twelve we have heard nothing, we will go to bed."

Emerson had come up with a sensible suggestion. The plan was precisely what I had been about to propose, for after all, we could not start out for the shop until we had heard the signal.

"That is a very reasonable compromise," I said. "As always, Emerson, I submit to your judgment."

There are worse ways of passing an hour than on Shepheard's terrace. We sat at a table near the railing, sipping our coffee and watching the passersby, for people keep late hours in the balmy clime of Egypt. The stars, thickly clustered, hung so low they appeared to be tangled in the branches of the trees, and they gave a light almost as bright as day. Flower sellers offered their wares—necklaces of jasmine, bouquets of rosebuds tied with bright ribbons. The scent of the flowers hung heavy and intoxicating in the warm night air. Emerson presented me with a nosegay and squeezed my hand. With the warm pressure of his fingers on mine, and his eyes speaking sentiments that required no words of ordinary speech; with the seductive breeze caressing my cheek and the scent of roses perfuming the night—I almost forgot my purpose.

But hark—what was that? High and clear above the moonlit cupolas, rising and falling in musical appeal—the cry of the muezzin! *"Allâhu akbar, allâhu akbar—lâ ilâha illa'llâh!"* God is great, God is great; there is no God but God.

I sprang to my feet. "I knew it! Quickly, Emerson, let us be off."

"Curse it," said Emerson. "Very well, Amelia. But when I get my hands on that fat villain he will be sorry he suggested this."

We had, of course, changed into our working attire before coming down to the terrace. Emerson changed because he hated evening dress; I changed because I had been certain all along we would be going to the Khan el Khaleel. And, as events proved, I was right. Emerson insists to this day that Abd el Atti never meant us to come, and that the spontaneous exclamation of the muezzin that night was pure coincidence. The absurdity of this should be readily apparent.

Be that as it may, we were on our way before the last testimonial of the religious person had faded into silence. We went on foot; it would have been inapropos to take a carriage to a secret rendezvous, and, in any case, no wheeled vehicle could have entered the narrow alleys of the Khan el Khaleel. Emerson set a rapid pace. He was eager to have the business over and done with. I was eager to reach the shop and learn what deadly secret threatened my old friend. For I had a certain fondness for Abd el Atti. He might be a scoundrel, but he was an engaging scoundrel.

After we had turned from the Muski into the narrower ways of the bazaar, the starlight was cut off by the houses looming high on either hand, and the farther we penetrated into the heart of the maze, the darker it became. The protruding balconies with their latticed wooden shutters jutted into the street, almost meeting overhead. Occasionally a lighted window spilled a golden glimmer onto the pathway, but most of the windows were dark. Parallel slits of light marked closed shutters. The darkness teemed with foul movement; rats glided behind heaps of refuse; lean, vicious stray dogs slunk into even narrower passageways as we approached. The rank stench of rotting fruit, human waste and infected air filled the tunnel-like street like a palpable liquid, clogging the nostrils and the lungs.

Emerson plunged on, splashing through puddles of unspeakable stuff and sometimes slipping on a melon rind or rotten orange. I stayed close behind him. This was the first time I had been in the old city at night without a servant carrying a torch. I am not easily daunted. Danger I can face unafraid, enemies I have confronted without losing my calm; but the stealthy, stinking silence began to overpower my mind. I was glad Emerson was with me, and even happier that he had not suggested I remain behind. In this, as in all our adventures, we were equal partners. Few men could have accepted that arrangement. Emerson is a remarkable man. But then, if he had not been a remarkable man, I would not have married him.

Except for the soft, sinister movements of the predators of the night, the silence was complete. In the modern street, where the tourists and those who catered to their whims still sought pleasure, there were lights and laughter, music and loud voices. The dwellers of the Khan el Khaleel were asleep or engaged in occupations that demanded dim lights and barred doors. As we proceeded I caught a whiff of sickening sweetness and saw a pallid streak of light through a shuttered window. A voice, muted by the thick mud-plaster walls, rose in a thin shriek of pain or ecstasy. The house was a *ghurza,* an opium den, where the *hashshahiin* lay wrapped in stuporous dreams. I bit back a cry as a dark form rushed through an opening ahead and vanished into a doorway, blending with the blackness there. Emerson chuckled. "The *nadurgiyya* was dozing. He ought to have heard us approaching before this."

He spoke softly; but oh, how wonderfully, blessedly comforting was that calm English voice! *"Nadurgiyya?"* I repeated.

"The lookout. He took us for police spies. The *ghurza* will close down until the supposed danger is past. Are you sorry you came, Peabody?"

The street was so narrow we could not walk side by side and so dark I could scarcely make out the vague outline of his form. I sensed, rather than saw, the hand stretched toward me. Clasping it, I replied truthfully, "Not at all, my dear Emerson. It is a most interesting and unusual experience. But I confess that if you were not with me I would be conscious of a certain trepidation."

"We are almost there," Emerson said. "If this is a wild-goose chase, Peabody, I will hold it over you for the rest of your life."

Like all the others, Abd el Atti's shop was dark and seemingly deserted. "What did I tell you?" Emerson said.

"We must go round to the back," I said.

"The back, Peabody? Do you take this for an English village, with lanes and kitchen doors?"

"Don't play games, Emerson. I am quite confident you know where the back entrance is located. There must be another entrance; some of Abd el Atti's clients would hardly choose to walk in the front door with their goods."

Emerson grunted. Holding my hand, he proceeded along the street for a distance and then drew me toward what appeared to be a blank wall. There was an opening, however, so narrow and opaque that it looked like a line drawn with the blackest of ink. My shoulders brushed the walls on the other side. Emerson had to sidle along sideways.

"Here it is," he said, after a moment.

"Where? I can't see a thing."

He directed my hand toward an invisible surface. I felt wood under my fingers. "There is no knocker," I said, groping.

"Nor a doorbell," Emerson said sarcastically. He tapped lightly.

There was no response. Emerson, never the most patient of men, let out an oath and struck his fist against the door.

The panel yielded. A scant inch, no more, and in utter silence it moved; and through the slit came a pallid light, so dim it did not penetrate the darkness where we stood.

"The devil," Emerson muttered.

I shared his sentiments. There was something strange and sinister about the movement of the door. From within came not the slightest whisper of sound. It was as if a pall of horror lay over the region, silencing even breath. More prosaically, the yielding of the portal held ominous implications. Either the person who had opened it was concealed behind it, or the door had not been latched in the first place. It was inconceivable that a merchant in that quarter would leave his shop unlocked at night, unless . . .

"Stand back, Peabody," Emerson ordered. He reinforced the command with an outthrust arm that flung me back against the wall with rather more force than was necessary. Before I could protest, he raised his foot and kicked the door.

If he had intended to pin a would-be assassin between door and inner wall he failed. The portal was so heavy it responded sluggishly to his attack, opening only halfway. Emerson cursed and clutched his foot.

I went to his side and looked in. A single lamp, one of the crude clay bowls that have been used since ancient times, lit the room; the flickering, smoking flame created an eerie illusion of surreptitious movement in the shadows. The place was in the wildest disorder. Abd el Atti was not noted for neatness, but something more alarming than sloth was responsible for the confusion that prevailed. A rickety wooden table had been overturned. The bits of pottery and glass littering the floor must have fallen from its surface, or from the shelves on the righthand wall, which were empty. Mingled with the broken pieces were scarabs and ushebtis, scraps of papyrus and linen, stone vessels, carvings, and even a wrapped mummy, half-hidden by a wooden packing case.

Emerson repeated his adjuration to the Prince of Evil and stepped boldly forward. I caught his arm. "Emerson, take care. I hypothesize that a struggle has ensued here."

"Either that or Abd el Atti has suffered a seizure at long last."

"Were that the case, his prostrate body would be visible."

"True." Emerson fondled the cleft in his chin, his invariable habit when deep in thought. "Your hypothesis seems more likely."

He tried to shake off my hold, but I persisted. "Presumably one of the combatants was our old friend. But the other—Emerson, he may be lying in wait, ready to attack."

"He would be a fool if he stayed," Emerson replied. "Even if he had been on the premises when we arrived, he had ample time to make good his escape through the front of the shop while we stood here debating. Besides, where would he hide? The only possible place . . ." He peered behind the door. "No, there is no one here. Come in and close the door. I don't like the look of this."

I followed his instructions. I felt more secure with the heavy door closed against the dangers of the night. Yet a sinking feeling had seized me; I could not shake off the impression that something dreadful lurked in that quiet, shadowy place.

"Perhaps Abd el Atti was not here after all," I said. "Two thieves fell out—or down—"

Emerson continued to worry his chin. "Impossible to tell if anything is missing. What a clutter! Good Gad, Amelia—look there, on the shelf. That fragment of painted relief—I saw it only two years ago in one of the tombs at El Bersheh. Confound the old rascal, he has no more morals than a jackal, robbing his own ancestors!"

"Emerson," I remonstrated, "this is not the time—"

"And there . . ." Emerson pounced on an object half-concealed by pottery shards. "A portrait panel—torn from the mummy—encaustic on wood . . ."

Only one thing can distract Emerson from his passion for antiquities. It did not seem appropriate to apply this distraction. I left him muttering and scrabbling in the debris; slowly, with dread impeding my every step, I approached the curtained doorway that led to the front room of the shop. I knew what I would find and was prepared, as I thought, for the worst; yet the sight that met my eyes when I drew the curtain aside froze my limbs and my vocal apparatus.

At first it was only a dark, shapeless mass that almost filled the tiny room. The dark thing moved, gently swaying, like a monster of the deep sluggishly responding to the slow movements of watery currents. A shimmer of gold, a flash of scarlet—my eyes, adjusting to the gloom, began to make out details—a hand, glittering with rings . . . A face. Unrecognizable as human, much less familiar. Black and bloated, the dark tongue protruding in ghastly mockery, the wide eyes suffused with blood . . .

A shriek of horror burst from my lips. Emerson was instantly at my side. His hands closed painfully over my shoulders. "Peabody, come away. Don't look."

But I had looked, and I knew the sight would haunt my dreams: Abd el Atti, hanging from the roofbeam of his own shop, swaying to and fro like some winged monster of the night.

Chapter Four

CLEARING my throat, I reassured my husband, "I am quite myself again, Emerson. I apologize for startling you."

"No apologies are necessary, my dear Peabody. What a horrible sight! He was grotesque enough in life, but this . . ."

"Should we not cut him down?"

"Impractical and unnecessary," Emerson said. "There is not a spark of life left in him. We will leave that unpleasant task to the authorities." I tried to put his hands away, and he went on, in mounting indignation, "You don't mean to play physician? I assure you, Peabody—"

"My dear Emerson, I have never pretended I could restore life to the dead. But before we summon the police I want to examine the situation."

Accustomed as I am to violent death, it cost me some effort to touch the poor flaccid hand. It was still warm. Impossible to calculate the time of death; the temperature in the closed room was stiflingly hot. But I deduced he had not been dead long. I struck several matches and examined the floor, averting my eyes from Abd el Atti's dreadful face.

"What the devil are you doing?" Emerson demanded, arms akimbo. "Let's get out of this hellish place. We will have to return to the hotel to call the police; people in this neighborhood don't respond to knocks on the door at night."

"Certainly." I had seen what I needed to know. I followed Emerson into the back room and let the curtain fall into place, concealing the horror within.

"Looking for clues?" Emerson inquired ironically, as I inspected the litter on the floor. The mummy portrait was not there. I made no comment; the piece had been stolen anyway, and it could not be in better hands than those of my husband.

"I don't know what I'm looking for," I replied. "It is hopeless, I suppose; there is no chance of finding a clear footprint in this debris. Ah! Emerson, look here. Isn't this a spot of blood?"

"The poor fellow died of strangulation, Peabody," Emerson exclaimed.

"Obviously, Emerson. But I am sure this blood—"

"It is probably paint."

". . . that this blood is that of the thief who . . ."

"What thief?"

". . . who cut himself during the fight," I continued, being accustomed to Emerson's rude habit of interrupting. "His foot, I expect. He trampled on a bit of broken pottery while struggling with Abd el Atti—"

Emerson seized me firmly by the hand. "Enough, Peabody. If you don't come with me, I will throw you over my shoulder and carry you."

"The passageway outside is too narrow," I pointed out. "Just one minute, Emerson."

He tugged me to my feet as my fingers closed over the object that had caught my attention. "It is a scrap of papyrus," I exclaimed.

Emerson led me from the room.

We had reached the broad stretch of the Muski before either of us spoke again. Even that popular thoroughfare was quiet, for the hour was exceedingly late; but the beneficent glow of starlight lifted our spirits as it illumined the scene. I drew a long breath. "Wait a minute, Emerson. I can't walk so fast. I am tired."

"I should think so, after such a night." But Emerson immediately slowed his pace and offered me his arm. We walked on side-by-side, and I did not scruple to lean on him. He likes me to lean on him. In a much milder tone he remarked, "You were right after all, Peabody. The poor old wretch did have something on his mind. A pity he decided to end it all before he talked to us."

"What are you saying?" I exclaimed. "Abd el Atti did not commit suicide. He was murdered."

"Amelia, that is the merest surmise. I confess I had expected you would concoct some wild theory. Sensationalism is your meat and drink. But you cannot—"

"Oh, Emerson, don't be ridiculous. You saw the murder room. Was there anything near the body—a table, a chair, a stool—on which Abd el Atti might have stood while he tied the noose around his neck?"

"Damnation," said Emerson.

"No doubt. He was murdered, Emerson—our old friend was foully slain. And after he had appealed to us to save him."

"Pray do not insult my intelligence by attempting to move me with such sentimental tosh," Emerson exclaimed furiously. "If Abd el Atti was murdered, the killer was one of his criminal associates. It has nothing to do with us. Only an unhappy coincidence—or, more accurately, your incurable habit of meddling in other people's business—put us on the spot at the wrong time. We will notify the police, as is our duty, and that will be the end of it. I have enough on my mind this year. I will not allow my professional activities to be interrupted. . . ."

I let him grumble on. Time would prove me right; the inexorable pressure of events would force our involvement. So why argue?

II

A few hours' sleep restored me to my usual vigor and spirits. When I awoke the sun was high in the heavens. My first act, even before drinking the tea the safragi brought me, was to open the door to the adjoining room. It was empty. A note, placed prominently on the table, explained that John and Ramses, not wishing to waken us, had gone out to explore the city. "Do not worry, sir and madam," John had written. "I will watch over Master Ramses."

Emerson was not reassured by the message. "You see what happens when you go off on your absurd adventures," he grumbled. "We overslept and now our helpless young son is wandering the streets of this wicked city, unprotected and vulnerable."

"I too am deeply concerned," I assured him. "I dare not imagine what Ramses can do to Cairo in the space of a few hours. No doubt we will soon be receiving delegations of outraged citizens, with bills for damages."

I spoke half in jest. I did expect a confrontation, not with Ramses's victims, but with the police; for though Emerson resolutely refused to discuss the murder of Abd el Atti, I felt sure our involvement with that affair was not over. And indeed the message came as we were finishing breakfast, which had been brought to our room. The white-robed safragi bowed almost to the floor as he delivered it. Would we, in our infinite condescension, come to the manager's office, where an agent of the police wished to consult us?

Emerson flung down his napkin. "There, you see? More delay, more vexation. It is all your fault, Amelia. Come along, let's get this over and done with."

Mr. Baehler, the manager of Shepheard's, rose to greet us as we entered his office. He was Swiss—a tall, handsome man with a mane of graying hair and an ingratiating smile.

My answering smile turned to a grimace when I saw the other persons who were present. I had expected to find a police official. I had not expected that the official would have in his custody the small and incredibly filthy person of my son.

Emerson was equally affected. He brushed past Mr. Baehler, ignoring the latter's outstretched hand, and snatched Ramses up in his arms. "Ramses! My dear boy! What are you doing here? Are you injured?"

Crushed to his father's bosom, Ramses was incapable of replying. Emerson turned an infuriated look upon the policeman. "How dare you, sir?"

"Control yourself, Emerson," I exclaimed. "You ought rather to thank this gentleman for escorting the boy home."

The police officer gave me a grateful look. He was a grizzled, heavyset man, with a complexion of beautiful coffee-brown. His excellent English and tidy uniform displayed the unmistakable British discipline that has transformed Egypt since her Majesty's government assumed beneficent control over that formerly benighted land.

"Thank you, ma'am," he said, touching his cap. "The young master is not hurt, I promise."

"So I see. I had anticipated, Inspector—is that the proper mode of address?—I had anticipated that you had come to question us concerning the murder last night."

"But I have, ma'am," was the respectful reply. "We found the young master at the shop of the dead man."

I sank into the chair Mr. Baehler held for me. Ramses said breathlessly, "Mama, dere is a matter I would prefer to discuss wit' you in private—"

"Silence!" I shouted.

"But, Mama, de cat Bastet—"

"Silence, I say!"

Silence ensued. Even Mr. Baehler, whose reputation for equanimity and social pose was unequaled, appeared at a loss. Slowly and deliberately I turned to focus my gaze on John, who stood flattened against the wall between a table and a tall carved chair. It was not possible for a person of John's size to be inconspicuous. But he was trying his best. When my eye fell upon him he stammered, "Ow, madam, Oi tried me best, indeed Oi did, but Oi didn't 'ave the least idear where we was until—"

"Watch your vowels," I said sternly. "You are reverting to the unacceptable verbal customs of the ambience from which Professor Emerson rescued you. Five years of my training ought to have eradicated all traces of your past."

John swallowed. His Adam's apple quivered violently. "I," he said slowly, "did not know where we was—where we were—until—"

"Dat is right, Mama," Ramses piped up. "It was not John's fault. He t'ought we were only exploring de bazaars."

Everyone spoke at once. Mr. Baehler implored we would settle our family disputes in private, since he was a busy man; the inspector remarked that he had work to do elsewhere; Emerson bellowed at John; John tried to defend himself, his vowels suffering dreadfully in the process; Ramses defended John. I silenced the uproar by rising impetuously to my feet.

"Enough! Inspector, I presume you have no further need of Ramses?"

"I do not," said the gentleman, with heartfelt sincerity.

"John, take Ramses upstairs and wash him. Remain in your room—both of you—until we come. No, Emerson, not a word."

I was, of course, obeyed to the letter. After the miscreants had departed, I resumed my chair. "Now," I said. "To business."

It was soon dispatched. To my exceeding annoyance I found that the policeman's view of the case coincided with that of Emerson. He could hardly refuse to listen to my interpretation, but from the glances that passed among the gentlemen, not to mention Emerson's constant interruptions, I knew my views would be disregarded. "A falling-out between thieves," was the inspector's summary. "Thank you, Professor and Mrs. Emerson, for your assistance."

"When you have located the suspect, I will come to the police station to identify him," I said.

"Suspect?" The inspector stared at me.

"The man I saw yesterday talking to Abd el Atti. You noted down the description I gave you?"

"Oh. Yes, ma'am, I did."

"That description would fit half the male population of Cairo," Emerson said disparagingly. "What you really require, Inspector, is an expert to evaluate the contents of the shop. Most of it is stolen property; it belongs by rights to the Department of Antiquities. Though heaven knows there is no one in that dusty barn of a museum who has the slightest notion of how to care for the exhibits."

"My friends," Mr. Baehler said piteously. "Forgive me—"

"Yes, of course," I said. "Emerson, Mr. Baehler is a busy man; I cannot imagine why you continue to take up his time. We will continue our discussion of the case elsewhere."

However, the inspector unaccountably refused to do this. He did not even accept Emerson's offer of assistance in cataloging the contents of the shop. Emerson would have followed him, arguing, had I not detained him.

"You can't go out on the street looking like that. Ramses has rubbed off on you. What is that blackish, sticky substance, do you suppose?"

Emerson glanced at the front of his coat. "It appears to be tar," he said in mild surprise. "Speaking of Ramses—"

"Yes," I said grimly. "Let us speak of, and to, that young man."

We found John and Ramses sitting side by side on the bed, like criminals awaiting sentence—though there was little sign of guilt on Ramses' freshly scrubbed countenance. "Mama," he began, "de cat Bastet—"

"Where is the cat?" I asked.

Ramses became quite purple in the face with frustration. "But dat is what I am endeavoring to explain, Mama. De cat Bastet has been mislaid. When de policeman took hold of me, radder more roughly dan de circumstances required, in my opinion—"

"Roughly, did you say?" Emerson's countenance reflected the same angry shade as that of his son. "Curse it, I knew I should have punched the villain in the jaw. Remain here, I will return as soon as I—"

"Wait, Emerson, wait!" I caught hold of his arm with both hands and dug my heels into the mat. As we struggled, I to hold on and Emerson to free himself, Ramses remarked thoughtfully, "I would not have kicked him in de shin if he had been more courteous. To refer to me as a meddlesome imp of Satan was uncalled for."

Emerson stopped struggling. "Hmmm," he said.

"Forget the policeman," I cried. "Forget the cat. She will return of her own accord, Ramses; she is, after all, a native of the country."

"De reputed ability of animals to cross great stretches of unknown country is exaggerated, in my opinion," said Ramses.

"You have too many opinions," I retorted severely. "What were you doing at Abd el Atti's establishment?"

I find myself incapable of reproducing Ramses' explanation. His style of speech was extremely prolix, and he appeared deliberately to select as many words as possible beginning with the diphthong "th." Nor was it a convincing explanation. Ramses said he had been curious to examine further several objects he had seen in the back room of the shop during his unauthorized visit the day before. When directly questioned, he admitted he had overheard us discussing our intention of visiting Abd el Atti that night. "I meant to go wit' you," he added accusingly, "but I could not stay awake, and you, Mama, did not waken me."

"I had no intention of taking you, Ramses."

"I suspected dat," said Ramses.

"What objects were you curious about?" his father asked.

"Never mind," I said. "Do you realize that the day is half gone? I have never known any group of people to waste so much time over inconsequential matters."

Emerson shot me a look that said, plain as speech, "And whose fault is it that we have wasted half the day?" He did not speak aloud, however, since we try not to criticize one another before Ramses. A united front is absolutely essential for survival in that quarter. Instead he groaned, "I cannot shake the dust of this abominable city off my shoes too soon. I had hoped to leave by the end of the week, but . . ."

"We can leave tomorrow if we get to work at once," I replied. "What remains to be done?"

There was not really a great deal. I agreed to take care of our travel arrangements and the dispatch of the supplies I had purchased. Emerson was to go to Aziyeh, the nearby village from which we recruited our skilled workers, to make the final plans for their travel to Mazghunah.

"Take him with you," I said, indicating Ramses.

"Certainly," said Emerson. "I had intended to do that. What about John?"

John had lumbered to his feet when I entered the room. He remained standing, stiff as a statue, throughout the discussion, without venturing to speak. His eyes, fixed unblinkingly on my face, held the same expression of mingled shame and hope I had often seen on the countenances of the dogs after they had misbehaved.

"Madam," he began, with the most meticulous attention to his vowels, "I wish to say—"

"Too much has been said already," I interrupted. "I don't blame you,

John. You are off your native turf, so to speak. In future I will define the perimeters of your wanderings more carefully."

"Yes, madam. Thank you, madam." John beamed. "Am I to go with Master Ramses and the professor, madam?"

"No. I need you. Is that all right with you, Emerson?"

Emerson, in his consummate innocence, said that it was quite all right with him.

And so, after a hasty meal, we separated to complete our assigned tasks. I was soon finished with mine. Europeans constantly complain about the dilatory habits of the East, but I fancy that is only an excuse for their own incompetence. I have never had the least difficulty getting people to do what I want them to do. It only requires a firm manner and a determination not to be distracted from the matter at hand. That is Emerson's trouble, and, in fact, the trouble with most men. They are easily distracted. I knew, for instance, that Emerson would spend the rest of the day on a project that could have been completed in three hours, travel time included. He would loll around smoking and *fahddling* (gossiping) with Abdullah, our old foreman; Ramses would come home with his stomach stuffed with insanitary sweeties and his precocious brain stuffed with new words, most of them indelicate. I was resigned to this. The alternative would have been to take Ramses with me.

John followed me with mute and meticulous devotion while I carried out my tasks. The faintest shade of apprehension crossed his ingenuous countenance when I directed the driver of the carriage to let us out near the entrance to the Khan el Khaleel, but he held his tongue until we were almost at our destination.

"Ow, madam," he began. "Oi promised the master—"

"Vowels, John," I said. "Mind your vowels."

John fell in behind me as I passed under the archway leading from the square. "Yes, madam. Madam, are we going to that there—to that place?"

"Quite right."

"But, madam—"

"If you promised Professor Emerson you would prevent me from going there, you ought to have known better. And he ought not to have extracted from you a promise you could not possibly keep." John let out a faint moan and I condescended to explain—something I seldom do. "The cat, John—Ramses' cat. The least we can do is search for the animal. It would break the boy's heart to leave it behind."

A scene of utter pandemonium met our eyes when we turned into the street before the shop. The narrow way was completely blocked by bodies, including those of several donkeys. Most of the people were men, though there were a few women, all of the humblest class, and all seemed intent on some spectacle ahead. They were laughing and talking, their bodies swaying as they tried to see over the heads of those in the front rank. Children wriggled through the crowd.

A few polite Arabic phrases, and the judicious application of my useful parasol to backs, shoulders and heads soon captured the attention of those nearest me. Obligingly they parted to let me pass.

Abd el Atti's shop was the focus of the crowd's interest. I had expected to find it locked and shuttered, with a constable on duty. Instead the place stood wide open, with not a policeman in sight. The small front room of the shop was filled with workmen wearing the cheap blue-and-white-striped robes of their class, and raglike turbans upon their heads. As soon as I saw what was going on I understood the amusement of the spectators. One workman would rush forward with a bundle in his arms, which he would load on the nearest donkey. Another workman would remove it. The process appeared to have all the futility of Penelope's weaving and unpicking of her tapestry, and at first I could not imagine what it all meant. Then I saw two people who stood nose to nose in the center of the room, shouting contradictory orders. One was a man, wearing a proper European suit and a bright red tarboosh. The other was a woman clad in dusty black from head to foot. In her agitation she had let fall her veil, disclosing a face as wrinkled as a currant and as malevolent as that of a witch in a German fairy tale. Her mouth gaped, showing toothless gums, as she alternatively shouted orders at the workmen and insults at her opponent.

It appeared to be the sort of situation that demanded the assistance of a sensible person. I applied the ferrule of my parasol briskly but impartially to the people blocking my way, and proceeded to the door of the shop. The old lady was the first to catch sight of me. She stopped in mid-word—a most improper word for anyone, much less a woman, to employ—and stared at me. The workmen dropped their bundles and gaped; the crowd murmured and swayed, watching expectantly; and the man in the tarboosh turned to face me.

"What is going on here?" I demanded. "This is the shop of Abd el Atti. Who are these people who are stealing his property?"

I had spoken in Arabic, but the man, identifying my nationality by my dress, replied in accented but fluent English. "I am no thief, missus. I am the son of the late Abd el Atti. May I ask your honored name?"

The last question was pronounced with a decided sneer, which vanished as soon as I gave my name. The old woman let out a high-pitched cackle of laughter. "It is the woman of the Father of Curses," she exclaimed. "The one they call Sitt Hakim. I have heard of you, Sitt. You will not let an old woman be robbed—an honorable wife be cheated of her inheritance?"

"You are the wife of Abd el Atti?" I asked in disbelief. This hideous old harridan? Abd el Atti, who was wealthy enough to purchase any number of young wives, and who had a keen appreciation of beauty?

"His chief wife," said the beldam. Belatedly recalling her bereaved state, she let out a sharp, unconvincing yelp of woe and stooped to scrape up a handful of dust, which she poured haphazardly over her head.

"Your mother?" I asked the man.

"Allah forbid," was the pious reply. "But I am the eldest living son, missus. I am taking the merchandise to my own shop; it is a fine shop, missus, on the Muski, a modern shop. Many English come to me; if you come, I will sell you beautiful things, very cheap—"

"Yes, yes; but that is not the question," I said, absently accepting the card he handed me. "You cannot take these things away now. The police are investigating your father's death. Didn't they tell you to leave the scene of the crime undisturbed?"

"Crime?" A singularly cynical smile transformed the man's face. His eyes narrowed to slits and his lips barely parted. "My unfortunate father has gone to make his peace with Allah. He had the wrong friends, missus. I knew that sooner or later one of them would remove him."

"And you don't call that a crime?"

The man only shrugged and rolled his eyes, in the ineffable and unanswerable fatalism of the East.

"In any case," I said, "you cannot remove anything from the shop. Replace all the objects, if you please, and lock the door."

The old woman's cacodemonic laughter broke out again. She began to shuffle her feet in a grotesque dance of triumph. "I knew the honored sitt would not let an old woman be robbed. The wisdom of the Prophet is yours, great lady. Accept an old woman's blessing. May you have many sons—many, many sons. . . ."

The idea was so appalling I think I turned pale. The man mistook my reaction for fear. He said in a grating voice, "You cannot make me do that, missus. You are not the police."

"Don't you talk that way to my lady," John said indignantly. "Madam, shall I punch him in the nose?"

A cheer, half-ironic, half-enthusiastic, broke out from those in the crowd who understood English. Evidently the son of Abd el Atti was not popular with the latter's neighbors.

"Certainly not," I said. "What is this talk of punching people? You must not attempt to imitate all your master's habits, John. Mr.—" I glanced at the card I held—"Mr. Aslimi will be reasonable, I am sure."

Mr. Aslimi had very little choice in the matter. The donkeys departed unencumbered, and although it is difficult to read the countenance of a donkey, they appeared pleased to be relieved of their burdens. The workmen left, cursing the paltriness of their pay, the crowd dispersed. I dismissed the dear old lady before she could repeat her ominous blessing. She went hopping off, cackling like a large black raven. Then I turned to Mr. Aslimi. He was an unpleasant individual, but

I could not help feeling some sympathy for anyone who had to deal with such a stepmother.

"If you will cooperate, Mr. Aslimi, I will do my best to plead your case with the authorities."

"How cooperate?" Aslimi asked cautiously.

"By answering my questions. How much do you know about your father's business?"

Well, of course he swore he knew nothing about any criminal connections. I expected him to say that, but my intuition (which is scarcely ever at fault) told me he was not directly involved with the antiquities gang—probably to his regret. He also denied any acquaintance with the suspicious character I had seen with Abd el Atti. This time my intuition assured me he was lying. If he did not know the man's identity, he had a good idea as to who it might have been.

I then asked to be allowed to search the shop. There were some fine and obviously illegal antiquities in various locked cupboards, but they were not my concern, and Aslimi's dour expression lightened perceptibly when I passed them by without comment. I found nothing that gave me a clue to the identity of Abd el Atti's murderer. The place had been trampled by many feet and thoroughly ransacked—and besides, I had no idea what I was looking for.

Nor was there any trace of the missing Bastet. Mr. Aslimi denied having seen her. This time I felt sure he was telling the truth.

We parted with protestations of goodwill that were false on both sides. I felt sure he would not venture to reopen the shop, since I had assured him I would notify the police of his activities.

As John and I retraced our steps through the crooked, shady streets, I kept on the lookout for a lithe, tawny form, but to no avail. There was no answer to my repeated cries, except for curious glances from passersby. I heard one say, in response to a question from his companion, "It is the name of one of the old gods. They are magicians of great power, she and her husband; no doubt she is pronouncing a curse on that—Aslimi."

Reaching the Muski we took a carriage at the entrance to the bazaar. John sat uneasily on the very edge of the seat. "Madam," he said.

"Yes?"

"Oi—I won't be mentioning this to the master, if you like."

"There is no reason why you should bring up the subject, John. But if you are asked a direct question, naturally you will tell the truth."

"I will?"

"Certainly. We were looking for the cat. Unfortunately we found no trace of her."

But when I entered my room the first thing I saw was the familiar feline shape, curled up on the foot of my bed. As I had predicted, Bastet had found her way home.

III

The sun was setting the gilded spires and minarets of Cairo ablaze when the wanderers returned, in precisely the state I had expected. Ramses rushed, as usual, to embrace me. I was wearing my oldest dressing gown in anticipation of this. I was the only person, aside from his Aunt Evelyn, with whom Ramses was so physically demonstrative. Sometimes I suspected him of doing it out of malice, for he was almost always covered with some noxious substance or other. On this occasion, however, he veered off at the last moment and flung himself on the cat.

"Where did you find her, Mama?"

I was flattered by his assumption that I was responsible, but truth compelled me to reply, "I did not find her, Ramses—though I did look for her. She found her own way back."

"That is a relief," said Emerson, smiling wanly. "Ramses was quite cut up about her. Keep her on the lead from now on, my boy."

"And put her down until after you have bathed," I added. "I spent an hour combing and cleaning her. You will get her dirty again."

Clutching the cat to his bosom, in flagrant disregard of this order, Ramses retired, with John in attendance. He (Ramses) smelled very peculiar. Goat, I believe.

Emerson also smelled of goat, and of the strong tobacco favored by the men of Aziyeh. He looked tired, and admitted as much when I questioned him. When I questioned him further, he admitted that Ramses' "boyish joie de vivre," as he put it, was responsible for his fatigue. Ramses had fallen out of a palm tree and into the river; he had been attacked and slightly trampled by a goat after attempting to loosen the rope around its neck, which he felt was too tight (the animal had either mistaken his motives or yielded to the irascibility of temper to which billy goats are traditionally prone); and had concluded the afternoon by consuming several pints of date wine, forbidden to devout Muslims, but brewed on the sly by some of the villagers.

"Strange," I said. "He did not appear to be inebriated."

"He rid himself of the wine almost immediately," said Emerson. "On the floor of Abdullah's house."

At my suggestion Emerson retired behind the screen to freshen up, while I called the safragi and ordered whiskey and soda for both of us.

As we sipped this refreshing beverage, we compared notes on the day's activities. The results were most satisfactory. All the necessary arrangements had been completed and we were ready to leave at dawn. I had spent the remainder of the afternoon packing and sealing up our boxes—or rather, supervising the hotel servants in that endeavor—so we could spend the evening in quiet enjoyment. It would be the last evening for many weeks that we would enjoy civilized amenities, and although I yield to no one in my appreciation of desert life, I intended to take advantage of wine and good food, hot baths and soft beds while they were available.

We took Ramses with us to dinner, though he was reluctant to part with Bastet. "Someone has hurt her," he said, looking accusingly at me. "Dere is a cut on her back, Mama—a sharp cut, like dat made by a knife."

"I saw it, and have attended to it, Ramses."

"But, Mama—"

"It is a wonder she has no more scars than that to show for her adventure. I only hope she has not . . ."

"Has not what, Mama?"

"Never mind." I stared at the cat, who stared back at me with enigmatic golden eyes. She did not appear to be in a state of amatory excitement. . . . Time, and only time, would tell.

For once Emerson did not grumble about being forced to dine out. Puffed with fatherly pride, he presented, "my son, Walter Peabody Emerson," to everyone he knew and several he did not know. I was rather proud of the boy myself. He was wearing Scottish dress, with a little kilt in the Emerson tartan. (Designed by myself, it is a tasteful blend of scarlet, forest-green and blue, with narrow yellow and purple stripes.)

All in all, it was a most pleasant evening, and when we retired to our rooms we sought our couch in serene contemplation of a day well spent and of useful work ahead.

The moon had set, and silvery starlight was the only illumination when I woke in the small hours of the morning. I was instantly alert. I never wake unless there is cause, and I soon identified the cause that had roused me on this occasion—a soft, stealthy sound in the corner of the room where our bags and boxes were piled, ready to be removed in the morning.

For an interval I lay perfectly still, allowing my eyes to adjust to the faint light, and straining to hear. Emerson's stertorous breathing interfered with this latter activity, but in the lulls between inspiration and expiration I could hear the thief scrabbling among our luggage.

I am accustomed to nocturnal alarms. For some reason they occur frequently with me. I hardly need say that I was not in the least afraid. The only question in my mind was how to apprehend the thief. There was no lock on our door. The presence of the safragi in the hallway was supposed to be sufficient to deter casual thieves, few of whom would have had the temerity to enter a place like Shepheard's. I felt certain that this unusual event was the result of my investigation into Abd el Atti's murder. It was a thrilling prospect. Here at last, in my very room, was a possible clue. It did not occur to me to awaken Emerson. He wakens noisily, with cries and gasps and thrashing about.

On several previous occasions I had fallen into the error of tangling myself up in the mosquito netting, thus giving a midnight invader a chance to escape. I was determined not to commit the same mistake. The filmy folds of the netting were tucked firmly under the mattress on all sides of the bed. I began tugging gently at the portion nearest my head, pulling it free an inch at a time. Emerson continued to snore. The thief continued to explore.

When the netting was loose as far down as I could reach without moving more than my arm, the crucial moment was upon me. Mentally I reviewed my plans. My parasol stood ready as always, propped against the head of the bed. The thief was in the corner farthest from the door. Speed rather than silence was now my aim. Gathering a handful of the netting, I gave it a sharp tug.

The whole cursed apparatus came tumbling down on me. Evidently the nails holding it to the ceiling had become weakened. As I struggled in vain to free myself, I heard, mingled with Emerson's bewildered curses, the sound of feet thudding across the floor. The door opened and closed.

"Curse it," I cried, forgetting myself in my frustration.

"Curse it," Emerson shouted. "What the devil . . ." And other even more forceful expressions of alarm.

My efforts to extricate myself were foiled by Emerson's frantic thrashing, which only succeeded in winding the netting more tightly about our limbs. When the sleepers in the next room rushed to the scene we were lying side by side, wrapped like a pair of matched mummies and incapable of movement of any kind. Emerson was still roaring out curses; and the look on John's face as he stood staring, his nightcap standing up in a peak and his bare shanks showing under the hem of his gown, moved me to a peal of hysterical laughter.

Emerson's breath finally gave out—he had inhaled a portion of the netting, which was wound around his face. In the blessed silence that followed I instructed John to put down the lamp before he dropped it and set the place on fire. The cat lowered her head and began sniffing about the room. The hair on her back stood up in a stiff ridge.

Ramses had taken in the situation with a look of mild inquiry. Now he disappeared into his own room and returned carrying some object that glittered in the light. Not until he approached close to the bed did I identify it. I let out a shriek.

"No, Ramses! Drop it. Drop it at once, do you hear?"

When I speak in that tone, Ramses does not argue. He dropped the knife. It was at least eight inches long, and polished to a wicked shine. "My intention," he began, "was to free you and Papa from de incumbrance dat in some wholly unaccountable manner seems to have—"

"I have no quarrel with your intentions, only with your methods." I managed to free one arm. It was not long before I had kicked off the netting, and I turned at once, with some anxiety, to Emerson. As I feared, his open mouth was stuffed with netting. His eyes bulged and his face had turned a portentous shade of mauve.

It took some little time to restore order. I resuscitated my wheezing spouse, confiscated the knife—a gift from Abdullah, which Ramses had not thought it expedient to mention—and ordered my son, my servant and my cat to return to their beds. Then, at last, I was able to turn my attention to the crime—for attempted burglary, I venture to assert, must be called a crime.

It was no use pursuing the thief. He had had time to cross half of Cairo by then. One look at the scene of his inquiries assured me he was a master at his illegal craft, for he had managed to create considerable havoc with a minimum of sound. He had not ventured to open any of the packing cases, for they had been nailed shut, but all our personal baggage had been searched. The contents lay in untidy heaps on the floor. A bottle of ink had lost its stopper, with disastrous consequences to my best shirtwaist.

Emerson, now fully restored but breathing loudly through his nose, pulled himself to a sitting position. Arms crossed, face engorged, he watched in grim silence for a time and then inquired gently, "Amelia, why are you crawling on all fours?"

"I am looking for clues, of course."

"Ah, yes. A calling card, perhaps. A fragment of cloth torn from our visitor's robe—a robe identical with those worn by half the population of Egypt. A lock of hair, courteously torn from his scalp in order to assist—"

"Sarcasm does not become you, Emerson," I said, continuing to crawl. And a tedious process it is, I might add, when the folds of one's nightgown keep bunching up under one's knees. Then I let out a cry of triumph. "Aha!"

"A photograph of the burglar's wife and children," Emerson went on, warming to his theme. "A letter, bearing his name and address—though there are no pockets in these robes, and few of the wearers can read and write—"

"A footprint," I said.

"A footprint," Emerson repeated. "Hobnailed boots, perhaps? Of an unusual pattern, made by only one bootmaker in all Cairo, who keeps records of his customers—"

"Correct," I said. "At least as to the boots. I doubt, however, that the pattern will prove to be unique. I will make inquiries, of course."

"What?" Emerson bounded from the bed. "Booted feet, did you say?"

"See for yourself. There is a clear print. He must have trod in the spilled ink. I am glad of the accident on that account, though I do not understand why there should have been a bottle of ink in my bag. I suppose Ramses put it there."

Now on all fours like myself, Emerson inspected the print. "There is no reason why a common sneak thief should not wear boots. If he were dressed in European clothing—or if he were European—he would find it easier to gain entry to the hotel. . . ." His voice trailed off in an indecisive manner.

"A common sneak thief would not dare enter the hotel, Emerson. Even if the safragi is asleep most of the time."

Emerson sat back on his haunches. "I know what you are thinking," he cried accusingly. "You will insist on some connection with the death of Abd el Atti."

"It would be a strange coincidence if the two events were not connected."

"Stranger coincidences have happened. What could he have been after?"

"The mummy portrait," I suggested.

Emerson looked uncomfortable. "I intend to hand it over to the Museum, Amelia."

"Of course."

"It is a handsome piece of work, but not valuable," Emerson mused, rubbing his chin. "Did you—er—rescue anything from the shop?"

"Only a scrap of papyrus, which appeared to be from the same manuscript as the one I obtained from Abd el Atti."

"Both together would not be worth the risk taken by the thief." Emerson seated himself. Elbow on his knee, chin on his hand, he might have sat as the model for M. Rodin's splendid statue, even to his costume—or, to put it as delicately as possible, the absence thereof. Emerson refuses to wear a nightshirt, and the new fad of pajamas has prompted a number of rude jests from him.

"The papyrus from which the fragments came might conceivably be of value," he said after a time. "Sayce was intrigued, though he tried to hide it—the devious fellow. We do not have the papyrus, though. Do we?"

"Emerson, you cut me to the quick. When have I ever deceived you about something of importance?"

"Quite often, Amelia. However, in this case I will take your word. You agree that we possess nothing that would explain a visit from an emissary of your imaginary Master Criminal?"

"Not to my knowledge. However—"

Emerson rose majestically to his feet. "The invasion was that of a common ordinary thief," he proclaimed, in orotund tones. "That is the end of it. Come to bed, Amelia."

Chapter Five

MAZGHUNAH.

Mazghunah! Mazghunah . . .

No, there is no magic in the name, punctuate it as one will. Not even a row of exclamation points can lend charm to such an uncouth collection of syllables. Giza, Sakkara, Dahshoor are no more euphonious, perhaps, but they evoke the lure of antiquity and exploration. Mazghunah has nothing whatever to recommend it.

It does possess a railway station, and we descended from the train to find that we were eagerly awaited. Towering above the spectators who had gathered on the platform was the stately form of our reis, Abdullah, who had gone on ahead to arrange for transport and accommodations. He is the most dignified of men, almost as tall as Emerson—that is to say, above the average Egyptian height—with a sweeping array of facial hair that turns a shade lighter every year, so that it will soon rival the snowy whiteness of his robe. Yet he has the energy of a young man, and when he saw us a broad smile lightened the solemnity of his bronzed countenance.

After our luggage had been loaded onto the donkeys Abdullah had selected, we mounted our own steeds. "Forward, Peabody," Emerson cried. "Forward, I say!"

Cheeks flushed and eyes glowing, he urged his donkey into a trot. It is impossible for a tall man to look heroic when mounted on one of these little beasts; but as I watched Emerson jog away, his elbows out and his knees well up, the smile that curved my lips was not one of derision. Emerson was in his element, happy as a man can be only when he has found his proper niche in life. Not even the disappointment of de Morgan's decision could crush that noble spirit.

The inundation was receding, but sheets of water still lay on the fields. Following the dikes of the primitive irrigation system, we rode on until suddenly the green of the trees and young crops gave way to the barren soil of the desert, in a line so sharp it appeared to have been drawn by a celestial hand. Ahead lay the scene of our winter's work.

Never will I forget the profound depression that seized me when I first beheld the site of Mazghunah. Beyond the low and barren hills bordering the cultivation, a vast expanse of rubble-strewn sand stretched westward as far as the eye could see. To the north, outlined bravely against the sky, were the two stone pyramids of Dahshoor, one regular in outline, the other marked by the curious change in the angle of the slope that has given it the name of the "Bent Pyramid." The contrast between these two magnificent monuments and the undulating sterility of our site was almost too painful to be endured. Emerson had halted; when I drew up beside him I saw that his eyes were fixed on the distant silhouettes and that a grimace of fury distorted his lips.

"Monster," he growled. "Villain! I will have my revenge; the day of reckoning cannot be far off!"

"Emerson," I said, putting my hand on his arm.

He turned to me with a smile of artificial sweetness.

"Yes, my dear. A charming spot, is it not?"

"Charming," I murmured.

"I believe I will just ride north and say good morning to our neighbor," Emerson said casually. "If you, my dear Peabody, will set up camp—"

"Set up camp?" I repeated. "Where? How? With what?"

To call the terrain in this part of Egypt desert is misleading, for it is not the sort of desert the reader may picture in his mind—vast sand dunes, rolling smoothly on to infinity without so much as a shrub or ridge of rock. This area was barren enough; but the ground was uneven, broken by pits and ridges and hollows, and every foot of the surface was strewn with debris—fragments of broken pottery, scraps of wood and other, less palatable evidences of occupation. My experienced eye at once identified it as a cemetery site. Beneath the rock surface lay hundreds of graves. All had been robbed in ancient times, for the scraps littering the ground were the remains of the goods buried with the dead—and the remains of the dead themselves.

Ramses got off his donkey. Squatting, he began sifting through the debris.

"Here, Master Ramses, leave that nasty rubbish alone," John exclaimed.

Ramses held up an object that looked like a broken branch. "It is a femuw," he said in a trembling voice. "Excuse me, Mama—a femur, I meant to say."

John let out a cry of disgust and tried to take the bone away from Ramses. I understood the emotion that had affected the child, and I said tolerantly, "Never mind, John. You cannot keep Ramses from digging here."

"That nasty rubbish is the object of our present quest," Emerson added. "Leave it, my son; you know the rule of excavation—never move anything until its location has been recorded."

Ramses rose obediently. The warm breeze of the desert ruffled his hair. His eyes glowed with the fervor of a pilgrim who has finally reached the Holy City.

II

Having persuaded Ramses to abandon his bones for the nonce, we rode on toward the northwest. Near a ridge of rock we found our men, who had come down the day before to select a campsite. There were ten of them in all, including Abdullah—old friends and experienced excavators, who would supervise the unskilled laborers we expected to hire locally. I returned their enthusiastic salutations, noting as I did so that the camp consisted of a fire pit and two tents. Questioning elicited the bland response, "But, Sitt, there is no other place."

On several of my expeditions I had set up housekeeping in an empty tomb. I recalled with particular pleasure the rock-cut tombs of El Amarna; I always say, there is nothing more commodious or convenient than a tomb, particularly that of a well-to-do person. Obviously no such amenity was available here.

I climbed to the top of the ridge. As I scrambled among the stones I gave thanks for one blessing at least—that I was no longer encumbered by the voluminous skirts and tight corsets that had been de rigueur when I first took up the study of Egyptology. My present working costume had been developed and refined by myself, and was wholly satisfactory, aesthetically and practically. It consisted of a broad-brimmed man's straw hat, a shirtwaist with long sleeves and a soft collar, and flowing Turkish trousers to the knee with stout boots and gaiters below the trousers. The uniform, if I may so designate it, was completed by an important accessory—a broad leather belt to which was attached a modification of the old-fashioned chatelaine. Instead of the scissors and keys housewives once attached to this device, my collection of useful tools included a hunting knife and a pistol, notepaper and pencil, matches and candles, a folding rule, a small flask of water, a pocket compass, and a sewing kit. Emerson claimed I jangled like a chained prisoner when I walked. He also objected to being jabbed in the ribs by knife, pistol, et cetera, when he embraced me. Yet I am certain the usefulness of each item will be readily apparent to the astute reader.

Abdullah followed me onto the hill. His face had the remote, meditative expression it wore when he was expecting a reprimand.

We were not far from the cultivation. A cluster of palms some half-mile distant betokened the presence of water, and among the palms I could see the low roofs of a village. Nearer at hand was the object I sought. I had caught a glimpse of it as we rode—the ruinous remains of a building of some sort. I pointed. "What is that, Abdullah?"

"It is a building, Sitt," said Abdullah, in tones of amazement. One would suppose he had never noticed the place before.

"Is it occupied, Abdullah?"

"I do not think it is, Sitt."

"Who owns it, Abdullah?"

Abdullah replied with an ineffable Arabic shrug. As I prepared to descend the far side of the ridge, he said quickly, "That is not a good place, Sitt Hakim."

"It has walls and part of a roof," I replied. "That is good enough for me."

"But, Sitt—"

"Abdullah, you know how your Muslim reticence annoys me. Speak out. What is wrong with the place?"

"It is filled with devils," said Abdullah.

"I see. Well, don't concern yourself about that. Emerson will cast the devils out."

I hailed the others and directed them to follow me. The closer we approached, the more pleased I was with my discovery, and the more puzzled by it. It was not an ordinary house; the extent of the walls, some tumbled, some still intact, suggested a structure of considerable size and complexity. There were no signs of recent habitation. The barren waste stretched all around, with never a tree or blade of grass.

The building materials were an odd mixture. Some of the walls were of mud brick, some of stone. A few blocks were as large as packing cases. "Stolen from our pyramids," Emerson grumbled. He pushed through a gap in the nearest wall. I need not say I was close behind.

The area within had been a courtyard, with rooms on three sides and a stout wall on the fourth. The wall and the southern range of rooms had fallen into ruin, but the remaining sections had survived, though most gaped open to the sky. A few pillars supported a roofed walkway along one side.

Emerson snapped his fingers. "It was a monastery, Peabody. Those were the monks' cells, and that ruin in the far corner must have been the church."

"How curious," I exclaimed.

"Not at all. There are many such abandoned sanctuaries in Egypt. This country was the home of monasticism, after all, and religious communities existed as early as the second century A.D. The nearest village, Dronkeh, is a Coptic settlement."

"You never told me that, Emerson."

"You never asked me, Peabody."

As we continued our tour of inspection I became conscious of a strange feeling of uneasiness. It was wholly unaccountable; the sun beamed down from a cloudless sky and, except for the occasional agitated rustle when we disturbed a lizard or scorpion from its peaceful nest, there was no sign of danger. Yet an air of brooding desolation lay over the place. Abdullah sensed it; he stayed close on Emerson's heels and his eyes kept darting from side to side.

"Why do you suppose it was abandoned?" I asked.

Emerson stroked his chin. Even his iron nerves seemed affected by the atmosphere; his brow was slightly furrowed as he replied, "It may be that the water supply failed. This structure is old, Peabody—a thousand years, perhaps more.

Long enough for the river to change its course, and for a deserted building to fall into ruin. Yet I think some of the destruction was deliberate. The church was solidly built, yet hardly one stone remains on another."

"There was fighting, I believe, between Muslims and Christians?"

"Pagan and Christian, Muslim and Christian, Christian and Christian. It is curious how religion arouses the most ferocious violence of which mankind is capable. The Copts destroyed the heathen temples and persecuted the worshipers of the old gods, they also slaughtered co-religionists who disagreed over subtle differences of dogma. After the Muslim conquest, the Copts were treated leniently at first, but their own intolerance finally tried the patience of the conquerors and they endured the same persecution they had inflicted on others."

"Well, it does not matter. This will make an admirable expedition house. For once we will have enough storage space."

"There is no water."

"It can be carried from the village." I took my pencil and began making a list. "Repair the roof; mend the walls; insert new doors and window frames; sweep—"

Abdullah coughed. "Cast out the afreets," he suggested.

"Yes, to be sure." I made another note.

"Afreets?" Emerson repeated. "Peabody, what the devil—"

I drew him aside and explained. "I see," he replied. "Well, I will perform any necessary rituals, but first perhaps we ought to go to the village and carry out the legal formalities."

I was happy to acquiesce to this most sensible suggestion. "We should not have any difficulty obtaining a lease," I said, as we walked side by side. "Since the place has been so long abandoned, it cannot be of importance to the villagers."

"I only hope the local priest does not believe in demons," said Emerson. "I don't mind putting on a show for Abdullah and the men, but one exorcism per day is my limit."

As soon as we were seen the villagers came pouring out of their houses. The usual cries of "Baksheesh!" were mingled with another adjuration—*"Ana Christian, Oh Hawadji*—I am a Christian, noble sir!"

"And therefore entitled to additional baksheesh," said Emerson, his lip curling. "Bah."

Most of the houses were clustered around the well. The church, with its modest little dome, was not much larger than the house next to it. "The parsonage," said Emerson, indicating this residence. "And there, if I am not mistaken, is the parson."

He stood in the doorway of his house—a tall, muscular man wearing the dark-blue turban that distinguishes Egyptian Christians. Once a prescribed article of dress for a despised minority, it is now worn as a matter of pride.

Instead of coming to greet us, the priest folded his arms and stood with head held high like a king waiting to receive petitioners. His figure was splendid. His face was all but invisible, adorned by the most remarkable assemblage of facial hair I had ever seen. It began at ear level, swept in an ebon wave across cheeks and upper lip, and flowed like a sable waterfall almost to his waist. His eyebrows were equally remarkable for their hirsute extravagance. They were the only feature that gave any indication of the owner's emotions, and at the moment their configuration was not encouraging, for a scowl darkened the pastoral brow.

At the priest's appearance most of the other villagers faded quietly away. Half a dozen men remained, loitering near the priest. They wore the same indigo turbans and the same suspicious scowls as their spiritual leader.

"The deacons," said Emerson with a grin.

He then launched into a speech of greeting in his most impeccable Arabic. I added a few well-chosen words. A long silence ensued. Then the priest's bearded lips parted and a voice growled a curt *"Sabakhum bil-kheir*—good morning."

In every Muslim household I had visited, the formal greeting was followed by an invitation to enter, for hospitality to strangers is enjoined by the Koran. We waited in vain for this courtesy from our co-religionist, if I may use that term loosely, and after an even longer silence the priest asked what we wanted.

This outraged Abdullah, who, though an admirable person in many ways, was not devoid of the Mussulman's prejudice against his Christian fellow-countrymen. Ever since he entered the village he had looked as if he smelled something bad. Now he exclaimed, "Unclean eaters of swine's flesh, how dare you treat a great lord in this way? Do you not know that this is Emerson, Father of Curses, and his chief wife, the learned and dangerous Lady Doctor? They honor your filthy village by entering it. Come away, Emerson; we do not need these low people to help with our work."

One of the "deacons" edged up to his leader and whispered in his ear. The priest's turban bobbed in acknowledgment. "The Father of Curses," he repeated, and then, slowly and deliberately, "I know you. I know your name."

A chill ran through my limbs. The phrase meant nothing to the priest, but all unknowingly he had repeated an ominous formula used by the priest-magicians of ancient Egypt. To know the name of a man or a god was to have power over him.

Abdullah found the comment offensive, though probably for other reasons. "Know his name? Who is there who does not know that great name? From the cataracts of the south to the swamps of the Delta—"

"Enough," Emerson said. His lips were twitching, but he kept a grave face, for laughter would have hurt Abdullah and offended the priest. "You know my name, Father? It is well. But I do not know yours."

"Father Girgis, priest of the church of Sitt Miriam in Dronkeh. Are you truly Emerson, the digger-up of dead man's bones? You are not a man of God?"

It was my turn to repress a smile. Emerson chose to ignore the second question. "I am that Emerson. I come here to dig, and I will hire men from the village. But if they do not want to work for me, I will go elsewhere."

The villagers had begun edging out into the open as the conversation proceeded. A low murmur arose from them when they heard the offer to work. All the fellahin, Muslim and Copt alike, are pitifully poor. The chance to earn what they considered munificent wages was not an offer to be missed.

"Wait," the priest said, as Emerson turned away. "If that is why you have come, we will talk."

So at last we were invited into the "manse," as Emerson called it. It was like all the other Egyptian houses we had seen, except that it was a trifle larger and slightly cleaner. The long divan that was the chief piece of furniture in the main room was covered with cheap, faded chintz, and the only ornament was a crucifix with a horribly lifelike image of Christ, smeared with red paint in lieu of blood.

At the priest's suggestion we were joined by a timid little walnut-colored gentleman who was introduced as the *sheikh el beled*—the mayor of the village. It was obvious that he was a mere figurehead, for he only squeaked acquiescence to everything the priest said until, the matter of employment having been settled, Emerson mentioned that we wanted to occupy the abandoned monastery. Then the mayor turned as pale as a man of his complexion can turn and blurted, "But, effendi, that is not possible."

"We will not profane the church," Emerson assured him. "We only want to use the rooms that were once storerooms and cells."

"But, great Lord, no one goes there," the mayor insisted. "It is accursed—a place of evil, haunted by afreets and devils."

"Accursed?" Emerson repeated incredulously. "The home of the holy monks?"

The mayor rolled his eyes. "Long ago all the holy men were foully murdered, Ó Father of Curses. Their spirits still haunt their house, hungry for revenge."

"We do not fear devils or vengeful ghosts," Emerson said courageously. "If that is your only objection, effendi, we will take possession immediately."

The mayor shook his head but did not protest further. The priest had listened with a sardonic smile. Now he said, "The house is yours, Father of Curses. May the restless spirits of the holy men requite you as you deserve."

III

Abdullah followed us along the village street, radiating disapproval as only Abdullah can. It felt like a chilly breeze on the back of my neck.

"We are going the wrong way," I said to Emerson. "We entered the village at the other end."

"I want to see the rest of the place," was the reply. "There is something strange going on here, Amelia. I am surprised your vaunted intuition did not catch the undercurrents."

"They would have been hard to miss," I replied haughtily. "The priest is patently hostile to outsiders. I hope he won't undermine our authority."

"Oh, I pay no attention to such persons." Emerson stepped over a mangy dog sprawled in the middle of the path. It growled at him and he said absently, "Good dog, then; nice fellow," before continuing, "It is not concern but curiosity that makes me wonder why the reverend gentleman should demonstrate such antagonism. I always have trouble with religious persons; they are so confoundedly superstitious, curse them. Yet the priest was rude to us even before he learned who we were. I wonder . . ."

His voice trailed off and he stood staring.

Half hidden by a splendid group of stately palms and partially removed from the rest of the village stood several houses. In contrast to the other hovels in that wretched place, these were in impeccable repair and freshly whitewashed. Even the dust before the doors looked as if it had been swept. Three of the houses were the usual small two- and three-room affairs. The fourth was somewhat larger and had undergone reconstruction. A stubby steeple graced the flat roof, and above the door was a sign in gilt letters on black. It read, "Chapel of the Holy Jerusalem."

As we stood in silent wonderment, the door of one of the smaller houses opened. An explosion of small boys burst out into the open, shouting and laughing with the joy of youths escaping from studies. As soon as they caught sight of us they darted at us, shouting for baksheesh. One minuscule cherub caught at my trousers and stared up at me with eyes like melting chocolate. "Baksheesh, Sitt," he lisped. "Ana Christian—ana *Brotestant!*"

"Good Gad," I said weakly.

Emerson put a hand to his head. "No," he cried passionately. "No. It is a delusion—it cannot be real. After all the other cruel blows of fate I have endured . . . Missionaries! Missionaries, Amelia!"

"Courage," I implored, as the swarthy infant continued to tug at my trousers. "Courage, Emerson. It could be worse."

Other children emerged from the door of the school—little girls, too timid to emulate the joie de vivre of their male counterparts. They were followed by another, taller form. For a moment he stood in the doorway blinking into the sunlight, and the rays of the noon-high orb set his silver-gilt hair to blazing like a halo. Then he saw us. A smile of ineffable sweetness spread over his handsome face and he raised a hand in greeting or in blessing.

Emerson collapsed onto a block of stone, like a man in the last throes of a fatal disease. "It is worse," he said in a sepulchral voice.

IV

"Boys, boys." The beautiful young man strode toward us, waving his arms. He spoke in Arabic, perfectly pronounced but slow and simple. "Stop it, boys. Go home now. Go to your mothers. Do not ask for baksheesh, it is not pleasing to God."

The youthful villains dispersed and their mentor turned his attention to us. At close range he was absolutely dazzling. His hair gleamed, his white teeth shone, and his face beamed with goodwill. Emerson continued to stare dazedly at him, so I felt it incumbent upon myself to address the amenities.

"I fear we must apologize for intruding on private property, sir. Allow me to introduce myself. I am Amelia Peabody Emerson—Mrs. Radcliffe Emerson—and this . . ."

"This block of wood" might have been an appropriate description, for all the response Emerson made, but the beautiful young man did not allow me to proceed. "You need no introduction, Mrs. Emerson; you and your distinguished husband are well known to all visitors in Cairo. It is an honor to welcome you. I was informed only yesterday that you would be coming."

The monolithic indifference or catatonia of Emerson was shattered. "Who informed you, pray?" he demanded.

"Why, it was M. de Morgan," said the young man innocently. "The director of the Antiquities Department. As you may know, he is working at Dahshoor, not far from—"

"I know the location of Dahshoor, young man," snapped Emerson. "But I don't know you. Who the devil are you?"

"Emerson!" I exclaimed. "Such language to a man of the cloth!"

"Pray don't apologize," said the young gentleman. "It is my fault, for not mentioning my name earlier. I am David Cabot—of the Boston Cabots."

This formula seemed to have some significance to him, but it meant nothing to me—nor, I hardly need add, to Emerson, who continued to glare at young Mr. Cabot, of the Boston Cabots.

"But I am forgetting my manners," the latter went on. "I am keeping you standing in the sun. Will you enter and meet my family?"

Knowing him to be unmarried, I assumed he was referring to his parents, but when I inquired he laughed and shook his head. "I refer to my spiritual family, Mrs. Emerson. My father in the Lord, the Reverend Ezekiel Jones, is the head of our little mission. His sister also labors in the vineyards of the Lord. It is almost time for our midday repast; will you honor our humble abode?"

I politely declined the invitation, explaining that the other members of our expedition were waiting for us, and we took our leave. Before we were quite out of earshot, Emerson said loudly, "You were confoundedly polite, Amelia."

"You make it sound like a crime! I felt it necessary to be overly cordial to compensate for your rudeness."

"Rude? I, rude?"

"Very."

"Well, I call it rude to walk into a man's house and order him to leave off worshiping his chosen god. What effrontery! Mr. Cabot and his 'father in the Lord' had better not try their tricks on ME."

"I hardly think even Mr. Cabot would try to convert YOU," I said, taking his arm. "Hurry, Emerson, we have been too long away. Goodness knows what mischief Ramses has got into by now."

But for once Ramses was innocent of wrongdoing. We found him squatting in the sand near the monastery, digging. Already a small pile of potsherds had rewarded his efforts. At the sight of his dedicated labors Emerson's expression lightened, and I hoped the irritation produced by the presence of the missionaries had been alleviated.

V

Shortly thereafter the arrival of a contingent of men from the village assured us that the priest did mean to cooperate with our endeavors. This first levy consisted of craftsmen—masons and brickmakers, carpenters and plasterers. Emerson beamed when he saw his augmented audience; he may and does deny it, but he loves putting on a theatrical performance. His exorcism that day was one of his best, despite the fact that he turned his ankle while capering around the house chanting poetry and prayers. The audience applauded enthusiastically and declared themselves relieved of all apprehension concerning evil spirits. Before long the place was swarming with activity, and I had high hopes that by nightfall we would have a roof over our heads and a cleared floor on which to place our camp cots, tables and chairs.

The men from Aziyeh did not fraternize with the villagers. Their professional skills and the parochialism of the peasant mentality, which regards a man from a village two miles off as a foreigner—not to mention the religious differences—made them view the "heretics" with haughty contempt. I knew there would be no trouble, however, for Abdullah was an excellent foreman and his men were guided by him. No less than four of them were his sons. They ranged in age from Feisal, a grizzled man with grown children of his own, to young Selim, a handsome lad of fourteen. He was obviously the apple of his father's eye and the adored Benjamin of the family. Indeed, his infectious boyish laughter and pleasant ways made him a favorite with all of us. In Egyptian terms he was already a man, and would soon take a wife, but since he was closer in age to Ramses than any of the others, the two soon struck up a friendship.

After I had watched the lad for a while and assured myself that my initial impression of his character was correct, I decided to appoint him as Ramses' official guide, servant and guard. John's unsuitability for the role was becoming only too apparent. He was always trying to prevent Ramses from doing harmless things—such as digging, which was, after all, our reason for being there—and allowing him to do other things, such as drinking unboiled water, that were not at all harmless. Besides, John was proving useful in other ways. He had picked up Arabic with surprising quickness and mingled readily with the men, displaying none of the insular prejudices that afflict many English persons, including some who ought to know better. As I swept sand from the large room, once the refectory of the monastery, that we had selected for our parlor, I could hear John chatting away in his ungrammatical but effective Arabic, and the other men laughing good-naturedly at his mistakes.

Late in the afternoon, when I emerged from the house to inspect the repairs on the roof, I saw a small procession advancing toward me. Leading it were two gentlemen mounted on donkeyback. The tall, graceful figure of Mr. Cabot was immediately recognizable. Beside him was another man wearing the same dark clerical garb and a straw boater. It was not until the caravan had come closer that I realized the third person was female.

My heart went out to the poor creature. She wore a high-necked, long-sleeved gown of dark calico, with skirts so full they almost hid the donkey. Only its head and tail protruded, with bizarre effect. One of the old-fashioned shovel bonnets—a style I had not seen in years—completely hid her face, and so enveloping was her attire it was impossible to tell whether she was dark or fair, young or old.

Mr. Cabot was the first to dismount. "We are here," he exclaimed.

"So I see," I replied, thanking heaven I had sent Emerson and Ramses out to survey the site.

"I have the honor," Mr. Cabot continued, "to present my revered mentor, the Reverend Ezekiel Jones."

There was nothing in the appearance of this person to justify the reverence and pride in Mr. Cabot's voice. He was of middle height, with the heavy shoulders and thick body of a working-man, and his coarse features would have been better hidden by a beard. His forehead was crossed by lowering dark brows as thick as my finger. His movements were awkward; he climbed awkwardly off his mount and awkwardly removed his hat. When he spoke I had some inkling as to why he commanded the admiration of his young acolyte. His voice was a mellow baritone, marred by an unfortunate American accent, but resonant and musical as a cello.

"How do, ma'am. We figured as how you could use some help. This here's my sister, Charity."

The woman had dismounted. Her brother grasped her by the shoulder and shoved her at me, like a merchant hawking his wares. "She's a hard worker and a handmaiden of the Lord," he went on. "You tell her what you want done."

A thrill of indignation passed through me. I offered the girl my hand. "How do you do, Miss Jones."

"We don't use worldly titles," her brother said. "Brother David here tends to forget that. Oh, it's all right, my friend, I know it's respect that prompts you—"

"It is indeed, sir," said "Brother David" earnestly.

"But I don't deserve respect, Brother. I'm just a miserable sinner like the rest of you. A few steps further up the road that leads to salvation, maybe, but a miserable sinner just the same."

The self-satisfied smile with which he proclaimed his humility made me want to shake him, but the young man gazed at him with melting admiration. "Sister Charity" stood with her hands folded at her waist and her head bowed. She looked like a silhouette cut out of black paper, lifeless and featureless.

I had been undecided as to whether to invite the visitors to enter the house; the decision was taken out of my hands by Brother Ezekiel. He walked in. I followed, to find that he had seated himself in the most comfortable chair the room contained.

"You've got quite a bit done," he said in obvious surprise. "Soon as you paint over that heathen image on the wall—"

"Heathen?" I exclaimed. "It is a Christian image, sir; a pair of matched saints, if I am not mistaken."

" 'Ye shall make unto yourselves no heathen images,' " Ezekiel intoned. His sonorous voice echoed hollowly.

"I am sorry I cannot offer you refreshment," I said. "As you see, we are not yet settled in."

This was an act of rudeness worthy of Emerson himself, for the portable stove was alight and the kettle was coming to the boil. As I was to learn, rudeness was no defense against Brother Ezekiel. "As a rule I don't hold with stimulants," he remarked coolly. "But I'll take a cup of tea with you. When in Rome, eh? I know you Britishers can't get on without it. You set down, ma'am. Charity'll tend to the tea. Well, go on, girl, where are your manners? Take off your bonnet. It ain't overly bright in here and I don't want you spilling nothing."

The room was bright enough for me to get a good look at the face displayed by the removal of the absurd bonnet. It was not a fashionable style of beauty. Her skin was extremely pale—not surprising, if she went about in that stovepipe of a bonnet—and the delicacy of her features, combined with her diminutive size, made her look like a child some years away from the bloom of womanhood. But when she glanced shyly at me, as if asking my permission to proceed, I was struck by the sweetness of her expression. Her eyes were her best feature, soft and dark, half veiled by extraordinarily long, curling lashes. Her abundant brown hair was strained back from her face into an ugly bun, but a few curls had escaped to caress her rounded cheeks.

I smiled at her before turning a less amiable look on her brother. "My servant will prepare the tea," I said. "John?"

I knew he had been listening. The new door into the courtyard had been hung, and it stood a trifle ajar. The door promptly opened, and I felt an almost maternal pride when he appeared. He was such a splendid specimen of young British manhood! The sleeves of his shirt were rolled high, displaying the muscular arms of a Hercules. He stood with stiff dignity, ready to receive my orders, and I felt sure that when he spoke his vowels would be in perfect order.

The response to my summons was never uttered. Vowels and consonants alike died in his throat. He had seen the girl.

A phrase of Mr. Tennyson's struck into my mind with the accuracy of an arrow thudding into the center of the target. "The curse is come upon me," cried the Lady of Shalott (a poor specimen of womanhood) when she first beheld Sir Launcelot. So might John have cried, had he been poetically inclined, when his eyes first beheld Charity Jones.

The girl was not unaware of his interest. It could not have been more apparent if he had shouted aloud. A faint, wild-rose flush warmed her cheeks and she lowered her eyes.

The lashes and the blush completed John's demoralization. How he managed to make and serve the tea I am sure I do not know, since he never took his eyes off the girl. I expected Brother Ezekiel to resent John's interest. Instead he watched the pair with a curious absence of expression, and spoke scarcely a word. Brother David's gentlemanly manners had never shown to better advantage. He carried on an animated conversation, describing with considerable humor some of the problems he and his colleague had encountered with the villagers.

I thought I would have to take John by the shoulders and turn him out of the room when he was finished, but on the third repetition of my dismissal he stumbled out. The door remained slightly ajar, however.

Mr. Jones finally rose. "We'll be getting back," he announced. "I'll come for Charity at sundown."

"No, you'll take her with you," I said. "I appreciate your offer of assistance, but I do not need it. My people have matters well in hand." The reverend started to object. I raised my voice and continued, "If I require domestic help I will hire it. I certainly will not permit this young lady to act as my scullery maid."

Ezekiel's face turned puce. Before he could speak, David said, "My dear Mrs. Emerson, your delicacy does you credit, but you do not understand our views. Honest labor is no disgrace. I myself would willingly roll up my sleeves and wield brush or broom. I know Charity feels the same."

"Oh, yes, gladly." It was the first time the girl had ventured to speak. Her voice was as soft as a breeze sighing through the leaves. And the look she gave young David spoke louder than words.

"No," I said.

"No?" Ezekiel repeated.

"No."

When I employ a certain tone and accompany it with a certain look, it is a brave man who dares contradict me. Brother Ezekiel was not a brave man. If he had been, his companion's sense of fitness would have intervened.

"We will take our leave then," he said with a graceful bow. "I hope our offer has not been misinterpreted."

"Not at all. It has only been declined. With thanks, of course."

"Humph," said Brother Ezekiel. "All right, then, if that's how you want it. Good-bye. I will see you in church on Sunday."

It was a statement, not a question, so I did not reply. "And your servant too," Ezekiel continued, glancing in a meaningful way at the partially open door. "We make nothing of the social distinctions you Britishers believe in. To us all men are brothers in the eyes of the Lord. The young man will be heartily welcome."

I took Brother Ezekiel by the arm and escorted him out of the house.

As I watched them ride away, the girl a modest distance behind the two men, such indignation flooded my being that I stamped my foot—a frustrating gesture in that region, since the sand muffled the sound. The wretched pastor was not only a religious bigot and a crude boor, he was no better than a panderer for his god. Seeing John's interest in Charity, he meant to make use of it in winning a convert. I almost wished Emerson had been there, to take the wretch by the collar and throw him out the door.

I described the encounter later to my husband as we sat before the door enjoying the magnificent display of sunset colors across the amber desert sands. Ramses was some distance away, still digging. He had amassed quite a sizable heap of potsherds and bones. The cat Bastet lay beside him. From time to time her whiskers quivered as the scent of roasting chicken from the kitchen reached her nostrils.

To my annoyance Emerson gave me scant sympathy. "It serves you right, Amelia. I told you you were too polite to that fellow."

"Nonsense. If you had met the Reverend Ezekiel Jones, you would realize that neither courtesy nor rudeness affects him in the slightest."

"Then," said Emerson coolly, "you should have drawn your pistol and ordered him to leave."

I adjusted the weapon in question. "You don't understand the situation, Emerson. I foresee trouble ahead. The girl is infatuated with young David, and John—our John—has taken a fancy to her. It is a classic triangle, Emerson."

"Hardly a triangle," said Emerson, with one of those coarse masculine snickers. "Unless the pretty young man takes a fancy to—"

"Emerson!"

"To someone else," Emerson concluded, with a guilty look at Ramses.

"Amelia, as usual you are letting your rampageous imagination run away with you. Now that your detectival instincts have been frustrated, by my removing you from the scene of Abd el Atti's death, you are inventing romantic intrigues. Why can't you confine your energies to the work that awaits us here? Forgo your fantasies, I beg. They are all in your own head."

Ramses glanced up from his digging. "John," he remarked, "is in de house reading de Bible."

VI

Alas, Ramses was correct. John *was* reading the Bible, and he continued to spend a great deal of his spare time in this depressing pursuit. The rest of his spare time was employed in mooning around the village (the expression is Emerson's) in hopes of catching a glimpse of his love. When he came back with a light step and an idiotic smile on his face I knew he had seen Charity; when he tramped heavily, looking as if his dog had died, I knew his vigil had been unrewarded.

The morning after the visit of the missionaries we completed our preliminary survey of the site. Its total length was about four miles, from the village of Bernasht to a line approximately half a mile south of the Bent Pyramid of Dahshoor. We found traces of many small cemeteries, from the Old Kingdom to Roman times. Almost all had been thoroughly ransacked. Two sunken areas, one approximately three miles south of the Bent Pyramid, the other a quarter of a mile north of the first, were thickly covered with limestone chips. These, Emerson announced, were the remains of the pyramids of Mazghunah.

I repeated the word in a hollow voice. "Pyramids?"

"Pyramids," Emerson said firmly. Clear on the horizon the monuments of Dahshoor rose in ironic commentary.

After luncheon Emerson declared his intention of paying a call on M. de Morgan. "We cannot begin work for another day or two," he explained glibly. "And Ramses ought to see Dahshoor. I had intended to take him to Giza and Sakkara, but we left Cairo in such haste the poor lad was not even allowed to visit the Museum."

"There will be ample time for sightseeing after the season," I replied, neatly folding my napkin.

"It is only courteous to call on our neighbor, Peabody."

"No doubt; but this is the first time I have ever seen you so conscious of propriety. Oh, very well," I added quickly. "If you insist, Emerson, we will go."

We took Selim with us, leaving John to superintend the renovation of our living quarters and Abdullah to conclude the survey. He knew Emerson's methods and was competent to carry them out; but it was a departure for Emerson to leave anyone else in charge. I knew it testified to the anguish of his spirit.

Despite the equanimity of temper for which I am well known, the closer we approached the noble monuments of Dahshoor, the more bitter was the emotion that choked me. With what indescribable yearning did I view the objects with which I had hoped to become intimately acquainted!

The two large pyramids of Dahshoor date from the same period of time as the Giza pyramids, and they are almost as large. They are built of white limestone, and this snowy covering exhibits bewitching changes of tint, according to the quality of the light—a mazy gold at sunset, a ghostly translucent pallor under the glow of the moon. Now, at a little past noon, the towering structures shone dazzlingly white against the deep blue of the sky.

There are three smaller pyramids at the site, built at a later period, when building skills had deteriorated. Constructed not of solid stone but of mud brick faced with stone, they lost their original pyramidal shape when the casing blocks were removed by their successors or by local peasants desirous of obtaining pre-cut building materials. Despite its ruined state, one of these brick pyramids—the southernmost—dominates the terrain, and from some aspects it appears to loom even larger than its stone neighbors. Stark and almost menacing it rose up as we approached, as dark as the great pyramids were pale. My eyes were increasingly drawn to it and finally I exclaimed, "What a strange and indeed sinister appearance that structure has, Emerson. Can it be a pyramid?"

Emerson had become increasingly morose as we neared Dahshoor. Now he replied grumpily, "You know perfectly well that it is, Peabody. I beg you will not humor me by pretending ignorance."

He was correct; I knew the monuments of Dahshoor as well as I knew the rooms of my own house. I felt I could have traversed the area blindfolded. Emerson's bad humor was due in no small part to the fact that he was aware of my poignant yearning and felt guilty—as well he might.

The Arabs called the dark structure the "Black Pyramid," and it merited the name, even though it more resembled a massive truncated tower. As we approached, signs of activity could be seen near the eastern side, where M. de Morgan was excavating. There was no sign of de Morgan, however, until Emerson's hail brought him out of the tent where he had been napping.

M. de Morgan was in his thirties. He had been a mining engineer before being appointed to head the Department of Antiquities, a position traditionally held by a citizen of France. He was a good-looking man, with regular features and a pair of luxuriant mustaches. Even though he had been roused suddenly from sleep his trousers were neatly creased, his Norfolk jacket buttoned, and his pith helmet in place—though of course he removed this latter object of dress when he saw me. Emerson's lip curled at the sight of this "foppishness"; he refused to wear a hat and usually went about with his sleeves rolled to the elbows and his shirt collar open.

I apologized for disturbing de Morgan. "Not at all, madame," he replied, yawning. "I was about to arise."

"High time, too," said my husband. "You will never get on if you follow this eastern custom of sleeping in the afternoon. Nor will you locate the burial chamber in that amateurish way—digging tunnels at random, instead of searching for the original opening to the substructure—"

With a forced laugh, de Morgan broke in. *"Mon vieux,* I refuse to discuss professional matters until I have greeted your charming lady. And this must be young Master Emerson—how do you do, my lad?"

"Very well, thank you," said Ramses. "May I go and look at de pyramid?"

"A true archaeologist already," said the Frenchman. *"Mais certainement, mon petit."*

I gestured at Selim, who had maintained a respectful distance, and he followed Ramses. De Morgan offered us chairs and something to drink. We were sipping wine when one of the tent flaps opened and another man appeared, yawning and stretching.

"By the Almighty," said Emerson in surprise. "It is that rascal Kalenischeff. What the devil is he doing here?"

De Morgan's eyebrows rose, but he said only, "He offered his services. One can always use an extra pair of hands, you know."

"He knows less about excavation than Ramses," said Emerson.

"I will be glad of Master Ramses' expertise," said de Morgan, smiling but clearly annoyed. "Ah, your highness—you have met Professor and Mrs. Emerson?"

Kalenischeff shook Emerson's hand, kissed mine, apologized for his disarray, asked after Ramses, commented on the heat and hoped that we were pleased with Mazghunah. Neither of us felt inclined to reply to this last remark. Kalenischeff put his monocle in his eye and ogled me in a familiar fashion. "At any rate, Madame lends beauty to an otherwise dismal site," he said. "What a fetching costume!"

"I did not come here to talk about women's clothing," said Emerson, scowling fiercely as the Russian studied my booted calves.

"Of course not," Kalenischeff said smoothly. "Any advice or assistance we can offer you—"

That is only a sample of the unsatisfactory tenor of the conversation. Every time Emerson tried to introduce a sensible subject, de Morgan talked about the weather or the Russian made some slighting suggestion. Needless to say, I burned with indignation at seeing my husband, so infinitely superior in all ways, insulted by these two, and finally I decided to suffer it no longer. I can, when necessary, raise my voice to a pitch and volume very trying to the ears, and impossible to ignore.

"I wish to talk to you about the illegal antiquities trade," I said.

Kalenischeff's monocle fell from his eye, de Morgan choked in mid-swallow, the servants jumped, and one dropped the glass he was holding. Having achieved my immediate goal of capturing the gentlemen's attention, I continued in a more moderate tone. "As director of Antiquities, monsieur, you are of course fully informed about the situation. What steps are you taking to halt this nefarious trade and imprison the practitioners?"

De Morgan cleared his throat. "The usual steps, madame."

"Now, monsieur, that will not suffice." I shook my finger playfully and raised my voice a notch or two. "You are not addressing an empty-headed lady tourist; you are talking to ME. I know more than you suppose. I know, for instance, that the extent of the trade has increased disastrously; that an unknown Master Criminal has entered the game—"

"The devil!" Kalenischeff cried. His monocle, which he had replaced, again fell from its place. "Er—your pardon, Madame Emerson . . ."

"You appear surprised," I said. "Is this information new to you, your highness?"

"There has always been illicit digging. But your talk of a Master Criminal . . ." He shrugged.

"His highness is correct," de Morgan said. "Admittedly there has been a slight increase in the illegal trade of late, but—forgive me, madame—the Master Criminal exists only in sensational fiction, and I have seen no evidence of a gang at work."

His denials proved to me that he was quite unfit for his responsible position. Kalenischeff was obviously hiding something. I felt I was on the verge of great discoveries, and was about to pursue my inquiries more forcibly when a shout arose. It held such a note of terror and alarm that we all started to our feet and ran in the direction from which it had come.

Selim lay flat on the ground, his arms flailing, his cries for help rising to a frenzied pitch. Such a cloud of sand surrounded him that we were quite close before I realized what the trouble was. The terrain, west of the pyramid base, was very uneven, covered with sunken hollows and raised ridges—certain evidence of ancient structures buried beneath the sand. From one such hollow an arm protruded, stiff as a tree branch. Around it Selim was digging furiously, and it required very little intelligence to deduce that *(A)*, the arm belonged to Ramses, and *(B)*, the rest of Ramses was under the sand.

Bellowing in horror, Emerson flung Selim aside. Instead of wasting time digging, he seized Ramses' wrist and gave a mighty heave. Ramses rose up out of the *souterrain* like a trout rising to a fly.

I stood leaning on my parasol while Emerson brushed the sand off his son, assisted halfheartedly by the others. When the worst of it was removed I uncorked my flask of water and offered it to Emerson, together with a clean white handkerchief.

"Pour the water over his face, Emerson. I observe he has had the sense to keep his eyes and mouth tightly shut, so the damage should not be extensive."

And so it proved. Emerson decided we had better take Ramses home. I agreed to the suggestion; the interruption had shattered the web I had been weaving around the villainous Russian, and there was no point in continuing. De Morgan did not attempt to detain us.

As we bade a reluctant farewell to Dahshoor, Selim tugged at my sleeve. "Sitt, I have failed you. Beat me, curse me!"

"Not at all, my boy," I replied. "It is quite impossible to prevent Ramses from falling into, or out of, objects. Your task is to rescue him or summon assistance, and you performed quite well. Without you, he might have smothered."

Selim's face cleared. Gratefully he kissed my hand.

Emerson, with Ramses, had drawn a short distance ahead. Overhearing what I had said, he stopped and waited for us.

"Quite right, Peabody. You have summed up the situation nicely. I have already cautioned Ramses to be more careful and—er—no more need be said on the subject."

"Humph," I said.

"All's well that ends well," Emerson insisted. "By the way, Peabody, what was the purpose of your quizzing de Morgan about antiquities thieves? The man is a perfect fool, you know. He is as ineffectual as his predecessor in office."

"I was about to question Kalenischeff about Abd el Atti's death when Ramses interrupted, Emerson."

"Interrupted? Interrupted! I suppose that is one way of putting it."

"Kalenischeff is a most suspicious character. Did you observe his reaction when I spoke of the Master Criminal?"

"If I had been wearing a monocle—"

"A most unlikely supposition, Emerson. I cannot imagine you wearing such an absurd accoutrement."

"If," Emerson repeated doggedly, "I had been wearing a monocle, I would have let it fall on hearing such a preposterous suggestion. I beg you will leave off playing detective, Amelia. That is all behind us now."

VII

Emerson was, of course, engaging in wishful thinking when he said our criminal investigations were ended. If he had stopped to consider the matter, he would have realized, as I did, that removal from Cairo did not mean we were removed from the case. The thief who had entered our hotel room had been led thither as a result of our involvement in Abd el Atti's death. I was as certain of that as I was of my own name. The thief had not found the object he was looking for. It must be something of considerable importance to him or he would not have risked entering a place as well guarded as Shepheard's. The conclusion? It should be obvious to any reasonable person. The thief would continue to search for the missing object. Sooner or later we would hear from him—another attempt at burglary, or an assault on one of us, or some other interesting attention. Since this had not occurred to Emerson, I did not feel obliged to point it out to him. He would only have fussed.

On the following day we were ready to begin work. Emerson had decided to start with a late cemetery. I tried to dissuade him, for I have no patience with martyrs.

"Emerson, you know quite well from the visible remains that this cemetery probably dates from Roman times. You hate late cemeteries. Why don't we work at the—er—pyramids? You may find subsidiary tombs, temples, a sub-structure—"

"No, Amelia. I agreed to excavate this site and I will excavate it, with a thoroughness and attention to detail that will set new standards for archaeological methodology. Never let it be said that an Emerson shirked his duty."

And off he marched, his shoulders squared and his eyes lifted to the horizon. He looked so splendid I didn't have the heart to point out the disadvantages of this posture; when one is striding bravely into the future one cannot watch one's footing. Sure enough, he stumbled into Ramses' pile of potsherds and went sprawling.

Ramses, who had been about to go after him, prudently retired behind my trousers. After a malignant glance in our direction Emerson got up and limped away.

"What is Papa going to do?" Ramses inquired.

"He is going to hire the workers. See, they are coming now."

A group of men had gathered around the table where Emerson now seated himself, with John at his side. We had decided to put John in charge of the work records, listing the names of the men as they were taken on, and keeping track of the hours they worked, plus additional money earned for important finds. Applicants continued to trickle in from the direction of the village. They were a somber group in their dark robes and blue turbans. Only the children lent some merriment to the scene. We would hire a number of the latter, both boys and girls, to carry away the baskets of sand the men filled as they dug.

Ramses studied the group and decided, correctly, that it promised to be a dull procedure. "I will help you, Mama," he announced.

"That is kind of you, Ramses. Wouldn't you rather finish your own excavation?"

Ramses gave the potsherds a disparaging glance. "I have finished it, to my own satisfaction. I was desirous of carrying out a sample dig, for, after all, I have had no experience at excavation, t'ough I am naturally conversant wit' de basic principles. However, it is apparent dat de site is devoid of interest. I believe I will turn my attention now—"

"For pity's sake, Ramses, don't lecture! I cannot imagine whence you derive your unfortunate habit of loquacity. There is no need to go on and on when someone asks you a simple question. Brevity, my boy, is not only the soul of wit, it is the essence of literary and verbal efficiency. Model yourself on my example, I beg, and from now on—"

I was interrupted, not by Ramses, who was listening intently, but by Bastet. She let out a long plaintive howl and bit me on the ankle. Fortunately my thick boots prevented her teeth from penetrating the skin.

In the pages of this private journal I will admit I made a mistake. I should not have interrupted Ramses when he spoke of his future plans.

I was fully occupied all that morning with domestic arrangements. Not until after the men resumed work after the midday break did I have time to look them over.

The first trench had been started. We had fifty men at work with picks and shovels, and as many children carrying away the detritus. The scene was familiar to me from previous seasons, and despite the fact that I expected nothing of interest to turn up, my spirits lifted at the well-loved scene—the picks of the men rising and falling rhythmically, the children scampering off with the loaded baskets, singing as they worked. I walked along the line, hoping someone would stop me to announce a find—a coffin or a cache of jewelry or a tomb. Not until I reached the end of the trench did I make the discovery.

One frequently hears, from English and European tourists, that all Egyptians look alike. This is nonsense, of course; Emerson calls it prejudice, and he is probably correct. I will admit, however, that the omnipresent, shapeless robes and turbans create an impression of uniformity. The facial hair to which our workers were addicted also added to the impression that they were all closely related to one another. Despite these handicaps, it was not five minutes before I had seen one particular face that made an electrifying impression on me.

I sped back to Emerson. "He is here," I exclaimed. "In section A-twenty-four. Come at once, Emerson."

Emerson, with a singularly sour expression on his face, was inspecting the first find of the day—a crude pottery lamp. He glowered. "Who is here, Amelia?"

I paused a moment for effect. "The man who was talking to Abd el Atti."

Emerson flung the lamp onto the ground. "What the devil are you talking about? What man?"

"You must remember. I described him to you. He spoke the gold sellers' argot, and when he saw me, he—"

"Are you out of your senses?" Emerson bellowed.

I seized his arm. "Come quickly, Emerson."

As we went, I explained. "He was a very ill-favored fellow, Emerson. I will never forget his face. Only ask yourself why he should turn up here, unless he is following us with some nefarious purpose in mind."

"Where is this villain?" Emerson inquired, with deceptive mildness.

"There." I pointed.

"You, there," Emerson called.

The man straightened. His eyes widened in simulated surprise. "You speak to me, effendi?"

"Yes, to you. What is your name?"

"Hamid, effendi."

"Ah, yes, I remember. You are not a local man."

"I come from Manawat, effendi, as I told you. We heard there was work here."

The answer came readily. The fellow's eyes never left Emerson's face. I considered this highly suspicious.

"Proceed discreetly, Emerson," I said in a low voice. "If accused, he may strike at you with his pick."

"Bah," said Emerson. "When were you last in Cairo, Hamid?"

"Cairo? I have never been there, effendi."

"Do you know Abd el Atti, the dealer in antiquities?"

"No, effendi."

Emerson gestured him to return to his work and drew me aside. "There, you see? You are imagining things again, Amelia."

"Of course he will deny everything, Emerson. You did not carry out a proper interrogation. But never mind; I didn't suppose we would wring a confession from the villain. I only wanted to draw your attention to him."

"Do me a favor," Emerson said. "Don't draw my attention to anyone, or anything, unless it has been dead at least a thousand years. This work is tedious enough. I do not need further aggravation." And off he marched, grumbling.

To be honest, I was beginning to regret I had acted so precipitately. I might have known Emerson would question my identification, and now I had let my suspect know I was suspicious of him. It would have been better to let him believe his disguise (of an indigo turban) had not been penetrated.

The damage was done. Perhaps, knowing my eyes were upon him, Hamid might be moved to rash action, such as a direct attack on one of us. Cheered by this reasoning, I returned to my work.

Yet I found it difficult to concentrate on what I was supposed to be doing. My gaze kept returning to the northern horizon, where the Dahshoor pyramids rose like mocking reminders of a forbidden paradise. Gazing upon them I knew how Eve must have felt when she looked back at the flowers and lush foliage of Eden, from which she was forever barred. (Another example of masculine duplicity, I might add. Adam was under no compulsion to eat of the fruit, and his attempt to shift the blame onto his trusting spouse was, to say the least, unmanly.)

Because of this distraction I was the first to see the approaching rider. Mounted on a spirited Arab stallion, he presented a handsome spectacle as he galloped across the waste. He drew up before me with a tug on the reins that made the horse rear, and removed his hat. The full effect of this performance was spoiled, for me, by the sight of the object de Morgan held before him on his saddle. The object was my son, sandy, sunburned, and sardonic. His look of bland innocence as he gazed down at me would have driven most mothers to mayhem.

Tenderly de Morgan lowered Ramses into my arms. I dropped him immediately and dusted off my hands. "Where did you find him?" I inquired.

"Midway between this place and my own excavations. In the middle of nowhere, to be precise. When I inquired of him where he thought he was going, he replied he had decided to pay me a visit. *C'est un enfant formidable!* Truly the son of my dear *collègue*—a splinter off the old English block of wood, *n'est pas?*"

Emerson came trotting up in time to hear the final compliment. The look he gave de Morgan would have withered a more sensitive man. De Morgan only smiled and twirled his mustaches. Then he began to congratulate Emerson on the intelligence, daring, and excellent French of his son.

"Humph, yes, no doubt," Emerson said. "Ramses, what the devil—that is to say, you must not wander off in this careless fashion."

"I was not wandering," Ramses protested. "I was aware at all times of my precise location. I confess I had underestimated de distance between dis place and Dahshoor. What I require, Papa, is a horse. Like dat one."

De Morgan laughed. "You would find it hard to control a steed like Mazeppa," he said, stroking the stallion's neck. "But a mount of some kind—yes, yes, that is reasonable."

"I beg you will not support my son in his ridiculous demands, monsieur," I said, giving Ramses a hard stare. "Ramses, where is Selim?"

"He accompanied me, of course," said Ramses. "But M. de Morgan would not let him come on de horse wit' us."

De Morgan continued to plead Ramses' case, probably because he saw how much his partisanship annoyed Emerson. "What harm can come to the lad, after all? He has only to follow the line of the cultivation. A little horse, madame— Professor—a pony, perhaps. The boy is welcome to visit me at any time. I do not doubt we will have more interesting—we will have interesting things to show him."

Emerson made a sound like a bull about to charge, but controlled himself. "Have you found the burial chamber yet?"

"We have only just begun our search," said de Morgan haughtily. "But since the burial chambers are generally located directly under the exact center of the pyramid square, it is only a matter of time."

"Not that it will matter," Emerson grunted. "Like all the others, it will have been robbed and you will find nothing."

"Who knows, *mon cher*? I have a feeling—here—" De Morgan thumped the breast of his well-tailored jacket—"that we will find great things this season. And you—what luck have you had?"

"Like you, we have only begun," I said, before Emerson could explode. "Will you come to the house, monsieur, and join us in a cup of tea?"

De Morgan declined, explaining that he had a dinner engagement. "As you know, Dahshoor is a popular stop for tourists. The dahabeeyah of the Countess of Westmoreland is there presently, and I am dining with her tonight."

This boast failed to wound Emerson; he was not at all impressed by titles, and considered dining out a painful chore, to be avoided whenever possible. But the Frenchman's other digs had hit the mark, and his final speech was designed to twist the knife in the wound. He wished us luck, told us to visit his excavations at any time, and repeated his invitation to Ramses. "You will come and learn how to conduct an excavation, *n'est pas, mon petit?*"

Ramses gazed worshipfully at the handsome figure on the great stallion. "T'ank you, monsieur, I would like dat."

With a bow to me and a mocking smile at Emerson, de Morgan wheeled the horse and rode off into the sunset. It was the wrong direction entirely, and I had to agree with Emerson when he muttered, "These cursed Frenchmen—anything for a grand gesture!"

Chapter Six

 IN the end Ramses got his way. After considering the matter, I decided it would be advisable for us to have some form of transport at hand, for the site was isolated and extensive. So we hired several donkeys, on a long-term lease, so to speak, and had the men build a shed for them near the ruins of the church. My first act upon coming into possession of the donkeys was, as usual, to strip off their filthy saddlecloths and wash them. It was not an easy task, since water had to be carried from the village, and the donkeys did not at all like being washed.

I will say for Ramses that he tried to be of use. However, he was more hindrance then help, falling over the water jars, getting more liquid on his own person than on the donkeys, and narrowly avoiding losing a finger to one irritated equine whose teeth he was trying to brush. The moment the animals were ready for locomotion he demanded the use of one.

"Certainly, my boy," his naive father replied.

"Where do you mean to go?" his more suspicious mother demanded.

"To Dahshoor, to visit M. de Morgan," said Ramses.

Emerson's face fell. He had been deeply wounded by Ramses' admiration for the dashing Frenchman. "I would rather you did not call on M. de Morgan,

Ramses. Not alone, at any rate. Papa will take you with him another time."

Instead of debating the matter, Ramses clasped his hands and raised imploring eyes to his father's troubled face. "Den, Papa, may I make a widdle excavation of my own? Just a widdle one, Papa?"

I cannot fully express in words the dark suspicion that filled my mind at this patent demonstration of duplicity. It had been months since Ramses had mispronounced the letter *l*. His father had been absurdly charmed by this speech defect; indeed, I am convinced that it originated with Emerson's addressing the infant Ramses in "baby-talk," as it is called. Before I could express my misgivings, Emerson beamed fondly at the innocent face turned up to his and said, "My dear boy, certainly you may. What a splendid idea! It will be excellent experience for you."

"And may I take one or two of de men to help me, Papa?"

"I was about to suggest it myself, Ramses. Let me see whom I can spare—besides Selim, of course."

They went off arm in arm, leaving me to wonder what Ramses was up to this time. Even my excellent imagination failed to provide an answer.

II

The cemetery *was* of Roman date. Need I say more? We found small rock-cut tombs, most of which had been robbed in ancient times. Our labors were rewarded (I use the word ironically) by a motley collection of rubbish the tomb robbers had scorned—cheap pottery jars, fragments of wooden boxes, and a few beads. Emerson recorded the scraps with dangerous calm and I filed them away in the storeroom. The unrobbed tombs did contain coffins, some of wood, some molded out of cartonnage (a variety of papier-mâché) and heavily varnished. We opened three of these coffins, but Emerson was forced to refuse Ramses' request that he be allowed to unwrap the mummies, since we had no facilities for that particular enterprise. Two of the mummies had painted portraits affixed to the head wrappings. These paintings, done in colored wax on thin panels of wood, were used in late times in lieu of the sculptured masks common earlier. Petrie had found a number of them, some exceedingly handsome, when he dug at Hawara, but our examples were crude and injured by damp. I hope I need not say that I treated these wretched specimens with the meticulous care I always employ, covering them with a fresh coating of beeswax to fix the colors and storing them in boxes padded with cotton wool, in the same manner I had employed with the portrait painting Emerson had rescued from Abd el Atti's shop. They compared poorly with the latter, which was that of a woman wearing elaborate earrings and a golden fillet. Her large dark eyes and expressive lips were drawn and shaded with an almost modern realism of technique.

On Sunday, which was our day of rest, John appeared in full regalia, knee breeches and all. His buttons had been polished to dazzling brightness. Respectfully he asked my permission to attend church services.

"But neither of the churches here are yours, John," I said, blinking at the buttons.

This rational observation had no effect on John, who continued to regard me with mute appeal, so I gave in. "Very well, John."

"I will go too," said Ramses. "I want to see de young lady dat John is—"

"That will do, Ramses."

"I also wish to observe de Coptic service," continued Ramses. "It is, I have been informed, an interesting survival of certain antique—"

"Yes, I know, Ramses. That is certainly an idea. We will all go."

Emerson looked up from his notes. "You are not including me, I hope."

"Not if you don't wish to go. But as Ramses has pointed out, the Coptic service—"

"Don't be a hypocrite, Peabody. It is not scholarly fervor that moves you; you also want to see John with the young lady he is—"

"That will do, Emerson," I said. John gave me a grateful look. He was bright red from the collar of his jacket to the curls on his brow.

Services at the Coptic church had already begun when we reached the village, though you would not have supposed it to be so from the babble of voices that could be heard within. From the grove of trees where the American mission was situated the tinny tolling of the bell called worshipers to the competing service. There was a peremptory note in its persistent summons, or so it seemed to me; it reminded me of the reverend's voice, and the half-formed idea that had come to me as we proceeded crystallized into a determination not to accede, even in appearance, to his demand that I attend his church.

"I am going to the Coptic service," I said. "Ramses, will you come with me or go with John?"

Somewhat to my surprise, Ramses indicated he would go with John. I had not believed vulgar curiosity would win over scholarly instincts. However, the decision suited me quite well. I informed the pair that we would meet at the well, and saw them proceed toward the chapel.

The interior of the Coptic church of Sitt Miriam (the Virgin, in our terms) was adorned with faded paintings of that lady and various saints. There were no seats or pews; the worshipers walked about chatting freely and appearing to pay no attention to the priest, who stood at the altar reciting prayers. The congregation was not large—twenty or thirty people, perhaps. I recognized several of the rough-looking men who had appeared to form the priest's entourage sanctimoniously saluting the pictures of the saints, but the face I had half-hoped to see was not among them. However, it did not surprise me to learn that Hamid was not a regular churchgoer.

I took up my position toward the back, near but not within the enclosure where the women were segregated. My advent had not gone unnoticed. Conversations halted for a moment and then broke out louder than before. The priest's glowing black eyes fixed themselves on me. He was too experienced a performer to interrupt his praying, but his voice rose in stronger accents. It sounded like a denunciation of something—possibly me—but I could not understand the words. Clearly this part of the service was in the ancient Coptic tongue, and I doubted that the priest and the congregation understood much more of it than I did. The prayers were memorized and repeated by rote.

Before long the priest switched to Arabic and I recognized that he was reading from one of the gospels. This went on for an interminable time. Finally he turned from the *heikal,* or altar, swinging a censer from which wafted the sickening smell of incense. He began to make his way through the congregation, blessing each individual by placing a hand upon his head and threatening him with the censer. I stood alone, the other worshipers having prudently edged away, and I wondered whether I would be ignored altogether or whether some particularly insulting snub was in train. Conceive of my surprise, therefore, when, having attended to every *man* present, the priest made his way rapidly toward me. Placing his hand heavily upon my head, he blessed me in the name of the Trinity, the Mother of God, and assorted saints. I thanked him, and was rewarded by a ripple of black beard that I took to betoken a smile.

When the priest had returned to the *heikal* I decided I had done my duty and could retire. The interior of the small edifice was foggy with cheap incense and I feared I was about to sneeze.

The sun was high in the heavens. I drew deep satisfying breaths of the warm but salubrious air and managed to conquer the sneeze. I then took off my hat and was distressed to find that my forebodings had been correct. Of fine yellow straw, to match my frock, the hat was draped with white lace and trimmed with a cluster of yellow roses, loops of yellow ribbon and two choux of white velvet. Clusters of artificial violets and leaves completed the modest decorations, and the entire ensemble was daintily draped with tulle. It was my favorite hat; it had been very expensive; and it had required a long search to find a hat that was not trimmed with dead birds or ostrich plumes. (I deplore the massacre of animals to feed female vanity.)

As the priest's hand pressed on my head I had heard a crunching sound. Now I saw the bows were crushed, the roses hung drunkenly from bent stems, and that the mark of a large, dirty hand was printed on the mashed tulle. The only consolation I could derive was that there was also a spot of blood on the tulle. Apparently one of my hat pins had pricked the ecclesiastical palm.

There was nothing to be done about the hat, so I replaced it on my head and looked about. The small square was deserted except for a pair of lean dogs and some chickens who had not been inspired to attend the service. As John and Ramses were nowhere to be seen, I walked toward the mission.

The church door stood open. From it came music—not the mellifluous strains of the organ or the sweet harmony of a trained choir, but motley voices bellowing out what I had to assume must be a hymn. I thought I recognized Ramses' piercing, offkey treble, but I could not make out any of the words. I sat down on the same rock Emerson had once used as a seat, and waited.

The sun rose higher and perspiration trickled down my back. The singing went on and on, the same monotonous tune repeated interminably. It was finally succeeded by the voice of Brother Ezekiel. I could hear him quite well. He prayed for the elect and for those still in the darkness of false belief (every inhabitant of the globe except the members of the Church of the Holy Jerusalem). I thought he would never stop praying. Eventually he did, and the congregation began to emerge.

The "Brotestants" appeared to be succeeding in their efforts at conversion, for Brother Ezekiel's audience was somewhat larger than that of the priest. Most, if not all, of the converts wore the dark Coptic turban. Christian missionaries had had little success in winning over Muslims, perhaps for ideological reasons and perhaps because the Egyptian government disapproved (in a number of effective and unpleasant ways) of apostates from the faith of Islam. No one cared what the Copts did; hence the higher conversion rate and the resentment of the Coptic hierarchy against missionaries. This resentment had, on several occasions, resulted in physical violence. When Emerson told me of these cases I exclaimed in disbelief, but my cynical husband only smiled contemptuously. "No one slaughters a co-religionist with quite as much enthusiasm as a Christian, my dear. Look at their history." I made no comment on this, for in fact I could think of nothing to say.

Among the worshipers wearing the blue turban was one I recognized. So Hamid was a convert! When he saw me he had the effrontery to salute me.

Eventually John came out of the church. His face was pink with pleasure—and probably with heat, for the temperature in the chapel must have been over one hundred degrees. He came running to me, babbling apologies: "It was a long service, madam."

"So I observed. Where is Ramses?"

"He was here," said John vaguely. "Madam, they have done me the honor to ask me to stay for dinner. May I, madam?"

I was about to reply with a decided negative when I saw the group coming toward me and forgot what I was going to say. Brother David, looking like a young saint, had given his arm to a lady—the same lady I had seen with him at Shepheard's. Her gown that morning was of bright violet silk in a broché design; the short coat had a cutaway front displaying an enormous white chiffon cravat that protruded a good twelve inches in front of her. The matching hat had not only ribbons and flowers, but an egret plume and a dead bird mounted with wings and tail uppermost, as if in flight.

Completing the trio was Ramses, his hand in that of the lady. He was

looking as pious as only Ramses can look when he is contemplating some reprehensible action, and he was smeared with dust from his once-white collar to his
buttoned boots. Ramses is the only person of my acquaintance who can get dirty
sitting perfectly still in a church.

The group bore down on me. They all spoke at once. Ramses greeted me,
Brother David reproached me for not coming into the chapel, and the lady cried,
in a voice as shrill as that of a magpie, *"Ach du lieber Gott,* what a pleasure it is!
The famous Frau Emerson, is it you? I have often of you heard and intended on
you to call and now you are here, in the flesh!"

"I fear you have the advantage of me," I replied.

"Allow me to present the Baroness Hohensteinbauergrunewald," said
Brother David. "She is—"

"A great admirer of the famous Frau Emerson and her so-distinguished
husband," shrieked the baroness, seizing my hand and crushing it in hers. "And
now the mother of the *liebe Kind* I find you are—it is too much of happiness! You
must me visit. I insist that you are coming. My dahabeeyah is at Dahshoor; I
inspect the pyramids, I entertain the distinguished archaeologists, I gather the
antiquities. This evening come you and the famous Professor Doctor Emerson to
dine, *nicht?"*

"Nicht," I said. "That is, I thank you, Baroness, but I am afraid—"

"You have another engagement?" The baroness's small muddy-brown
eyes twinkled. She nudged me familiarly. "No, you have not another engagement.
What could you do in this desert? You will come. A dinner party I will have for
the famous archaeologists. Brother David, he will come also." The young man
nodded, smiling, and the baroness continued, "I stay only three days at Dahshoor.
I make the Nile cruise. So you come tonight. To the famous Professor Doctor
Emerson I show my collection of antiquities. I have mummies, scarabs,
papyrus—"

"Papyrus?" I exclaimed.

"Yes, many. So now you come, eh? I will the young Ramses with me take,
he wishes to see my dahabeeyah. Then at night you will come and fetch him.
Good!"

I gave Ramses a searching look. He clasped his hands. "Oh, Mama, may
I go wit' de lady?"

"You are too untidy—" I began.

The baroness guffawed. "So a small boy should be, *nicht?* I will take good
care of him. I am a mama, I know a mama's heart." She rumpled his ebony curls.
Ramses' face took on the fixed look that usually preceded a rude remark. He
loathed having his curls rumpled. But he remained silent, and my suspicions as to
his ulterior motives, whatever they might be, were strengthened.

Before I could frame further objections the baroness started, and said in
what is vulgarly called a pig's whisper, *"Ach,* he comes, *der Pfarrer.* Too much

he talks already. I escape. I come only to see Brother David, because he is so beautiful, but *der Pfarrer* I do not like. Come, *Bübchen,* we run away."

She suited the action to the words, dragging Ramses with her.

Brother Ezekiel had emerged from the chapel. Behind him was Charity, hands clasped and face obscured by the bonnet. At the sight of her John jumped as if a bee had stung him. "Madam," he groaned piteously, "may I—"

"Very well," I said.

The baroness was certainly one of the most vulgar women I had ever met, but her instincts were basically sound. I also wished to run away from Brother Ezekiel. As I beat a hasty retreat I felt as if I had tossed John to him like a bone to a lion, in order to make good my escape. At least John was a willing martyr.

So the baroness had papyri. In my opinion that fact justified a visit. Emerson would not be pleased, though. I had lost John to the missionaries and Ramses to the baroness, and I had committed my husband to a social call of the sort he particularly abominated. However, there was one mitigating circumstance. We would be alone in the house that afternoon, and I had no doubt I could persuade Emerson to do his duty.

III

Emerson was duly persuaded. He refused to wear proper evening dress, and I did not insist, for I had discovered that my red velvet gown was not suited to riding donkey-back. I put on my best Turkish trousers and we set off, accompanied by Selim and Daoud.

Bastet had been even more annoyed than Emerson to learn I had not brought Ramses back with me. We had shut her in one of the empty storerooms to prevent her from attending church with us; when I let her out she addressed me in raucous complaint and bolted out of the house. She had not returned by the time we left, nor had John.

"Something must be done about this nonsense, Amelia," Emerson declared, as we jogged northward. "I won't have John turning into a Brother of Jerusalem. I thought he had more intelligence. I am disappointed in him."

"He has not been converted by Brother Ezekiel, you booby," I said affectionately. "He is in love, and as you ought to know, intelligence is no defense against that perilous condition."

Instead of responding to this tender remark, Emerson only grunted.

It was another of those perfect desert evenings. A cool breeze swept away the heat of the day. The western sky was awash with crimson and gold, while the heavens above our heads had the clear translucence of a deep-blue china bowl. Golden in the rays of the setting sun, the slopes of the great pyramids of Dahshoor rose like stairways to heaven. Yet the somber tower of the Black Pyramid dominated the scene. Because of its position it appeared as high or higher than the nearby southern stone pyramid.

We passed close by its base on our way to the riverbank. The ground was littered with chips of white limestone, the remains of the casing blocks that had once covered the brick core. The previous season de Morgan had uncovered the ruins of the enclosure wall and the funerary chapel next to the pyramid. A few fallen columns and fragments of bas-relief were all that remained above the surface of the ground. So much for futile human vanity; in a few years the relentless sand would swallow up the signs of de Morgan's work as it had covered the structures designed to ensure the immortality of the pharaoh. The site was deserted. De Morgan was staying at Menyat Dahshoor, the nearest village.

We rode on, following the lengthening shadow of the pyramid toward the river. Several dahabeeyahs rocked gently at anchor, but it was easy to distinguish that of the baroness, since the German flag flew at the bow. A freshly painted plaque displayed the vessel's name: *Cleopatra*. It was precisely the sort of trite, obvious name I would have expected the baroness to select.

A gentle nostalgia suffused me when I set foot on the deck. There is no more delightful means of travel than these houseboats; the Nile steamers of Mr. Cook, which have almost replaced them, cannot compare in comfort and charm.

The main salon was in the front of the boat, with a row of wide windows following the curve of the bow. The baroness's dragoman threw open the door and announced us, and we stepped into a chamber swimming with sunset light and furnished with garish elegance. A wide divan covered with cushions filled one end of the room, and upon it, in more than oriental splendor, reclined the baroness. Golden chains twined the dusky masses of her unbound hair, and golden bracelets chimed when she raised a hand in greeting. Her snowy robes were of the finest chiffon; a heavy necklace or collar, of carnelian and turquoise set in gold, covered her breast. I assumed that the absurd costume was meant to conjure up the fabulous queen after whom the boat was named, but I could not help being reminded of the late and not much lamented Madame Berengeria, who had also affected ancient Egyptian costume, laboring as she did under the impression that she was the reincarnation of several long-dead queens. Poor Berengeria would have turned green with envy at the magnificence of the baroness's garb, for her bracelets were of pure gold and the collar around her neck appeared to be a genuine antiquity.

From Emerson, behind me, came sounds of imminent strangulation. I turned to find that his apoplectic gaze was fixed, not on the lady's ample charms, but upon another object. It was a handsome mummy case, gleaming with varnish, that stood carelessly propped against the grand piano like some outré parlor ornament. A table was covered with an equally casual display of antiquities— scarabs, ushebtis, vessels of pottery and stone. On another table were several papyrus scrolls.

The baroness began to writhe. After a moment I realized her movements were not those of a peculiar, recumbent dance, but merely an attempt to rise from the couch, which was low and soft. Succeeding in this, she swept forward to welcome us. Since Emerson made no move to take the hand she held under his nose, she snatched his. The vigorous shaking she gave it seemed to wake him from his stupor. His eyes focused in a malignant glare upon her conspicuous bosom, and he inquired, "Madam, do you realize the object you have slung across your chest is a priceless antiquity?"

The baroness rolled her eyes and covered the collar with ringed hands. "*Ach,* the monster! Would you tear it from my helpless body?"

"Not at all," Emerson replied. "Rough handling might damage the collar."

The baroness burst into a roar of laughter. "It is the truth, what they say about Emerson the most distinguished. They have of you me warned, that you would scold—"

"For heaven's sake, madam, speak German," Emerson interrupted, his scowl deepening.

The lady continued in that language. "Yes, yes, everyone speaks of Professor Emerson; they have told me you would scold me for my poor little antiquities. M. de Morgan is not so unkind as you."

She proceeded to introduce the other guests. If she had deliberately selected a group designed to vex Emerson, she could hardly have done better—de Morgan, Kalenischeff (in faultless evening dress, complete with ribbon and monocle), Brother David, and three of what Emerson called "confounded tourists," from the other dahabeeyahs. The only memorable remark made by any of the tourists the entire evening came from one of the English ladies, who remarked in a languid drawl, "But the ruins are so dilapidated! Why doesn't someone repair them?"

The one person I expected to see was not present, and during a lull in the ensuing conversation I inquired of the baroness, "Where is Ramses?"

"Locked in one of the guest chambers," was the reply. "Oh, do not concern yourself, Frau Emerson; he is happily engaged with a papyrus. But it was necessary for me to confine him. Already he has fallen overboard and been bitten by a lion—"

"Lion?" Emerson turned, with a cry, from the granite statue of Isis he had been examining.

"My lion cub," the baroness explained. "I bought the adorable little creature from a dealer in Cairo."

"Ah," I said, enlightened. "Ramses was no doubt attempting to free the animal. Did he succeed?"

"Fortunately we were able to recapture it," the baroness replied.

I was sorry to hear that. Ramses would undoubtedly try again.

The baroness reassured my snarling husband. The bite had not been deep and medical attention had been promptly applied. It was tacitly agreed that we would leave Ramses where he was until it was time to take him home. Emerson did not insist. He had other things on his mind.

These were, I hardly need say, the illicit antiquities collected by the baroness. He kept reverting to the subject despite the efforts of the others to keep the conversation on a light social plane, and after we had dined he finally succeeded in delivering his lecture. Striding up and down the salon, waving his arms, he shouted anathemas while the baroness grinned and rolled her eyes.

"If tourists would stop buying from these dealers, they would have to go out of business," he cried. "The looting of tombs and cemeteries would stop. Look at this." He pointed an accusing finger at the mummy case. "Who knows what vital evidence the tomb robber lost when he removed this mummy from its resting place?"

The baroness gave me a conspiratorial smile. "But he is magnificent, the professor. Such passion! I congratulate you, my dear."

"I fear I must add my reproaches to those of the professor." The statement was so unexpected it halted Emerson's lecture and turned all eyes toward the speaker. David continued, in the same soft voice, "Carrying human remains about as if they were cordwood is a deplorable custom. As a man of the cloth, I cannot condone it."

"But this poor corpse was a pagan," said Kalenischeff, smiling cynically. "I thought you men of the cloth were only concerned about Christian remains."

"Pagan or Christian, all men are the children of God," was the reply. All the ladies present—except myself—let out sighs of admiration, and David went on, "Of course, if I believed the remains were those of a fellow-Christian, however misled by false dogma, I would be forced to expostulate more forcibly. I could not permit—"

"I thought he was a Christian," the baroness interrupted. "The dealer from whom I bought him said so."

A general outcry arose. The baroness shrugged. "What is the difference? They are all the same, dry bones and flesh—the cast-off garments of the soul."

This shrewd hit—it was shrewd, I admit—was wasted on David, whose German was obviously poor. He looked puzzled, and de Morgan said soothingly, in the tongue of Shakespeare, "No, there is no question of such a thing. I fear the dealer deceived you, Baroness."

"*Verdammter* pig-dog," said the baroness calmly. "How can you be sure, monsieur?"

De Morgan started to reply, but Emerson beat him to it. "By the style and decoration of the mummy case. The hieroglyphic inscriptions identify the owner as a man named Thermoutharin. He was clearly a worshiper of the old gods; the scenes in gilt relief show Anubis and Isis, Osiris and Thoth, performing the ceremony of embalming the dead."

"It is of the Ptolemaic period," said de Morgan.

"No, no, later. The first or second century A.D."

De Morgan's lean cheekbones flushed with annoyance at Emerson's dogmatic tone, but he was too much of a gentleman to debate the point. It was young David Cabot who peppered my husband with questions—the meaning of this sign or that, the significance of the inscriptions, and so on. I was surprised at his interest, but I saw nothing sinister in it—then.

Before long the baroness became bored with a conversation of which she was not the subject. *"Ach!"* she exclaimed, clapping her hands. "So much fuss over an ugly mummy! If you feel so strongly, Professor, you may have it. I give it as a gift. Unless Brother David wants to take it, to bury it with Christian rites."

"Not I," David said. "The professor has convinced me; it is pagan."

"Nor I," said Emerson. "I have enough damned—that is, er . . . Give it to the Museum, Baroness."

"I will consider doing so," said the lady, "if it will win your approval, Professor."

I could have told her that her elephantine flirtatiousness would have no effect on Emerson. Tiring finally of a game in which she was the only player, she invited her guests to view her new pet, which was kept in a cage on the deck. Emerson and I declined; and when the others had gone, I turned to my unhappy spouse. "You have done your duty like an English gentleman, Emerson. I am ready to leave whenever you are."

"I never wanted to come in the first place, Peabody, as you know. As I suspected, my martyrdom was in vain. The confounded woman has no demotic papyri."

"I know. But perhaps your appeals on behalf of antiquities will affect not only the baroness but the other tourists who were present."

Emerson snorted. "Don't be naive, Peabody. Let us go, eh? If I remain any longer in this storehouse of disaster, I will choke."

"Very well, my dear. As always, I bow to your wishes."

"Bah," said Emerson. "Where do you suppose that dreadful female has stowed our poor child?"

It was not difficult to locate Ramses. One of the baroness's servants stood on guard before the door. He salaamed deeply when he saw us and produced the key.

Darkness had fallen, but the room was well lighted by two hanging lamps. Their beams fell upon a table well supplied with food and drink, and upon another table that held a papyrus scroll, partially unrolled. There was no sign of Ramses.

"Curse it," Emerson said furiously. "I'll wager she neglected to nail the porthole shut." He pulled aside the drapery that concealed the aforementioned orifice, and fell back with a cry. Hanging from the wall, like a stuffed hunting trophy, was a small headless body culminating in shabby brown buttoned boots. The legs were quite limp.

Accustomed as I was to finding Ramses in a variety of peculiar positions, this one was sufficiently unusual to induce a momentary constriction of the chest that kept me mute. Before I could recover myself, a far-off, strangely muffled but familiar voice remarked, "Good evening, Mama. Good evening, Papa. Will you be so good as to pull me in?"

He had stuck, in actuality, somewhere around the midsection, owing to the fact that the pockets of his little suit were filled with rocks. "It was a singular miscalculation on my part," Ramses remarked somewhat breathlessly, as Emerson set him on his feet. "I counted on de fact, which I have often had occasion to establish t'rough experiment, dat where de head and shoulders can pass, de rest of de body can follow. I had forgotten about de rocks, which are interesting specimens of de geological history of—"

"Why did you not pull yourself back into the room?" I inquired curiously, as Emerson, still pale with alarm, ran agitated hands over the child's frame.

"De problem lies in my unfortunate lack of inches," Ramses explained. "My arms were not long enough to obtain sufficient purchase on de side of de vessel."

He would have gone on at some length had I not interrupted him. "And the papyrus?" I asked.

Ramses gave it a disparaging glance. "An undistinguished example of a twentiet'-dynasty mortuary text. De lady has no demotic papyri, Mama."

We found the rest of the party still on deck. The ladies crouched before the cage in which the lion cub prowled restlessly, growling and snapping. I kept firm hold of Ramses' arm while we made our excuses and thanked our hostess. At least I thanked her; Emerson only snorted.

Brother David announced his intention of riding back with us. "I must arise at dawn," he intoned. "This has been a delightful interlude, but my Master calls."

The baroness extended her hand and the young man bent over it with graceful respect. "Humph," said Emerson, as we left him to complete his farewells. "I presume the interval has been lucrative as well as delightful. He wouldn't be ready to leave if he had not accomplished what he came for."

"What was dat?" Ramses asked interestedly.

"Money, of course. Donations to the church. That is Brother David's role, I fancy—seducing susceptible ladies."

"Emerson, please," I exclaimed.

"Not literally," Emerson admitted. "At least I don't suppose so."

"What is de literal meaning of dat word?" Ramses inquired. "De dictionary is particularly obscure on dat point."

Emerson changed the subject.

After we had mounted, Emerson set off at a great pace in an effort to avoid David's company, but the young man was not to be got rid of so easily. Before the pair trotted beyond earshot I heard him say, "Pray explain to me, Professor, how a man of your superior intelligence can be so indifferent to that one great question which must supersede all other intellectual inquiries. . . ."

Ramses and I followed at a gentler pace. He seemed deep in thought, and after a time I asked, "Where did the lion cub bite you?"

"He did not bite me. His toot' scratched my hand when I pulled him from de cage."

"That was not a sensible thing to do, Ramses."

"Dat," said Ramses, "was not de issue, Mama."

"I am not referring to your ill-advised attempt to free the animal from captivity. It appears to be a very young lion. Its chances of survival in a region where there are no others of its kind would be slim."

Ramses was silent for a moment. Then he said thoughtfully, "I confess dat objection had not occurred to me. T'ank you for bringing it to my attention."

"You are welcome," I replied, congratulating myself on having headed Ramses off in the neatest possible manner. He scarcely ever disobeyed a direct command, but on those few occasions when he had done so, he had appealed to moral considerations as an excuse for failing to comply. I suspected the well-being of an animal would seem to him a sufficient excuse. By pointing out that he would only be worsening the unfortunate lion's condition I had, as I believed, forestalled a second attempt at liberation.

How true it is that there are none so blind as those who will not see!

The night was utterly silent; the contentious missionary and his would-be prey had drawn far ahead. Sand muffled the hoof-beats of our steeds. We might have been a pair of ancient Egyptian dead seeking the paradise of Amenti, for I was absorbed in self-congratulation and Ramses was abnormally silent. Glancing at him, I was struck by an odd little chill, for the profile outlined against the paler background of the sandy waste was alarmingly like that of his namesake—beaky nose, prominent chin, lowering brow. At least it resembled the mummy of his namesake; one presumes that centuries of desiccation have not improved the looks of the pharaoh.

When we reached the house David bade us good night and rode off toward the village. It did not improve Emerson's spirits to find the house dark and apparently deserted. John was there, however. We found him in his own room reading the Bible, and Emerson's language, when he beheld that sacred Book, was absolutely disgraceful.

Next morning John was most apologetic about his lapse. "I know I ought to 'ave 'ad your beds made up and the kettle on the boil," he said. "It won't 'appen again, madam. Duty to one's superior is wot a man must do in this world, so long as it don't conflict with one's duty to—"

"Yes, yes, John, that is quite all right," I said, seeing Emerson's countenance redden. "I shall want you to help me with photography this morning, so hurry and clear away the breakfast things. Ramses, you must—what on earth is the matter with you? I believe your chin is in your porridge. Take it out at once."

Ramses wiped his chin. I looked at him suspiciously, but before I could pursue my inquiries Emerson threw down his napkin and rose, kicking his chair out of the way as is his impetuous habit.

"We are late," he announced. "That is what happens when one allows social stupidities to interfere with work. Come along, Peabody."

So the day began. Emerson had moved the men to a site farther north and west, where the irregular terrain suggested the presence of another cemetery. So it proved to be. The graves were quite unlike those of the Roman cemetery. These were simple interments; the bodies were enclosed only in coarse linen shrouds bound in crisscross fashion with red-and-white striped cords. The grave goods included a few crude stelae with incised crosses and other Christian insignia, proving what we had suspected from the nature of the burials themselves—that they were those of Copts. They were very old Copts, and I hoped this consideration would prevent the priest from protesting. He had left us strictly alone, but I feared he might object to our excavating a Christian cemetery. Emerson of course pooh-poohed this possibility; we would handle the bodies with the reverence we accorded all human remains and even rebury them if the priest desired. First, however, he wanted to study them, and if any superstitious ignoramus objected, he could take himself and his superstitions to Perdition or Gehenna.

Emerson wanted photographs of the graves before we removed the contents. That was my task that morning, and with John's help I carried the camera, tripod, plates and other impedimenta to the site. We had to wait until the sun was high enough to illumine the sunken pits, and as we stood in enforced idleness I asked, "Did you enjoy yourself on your day out, John?"

"Oh yes, madam. There was another service in the evening. Sister Charity sang divinely that touching 'ymn, 'Washed in the blood of the Lamb.' "

"And was it a good dinner?"

"Oh yes, madam. Sister Charity is a good cook."

I recognized one of the symptoms of extreme infatuation—the need to repeat the name of the beloved at frequent intervals. "I hope you are not thinking of being converted, John. You know Professor Emerson won't stand for it."

The old John would have burst into protestations of undying loyalty. The new, corrupted John looked grave. "I would give me life's blood for the professor, madam. The day he caught me trying to steal 'is watch in front of the British Museum he saved me from a life of sin and vice. I will never forget his kindness in punching me in the jaw and ordering me to accompany him to Kent, when any other gentleman would 'ave 'ad me taken in charge."

His lips quivered as he spoke. I gave him a friendly pat on the arm. "You certainly could not have continued your career as a pickpocket much longer, John.

Considering your conspicuous size and your—if you will forgive me for mention-ing it—your growing clumsiness, you were bound to be caught."

"Growing is the word, madam. You wouldn't believe what a small, agile nipper I was when I took up the trade. But that is all in the past, thank 'eaven."

"And Professor Emerson."

"And the professor. Yet, madam, though I revere him and would, as I mentioned, shed the last drop of blood in me body for him, or you, or Master Ramses, I cannot endanger me soul for any mortal creature. A man's conscience is—"

"Rubbish," I said. "If you must quote, John, quote Scripture. It has a literary quality, at least, that Brother Ezekiel's pronouncements lack."

John removed his hat and scratched his head. "It does 'ave that, madam. Sometimes I wish as 'ow it didn't 'ave so much. But I'm determined to fight me way through the Good Book, madam, no matter 'ow long it takes."

"How far have you got?"

"Leviticus," said John with a deep sigh. "Genesis and Exodus wasn't so bad, they tore right along most of the time. But Leviticus will be my downfall, madam."

"Skip over it," I suggested sympathetically.

"Oh no, madam, I can't do that."

A wordless shout from my husband, some little distance away, recalled me to my duties, and I indicated to John that we would begin photographing. Scarcely had I inserted the plate in the camera, however, when I realized Emerson's hail had been designed to draw my attention to an approaching rider. His blue-and-white striped robe ballooning out in the wind, he rode directly to me and fell off the donkey. Gasping theatrically, he handed me a note and then collapsed face down in the sand.

Since the donkey had been doing all the work, I ignored this demonstra-tion. While John bent over the fallen man with expressions of concern I opened the note.

The writer was obviously another frustrated thespian. There was no saluta-tion or signature, but the passionate and scarcely legible scrawl could only have been penned by one person of my acquaintance. "Come to me at once," it read. "Disaster, ruin, destruction!"

With my toe I nudged the fallen messenger, who seemed to have fallen into a refreshing sleep. "Have you come from the German lady?" I asked.

The man rolled over and sat up, none the worse for wear. He nodded vigorously. "She sends for you, Sitt Hakim, and for Emerson Effendi."

"What has happened? Is the lady injured?"

The messenger was scarcely more coherent than the message. I was still endeavoring to get some sense out of him when Emerson came up. I handed him the note and explained the situation. "We had better go, Emerson."

"Not I," said Emerson.

"It isn't necessary for both of us to respond," I agreed. "Do you take charge of the photography while I—"

"Curse it, Peabody," Emerson cried. "Will you let this absurd woman interrupt our work again?"

It ended in both of us going. Emerson claimed he dared not let me out of his sight, but in fact he was as bored with our pitiful excavation as I was.

And of course one owes a duty to one's fellow man—and woman.

As we rode across the desert, my spirits rose—not, as evil-minded persons have suggested, at the prospect of interfering in matters which were not my concern, but at the imminence of the exquisite Dahshoor pyramids. My spirits were bound to them by an almost physical thread; the nearer I came the gladder I felt, the farther I went the more that tenuous thread was stretched, almost to the point of pain.

The baroness's dahabeeyah was the only one at the dock. We were led at once to the lady, who was reclining on a couch on deck, under an awning. She was wearing a most peculiar garment, part negligee, part tea gown, shell-pink in color and covered with frills. Sitting beside her was M. de Morgan, holding her hand—or rather, having his hand held by her.

"Ah, mon cher collègue," he said with obvious relief. "At last you have come."

"We only received the message a short time ago," I said. "What has happened?"

"Murder, slaughter, invasion!" shrieked the baroness, throwing herself about on the couch.

"Robbery," said de Morgan succinctly. "Someone broke into the salon last night and stole several of the baroness's antiquities."

I glanced at Emerson. Hands on hips, he studied the baroness and her protector with impartial disgust. "Is that all?" he said. "Come, Peabody, let us get back to work."

"No, no, you must help me," the baroness exclaimed. "I call for you—the great solvers of mysteries, the great archaeologists. You must protect me. Someone wishes to murder me—assault me—"

"Come, come, Baroness, control yourself," I said. "Why was not the robbery discovered earlier? It is almost midday."

"But that is when I rise," the baroness explained guilelessly. "My servants woke me when they found out what had happened. They are lazy swine-dogs, those servants; they should have been cleaning the salon at sunrise."

"When the mistress is slack, the servants will be lazy," I said. "It is most unfortunate. Several of the possible suspects have already left the scene."

De Morgan let out a French expletive. *"Mais, chère madame,* you cannot be referring to the people of quality whose dahabeeyahs were moored here? Such people are not thieves."

I could not help smiling at this credulous statement, but I said only, "One never knows, does one? First let us have a look at the scene of the crime."

"It has not been disturbed," said the baroness, scrambling eagerly up from the couch. "I ordered that it be left just as it was until the great solvers of mysteries came."

It was easy to see how the thieves had entered. The wide windows in the bow stood open and the cushions of the couch had been crushed by several pairs of feet. Unfortunately the marks were amorphous in the extreme, and as I examined them with my pocket lens I found myself wishing, for once, that Egypt enjoyed our damp English climate. Dry sand does not leave footprints.

I turned to my husband. "You can say what is missing, Emerson. I fancy you studied the antiquities even more closely than I."

"It should be obvious," said Emerson morosely. "What was last night the most conspicuous article in the room?"

The grand piano was the answer, but that was not what Emerson meant. "The mummy case," I replied. "Yes, I saw at once it was no longer present. What else, Emerson?"

"A lapis scarab and a statuette of Isis nursing the infant Horus."

"That is all?"

"That is all. They were," Emerson added feelingly, "the finest objects in the collection."

Further examination of the room provided nothing of interest, so we proceeded to question the servants. The baroness began shrieking accusations and, as might have been expected, every face looked guilty as Cain.

I silenced the woman with a few well-chosen words and directed Emerson to question the men, which he did with his usual efficiency. One and all denied complicity. One and all had slept through the night; and when the dragoman suggested that djinns must have been responsible, the others quickly agreed.

De Morgan glanced at the sun, now high overhead. "I must return to my excavations, madame. I advise you to call in the local authorities. They will deal with your servants."

A howl of anguish broke out from the huddled group of men. They knew only too well how local authorities dealt with suspects. With a reassuring gesture I turned to the baroness. "I forbid it," I cried.

"You forbid it?" De Morgan lifted his eyebrows.

"And so do I," Emerson said, stepping to my side. "You know as well as I do, de Morgan, that the favorite method of interrogation hereabouts consists of beating the suspects on the soles of their feet until they confess. They are presumed guilty until proven innocent. However," he added, scowling at de Morgan, "that assumption may not seem unreasonable to a citizen of the French Republic, with its antiquated Napoleonic Code."

De Morgan flung up his arms. "I wash my hands of the whole affair! Already I have wasted half a day. Do as you wish."

"I fully intend to," Emerson replied. *"Bonjour, monsieur."*

After de Morgan had stamped off, cursing quietly in his own tongue, Emerson addressed the baroness. "You understand, madam," he said, squaring his splendid shoulders, "that if you call the police, Mrs. Emerson and I will not assist you."

The baroness was more moved by the shoulders than by the threat. Eyes slightly glazed, she stood staring at my husband's stalwart form until I nudged her with my indispensable parasol. "What?" she mumbled, starting. "The police— who wants them? What is missing, after all? Nothing I cannot easily replace."

"I congratulate you on your good sense," said Emerson. "There is no need for you to concern yourself further at this time; if you would care to retire—"

"But no, you do not understand!" The appalling woman actually seized him by the arm and thrust her face into his. "The stolen objects are unimportant. But what of me? I am afraid for my life, for my virtue—"

"I really don't think you need worry about that," I said.

"You will protect me—a poor helpless *Mädchen?"* the baroness insisted. Her fingers stroked Emerson's biceps. Emerson's biceps are quite remarkable, but I allow no one except myself to admire them in that fashion.

"I will protect you, Baroness," I said firmly. "That is our customary arrangement when my husband and I are engaged in detectival pursuits. He pursues, I protect the ladies."

"Yes, quite right," said Emerson, shifting uneasily from one foot to the other. "I will leave you with Mrs. Emerson, madam, and I will—I will go and—I will inquire—"

The baroness released her hold and Emerson beat a hasty retreat. "You are in no danger," I said. "Unless you have information you have not disclosed."

"No." The baroness grinned knowingly at me. "He is a very handsome man, your husband. *Mucho macho,* as the Spanish say."

"Do they really?"

"But I do not waste time on a hopeless cause," the baroness continued. "I see that he is tied firmly to the apron strings of his good English *Frau.* I shall leave Dahshoor tomorrow."

"What of Brother David?" I asked maliciously. "He is not tied to a woman's apron strings—unless Miss Charity has captured his heart."

"That pale, washed-out child?" The baroness snorted. "No, no, she adores him, but he is indifferent to her. She has nothing to offer him. Make no mistake, Frau Emerson, the beautiful young man is only saintly in his face and figure. He has, as the French say, an eye *pour le main chance."*

The baroness's French and Spanish were as fractured as her English, but I fancied she was not as ignorant of human nature as she was of languages. She went on with mounting indignation, "I have sent for him today, to come to my rescue, and does he come? No, he does not. And a large donation I have made to his church."

So Emerson's surmise had been correct! I said, "You do Brother David an injustice, Baroness. Here he is now."

She turned. *"Herr Gott,"* she exclaimed. "He has brought the ugly *Pfarrer* with him."

"It is the other way around, I fancy."

"I escape," the baroness said loudly. "I run away. Tell them I can see no one." But in stepping forward she tripped on her flounces and fell in a disheveled heap upon the couch. Brother Ezekiel pounced on her before she could rise. Fumbling in the pile of agitated ruffles, he pulled out a hand, which he seized firmly in his big hairy fists.

"Dear sister, I rejoice that you are not harmed. Let us bow our heads and thank God for this merciful escape. Heavenly Father, let the weight of your wrath fall on the villains who have perpetrated this deed; mash 'em flat to the dust, O Lord, lay 'em low as you did the Amalekites and the Jebusites and the . . ."

The polysyllabic catalog rolled on. "Good morning, Brother David," I said. "I am glad you are here; I can leave the baroness to you."

"You can indeed," David assured me, his mild blue eyes beaming. "The tender and womanly compassion that is so peculiarly your own does you credit, Mrs. Emerson, but there is no need for you to remain."

The baroness lay quite still. I could see her face; her eyes were closed and she appeared to be asleep, though how she could have slept through Brother Ezekiel's voice I cannot imagine. ". . . and the kings of Midian, namely Evi and Rekem and Zur and Hur . . ."

I found Emerson surrounded by the servants and the members of the crew. He was haranguing them in Arabic, to which they listened with fascinated attention. Arabs do love a skilled orator. Seeing me, he concluded his speech. "You know me, my brothers; you know I do not lie, and that I protect all honest men. Think well on what I have said."

"What did you say?" I inquired as we walked away, followed by the respectful farewells of the audience: "Allah preserve thee; the mercy and blessing of Allah be with thee."

"Oh, the usual thing, Peabody. I don't believe any of the men were directly involved in the robbery, but they must have been bribed to remain silent. An object the size of that mummy case could not have been removed from the salon without waking someone."

"Bribed—or intimidated? I sense the sinister shadow of the Master Criminal, Emerson. How far his evil web must stretch!"

"I warn you, Peabody, I will not be responsible if you go on talking of webs and shadows and Master Criminals. This is a case of sordid, commonplace thievery. It can have no connection—"

"Like a giant spider weaving his tangled strands into a net that snares rich and poor, guilty and innocent—"

Emerson leaped onto his donkey and urged it into a trot.

We had left the cultivation far behind before his countenance regained its customary placidity. I refrained from further discussion, knowing that sooner or later he would acknowledge the accuracy of my analysis. Sure enough, it was not long before he remarked musingly, "All the same, the case has one or two curious features. Why should thieves go to so much trouble to make off with an ordinary Romano-Egyptian mummy case? It was that of a commoner; there could be no expectation of finding jewelry or valuable amulets among the wrappings."

"What of the other objects that were taken?" I asked.

"That is what makes the situation even more curious, Peabody. Two other things were taken—the scarab and the statuette. They were the most valuable objects in the collection. The statuette was particularly fine, late Eighteenth Dynasty, if I am not mistaken. One might suppose that the thief was an expert in his unsavory trade, since he knew the valuable from the valueless. Yet there were other items, small and easily portable, that might have fetched a decent price, and the thieves left them in order to expend enormous effort on removing a worthless mummy case."

"You have forgotten to mention one item that was taken," I said. "Or perhaps you did not observe it was missing."

"What are you talking about, Peabody? I missed nothing."

"Yes, Emerson, you did."

"No, Peabody, I did not."

"The lion cub, Emerson. The cage was empty."

Emerson's hands released their grip on the reins. His donkey came to a halt. I reined up beside him.

"Empty," he repeated stupidly.

"The door had been closed and the cage pushed aside, but I observed it closely and I can assure you—"

"Oh, good Gad!" Emerson looked at me in consternation. "Peabody! Your own innocent child . . . You don't suspect . . . Ramses could not possibly have carried off that heavy mummy case. Besides, he has better taste than to steal something like that."

"I have long since given up trying to anticipate what Ramses can and cannot do," I replied, with considerable heat. "Your second point has some merit; but Ramses' motives are as obscure as his capabilities are remarkable. I never know what the devil the child has in mind."

"Language, Peabody, language."

I took a grip on myself. "You are right. Thank you for reminding me, Emerson."

"You are quite welcome, Peabody."

He took up his reins and we went on in pensive silence. Then Emerson said uneasily, "Where do you suppose he has put it?"

"What, the mummy case?"

"No, curse it. The lion cub."

"We will soon find out."

"You don't believe he was involved in the other theft, do you, Amelia?" Emerson's voice was piteous.

"No, of course not. I know the identity of the thief. As soon as I have dealt with Ramses I will take him into custody."

Chapter Seven

THE lion cub was in Ramses' room. Ramses was sitting on the floor teasing it with a nasty-looking bit of raw meat when we burst in. He looked up with a frown and said reproachfully, "You did not knock, Mama and Papa. You know dat my privacy is important to me."

"What would you have done if we had knocked?" Emerson asked.

"I would have put de lion under de bed," said Ramses.

"But how could you possibly suppose—" Emerson began. I joggled him with my elbow. "Emerson, you are letting Ramses get you off the track again. He always does it and you always succumb. Ramses."

"Yes, Mama?" The cub rolled itself into a furry ball around his fist.

"I told you not to . . ." But there I was forced to stop to reconsider. I had not told Ramses he must not steal the baroness's lion. He waited politely for me to finish, and I said weakly, "I told you not to wander off alone."

"But I did not, Mama. Selim went wit' me. He carried de lion cub. My donkey would not let me take it up wit' me."

I had seen Selim that morning, but now that I thought about it I realized he had been careful to let me see only his back. No doubt his face and hands bore evidence of the cub's reluctance to be carried.

I squatted down on the floor to examine the animal more closely. It certainly appeared to be in good health and spirits. In a purely investigative manner, to check the condition of its fur, I tickled the back of its head.

"I am training it to hunt for itself," Ramses explained, dragging the loathsome morsel across the cub's rounded stomach. Apparently it had had enough to eat, for it ignored the meat and began licking my fingers.

"What are you going to do with it?" Emerson inquired, sitting down on the floor. The cub transferred its attentions to his fingers, and he chuckled. "It's an engaging little creature."

"All small creatures are engaging," I replied coldly. The cub climbed onto my lap and nuzzled into my skirt. "But one day this small creature will be big enough to swallow you in two bites, Ramses. No, lion, I am not your mother. There is nothing for you there. You had better find it some milk, Ramses."

"Yes, Mama, I will. T'ank you, Mama, I had not t'ought of dat."

"And don't try your tricks with me, Ramses. I am not susceptible to charming young animals of any species. I am really disappointed in you. I had hoped you possessed a greater sense of responsibility. You have taken this helpless creature . . ." The cub, frustrated in its quest for sustenance, sank its sharp little teeth into the upper portion of my leg, and I broke off with a yelp. Emerson removed it and began playing with it while I continued, ". . . this helpless creature into your charge, and you are incapable of giving it the care it requires. I fondly hope you do not entertain any notion that you can persuade your father and me to take it home with us."

"Oh no, Mama," said Ramses, wide-eyed. Emerson trailed the meat across the floor and chortled when the cub pounced on it.

"I am glad you realize that. We cannot always be bringing animals back from Egypt. The cat Bastet . . . Good heavens, what about the cat? She won't tolerate this infantile intruder for a moment."

"She likes it," said Ramses.

The cat Bastet lay atop the packing case Ramses used as a cupboard. Paws folded beneath her smooth breast, she watched the antics of the cub with what appeared to be an expression of benevolent interest.

"Well, well," said Emerson, getting to his feet. "We will think of something, Ramses."

"I have already t'ought, Papa. I am going to give it to Aunt Evelyn and Uncle Walter. Dere is ample space for a menagerie at Chalfont, conducted on de latest scientific principles, and wit' a veterinarian in constant attendance—"

"That is the most appalling suggestion I have ever heard," I exclaimed. "Ramses, I am thoroughly disaffected with you. Consider yourself confined to your room until further notice. No—that won't do. You must repair some small part of the havoc you have wrought. Go immediately and fetch Selim."

Ramses ran for the door. I sank into a chair. It was the first time—though certainly not the last—that I began to have serious doubts as to my capability of carrying out the task I had so unthinkingly assumed. I have dealt with murderers, thieves and brigands of all kinds; but I suspected Ramses might be too much even for me.

These doubts soon passed, naturally, as I attacked the immediate problems with my habitual efficiency. After lecturing Selim and painting iodine on his scratches—his face resembled that of a Red Indian ready for the warpath when I finished—I set one of the men to building a cage, another to the task of constructing a heavy wooden screen for Ramses' window, and a third to the village to purchase a goat of the proper gender and lactiferous condition. Emerson protested the decimation of his work force, but not with his usual vehemence; and when I escorted Ramses into the parlor and sat him down on a footstool, Emerson took a chair next to mine with an expression of unusual gravity on his face.

I confess my own heart was lightened when Ramses declared, with a wholly convincing show of candor, that he knew nothing of the theft of the baroness's antiquities.

"I would not take dat rubbishy mummy case," he exclaimed. "I am deeply hurt, Mama, dat you should t'ink me capable of such ignorance."

I exchanged glances with Emerson. The relieved twinkle in his fine blue eyes brought a reluctant answering smile to my lips. "You observe he is not offended that we questioned his honesty, only his intelligence," I said.

"Stealing is wrong," said Ramses virtuously. "It says so in de Scripture."

"Accept my apologies for doubting you, my son," said Emerson. "You know, you might have pointed out that you lacked the strength to handle the object in question, even with Selim's help."

"Oh, dat would not have been a sufficient defense, Papa. Dere are met'ods of dealing wit' dat difficulty." And his face took on such a look of portentous calculation, I felt a shudder run through me.

Emerson said hastily, "Never mind, Ramses. Did you observe any suspicious activities at the dahabeeyah last night? Other than your own, that is."

Ramses had nothing useful to offer on this subject. His visit to the baroness's boat had taken place shortly after midnight, and he was reasonably certain that at that time the break-in had not taken place. The watchman had been sound asleep and snoring. Upon being questioned further, Ramses admitted that one of the crewmen had awakened. "I had de misfortune of treading upon his hand." A finger to the lips and a coin dropped into the abused hand had kept the grinning witness quiet.

"And I know which one of the men it was," growled Emerson. "He was laughing behind his hand the whole time I was questioning him about burglars. Curse it, Ramses. . . ."

"I am very hungry, Mama," Ramses remarked. "May I go and see if de cook has luncheon ready?"

I acquiesced, for I wished to talk to Emerson alone. "It appears that the break-in took place after midnight," I began.

"A logical conclusion, Peabody. But, if you will forgive my mentioning it, the fact is not particularly useful."

"I never said it was, Emerson."

Emerson leaned back and crossed his legs. "I suppose you have fixed on Hamid as the burglar?"

"Are not the circumstances suspicious, Emerson? Hamid was on the scene when Abd el Atti met his death. . . . Oh, you need not wriggle your eyebrows at me in that supercilious fashion, you know what I mean—we can't prove he was in the shop that night, but he was in Cairo, and he was involved in some shady negotiation with Abd el Atti. A few days later he turns up here, with some specious excuse about looking for work—and the baroness is robbed."

"Weak," said Emerson judiciously. "Very weak, Peabody. But knowing you, I am surprised you have not already put your suspect under arrest."

"I have had time to reconsider my first impulse, Emerson. What good would it do to apprehend the man? As yet we have no physical evidence connecting him to either crime, and naturally he will deny everything. The most sensible course is to ignore him, and watch his every movement. Sooner or later he will do something criminal, and we will catch him in the act."

"Watch him, Peabody? Follow him, you mean? If you think I am going to spend the night squatting behind a palm tree watching Hamid snore, you are sadly mistaken."

"That is a difficulty. You need your sleep, Emerson, and so do I."

"Sleep," said Emerson, "is not the only nocturnal activity of which I do not mean to be deprived."

"We might take it in turn," I mused. "In a turban and robe I could pass for a man—"

"The activity to which I referred requires that both of us be present, Peabody."

"My dear Emerson—"

"My darling Peabody—"

But at that point we were interrupted by Ramses, returning from the kitchen with the roasted chicken that had been prepared for us, and I had to mention several excellent reasons why it should be fed to us instead of to the lion.

II

Emerson's objections to our keeping a watch on Hamid, though frivolous, had merit. I therefore considered alternatives. The most obvious alternative was John, and when we returned to the dig after luncheon I was pleased to observe that he had carried out his responsibilities with skill and dedication. I had given him some instruction in the use of the camera; although we would have to wait until the plates were developed to be sure he had carried out the procedure correctly, his description of the method he had followed seemed correct. I took several more photographs to be on the safe side, and then our most skilled workmen were set to work clearing the graves. As the fragile and pitiful remains were carried carefully to the house I congratulated myself on our luck in having found such an admirable place. Never before, on any expedition, had I had enough storage space. Thanks to the old monks, I could now classify our finds in a proper methodical manner—pottery in one room, Roman mummies in another, and so on.

Hamid was working even more lethargically than usual. Naturally he would be tired if he had helped transport a weighty object the night before. Where the devil had he put the thing? I wondered. The mummy case was over seven feet long. Hamid was a stranger in the village, he had no house of his own. But there were hiding places aplenty in the desert—abandoned tombs, sunken pits, and the sand itself. Or the mummy case might have been loaded onto a small boat and carried away by water. There were many answers to the question of where it might have been hidden, but none to the most difficult question: Why take it in the first place?

Finally I reached a decision. "John," I said. "I have a task for you—one requiring unusual intelligence and devotion."

The young man drew himself up to his full height. "Anything, madam."

"Thank you, John. I felt sure I could count on you. I suspect one of our workers is a vicious criminal. During the day he will be under my watchful eye, but at night I cannot watch him. I want you to be my eyes. Find out where he is living. Take up a position nearby. If he leaves during the night, follow him. Do not let your presence be known, only observe what he does and report back to me. Can you do this?"

John scratched his head. "Well, madam, I will certainly try. But I see certain difficulties."

"Such as?"

"Won't he see me if I am standing outside 'is 'ouse when he comes out?"

"Don't be absurd, John. He will not see you because you will be in hiding."

"Where, madam?"

"Where? Well—er—there must be a tree or a wall or something of that sort nearby. Use your imagination, John."

"Yes, madam," John said doubtfully.

"What other difficulties do you anticipate?"

"Supposing someone sees me behind the tree and asks what I'm doing there?"

"If you are sufficiently well hidden, you will not be seen. Good heavens, John, have you no resources?"

"I don't think so, madam. But I will do me best, which is all a man can do. Which of the chaps is it?"

I started to point, then thought better of it. "That one. Third from the end—no, curse it, second. . . . He keeps changing position."

"You don't mean Brother 'amid, madam?"

"Brother Hamid? Yes, John, I believe I do mean Brother Hamid. He is really a convert, then?"

"Yes, madam, and I know where he lives, for he sleeps in a storeroom behind the mission house. But, madam, I'm sure you are mistaken about 'im being a criminal. Brother Ezekiel has quite taken to 'im, and Brother Ezekiel could not take to a criminal, madam."

"Brother Ezekiel is no more immune than other men to the blandishments of a hypocrite." John gave me a blank stare, so I elaborated. "Godly persons are more vulnerable than most to the machinations of the ungodly."

"I don't understand all them long words, madam, but I think I take your meaning," John replied. "Brother Ezekiel is too trusting."

"That is a quality of saints, John," I said. "Martyrdom is often the result of excessive gullibility."

Whether John comprehended this I cannot say, but he appeared to be convinced. No doubt he had also realized that spying on Hamid would bring him closer to Charity. Squaring his shoulders, he exclaimed, "I will do just what you say, madam. Shall I 'ave a disguise, do you think?"

"That is an excellent suggestion, John. I am happy to see that you are entering into the spirit of the thing. I will borrow a robe and turban from Abdullah; he is the only one of the men who is anything near your height."

John went off to assist Emerson and I remained where I was, keeping a close but unobtrusive watch over Hamid. After a while Abdullah came up to me. "What is the man doing, Sitt, that you watch him so closely?" he asked.

"What man, Abdullah? You are mistaken. I am not watching him."

"Oh." Delicately Abdullah scratched his bearded chin. "I was in error. I thought your keen eyes were fixed upon the foreigner—the man from Manawat."

"No, not at all. . . . What do you know about him, Abdullah?"

The reis replied promptly, "He has not worked with his hands, Sitt Hakim. They are sore and bleeding from the pick."

"How does he get on with the other men?"

"He has no friends among them. Those of the village who remain faithful to the priest are angry with the ones who have gone over to the Americans. But he does not even talk to the other new 'Brotestants.' Shall I dismiss him, Sitt? There are others who would like the work."

"No, don't do that. Only keep a close watch on him." I lowered my voice. "I have reason to think Hamid is a criminal, Abdullah; perhaps a murderer."

"Oh, Sitt." Abdullah clasped his hands. "Not again, honored Sitt! We come to excavate, to work; I beg you, Sitt, do not do it again."

"What do you mean, Abdullah?"

"I feared it would happen," the reis muttered, passing a shaking hand over his lofty brow. "A village of unbelievers, hateful to Allah; a curse on the very house where we dwell—"

"But we have lifted the curse, Abdullah."

"No, Sitt, no. The restless spirits of the dead are still there. Daoud saw one of them only last night."

I had been expecting something of the sort—or if I had not expected it,

I was not surprised that it had occurred. As Emerson says, most men are superstitious, but Egyptians have more reason to believe in ghosts than do men of other nations. Is it any wonder the descendants of the pharaohs feel the presence of gods who were worshiped for over three thousand years? Add to them the pantheons of Christianity and Islam, and you have a formidable phalanx of mixed demons.

I was about to explain this to Abdullah when we were interrupted by a hail from Emerson. "Peabody! Oh, Peee-body! Come here, will you?"

"I will talk with you later," I said to Abdullah. "Don't yield to fear, my friend; you know the Father of Curses is a match for any evil spirit."

"Hmmm," said Abdullah.

We had moved the scene of our operations again that afternoon. As Emerson put it (rather unfortunately, in my opinion) we had enough moldy Christian bones to last us. What we were doing, in archaeological terms, was making a series of trial trenches across the area in order to establish the general nature of the remains. Critical persons, unacquainted with the methods of the profession, have described this as poking around in the hope of finding something interesting, but of course that is not the case.

I found Emerson standing atop a ridge of rock staring down at something below. John was with him. "Ah, Peabody," said my husband. "Just have a look at this, will you?"

Taking the hand he offered, I stepped up onto the ridge. At first glance there was nothing to justify his interest. Half buried in the sand, half exposed by the picks of the workers, was a wrapped mummy. The intricacy of the bandaging indicated that it was another Ptolemaic or Roman mummy, of which we already had a sufficiency.

"Oh dear," I said sympathetically. "Another cursed Roman cemetery."

"I do not think so. We are still on the edge of the Christian cemetery; two other burials of that nature have turned up."

John cleared his throat. "Sir. I have been wanting to speak to you about that. These 'ere pore Christians—"

"Not now, John," Emerson said irritably.

"But, sir, it ain't right to dig them up as if they was 'eathens. If we was in England—"

"We are not in England," Emerson replied. "Well, Peabody?"

"It is curious," I agreed. "One would expect such a carefully wrapped mummy to possess a coffin or a sarcophagus."

"Precisely, my dear Peabody."

"Was that how it was found?"

"You see it," Emerson replied, "just as the men found it—a scant two feet below the surface."

"These intrusions do sometimes occur, Emerson. Do you want me to take a photograph?"

Emerson stroked his chin and then replied, "I think not, Peabody. I will make a note of its location and we will see what turns up as the work progresses."

"Sir," John said. "These 'ere Christians—"

"Hold your tongue, John, and hand me that brush."

"It is almost time for tea, Emerson," I said. "Will you come?"

"Bah," said Emerson.

Taking this for acquiescence, I made my way back to the house. Ramses was not in his room. The lion cub ran to greet me when I opened the door, and as I tickled it under its chin I noticed it had eaten Ramses' house slippers and reduced his nightshirt to shreds. Restoring it to the cage, over its piteous objections, I returned to the parlor and put the kettle on.

We took tea alfresco, as the Italians say, arranging tables and chairs in a space cleared for that purpose before the house. The bits of sand that occasionally sprinkled tea and bread were a small inconvenience to pay for the fresh air and splendid view.

When Emerson joined me he was grumbling as usual. "How often have I told you, Amelia, that this ritual is absurd? Afternoon tea is all very well at home, but to interrupt one's work when in the field . . ." He seized the cup I handed him, drained it in a gulp, and returned it to me. "Petrie does not stop for tea. I won't do it, I tell you. This is the last time."

He said the same thing every day. I refilled his cup and said what I said every day, namely that an interval of refreshment increased efficiency, and that it was necessary to replenish the moisture lost from the body during the heat of the afternoon.

"Where is Ramses?" Emerson asked.

"He is late," I replied. "As to precisely where he may be, I cannot answer, thanks to your refusal to let me supervise his activities. You spoil the boy, Emerson. How many children of his age have their own archaeological excavations?"

"He wants to surprise us, Peabody. It would be cruel to thwart his innocent pleasures. . . . Ah, here he is. How very tidy you are this evening, Ramses."

Not only was he tidy, he was clean. His hair curled into tight ringlets when damp. Drops of water still sparkled in the sable coils. I was so pleased at this demonstration of conformity—for bathing was not something Ramses often engaged in of his own free will—that I did not scold him for being late or even object to the presence of the lion. Ramses secured its lead to a stone stub and began devouring bread and butter.

It was a pleasant domestic interlude; and I confess I shared Emerson's sentiments when he let out an exclamation of annoyance. "Curse it, we are going to be interrupted again. Doesn't that Frenchman do anything except pay social calls?"

The approaching figure was indeed that of de Morgan, mounted on his beautiful steed. "Ramses," I began.

"Yes, Mama. I t'ink dat de lion has had sufficient fresh air for de present." There was only time for him to thrust it into the house and close the door before de Morgan was with us.

After greetings had been exchanged and de Morgan had accepted a cup of tea, he asked how our work was going.

"Splendidly," I replied. "We have completed a survey of the area and are proceeding with trial excavations. Cemeteries of the Roman and Christian periods have been discovered."

"My commiseration, dear friends," de Morgan exclaimed. "But perhaps you will come upon something more interesting in time."

"Commiseration is not needed, monsieur," I replied. "We dote on Roman cemeteries."

"Then you will no doubt be pleased to receive another Roman mummy," said de Morgan, twirling his mustache.

"What the devil do you mean?" Emerson demanded.

"That is the reason for my visit," de Morgan replied, a Machiavellian smile curving his lips. "The stolen mummy case has been discovered. The thieves abandoned it a few kilometers from my camp, where it was found this afternoon."

"How very strange," I said.

"No, it is easy to understand," said de Morgan patronizingly. "These thieves are ignorant people. They committed an error, taking the mummy case; having discovered its worthlessness and tiring of its weight, they simply abandoned it."

Emerson shot the Frenchman a look of blistering contempt. I said, "No doubt the baroness is glad to have her relic back."

"She will have nothing to do with it." De Morgan shook his head. "*Les femmes*, they are always illogical. . . . That is, madame, I do not refer to you, you understand—"

"I should hope not, monsieur."

" 'Take it away,' she cries, waving her arms. 'Give it to Herr Professor Emerson, who has scolded me. I want nothing more to do with it, it has brought me terror and distress.' So," de Morgan concluded, "my men will fetch it to you later."

"Thank you very much," said Emerson between clenched teeth.

"Not at all." De Morgan patted the damp curls of Ramses, who was crouched at his feet like a puppy. "And how is your study of mummies progressing, *mon petit?*"

"I have given it up for de present," said Ramses. "I find I lack de proper instruments for such research. Accurate measurements of cranial capacity and bone development are necessary if one is to reach meaningful conclusions regarding de racial and physical—"

De Morgan interrupted with a hearty laugh. "Never mind, *petit chou;* if you are bored with your papa's excavations you may visit me. Tomorrow I begin a new tunnel which will surely lead me to the burial chamber."

Emerson's countenance writhed. Catching my eye, he said in a muffled voice, "Excuse me, Amelia. I must—I must—"

And, leaping from his chair, he vanished around the corner of the house.

"I take my leave of you, madame," said de Morgan, rising. "I came only to tell you that the stolen property has been recovered and to give you the baroness's farewells. She sails at dawn."

"Good," I exclaimed. "That is—I am glad she is recovered enough to continue her journey."

"I thought you might feel that way," said de Morgan with a smile. "You know that her little pet escaped after all?"

"Did it?"

For the past several minutes a muffled undercurrent of thumps and growls had issued from the house. De Morgan's smile broadened. "Yes, it did. Possibly the thieves opened the cage by mistake. Ah, well; it is a small matter."

"Quite," I said, as a howl of feline frustration arose and claws attacked the inside of the door.

After de Morgan had left, grinning like a Gallic idiot, I went in search of Emerson. I found him methodically kicking the foundations of the house, and led him back to the dig.

The rest of the day went quietly, and Emerson's temper gradually subsided under the soothing influence of professional activity. After dinner he sat down to write up his journal of the day's work, assisted by Ramses, while John and I went to the darkroom and developed the plates we had taken that day. Some had turned out quite well. Others were very blurred. John tried to take the credit for the good ones, but I soon set him straight on that, and pointed out where he had gone astray in focusing the camera.

We returned to the sitting room. The cat Bastet was sitting on top of Emerson's papers. Emerson absently lifted her up whenever he added a finished sheet to the pile. The lion cub was chewing on Emerson's bootlace. As I entered, the front door opened and Ramses appeared. He had got into the habit of spending the evening with Abdullah and the other men from Aziyeh, in order to practice his Arabic, as he claimed. I had reservations about this, but felt sure Abdullah would prevent the men from adding too extensively to Ramses' collection of colloquialisms. I was pleased that he got on well with them. Abdullah said they enjoyed his company. I suppose he could hardly say anything else.

"Time for bed, Ramses," I said.

"Yes, Mama." He unwound the cub's leash from the legs of the table and those of his father. "I will walk de lion and den retire."

"You don't believe you can train that creature as you would a dog, do you?" I asked, in mingled amusement and exasperation.

"De experiment has never been tried, to my knowledge, Mama. I consider it wort' a try."

"Oh, very well. Put the lion in its cage before you get into bed. Make sure the shutter is tightly fastened—"

"Yes, Mama. Mama?"

"What is it, Ramses?"

He stood holding the leash, his grave dark eyes fixed on my face. "I would like to say, Mama, dat I am fully cognizant of your support and forbearance regarding de lion. I will endeavor to discover some way of proving my gratitude."

"Please don't," I exclaimed. "I appreciate your remarks, Ramses, but you can best express your gratitude by being a good little boy and obeying your mama's orders."

"Yes, Mama. Good night, Mama. Good night, John. Good night, de cat Bastet. Good night, Papa."

"Good night, my dearest boy," Emerson replied. "Sleep well."

After Ramses had gone and John had carried the tray of pottery shards to the storeroom, Emerson put down his pen and looked reproachfully at me. "Amelia, that was a very manly and loving apology you received from Ramses."

"It did not sound like an apology to me," I replied. "And when Ramses offers to do something for me, my blood runs cold in anticipation."

Emerson threw down his pen. "Curse it, Amelia, I don't understand you. Heaven knows you are an excellent mother—"

"I try to be, Emerson."

"You are, my dear, you are. Ramses does you credit. But can't you be more—more—"

"More what, Emerson?"

"More affectionate? You are always snapping at the boy."

"I am not a demonstrative person, Emerson."

"I have reason to know better," said Emerson, giving me a meaningful look.

"That is a different matter altogether. Naturally I am fond of Ramses, but I will never be one of those doting mamas who allow maternal affection to blind them to the flaws of character and behavior demonstrated by a child."

John returned at this point in the discussion. "Madam," he exclaimed, "there is a great 'uge mummy case in the courtyard. What shall I do with it?"

"It must be the baroness's mummy case," I said. "I suppose M. de Morgan's men simply dropped it and left. How vexatious! What shall we do with it, Emerson?"

"Throw the cursed thing out," Emerson replied, returning to his writing.

"We will put it with the others," I said. "Come along, John, I will unlock the storeroom."

The moon had not yet risen, but the varnished surface of the mummy case glimmered darkly in the brilliant starlight. I unlocked the door and John hoisted the coffin into his arms, as effortlessly as if it had been an empty paper shell. I was reminded of that Italian mountebank Belzoni, a former circus strongman who had turned to archaeology. He had been one of the first to excavate in Egypt, but his methods could hardly be called scientific, for among other sins he had employed gunpowder to blast his way into closed pyramids.

The storeroom was full of coffins and we had to shift several of them to find a place for the newcomer. It would have been more practical, perhaps, to open another room, but I always like to keep objects of the same type together. When the thing had been stowed away, John said, "Would you be wanting me to go to spy on Brother 'amid now, madam?"

I gave him the disguise I had procured for him. Abdullah's spare robe barely reached his shins, and the boots showing under the hem of the garment looked rather peculiar. John offered to remove them, but I decided against it. His feet were not hardened like those of the Egyptians, and if he trod on something sharp and painful he might let out a cry that would alert Hamid to his presence. I wound the turban around his head and then stood back to study the effect.

It was not convincing. However, we had done the best we could. I sent John on his way and returned to Emerson. He was curious as to why John had retired so early, but I was able to distract him without difficulty.

It seemed as if I had slept for only a few hours (which was in fact the case) when I was awakened by a furious pounding at the door. For once I was not impeded by a mosquito netting. At that season, in the desert, the noxious insects do not present a problem. Springing from the bed, I seized my parasol and assumed a posture of defense. Then I recognized the voice that was calling my name.

Emerson was swearing and flailing around in the bed when I flung the door open. The first streaks of dawn warmed the sky, but the courtyard was still deep in shadow. Yet there was no mistaking the large form that confronted me. Even if I had not recognized John's voice, I would have recognized his shape. That shape was, however, oddly distorted, and after a moment I realized that he held a smaller, slighter body closely clasped in his arms.

"Who the devil have you got there?" I asked, forgetting my usual adherence to proper language in my surprise.

"Sister Charity, madam," said John.

"Will you please ask him to let me down, ma'am?" the girl asked faintly. "I am not injured, but Brother John insists—"

"Don't move, either of you," I interrupted. "This is a most unprecedented situation, and before I can assess it properly I must have light." A vehement curse from the direction of the nuptial couch reminded me of something I had momentarily overlooked and I added quickly, "Emerson, pray remain recumbent and wrapped in the blanket. There is a lady present."

"Curse it, curse it, curse it," Emerson cried passionately. "Amelia—"

"Yes, my dear, I have the matter well in hand," I replied soothingly. "Just a moment till I light the lamp. . . . There. Now we will see what is going on."

First I made certain Emerson was not in a state that would cause embarrassment to him or to anyone else. Only his head protruded from the sheet he had wrapped around himself. The expression on his face did his handsome features no justice.

John's turban had come unwound and hung down his back. His once snowy robe was ripped half off; the tattered remnants were blackened by what I first took to be dried blood. A closer examination proved that the stains were those of smoke and charring. His face was equally smudged, but the broad smile on his lips and the steady beam of his blue eyes assured me he had taken no hurt.

The girl was also disheveled but unmarked by fire. Her mousy brown hair tumbled over her shoulders and her face was flushed with excitement and embarrassment as she struggled to free herself from the brawny arms that clasped her. Her feet were bare. She wore a garment of voluminous cut and dismal color, dark blue or black, that covered her from the base of her throat to her ankles. It had long tight sleeves. A nightcap dangled from her neck by its strings.

"Please, ma'am, tell him to put me down," she gasped.

"All in due time," I assured her. "Now, John, you may tell me what has happened."

"There was a fire, madam."

"I deduced as much, John. Where was the fire?"

It is expedient to summarize John's statement, which had to be extracted from him sentence by sentence. He had been hiding among the palms near the chapel when he had seen a tongue of flame rise from behind that edifice. His cries had aroused the men, and with their assistance he had succeeded in quenching the conflagration before it did much damage. No help had come from the village; indeed the place had remained suspiciously dark and silent, though the shouts of the missionaries must have been heard. A search of the area revealed no sign of the arsonist. The fire had been deliberately set, getting its start in a pile of dry branches and palm fronds heaped against the foundation of the little church. Once the flames were extinguished, John had seized the girl and carried her off.

"What the devil for?" cried Emerson, from the bed.

"To bring her to Mrs. Emerson, of course," John replied, his eyes widening.

Emerson subsided with a curse. "Of course. Everyone brings everything to Mrs. Emerson. Lions, mummy cases, miscellaneous young ladies—"

"And quite right, too," I said. "Pay no attention to Professor Emerson, my dear Miss Charity. He would welcome you with the kindness that is his most conspicuous characteristic were he not a trifle out of sorts because—"

"I beg you will not explain, Amelia," said my husband in tones of freezing disapproval. "Er—hem. I am not objecting to the presence of Miss Charity, but to the invasion that will inevitably follow. Would it be too much to ask, Amelia, that the young person be removed so that I may assume my trousers? A man is at a decided disadvantage when he receives irate brothers and indignant lovers wrapped in a sheet."

My dear Emerson was himself again, and I was happy to accede to this reasonable request. "Certainly, my dear," I replied. "John, take the young lady to your room."

The girl shrieked and resumed her struggles. "It is the only room fit for habitation that is presently available," I explained, somewhat irritated at this excessive display of sensibility. "Wait a moment until I find my slippers and I will accompany you. Curse it, where are they?"

"Madam!" John exclaimed.

"You will excuse my language," I said, kneeling to look under the bed. "Ah, here they are. Just as I suspected—Ramses has let the lion in the room, after I strictly forbade it."

"Lion?" Charity gasped. "Did you say . . ."

"You see how they are chewed. I told that child . . . Dear me, I believe the girl has fainted. Just as well. Take her along, John, I will follow."

The ensuing hour was a period of unprecedented confusion, but I recall it without chagrin; I rise to my true powers in periods of confusion. Ramses had been awakened by the noise. He and the cat and the lion followed us to John's room, spouting questions (in the case of Ramses) and attacking the tatters of John's robe (in the case of the lion). I ordered all three back to Ramses' room, and after John had placed the girl on his cot, directed him to withdraw to the same location. The only one who refused to obey was the cat Bastet. Squatting on the floor by the bed, she watched interestedly as I sought to restore Charity to her senses.

As soon as she recovered she insisted, almost hysterically, upon leaving the room. Apparently the very idea of being in a young man's bedchamber in her nightgown was indelicate. I had ascertained that she was unharmed, so I gave in to her foolish insistence, and when we reached the parlor she became calmer.

The expected invasion had not yet occurred, but I felt sure Emerson was right; the outraged brother would come in search of his sister, and Brother David would undoubtedly be with him, though Emerson's designation of the latter as Charity's lover was only another example of Emerson's failure to comprehend the subtler currents of the human heart. I decided I had better take advantage of this opportunity to talk with the girl alone, and I got straight to the point.

"You must not be angry with John, Miss Charity. His action was precipitate and thoughtless, but his motives were of the best. His only concern was for your safety."

"I see that now." The girl brushed the waving locks from her face. "But it was a terrifying experience—the shouting, and the flames—then to be seized like that, without warning. . . . I have never—it is the first time a man . . ."

"I daresay. You have missed a great many things, Miss Charity. Most ill-advised, in my opinion. But never mind that. Don't you like John?"

"He is very kind," the girl said slowly. "But very, very large."

"But that can be an advantage, don't you think?" Charity stared at me in bewilderment, and I went on, "No, you would not know. But let me assure you, as a respectable married woman, that the combination of physical strength and moral sensibility, combined with tenderness of heart, is exactly what is wanted in a husband. The combination is rare, I confess, but when one encounters it—"

"Tactful as always, Amelia," said a voice from the doorway.

"Ah, there you are, Emerson. I was just explaining to Miss Charity—"

"I heard you." Emerson came into the room, buttoning his shirt. "Your tactics rather resemble those of a battering ram, my dear. Why don't you make the tea and leave the poor girl alone?"

"The tea is ready. But, Emerson—"

"Please, Amelia. I believe I hear the approach of the invasion I mentioned, and if I don't have my tea before I face it . . ."

The girl had shrunk down into her chair, her arms clutching her body and her face averted, though Emerson politely refrained from looking at her. When the strident accents of Brother Ezekiel were heard she looked as if she were trying to squeeze her body into the framework of the chair.

Emerson hastily gulped his tea, and I went to the door to see whom the visitor was addressing. As I might have expected, it was Ramses.

"I told you to stay in your room," I said.

"You told me to go to my room, but you did not say to stay dere. Seeing dis person approaching, I felt it would be advisable for someone to meet him in order to—"

"Talks a blue streak, don't he?" Brother Ezekiel slid clumsily off his donkey and fixed Ramses with a critical stare. "Sonny, don't you know children should be seen and not heard?"

"No, I don't," Ramses replied. "Dat is to say, sir, I have heard dat sentiment expressed more dan once, but it is no more dan an opinion and it is not based on sound t'eories of—"

"That will do, Ramses," I said, with a sigh. "Brother Ezekiel, will you come in? Your sister is here, safe and sound."

"So you say." Brother Ezekiel pushed past me. "Well, she's here, at any rate. Charity, where's your penknife?"

The girl rose. Head bowed, she murmured from under the hair that veiled her face, "Under my pillow, brother. There was such confusion I forgot—"

"Didn't I tell you never to take a step without that weapon?" Brother Ezekiel thundered.

"I am guilty, brother."

"Yes, you are. And you'll be punished."

"A moment, sir." Emerson spoke in the purring rumble that often deceived persons unfamiliar with his temperament into believing he was in an affable mood. "I don't believe we have been formally introduced."

"It ain't my fault if we wasn't," Ezekiel replied. "At least this here unfortunate event gives me a chance to talk to you, Professor. I know who you are and you know me; let's skip the formalities, I don't hold with 'em." He sat down.

"Have a chair," Emerson said.

"I already have one. I could fancy a cup of tea, if you ain't got coffee."

"By all means." Emerson offered him a cup. I resignedly awaited the explosion I knew was coming. The longer Emerson's appearance of mildness continued, the louder the eventual explosion would be.

"Do I understand," Emerson continued blandly, "that Miss Charity goes about armed with a knife? Let me assure you, Mr. Jones, that such precautions are not necessary. This is a peaceful country, and I doubt that she is capable of using such a weapon."

"She'd be able to use it on herself," Brother Ezekiel retorted. "And that's what she was supposed to do before she let a male critter lay hands on her."

"Good Gad," I cried. "This is not ancient Rome, sir."

I expected the allusion would be lost on Ezekiel, but to my surprise he replied, "They was heathens, but that Lucretia female knew the value of a woman's purity. Well, in this case no harm done. I come to fetch her home, but long as I'm here I may as well tell you what's on my mind."

"By all means unburden yourself," Emerson said earnestly. "I doubt that the organ you mention can stand any undue weight."

"What? It's about the Christian cemetery you've been digging up. You'll have to stop it, Professor. They were heretics, but they was laid to rest in the Lord."

I braced myself for the explosion. It did not come. Emerson's eyebrows rose. "Heretics?" he repeated.

"Monophysites," said Brother Ezekiel.

I had believed Emerson's eyebrows could rise no higher, but I was wrong. Mistaking the cause of his surprise, Brother Ezekiel enlightened him.

"Our Lord and Saviour, Professor, has a double nature—the human and the divine are mingled in him. 'Twas all laid down by the Council of Chalcedon, anno Domini 451. That's doctrine, and there's no getting around it. These Copts wouldn't accept it, though. They followed Eutyches, who insisted on the absorption of the human part of Christ by the divine into one composite nature. Hence, sir, the term Monophysite."

"I am familiar with the term and its meaning," Emerson said.

"Oh? Well, but that ain't the issue. They may of been heretics, but they was Christians, of a sort, and I demand you leave their graves alone."

The twinkle of amusement in Emerson's eyes was replaced by a fiery glow, and I decided to intervene. "Your sister is on the verge of fainting, Brother Ezekiel. If you don't take steps to relieve her, I shall. Charity—sit down!" Charity sat down. Brother Ezekiel stood up. "Come along, girl, a hand-maiden of the Lord has no business swooning. I've said my say, now I'll go." "Not just yet," said Emerson. "I haven't had my say. Mr. Jones—" "Brother Ezekiel, sir."

Emerson shook his head. "Really, you cannot expect me to employ that absurd affectation. You are not my brother. You are, however, a fellow human being, and I feel it my duty to warn you. You have aroused considerable resentment in the village; last night's fire may not be the last demonstration of that resentment."

Brother Ezekiel raised his eyes to heaven. "If the glorious crown of the martyr is to be mine, O Lord, make me worthy!"

"If it weren't such an entertaining idiot it would make me angry," Emerson muttered as if to himself. "See here, sir; you are doing everything possible to increase the justifiable annoyance of the local priest, whose flock you are stealing away—"

"I seek to save them from the fires of hell," Ezekiel explained. "They are all damned—"

Emerson's voice rose to a roar. "They may be damned, but you will be dead! It would not be the first time Protestant missions have been attacked. Court danger as you will, but you have no right to risk your innocent converts and your sister."

"God's will be done," Ezekiel said.

"No doubt," Emerson agreed. "Oh, get out of here, you little maniac, before I throw you out. Miss Charity, if at any time you need our help, we are here, at your command. Send word by John or any other messenger."

Then I realized that in his own peculiar way Ezekiel had exhibited a variety of self-control comparable to that of my husband. Emerson's final insult cracked the missionary's calm facade. A thunderous scowl darkened his brow. But before he could express in words the outrage that filled him, another sound was heard— the sound of a low, menacing growl. I thought Ramses might have let the lion cub out, and looked around. But the source of the growl was Bastet, who had appeared out of nowhere in that unnerving way of hers. Crouched on the table near Emerson, she lashed her tail and rumbled low in her throat, sensing the anger that filled the room and prepared to defend her master.

Charity let out a thin cry. "Take it away—oh, please, take it away."

"You must conquer this weakness, Charity," said Brother David, shaking his head. "There is nothing more harmless than an amiable domestic cat. . . ." He put out a hand to Bastet. She spat at him. He stepped hastily back. "An amiable domestic cat," he repeated, less confidently.

Charity retreated, step by stumbling step, her wide eyes fixed on the cat's sharp white snarl. "You know I would do anything to please you, brother. I have tried. But I cannot—I cannot—"

Observing her pallor and the perspiration that bedewed her brow, I realized her terror was as genuine as it was unusual. No wonder the mere mention of the lion had caused her to lose consciousness!

I glanced at Ramses, who was sitting quietly in a corner. I had fully expected a comment—or, more likely, a long-winded speech—from him before this. No doubt he knew I would order him out of the room if he ventured to speak. "Take the cat away, Ramses," I said.

"But, Mama—"

"Never mind, we're leaving," snapped Ezekiel. The look he gave Bastet showed that he found Charity's fear as hard to comprehend as Brother David's affection for such creatures. Then he turned to Emerson. "Don't concern yourself about my sister, Professor, she's been taught right; she knows a woman's place. I remind you, sir, of First Corinthians, Chapter fourteen, Verses thirty-four and thirty-five: 'Let your women keep silence . . . for it is not permitted unto them to speak. . . . And if they will learn any thing, let them ask their husbands at home.' You'd best apply that in your own household, Professor, before you start interfering with them that knows better."

When he and his entourage had gone, Emerson burst into a great roar of laughter. "Henpeckery!" he shouted cheerfully. "The old charge of henpeckery. Will I never live it down?"

I stood on tiptoe and threw my arms about his neck. "Emerson," I said, "have I had occasion in the recent past to mention that my feelings for you are of the warmest nature?"

My husband returned my embrace. "You mentioned it in passing a few hours ago, but if you would care to enlarge upon the subject . . ."

But after an all-too-brief interval he gently put me aside. "All the same, Peabody," he said seriously, "we cannot let those fools rush headlong to destruction without trying to stop them."

"Are matters that serious, do you think?"

"I fear so." He added, with a refreshing touch of malice, "You have been too busy playing detective to notice what has been going on. Already there is a visible division among our workers; the converts are shunned by their fellows, and Abdullah has reported several cases of fisticuffs. I really believe that wretched preacher wants to achieve martyrdom."

"Surely there is no danger of that, Emerson. Not in this day and age."

"Let us hope not. What the devil, we have wasted too much time on the creature. The men will be on the dig. I must go."

With a hasty embrace he departed, and I sat down to have another cup of tea. Scarcely had I taken a seat, however, before a cry of outraged fury reached my ears. I recognized the beloved voice and hastened to rush to his side, fearing I know not what—some fresh outrage from Brother Ezekiel, perhaps.

The pastor had gone, and Emerson was nowhere in sight. The volume of his complaints led me to him, on the far side of the house. I do not believe I had inspected that region since the day of our arrival, when I had made a circuit of the walls to see where repairs were needed. On that occasion the walls had been intact, if aged. Now a gaping hole confronted my astonished eyes. Emerson was stamping up and down waving his arms and shouting at Abdullah, who listened with an air of injured dignity. Seeing me, Emerson turned his reproaches on a new object.

"What kind of housekeeping do you call this, Peabody?"

I pointed out the injustice of the charge in a few brisk but well-chosen words. Emerson mopped his brow. "Pardon my language, Peabody. It has been a trying morning. And now this!"

"What is it?" I asked.

"It is a hole, Peabody. A hole in the wall of one of our storage rooms."

"Oh, Emerson, I can see that! How did it come there?"

"I do not know, Peabody. Perhaps Ramses has stolen an elephant and attempted to confine it in the room."

I ignored this misplaced attempt at humor. "The wall is old, and some of the mortar has fallen out. Perhaps it simply collapsed."

"Don't talk like an idiot, Peabody!" Emerson shouted.

"Don't shout at me, Emerson!"

Abdullah's head had been moving back and forth like someone watching a tennis match. Now he remarked, not quite sotto voce, "It is good to see them so friendly together. But of course it was the spirit of the old priest, trying to get back into his house from which the Father of Curses expelled him."

"Abdullah, you know that is nonsense," I said.

"Quite right," Emerson agreed. "When I expel a spirit, he stays expelled."

Abdullah grinned. Emerson wiped his forehead with his sleeve and said in a resigned voice, "Let's see what the damage is. Which of the storerooms is this, Amelia? I cannot quite get my bearings."

I counted windows. "This is the room where I keep the mummy cases, Emerson. The ones from the Roman cemetery."

Emerson struck himself heavily on the brow. "There is some strange fatality in this," he muttered. "Abdullah, go to the dig and get the men started. Come around to the door, Peabody, and we will see what is—or is not—inside."

We did as he suggested. The coffins had been jumbled about, but I noticed that none of the bricks had fallen inside—which cast a doubt on my theory of a spontaneous fall. I had not really believed it, of course. The bricks had been removed one by one until a sufficiently large opening was made. It would not have been difficult to do. The mortar was old and crumbling.

". . . five, six, seven," Emerson counted. "They are all here, Amelia."

I cleared my throat. "Emerson . . ."

"Oh, curse it," Emerson exclaimed. "Don't tell me—you put the baroness's mummy case in this room."

"It seemed the logical place, Emerson."

"Then there ought to be eight mummy cases here."

"My reckoning agrees with yours, Emerson."

"One is missing."

"It seems a reasonable conclusion."

Emerson's fingers clawed at his chin. "Fetch John," he said. I turned to obey; this was not the time to cavil at an unnecessarily peremptory tone. From one of the doors along the line of cells a head protruded. "May I come out, Mama?" Ramses inquired.

"You may as well. Find John."

"He is here, Mama."

The pair soon joined us and Emerson, with John's help, began removing the mummy cases from the storeroom. When they were lined up in a grisly row, Emerson looked them over.

"These are the coffins we found, Peabody," he announced. "It must be the one belonging to the baroness that has been stolen—again."

"Wrong, Emerson. That"—I pointed—"is the mummy case John and I put in this room last night. I remember the patch of missing varnish on the foot, and also the relative location, which I noted when you removed them."

"Wrong, Peabody. I know each and every one of these mummy cases. I could as easily be mistaken as to the identity of my own mother."

"Since you haven't seen the dear old lady for fifteen years, you might easily make such a mistake."

"Never mind my mother," Emerson retorted. "I can't imagine why we brought her into this. If you don't believe me, Peabody, we will check my notes. I made careful descriptions of the coffins, as I always do."

"No, no, my dear Emerson, I need no such verification; your memory is always accurate. But I am equally certain that this"—again I pointed—"is the mummy case brought to us last night."

"De conclusion is obvious, surely," piped Ramses. "De mummy case brought here last night, purportedly de one stolen from de lady, was not in fact de one stolen from—"

"I assure you, Ramses, that possibility had not escaped either of us," I replied with some asperity.

"De inevitable corollary," Ramses went on, "is dat—"

"Pray be silent for a moment, Ramses," Emerson begged, clutching his ambrosial locks with both hands. "Let me think. What with mummy cases whizzing in and out of my life like express trains . . . There were originally seven mummy cases in this room."

I murmured an encouraging "Quite right, Emerson," and fixed Ramses with a look that stilled the words hovering on his lips.

"Seven," Emerson repeated painfully. "Last night another mummy case was placed in this room. Eight. You didn't happen to notice, Peabody, how many—"

"I am afraid not, Emerson. It was dark and we were in a hurry."

"The baroness's mummy case was stolen," Emerson continued. "A mummy case believed to be that mummy case was handed over to us. You are certain that this"—he pointed—"was the mummy case in question. We must assume, then, that the mummy case we received was not the mummy case belonging to the baroness, but another mummy case, derived God knows whence."

"But we know whence," cried Ramses, unable to contain himself any longer. "Papa is correct; we have here de original mummy case discovered by our men. De one returned to us was our own. A t'ief must have removed it from dis room earlier."

"A what?" I asked.

"A robber," said Ramses.

"Who replaced the bricks after he had stolen the mummy case from us. Yes," Emerson agreed. "It could have been done. The thief then carried the stolen mummy case out into the desert, where he abandoned it. That incompetent idiot de Morgan, who would not recognize his own mummy case if it walked up and bade him 'Bonjour,' assumed that the one found by his men was the one belonging to the baroness. Apparently that is what the thief did—but why the devil should he do it?"

This time I was determined that Ramses should not get ahead of me. "In the hope, which proved justified, that the search for the baroness's mummy case would be abandoned."

"Humph," said Emerson. "My question was purely rhetorical, Peabody. Had you not interrupted, I would have proposed that very solution. May I request that you all remain silent and allow me to work out this problem step by step in logical fashion?"

"Certainly, my dear Emerson."

"Certainly, Papa."

"Certainly, sir." John added in a bewildered voice, "I don't 'ave the faintest notion of what anyone is talking about, sir."

Emerson cleared his throat pontifically. "Very well. We will begin with the hypothesis that the thief stole one of our mummy cases in order to substitute it for the one belonging to the baroness. He went to the considerable trouble of replacing the bricks in the wall so the theft would not be noticed. Why then did he demolish the wall last night?"

He fixed Ramses with such an awful look that the child closed his mouth with an audible snap. Emerson continued, "Not to return the stolen mummy case. There are only seven here, the same number we had originally. Two possibilities suggest themselves. Either the thief wished to recover some object he had concealed in the storeroom on the occasion when he removed our mummy case, or he wished to draw our attention to his activities."

He paused. Those of us in the audience remained respectfully silent. A look of childish pleasure spread over Emerson's face. "If any of you have alternative hypotheses to suggest, you may speak," he said graciously.

My abominable child beat me to the punch again. "Perhaps some second party, oder dan de original t'ief, wished to expose de villain's act of pilferage."

Emerson shook his head vehemently. "I refuse to introduce another unknown villain, Ramses. One is enough."

"I favor the first of your hypotheses, Emerson," I said. "It was necessary to find a hiding place for the baroness's mummy case. What better place than among others of the same? I believe the thief put her mummy case in the storage room and took one of ours. Last night he broke in again and removed the first mummy case."

"I have a feeling," said Emerson conversationally, "that if I hear the words 'mummy case' again, a blood vessel will burst in my brain. Peabody, your theory is perfectly reasonable, except for one small point. There is no reason why anyone with an ounce of sense would steal the baroness's mum—property in the first place, much less go through these fantastic convolutions with it."

We stared bemusedly at one another. John scratched his head. Finally Ramses said thoughtfully, "I can t'ink of several possibilities, Papa. But it is a capital mistake to t'eorize wit' insufficient data."

"Well put, Ramses," Emerson said approvingly.

"De statement is not original, Papa."

"Never mind. Let us forsake theories and take action. Peabody, I have come around to your way of thinking. Hamid is the only suspicious character hereabouts. Let us question Hamid."

But Hamid was not on the dig. He had not reported for work that morning, and all the men denied having seen him.

"What did I tell you?" I cried. "He has flown. Does not that prove his guilt?"

"It proves nothing except that he is not here," Emerson replied waspishly. "Perhaps he has accomplished his purpose, whatever the devil that might have been, and has departed. So much the better. I can get on with my work in peace."

"But, Emerson—"

Emerson rounded on me and wagged his finger under my nose. "Work, Peabody—work! Is the word familiar to you? I know you find our activities tedious; I know you yearn for pyramids and sneer at cemeteries—"

"Emerson, I never said—"

"You thought it. I saw you thinking it."

"I was not alone if I did."

Emerson threw his arm around my shoulders, careless of the men working nearby. A low murmur of amusement rose from them. "Right as always, Peabody. I find our present excavations boring too. I am taking out my bad humor on you."

"Couldn't we start work on the pyramids here, Emerson? They are poor things, but our own."

"You know my methods, Peabody. One thing at a time. I will not be distracted from duty by the siren call of—er—pyramids."

III

For the next few days it appeared that Emerson's hopes regarding Hamid were justified. There were no further attacks on the missionaries or on our property, and one evening, when I inadvertently used the phrase "mummy case," Emerson scarcely flinched. I let him enjoy his illusory sense of tranquillity, but I knew, with that intuitive intelligence upon which I have often been commended, that the peace could not last—that the calm was only a thin surface over a seething caldron of passions that must eventually erupt.

Our decision to allow Ramses his own excavation had been a success. He was gone all day, taking his noon meal with him, and always returned in time for tea. One evening he was late, however, and I was about to send someone out to look for him when I caught a glimpse of a small form scuttling with an odd crablike motion along the shaded cloister. He was carrying something, wrapped in his shirt. I knew the cloth enclosing the bundle was his shirt because he was not wearing the garment.

"Ramses!" I called.

Ramses ducked into his room, but promptly reappeared.

"How many times have I told you not to remove any of your outer garments without sufficient cause?" I inquired.

"Very many times, Mama."

"What have you got there?"

"Some t'ings I found when I was excavating, Mama."

"May I see them?"

"I would radder you did not, Mama, at present."

I was about to insist when Emerson, who had joined me, said softly, "A moment, Peabody."

He drew me aside. "Ramses wants to keep his discoveries for a surprise," he explained. "You wouldn't want to disappoint the dear little chap, would you?"

This was not a question I could answer fully, under the circumstances, so I remained silent. A fond smile spread across Emerson's face. "He has been collecting potsherds and his favorite bones, I expect. You must exclaim over them and admire them, Amelia, when we are invited to view the display."

"Naturally I will do my duty, Emerson. When did you ever know me to fail?" I turned back to Ramses, who stood waiting outside his room, and dismissed him with a gesture. He went in at once and closed the door.

Whatever the nature of Ramses' discoveries, they could not have been poorer than our own. We had found a small family burial ground dating from the Fourth or Fifth Dynasty, but the humble little tombs contained no funeral goods worthy of preserving, and the ground in that part of the site was so damp the bones were of the consistency of thick mud. Even now I cannot recall that period without a pall of ennui settling over me.

Fortunately this miserable state of uneventfulness was not to last long. The first intimation of a new outbreak of violence was innocent enough—or so it seemed at the time. We were sitting in the parlor after our simple supper, Emerson and I. He was writing up his notes and I was fitting together my eleventh Roman amphora—a form of vessel I have never admired. Ramses was in his room, engaged in some mysterious endeavor; John was in his room trying to finish Leviticus. The lion club played at my feet, finishing off my house slippers. Since it had already eaten one, I decided it might as well have the other. Bastet lay on the table next to Emerson's papers, her eyes slitted and her rare purr echoing in the quiet room.

"I believe I must make a trip to Cairo soon," I remarked.

Emerson threw his pen down. "I knew this was coming. Peabody, I absolutely forbid you to prowl the bazaars looking for murderers. Everything is peaceful just now and I won't have you—"

"Emerson, I cannot imagine where you get such ideas. I need to shop, that is all. We have not a pair of house slippers among us, and my store of bismuth is getting low. All these people seem to suffer from stomach complaints."

"If you didn't deal it out so lavishly, you would not be running out of it."

Our amiable discussion was developing nicely when we were interrupted from a hail without. Since the breaking in at the storeroom, Abdullah had taken it upon himself to set a guard on the house. He or one of his sons slept near the door every night. I was touched by this gesture, all the more so because I knew Abdullah was not completely convinced that Emerson had got rid of all the evil spirits.

Hearing him call out, we both went to the door. Two forms were approaching. In the light of the torch Abdullah held high I soon recognized friends. "It is the reverend and Mr. Wilberforce," I exclaimed. "What a surprise!"

"I am only surprised they haven't come before," Emerson grumbled. "It has been three or four days since we had callers; I was beginning to entertain the fond delusion we might be allowed to get on with our work in peace."

The presence of our visitors was soon explained. "We moored this morning at Dahshoor," the Reverend Sayce declared, "and spent the afternoon with de Morgan. Since we must be on our way again in the morning, we decided to ride over and call on you tonight."

"How very kind of you," I said, elbowing Emerson in the ribs to keep him from contradicting the statement. "Welcome to our humble quarters."

"Not so humble," said the American, with an approving glance at the cozy scene. "You have the true womanly knack, Mrs. Amelia, of making any abode seem homelike. I congratulate—good heavens!" He leaped backward, just in time to prevent the lion cub from seizing his foot. He was wearing elegant tassled gaiters, and I could hardly blame the young creature for being interested in this new form of fashion.

I seized the lion and tied its lead to a table leg. Mr. Wilberforce took a chair as far from it as possible, and the reverend said, "Can that be the lion belonging to the baroness? We heard it had been lost."

"Ramses found it," I explained. I do not believe in telling falsehoods unless it is absolutely necessary. The statement was true. There was no reason to explain where Ramses had found the lion.

The conversation turned to de Morgan's discoveries, and Emerson sat chewing his lip in silent aggravation. "There is no doubt," said the Reverend Sayce, "that the southern brick pyramid was built by King Amenemhet the Third of the Twelfth Dynasty. De Morgan has found a number of fine private tombs of that period. He has added volumes to our knowledge of the Middle Kingdom."

"How nice," I said.

Conversation languished thereafter. Not even the reverend had the courage to ask Emerson how his work was progressing. Finally Mr. Wilberforce said, "To tell the truth, my friends, we had a particular reason for calling. We have been a trifle concerned for your safety."

Emerson looked offended. "Good Gad, Wilberforce, what do you mean? I am perfectly capable of protecting myself and my family."

"But a number of alarming events have occurred in your neighborhood," Wilberforce said. "We heard of the burglary of the baroness's dahabeeyah. The day before we left Cairo we met Mr. David Cabot, who told us of the attack on the mission."

"Hardly an attack," Emerson said. "Some malcontent had set a fire behind the chapel; but even if that edifice had been totally destroyed, which was unlikely, no harm would have come to anyone."

"Still, it is an ominous sign," Sayce said. "And Mr. Cabot admitted there is growing animosity among the villagers."

"Have you met Brother Ezekiel?" Emerson inquired.

Wilberforce laughed. "I take your point, Professor. If I were inclined toward arson, his is the first establishment I would set a match to."

"It is not a joking matter, Wilberforce," the reverend said gravely. "I have no sympathy for the creed or the practices of the Brothers of Jerusalem, but I would not like to see any of them injured. Besides, they give all Christian missionaries a bad name with their tactless behavior."

"I think you overestimate the danger, gentlemen," Emerson replied. "I am keeping an eye on the situation, and I can assure you no one will dare make a hostile move while I am on the scene." His large white teeth snapped together as he concluded. Sayce shook his head but said no more.

Shortly thereafter the two gentlemen rose to depart, claiming they must make an early start. Not until they were at the door, hats in hand, did Sayce clear his throat and remark, "There is one other little matter I meant to discuss with you, Mrs. Emerson. It almost slipped my mind; such a trivial thing. . . . That bit of papyrus you showed me—do you still have it?"

"Yes," I said.

"Might I prevail upon you to part with it? I have been considering the part of the text I managed to translate, and I believe it may hold some small interest to a student of biblical history."

"To be honest, I would not be able to put my hand on it just at the moment," I admitted. "I have not had occasion to look at it since we left Cairo."

"But you do have it?" The reverend's tone was oddly intense.

"Yes, to be sure. It is somewhere about."

"I would not want to trouble you—"

"Then don't," said Emerson, who had been watching the little man curiously. "You don't expect Mrs. Emerson to turn out all her boxes and bags at this hour of the night, I suppose."

"Certainly not. I only thought—"

"Look in again on your way upriver," Emerson said, like a genial host suggesting a call, "when you are in the neighborhood." "We will try to locate the scrap and then consider your request."

And with this the reverend had to be content, though he did not look pleased.

We stood in the door watching our visitors ride away. Stars spangled the heavens in glorious abandon and the desert lay silver under the moon. Emerson's arm stole around my waist. "Peabody."

"Yes, my dear Emerson?"

"I am a selfish brute, Peabody."

"My dear Emerson!"

Emerson drew me inside and closed the door. "Though thwarted in your heart's desire, you defend me nobly. When you told de Morgan the other day that you doted on Roman mummies, I could hardly contain my emotion."

"It is kind of you to say so, Emerson. And now, if you will excuse me, I had better finish my amphora."

"Damn the amphora," Emerson cried. "No more Roman pots or mummies, Peabody. Tomorrow we begin on our pyramids. To be sure, they are not much in the way of pyramids, but they will be an improvement over what we have been doing."

"Emerson, do you mean it?"

"It is only your due, my dear Peabody. Spite and selfishness alone kept me from beginning on them long ago. You deserve pyramids, and pyramids you will have!"

Emotion choked me. I could only sigh and gaze at him with the whole-hearted admiration his affectionate gesture deserved. His eyes sparkling like sapphires, Emerson put out his hand and extinguished the lamp.

Chapter Eight

EMERSON'S demonstrations of marital affection are of so tempestuous a nature that as a rule we succumb quickly to slumber when they are concluded. On this occasion, however, I found myself unaccountably wakeful long after my spouse's placid breathing testified to the depths of his repose. Starlight glimmered at the open window, and the cool night breeze caressed my face. Far off in the stilly night the lonely howl of a jackal rose like the lament of a wandering spirit.

But hark—closer at hand though scarcely louder—another sound! I sat up, pushing my hair back from my face. It came again; a soft scraping, a scarcely audible thud—and then—oh heavens!—a cacophony of screams scarcely human in their intensity. They were not human. They were the cries of a lion.

I sprang from bed. Despite my agitation a sense of triumph filled me. For once a nocturnal disturbance had found me awake and ready; for once no cursed netting interfered with my prompt response to the call of danger. I snatched my parasol and ran to the door. Emerson was awake and swearing. "Your trousers, Emerson," I shouted. "Pray do not forget your trousers."

Since there was only one lion on the premises, it was not difficult for me to deduce whence the sound came. Ramses' room was next to ours. On this occasion I did not knock.

The room was dark. The light from the window was cut off by a writhing form that filled the entire aperture. Without delaying an instant, I began beating it with my parasol. Unfortunately the blows fell upon the wrong end of the intruder, whose head and shoulders were already out of the window. Stimulated, no doubt, by the thrashing, it redoubled its efforts and made good its escape. I would have followed, but at that moment an excruciating pain shot through my left ankle and I lost my balance, falling heavily to the floor.

The household was now aroused. Shouts and cries of alarm came from all directions. Emerson was the first to arrive on the scene. Rushing headlong into the room, he tripped over my recumbent form and crushed the breath out of me.

Next to appear was John, a lamp in one hand and a stout stick in the other. I would have commended him for thinking of the lamp if I had had the breath to speak, for by its light he was able to recognize us just in time to arrest the blow of the cudgel which he had aimed at Emerson's anatomy. The lion cub continued to gnaw at my foot. It had identified me, I believe, after the first impulsive attack, and was now merely playing, but its teeth were extremely sharp.

Emerson struggled to his feet. "Ramses!" he shouted. "Ramses, where are you?"

It struck me then that I had not heard from Ramses, which was unusual. His cot was a mass of tumbled blankets, but the boy himself was nowhere to be seen.

"Ra-a-amses!" Emerson shrieked, his face purpling.

"I am under de cot," said a faint voice.

Sure enough, he was. Emerson yanked him out and unrolled the sheet in which he had been wrapped so tightly that it had the effect of a straitjacket. Crooning endearments, he pressed the boy to his breast. "Speak to me, Ramses. Are you hurt? What has been done to you? Ramses, my son . . ."

Having heard Ramses speak, I had no apprehension concerning his safety. I therefore returned the lion to its cage before saying calmly, "Emerson, he cannot talk because you are squeezing the breath out of him. Release your grip, I beg you."

"T'ank you, Mama," said Ramses breathlessly. "Between de sheet, which I only now succeeded in getting off from over my mout', and Papa's embrace, which t'ough it is appreciated for de sentiment dat prompted it, neverdeless—"

"Good Gad, Ramses," I exclaimed. "For once will you give over your rhetorical orotundities and get to the point? What happened?"

"I can only guess as to de origin of de difficulty, since I was soundly sleeping," said Ramses. "But I presume a person removed de screen and entered by way of de window. I did not awaken until he—or she, for I was not able to determine de gender of de intruder—was wrapping me in de sheet. In my attempt to free myself I fell off de cot and somehow, I cannot tell how, found myself beneat' dat object of furniture."

Being somewhat short of breath, he had to pause at this point, and I demanded, "How did the lion cub get out of its cage?"

Ramses looked at the cage. In the manner of all small creatures the cub had rolled itself into a furry ball and dropped off to sleep.

"Apparently I neglected to close de door of de cage," said Ramses.

"And very fortunate it was, too," said Emerson. "I shudder to think what would have happened if the noble beast had not warned us you were in danger."

"It could have roused us just as effectively in the cage as out of it," I said. "The only person it seems to have attacked is me; and if it had not done so I might have succeeded in apprehending the burglar."

Father and son looked at me, and then at one another. "These women!" they seemed to remark, in silent unanimity. "They are always complaining about something."

II

Next morning at breakfast I reminded Emerson of his promise to give me a pyramid. He looked at me reproachfully. "I do not need to be reminded, Amelia. An Emerson never breaks his word. But we can't begin today. I need to do a preliminary survey of the surrounding area and close down our excavations at the cemetery."

"Oh, quite, my dear Emerson. But please don't bring me any more bones. The last lot was frightfully brittle. I set them in a stiff jelly to remove the salt, but I am running short of suitable containers."

"We have not the proper facilities to deal with bones," Emerson admitted. "To expose them without being able to preserve them would be a violation of my principles of excavation."

"Brother Ezekiel will be pleased you have given up the cemetery," I said, helping Emerson to marmalade.

"I only hope he won't think I was influenced by his outrageous demands." Emerson looked sheepish. "I went on with the cemeteries longer than I ought to have done only because he told me to stop."

"Since it will be several days before we can begin on the pyramids, I may as well make my trip to Cairo at once."

"Go away, now?" Emerson cried. "After the murderous attack on our son last night?"

"I must go, Emerson. The lion has eaten every pair of slippers we own. There is no question of leaving Ramses unprotected; I can go and come in the same day. Besides, I don't believe an assault on Ramses was intended. The intruder was after something—was, in short, a burglar, not a murderer."

"After something? In Ramses' room?"

"He may have mistaken the window. Or used it as a means of reaching the storage rooms, which are windowless, or the parlor, whose outer door was guarded by Abdullah."

"And a fine help Abdullah was," Emerson grunted. "He must have been dead asleep or he would not have been so late in arriving on the scene. Well, well, if you are determined to go, you will go—but I entertain some doubts as to your real motive. Slippers, indeed! Don't deny it, Amelia—you are still on the trail of your imaginary Master Criminal."

"We had better devote some attention to criminals, master or otherwise; they are giving us their full attention. How many more of these burglarious episodes must we endure?"

Emerson shrugged. "Do as you like, Amelia. You will in any case. Only try not to be assaulted, kidnapped, or murdered, if you can possibly do so."

Somewhat to my surprise, Ramses refused to accompany me. (The invitation was proffered by his father, not by me.)

"So long as you are going, Mama," he said, "will you bring me back a Coptic dictionary?"

"I don't know that there is such a thing, Ramses."

"Herr Steindorff has just published a *Koptische Grammatik mit Chrestomathie, Wörterverzeichnis und Literatur.* Should that work be unobtainable, dere is de elementary Coptic grammar and glossary in Arabic of Al-Bakurah al-shakiyyah, or de *Vocabularium Coptico-Latinum* of Gustav Parthey—"

"I will see what I can do," I said, unable to bear any more multilingual titles.

"T'ank you, Mama."

"What do you want with a Coptic dictionary?" Emerson asked.

"Dere are a few words on de fragment of papyrus Mama found dat continue to elude me."

"Good heavens, the Coptic papyrus," I exclaimed. "I keep forgetting about it. Mr. Sayce was asking about it only last night—"

"He shan't have it," Emerson declared.

"Don't be spiteful, Emerson. I wonder what I did with the other scrap I found the night Abd el Atti was killed."

"Anodder fragment, Mama?" Ramses asked.

"It appeared to be from the same manuscript, but it was much smaller."

Ramses' face became taut with excitement. "I would like to have it, Mama."

"I don't remember where I put it, Ramses."

"But, Mama—"

"If you are a good little boy and do everything your Papa tells you, Mama will give you your treat when she returns."

III

I regretted my promise to Ramses, for I had a great deal to do, and finding a given book in the shops devoted to that trade is a time-consuming process. Instead of being neatly arranged on shelves, the merchandise is piled in stacks; and since the bookdealers are scholarly gentlemen whose shops are frequented by the learned world of Cairo, I was tempted to linger and talk. I managed to find one of the volumes Ramses had requested. Then I left the Sharia 'el Halwagi and went to the bazaar of the shoemakers, where I purchased a dozen pair of slippers, two each for myself, Ramses and Emerson, and six for the lion. I hoped, by the time he had finished these, he would have done cutting his teeth.

Then, and only then, did I go to the Khan el Khaleel.

Abd el Atti's shop was closed and shuttered. No one answered, even when I went to the back door and hammered on it. Somewhat disheartened, I turned away. I had the address of Mr. Aslimi's shop on the Muski and I was about to go in that direction when another idea occurred to me. I went on past the fountain and under an ancient arch, farther into the bazaar.

Kriticas was the best-known antiquities dealer in Cairo, a rival of Abd el Atti's and an old friend. He greeted me with mingled pleasure and reproach. "I understand you are looking for demotic papyri, Mrs. Emerson. Why did you not come to me?"

"I would have done, Mr. Kriticas, had I not been distracted by the death of Abd el Atti, of which I am sure you have heard."

"Ah, yes." Kriticas' noble Greek brow furrowed. "A sad tragedy, to be sure. Now I happen to have an excellent specimen of a Twenty-Sixth Dynasty papyrus. . . ."

I examined the merchandise, drank the coffee he pressed upon me, and inquired after his family before saying casually, "I see that Abd el Atti's shop is closed. Who is the new owner—his son, or that charming old lady his wife?"

Kriticas had a characteristic silent laugh; his whole body shook, but not a sound came from his bearded lips. "You have met the lady?"

"Yes. She appears to be a very determined woman."

"Yes, one might say that. She has no legal claim, of course. She has been acting on behalf of her son, Hassan. He is a bad hat, as you English say; a user of drugs, often in trouble with the police. But you know how these mothers are; the worse a son, the more they dote on him."

"Hmmm," I said.

"Her cause was hopeless from the start," Kriticas went on. "Abd el Atti disinherited Hassan several years ago. No doubt he is in fresh trouble of some kind; he has not been seen for several weeks."

The idea that popped into my mind was so obvious I wondered I had not thought of it before. "I think I may have seen him," I said. "Is he of medium height, with scanty eyebrows and a missing front tooth?"

"He and a hundred thousand other Egyptians," said Kriticas, with his silent laugh. "Now, Mrs. Emerson, this papyrus is particularly fine. I have a buyer for it, but if you want it . . ."

I bought the papyrus, after considerable bargaining. The transaction put Kriticas in a good humor and lowered his guard; and that was when I struck! "Is this papyrus one of the spoils of the Master, by any chance?"

I used the *siim issaagha* word. Kriticas' eyelids flickered. "I beg your pardon, Mrs. Emerson?"

"You know the argot as well as I," I said. "Never mind, Mr. Kriticas. You have your own reasons for remaining silent, but remember, Emerson and I are your friends. If you ever need our help you have only to ask."

The dignified Greek pursed his lips. "Did you say the same to Abd el Atti?" he asked.

IV

I took luncheon at Shepheard's. Emerson would have considered this a waste of time, but Emerson would have been mistaken. The hotel is the center of social life in Cairo, and I hoped to hear news about a number of individuals in whose activities I was interested. This proved to be the case. Mr. Baehler caught sight of me and—upon observing I was alone—joined me for an aperitif, and filled me in on the gossip. After he had gone I was taking coffee on the terrace when I caught sight of a familiar face. He pretended not to see me, but I rose and waved my parasol. "Prince Kalenischeff! Your highness!"

He affected great surprise at seeing me and was persuaded to take a seat at my table. "I thought you never left the side of your distinguished husband," he said.

"I am equally surprised to see you, your highness. I trust nothing is amiss at Dahshoor?"

This sample of the inanity of our conversation will suffice, I believe. I let him talk, waiting for the opportunity to insinuate a subtle but significant question. I did not notice that he was gradually oozing closer and closer until something touched my foot.

"I was in the Khan el Khaleel this morning," I said, moving my foot away.

"What a coincidence. So was I," said Kalenischeff. "It is a pity we did not meet earlier. I might have had the pleasure of offering you luncheon."

This time it was not a foot but a hand that, under cover of the tablecloth, made contact with one of my extremities. Again I moved away; again the chair of Prince Kalenischeff inched closer. "I have a charming little *pied-a-terre* here in

Cairo," he went on, leering at me through his monocle. "Since we are too late for luncheon—what about tea?"

Hand and foot together intruded upon my person.

I will go to considerable lengths in my quest for truth and justice, but there are limits. I had left my useful chatelaine and its tools at home, but my trusty parasol was at my side. Raising it, I brought the steel tip down on the prince's foot.

Kalenischeff's monocle dropped from his eye and his mouth opened wide, but he did not scream aloud. I rose. "Good day, your highness. I will miss my train if I stay any longer."

All in all it had been a most productive day. I could hardly wait to tell Emerson of my discoveries. (The encounter with Kalenischeff would have to be edited, or Emerson would rush off to Dahshoor and commit various violent indignities upon the prince's person.) The most important discovery was that the man we knew as Hamid was really Abd el Atti's renegade son. But was Hamid guilty of the dastardly sin of patricide? At first the idea pleased me, but the more I thought about it, the more my enthusiasm cooled. I could visualize a quarrel—angry words—blows struck in the heat of passion. But I could not visualize Hamid, who was not notably muscular, making the perverse and terrible effort of hanging his father's huge body from the roof of the shop. In fact, this was one of the more curious aspects of the case. Why would anyone, muscular or not, make that effort? The most superficial examination would show that Abd el Atti had not committed suicide.

I amused myself during the train journey speculating on these matters. The sun had not yet set when I reached the house. I expected Emerson would be on the dig. Conceive of my surprise, therefore, to find him in the parlor with Ramses on his knee. A thrill of apprehensive inquiry pervaded my being, but the news I brought could not be contained.

"Emerson," I cried. "I have discovered who Hamid really is."

"Was," said Emerson.

"I beg your pardon?"

"Was. Ramses has just discovered his remains, torn and dismembered by jackals."

V

I was bitterly chagrined. Now we would never be able to question Hamid. I sat down and stripped off my gloves. "I begin to wonder about you, Ramses," I said. "How did you come to make such a discovery?"

"It was de cat Bastet, in fact," said Ramses calmly. "I have been training her to fetch for me. She is particularly interested in bones, which is not surprising, considering dat she is a carnivore; and I consider it a testimonial to my met'ods as well as to de intelligence of de cat Bastet dat she has been able to overcome her instinctive—"

"Say no more, dear boy," Emerson exclaimed. "Amelia, how can you ask Ramses to discuss a subject that has struck him dumb with horror?"

"I am not at all horrified," said Ramses, squirming in his father's affectionate grasp. "A student of physiology must develop a detached attitude toward specimens dat are de object of his research. I have been endeavoring to explain dis to Papa, but to no avail."

Emerson's arms relaxed and Ramses slipped out of his hold. "I saw at once, from de freshness of de specimen, dat despite de desiccation dat is de inevitable consequence of dis climate, it was dat of an individual who had recently met his demise. De cat Bastet led me to de place where de odder parts of de—"

"Enough, Ramses," I said. "Emerson, where are the—er—remains?"

"I had them fetched back here."

"That was an error. I would like to have examined them in situ."

"You would not like to have examined them at all," said Emerson. "The word 'remains' is apt, Amelia."

"I examined dem carefully, Mama," Ramses said consolingly. "De body was unclot'ed. It had been dead for several days. Dere were no marks upon it except for extensive bruising around de neck. A rope tied tightly about dat part of de anatomy may have accounted for some of de contusions, but it is my opinion dat manual strangulation was de cause of deat'."

"Very good, Ramses," I said. "What steps have you taken, Emerson?"

"I have sent for the local chief of police."

"Good. If you will excuse me, I will go and change my clothes."

As I left I heard Ramses say, "May I remark, Papa, dat alt'ough your consideration for my sensitivities was quite unnecessary, I am not wit'out a proper appreciation of de sentiment dat prompted it."

VI

The *mudir* was of no use whatever, but since I had not expected he would be, I was not put out. Viewing the remains—and I must confess that the word was, as Emerson had suggested, decidedly apropos—he stroked his silky beard and murmured, "*Alhamdullilah.* What will these unbelievers do next?"

"We are hoping, effendi, that you will tell us what this unbeliever did last," said Emerson courteously.

"It appears, O Father of Curses, that he hanged himself."

"And then walked out into the desert to bury himself?"

"The Father of Curses jests with his servant," said the *mudir* gravely. "A friend must have performed that office for him. Only the friend did not do a thorough job of it."

"Nonsense," I exclaimed. "The man was murdered."

"That is another possibility. If the sitt desires, I will question the other unbelievers."

He was obviously puzzled by our interest in the affair. It was nothing to him if unbelievers chose to murder one another and he could not understand why the death of a peasant, who was not even one of our servants, should concern us. Since I had no desire to see the villagers lined up and beaten in the local version of police interrogation, I declined his offer. Nor was I tempted to explain that Hamid was no Copt, nor a local resident. The story would only have confused the solemn old gentleman even more.

So we bade him farewell and watched him ride away, followed by his entourage of ragged, barefoot constables. I was about to return to the house when Emerson, leaning with folded arms against the door, said, "We may as well wait here, Amelia. The next delegation should be arriving at any moment."

"Whom are you expecting?"

"Jones—whom else? He will have heard the news by now; I dismissed the men, since it is almost sunset, and there was no getting any work out of them once they learned what had happened."

Sure enough, it was not long before a familiar procession appeared in the distance. The two men rode side by side. It was not until they had drawn closer that I saw the third donkey and its rider. "Good heavens," I exclaimed. "He has brought Miss Charity. Emerson, you don't suppose that dreadful man expects her to—to—"

"Lay out the remains? Even Brother Ezekiel would hardly go so far as that, I fancy. He likes to have the girl tagging at his heels like an obedient hound."

Brother David urged his mount to a gallop and was soon before us. "Is it true?" he asked in agitated tones. "Is Brother Hamid . . ."

"Dead," Emerson said cheerfully. "Quite dead. Very dead indeed. Unquestionably dead and . . ." The others had come up by then and he broke off. Charity had heard, however; her small calloused hands gripped the reins so tightly, her knuckles whitened. No other sign of emotion was apparent, for her face, as usual, was shadowed by the brim of her bonnet.

Ezekiel dismounted. "We have come to take our poor brother back for burial," he announced. "And to call down the wrath of the Lord on his murderer."

"I suppose you could fancy a cup of tea," I said.

Ezekiel hesitated. "It will lubricate your vocal cords," Emerson said hospitably. "And strengthen the volume of your anathemas."

Smiling to myself, I led the way into the parlor. Emerson might complain all he liked about my detective interests, but he was not immune to the fever. Here was a chance to find out from the missionaries what they knew about their 'convert.' "

I had intended to spare John the embarrassment of appearing, after his unorthodox behavior following the fire, but the presence of Charity sent out invisible tentacles that wrapped round his heart and drew him inexorably to her. Shortly he appeared, wreathed in blushes, to ask if he might serve us. To send him away would have been to wound him, so I acquiesced and resigned myself to watching him fall over the furniture and spill the tea, for he never took his eyes off the object of his affections.

The discussion turned at once to Hamid's death. "Poor fellow," David said mournfully. "You did him an injustice, Brother, when you said he had run away."

"I did," Ezekiel acknowledged. Then he looked around at the rest of us as if expecting admiration for his admission of fallibility. Presumably he got enough of it from Brother David to satisfy him, for he went on in the same rotund, self-satisfied voice, "He was a true vessel of grace."

"A fine man," Brother David said.

"He will be greatly missed."

"One of the elect."

"I never liked him."

The interruption of the litany by this critical remark was almost as surprising as its source; the words issued from under Charity's black bonnet. Her brother turned a look of outraged astonishment upon her and she went on defiantly. "He was too obsequious, too fawning. And sometimes, when you were not looking at him, he would smile to himself in a sneering way."

"Charity, Charity," Brother David said gently. "You are forgetting your name."

The girl's slight, dark-robed form turned toward him as a flower seeks the sun. She clasped her hands. "You are right, Brother David. Forgive me."

"Only God can do that, my dear."

Emerson, who had been watching the exchange with undisguised amusement, now tired of the diversion. "When did you see the fellow last?" he asked.

All agreed that Hamid had not been seen since the night of the fire. He had taken his evening meal with the other converts before retiring to his humble pallet. Brother David claimed to have caught a glimpse of him during the confusion later, but Brother Ezekiel insisted Hamid had been conspicuous by his absence among those attempting to put out the flames. When he failed to appear the following morning, it was discovered that his scanty possessions were also gone. "We assumed he had gone back to his village," David said. "Sometimes our converts are . . . Sometimes they do not—er—"

"Yes, quite," said Emerson. "Your naïveté amazes me, gentlemen. Leaving aside the question of conversion, to introduce into your home a complete stranger, without credentials or local references . . ."

"We are all brothers in the Lord," Ezekiel proclaimed.

"That is your opinion," Emerson retorted. "In this case Miss Charity appears to have had better sense than either of you men. Your 'brother' was not a Copt but a Muslim; he did not come from a neighboring village but from the underworld of Cairo; he was a liar, most probably a thief, and very possibly a murderer."

Had Emerson consulted me beforehand, I would have advised against betraying this information—which, the reader will note, he implied he had discovered. However, the blunt announcement had the result of enabling me to study its effect on the missionaries. Since it is my practice to suspect everyone, without exception, I had naturally wondered whether one of them had murdered Hamid—for reasons which were at that time irrelevant to the inquiry. But their astonishment appeared genuine. Brother's David's expression was one of polite incredulity. Brother Ezekiel was thunderstruck. His heavy jaw dropped and for a few seconds he could only sputter unintelligibly. "What—where—how did you—"

"There is no doubt about it," Emerson said. "He was a thorough rascal, and he took you in very nicely."

"You accuse the poor chap of being a thief," said Brother David. "Since he is no longer here to defend himself, I must do it for him. Do you accuse him of robbing you?"

"He stole nothing from us. That is . . . ." A shade of vexation crossed Emerson's face. I knew he was thinking of the peripatetic mummy cases. He decided not to attempt to explain this. Instead he said, "He was responsible for the theft of the baroness's antiquities."

"How do you know that, sir?" Brother Ezekiel demanded.

"Mrs. Emerson and I have our methods," Emerson replied.

"But at least one of the missing objects was recovered," Ezekiel said.

"That was an error. The mummy—" Emerson's voice caught, but he got the word out. "The mummy case was not the one belonging to the baroness. It is still unaccounted for. But we are on the track of it; it won't be long before we locate it."

Brother David rose to his full height. "Forgive me, Professor, but I cannot listen to accusations against the dead. Our servants must have arrived by now; if you will show me where our unfortunate brother lies, we will take him away with us."

"Certainly. I will also lend you a sack in which to carry him."

The sun was setting in fiery splendor when the funeral procession made its way toward the village, in somber outline against the darkening blue of the eastern sky. We had been bidden to attend the obsequies of "our dear brother" on the following morning, an invitation to which Emerson replied with sincere astonishment. "Sir, you must be out of your mind to suggest such a thing."

John had lit the lamps when we returned to the parlor. Ramses was there too. He had been eavesdropping, for he said at once, "Papa, I would like to attend de funeral."

"Why on earth would you want to do that?" Emerson asked.

"Dere is a variety of folktale dat claims dat de murderer is drawn to de funeral services of his victim. I suspect dat is pure legend, but a truly scientific mind does not dismiss a t'eory simply because it—"

"Ramses, I am surprised at you," Emerson said. "Scientific inquiry is one thing, but there is a form of morbid curiosity—to which, I regret to say, certain adult persons who ought to know better are also prone . . ."

Here he stopped, having got himself into a hopeless grammatical tangle. I said icily, "Yes, Emerson? Do go on."

"Bah," said Emerson. "Er—I was about to suggest an alternative form of amusement. Instead of attending the obsequies we might go to Dahshoor and harass—I mean, visit—de Morgan."

"An excellent idea, Emerson," I said. "But there is no reason why we cannot do both. The funeral is early in the morning, and after that we can ride to Dahshoor."

Somewhat to my surprise Emerson agreed to this proposal. Ramses was also kind enough to consent. Later, after Ramses had been sent to bed and John had retired to his room—he had finally finished Leviticus and was now deep in the even greater intricacies of Numbers—I said to my husband, "I commend you on your self-control, Emerson. You didn't once lose your temper with Brother Ezekiel."

"He isn't worth my anger." Emerson pushed his notebook aside. "In fact, I find the creature quite entertaining. He is the most absurd person I have encountered recently."

"Do you think he murdered Hamid?"

Emerson stared. "Why the devil should he?"

"Emerson, you are always worrying about motive. You ought to know by now that is not the way to solve a case." Emerson continued to gape at me. I continued, "I can think of several reasons why Brother Ezekiel might exterminate Hamid. The man may have made unwelcome advances to Miss Charity—Ezekiel is such a prude he would interpret a polite greeting as an unwelcome advance. Or Ezekiel may have discovered that Hamid was not sincere in his conversion."

"Peabody—" Emerson began in an ominous tone.

"I have made a few notes on the case." I opened my own notebook. "We know now that Hamid was the disinherited son of Abd el Atti and that he was a member of the criminal ring of antiquities thieves. I agree with you that a falling-out among thieves is the most likely explanation of his murder. These secret societies are devilish things. If Hamid had betrayed his oath—sworn in secret ceremonies and sealed in his own blood—"

"Peabody, you never cease to astonish me. When do you find time to read such trash?"

Recognizing this as a rhetorical question, I did not answer it. "Drug takers are notoriously unreliable; the Master Criminal may have concluded Hamid was dangerous, and ordered him executed."

"I believe this is our first Master Criminal, is it not? I don't care for them, Peabody. The noble amateur villain is much more to my taste."

"Or—which is, in my opinion, more likely—Hamid decided to set up in business for himself, thus robbing the ring of the profits to which they believed themselves entitled. The Master Criminal is unquestionably the most likely suspect."

"Oh, quite." Emerson folded his arms. "I suppose you have deduced the identity of this mysterious—one might almost say apocryphal—figure?"

"Hardly apocryphal, Emerson. We can now be certain that more than one evildoer is involved, for Hamid was not the person who entered Ramses' room last night. He had been dead for several days, probably since the night of the fire."

"Humph," said Emerson. "I grant you a gang, Peabody—though that is stretching the evidence. But a Master Criminal?"

"A gang must have a leader, Emerson. Naturally I have given some thought as to who he may be." I turned over a page of my notebook. "Now pray don't interrupt me again. This is a complex problem and you will confuse me."

"I wouldn't do that for the world," said Emerson.

"The Master Criminal is obviously not what he seems."

"Brilliant, Peabody."

"Please, Emerson. What I mean to say is that he—or she—for one must not denigrate the natural talents of the so-called weaker sex. . . . Where was I?"

"I have no idea, Peabody."

"The Master Criminal undoubtedly has another persona. He or she may be in outward appearance the most respectable of individuals. A missionary—a Russian nobleman—a German baroness—an archaeologist. . . ."

"Humph," said Emerson. "I assure you, Peabody, I am not your Master Criminal. I claim an alibi. You know where I am at night."

"I never suspected you, Emerson."

"I am relieved to hear it, Peabody."

"Let us take the suspects in order. First, Brother Ezekiel. What do we know of him before he appeared at Mazghunah this year? I don't doubt that the Brothers of the Holy Jerusalem are a legitimate sect, but they seem only too ready to accept plausible scoundrels into their ranks. The entire mission staff may be involved—Brother David as the liaison between Ezekiel and the Cairo underworld, and Miss Charity as a decoy. Her presence adds a look of innocence to the group."

Emerson's interest was growing, but he tried to hide it. "There it is again, Peabody—your weakness for young persons of pleasant appearance. Miss Charity herself may be the Master Criminal. There certainly is no less likely suspect."

"Oh, I don't deny she may be criminally involved, Emerson. She is almost too good to be true—a caricature of a pious young American lady. Or Brother David may be the head of the gang, with Ezekiel as his dupe or his confederate. However, I consider Prince Kalenischeff to be just as suspicious. His reputation is none of the best. His title is questionable, his source of income unknown. And Slavs, in my opinion, are very unstable persons."

"And Germans, Peabody?"

"Bismarck, Emerson—I remind you of Bismarck. And the Kaiser has been extremely rude to his grandmama."

"A palpable hit, Peabody." Emerson rubbed his chin thoughtfully. "I confess the idea of the baroness being a Master Criminal delights me. However, she is probably in Luxor by now. A successful leader of criminals should supervise her henchmen more closely."

"Ah, but she is not at Luxor," I cried triumphantly. "I spent the afternoon at Shepheard's, catching up on the news. The baroness's dahabeeyah went aground at Minieh, two days after she left Dahshoor. She returned to Cairo by train and is now staying at that new hotel near the pyramids—Mena House. Giza is only two hours from Dahshoor by donkey, less by train."

"The theft of her antiquities was a blind, then, to remove suspicion from her?"

"Possible but not probable; she was not under suspicion at that time—at least not by us. I consider it more likely that the theft was an act of rebellion by Hamid. If, that is, the baroness is the Master Criminal."

"And who is your archaeologist suspect? Surely not our distinguished neighbor."

"What better disguise could a Master Criminal adopt? An archaeologist has the most legitimate of excuses for excavation, and the best possible means of learning of new discoveries. As inspector general, M. de Morgan can control all other excavators, heading them away from sites that promise to yield valuable objects. He worked at Dahshoor, where there are Twelfth Dynasty tombs, last spring; and last summer we first heard of the Twelfth Dynasty pectoral appearing on the market."

Emerson's face took on a far-off look; his brilliant blue eyes softened. Then he shook his head. "No, Peabody. We must not be led astray by wishful thinking. There must be some other way of getting de Morgan to give us Dahshoor besides putting him in prison. Your suggestion of a criminal archaeologist has intriguing aspects, however. And de Morgan is not the only excavator of my acquaintance who has displayed weakness of character."

"I do not for a moment believe that Mr. Petrie is the Master Criminal, Emerson."

"Humph," said Emerson.

Though we discussed suspects a while longer, we could add nothing to the list I had made. Emerson's suggestions—the Reverend Sayce, Chauncy Murch, the Protestant missionary at Luxor, and M. Maspero, distinguished former head of the Antiquities Department—were too ridiculous to be considered. As I pointed out to him, theories are one thing, wild improvisation is quite another. I hoped that the morrow's projected visit to Dahshoor would enable us to learn more. Kalenischeff was still there, purportedly assisting de Morgan, and I promised myself another interview with that gentleman.

It was rather late before we got to sleep, and although my famous instinct brought me instantly alert at the sound of a soft scratching at the window, I was not quite as wide-awake as I ought to have been. I was about to strike with my parasol at the dark bulk looming at the open window when I recognized the voice repeating my name.

"Abdullah?" I replied. "Is it you?"

"Come out, Sitt Hakim. Something is happening."

It took only a moment to throw on my robe. Finding my slippers took a little longer; I had been forced to hide them to keep Ramses from feeding them to the lion, and in the muzziness of lingering sleep I could not recall where I had put them. At last I joined Abdullah outside the house.

"Look there," he said, pointing.

Far to the northeast a bright pillar of flame soared heavenward. There was something so uncanny about the scene—the utter stillness of the night, unbroken even by the lament of jackals—the vast empty waste, cold under the moon—that I stood motionless for a moment. The distant flame might have been the sacrificial fire of some diabolic cult.

I reminded myself that this was the nineteenth century A.D., not ancient Egypt, and my usual good sense reasserted itself. At least the mission was not under attack; the fire was somewhere in the desert. "Quickly," I exclaimed. "We must locate the spot before the flames die down."

"Should we not waken the Father of Curses?" Abdullah asked nervously.

"It will take too long. Hurry, Abdullah."

The site of the blaze was not as distant as it had appeared, but the flames had died to a sullen glow before we reached it. As we stood gazing at the molten remains Abdullah hunched his shoulders and shot a quick glance behind him. I sympathized with his feelings. The ambience was eerie in the extreme, and the smoldering embers were gruesomely suggestive of the contours of a human form.

The sound of heavy breathing and running footsteps made us both start. Abdullah knew Emerson's habits as well as I; he prudently got behind me, and I was able to prevent Emerson from hurling himself at the throat of—as he believed—my abductor. When the situation was explained, Emerson shook himself like a large dog. "I wish you wouldn't do this to me, Peabody," he complained. "When I reached out for you and found you gone I feared the worst."

He had paused only long enough to assume his trousers. His broad chest heaved with the speed of his running and his tumbled locks curled about his brow. With an effort I conquered my emotions and recounted the cause of my departure.

"Hmmm," said Emerson, studying the dying coals. "They have an ominous shape, do they not?"

"Less so now than before. But it cannot have been a human body, Emerson. Flesh and bone would not be so completely consumed."

"Quite right, Peabody." Emerson knelt and reached out a hand. "Ouch," he exclaimed, putting his fingers to his mouth.

"Be careful, my dear Emerson."

"Immediate action is imperative, Peabody. The object is almost entirely reduced to ash. A few more moments . . ." He succeeded in snatching up a small fragment, scarcely two inches across. It crumbled even more as he tossed it from hand to hand, but he had seen enough.

"I fancy we have found the missing mummy case, Peabody."

"Are you certain?"

"There are traces of brown varnish here. I suppose it could be one of ours—"

"No one has approached our house tonight," Abdullah assured him.

"Then it must be the one belonging to the baroness," I said.

"Not necessarily," Emerson said morosely. "There must be four or five thousand of the cursed things that have not yet passed through our hands."

"Pray do not yield to despair, Emerson," I advised. "Or to levity—if that was your intention. I have no doubt this is the mummy case we have been seeking. What a pity there is so little left of it."

"It is not surprising it should burn so readily, since it was composed of varnish and papier-mâché, both highly flammable."

"But, Emerson, why would a thief go to so much trouble to obtain this article, only to destroy it?"

He had no answer. We gazed at one another in silent surmise, while the sun rose slowly in the east.

I was pleased with the appearance of our little party when we set out for the funeral service. John's scrubbed cheeks shone like polished apples, and Ramses had an air of deceptive innocence in his little Eton jacket and short trousers. Emerson snorted when I suggested he put on a cravat, but Emerson can never appear less than magnificent; and I fancy I looked my usual respectable self, though the fact that we planned to proceed directly from the village to Dahshoor necessitated a less formal costume than I would ordinarily have assumed when attending religious services.

Emerson flatly refused to enter the chapel. We left him sitting on his favorite block of stone, back ramrod-straight, hands on knees in the very pose of an Egyptian pharaoh enthroned.

The service was less prolonged than I expected, possibly because Brother Ezekiel's command of Arabic was not extensive, and possibly because his new-founded doubts as to Hamid's character curtailed the fervor of his eulogy. A few lugubrious hymns were sung—John and Ramses joined in, to disastrous effect—and then half a dozen stalwart converts shouldered the rough wooden coffin and the company straggled out after them.

A considerable crowd had assembled outside the chapel. At first I thought they had come to watch, or even protest, the ceremonies of the intruders. Then I saw that all were laughing or smiling, and I realized that they were gathered around my husband, who was chatting with all the graciousness of his ancient model holding court. Emerson has, I regret to say, an extensive store of Arabic jokes, many of them extremely vulgar, which he keeps for masculine company. Catching sight of me, he broke off in the middle of a word and rose to his feet.

Trailed by the spectators, we followed the coffin through the grove of palm trees to the edge of the cultivation. I assumed Brother Ezekiel had marked the spot for a cemetery, but there was no symbol of that purpose except for the grimly significant hole in the ground. No fence enclosed the area, no religious symbol marked it. It was a desolate and forbidding final resting place; only too appropriate, I feared, for the wretched man whose bones were to lie there.

His Bible open in his hands, Brother Ezekiel stood at the head of the grave with David beside him and Charity the customary two paces to the rear. John began edging toward her. I poked him with my parasol and shook my head, frowning. Ordinarily I am sympathetic to romantic feelings, but this was not the time or the place.

The somber message of Isaiah sounded even more dismal in Ezekiel's guttural Arabic. "All flesh is grass, and all the goodliness thereof is as the flower of the field. The grass withereth, the flower fadeth: because the spirit of the Lord bloweth upon it."

Ezekiel did not proceed to the comfort of the following verses, with their assurance of immortality in the grace of God. Instead he closed the Book with a slam and began to speak extemporaneously.

I was anxious to be on our way, so I paid little attention to his words until I felt the muscles of Emerson's arm stiffen under my hand. Then I realized that Ezekiel's eulogy had turned into a tirade, stumbling but passionate—a bitter denunciation of the Coptic Church, its beliefs and its local representative.

A murmur of anger arose, like the first wind of a storm through dry grasses. David turned to look with surprise and alarm at his associate. Emerson cleared his throat loudly. "I would like to say a few words," he called out.

His voice stilled the mutter of the crowd and Brother Ezekiel broke off. Before he could draw breath, Emerson launched into a flowery speech. He was not hypocrite enough to praise Hamid, of whom he said only that he had worked for us, so that we felt the need to acknowledge his passing. He went on to quote the Koran and the Bible on the sin of murder, and proclaimed his intention of bringing the killer to justice. Then he dismissed the audience with the blessing of

God, Allah, Jehovah, Christ and Mohammed—which pretty well covered all possibilities.

The listeners slowly dispersed, with the exception of the few who had been designated as grave diggers. They began shoveling sand into the pit and Emerson confronted the angry preacher. "Are you out of your mind?" he demanded. "Are you trying to start a small war here?"

"I spoke the truth as I saw it," Ezekiel said.

Emerson dismissed him with a look of scorn. "Try to contain your friend's candor," he said to David, "or you will find yourself burning with your church."

Without waiting for a reply, he strode away. I had to run to catch him up. "Where are you going, Emerson? We left the donkeys at the chapel."

"To see the priest. Word of the affair has already reached him, I fear, but we will do what we can to mitigate its effect."

The priest refused to see us. According to the hard-faced disciple who responded to our call, he was absorbed in prayer and could not be disturbed. We turned reluctantly away. "I don't like this, Peabody," Emerson said gravely.

"You don't believe we are in danger, Emerson?"

"We? Danger?" Emerson laughed. "He would hardly venture to threaten us, my dear Peabody. But the lunatics at the mission are another story, and Ezekiel seems bent on starting trouble."

"The priest was courteous enough to me the other day. At least," I added, thinking ruefully of my ruined chapeau, "he meant to be courteous."

"Ah, but that was before we began entertaining his rival to tea and encouraging our servant to patronize the other establishment. Never mind, Peabody, there is no cause for alarm at present; I will call on the priest another day."

John returned to the house and Ramses, Emerson and I set out for Dahshoor. As we rode along the edge of the fields, the first of the Dashsoor monuments we encountered was the Black Pyramid. Ramses, who had been silent up to that time, began to chatter about Egyptian verb forms, and Emerson, whose strength lay in excavation rather than in philology, was at something of an embarrassment. We drew near the base of the pyramid and he stopped, with an exclamation of surprise. "What the devil, Peabody—someone has been digging here."

"Well, of course, Emerson."

"I am not referring to de Morgan's incompetent probing, Peabody. These are fresh excavations."

I saw nothing unusual, but Emerson's expert eye cannot be gainsaid. I acknowledged as much, adding casually, "Perhaps some of the villagers from Menyat Dahshoor are doing a little illicit digging."

"Practically under de Morgan's eye? Well, but he would not notice if they carried the pyramid itself away."

"He is a very forceful individual," said Ramses in his piping voice. "All de Arabs are afraid of him."

Emerson, who had been studying the tumbled terrain with a thoughtful frown, replied to his son, "They are afraid of the *mudir* and his bullwhip, Ramses. English gentlemen do not employ such threats—nor are they necessary. You must win the respect of your subordinates by treating them with absolute fairness. Of course it helps to have an inherently dominant personality and a character both strong and just, commanding and yet tolerant. . . ."

We found the workers sprawled in the shade taking their midday rest. De Morgan was not there. We were informed that he was at the southern stone pyramid, with his guest, who had expressed an interest in seeing that structure. So we turned our steeds in that direction, and found de Morgan at luncheon. At the sight of the table, which was covered with a linen cloth and furnished with china and crystal wineglasses, Emerson let out a sound of disgust. I paid no heed; the near proximity of the noble monument in all its glory induced a rapture that overcame all else.

Emerson immediately began berating de Morgan for taking so much time from his work. "You leave the men unsupervised," he declared. "They have every opportunity to make off with their finds."

"But, *mon vieux,*" said de Morgan, twirling his mustache, "you are also away from the scene of your labors, *non?*"

"We were attending a funeral," Emerson said. "I presume you heard of the mysterious death of one of our men?"

"I confess," de Morgan said superciliously, "that I take little interest in the affairs of the natives."

"He was not one of the local people," I said. "We have reason to believe he was a criminal of the deepest dye—a member of the gang of antiquities thieves."

"Criminals? Thieves?" De Morgan smiled. "You insist upon your interesting fictions, madame."

"Hardly fictions, monsieur. We have learned that the murdered man was in reality the son of Abd el Atti." I turned abruptly to Prince Kalenischeff. "You knew him, did you not?"

But the sinister Russian was not to be caught so easily. His arched brows lifted infinitesimally. "Abd el Atti? The name is familiar, but . . . Was he by chance an antiquities dealer?"

"Was, your highness; your use of the past tense is correct. Abd el Atti is no more."

"Ah yes, it comes back to me now. I believe I heard of his death when I was last in Cairo."

"He was murdered!"

"Indeed?" The prince fixed his monocle more firmly in his eyesocket. "I fear I share M. de Morgan's disinterest in the affairs of the natives."

I realized it would be more difficult than I had thought to trick Kalenischeff into a damaging admission. He was an accomplished liar. Also, I found myself increasingly distracted as the conversation went on. I soon realized what the problem was. Once again detective fever warred with my passion for archaeology. It was not hard to keep the latter within reasonable bounds when the distraction consisted of decadent Roman mummies and scraps of pottery; but in the shadow of a pyramid—not any pyramid, but one of the most majestic giants in all of Egypt—other interests were subdued, as the brilliance of the sun dims the light of a lamp. My breathing became quick and shallow, my face burned. When finally de Morgan patted his lips daintily with his napkin and offered us coffee I said, as casually as I could, "Thank you, monsieur, but I believe I will go into the pyramid instead."

"Into the pyramid?" De Morgan paused in the act of rising, his eyes wide with astonishment. "Madame, you cannot be serious."

"Mrs. Emerson never jokes about pyramids," said my husband.

"Certainly not," I agreed.

"But, madame . . . The passages are dark, dirty, hot. . . ."

"They are open, I believe? Perring and Vyse explored them over sixty years ago."

"Yes, certainly, but . . . There are bats, madame."

"Bats do not bodder my mudder," said Ramses.

"Pardon?" said de Morgan, quite at a loss.

"Bats do not bother me," I translated. "Nor do any of the other difficulties you mentioned."

"If you are determined, madame, I will of course send one of my men along with a torch," de Morgan said doubtfully. "Professor—you do not object?"

Emerson folded his arms and leaned back in his chair. "I never object to any of Mrs. Emerson's schemes. It would be a waste of time and energy."

De Morgan said, "Humph," in almost Emerson's tone. "Very well, madame, if you insist. You may take your son with you as guide," he added, with a sidelong glance at Ramses. "He is quite familiar with the interior of that particular pyramid."

Emerson swallowed the wrong way and burst into a fit of coughing. I looked at Ramses, who looked back at me with a face as enigmatic as that of the great Sphinx. "You have explored the Bent Pyramid, Ramses?" I asked, in a very quiet voice.

"But of a certainty, madame," said de Morgan. "My men were some time searching for the little . . . fellow. Fortunately one of them saw him enter, otherwise we might not have found him in time to save him."

"As I endeavored to explain, monsieur, I was not in need of rescue," said Ramses. "I could have retraced my steps at any time, and had every intention of doing so once my research was completed."

I felt certain this statement was correct. Ramses had an uncanny sense of direction and as many lives as a cat is reputed to have—though by now, I imagined, he had used up several of them.

I said, "I should have known. One day when you returned home and took a bath without being told to do so—"

"De odor of bat droppings is extremely pervasive," Ramses said.

"Did I not forbid you to explore the interiors of pyramids?"

"No, Mama, I am certain you never uttered dat specific prohibition. Had you done so, I would of course—"

"Never mind. Since you know the way, you may as well come with me."

We left the others at table and sought the entrance, with one of de Morgan's men in attendance. I was extremely vexed with Ramses. I could not punish him for disobeying me, since it had not occurred to me to forbid him to explore pyramids. That omission at least could be remedied, though I felt sure Ramses would immediately find some other activity I had not thought of prohibiting.

"Ramses," I said. "You are not to go into any more pyramids, do you understand?"

"Unless it is wit' you and Papa?" Ramses suggested.

"Well—yes, I suppose I must make that exception, since it applies to the present situation."

The entrance to the interior of the pyramid was on the north side, thirty-nine feet from the ground. Thanks to the unusual slope, the climb was not as difficult as it appeared; at close range the seemingly smooth facing was seen to have innumerable cracks and breaks that provided holds for fingers and toes. Ramses went up like a monkey.

At the opening the guide lit his torch and preceded me into a narrow, low-roofed corridor that descended at a moderate gradient. The air became increasingly close and hot as we went on, down, down, ever down, into breathless darkness. I remembered from my reading that the corridor was almost two hundred and fifty feet long. It seemed longer. Finally it leveled out; then we found ourselves in a narrow but lofty vestibule whose ceiling was shrouded in shadows— and in bats. They set up an agitated squeaking, and began to stir uneasily; it was necessary for me to reassure them before they settled down again.

I was familiar with the general plan of the place from my reading, but Ramses had to point out the exit from this vestibule, which was more than twenty feet above the floor, in the southern wall of the chamber. Another room, with a fine corbeled ceiling—another passage . . . It was absolutely delightful, and I was enjoying myself immensely when the guide started to whine. The torch was burning low for lack of air; he was choking; he had sprained his ankle on the rubble littering the floor; and so on. I ignored his request that we turn back, but I was a trifle short of breath myself, so I suggested we sit down and rest for a while.

We were in one of the upper corridors near a great portcullis stone, which had been designed to block the passage and prevent robbers from reaching the burial chamber. For some reason it had never been lowered into place, and it provided a convenient back rest.

As we sat there, the full wonder and mystery of the place overshadowed me. We were not the first to penetrate that mystery; several modern archaeologists had entered the pyramid, and three thousand years before that, a group of hardy robbers had braved the physical dangers and the curses of the dead to rob the pharaoh of his treasures. When those intrepid but unscientific explorers, Perring and Vyse, explored the passages in 1839, they found only scraps of wood and baskets, and a few mummified bats, inside a wooden box. There was no sarcophagus and no royal mummy. Since Pharaoh Snefru, to whom the pyramid belonged, had another tomb, he may never have rested here; but something of value must have occupied the now-empty chambers or the ancient thieves would not have broken into them, with baskets to carry away their loot.

As I mused in blissful enjoyment, with the perspiration dripping from my nose and chin, there occurred the most uncanny event of that entire season. The stifling air was suddenly stirred by a breeze, which rose in an instant to a gusty wind. It felt cold against our sweating bodies. The torch flickered wildly and went out. Darkness closed in upon us—a darkness filled with movement. The guide let out a howl that echoed gruesomely.

I ordered him to be quiet. "Good Gad, Ramses," I said excitedly. "I have read of this phenomenon, but I never thought I would be fortunate enough to experience it myself."

"I believe Perring and Vyse mention it," said the high, piping voice of my annoyingly well-informed son, close beside me. "It is indeed a curious phenomenon, Mama, leading one to de suspicion dat dere are passageways and exists to de exterior as yet undiscovered."

"I had reached that conclusion myself, Ramses."

"It was in de investigation of dat t'eory I was engaged when M. de Morgan's men interrupted me. One of dem had de effrontery to shake me, Mama. I spoke to M. de Morgan about it, but he only laughed and said—"

"I don't want to know what he said, Ramses."

The wind subsided as suddenly as it had begun. In the silence I could hear our guide's teeth chattering. "Sitt," he moaned, "oh, Sitt, we must go at once. The djinns are awake and looking for us. We will die here in the darkness and our souls will be eaten."

"We could continue de search for de unknown opening, Mama," said Ramses.

To say that I was tempted is like saying a starving man is a trifle peckish. Common sense prevailed, however. The search Ramses proposed would be the work of days, possibly weeks, and it could not be carried out without advance preparation. I had lost all track of time, as I am inclined to do when I am enjoying myself, but I suspected we had been gone longer than we ought to have been. I was therefore forced to refuse Ramses' request; and after I had relit the torch (a supply of matches, in a waterproof tin box, is part of my supplies), we retraced our steps.

Ramses must have sensed the pain that filled my heart, for as I was crawling up the last long passageway he said, "It is too bad Papa was not able to obtain de firman for Dahshoor, Mama."

"No one is perfect, Ramses, not even your papa. Had he allowed ME to deal with M. de Morgan . . . But that is over and done with."

"Yes, Mama. But you would like to have dis site, would you not?"

"It would be futile for me to deny it, Ramses. But never forget that your papa is the greatest living Egyptologist, even if he is somewhat lacking in tact."

Emerson kept a discreet distance from us as we rode back to Mazghunah. As Ramses had noted, the smell of bat droppings is extremely pervasive and unpleasant. I knew it was Emerson's sense of smell, not his affections, that dictated the removal. After a while he called out, "Did you have a pleasant time, Peabody?"

"Yes, thank you, my dear Emerson. Very pleasant."

Emerson touched his donkey and the animal sidled nearer. "You know I would have got you Dahshoor if I could, Peabody."

"I know that, Emerson."

There was a stiff breeze blowing from the south. Emerson's nose wrinkled and he let his donkey fall behind. "Don't you want to know what I learned from the sinister Russian while you were gadding about inside the pyramid?" he called.

"I would like to know, Papa," cried Ramses, turning his donkey. Emerson hastily covered his face with his sleeve. "Later, Ramses, later. Why don't you ride with your mama?"

VII

Emerson's hints of Russian revelations were only intended to pique my curiosity, as he finally admitted. But after we had dined and Ramses had gone to his room, Emerson seated himself at the table, folded his hands, and regarded me seriously.

"We must talk, Peabody. The time has come for us to face a painful truth. I have reason to believe that we are involved with a sinister criminal conspiracy."

"Emerson," I exclaimed. "You astonish me!"

My husband shot me a sour glance. "Sarcasm does not become you any more than it does me, Peabody. Until recently your wild theories were no more than that. The repeated invasions of our premises, however, indicate that for some reason as yet unknown we are the objects of active malice. Even more significant is the fact that someone has been digging near the Black Pyramid. And," he added, frowning, "if you use the words 'Master Criminal' . . ."

"We may as well call him that in lieu of a less distinctive pseudonym, Emerson."

"Humph," said Emerson.

"Then you agree that our burglaries were committed by the gang of antiquities thieves?

"Wait." Emerson raised a magisterial hand. "For once, Peabody, let us work out this problem step by step, in strictly logical fashion, instead of leaping across an abyss of speculation onto an unstable stepping-stone of theory."

I took up my mending. Emerson's shirts always need to have buttons sewn on. "Proceed, my dear Emerson."

"Point number one: illicit digging at Dahshoor. You may recall my mentioning that one of the objects to come on the market recently was a Twelfth Dynasty pectoral, with a royal cartouche. Dahshoor has three Twelfth Dynasty pyramids, the Black Pyramid being one of them. There are other royal tombs of that period in Egypt; but, given the evidence of recent excavation, I think there is a strong presumption that the pectoral came from that site."

"I agree, Emerson. And the thieves have not finished, so there may be other tombs—"

"Point number two," Emerson said loudly. "Abd el Atti's association with the Master . . . with the gang. His death, the presence of his renegade son here at Mazghunah, the latter's murder, support this connection. Do you agree?"

"Since it was I who first put forth that theory, I do agree."

"Humph," said Emerson. "But from here on, Peabody, we are adrift in a sea of conjecture. What possible interest could these villains have in an innocent party like ours? Their aim cannot be to silence us; neither of us saw anything that would identify the murderer of Abd el Atti—"

"We may have observed a clue without recognizing its significance."

"The fact remains, Peabody, that no attacks have been made on our persons. It seems clear that these people are looking for something we have in our possession—or that they believe we have in our possession."

"I believe you have hit it, Emerson," I exclaimed. "We know we have nothing of value; the mummy portrait was attractive, but not worth a great deal, and the papyrus fragments are completely worthless. Do you suppose something else was missing from the shop—sold, hidden away, or stolen by a third party— and that the gang attributes its loss to us?"

"It is a plausible theory," Emerson admitted. "I have a fairly clear memory of the objects that were scattered around the shop that night. It is a pity you did not get into the back room on your first visit; we might then compare inventories."

"I didn't but Ramses did. Shall we ask him?"

"I hate to involve the lad in this dirty business, Amelia. I waited until he had retired before discussing it."

"Emerson, you underestimate Ramses. In the past weeks he has been taken in custody by the police, half-stifled in a sheet, and buried in the sand; he has stolen a lion and examined a body in an unpleasant state of disrepair, without turning a hair."

Emerson demurred no longer. Detective fever burned as bright in his manly chest as it did in my bosom. I felt sure Ramses was not in bed, and the slit of light under his door proved me correct.

Emerson knocked. After a moment the door opened and Ramses' tousled head appeared. He was in his nightgown, but his lamp was alight and there was a heap of papers on the table that served as his desk. The Coptic grammar was open.

Emerson explained his idea. Ramses nodded. "I believe I can supply de information, Papa. Shall we retire to de parlor?"

At my suggestion Ramses put on his dressing gown and one of his slippers. The other was nowhere to be found, and I was glad I had kept one pair in reserve. After Emerson had detached the lion cub from his bootlace we retired to the parlor, with Bastet following. Emerson took up his pen. Ramses closed his eyes and began.

"A heart scarab of blue faience, with a prayer to Osiris; a tray of mixed beads, cylindrical; a piece of linen approximately ten centimeters by forty, wit' a hieratic docket reading 'Year twenty, day four of the inundation. . . .' "

I picked up my mending. We had obviously underestimated Ramses' powers of visual recall.

His voice droned on. "Fragments of a coffin of de Roman period, consisting of de foot and portions of de upper back; anodder coffin, Twenty-First Dynasty, belonging to Isebaket, priestess of Hathor. . . ."

It was a good twenty minutes later before he stopped talking and opened his eyes. "Dat is all I can recall, Papa."

"Very good, my boy. You are certain there were no pieces of jewelry, aside from cheap beads?"

"Small objects of value would be in de locked cupboards, Papa. I did not attempt to open dem, since Mama had forbidden me to touch anyt'ing."

"And because such an act would have been illegal, immoral, and unprincipled," I suggested.

"Yes, Mama."

"It is a pity you didn't, though," Emerson remarked.

"Can you remember what items from Ramses' list were missing?" I asked. "Not that it would necessarily prove anything; Abd el Atti might have sold them during the afternoon."

"True." Emerson looked at the list.

"I don't remember seeing any mummy cases," I said.

Emerson threw the list across the room. The cat Bastet pounced on it and batted it back and forth. "I do not want to talk about mummy cases, Peabody!"

"Yet dey continue to intrude, do dey not?" Ramses said. "I believe we must consider de mummy case of de baroness as vital to de solution. Until we can explain dat, we are at sea."

"I agree, Ramses," I said. "And I have an idea."

Ramses slid down off his chair and went to retrieve the list from Bastet. Emerson looked off into space. Neither asked me to explain my idea; so I proceeded.

"We have concluded, have we not, that someone has found treasure at Dahshoor and hopes to find more."

Emerson shook his head. "A possibility only, Peabody."

"But when you have eliminated de impossible, whatever remains, however improbable, must be de trut'," said Ramses, returning to his chair.

"Very good, Ramses," exclaimed his father. "How pithy you are becoming."

"It is not original, Papa."

"Never mind," I said impatiently. "Gold and jewels are sufficient causes of violence, as the history of mankind unhappily demonstrates; but a commonplace mummy case is not. But what, I ask, is a mummy case?" I paused for effect. My husband and son regarded me in stony silence. "It is a container," I cried. "Normally it contains a human body, but what if this mummy case were used as a hiding place for small, stolen antiquities? The baroness would have taken it away with her, out of the country, and it is most unlikely that the authorities would have inspected it. She purchased her antiquities openly and no doubt has the proper papers."

"That explanation had of course occurred to me," said Emerson, stroking his chin. "But why did the thieves steal the mummy case back from her if they meant her to smuggle their stolen goods out of the country?"

"Because *we* were interested in it," I explained. "Don't you see, Emerson? The baroness is a woman of volatile and impetuous character and she was trying to make an impression on you. She offered the mummy case to you upon one occasion; though she spoke half in jest, there was a chance she might have gone through with the plan. The thieves had to retrieve it. They extracted the stolen goods and destroyed the mummy case, having no more use for it."

"I perceive several difficulties wit' dat explanation, Mama," said Ramses.

"Hush, Ramses." Emerson pondered. "If that idea is correct, Peabody, the baroness cannot be the Master Criminal."

"I suppose you are right, Emerson."

"Cheer up, Peabody, it is only an idea. We may yet think of something that proves the baroness guilty." Emerson grinned at me.

"The baroness was only one of our suspects," I replied. "Several of the others were present that evening, when the baroness offered you the mummy case. Or one of the servants—if he was in the pay of the Master Criminal he could have warned his superior that the hiding place was no longer safe."

"But who is that unknown superior? (If you have no objection, Peabody, I prefer that term to 'Master Criminal,' which smacks too strongly of the type of sensational literature to which I object.) Our deductions may be valid so far as they go, but we are still in the dark as to the identity of the person who is behind all this."

"We will catch him, Emerson," I said reassuringly. "We have never failed yet."

Emerson did not reply. Ramses sat swinging his feet—one bare, one enclosed in a red morocco slipper—and looking pensive. After an interval Emerson said, "We may as well give it up for the time being. Off to bed, my boy; it is very late. I regret having kept you from your rest."

"Dere is no need to apologize, Papa. I found de discussion most stimulating. Good night, Mama. Good night, Papa. Come along, de cat Bastet."

We replied in kind—Emerson and I in words, Bastet by falling in behind Ramses as he walked to the door. Just before it closed behind him I heard him say musingly, "What is a mummy case? A most provocative question. . . . What indeed is a mummy case? A mummy case is . . . A mummy case . . ."

I began to agree with Emerson, that I would rather not hear those words again.

Chapter Nine

THE following day saw the moment I had awaited so long—the beginning of work on our pyramids (or, to be precise, our pyramid, Emerson having selected the northernmost of the two). Dare I confess the truth? I believe I do dare. Though a measurable improvement over Roman mummies and Christian bones, the pitiful excuse for a pyramid I saw before me held little charm. Too late, alas, I knew I should not have yielded to the temptation to explore the Bent Pyramid, well-nigh irresistible as that temptation had been.

Nor was Emerson his usual cheerful self. Something was troubling him—my affectionate perception told me that—but it was not until that evening, when we set to work recording the activities of the day, that he deigned to confide in me.

We worked in silence for some time, at opposite ends of the long table, with the lamp shedding a pool of brightness between us. From time to time I glanced at Emerson, but always found him writing busily. All at once my labors were interrupted by a loud "Curse it!" and the whiz of a missile through the air. The pen hit the wall with a spattering of ink, and fell to the floor.

I looked up. Emerson's elbows were on the table. His hands clutched his hair. "What is wrong, Emerson?" I asked.

"I cannot concentrate, Peabody. Something is nagging at my mind. I felt sure you would sense my distraction, but every time I looked at you you were busy writing, and I did not want to interrupt."

"But I felt the same," I cried eagerly. "Our mental communication is truly remarkable, Emerson. I have noticed it often. What is troubling you?"

"Do you remember the intrusive mummy we found a few days after the robbery of the dahabeeyah?"

I had to think for a few moments before the memory returned. "I believe I do. On the edge of the Christian cemetery, was it not?"

"Yes. I wondered at the time. . . ." Emerson leaped to his feet. "Do you recall where you put it?"

"Certainly. Nothing is stored away in *my* expedition house without my having a distinct . . . Emerson! I believe I know what you are thinking."

We collided in the doorway. "Just a moment," I said breathlessly. "Let us not be precipitate. Fetch a light and I will call John; we will need to move a few objects to reach the mummy."

With John's assistance we removed the mummy from its shelf and carried it back to the parlor. Emerson cleared the table by the simple expedient of sweeping his papers onto the floor, and the mummy was placed on its surface.

"Now," said Emerson. "Look at it, Peabody."

There was nothing out of the ordinary about the mummy, except for the arrangement of the wrappings. Instead of being wound haphazardly around the body, the strips of linen were arranged in complex patterns of intersecting lozenges. It was this technique, among other factors, that had enabled Emerson to date it. So ornate were some of the designs I had sometimes wondered whether there were pattern books to which the embalmers might refer. Some mummies of that period had cartonnage masks. Others had painted panels with a portrait of the deceased laid over the bandaged head. In the case of our mummy there was neither mask nor portrait panel, only a shapeless expanse of bandages.

"It has been removed," said Emerson, as I ran an inquiring hand over this part of the mummy.

"I believe you are right, Emerson. There are streaks of glue, or some other adhesive, remaining, and the bandages seem to have been disturbed."

"And," Emerson concluded, "here it is."

Over the featureless head he laid the portrait panel he had rescued from Abd el Atti's shop.

John gasped. The painting, which was remarkably lifelike, animated the whole anonymous bundle and changed its character. A woman lay before us, swathed in grave clothes. Her great liquid dark eyes seemed to return our curious stares with an expression of gentle inquiry; the curved lips smiled at our consternation.

"Two pieces of the puzzle," said Emerson. "All we need now is a coffin."

"It is destroyed—burned," I said certainly. "This is the baroness's mummy, Emerson."

"I believe so, Peabody. As I watched the coffin burn the other night, I was struck by the fact that it was so quickly consumed, with little remaining except ashes. Certainly these mummified bodies, saturated with bitumen, burn readily, but there ought to have been some sign of its presence—a scrap of bone or the remains of an amulet. John—"

The young man jumped. His eyes were fixed in horrified fascination on the mummy. "Sir," he stuttered.

"You put the mummy case in the storeroom. Did you notice any difference in the weight, compared to the ones you had handled before?"

"It was not so heavy as the others," John said.

"Why the devil didn't you say so?" I demanded.

"Now, Peabody, don't scold the boy. He is not accustomed to handling mummy cases; one cannot expect him to realize that the fact was significant."

"True. I apologize, John."

"Oh, madam—" John broke off with a gulp. His eyes widened till the whites showed around the pupils. Emerson had picked up a knife and poised it over the breast of the mummy. "Oh, sir—oh, my goodness—sir—"

"I don't want to disturb the pattern of the bandaging," Emerson explained. "The fabric closest to the body is probably set in a solid mass anyway." The muscles on his forearms stood out as he forced the knife through the layers of linen.

John yelped and covered his eyes with his hands.

"Hmmm," said Emerson, cutting delicately. "Here's one—a *djed* pillar in blue faience. The heart scarab should be nearby. . . . Yes, and a rather good specimen too. Green feldspar."

"He is looking for amulets," I told John. "Magical objects, you know. Quantities of them were wrapped in with the bandages. The *djed* pillar indicated stability, the heart scarab insured that the heart—the seat of the intelligence—would not be taken away by demons. These two amulets are almost always found in the chest area—"

"Don't tell me about it, madam," John begged, pressing his hands tightly over his eyes.

Emerson threw down the knife. "There is no need to dismember the specimen further. Doubtless we would find more amulets and ornaments—the lady appears to have been moderately well-to-do—but the point has been made, I believe."

I nodded. "The mummy and its accoutrements are as unremarkable as the coffin. How very vexing! Come, come, John, Professor Emerson is finished; don't stand there like a model posing for a statue of horror."

John uncovered his eyes, but kept them resolutely turned away from the mummy. "I beg pardon, sir and madam. It was just—she looks so real, lying there like that."

Now there seemed to be a look of mild reproach in the luminous dark eyes. I picked up a coverlet from the sofa and tossed it over the mutilated body. John let out a sigh of relief. "Thank you, madam. May I take her back to the storeroom now?"

" 'It,' not 'she,' " Emerson said shortly. "You will never make an archaeologist, John, if you allow such bathetic thoughts to intrude."

"Thank you, sir, but I don't want to be an archaeologist. Not that it isn't useful work, sir, I don't say that; but I don't think I 'ave the temperament for it."

"I am afraid you are right, John. It is a pity you cannot emulate ME. These are only specimens; they have no identity; one must regard them with calm dispassion and not allow sentimentality to affect one." He had stretched out his hand to remove the portrait panel. For a moment his fingers hovered. Then he said, "Fasten it on, Amelia, or it will fall and be broken when the mummy is moved."

It would have been simpler to return the panel to the padded box I had prepared for it, but I did not make that suggestion. I placed the padding carefully over the portrait and bound it in place with strips of cloth. Wrapping the coverlet around the mummy, John lifted it in his arms.

Lamp in hand, I accompanied him as he carried it back to the storeroom. If I may say so, the subject was worthy of one of our finest painters—the somber shadows of the ruined cloister, the single bright circle of lamplight, and the mighty form of the young man pacing in measured strides with the white-wrapped form held to his breast. I was not unsympathetic with John's mood, but I did hope he was not about to transfer his affections from Charity to the mummy. Charity had not encouraged him, but there can be no more unresponsive recipient of love than a woman who has been dead for seventeen hundred years, give or take a century.

After I had locked the door I thanked John and told him he could now retire. He said hesitantly, "If it would not be an inconvenience, madam—could I sit with you and the professor for a while?"

"Certainly, John; you know you are always welcome. But I thought you were occupied with Leviticus."

"Numbers, madam; I had got as far as Numbers. I don't think, madam, I will ever get past Numbers."

"Don't lose heart; you can succeed at anything if you try." To be honest, my encouragement was a trifle abstracted. John's romantic and religious problems had begun to bore me, and I had more pressing matters on my mind.

As we passed Ramses' door I saw the too-familiar slit of light beneath it. I was surprised he had not popped his head out to ask what we were doing, for he was usually as curious as a magpie. I tapped on the door. "Lights out, Ramses. It is past your bedtime."

"I am working on somet'ing, Mama. May I have a half-hour's grace, please?"

"What are you working on?"

There was a pause. "The Coptic manuscript, Mama," he said at last.

"You will ruin your eyes studying that faded script by lamplight. Oh, very well; half an hour, no more."

"T'ank you, Mama. Good night, Mama. Good night, John."

"Good night, Master Ramses."

"I wonder how he knew you were with me," I said musingly.

When we returned to the parlor Emerson was gathering his scattered papers. "What a mess," he grumbled. "Give me a hand, will you, John?"

John hastened to oblige. The papers having been restored to the table, he asked eagerly, "Is there anything I can do for you, sir?"

"No, thank you; I will have to sort them myself. Go back to your Bible, John—and much good may it do you."

John gave me a look of appeal and I said, "John wants to sit with us awhile, Emerson. Proceed, John. Sit."

John sat. He sat on the edge of the chair, hands on his knees and eyes fixed on Emerson. It was impossible to work with that silent monument present; I was not surprised when after a time Emerson put down his pen and commented, "You appear to be at loose ends, John. You have about you a certain air of indecision. Is something troubling you?"

I knew John would not confide in him. The poor lad had been subjected to many derisive comments on the subject of religion, and although Emerson had been—for Emerson—fairly considerate about John's romantic yearnings, his generally sardonic look and manner was not of the sort that would inspire a young lover to pour out the (usually insipid) sentiments that fill his heart. Emerson's attachment to me is romantic, but it is never insipid.

John scratched his head. "Well, sir . . ."

"The young lady, I suppose. Give it up, John. You will never make headway there; she has given her heart to Brothers David and Ezekiel, and to Jesus—not necessarily in that order."

"Emerson, you are being rude," I said.

"I am never rude," Emerson said indignantly. "I am consoling John and assisting him to a better understanding. If he wishes to persist in his absurd attachment I won't stand in his way. Have I stood in his way? Have I prevented his wandering off to the mission half the evenings in the week? What do you do there, John?"

"Well, sir, we talk, sir. It is what Brother Ezekiel calls the hour of social intercourse."

Emerson's mouth widened into a grin. I coughed in a pointed manner; catching my eye, he refrained from comment, and John went on, "Brother Ezekiel speaks of his boyhood days. His mother, sir, must have been a regular saint. He can't tell how many switches she wore out on him—beating the devils out, you know, sir. I tell them about what's going on here—"

"You gossip about us?" Emerson demanded in awful tones.

"Oh, no, sir, I would never gossip about you and Mrs. Emerson. Only the little things that happen, and Master Ramses' adventures, like . . . Brother David explains Scripture and helps me with my reading."

"And what does Charity talk about?" I asked.

"She don't talk, madam, she sits and sews—shirts for the children and for Brother Ezekiel."

"It sounds very dull," said Emerson.

"Well no, sir, I won't say dull; but it ain't exactly lively, if you understand me."

"Aha!" Emerson burst out laughing. "Amelia, I believe I detect the first crack in the devotional facade. There may be hope for the lad yet. John, you had better spend your evenings with Abdullah and the men, improving your Arabic. Their conversation is a good deal more lively."

"No, sir, I can't do that. To tell the truth, sir, I'm worried about the reverends. There ain't so many converts as there was. One of the children threw a stone at Sister Charity t'other day. And there's been other things."

"Humph." Emerson stroked his chin. "You confirm my own fears, John. Something will have to be done about it. Well, my lad, I'm glad you unburdened yourself. Off to bed with you now; Mrs. Emerson and I will deal with the matter."

After John had gone, Emerson said complacently, "I knew he had something on his mind. You see, Amelia, a little tact, a little sympathy are all that is needed to win the confidence of an unassuming lad like John."

"Humph," I said. "What are you going to do, Emerson?"

"Steps must be taken," said Emerson, firmly but vaguely. "I do wish people would work out their own problems and not expect me to rescue them. No more, Amelia; I have work to do."

His pen began driving across the page. I picked up my pen; but instead of the scale drawing of the pottery fragments I was making, a vision intruded between my sight and the page—that of a painted woman's face with liquid dark eyes and a faint, enigmatic smile.

How could I concentrate on pots or even pyramids when an unsolved crime demanded my attention? The very perplexity of the problem held an unholy fascination; for I felt sure all the scraps of fact fit into a pattern, if I could only make it out. Mummy and mummy case, portrait panel and Twelfth Dynasty pectoral, murder, burglary, arson. . . . All parts of a single underlying plot.

Before me on the table lay the lists Emerson had made of the contents of Abd el Atti's shop. I put out a cautious hand. Emerson did not look up. I drew the lists to me.

It came, not as a dazzling burst of mental illumination, but as a tiny pinhole of light. Slowly it widened, meeting another crack of understanding here, connecting with something else there. . . .

The scratch of Emerson's pen stopped. I looked up to find him watching me. "At it again, Amelia?"

"I think I have it, Emerson. The clue is here." I held up the lists.

"One of the clues, Peabody."

"You have a new theory, Emerson?"

"More than a theory, my dear. I know who murdered Hamid and Abd el Atti."

"So do I, Emerson."

Emerson smiled. "I expected you would say that, Peabody. Well, well; shall we enter into another of those amiable competitions—sealed envelopes, to be opened after we have apprehended the killer?"

"My dear Emerson, there is no need of that. I would never doubt your word. A simple statement to the effect that you knew all along will suffice—accompanied, of course, by an explanation of how you arrived at the answer."

Emerson reflected, but the advantages of the arrangement were so obvious that he did not reflect long. A humorous twinkle brightened his blue eyes as he nodded agreement. "I can hardly do less than return the compliment. Your hand on it, my dear Peabody!"

II

I spoke no more and no less than the truth when I told Emerson I had discovered the identity of the murderer; however, in the privacy of these pages I will admit that a few of the details still eluded me. I was pondering how best to acquire the necessary information when an event occurred that gave me the chance I needed. I refer to the discovery of the entrance to our pyramid.

So bright was the flame of detective fever that that statement, which would ordinarily be adorned by several exclamation marks, is presented as a simple fact. I was not entirely unmoved, never believe that; the sight of the dark hole gaping in the ground roused a brief spurt of enthusiasm and only Emerson's strong arm, plucking me back, prevented me from entering at once.

After a brief examination he emerged covered with dust and gasping for breath. "It is in wretched condition, Peabody. Some of the stones lining the passageways have collapsed. They will have to be shored up before any of us goes farther in."

His eyes moved over the group of workmen, all of whom were as excited as he. One man bounced up and down on his toes, waving his arms. Mohammed was short and fat, with small, pudgy hands; but those hands had a delicacy of touch unequaled by any others in the group. He was a carpenter by trade, when he was not employed by us—the best possible man for the task that awaited us—and he knew it.

Emerson grinned companionably at him. "Be careful, Mohammed. There are some planks remaining from the construction of the donkey shed, I believe; start with those. I will go to the village and find more."

"You could send one of the men," I remarked, as we walked away, leaving Abdullah shouting orders.

"So I could," said Emerson agreeably.

"I will go with you."

"I rather thought you might, Peabody."

"And afterwards, a call on M. de Morgan?"

"We are as one, Peabody. A final roundup of our suspects, eh?"

"Suspects, Emerson? You said you knew the answer."

"Ah, but this is a complex matter, Peabody—a criminal conspiracy, no less. Several people may be involved."

"Quite true, Emerson."

Emerson grinned and gave me an affectionate pat on the back. "I also intend to have a word with the missionaries. I promised John I would. . . . Just a moment, Peabody. Where is Ramses?"

He was, as Emerson had feared, in the thick of the group clustered around the entrance to the pyramid. Emerson took him aside. "You heard me warn Mohammed to be careful?"

"Yes, Papa. I was only—"

Emerson took him by the collar. "Mohammed is our most skilled carpenter," he said, emphasizing each word with a gentle shake. "The task will be dangerous, even for him. You are not under any circumstances to attempt to assist him or go one step into that or any other passageway. Is that clear, my boy?"

"Yes, Papa."

Emerson released his grip. "Will you come with us, Ramses?"

"No, Papa, I think not. I will just go and do a little digging. I will take Selim, of course."

"Don't go far."

"Oh, no, Papa."

I had not been in the village for several days. Outwardly it looked normal enough—the group of women gathered around the well filling the huge jars they carried with such apparent ease atop their heads, the men lounging in the shade, the stray dogs sprawled in the dust of the path. But the greetings were strangely subdued, and none of the children accosted us with their perennial and pitiful demands for baksheesh.

Emerson went straight to the house of the priest. At first it appeared we would be refused entrance. The guard—one of the "deacons," as Emerson called them—insisted the priest was still praying. Then the door opened.

"You fail in courtesy to guests, my son," said the deep voice of the priest. "Bid them enter and honor my house."

When we had seated ourselves on the divan the priest asked how he could serve us. Emerson explained our need of wooden planks, and the priest nodded. "They shall be found. I hope your walls have not fallen down—your roof given way—your peace disturbed, in that ill-omened place?"

"It is the pyramid that has fallen down," Emerson replied. "We have had troubles at the monastery, to be sure, but they were not caused by demons; they were the work of evil men."

The priest shook his head sympathetically. I almost expected him to click his tongue.

"You did not know of these things?" Emerson persisted. "The breaking into my house, the attack on my son?"

"It is unfortunate," the priest said.

" 'Unfortunate' is not the word. A man murdered, a fire at the mission—it seems, Father, that there have been too many 'unfortunate' happenings."

Even in the shadows where he sat I saw the flash of the priest's eyes. "Since the coming of the men of God. We had no trouble before they came."

"They did not set the fire," Emerson said. "They did not break into my house."

"You think my people did these things? I tell you, it is the men of God who are responsible. They must go. They cannot stay here."

"I know there has been provocation, Father," Emerson said. "I beg you—I warn you—do not let yourself be provoked."

"Do you take me for a fool?" the priest asked bitterly. "We are no more than slaves in this country, tolerated only so long as we do nothing. If I lifted my hand against the men of God, I and all my people would die."

"That is true," I said.

The priest rose. "You come here and accuse me of violence and crime. I tell you again—look to the men of God for answers to your questions. Find out for yourself what kind of men they are. They must leave this place. Tell them."

We could not have been more firmly dismissed. Emerson bowed in silence, and I felt a certain . . . well, perhaps embarrassment is the proper word. For the first time I could see the priest's point of view. The strangers had moved into his town, told his people they were wrong, threatened his spiritual authority; and he had no recourse, for the strangers were protected by the government. A way of life centuries old was passing; and he was helpless to prevent it.

We walked away from the priest's house. Emerson said, "Perhaps we can persuade Brother Ezekiel to set up headquarters elsewhere."

"It will require superhuman tact to persuade him, Emerson. The slightest hint that he may be in danger will only make him more determined to stay."

"Tact, or a direct order from the Almighty." Emerson's face brightened. "I wonder . . ."

"Put it out of your head, Emerson. Your simple parlor magic may work with our people, but I do not believe you can deceive Brother Ezekiel into taking your voice for that of Another."

The mission was a scene of utter tranquillity. School was in session. The drone of voices came through the open windows like the buzz of bees on a lazy summer afternoon. The shadows of palm and tamarisk lay cool upon the ground; and in a shady corner a sewing class was in progress. The little girls sat with their bare feet modestly tucked under their somber robes and their shining black heads bent over their work. Perched on the block that had served Emerson as a seat, Charity was reading aloud from the Arabic translation of the New Testament. Her gown was of the same dark print she always wore, and perspiration sparkled on her face, but for once she was without the hideous bonnet. Her pronunciation was poor; but her voice was soft and sweet, and the beautiful old story took on added charm because she read it with such feeling. " 'And Jesus said, "Let the little children come to me; for the Kingdom of Heaven is theirs." ' "

I felt as if I were seeing the other side of the argument the priest had presented so eloquently. Brother Ezekiel was the most irritating man in the world and, in my opinion, wholly unfit for the profession he had embraced; but the missionaries were performing a worthwhile task, particularly with the ignorant and ignored little girls. Coptic women were no better off than their Muslim sisters. If the missionaries did nothing else, they might be the salvation of the women of Egypt.

I think even Emerson was moved, though one would not have known it from his expression. Few people see Emerson's softer side; in fact, some people deny that he has one.

It was not the time for sentiment, however. I repressed my emotions and Emerson said in a low voice, "We are in luck. Here's our chance to talk to the girl alone."

I cleared my throat loudly. There was a serpent in the little Paradise after all; the harmless sound made Charity start violently and look around with fear writ large upon her face. I stepped out from the shadow of the trees. "It is only I, Miss Charity. And Professor Emerson with me. Resume your seat, I beg, and let us have a little chat."

She sank down upon the stone from which she had risen in her alarm. "You may go home now, girls," I said. "Class is over."

One of the youngsters began the old cry of baksheesh, but cut it off after glancing at Charity. I took a seat beside the girl. "I apologize for startling you," I said.

Emerson made an impatient gesture. "We are wasting time, Peabody. Heaven knows how soon we will be interrupted. What are you afraid of, child?"

He knelt beside her. I expected she would flinch away, but something in the stern face so near her own seemed to give her courage. She even smiled faintly. "I was absorbed in that wonderful story, Professor. I was not expecting anyone—"

"Bah!" Emerson exclaimed. "Doesn't your creed tell you that lying is a sin, Miss Charity?"

"It was the truth, sir."

"A half-truth at best. This village is no longer safe, child. Can't you persuade your brother to go elsewhere?"

The girl lifted her head. "You see what we are doing here, sir. Can we admit defeat—can we abandon these helpless infidels?"

I caught the eye of one of the infidels, who was peeking at us from behind a tree trunk. She gave me a wide impudent grin. I shook my head, smiling.

Emerson shook his head, frowning. "You are in danger, and I believe you know it. Is there no way . . . What is it, Peabody?"

"Someone is watching from the window of the house," I reported. "I saw the curtain move. Yes, curse it—the door is opening; he is coming."

"Curse it," Emerson repeated. "Don't get up, Miss Charity; listen to me. There may come a time when you need our help. Send to us, at any hour of the day or night."

Charity did not reply. Brother Ezekiel was almost upon us.

"Well, if it isn't the professor and his worthy helpmeet," he said. "What are you setting there for, Charity? Why don't you invite them to come in?"

Charity rose like a puppet pulled by strings. "I am neglectful," she said. "Forgive me, brother."

"Not at all," said Emerson, though the apology had not been intended for him. "We were just—er—passing by."

"You will come into my house," Brother Ezekiel said solemnly. "We will break bread together. Charity, summon Brother David."

"Yes, brother." She glided off, hands clasped, head bowed, and we followed her brother into the house.

I had always thought the expression "painfully clean" a figure of speech. The small parlor into which we were ushered made me wince, it was so bare, so blazingly whitewashed, so agonizingly spare of comfort. A few straight chairs, a table upon which were several candles and a Greek New Testament; no rug on the floor nor cloth on the table nor picture on the wall, not even one of the hideous religious chromos I had seen in homes of other religious persons. The Brethren of the Holy Jerusalem appeared to take the Bible literally, including the injunction against graven images. The only attractive piece of furniture in the room was a bookcase; I was drawn to it as a person coming in from the cold is drawn to a fire.

Most of the books were ponderous theological tomes in several languages, or collections of sermons.

We were soon joined by Brother David. I had not seen him for some time, and the change in him made me stare. His black suit hung loosely on his frame; the glowing marble of his skin had a sickly cast, and his eyes were sunk in their sockets. My inquiries after his health were sincere. He smiled unconvincingly. "Indeed, I am quite well, Mrs. Emerson. Only a little tired. I am not accustomed to the—to the heat."

I exchanged an expressive look with Emerson. We were now well into the winter season, and the climate was superb—cool enough after sunset to make a wrap necessary and pleasantly warm during the day.

Brother Ezekiel appeared to be in an unusually affable mood. Rubbing his hands, he declared, "Charity is getting the food ready. You'll have a bite with us."

"We cannot stay," I said. "We found the entrance to the pyramid this morning and our men are at work shoring up parts of the passageway that have collapsed. We ought to be there."

I had unconsciously turned to Brother David as I made this explanation; it was his colleague who replied, and his words explained some of his good humor. "Yes, we heard you had stopped digging at the cemetery. I'm glad you took my words to heart, friends. You committed a grievous error, but your hearts were not of adamant; you did right in the end."

Emerson's eyes flashed, but he can control his temper when it serves his purpose. "Er—yes. Mr. Jones, we came to talk to you about a serious matter. There have been a number of distressing incidents, not only here but in our house."

"You are referring to the death of poor Brother Hamid?" David asked.

"In the past ten days," said Emerson, "there has been a murder, three burglaries, a fire here at the mission and another mysterious fire in the desert. I understand Miss Charity was also attacked."

"Some naughty child—" Brother David began.

"It was no child who broke into my son's room."

"Are you implying that these incidents are connected?" Brother David asked doubtfully. "How can that be? The criminal acts committed against you— and the baroness—have nothing to do with us. Our own small difficulties are of the sort we have come to expect; the hearts of those who wander in darkness are of flint, but eventually our gentle persuasion will—"

Emerson cut him off with a loud "Bah!" He went on, "I warned you before. I warn you again. The dangers that threaten us all may not be entirely of your making, but you are not improving matters by your intemperate behavior. Leave off attacking the priest, or find another place in which to employ your gentle persuasion."

Brother Ezekiel only smiled smugly and emitted a string of pompous references to truth, duty, salvation and the glorious crown of the martyr. The final item cast a deeper gloom over Brother David's morose countenance, but he remained silent.

Emerson turned to me. "We are wasting our time, Amelia. Let us go."

"I bear no malice," Brother Ezekiel assured him. "The meek shall inherit the earth, and I stand ready at all times to pour the refreshing water of salvation on the spirit of the haughty. You have only to ask and it will be given unto you, for there is no way to the Father but through me. Come to me at any hour, Brother Emerson."

Fortunately Emerson was at the door when he heard this affectionate epithet, and I was able to propel him out with a hard shove.

We had not gone far when we heard footsteps, and turned to see Brother David running toward us.

"Do you really think we are in danger?" he panted.

Emerson's eyebrows rose. "What the devil do you suppose I came here for if not to warn you of that? It was not for the pleasure of Jones's company, I assure you."

"But surely you overestimate the peril," the young man persisted. "Brother Ezekiel's zeal sometimes overcomes his sense of caution. The saints of the Lord do not know fear—"

"But we weaker vessels do," Emerson said drily. "Don't be ashamed to admit it, Mr. Cabot."

"I am concerned," David admitted. "But I tell you, Professor, the incidents you mentioned cannot be the result of our labors here."

"What is your theory?" Emerson asked, watching him keenly.

David flung out his hands in a despairing gesture. "It can only be that, by an unhappy accident, we have stumbled into the midst of some sinister conspiracy."

"An interesting idea," said Emerson.

"But what can we do?"

"Leave," Emerson said tersely.

"That is impossible. Brother Ezekiel would never consent—"

"Then let him stay and roast," said Emerson impatiently. "Take the young woman and go. That idea does not appeal to you? Think it over. If common sense triumphs over your devotion to your leader, we will assist you in any way possible. But the decision must be yours."

"Yes, of course," David said unhappily. He stood twisting his hands, the very picture of guilt and indecision.

We walked back to the fountain, where we had left the donkeys. As we rode away Emerson said, "An interesting encounter, Peabody. Cabot knows more than he is telling. Would you care to hazard a guess as to the nature of the guilty secret that lies hidden in his heart?"

"Nonsense, Emerson. It is not guilt but terror that affects him. He is suffering all the torments of cowardice—afraid to go and afraid to stay. I am sadly disappointed in the young man. What a pity that his manly face and figure do not indicate his real character."

"So that is the way your theories tend, is it?"

"I will say no more at the present time," I replied. "Let us assume, however, just for the sake of argument, that the missionaries are innocent but stupid. Your attempt at persuasion has failed, as I knew it would; do you intend to take any further steps to save them?"

"I suppose I might talk to Murch or another of the Protestant missionaries, and endeavor to find the home base of the Brothers of Jerusalem. Ezekiel's superiors ought to know what is going on here. But I have a feeling, Peabody, that other events are about to transpire that will make such a step unnecessary."

I felt the same. But neither of us knew how imminent were those events, or how dreadful would be their consequences, not only to the missionaries but to ourselves and those we held dear.

III

Though in one sense our visit had not borne fruit, it had not been entirely without value insofar as our criminal investigations were concerned. I had confirmed one of my suspicions. I wondered if Emerson's thoughts tended along the same line. He looked rather pleased with himself, so I was afraid they did.

We were not so lucky with our second group of suspects. De Morgan was not in camp, and his men were sprawled in the shade, resting and smoking. Emerson's roar made them scramble to their feet. The foreman came running to greet us. He hung his head when Emerson began lecturing him, but said that the effendi had given them leave to stop work; it was the time of the midday rest period. The effendi had gone to visit the lady on the dahabeeyah.

"What lady?" I asked.

"You know her, Sitt. The German lady who was here before. She has returned. It is said," the headman added naively, "that she wishes to give the effendi much money for his work. Will you go there also, to get money from the lady?"

"No," Emerson said hastily.

"No," I agreed. "When will M. de Morgan return?"

"Only Allah knows, Sitt. Will you wait for him?"

"Shall we, Emerson?" I asked.

"Hmmm." Emerson rubbed his chin. "I think I will just have a quick look around. You might wait in the tent, Amelia."

"But, Emerson, I also want to—"

"You might wait in the tent of M. de Morgan, Peabody."

"Oh. Oh, yes. That is an excellent idea, Emerson."

It seemed like an excellent idea then, but it did not prove to be so, except in a negative sense. I discovered that M. de Morgan was a tidy man, which I had already suspected, and that his notes were not well organized, which I had also suspected. However, there was nothing in the notes, or in the packing cases that served as storage cupboards, that should not have been there. I had never considered de Morgan a serious suspect, of course.

I felt a little uncomfortable searching the place, but told myself that all is fair in love, war and detective work. I then put my head in the next tent, which was presumably occupied by Prince Kalenischeff, but it was even more barren of clues. In fact, it was bare. There was no sign of his personal possessions.

I found Emerson squatting by one of M. de Morgan's tunnels, peering into the depths and lecturing the foreman. "Look at this, Peabody," he cried. "He has hopelessly disturbed the stratification. How the devil the man expects—"

"If you have finished, we had better return," I said.

"That wall is almost certainly of the Old Kingdom, and he has cut straight through without . . . What? Oh yes. Let us be off."

The head man's dour expression lightened. He had been deprived of most of his rest period; he saw hopes of enjoying a part of it, at least.

"Where is the other gentleman?" I asked.

"The One with the Glass Eye? He is gone, Sitt. He sails with the lady tomorrow."

"Aha," said Emerson.

"Aha," I repeated.

We mounted our donkeys. "Thank goodness that is over," Emerson said. "I have learned what I needed to know and can wind this business up in short order."

"What did you learn from the foreman, Emerson?"

"What did you find in the tent, Peabody?"

"Slow down, if you please. I cannot talk or think while bouncing up and down on a donkey."

Emerson obliged. "Well? Fair is fair, Peabody."

"Oh, certainly, Emerson. But I have nothing to contribute. Only the fact that Kalenischeff has left, which I deduced from the absence of his luggage."

"Nothing suspicious among de Morgan's gear?"

"Not a thing."

Disappointment lengthened Emerson's face. "Ah, well, I feared it was too good to be true. He is making little headway with his excavations. No sign of the burial chamber, and the nearby private tombs have all been robbed—stripped of everything, even the mummies."

"I never really suspected him, Emerson."

"Neither did I, Peabody."

IV

When we reached Mazghunah we found that work had stopped. The passage was in such poor condition it could not be dug out. Mohammed had narrowly escaped being buried alive when the shattered walls gave way; and, after he had examined the situation, Emerson commended Abdullah on his good sense in halting further attempts.

"I feared from the start this would eventuate," he told me. "We will have to clear the entire area and get at the chambers of the substructure from above. The superstructure has entirely disappeared, except for that small mass of brickwork on the north side. Apparently the subterranean passageways have collapsed; you saw how the ground above has sunk in."

"I am sure you are right, Emerson."

"My heartfelt apologies, Peabody. I know how you love crawling on your hands and knees through dark, stifling tunnels; but in this case . . ."

"My dear Emerson, it is not your fault that the pyramid is in disrepair. We must not risk our men on a hopeless task."

My cheerful tone did not deceive my husband, but I kept the smile fixed on my face until he had left me. Only then did I allow my countenance to reflect the disappointment that filled my heart. I had resigned myself to a sunken pit in place of a towering pyramid, but I had hoped for a substructure. In some pyramids the burial chamber and the passages leading to it were built into the pyramid itself. The internal chambers of others were dug wholly or in part into the rock of the plateau on which the pyramid stood. Ours was one of the latter type, but now my dreams of exploring its mysterious interior were over.

Ramses heard the tragic news with his customary appearance of equanimity, remarking only, "I surmised as much when de wall fell on Mohammed." I had begun to believe he might have inherited my enthusiasm for pyramids, but this phlegmatic reaction cast grave doubts on such a hypothesis. He did not join us when we returned to work after a hasty luncheon.

Early in the afternoon the men came on a portion of wall over forty inches thick. Deducing that this was part of the enclosure wall of the pyramid, and that its outline defined the extent of the pyramid foundations, Emerson set the crew to work tracing its four sides. I could see it would take several weeks to clear the entire enclosure, for the loose sand kept trickling back into the trenches almost as fast as it was dug out.

Ramses went to his room immediately after supper, while Emerson and I turned to the clerical and recording chores that are a necessary if boring part of any archaeological expedition. The next day was payday; with John's assistance Emerson began totaling the men's wages, which varied according to the hours each had put in, the type of work, and the rewards given for objects found. Our evenings had been so lively, with burglaries and detective investigations, that to pass one quietly was an anticlimax. I found myself yawning over my work and was about to suggest we retire early when I heard voices outside.

One was the voice of our loyal Abdullah, raised in peremptory challenge. The other was softer; I could not make out the words it spoke. After a moment Abdullah knocked at the door.

"A man brought this, Sitt," he said, handing me a folded paper.

"What man?"

Abdullah shrugged. "One of the infidels."

"Thank you, my friend."

Abdullah bowed and withdrew.

"Well, Peabody, what is it?" Emerson asked, adding a finished page to the stack of pay sheets.

"It appears to be a note. It is addressed to me. I don't recognize the writing, but I think I can guess—"

"Stop guessing and open it," Emerson said impatiently.

I shook off the strange apprehension that had seized me. Never before had I had so strong a sensation of evil—of some monstrous shadow waiting in the darkness with fangs bared. And all from a folded sheet of paper!

Something in my expression as I read alerted the others. Emerson threw down his pen and rose. John sat staring, mute and expectant.

"It is from Charity," I said. "Your warning was not in vain after all, Emerson. She asks for our help."

"When?"

"Now. This very night."

John leaped to his feet. "Wot 'as 'appened?" he cried, wringing his hands. "Where is she? Is she in danger?"

"Now, John, calm yourself. She is in no immediate danger. She asks us to meet her . . ." I checked myself. John's staring eyes and pallid cheeks testified to the depth of his concern. I did not want him running to the mission to rescue his lady; he had already displayed an unfortunate propensity for unnecessary rescues. I said, "Go to your room, John."

"You can't talk to him as if he were Ramses," said Emerson. "Speaking of Ramses—"

"Yes, quite. I follow you, Emerson. John, I assure you there is no need for alarm. We will meet the young lady and listen to her story. If in our opinion there is the slightest cause for concern as to her safety, we will fetch her here."

"You'll come at once and tell me what 'as 'appened, madam," John implored.

"Of course. Run along now."

John departed, with dragging steps and backward looks. I handed Emerson the note.

"Midnight," Emerson muttered. "Why do all persons in distress pick on midnight? It is a damned inconvenient hour, too early to get some sleep before-hand and too late to—"

"Sssh. I don't want anyone to overhear. Especially Ramses."

"She does not appear to have any sense of imminent peril," Emerson said, reading on. "But she is obviously distressed. What, do you suppose, is this 'terrible thing' she has discovered?"

"I have an idea, I think."

"Oh yes, so do I. I only wondered whether she had discovered what *I* already know."

It lacked an hour till the time of the assignation. We employed it in putting Ramses to bed. He was in an aggravating mood, inventing one distraction after another in order to detain us. "I have deciphered de Coptic, Mama," was his final effort. "Do you want to know what it says?"

"Not now, Ramses. Tomorrow."

"It is very interesting, Mama. Dere is a mention on de smaller fragment of de son of—"

" 'The Son of God' is one of the appellations of Jesus," I explained. "Your religious training has been sadly neglected, Ramses. It is an omission I mean to remedy for, whatever are your dear papa's opinions on the subject, an English gentleman should be familiar with the rudiments, at least, of Anglican doctrine. Hop into bed, now."

"Yes, Mama. De gospel according to Saint Thomas—"

"That is just what I mean, Ramses. There is no gospel of Saint Thomas. Matthew, Mark, Luke and John. . . . There is a pretty little prayer that begins with the names of the Evangelists; I will teach it to you. But not now. Good night, my son."

"Good night, Mama," Ramses said resignedly.

The remaining time passed very slowly. I was intensely curious to hear what Charity would say. Finally Emerson decided we should leave. Abdullah had fallen asleep, but he woke instantly when we opened the door. Emerson explained we were going for a stroll and would be back before long.

"I wonder why she chose such a remote spot," he said, as we set out across the moonlit sands.

"She could hardly arrange to meet us in the village, Emerson. And she knows we have been working at the pyramid."

My heart beat fast as we approached the sunken area. The trenches of our excavations cast dark shadows against the pale ground. At first there was no sign of a living form. Then something moved. I caught Emerson's arm. "It is she! I would know that shape anywhere, especially that horrid bonnet."

For an instant she stood motionless as a black paper silhouette, slender and featureless. One arm lifted. The dark form glided silently away.

"She is beckoning us to follow," I exclaimed.

"So I see."

"Where the devil is she going?"

"No doubt she will explain when we catch her up."

Emerson increased his pace. I had to trot to keep up with him, yet the distance between us and the slender form ahead never grew less.

"Curse it," Emerson said. "This is ridiculous, Amelia. Is she going to run all the way to Dahshoor? I will give her a hail."

"No, don't do that! Even a low voice carries a long distance here; a shout would waken everyone for a mile around."

"Well, damnation, we have been walking for a mile."

"Hardly that, Emerson."

We went on for a time in silence. I began to share Emerson's annoyance, and yet there was something uncanny about that silent pursuit across the quiet sand. Ever retreating yet ever beckoning us onward, the figure ahead seemed not a living woman but a symbol of mysterious fate.

"Can she have mistaken us for someone else?" I panted.

"Impossible. The night is bright as day and we are, if I may say so, quite distinctive in appearance. Especially you, in those bloomers."

"They are not bloomers. They are Turkish trousers."

"And you are clashing like a German brass band."

"One never knows . . . when one will need . . ."

"Save your breath, Peabody. Ah—there—she is turning east, toward the cultivation."

One lone palm, a giant of its kind, had invaded the rim of the waterless desert. The slim shadow vanished into its shade. Emerson broke into a trot and I into a run.

She was there. She awaited us. Her head turned.

Then from out of the very ground, or so it seemed, three ghostly forms emerged. Barely visible against the darkness, they moved with the speed and ferocity of the afreets they resembled. My hand went to my belt—too late! They were upon us. I heard Emerson's shout and the smack of his fist on flesh. Rough hands seized me; I was flung to the ground.

Chapter Ten

SO sweet, submissive Charity was in reality the Master Criminal, mistress of vicious thugs! I proceeded no further with my reflections on the case, for other considerations supervened: for one, a large foot planted in the small of my back holding me prostrate while rough hands stuffed a gag into my mouth and rapidly enclosed my body with cords. Even more distracting than physical discomfort was my apprehension concerning Emerson. No longer did the sounds of complaint and struggle reach my ears. The miscreants must have rendered him unconscious—or worse. . . . But no; I could not, I would not, entertain that ghastly thought.

One of the villains picked me up and tossed me over his shoulder. The muscular arm holding my lower limbs warned me of the futility of attempting to escape; I bent all my efforts instead to twisting my neck far enough to get a glimpse of Emerson. As my captor set out across the sands, I was finally rewarded in this endeavor, but what I saw was far from reassuring. Close behind came a pair of bare feet and a ragged robe. I could see no more of the second villain than that, owing to my unconventional posture, but behind the feet a lax, limp hand trailed through the sand. They were carrying him. Surely that must mean my dear Emerson yet lived. I clung to that thought while endeavoring to discern some sign of animation, however faint, in the member.

I could look no more. The discomfort of strained neck muscles forced me to relax. This brought my face in close proximity with the dirty robe covering my captor's body, and I was conscious of a strange odor, even more unpleasant than that of unwashed flesh. I knew that smell. It was the unmistakable stench of bat droppings.

I could see only a small expanse of the desert floor, but I am not a trained archaeologist for nothing; the nature of the debris that, before long, cluttered the surface told me of my location. We were approaching the Black Pyramid. My kidnapper came to a stop before a gaping hole in the ground. If I had not been incapable of speech I would have cried, "Good Gad," or something equally indicative of surprise; for that hole had not been in existence earlier. I did not like the look of it. I resumed my struggles. The wretch replied by dropping me onto the ground. Emerson lay beside me. His eyes were closed, but he looked quite peaceful. Most marvelous of all was the rise and fall of his massive breast. He lived! Thank heaven, he lived!

But for how long? This unpleasant question inevitably arose, and ensuing events made the answer seem highly doubtful. The man who had been carrying me seized me by the collar and started into the hole, dragging me after him.

It was not a grave pit, then, but a structure considerably more extensive. A wild surmise rose and strengthened as we went on into the darkness. I deduced the presence of a flight of steps leading downward, from the impression they made upon my helpless form. At the bottom of the stairs my captor paused to light a candle; then we went on, more rapidly than before, and in the same manner. In justice to the fellow who transported me in such an uncomfortable manner I must admit he had little choice; the ceiling of the passage was so low he had to bend double, and it would have been impossible for him to carry me.

The thieves had discovered the entrance to the interior chambers of the pyramid, which de Morgan had sought in vain. A thrill of archaeological fervor overcame my mental and physical distress. It soon faded, however, for even a lover of pyramids cannot enjoy being in one when she is in the position I then occupied—my collar choking me, the stones of the floor bruising my lower back. Another discomfort soon took precedence. The floor of the passageway was thick with sand and disintegrated bat manure. This rose in a cloud as we proceeded, and being so low to the floor, I found it increasingly hard to breathe.

The candle held by my kidnapper gave little light to my own surroundings. A twinkling starry point behind indicated the presence of the others. Were they still transporting my unconscious spouse, or had they flung his corpse into an empty tomb?

Decayed bat droppings are not precisely poisonous, but they cannot be breathed in too long without ill effect. My head began to swim. I was barely aware of being raised and dragged, or carried, up a wooden ladder. This occurred several times, and I verily believe that but for these intervals I would have been overcome by the effluvium of the excretions of the flying mammals. I had lost all sense of direction, despite my efforts to make a mental map of the path we followed. The passageways formed a veritable maze, designed to confuse tomb robbers as to the location of the king's burial chamber. It succeeded in confusing me, at any rate, but in my defense it must be said that my position was not conducive to clear thinking.

Finally the villain came to a stop. My eyes were streaming with tears from the irritation of the dusty dung. The man bent over me. I did not want him to think I was weeping from fear or weakness, so I blinked the tears away and frowned—that being the only expression of disapprobation available to me at that time. An unpleasant smile spread over his face, which shone like greased mahogany in the dim light. He held the candle in one hand. In the other hand was a long knife, polished to razor sharpness. The light ran in glimmering streaks along the blade.

Two quick slashes, and a sharp shove. . . . I toppled—tried to cry out—fell, helpless and blind, into impenetrable darkness.

An individual who has been kidnapped, bound and gagged, suffocated and tossed into a seemingly bottomless pit in the heart of an unexplored pyramid—that individual is a fool if she is not afraid. I am not a fool. I was terrified. In the Stygian blackness the pit seemed a chasm into infinite depths where the monsters of the abyss lay waiting to devour the bodies and souls of the dead. One part of my frozen brain knew better, of course, but that part was well aware that the bottom of the pit was undoubtedly floored with stone, against which my bones would be broken to splinters.

I now believe the tales of those who claim to have relived their entire lives in the space of a few seconds, for those thoughts and others that do not merit description flashed through my mind in the moments that elapsed before I reached the bottom of the pit. To my astonishment I found it was covered with water. Under the water was mud and under the mud was stone. The presence of the water and the mud broke my fall, though it was hard enough to bruise me and knock the breath clean out of me. Not until I made instinctive swimming motions did I realize that my limbs had been freed. Swimming was unnecessary; the water and underlying slime were scarcely three feet deep. After I had gained my feet my first act was to pluck the gag from my mouth. It was saturated with water and tasted foul, but it had prevented me from swallowing the revolting liquid.

Scarcely had I gained an upright position when I was thrown back into the water by the impact of a heavy object that narrowly missed me and sent a fountain of spray high in the air. Without an instant's hesitation I dropped to my hands and knees and began feeling about. My groping hands encountered a substance that felt like the fur of a drowned animal, slippery with slime and water, but I knew the feel of it, wet or dry, muddy or slimy; and thanking heaven for Emerson's thick, healthy head of hair, I twisted both hands in it and dragged his head up from under the water. The angelic choir will sound no sweeter to me than the sputtering and cursing that told me Emerson was alive and conscious. Presumably the water on his face had brought him around.

His first act, after spitting out the mud that had filled his mouth, was to aim a blow at my jaw. I had expected this, so I was able to avoid it, while announcing my identity in the loudest possible voice.

"Peabody!" Emerson gurgled. "Is it you? Thank God! But where the devil are we?"

"Inside the Black Pyramid, Emerson. Or rather, under it; for though overcome by bat effluvium and other physical inconveniences, I am certain the general direction of the passageway was—"

During my reply Emerson had located my face by feeling around; he put an end to the speech by placing his mouth firmly over mine. He tasted quite nasty, but I did not mind.

Eventually Emerson stopped kissing me and remarked, "Well, Peabody, we are in a pretty fix. The last thing I remember is an explosion somewhere around the base of my skull. I take it you did not have the same experience; or are you merely producing one of your imaginative hypotheses when you claim we are inside the pyramid? I have never been in one that was as wet as this."

"I was gagged and bound, but not unconscious. Emerson, they have found the entrance! It is not on the north side, where de Morgan looked, but at ground level near the southwest corner. No wonder he could not find it." A critical clearing of the throat from the darkness beside me reminded me that I was wandering off the subject, so I went on, "I suspect we are in the burial chamber itself. This pyramid is quite near the cultivation, if you recall; the recent inundation must have flooded the lower sections."

"I don't understand the point of this," Emerson said, in almost his normal voice. "Why did they not murder us? You can, I presume, find the way out."

"I hope so, Emerson. But this is a very confusing pyramid—a maze, one might say. And I was not at my best. The kidnapper dragged me most of the way and my—er—my body kept bumping on the stones, and—"

"Grrr," said Emerson fiercely. "Dragged you, you say? The villain! I will have his liver for that when I catch up with him. Never mind, Peabody; I would back you against any pyramid ever built."

"Thank you, my dear Emerson," I replied with considerable emotion. "First, though, we must have a look at our surroundings."

"I don't see how we are going to manage that, Peabody. Unless you can see in the dark, like the cat Bastet."

"According to Ramses, that is a folktale. Even cats require a small amount of light in order to see, and this darkness is almost palpable. Wait, Emerson, don't go splashing about; I will strike a light."

"All this banging on the posterior has weakened my poor darling's wits," Emerson muttered to himself. "Peabody, you cannot—"

The tiny flame of the match reflected in twin images in his wide eyes. "Hold the box," I instructed. "I need both hands for the candle. There. That is better, is it not?"

Standing in muddy water up to his hips, a purpling bruise disfiguring his brow and another, presumably, rising on the back of his head, Emerson nevertheless managed a broad and cheerful smile. "Never again will I sneer at your beltful of tools, Peabody."

"I am happy to find that the manufacturer's claim of the waterproof quality of the tin box was not exaggerated. We must not take chances with our precious matches; close the box carefully, if you please, and put it in your shirt pocket."

Emerson did so. Then at last we had leisure to look about us.

Our poor little candle flame was almost overcome by the vast gloom of the chamber. It illuminated only our drawn faces and dank, dripping locks. At the farthest edge of the bright circle a dim-looming object could be made out, rising like an island from the watery surface. Toward this we made our way.

"It is the royal sarcophagus," said Emerson unnecessarily. "And it is open. Curse it; we are not the first to find the pharaoh's final resting place, Peabody."

"The lid must be on the—oh dear—yes, it is. I have just stubbed my toe on it."

The red granite sides of the sarcophagus were as high as Emerson's head. Seizing me by the waist, he lifted me so I could perch on the ledgelike rim; it was fully a foot thick and made a commodious if uncomfortable seat.

"Let me have the candle," he said. "I will make a circuit of the walls."

He splashed through the water to the nearer side of the chamber. The walls shone in the candlelight as smoothly as if they had been cut from a single block of stone. My heart sank at the sight of the unbroken surface, but I summoned up a firm voice as I called to Emerson, "Hold the candle higher, my dear; I fell some considerable distance before striking the water."

"No doubt it seemed farther than it was," Emerson replied, but he complied with the suggestion. He had gone around two of the walls and was midway down the third before a darker shadow was visible high above the glow of the light. Emerson held the candle above his head.

He stood still as a statue, which in the dim light he rather resembled. His wet garments molded his muscular body and the candlelight brought the muscles and tendons of his upraised arm into shaded outline. The sight was one that will remain printed on my brain—the solemn grandeur of his pose, the funereal gloom of the surroundings—and the knowledge that the opening of the shaft which was our only hope of escape was far out of reach. Emerson is six feet tall; I am five feet and a bit. The hole was a good sixteen feet from the floor.

Emerson knew the truth as well as I. It was several moments before he lowered his arm and returned to my side. "I make it sixteen feet," he said calmly.

"It is nearer seventeen, surely."

"Five feet one inch and six feet—add the length of your arms—"

"And subtract the distance from the top of my head to my shoulders. . . ." In spite of the gravity of the situation I burst out laughing, the calculations sounded so absurd.

Emerson joined in, the echoes of his hearty mirth rebounding ghostily around the chamber. "We may as well try it, Peabody."

We had neglected to deduct the distance from the top of his head to his shoulders. When I stood upon the latter, my fingertips were a good three feet below the lip of the opening. I reported this to Emerson. "Humph," he said thoughtfully. "Supposing you stood on top of my head?"

"That would only give us another twelve or thirteen inches, Emerson. Not nearly enough."

His hands closed over my ankles. "I will lift you at arms' length, Peabody. Can you keep your knees rigid and maintain your balance by leaning toward the wall?"

"Certainly, my dear. When I was a child my highest ambition was to be an acrobat in a fair. Are you sure you can do it?"

"You are a mere feather, my dear Peabody. And if you can be an acrobat, I can aspire to the position of circus strongman. Who knows, if we ever tire of archaeology we can turn to another profession."

"Slowly, please, my dear."

"But of course, Peabody."

I believe I have had occasion to mention Emerson's impressive muscular development, but never before had I realized the full extent of his strength. A gasp escaped my lips when I felt nothing but empty air under the soles of my boots, but my initial trepidation was quickly succeeded by a thrill of pure excitement. I heard Emerson's breath catch and fancied I could almost hear his muscles crack. Slowly I rose higher. It was like flying—one of the most interesting experiences I have ever had.

I was afraid to tilt my head back in order to look up; the slightest movement might have destroyed the precarious balance Emerson and I were maintaining between us. When the upward movement finally ceased, there was nothing under my outstretched hands but the same cold, smooth stone. Emerson let out an inquiring grunt. I looked up.

"Three inches, Emerson. Can you—"

"Ugh," Emerson said decidedly.

"Lower me, then. We shall have to think of something else."

Going down was considerably less pleasant than going up. It was not only the consciousness of failure that weakened my knees, it was the ominous quivering of the arms that supported me. When my feet once more found secure footing on the brawny shoulders of my heroic spouse I leaned against the wall and let out a deep breath. It was as well I did so, for one of Emerson's hands lost its grip and I feared we were both going to topple over backwards.

"Sorry, Peabody," he said, taking a firmer hold. "Cramp."

"Small wonder, my dear Emerson. Don't bother to lower me, I will just let myself down bit by bit."

Somehow he found strength enough to laugh. "I will play Saint Christopher and carry you back to the sarcophagus. Sit on my shoulders."

After he had returned me to my seat he hoisted himself up beside me. We sat side by side, our feet dangling till Emerson got his breath back. "Have you still got the matchbox, Emerson?" I asked.

"You may be sure I have, Peabody. That little tin box is more precious to us now than gold."

"Let me have it, then, and I will button it into my shirt pocket. Then, if you agree, I will blow out the candle. I only have the one, you see."

He nodded, his face somber. The dark closed in upon us, but I did not mind; Emerson's arm was around me and my head rested on his shoulder. For some time we did not speak. Then a sepulchral voice remarked, "We will die in one another's arms, Peabody."

He seemed to find this thought consoling. "Nonsense, my dear Emerson," I said briskly. "Do not abandon hope. We have not yet begun to fight, as one of our heroes said."

"I believe it was an American hero who said it, Peabody."

"Irrelevant, my dear Emerson. It is the spirit of pluck I mean to conjure up."

"But when I die, Peabody, I would like the condition I mentioned to prevail."

"And I, my dearest Emerson. But I have no intention of dying for a long time. Let us turn our brains to the problem and see if we can't think of a way out."

"There is always the possibility of rescue," Emerson said.

"You need not attempt to raise my spirits by false hopes, Emerson. To be sure, I did wonder why our kidnappers would carry us here instead of murdering us outright; but they knew our chance of escape was almost nil. They won't come back. As for rescue from anyone else—to the best of my knowledge, no archaeologist has succeeded in locating the entrance. The villains will have filled in the hole they dug; do you suppose de Morgan can find it? He has no reason to look, for even after our disappearance is discovered, no one will think of searching for us here."

"De Morgan is certainly the least likely person to find an entrance to a pyramid," Emerson agreed. He added, "Peabody, I adore you and I meant it when I said I would not be averse to dying in your arms, but you do have a habit of running on and on, which is particularly trying at a time like this."

My dear Emerson was trying to cheer me with that teasing comment; I gave him an affectionate squeeze to show I understood. "Be that as it may," I said, "we had better not depend on outside help. What we need is something to stand on. A mere three inches shall not defeat us, Emerson."

"We can't move the sarcophagus. It must weigh half a ton."

"More, I fancy. And the cover is probably several hundred pounds in weight. But there may be other objects in the chamber, hidden under the mud. An alabaster canopic chest or cosmetic box—anything made of stone. Wooden objects would be rotted by time and immersion."

"We will have a look," Emerson agreed. "But first let us ascertain whether there are any other possibilities."

"Another entrance, for instance? That is certainly something we must investigate. A pity the ceiling is so high. It will be hard to see a crack or crevice, with only a candle for light."

"At any rate, we know there is no opening at floor level. Had that been the case, the water would have drained out."

Silence followed, as we bent our mind to the problem. Then Emerson chuckled. "This will do Petrie one in the eye," he said vulgarly. "He ran into something of the same sort at Hawara, if you remember. You know how he brags endlessly of how he cleared the chamber of the pyramid by sloshing around underwater and shoving things onto a hoe with his bare toes."

"He found a number of fine objects," I said. "The alabaster altar of Princess Ptahneferu—"

"Something of that nature would make an admirable box on which to stand."

"Alabaster dishes and bowls. . . . Only think, Emerson, what we might find here."

"Don't let archaeological fever get the better of you, Peabody. Even if . . . Even when we get out of here, we will not have the right to excavate. It is de Morgan's pyramid, not ours."

"He can't object if we make a few discoveries while seeking a means of escape. That is our main purpose, is it not—escape?"

"Oh, certainly," Emerson agreed.

"I fear the writing implements attached to my belt have been rendered useless by the water. My pocket rule is functional, however; we will have to make mental notes of the location of anything we might find. That should not be difficult."

"You are a remarkable woman, Peabody. Few individuals, male or female, could think about antiquities while engaged in a struggle for survival."

"Your approbation pleases me more than I can say, Emerson. May I return the compliment?"

"Thank you, my dear Peabody. We will return to that subject later in—let us hope—more salubrious surroundings. Now, before you light the candle, let us be sure we have our strategy clearly in mind."

I was about to reply when I saw something that made me wonder if my brain was not beginning to weaken. It was only the faintest suggestion of light; but in that dank darkness, so thick it seemed to press against one's staring eyeballs, even a natural phenomenon carries sinister suggestions. The pale glow strengthened. It came from high in the wall—from the opening of the corridor. I pinched Emerson.

"Look," I hissed.

"I see it," he replied in equally subdued tones. "Quick, Peabody, down into the water."

He slid off the sarcophagus. With his assistance I followed suit. "Is it the villains returning, do you think?" I breathed.

"It can be no one else. Get behind the sarcophagus, Peabody. Keep out of sight and don't make a sound."

I heard the soft susurration of the water as he waded slowly away from me. There was no need for him to explain; my dear Emerson and I understand one another without words. The criminals had returned to make sure we were deceased, or to taunt us in our agony; if they saw no trace of us, they might be moved to descend, in order to search for our bodies. There was a slight hope of escape in that, if they lowered a rope or a rope ladder, and Emerson could seize it. I crouched low behind the shelter of the great stone box, braced and ready for whatever action suggested itself.

The opening was now a glowing yellow. Something showed silhouetted against the light. I could not see Emerson, but I knew he was pressed against the wall, under the shaft. My fingers closed around the handle of my knife.

Then occurred the most astonishing event of that astonishing evening. A voice spoke—a voice I knew, pronouncing a name only one individual in all the world employs for me. So great was my wonderment that I stood erect, banging my head painfully on the rim of the sarcophagus; and in that same instant, as I reeled and tried to collect my wits, the light went out, a voice shouted in alarm and horror, and something splashed heavily into the water not far away.

My initial impulse was to rush into action. But reason prevailed, as I hope it always does with me. I knew from the sounds of splashing, cursing and heavy breathing that Emerson was doing all he could to locate the fallen object; my intervention would only impede his search. My first act, therefore, was to strike a match and light the candle, which I anchored carefully in a pool of its own grease on the wide rim of the sarcophagus. Then and only then did I look to see whether Emerson's quest had been successful.

He had risen from the water. In his arms was a muddy, dripping object. It moved; it was living. I groped for appropriate words.

"Ramses," I said. "I thought I told you you were never to go into any more pyramids."

Chapter Eleven

"YOU said I might go in if you and Papa were wit' me," said Ramses.
"So I did. Your reasoning is Jesuitical, Ramses; I see we will have to have a talk about it one day. However . . ." I stopped. Had Ramses emphasized, ever so slightly, the preposition "in"? As I explained earlier, the chambers and passages of pyramids are sometimes internal, sometimes subterranean. Surely not even Ramses' diabolically devious mind would be capable of a distinction so Machiavellian. . . . I promised myself I must explore that suspicion at a more appropriate time.

"However," I resumed, "I appreciate your motives, Ramses, and—Emerson, will you please put the boy down and stop babbling?"

Emerson interrupted his mumbled endearments. "I cannot put him down, Peabody. His mouth would be underwater."

"That is true. Fetch him here, then. He can sit on the sarcophagus."

I kept a precautionary hand on the candle when Ramses was set down beside it. He was a dreadful spectacle. A coating of dark mud covered him from head to foot. But I had seen him looking worse, and the bright eyes that peered at me from the mask of slime were alert and steady.

"As I was saying, Ramses, I appreciate your motives in coming to our rescue, as I suppose you intended. But I must point out that jumping into the pit with us was not helpful."

"I did not jump, Mama, I slipped. I brought a rope, t'inking dere would be some point of attachment in de passageway by means of which I might be able to—"

"I follow your reasoning, Ramses. But if the rope is, as I suppose, down here with you, it cannot be of great assistance."

"Dat was an unfortunate mishap," Ramses admitted.

"My boy, my boy," Emerson said mournfully. "I had consoled myself with the expectation that you would carry on the name of Emerson to glory and scientific achievement. Now we will all perish in one another's—"

"Please, Emerson," I said. "We have already discussed that. I don't suppose it occurred to you, Ramses, to fetch help instead of rushing in where angels fear to tread?"

"I was in some haste and concerned for your safety," said Ramses, swinging his feet and dripping. "However, I did leave a message."

"With whom?" Emerson asked hopefully.

"Well, you see, de circumstances were confusing," Ramses said calmly. "I had followed you when you slipped out of de house—I debated wit' myself for some little time before doing so, but could not recall, Mama, dat you had specifically forbidden me to follow you and Papa when you slipped out of de—"

"Good Gad," I said helplessly.

"Pray don't interrupt the boy, Peabody," Emerson said. "His narrative may yet contain information of practical interest to us in our present situation. Skip over your struggles with your conscience, Ramses, if you please; you may take it that for now there will be no recriminations."

"T'ank you, Papa. I was not far away, in concealment, when de men struck you and captured Mama. I could not go for help at dat time since it was expedient dat I discover where dey were taking you. Nor could I abandon you after you were dragged into de substructure of de pyramid, for I feared dey might dispatch you fort'wit'. Dere was only time for me to snatch up a coil of rope from de equipment dey had brought wit' dem, and scribble a brief message, before I followed."

"The message, Ramses," I said between my teeth. "Where did you leave the message?"

"I tied it to de collar of de cat Bastet."

"To de collar of de—"

"She had accompanied me, of course. I could hardly leave it lying on de ground, Mama," Ramses added in an injured tone—my comment, though brief, had admittedly held a note of criticism. "Even if it was not found by de villains, its chances of being discovered by someone would have been slight in de extreme."

"Do you mean," Emerson demanded, "that you have been inside the pyramid all this time? How did you elude the criminals when they returned?"

"And why did it take you so long to reach this place?" I added.

Ramses settled himself more comfortably. "Bot' questions will be answered if you will allow me to proceed wit' de narrative in an orderly fashion. I heard splashes, and surmised dat dey had t'rown you into de burial chamber. I also heard Papa cry out, which relieved my anxiety as to his survival. When de men came back I had to hide in one of de side passages. Dese passages are not all in good condition, as you may perhaps have observed. De route used by de criminals has been shored up by timbers, but some of de side passages are less secure. De one I selected, *faute de mieux,* I might add, collapsed. I was some time extricating myself."

"Good heavens," Emerson gasped. "My dear child—"

"You have not heard de worst, Papa. Upon reaching de main passage again I decided to return to de outside world and summon assistance. You may imagine my consternation when I discovered dat de way was blocked—deliberately, I believe, by the removal of the timbers that had supported de stones lining de passage. Dere was not'ing for it but return to you, but it took some little time owing to de state of perturbation dat afflicted me and de fact dat, because of dis emotional disability, I had forgotten dat, in emulation of Mama's admirable custom, I always carry wit' me a box of matches and a candle, among oder useful equipment. But I fear I lost dem when I fell into de water."

For once Ramses had succeeded in finishing a statement without being interrupted. It was less diffuse than usual, though it might certainly have profited by judicious editing. However, my silence was the result of considerable emotion. It appeared we were doomed, unless the message tied to the cat's collar was found before she chewed it off or lost it. Among other emotions—I confess it without shame—was maternal pride. Ramses had displayed the qualities I might have expected from a descendant of the Emersons and the Peabodys. I might even have told him so had not Emerson begun showering him with profuse compliments. Ramses' smug look as he sat there swinging his legs convinced me he had had quite enough commendation.

"You have done well, Ramses, but it is necessary to do better," I said. "We must get out of this chamber."

"Why?" Emerson inquired. "If the passage is blocked, we can't get out of the pyramid."

"For one thing, it is very damp here. Without a flannel belt, which you refuse to wear, there is the danger of catarrh."

"The danger of having one of the passageways fall in on us strikes me as more life-threatening, Peabody. We will be safer here, while we await rescue."

"We may wait a long time, Emerson. The cat Bastet will eventually return to the house, no doubt, but Ramses' note may be lost before then."

"And also," Ramses added, "if we wish to apprehend de miscreants, we cannot wait. Dey are planning to leave at dawn. I heard dem say so."

"But if the passage is blocked—"

"Dere is anodder way out, Papa."

"I beg your pardon, Ramses?"

"It leads to a vestibule beside de pyramid containing several subsidiary tombs of members of de royal family. It was de means by which I originally entered dis pyramid. And," Ramses added hastily, "if Mama will allow me to postpone de explanation of dat circumstance until a more propitious moment, we would be better employed in ascertaining whedder dat entrance is still open."

"Quite right, my boy." Emerson squared his shoulders and flexed his biceps. "Our first problem, then, is to find some object on which to stand. Your mama and I were about to begin that search when you—er—joined us."

"No, Emerson," I said. "We must first find the rope Ramses so carelessly let fall."

"But, Peabody—"

"Think, Emerson. We lacked, initially, three feet of height. Here is an object over three feet long." I indicated Ramses, who returned my gaze with an owlish stare.

"Ha!" Emerson cried. The echoes repeated the syllable in an eerie imitation of laughter. "Correct as always, my dear Peabody."

Ramses' offer of diving to look for the rope was unanimously refused. It did not take Emerson long to locate it. The rope, tied in a coil, had fallen straight down from the opening and sunk to the bottom of the mud, from which Emerson finally drew it. We could not dry it, but we rinsed off the worst of the slime, which would render it slippery and dangerous to climb. Then we once more formed our human ladder, with Ramses at the top. The procedure was almost laughably easy now. Ramses swarmed up our bodies with the agility of a monkey. Once his hands had closed over the rim of the hole, I was able to assist him by pushing on the most conveniently located portion of his anatomy, and he was soon in the passage.

It was then necessary for us to wait while Ramses lit the candle and attempted to locate some protruding stub of stone around which the rope could be tied; for it was clearly impossible for him to support my weight. This was the part of the business that worried me most. Given the decaying condition of the interior stonework, there was a danger that the wall might give way if excessive strain were put upon any of the stones that lined it. Unlike the larger pyramids of Dahshoor, this later structure was not built of stone throughout, but of brick faced with stone. The shapelessness of the exterior demonstrated what could happen when the facing stones were removed.

I could hear the boy moving cautiously along the passage and was happy to note that he was taking his time in selecting a suitable support. Glad as I was to be leaving the burial chamber, I was somewhat disappointed that Emerson and I had been foiled in our hopes of exploring that room. We would never have the chance now.

Ramses finally announced that he had located a protruding stone he considered suitable. "It won't stand much strain, Mama," he called. "You will have to be quick."

The section of rope that hung beside me twitched and wriggled, for all the world like a snake. Breathing a wordless prayer to whatever Deity guides our ends I seized the rope. Emerson flung me up as high as he could manage. For one long moment I hung supported only by the frail strand between my hands. I felt the line sag ominously; then my boot found a purchase, slight but sufficient, against the wall; my left hand closed over the edge of the opening; and after a brief but exciting scramble I drew myself into (temporary) safety.

I announced my success to Ramses and Emerson, both of whom replied with suitable congratulations. "You may give me the candle now, Ramses," I said.

He dropped it, of course. After I had retrieved it, and the matches, I struck a light and turned to examine the support he had found.

It was not an encouraging sight. Several of the stones in the lower portion of the wall had buckled under the pressure of the bricks beyond. Around one of the protruding edges Ramses had looped the rope—*faute de mieux,* as he might have said, for there was nothing else that would serve. I had depended on the rope as little as possible, but Emerson would have to use it for most of his ascent, and his weight was considerably greater than mine. There was a distinct possibility that the loosened block might be pulled completely out by the strain, which would not only precipitate Emerson back into the water but would bring the wall toppling down. I seriously considered asking him to remain below until we could fetch help. The only reason I did not do so was because I knew he would become bored with waiting and try to climb the rope anyway. He is not and has never been a patient man.

"I am coming up, Peabody," he shouted.

"Just a moment, Emerson." I sat down on the floor with my back against the loosened block and my feet braced against the opposite wall. "Ramses," I said. "Proceed along the passage, around the next corner."

I fully expected another of those eternal "But, Mama"s. Instead Ramses said quietly, "Very well," and went trotting off. I waited until he was out of sight and then called to Emerson to proceed.

The ensuing moments were not among the most comfortable I have undergone. As I had feared, Emerson's tugging and jerking of the rope had a deleterious effect on the block that held it, and though I pressed against the stone with every ounce of strength I possessed, it outweighted me by some six hundred pounds. The cursed thing gave a centimeter or so every time Emerson's hands took a fresh hold on the rope, and it made an obscene groaning sound as it rubbed against the adjoining surface. The softest, gentlest touch on my hand, which was pressed against the floor, almost brought a cry to my lips—but, I hope I need not add, that cry was suppressed before it found utterance. The touch was that of sand—the crumbled substance of ancient mud brick—trickling slowly and horribly from the widening crack.

It seemed hours before I finally saw his shaggy, slime-smeared head appear at the opening. By that time the pressure of the stone against my back had raised my knees to an acute angle from the floor. I was afraid to speak aloud; it seemed as if the slightest vibration would push the block past the delicate point on which it hung balanced.

"Emerson," I whispered. "Don't delay an instant, but follow me. On hands and knees, if you please, and with the most felicitous combination of speed and delicacy of movement."

Once again I had reason to bless the unity of spirit that binds my husband and me. Without question he at once obeyed. I abandoned my strained position and with aching back and pounding heart crawled ahead of him down the passage. When we turned the corner and reached the place where Ramses was waiting, I felt it was safe to stop for a brief rest.

If this were a sensational novel instead of an autobiography, I would report that the wall collapsed just as we scrambled to safety. However, it did not. I remain convinced that the peril was imminent, despite the assurances of those who examined the spot later and insisted that the stone would have moved no farther.

But to resume. Like the preceding section, this part of the passageway was lined with blocks of limestone. It was barely four feet high. Even Ramses had to duck his head. I wiped my bleeding hands on my trousers, tucked my shirtwaist in, and tidied my hair, which had been sadly disarranged. "Lead on, Ramses," I said. "That is—are you fully recovered, Emerson?"

"I may never fully recover," said Emerson, still prone. "But I am ready to go on. First let me retrieve the rope. We may need it."

"No! We must do without the rope, Emerson. It is a miracle the wall has not collapsed. I won't let you go back there."

"A rope will not be required," said Ramses. "At least . . . I hope it will not."

With that doubtful assurance we had to be content.

There were several places in which we might have made good use of a rope, for the ancient architects had used every trick they could think of to foil grave robbers, from gaping pits in the floor to concealed entrances high in the walls. Fortunately for us, the long-dead thieves had been shrewder than the architects. I never believed I would think kindly of these ghouls who had looted the treasures buried with the pharaohs, foiling modern archaeologists in their quest for knowledge; but as I scrambled around a huge portcullis stone, through the narrow tunnel dug by the invaders of the pyramid, I blessed their greedy and ambitious souls.

I also blessed Ramses' uncanny sense of direction. The maze-like corridors and chambers turned and twisted, some ending in blind alleys, but he led us unerringly toward his goal. "I believe we can assume that these complex substructures are typical of Twelfth Dynasty pyramids," I remarked to Emerson, as we crawled along single-file. "This example resembles the one at Hawara that Petrie explored in '87."

"It seems a reasonable assumption," was the reply. "I suspect our pyramid is of the same period, so it will probably have a similar substructure. A pity we have not been able to find an inscription naming the pharaoh for whom it was built."

"We may yet find it, Emerson. I think this must be earlier than ours. It is more sturdily built—"

At this point I was struck smartly on the head by a mass of mixed mud brick and sand falling from a gap in the ceiling and had to save my breath for moving more rapidly. Emerson also quickened his pace, and we did not resume our conversation until we had gone a little distance.

It may seem strange to some that we should carry on a scholarly discussion at a time when our sole preoccupation should have been bent toward escape from deadly peril. Yet the act of crawling does not in itself engage all the critical faculties, and what better way to pass the time than in conversation? Archaeological passion burns brightly in our family, thank heaven, and I sincerely trust that my penultimate breath will be employed in speculating on the latest Egyptological theories. The ultimate breath, I hardly need say, will be reserved for the affectionate descendants who stand by my couch.

The fall of rubble that raised another lump on my aching head was not the only such peril we had to contend with. In several places the stone lining of the corridor had given way. One place was almost completely blocked, with only a narrow tunnel through at one side of the fallen stones. Ramses became very quiet at this point—he had been lecturing us about the construction of Middle Kingdom pyramids—and looked even more enigmatic than usual as we carefully widened the tunnel to permit our larger bodies to pass. I said nothing; I had determined to reserve my remarks on his mendacious behavior until after the other criminals had been dealt with.

Except for such occurrences and Ramses' falling into a pit (from which Emerson drew him up by means of my waist flannel—proving once again the usefulness of this article of dress), we had no real difficulty until we reached the end of our underground journey. A long, straight passageway led into a sizable chamber cut in the rock. It, too, had been robbed in antiquity (at least I assumed so at the time); for it contained nothing but an empty stone sarcophagus. Here at last we were able to stand upright, and Ramses directed Emerson to hold his candle up toward the roof.

One of the stones was missing. "It is de opening of de shaft from de surface," said Ramses. "De depth is not great—twelve feet eight inches, to be precise. My only concern is dat de stone I placed atop de surface opening of de shaft may be too heavy for Papa to move. It took bot' Selim and Hassan to put it dere."

I promised myself an interview with Selim and Hassan later. "What do you think, Emerson?" I asked.

Emerson's fingers rasped across his unshaven chin. "I can but try, Peabody. After all we have been through I don't mean to let a mere stone stop me."

The shaft was so narrow he could climb by bracing his back against one side and his feet against another—chimney climbing, I believe the process is called. It was an awkward position from which to exert pressure on a considerable weight, and Emerson's grunts and groans testified to the effort he was putting forth. "Try sliding it to one side instead of lifting it, Emerson," I called.

"What the devil do you think I am doing?" was the reply. "It is hard to get a grip on the cursed thing. . . . Ah, there. I believe—"

His speech was interrupted by a shower of sand, some of which sprinkled my upturned face. The bulk of it, unfortunately, fell full on Emerson's head. I have seldom heard such a rich wealth of invective, even from Emerson. "You should have kept your mouth closed, my dear," I said. "——— ——— ———," said Emerson.

"I had to spread sand on de stone," Ramses explained, "in order to conceal de location of de—"

A positive avalanche of sand and pebbles put an end to this inapropos remark. Emerson continued to curse inventively as he put his back into his task; no doubt mental irritability and physical discomfort gave him additional strength. At last the downpour slowed to a trickle. "Look out below," Emerson cried grittily. "I am coming down."

He descended with a rush and a thud. The candle flame quivered in my hand as I contemplated him; sand coated every inch of his body, sticking to the perspiration and slimy water. From the stony mask of his face two red-rimmed eyes blazed blue sparks.

"Oh, my dear," I said sympathetically. "Let me bathe your eyes. This little flask of water, which I always carry with me . . ."

Emerson's tightly pressed lips parted. He spat out a mouthful of mud and remarked, "Not now, Peabody. I feel my usually equable temper beginning to fray. You first. Let me give you a hand up."

He assisted me into the mouth of the shaft. It was not the first time in our adventures I had ascended a narrow fissure in such a fashion, but for a moment I was unable to move. A few feet above me was a square of deep-blue velvet strewn with sparkling gems. It looked so close I felt I could reach up and touch it. My shaken mind refused to recognize it for what it was—the night sky, which I had wondered if I would ever see again.

Then a querulous question from Emerson, below, reminded me of my objective, and I began my final labor. Not until I lay at full length upon the hard desert floor, with the night breeze cooling my flushed face, did I fully realize our dreadful ordeal was over.

I raised my head. Three feet away, silent in the moonlight, an amber statue sat motionless, staring at me with slitted eyes. So might the ancient goddess of love and beauty welcome a devotee after his journey through the perilous paths of the underworld.

The cat Bastet and I communed in silence. There was considerable criticism in my mind, mild curiosity in hers, to judge by the placidity of her expression. She tilted her head inquiringly. I snapped, "He will be with you in a moment."

Ramses soon emerged. His fingers and toes found purchases in the stones of the shaft I had not even seen. When I dragged him out, the cat Bastet mewed and trotted to him. She began busily licking his head, spitting irritably between licks. After Emerson had pulled himself from the shaft he shook himself like a large dog. Sand flew in all directions.

The ruined mound of the Black Pyramid rose up beside us. We were on its north side. To the west, calm in the starlight, stood the silver slopes of the Bent Pyramid, with its more conventional neighbor visible farther north. Silence and peace brooded over the scene. Eastward, where the village of Menyat Dahshoor lay amid the palm groves and tilled fields, there was not a light to be seen. It must be late; but not so late as I had feared, for the eastern sky still waited in darkness for the coming of dawn.

The cat Bastet had given up her attempt to clean Ramses. She was an intelligent animal and had no doubt realized that only prolonged immersion would have the desired effect. The same had to be said about Ramses' parents. Emerson looked like a crumbling sandstone statue, and as for myself . . . I decided not to think about it.

I reached for the cat. A ragged scrap of paper was still attached to her collar. "Half of the note is still here," I said. "It is just as well we decided not to wait to be rescued."

"Furder training would seem to be indicated," said Ramses. "I had only begun dis aspect of de program, since I had no reason to anticipate dat an emergency would—"

"We have a good three-mile walk ahead of us," Emerson interrupted. "Let us be off."

"Are you up to it, Emerson? We are closer to Menyat Dahshoor; perhaps we ought to arouse de Morgan and request his assistance. He could supply us with donkeys and men."

"Be honest, Peabody—you are no more keen than I to go crawling to de Morgan for help."

"But, my dear, you must be tired."

Emerson thumped himself on the chest. "I have never felt better. The air is like wine, particularly after the noisome substitute for air we have been breathing. But you, my dear Peabody—perhaps you ought to go to Dahshoor. You are shivering."

"I will not leave you, Emerson. Where you go, I go."

"I expected you would say that," Emerson replied, his sandy mask cracking in a fond smile. "Excelsior, then. Ramses, put down the cat and Papa will carry you."

The assorted bruises and aches that had stiffened as we stood talking were soon forgotten. Brisk walking warmed us and the pleasures of familial intimacy were never more keenly felt. Had I not been anxious to come to grips with the villains who had attempted to exterminate us, I might have wished that stroll to be prolonged.

Our plans were soon made. They were simple: to collect our loyal men and procure a fresh supply of firearms (my pistol, being choked with mud, was unusable) before proceeding to the village to arrest the Master Criminal.

"We must catch him unawares," I said. "He is desperate and may be armed."

"He?" Emerson said. "Miss Charity is not your choice for the role?"

I had had time to revise my first hasty impression, so I replied, "We never saw the face of the elusive figure, Emerson. Any young person, male or female, could have worn Charity's dress, and that unfashionable bonnet concealed the person's features as effectively as a mask could do. Nor does the message I received incriminate her, for I have never seen her handwriting. Anyone could have written that note."

"Not anyone, Peabody."

"Correct, Emerson. If the note was a forgery, as I believe, it could only have been penned by Brother Ezekiel or Brother David."

"Which have you settled on?" Emerson asked.

We were now so close to concluding the case that further equivocation seemed futile. "Brother Ezekiel, of course," I said.

"I disagree. Brother David."

"You only choose him because you dislike his manners."

"People who live in glass houses, Peabody. You have a weakness for pretty young men with smooth tongues. Whereas Brother Ezekiel—"

"All the clues point to him, Emerson."

"Quite the contrary, Peabody. They point to Brother David."

"Would you care to explicate, Emerson?"

"Not just at present, Peabody. There are one or two minor questions to be resolved. What about you?"

"I am also undecided about a few exceedingly unimportant details, Emerson."

So the discussion ended. Ramses' attempt to offer his views was rejected by mutual consent, and we went on in silence. It was fortunate that we did. Sounds carry some distance in the desert, and we were close to the house when Emerson, who had been casting increasingly anxious glances about, came to a sudden stop.

"Ramses," he said softly, "did you leave a light in your room?"

"No, Papa."

"Nor did we. Look."

Two squares of yellow broke the darkness of the house. Emerson took my arm and pulled me to the ground. Ramses slipped from his shoulders and crouched beside us.

"John may have discovered Ramses' absence and be looking for him," I suggested.

"In utter silence? And where is Abdullah? I have an uneasy feeling about this, Peabody."

"I think I see Abdullah—there, to the left of the door. He seems to be asleep."

I half rose, for a better look. Emerson held me down.

Around the corner of the wall, from the direction of the ruined church, came a dark and ghostly shape. Flitting from shadow to deeper shadow, it passed the sleeping form of Abdullah and vanished into the house.

I reminded myself that bare feet on sand make no sound, and that most of the villagers wore dark robes. If Abdullah had seen the form, he would have been certain that the spirit of one of the murdered monks had returned.

On hands and knees we crept forward. The huddled form was indeed that of our loyal reis; he did not stir, even when Emerson shook him gently. It was with a sense of infinite relief that I heard Emerson say, "Drugged. Hashish, from the smell of it. He'll be none the worse in the morning."

In the same whisper I said, "Do we assume our other men are in the same condition?"

"Or worse," was the grim reply. "Give me your pistol, Peabody."

"You dare not fire it, Emerson. The mud—"

"I know. I can only bluff. Will you stay here?"

"No, Emerson, I will not."

"Then Ramses must be the lookout." Turning to the boy he went on, "You understand, Ramses, that if your mama and I do not succeed in overpowering the intruders, you will have to go for help."

"But, Papa—"

My nerves were a trifle strained. I seized Ramses by his thin shoulders and shook him till his teeth rattled. "You heard your papa. Wait fifteen minutes. If we have not summoned you by then, set out for Dahshoor as fast as you can go. And if you say one word, Mama will slap you."

Ramses scuttled off into concealment without so much as a "Yes, Mama." Like me, he is a literal-minded person.

"Really, Peabody, must you be so brusque?" Emerson inquired. "The lad has performed prodigies of devotion and skill tonight; some slight show of appreciation—"

"Will be rendered at the proper time and in the proper manner. Ramses knows I am not emotional. He does not expect it. Now, Emerson, let us not waste any more time. What the devil can they be doing in Ramses' room?"

Whatever it was, they were still at it when we reached the courtyard. The door of Ramses' room stood open, and we could hear voices. Obviously they did not fear interruption. Our men must be prisoners, as Emerson had suggested. And John—what had they done with poor John?

We moved noiselessly, close to the wall, until we stood behind the door, which opened out into the courtyard. Concealed behind it, Emerson applied his eye to the crack. I followed suit, on a lower level.

We could see one end of the room—the table that served Ramses as a desk, the screened window, the cage containing the lion cub, and the lower part of the bed, which had been overturned. Blankets and sheets lay in a tumbled heap. There were two men visible, both wearing the dark-blue turbans customary in the village. No, they did not fear interruption; not only had they left the door wide open but they were making a considerable amount of noise. The sounds of voices uttering expletives indicative of frustration and anger were interspersed with the crashes of the objects they overturned in their search and by the frantic yelps and growls of the lion. One of the men kicked the cage in passing. I ground my teeth. Nothing angers me so much as cruelty to an animal.

My hand closed over the handle of my parasol. We had no other weapon; our pistols were in our bedchamber, which was also occupied by the uninvited visitors. Fortunately I had left the parasol in the parlor the night before. I stood on tiptoe and applied my mouth to Emerson's ear. "There are only two of them," I breathed. "Now, Emerson?"

"Now."

I am sure our attack would have been a complete success had not Emerson got in my way. There was a little confusion in the doorway, as both of us tried to enter at once. By the time I regained my feet, and my parasol, I was distressed to note that one of the men was pointing a pistol at us.

His features were vaguely familiar. I thought I had seen him among the "deacons" who served the priest. The other man was a complete stranger, and when he spoke I recognized the Cairene accent.

"You are hard to kill, O Father of Curses. Shall we see if a bullet can do what burial alive could not?"

As if in response the little lion gave a piercing wail. The other villain gave the cage a vicious kick.

Then a voice replied to what I had believed to be a rhetorical question. It came from the end of the room we had not been able to see and it spoke the purest classical Arabic-Egyptian. "There will be no killing unless Emerson leaves us no choice. And do not kick the cage. Did not the Prophet cut off his sleeve rather than disturb his sleeping cat?"

The speaker stepped forward into the illumination cast by the lamp on the table. Dark turban, black robe, black beard—and the features of Father Girgis of the church of Sitt Miriam.

In my astonishment I almost let my parasol fall from my hand. "You? You are the Master Criminal?"

He laughed and replied, in English as unaccented as his Arabic had been, "A melodramatic term, Mrs. Emerson. I am only the chairman of a business organization with whose operations you and your family have been interfering."

Hands raised, eyes watchful, Emerson said calmly, "You speak excellent English. Is that, by any chance, your nationality?"

The "priest" smiled. "I speak most of the European languages with equal facility. Speculate, Professor—speculate! You are a determined pair of busybodies. If you had kept out of my way, you would not be in danger."

"I suppose tossing us into a pyramid and sealing the entrance was not dangerous," I said tartly.

"I would have taken steps to ensure your release once we had left the region, Mrs. Emerson. Murder is not my business."

"What of the priest of Dronkeh? I am sure the Patriarch in Cairo has no idea that his local representative has been replaced. What have you done with the poor man?"

A flash of white teeth broke the blackness of that extraordinary beard. "The dear old gentleman is an honored prisoner. He is learning first-hand of the worldly pleasures he has abjured. I assure you, the only dangers he faces are spiritual."

"And Hamid?"

A spark glimmered darkly in the deep-set eyes. "I would have executed the traitor, yes. But I did not. Another's vengeance reached him before mine."

"You don't expect me to believe that, I hope?"

"Amelia," said my husband, "there is surely no profit in annoying this— er—this gentleman."

"It doesn't matter, Professor. I don't care whether Mrs. Emerson believes me or not. I am here on business. I was looking for a certain item. . . ."

"That?" I raised my parasol to point, and both the Copts (or pseudo-

Copts) jumped. Their leader swore at them. Then he answered my question.

"I am not such a fool as to waste my time over a fragment of Coptic manuscript, Mrs. Emerson. No. I came for this."

He drew the box from the breast of his robe and removed the lid.

Lamplight caressed the gleaming gold and the soft glow of turquoise, the royal blue of lapis lazuli, the red-orange of carnelian. I caught my breath. "The Twelfth Dynasty pectoral!"

"Another Twelfth Dynasty pectoral," the priest corrected. "With its necklace of gold and carnelian beads, and a set of matching bracelets. The parure of a princess of the Middle Kingdom, hidden so well under the floor of her tomb that it escaped the tomb robbers who looted her mummy. It is the second such cache we have found at Dahshoor, Mrs. Emerson, and were it not for that interfering brat your son, we would perhaps have found others. He has been digging around all the Dahshoor pyramids for the past weeks. One of my men was watching when he found the princess's tomb and removed these ornaments, but we refrained from repossessing them because we hoped he would abandon his pursuits and leave us to go on with our work in peace. That hope has not been realized. You spoil the child, Mrs. Emerson; how many boys of that age are allowed to excavate on their own?"

I was about to reply when I saw something that made my blood run cold. It was a face, pressed against the barred window, and set in a hideous grimace. I might not have recognized it, had it not been for the nasal appendage that protruded into the space between two bars. Ramses!

The priest went on. "Such, however, are the unavoidable vicissitudes of my profession. Now I must beg you to excuse me. I must notify the men who are searching your room that the objects I wanted have been found. This, then, is farewell. I trust we may not meet again."

He strode toward the door.

His men watched him go. Emerson's back was to the window. I was the only one who saw the framework of wooden bars shiver and give way. Silently it swung out—and then I knew how Ramses had come and gone by night without being observed. I was helpless. I could not order him away without calling attention to his presence. I could only avert my eyes and plan the indignities I hoped to perpetrate upon his person.

Neither Emerson nor I had replied to that last taunt, though I knew the same thought was in both our minds: "We will meet again, never fear; for I will make it my business to hunt you down and put an end to your nefarious activities." Emerson always has to have the last word, however. The priest was at the door when my husband shouted, "Are you leaving us to be slaughtered by your henchmen? I might have known you would leave the dirty work to others; but our blood will be on your head, you villain!"

"My dear Professor, not a drop of your blood will be shed if you accept the inevitable. My men have orders to bind and—" Turning, the priest broke off with a gasp.

Ramses fell into the room. He picked himself up off the floor and started forward. "Give it back to me," he said, in a growl that was terrifyingly like that of his father.

The priest laughed contemptuously. "Imp of Satan! Seize him, Mustafa."

With a malevolent grin the man he addressed threw out a careless arm. The blow caught Ramses across the midsection and lifted him clean off his feet. His body hit the wall with a horrible crash; he fell in a heap and lay motionless.

I heard Emerson's roar, and the crack of a pistol. I saw nothing. Inky blackness engulfed me, like a cloud of thick smoke shot with bursts of flame. A great rushing filled my ears, like the thunder of an avalanche. . . .

After an immeasurable interval I became aware of hands clasping me and a voice calling my name. "Peabody! Peabody, for God's sake . . ."

The mists before my eyes cleared. I was still on my feet, parasol in hand, and Emerson was shaking me.

Ramses sat bolt upright, his back against the wall, his hands braced on the floor, his legs sticking straight out. His mouth hung open; his eyes were popping.

"You are alive," I said.

Ramses nodded. For once in his life he seemed incapable of speech.

On Emerson's face I saw the same expression of incredulous horror. Yet there was no reason for alarm; one villain lay face down on the floor, his arms over his head. The second huddled in a corner, babbling incoherently. The priest was gone.

"You seem to have the situation well in hand, Emerson," I said, wondering why my voice sounded so hoarse. "My congratulations."

"I didn't do it," Emerson said. "You did."

"What are you saying, Emerson?"

Emerson released me and staggered back. He dropped heavily onto the tumbled blankets. "There is blood on your parasol, Peabody."

I realized that I was holding the instrument poised, as if to strike. There was certainly some viscous substance on the steel-dark tip. A drop formed and fell as I stared.

"Berserk," Emerson went on, shaking his head dazedly. "That is the term. . . . A berserker rage. I have heard it described. One could almost believe in the old legends, that the one possessed is impervious to blows, weapons, bullets. . . . The maternal instinct, roused to fury—the tigress defending her cub. . . ."

I cleared my throat. "Emerson, I cannot imagine what you are talking about. Tear one of the sheets into strips, and we will tie up the criminals before going out to rescue our men."

*   *   *

The rescue proved to be unnecessary. While we were binding the two thugs (who were in a peculiar state of trembling paralysis and gave us no trouble), our men from Aziyeh rushed into the house in an agitated and vociferous body. They had been unaware of danger until one of them awoke to find himself held at gunpoint by "a cursed Christian," as Ali naively expressed it. Emerson hastened to clear the name of the Copts. The expression "Master Criminal" confused Ali at first; after further explanations he proceeded with his narrative.

"When I saw the gun I cried out and woke the others. The man told us not to move, Sitt Hakim, so we did not; it was a Mauser repeating rifle, you understand. Yet we would have come if we had known you were in danger; indeed, we were about to rush the villain, risking our lives in your service, when out of the night a man appeared, waving his arms and crying out. . . ."

I knew it must have been the priest from Ali's description. "He had a long black beard, Sitt, and a cross hanging at his waist. There was blood all down his face and he was screaming in a high voice, like a frightened woman."

Emerson shot me a glance from under his brows, which I chose to ignore. "Go on, Ali."

Ali put a finger under his turban and scratched his head. "They ran away, Sitt, both of them. We were so surprised we could not think what to do. We talked for a while and Daoud said we should stay where we were, in case the man with the gun was hiding, watching us—"

Daoud squirmed and started to protest. I reassured him, and Ali finished his story. "Mohammed and I said, no, we must find you and make sure you were safe. So we came. Our honored father is very drunk on hashish, Sitt."

Abdullah looked so happy it seemed a shame to rouse him. So we carried him in and put him to bed, with Ali to watch over him. I ordered another of the men to go with Ramses to put his room in order.

Ramses lingered. To his meager breast he still clutched the box containing the pectoral. "Do you wish to talk to me, Mama?"

"I will have a great many things to say to you later, Ramses. Now go and do as I order."

"One question," said Emerson, absently scratching his now excessive beard. "What the devil induced you to climb in that window, Ramses? I thought I told you to go for help."

"De criminal was about to steal my pectoral," Ramses replied. "It is MINE. I found it."

"But, my dear boy, it was horribly dangerous," Emerson exclaimed. "You cannot go about demanding your rightful property from thieves; they are not amenable to such appeals."

"It was not dangerous," Ramses said serenely. "I knew you and Mama would not allow de men to harm me."

Emerson cleared his throat noisily and passed his sleeve across his eyes.

Ramses and I exchanged a long, steady look. "Go to bed, Ramses," I said.

"Yes, Mama. Good night, Mama. Good night, Papa."

"Good night, my dear boy."

Beneath his muscular exterior Emerson is a very sentimental person. I tactfully looked elsewhere while he wiped his eyes and got his face under control. Then he said, "Peabody, that was the most magnificent testimonial any child ever gave his parents. Could you not have responded more warmly?"

"Never mind, Emerson. Ramses and I understand one another perfectly."

"Humph," said Emerson. "Well, my dear, what next?"

"John," I said. "He must certainly be next."

"John? John! Good Gad, my dear, you are right. Where is the poor fellow?"

Emerson sprang to his feet. I waved him back into his chair, for despite his extraordinary stamina he was showing signs of fatigue. "There is only one place he can be, Emerson. But before we go in search of him I insist upon a bath and a change of clothing. There is no further danger in delay; if harm was intended, it must already have befallen him. Let us pray that the killer of Hamid and Abd el Atti has spared the lad."

Emerson's eyes narrowed. His concern for his unhappy servant was wholly sincere, but for the moment another matter had taken precedence. "Aha," he said. "So you believed that villain when he disclaimed responsibility for the murders?"

"Why should he lie? We had caught him red-handed. No, Emerson, the priest—or, if you prefer, the Master Criminal—is unquestionably a villain of the deepest dye and I am certain he has several murders on his conscience (if he possesses such an organ, which is doubtful); but he did not kill Abd el Atti and Hamid."

"Amelia."

"Yes, Emerson?"

"Did you suspect the priest? Be honest."

"No, Emerson, I did not. Did you?"

"No, Peabody, I did not."

"But I was not altogether wrong," I continued. "The person I suspected of being the Master Criminal is the murderer. It is a meaningless distinction, actually."

"Curse it, Peabody, you never give up, do you? Hurry with your bath, then, and we will go to the mission and apprehend Brother David."

"Brother Ezekiel," I said, and left the room before Emerson could reply.

Chapter Twelve

THE sun was well above the horizon before we were ready to set forth on our errand of justice and—I hoped—mercy. The morning air was clear and fresh; the eastern sky flaunted the exquisite golden glow of a desert sunrise. Yet we walked with dragging steps, oblivious for once to the marvels of nature. I did not anticipate danger, but the interview promised to be a painful one, and I was filled with apprehension for poor John.

He had gone to the mission, of course. I could not blame him for disobeying my express command; when we failed to return he must have feared for us as well as for his beloved. Since I had not told him where we were to meet the girl, he would search for her in the most obvious place.

Arriving, he had found . . . what? What scene of horror or massacre had met his astonished eyes, and made it necessary for the killer to add another crime to his list? That John had failed to return made it certain he had been prevented from returning; but was it murder or kidnapping that had prevented him? Whatever had happened had happened hours before. If John was no more, we could only avenge him. If he was held prisoner, we would be in time to save him.

One of my first acts, even before bathing and changing into fresh attire, had been to dispatch a message to de Morgan. I mentioned this to Emerson, hoping to cheer him, for his expression as he tramped along was gloomy in the extreme.

He only grunted. "De Morgan has no evidence on which to arrest Kalenischeff, Peabody. Even if the rascal has stolen antiquities, he is under the protection of the baroness. It would take a direct order from Cromer to interfere with such a distinguished visitor."

"Kalenischeff must be one of the gang, Emerson. It is too much of a coincidence that he should be leaving Dahshoor at the same time as the Master Criminal."

"Oh, I agree. His job was to act as spotter. If de Morgan found anything of interest, Kalenischeff would notify his leader. But we will never prove it,

Peabody, nor even convince de Morgan that he was taken in."

"It appears that this is one of those cases where everyone is guilty," I said.

"You exaggerate, Peabody. The baroness was duped; de Morgan is innocent of everything except congenital stupidity; and of the three at the mission, only one is guilty."

"Ah, do you think so? What about two out of three?"

The challenge roused Emerson from his depression. "Which two—or which one?"

"I did not say two were guilty. I only present it as a possibility."

"Are you sticking to your guns, then? Ezekiel?"

"Er—yes."

"It was at Brother David that Bastet spat, Peabody."

I was sorry he had noticed that. I had had some difficulty fitting it into my theory and had finally decided to ignore it altogether. "The incident was meaningless, Emerson. Bastet was in a bad mood—"

"And why was she in a bad mood, Peabody? Her keen sense of smell had recognized the spoor of the man who had been in Abd el Atti's shop—"

"You are becoming as fanciful as Ramses where that cat is concerned, Emerson. Oh, I don't doubt that was what the child intended when he returned to the shop and found out that Abd el Atti had been murdered; he is only a little boy, and does not understand that animals can't be trained to do what he wants. But if you are naive enough to suppose that Bastet tracked the murderer through the extensive and odorous byways of Cairo and that, many days thereafter, recalled the scent of the individual who threw a boot or some other missile at her—"

"Humph," said Emerson.

It did sound absurd, when put into words. But I wondered. Brother David had not been the only stranger present that day.

The village ought to have been teeming with activity, for the working day in such places begins at dawn. Not a soul was to be seen. Even the dogs had slunk into hiding. Not until we reached the well did a timid voice call out to us. Then I realized that behind every window were watching eyes, and that the doors stood a trifle ajar. One of them opened cautiously and a head appeared. It was that of the shy little *sheikh el beled*. We stopped and waited, and finally he summoned up courage to emerge.

"The peace of God be upon you," he said.

"And upon you," Emerson said automatically. Then he added, "Curse it, I have no time for this sort of thing. What the devil has happened here?"

"I do not know, effendi," the mayor said. "Will you protect us? There was much shouting and shooting in the night—"

"Oh, heavens," I exclaimed. "Poor John!"

"He is just making a good story of it," Emerson said in English; but he looked grave. "Shooting, your honor?"

"One shot," the mayor admitted. "One, at least. . . . And when we woke this morning, the priest was gone and all his friends with him; and the sacred vessels are gone too. They were very old and very precious to us. Has he taken them to Cairo to be repaired, perhaps? Why did he tell no one he was going?"

"He is half right," said Emerson. "I don't doubt that the sacred vessels are on their way to Cairo by now."

"I ought to have anticipated this," I said in some chagrin. "To be honest, Emerson, I did not notice the vessels when I attended the service."

This exchange had been in English. The little man looked timidly from me to Emerson. Emerson patted him on the back. "Be of good cheer, my friend," he said in Arabic. "Go back to your house and wait. It will all be explained to you later."

We went on through the deathly silence. "I have the direct forebodings, Emerson," I murmured.

"I expected you would, Peabody."

"If we have brought that boy to his death, I will never forgive myself."

"It was my idea to bring him, Peabody." That was all Emerson said, but his haggard look expressed the depth of his remorse.

"Oh no, my dear. I agreed; it was as much my fault as yours."

"Well, let us not borrow trouble, Peabody," Emerson said, squaring his shoulders and exhibiting the dauntless spirit I expected.

We reached the open space before the mission. The small neat buildings looked peaceful enough, but the same brooding silence hung over the place.

"Let us hurry," I said. "I can bear the suspense no longer."

"Wait." Emerson drew me into concealment among the trees. "Whatever awaits us in that ominous place, there is one thing we know we will find—a raving madman. Our theories agree on that, at least?"

I nodded. "Then it behooves us to behave with extreme circumspection," Emerson said. "We don't want to push the fellow into a rash act."

"You are correct as always, Emerson. But I cannot wait much longer."

"You won't have to." Emerson's voice dropped to a thrilling whisper. "By heaven, there he is—as unconcerned as if he were not a murderer twice over. Amazing how normal he looks; but that is often true of madmen."

He spoke of Brother David. The young man did not appear mad, but neither was he unconcerned. He stood just outside the door of the house looking nervously from side to side. After a long, suspicious survey of the scene, he summoned the courage to proceed. Emerson waited until he had got halfway across the clearing; then, with a roar, he bounded out of concealment.

When I reached them, Brother David was flat on his back and Emerson was sitting on his chest. "I have him safe," my husband cried. "There is nothing to be afraid of, Peabody. What have you done with my servant, you rascal?"

I said, "He can't answer, Emerson; you are squeezing the breath out of him. Get off him, why don't you."

Emerson shifted his weight. David took a long shuddering breath. "Professor?" he gasped. "Is it you?"

"Who the devil did you think it was?"

"That fiendish priest, or one of his adherents—we are beset with enemies, Professor. Thank God you are here. I was just going to try to reach you, to ask for your help."

"Ha," said Emerson skeptically. "What have you done with John?"

"Brother John? Why, nothing. Has he disappeared?"

No theatrical person could have counterfeited the bewilderment on the young man's face, but Emerson is notoriously hard to convince, once he has set his mind on something. "Of course he has disappeared! He is here—you have kidnapped him, or worse. . . . What of the shots in the night, you wretch?" Seizing David by his collar, he shook him like a mastiff worrying a rat.

"For heaven's sake, stop asking him questions and then preventing him from answering," I exclaimed.

Emerson let go of the young man's collar. David's head hit the sand with a thud and his eyes rolled up in his head. "What was it you asked? . . . I am not quite myself. . . . Shots in the night. Oh, yes—Brother Ezekiel was forced to fire his revolver at a would-be thief. He fired high, of course, only to frighten the fellow off."

"Brother Ezekiel." Emerson fingered his chin and glanced at me. "Hmmm. Where is Brother Ezekiel? He is usually the first on the scene."

"He is at prayer, in his study. He is asking the Almighty to defend his saints against the enemies that surround them."

Still astride his victim, Emerson studied him intently while he continued to stroke the dimple in his chin. "You were right, Amelia," he said at last. "I concede defeat. This helpless weakling is not a murderer."

Rising, he lifted David to his feet. "Mr. Cabot, your leader is a dangerous maniac. For his own sake, as well as the sake of others, he must be put under restraint. Follow me."

The moment he released his hold, David scuttled away. The door of the church opened and banged shut. A pale face peered out from one of the windows.

"Leave him be, Emerson," I said in disgust. "If you were mistaken about the creature, so was I. He will only be in our way. Let us smoke the murderer from his lair. I only hope we are not too late."

The advantage of surprise now being lost, we proceeded without further ado to the house. The front door stood open as David had left it. There was no one in the parlor; it was as barren and cheerless as before. The Greek Testament was no longer on the table.

"Which do you suppose is his study?" Emerson asked, contemplating the pair of doors at the back of the room.

"There is only one way to find out." Carefully I turned the knob of the right-hand door. The small chamber within was obviously Charity's bedroom. The bonnet, and a gown of the familiar dark calico, hung from pegs on the wall. There was nothing else in the room except a cot as narrow and probably as hard as a plank. A single thin coverlet was thrown back, as if the sleeper had risen in haste. I closed the door. "That one," I said, indicating the other door.

We had spoken softly, but some sound of our presence ought, by then, have reached the ears of a listener. I began to wonder if the house were inhabited after all. Or were the occupants of that silent room lying dead in their gore?

I drew my pistol. "Stand back, Emerson."

"Certainly not, Peabody. You are going about it the wrong way." He knocked gently at the door.

To my astonishment a voice promptly replied. "I told you, Brother David, to leave me be. I am speaking with my Father."

Emerson rolled his eyes expressively. "It is not Brother David. It is I—Emerson."

"Professor?" There was a pause. "Come in."

Emerson opened the door.

Prepared as I was for any ghastly sight—priding myself as I do on my aplomb under all circumstances—even I was struck dumb by the sight that confronted me. My eyes went first to John, who sat on the edge of the bed. A bloody bandage encircled his brow, but his eyes were open—staring wildly, in fact—and he did not appear seriously injured. I breathed a sincere but necessarily brief prayer of thanksgiving.

One of the two chairs was occupied by Charity. She appeared to be in a trance; her white face was utterly expressionless and she did not look up when the door opened. Brother Ezekiel sat at the table, an open book before him and a pistol in his hand. It was pointed at John.

"Come in, brother and sister," he said calmly. "You are just in time. I have been wrestling with the demons that possess this unfortunate young man. There wasn't any swine to cast 'em into, you see. I figure the only way to get rid of 'em is to shoot him, but first he must acknowledge his Saviour. I wouldn't want his soul to burn in hell."

"That is most considerate of you," said Emerson, with equal coolness. "Why don't I fetch a goat—or a dog? You can cast the demons into it."

"Afraid that won't do," said Ezekiel, shaking his head. "See, Professor, you have got a few demons in you too. I'll have to deal with 'em before I let you out of here or they might lead you astray."

"Mr. Jones—"

"That's not the way to talk to me, my son. Call me by my right name. For I am the Annointed One, whose coming to redeem Israel was foretold by the prophets."

"Good Gad," I said involuntarily.

Emerson grimaced at me, and Ezekiel said, "She's got more demons than any of 'em. Come in, sister, and acknowledge your Lord and Saviour."

My pistol was in my hand, hidden by the voluminous folds of my trousers, but I never thought of using it. How long had the madness been festering in his poor warped brain? He had maintained a semblance of normalcy till now.

Emerson edged into the room. "That's far enough," said Ezekiel. "Now you, sister. Come in."

I could not think what to do. The room was so small the madman was bound to hit someone if he pulled the trigger, and he might pull it if he were physically attacked. It seemed equally dangerous and fruitless to reason with him. Then something moved at the open window. Was it rescue—reinforcements? No. It was David, wild-eyed and pale with fright. We could not count on assistance from him.

Emerson saw him too, and with the brilliance that always marks his actions, seized the only possible advantage from his presence. "Look there, at the window," he cried. As Ezekiel turned, Emerson leaped.

The gun went off. The bullet struck harmlessly into the ceiling. David shrieked and vanished. John jumped to his feet and promptly sat down again as his knees gave way. Charity slid fainting from her chair. Emerson tossed me the gun and enveloped Brother Ezekiel in a tight embrace. Footsteps sounded in the outer room. *"Nom du nom du nom,"* de Morgan ejaculated. "What has transpired here?"

Behind the Frenchman was my son Ramses.

"It was de Coptic manuscript after all," Ramses said, some time later. Ezekiel was under guard and his victims had been attended to; we were once more in our own home and John, though pale and shaken, had insisted on making tea.

"Quel manuscrit coptique?" de Morgan demanded. "I understand nothing of this—nothing! It is of a madness unexampled. Master Criminals, manuscripts, raving missionaries. . . ."

I explained about the Coptic manuscript. "I knew all along it must be involved," I said. "But I could not think what to make of it. The trouble was—"

"That two different groups of criminals were at work," said Emerson. "The first was the gang of antiquities thieves. They had discovered a cache of royal jewelry at Dahshoor and were searching for more. Their leader took the place of the village priest at Dronkeh in order to supervise their illicit digging—"

"But the thieves fell out, as such persons are wont to do," I went on. "Hamid, who was a minor member of the gang, was not content with his share of the profits. He saw an opportunity to rob the thieves and sell some of his finds himself. He persuaded his father to market them. And among these objects—"

"Was the mummy case purchased by the baroness," Emerson interrupted.

"No, no, my dear. There were *two* mummy cases. From that fact arose much of the confusion. Both are now destroyed, but I fancy they were twin coffins, made at the same time by the same craftsman. Belonging, I do not doubt, to a husband and wife who wished to express their mutual affection by eventually occupying identical—"

"Never mind that, Amelia," Emerson growled. "The point is that they were made of the same materials—waste linen and old papyrus, dampened and molded into shape before being painted. Such cartonnage coffins are common; fragments of Greek manuscripts have been found in some. We should have realized that our papyrus scraps came from such a source."

"My dear Emerson, you do yourself an injustice," I said. "Our papyrus was Coptic, not Greek; Christian, not pagan. The baroness's mummy case obviously belonged to a worshipper of the old gods. It was early Roman in date, and Christianity did not become the official religion of the Empire until 330 A.D., under Constantine the Great. Yet the Coptic Church was established in the first century, and Egyptian Christians survived, though subjected to cruel persecution, until—"

"Until they got the chance to persecute everyone else," said Emerson.

"I beg you will refrain from expressing your unorthodox religious opinions just now, Emerson. I am endeavoring to explain that Christian writings of the first and second centuries did exist, and that it would be natural for a pagan to consider them waste paper, fit to be used in the construction of a coffin."

"Granted, granted," de Morgan said, before Emerson could pursue his argument. "I will grant anything you like, madame, if you will only get on with your story. This business of the twin coffins—"

"It is really very simple," I said, with a kindly smile. "Abd el Atti gained possession of the two mummy cases; they came, of course, from the same tomb. One, belonging to the wife, may have been damaged to begin with. Abd el Atti realized the papyrus used in its construction contained Coptic writing. Being a shrewd old rascal, he understood the nature of his find—"

"And looked for a customer who would appreciate its value," Emerson broke in. "Unluckily for him, the clergyman he approached was a religious fanatic. Ezekiel Jones was no mean scholar. His crude manners and speech caused us to underestimate him, but there were, in fact, a number of indications of his intellectual ability, including his knowledge of Greek. He translated the manuscript Abd el Atti sold him, and the startling revelations in the text drove him over the brink into madness. He determined to destroy the blasphemous manuscript. But it was incomplete. He visited Abd el Atti on the night of the murder. . . ."

Emerson's breath gave out, and I took up the story. "He went there in search of the rest of the manuscript. No doubt he had harassed and threatened Abd el Atti; the old man was in deadly fear—not, as I had supposed, of his criminal associates, but of the unbeliever who was behaving so strangely. On that last night Abd el Atti admitted to Ezekiel that there had been two coffins, one of which had been sold to the baroness. He also told Ezekiel I had a fragment from the first coffin. Ezekiel went berserk. He strangled the old man then and there—"

"And hanged him from the roofbeam," Emerson said grimly. "There was always a suggestion of ritual murder in that, for why go to the trouble of hanging a man who is already dead? I took it for some ceremony of the gang Abd el Atti had betrayed; but did not Judas, the greatest of traitors, hang himself, and was not David's treacherous and beloved son Absalom found hanging from a tree? In Ezekiel's darkening mind it was the proper treatment for a blasphemer."

"Ezekiel broke into our room at Shepheard's hoping to retrieve the fragment," I went on. "He had removed the remaining pieces of the first mummy case from Abd el Atti's shop the night of the murder. He was not interested in the mummy; along with other items it was knocked over and the painted panel fastened to it was dislodged from the wrappings. That was the painting Emerson—"

"Ahem," said Emerson loudly. "So much for the first coffin and mummy. The second, that of Thermoutharin, was in the salon of the baroness's dahabeeyah. Ezekiel knew his holy mission would not be complete until he had obtained and destroyed it. There was a strong possibility that it contained the remainder of the blasphemous manuscript."

"That clumsy fellow broke into the baroness's cabin and single-handedly carried off the mummy case?" de Morgan asked incredulously.

Emerson beat me to the draw, as the American idiom has it. "No, that was Hamid, with the help of a few confederates. He knew how desperately Ezekiel wanted the mummy case. He discarded the mummy itself, since it was worthless—and heavy—but he removed the painted portrait in an effort to render the mummy anonymous. I don't know what has become of that painting. Perhaps Hamid sold it to a passing tourist. The portrait we had, that of—er—Mrs. Thermoutharin, appeared to fit the mummy of her husband, because they were the same size."

It was my turn to speak. "Hamid probably took the other objects he had stolen from the baroness directly to his leader as proof of his loyalty; but the leader, who is no fool, was bound to wonder what he had done with the mummy case and why he had stolen it in the first place. Hamid could invent some lie to explain the latter question—he had been mistaken about its value, he had believed it contained valuable jewels—that sort of thing. But he had to account for its disappearance. His tricks with the mummy cases coming and going were designed to confuse his leader as well as us."

"It was clever of him to conceal his prize among others of the same sort," Emerson said grudgingly. "The old 'Purloined Letter' device. He put it in our storeroom and carried one of our coffins into the desert. Later, after Ezekiel had agreed to buy it, he removed it from the storeroom. Ezekiel had no intention of paying him; he had no more money, but he had his murderous hands. The rope around Hamid's neck was a symbolic gesture. Ezekiel could hardly hang the man from the roof-beam of his own house."

"He was still clinging to the rags of sanity then," I remarked.

"You are mixing your metaphors, Peabody, I believe. His hold on reality was weakening every day. But he had sense enough to know he could not hide the mummy case indefinitely. He destroyed it by fire a few days later. That was his real aim, after all—to destroy the manuscript. That," Emerson added nonchalantly, "was one of the vital clues. The Master Criminal—curse it, I mean the leader of the gang—would have no reason to steal an antiquity only to destroy it."

De Morgan could contain himself no longer. "But what was it?" he cried. "What was this terrible manuscript that drove a man to murder?"

There was a brief pause, fraught with drama. Then Emerson turned to Ramses, who had been an interested spectator. "Very well, my boy; not even your mama can deny that you have a right to speak. What was in the manuscript?"

Ramses cleared his throat. "You understand dat I can only t'eorize, since de fragments remaining are only a small fraction of de whole. However—"

"Ramses," I said gently.

"Yes, Mama, I will be brief. I t'ink dat de manuscript is a copy of a lost gospel, written by Didymus Thomas, one of de apostles. Dat much could be surmised from de first fragment. It is de second fragment, found by Mama later, dat may provide an explanation for de madness of Brudder Ezekiel."

"Ramses," said Emerson.

"Yes, Papa. It contained t'ree words. Dey are: 'de son of Jesus.' "

"Nom de Dieu," de Morgan gasped.

"You are quick, monsieur," I said. "You see the significance of those words."

"They may not mean what we think," de Morgan muttered, passing a trembling hand across his brow. "They cannot mean what we think."

"But we may reasonably conclude from the actions of Brother Ezekiel that the lost gospel contained matter he would consider blasphemous and heretical— matter that must never come to light. It is not unheard of even for supposedly sane scholars to suppress data that does not agree with their pet theories. Imagine the effect of such information on a man whose brain was already reeling; who suffered from incipient megalomania."

"You must be right," said de Morgan. "There is no other explanation that fits the facts. *Mais, quel mélodrame!* You are a true heroine, madame; the murderer seized, the thieves routed. . . . I congratulate you from my heart."

I stretched out a hand to Emerson. "Congratulate us both, monsieur. We work together."

"Admirable," said the Frenchman politely. "Well, I must return to work. I only hope the thieves have left me something to discover. What a coup it would be if I could find such a cache!"

"I wish you luck," I said politely. Emerson said nothing.

"Yes, a veritable coup." De Morgan sighed. "My picture would be in the *Illustrated London News,"* he explained, rather pathetically. "I have always wanted to be in the *Illustrated London News.* Schliemann has been in the *Illustrated London News.* Petrie has been in the *Illustrated London News.* Why not de Morgan?"

"Why not indeed?" I said. Emerson said nothing.

De Morgan rose and picked up his hat. "Oh, but madame, there is one little thing you have not explained. Your escape from the pyramid was truly marvelous. Accept my felicitations on that escape, by the way; I do not believe I expressed them earlier. But I do not understand why the Master—the leader of the gang—should put you there in the first place. It was the evil Hamid and the insane Ezekiel who were responsible for the other attacks on you, searching for the mummy case and the papyrus. Was the Master—the leader of the gang—also looking for the papyrus?"

Ramses stopped swinging his feet and became very still. Emerson cleared his throat. De Morgan looked inquiringly at him. "A slight touch of catarrh," Emerson explained. "Hem."

De Morgan stood waiting. "It seems," I said, "that the leader—the Master Criminal—was under the impression we had some other valuables."

"Ah." De Morgan nodded. "Even Master Criminals are sometimes wrong. They suspect everyone, the rascals. *Au revoir, madame. Adieu, professor.* Come soon to visit me, *mon petit* Ramses."

After the Frenchman had gone out I turned a critical eye on my son. "You must give it back, Ramses."

"Yes, Mama. I suppose I must. T'ank you for allowing me to arrange de matter wit' de least possible embarrassment to myself."

"And to me," Emerson muttered.

"I will go and talk to him immediately," said Ramses.

He suited the action to the word.

De Morgan had mounted his horse. He smiled at the small figure trotting toward him and waited. Ramses caught hold of the stirrup and began to speak. De Morgan's smile faded. He interrupted Ramses with a comment that was clearly audible even at that distance, and reached out for him. Ramses skipped back and went on talking. After a time a curious change came over the Frenchman's face. He listened a while longer; then he dismounted, and squatted down so that his face was close to Ramses.' An earnest and seemingly amicable dialogue ensued. It went on so long that Emerson, standing beside me, began to mutter. "What are they talking about? If he threatens Ramses—"

"He has every right to beat him to a jelly," I said.

Yet when the conversation ended, de Morgan appeared more puzzled than angry. He mounted. Ramses saluted him courteously and started back toward the house. Instead of riding off, de Morgan sat staring after Ramses. His hand moved in a quick furtive gesture. Had I not known better, I would have sworn the cultured, educated director of the Antiquities Department had made the sign of the evil eye—the protection against diabolic spirits.

II

What was in the lost gospel of Didymus Thomas? We will never know the answer, although Emerson often engages in ribald and unseemly speculation. "Does he describe the trick the disciples played on the Romans, to make them believe a man had risen from the dead? Was Jesus married and the father of children? And what exactly was his relationship with Mary Magdalen?"

Brother Ezekiel, the only living person who actually read part of the lost gospel, will never tell us what it contained. He is a raving lunatic; and I have heard that he wanders the corridors of his home near Boston, Massachusetts, dressed in a simple homespun robe, blessing his attendants. He calls himself the Messiah. He is tended by his devoted sister and his sorrowing disciple, and I suppose that one day—if it has not already occurred—Charity and Brother David will be wed. They have in common not only their devotion to a madman but their invincible stupidity. Some persons cannot be rescued, even by me.

John was sure his heart was broken. He went about for weeks with his large brown hand pressed to the precise center of his breast, where he erroneously believed that organ was located. However, one of the housemaids is a charming girl, with mouse-brown hair and a dimple in her cheek, and I begin to detect signs of convalescence.

We left Egypt in March and returned to England to greet our newest nephew. Mother and infant survived the ordeal in excellent condition. We had uncovered the substructure of our pyramid before we left, and although no remarkable discoveries were made I became quite attached to the place. I was able to abandon it with equanimity, however, since de Morgan had offered us the firman for Dahshoor the following year. He was not very gracious about it, but that was of small concern to me. That half-submerged chamber in the heart of the Black Pyramid—I felt sure that under the dark water something fascinating awaited us.

It was not until after we had returned to England that we learned of de Morgan's remarkable discovery of the jewels of the princesses, near the pyramid of Senusret III. It was featured in the *Illustrated London News*, with a flattering engraving of de Morgan, mustache and all, holding up the crown of Princess Khnumit before the audience he had invited to admire his discovery. I could not but agree with Emerson when he flung the paper aside with a critical "These Frenchmen will do anything to get in the newspaper."

One of the necklaces on the mummy of the princess bore a striking resemblance to the one Ramses had found. I remembered the long conversation between Ramses and de Morgan; the sudden concession of the Frenchman to our wishes; and I wondered. . . .

The lion seems to have settled in very nicely at Chalfont. Walter has suggested we bring back a young female next time.